S. J. Michaels lives in Ireland and is the author of one previous novel, *Summary Justice* – 'one of the best terrorist thrillers ever to come out of Northern Ireland'.

D1464823

Also by S. J. Michaels in Pan Books

SUMMARY JUSTICE

S. J. MICHAELS

DIEBACK

PAN BOOKS
IN ASSOCIATION WITH MACMILLAN LONDON

First published 1991 by Macmillan London Limited
This edition published 1992 by Pan Books Ltd
Cavaye Place, London SW10 9PG
in association with Macmillan London Limited

1 3 5 7 9 8 6 4 2

ISBN 0 330 31874 8

Photypeset by Intype, London
Printed and bound in Great Britain by
Clays Ltd, St Ives plc

For my daughters,
Katrina, Oonagh, and Victoria,
with love

ACKNOWLEDGEMENTS

The author gratefully acknowledges the authoritative guidance of Eddie Baird regarding firearms and explosives. A particular debt of gratitude is due to Ljudmila Gilmour and Kay Aiken for their help and stalwart support. Finally, but not least, mention must be made of the expert assistance received from Archie Smyth and Larne Information Technology Centre.

GLOSSARY

AEW	Airborne Early Warning
CIA	US Central Intelligence Agency
FBI	US Federal Bureau of Investigation
GCHQ	British Government Communications Headquarters (Primary Function: Electronic Interception)
GRU	Glavnoye Razvedyvatelnoye Upravleniye (Soviet Military Intelligence)
HQNI	British Army Headquarters, Northern Ireland (based at Lisburn, County Down)
IWS	Individual Weapon Sight (used for night vision purposes, it works by intensifying the imagery and operates by using all available light sources, such as moonlight)
KGB	Komitet Gosudarstvennoi Bezopasnosti (Soviet Committee for State Security)
KOMSOMOL	Young Communist League
MI5	British Security Service (Primary Function: Domestic Counterintelligence)
MI6	British Secret Intelligence Service (Primary Function: Foreign Counterintelligence)
NASA	National Aeronautics and Space Administration (USA)

NKVD	Narodny Kommissariat Vnutrennikh Del (Soviet People's Commissariat of Internal Affairs: the forerunner of the KGB)
NORAD	North American Air Defence
NSA	USA National Security Agency (Primary Function: Electronic Interception)
ORBATS	British Intelligence slang for the terminology given to describe 'the organization and battalion command structure' of individual terrorist groups
QRF	British Army 'Quick Reaction Force' (normally airborne)
SAS	Special Air Service
SIB	British Army 'Special Investigation Branch' (the investigative section of the Royal Military Police)
SITREP	Army slang for 'Situation Report'
TCG	RUC Special Branch 'Tactical Control Group' (based regionally throughout Northern Ireland to co-ordinate covert operations and deployment involving specialist police and military units)
YO	British army slang for 'young officer'

PART ONE

THE GATHERING STORM

IRELAND
Good Friday

It was cold and black, and the wind whistled through the grave-yard like a wailing banshee. The solitary figure moved through the rows of broken and fallen headstones and hurried towards the old cemetery wall. No one noticed; only the cemetery cat squeaked out at the passing figure, then was gone. A quicker movement now, a renewed urgency in the pace.

The decaying crypt lay open as always. Suddenly the wind picked up again, and the surrounding trees began to swirl and dance – the sound of a dozen tormented crying souls, bending and swaying. Then the figure vanished, hobbling unsteadily down the wet and broken steps into the pitch blackness of the crypt. A small pencil light was switched on, illuminating the way to the third coffin set at the back of the vault. The lid creaked open, cobwebs stretching to breaking-point and then further as the lid was opened more fully. The pencil light shone into the coffin now. The old Uher tape recorder, wrapped in green plastic, lay across the corpse's femurs, denuded of all flesh and clothing a century before.

Twenty minutes later, in an old dilapidated farmhouse next to the cemetery, the tape recorder was fitted to a light bulb connection and switched on. But it never recorded; it never would. The spool tape was loaded, and, as the crystals warmed up, the recorder was finally connected to the television aerial. Apart from the reconnected electricity supply, the aerial was perhaps the only other thing that still worked around the dis-used farmhouse. A single white light flashed on the machine, then the tape began to whir round. Ten seconds later the burst transmission was sent out.

The duty cipher officer was initially alerted from his unofficial forty winks by the audible alarm on the panel in front of him. He shook his head and started to focus on the computerized controls. Captain Sergei Petrov's eyes widened as the visual display unit began to flash wildly. It was almost 3 a.m., and he'd been on duty for ten hours already, the majority of which time he had had to spend in isolation in the computer communications centre of Soviet Military Intelligence. He smacked the keys on his terminal, repeating the sequence twice over, but he still got the same answer. Someone had just transmitted a Field Radio Signal to Moscow from somewhere in Western Europe, using a totally obsolete frequency. He rubbed his tired eyes; he knew he wouldn't get back to sleep again that night.

EASTERN LIBYA

The burning midday sun beat down on the camp. The tall swarthy man in the blue denim suit stood outside the corrugated-tin hut with its sand-coloured curved roof which ran straight down into three rows of sandbags surrounding the perimeter of the building. It was only one of ten such structures stretching across the terrorist training-camp. He checked his wrist-watch and looked up; it was almost time. Then he turned and walked back inside.

A hundred miles above, the circling Soviet Spysat locked into position. The satellite communications control centre at Viliuisk in Siberia had already reprogrammed the satellite days before. Now the blocking mechanisms were introduced. Even if a hostile satellite wanted to, it would never detect the activity far below in the Libyan desert; and to Soviet Military Intelligence the enemy was still real, no matter what the Kremlin said or did.

The tall, swarthy man with the straggly, unkempt hair was

4

working at his desk when a knock on the door alerted him. He turned around slowly.

'George?' The man's French accent was clearly evident.

The tall Arab looked at the young blond-haired Frenchman in the military bush-shirt and desert-pattern camouflage-trousers as he handed him a strip of paper.

'It just came into the communications room,' he continued in English.

The Arab stared at the inch-wide strip of paper, a printout from the teleprinter radio room. It said just two words: 'Autumn Harvest.'

'They are coming back from the exercise now,' continued the Frenchman.

'Then, we shall go and meet them, François.' The Arab grinned; his yellow and badly spaced teeth seemed more prominent than ever.

The two men travelled under the hot desert sun in an open-backed Land-Rover, leaving in their wake a small dust-cloud rising over forty feet off the desert floor. Just over the first rise the Land-Rover halted.

'There they are now.' The Frenchman pointed towards the south-west where a small cloud of dust rose up high into the still air. At first the images shimmered like desert mirages, then they quickly solidified. Six sand-coloured dune-buggies roared across the desert floor almost abreast of each other.

'What was the word back from Oberon?' enquired George.

'The Greek says they took the target with no difficulty,' replied François, clearly excited.

'Time?'

'Twelve minutes in all. Casualty assessment for us was three per cent; the enemy estimate is total, over one hundred killed or wounded.' François smiled across to his leader. 'They are ready.'

'But are *you*?' replied George, crushing the Frenchman's confidence to the ground. Without waiting for a response he continued: 'Just as well we didn't let them kill any more; otherwise I'd have had the Libyan President on my neck before sunset.'

The Frenchman kept quiet; he knew better. He watched as

George stepped out of the vehicle. A scorpion moved across the sand just in front of the Arab; he stepped on it, instantly crushing it with his boot, then paused to watch it squirm and twist underfoot.

'From tomorrow the training-camp here will start to be dismantled. By the end of the week our group will have moved to our new training-camp in Cyprus.' George spoke without looking at the Frenchman; he was intently watching the approaching vehicles as they raced across the desert towards him. 'There you will receive the specialist training you specified as essential in your original proposal for Autumn Harvest, along with a few additional aspects we feel may be necessary.'

'How long will it take?' asked the Frenchman.

As if ignoring the question, George continued: 'Then you will be told how you fit into the overall plan of things.'

The Frenchman was totally surprised by the revelation of any amendment to his original plan. 'I don't understand. The plan was complete; it did not require any variation.'

'But the ending wasn't enough, François.' George turned to face his second-in-command. 'We are going for the gold rather than the silver medal.' There was just the hint of a grin on his lean face.

The Frenchman kept silent; the new permutations flashed across his mind. He was a survivor. Even from the first day he had chosen his violent path towards revolution, he had always ensured that he alone was in complete control; anything unknown in a plan was dangerous, no matter how small or insignificant it seemed. His mind raced now; the Arab was telling him of some additional factor in the plan, a factor that could already have been discovered and infiltrated by any one of a number of security organizations, every one of them hungry for terrorist blood.

They waited in silence for several more minutes before the dune-buggies pulled up in front of them. As they each braked, their occupants, dressed in the combat uniform of the Soviet Airborne Division, scrambled off and stood forming a continuous line stretching in front of their vehicles. A small, muscular man dressed in the uniform of a Soviet colonel walked through the line, brushing against the dusty shoulder of one of his men as he moved up the slight incline to face the Arab. He stood to attention and saluted.

'Comrade, we achieved our objective.' The officer spoke in Russian.

George nodded, before addressing the entire group of thirty young men and women.

'We are many organizations.' He spoke in English as he looked down the line before him. 'The RAF from Germany, ETA from Spain, the PLO and PFLP, Action Directe, PIRA and INLF from Ireland, not forgetting my own Hezbollah; but now we are one group, one fighting unit, and with one purpose.' All eyes were fixed on him now, not an eyelid-movement anywhere. 'Autumn Harvest is on! We go! We go!' he screamed.

The last part of his statement was lost in the roar of excitement and applause from the group. Berets were thrown skywards as men began to jump for joy. A few began to dance wildly; a babel of perhaps five or six different languages began to scream statements of approval. The Arab stood looking on impassively as the adulation continued. The man in the Soviet colonel's uniform moved over to François. 'That's something we'll have to sort out: a common language of understanding!'

'Russian sounds fine to me, comrade!' responded François. They laughed and looked towards the ecstatic group and waved together. George was already among them shaking hands and being kissed. Some of the PLO began to shoot off their rifles skywards. The roar of approval reached a new peak. Autumn Harvest was now a reality, and soon the world would shake to their tune.

NOGINSK MILITARY PRISON, EASTERN OUTSKIRTS OF MOSCOW
Nineteen days later

It had been so long since he had eaten that his stomach no longer reacted to the thought of food, but even momentary pleasant images were hard to sustain when the mind was constantly preoccupied with the certain knowledge of some further torture. At first they had only questioned him, and he still ate, although he had not been permitted to fall asleep. Then the food stopped, and so did the niceties.

It all began with a punching session, followed by a brief recovery period before a further beating, this time with sticks. They were no longer asking him the endless stupid questions – not that he knew the answers in any case; they were breaking him in body and spirit. Then the beating sessions became inter-mingled with the electric treatment, administered by way of probes placed on his genitals and his spinal column. After strapping him face down on to a wooden bench, they roughly inserted a probe half-way down his spine; another probe punc-tured his skin at his scrotum. The shocks varied; he could never anticipate the tingle of a mild voltage or the sudden agony of a more powerful charge that automatically punctured his body into spasms as he was pushed faced down against the flat wooden board, his wrists and ankles tearing at the leather straps until he bled.

The torture all seemed endless; that was the worst of it. Death became a welcome prospect and friend, but a friend that kept eluding him. After his torturers had done their worst, to the point of almost killing him, Sergei Petrov was dragged back to his dirty little cell with its damp walls and acrid stench. That the previous occupant had died and rotted in that cell seemed the only reasonable explanation for the vile atmosphere. Per-haps he, too, was destined for the same fate, dying alone and afraid, for he had heard many strange stories about the infa-mous Noginsk Military Prison. Indeed, he had personally con-veyed many of the prison's previous guests to the inner walls of the place; the fact that he never set eyes on them or heard of them again never mattered – at least, not until now.

But that was all in another world. Now he was alone, no access to family or to the outside world, no appeal to some superior officer, no one to intercede and tell them it was all a big mistake. Yes, he had almost convinced himself that they had forgotten about prisoner number 231, until the cell door reopened that morning and he was dragged along the corridor into what seemed to be a communal shower room, white tiles

8

covering the floor and stretching up the walls to a height of nine feet, above which the decaying plaster, discoloured by years of moisture and condensation, painted strange patterns on his mind. Through squinting eyes he could just make out the rows of shower pipes stretching around the walls and the slight undulation of the floor as it splayed into grill-covered gullies that ran long the bottom of the shower walls.

Only when he was pulled into the adjoining room did his fear begin to surge anew. In the centre of another white-walled room was a large cast-iron bath, beside which stood a guard dressed in a white plastic overall. The metal door slammed shut behind him. He gritted his teeth in response, trying to control his shaking head. The guard in the white overalls stooped over the bath and removed a flexible rubber pipe, still gushing water.

'*Poshel K. Chirtu!*' he cried out.

Before the prisoner could scream, powerful hands lifted him from either side, submerging him face down into the bath's icy water. He tried to move, to get out, but someone was pushing down heavily on his back now. He tried moving his arms under his body, but they were pinned down on either side of his legs. Now also his thighs were being held tightly against the bottom of the bath. He began thrashing his legs, but it was no use; he had no grip. In sheer panic Petrov tried to scream; water rushed into his mouth as the last air was expelled from his lungs. He swallowed, almost retching, then more water. He began to feel his eyes bulge and his chest expand even against the pressure of the guard's weight on his back. No memory of his life flashed past, just sheer terror and panic.

Now, at the moment of death, they had finally broken him, for if his torturers had taken the time to give him a psychiatric test instead of beating him senseless they would have discovered his real weakness. To some it was snakes or spiders, to others it was a fear of heights or enclosed spaces, but Petrov's greatest fear was of drowning. Even as a young soldier he had remained the only man in his infantry company not to pass the elementary swimming course.

He began to pass out, choking giving way to the body's acceptance of the end. The noise of his own retching aroused

9

him before the pain of his stomach contractions registered. Through blurred vision and distorted hearing he could just sense the presence of two guards standing several feet from him. He tried to get up but fell backwards on to the wet floor, banging his head on the tiled surface. A doctor quickly checked his pulse and chest before beckoning the two guards to set him on a wooden chair now standing close to the iron bath. Then the questioning started. Always the same things, over and over again. 'What do you know? Who did you tell?' Just as before, he was eager to answer, to explain their mistake, but now with a renewed eagerness and to avoid re-immersion in the bath. But his efforts were pointless. They were determined to use the bath again, and again and again. They knew of his fear all right; they had always known. The electric shocks, the beatings, the drugs were just for their 'amusement'. He lost count of the number of times they submerged him; towards the end he no longer struggled, no longer fought to hold his breath, but rather beckoned unconsciousness and the instant pleasant possibility of death. When he reopened his eyes the bright lights no longer blinded him; the air was stale and damp, familiar. Even so, it took him several minutes to realize that he had been returned to the cell and was now sprawled on the cold floor. After an indeterminate period he climbed painfully on to the barren wooden bed and tried to fall asleep. Again, just as before, sleep eluded him; thoughts of why they had done this to him kept his mind from rest. He recalled again that horribly fateful night at the communications centre, the day before his arrest . . .

The communications centre for Glavnoye Razvedyvatelnoye Upravleniye, the official title for Soviet Military Intelligence, but more commonly known by its initials GRU, is a self-contained complex, built mainly underground and situated in the outer suburbs of Moscow. Part of the communications establishment is known simply as 'Section Six', responsible for the reception of all Field Radio Signals in the northern hemisphere. 'Field Radio Signals' is the common term used for all data received from Soviet agents active in the field of intelligence-gathering, especially in the Western Alliance countries. The information is passed to the GRU communications centre via tiny high-powered transmitters which operate in conjunction with established satellite communications channels. The message is prepared in advance and then typed into the memory store of the transmitter. Once stored it is yet again transformed by means of binary principles, and after a few seconds the operator is then ready to transmit his recoded message which is discharged in a single 'burst' at automatic and lightning speed. Within milliseconds it is safely inside a decoding machine in Moscow Centre; thus, there is little prospect of the enemy ever obtaining a 'fix' on the agent's position, reducing the chances of any enemy interception.

It had been at 4.02 that April morning when the senior duty cipher officer was disturbed from his nap by the audible warning signal on his master control-panel. A message had been received by one of the decoding machines from somewhere in the West. He hesitated, setting aside his pencil and note-pad before typing an entry into his computer terminal. It took several seconds for the response to flash on to the VDU. A series of numbers in six-figure columns appeared on the screen. Sergei Petrov stared at the configuration.

179435	281934	727680
041892	397845	919560
593146	728109	024195
472913	670405	350468
736508	518524	491701

OPUS 49 – 437291 – OMEGA

He stared at the flashing code-verification. Omega was the highest classification in existence, but he had never heard of Opus 49 before; it was not in his directory. He rubbed the tiredness from his eyes before typing an entry into the computer again. He had made an error, easy to do after spending ten hours of a twelve-hour shift on your own. He had almost convinced himself that it was a mistake, and he repeated his check; but again, for a third time, he got the same response. He studied the keyboard. He had not made any mistake. It was impossible! Yet the evidence was before his eyes. Someone had linked into the highly secret computer system using an unlisted code-classification! He lifted the telephone and punched the three-digit number on the side-console. The line burred for several seconds before being answered.

'Comrade Major? This is Captain Petrov. Can you come to the main cipher room right away?'

The reply was snapped, the line went dead. The duty GRU officer, a passed-over major called Bulganin, was well known for his coarse if not ignorant attitude, especially when awakened from an unofficial slumber in the duty officer's quarters. His pale and angry face soon cleared when he was confronted with the facts.

'Are you sure, Petrov?' he queried, examining more closely the visual display unit before him.

'It is my job to be sure, Comrade Major. This code-classification is not in the directory. I've never seen anything like it before, except once in a training exercise and that was back in my earliest days in intelligence!' exclaimed Petrov.

'And you are certain it has Omega status?'

'See for yourself, comrade.' Petrov pointed towards the VDU; the only successful interrogation the computer's brain could determine was the security status of the message, the highest in the Soviet Union.

'What does it say? What is the message anyway? And who is this 437291?' continued Bulganin, staring at the flashing Omega symbol on the screen.

'I'm sorry, Comrade Major, but even I cannot tell you that at this stage. Each message-code has a different formula for decoding; in present-day codes, as you know, this is included in the message and fed into our mainframe computer, following which I or my staff set about the final product, but in this case there is no such formula.'

The major spun the cipher officer sharply around in his swivel chair until he was staring him fully in the face. He then bent down menacingly within an inch of Petrov's face.

'Let me get this straight! Are you telling me that you can't decode this blasted message?' Petrov could feel the major's spittle splash over his face; the smell of his foul breath was unavoidable. Bulganin eased back and stood away from the little officer as another thought crossed his mind. 'Tell me.

Could this be some sort of training exercise to catch us out in our efficiency?'

'Perhaps, comrade.' Petrov inwardly smiled; he knew exactly what the office bully meant. It was his job, as chief duty cipher officer, to decode the information, and he knew he could probably do it given more time, but it was the duty officer's responsibility to disseminate the information and it was becoming obvious that Bulganin was lacking a great deal in confidence. Bulganin continued to stare at Petrov; the cipher officer could almost smell the man's contempt towards him.

'Are you telling me everything, Petrov? Is this some sort of game to test me? Well! Is it?' He snarled like a dog.

Petrov quickly assessed the situation; it would be dangerous to antagonize Bulganin further. He knew just how easily transfers to obscure locations were arranged and he had never been further east than the Urals, nor did he have any desire to be.

'I know no more than you, Comrade Major . . . I think I can decode this, but it will take some time.'

'How much time?'

Petrov studied the VDU for a moment. 'If my calculations are correct, and I can gain immediate access to the archives at this unearthly hour, I can crack it maybe inside two hours.'

'You have until six o'clock, comrade.' The major looked at his watch. 'Just make sure you do. I want to get to the bottom of this matter before the day-shift arrives, understand?'

The last statement was wasted on Petrov. A bell was already ringing inside his head. This message was no test. It was important; all his senses told him that. Somehow he would break the code, and nothing short of awakening the comrades of the Central Committee was going to stop him; but the task of decoding proved much harder than Sergei Petrov could ever have imagined. After a preliminary search through the archives and computer retrieval system, he drew a complete blank. Then he tried all available information relating to Omega section. Again nothing.

He engaged his own computer, attempting the interrogation manually. He found it was a code within a code, not an uncommon feature, but in this case with a marked difference: the reference signal at the end of the message was not a sender classification; it was the coding for the person in GRU to whom the message was addressed. Petrov scratched his forehead. The system had been completely revised over twelve years previously after a series of security leaks. No one any longer used this format. From the retrieval system he obtained access to the appropriate security section. It was impossible. He had to go to the computer archive section himself. Forty minutes later he found something: the recipient's identity locked away in the memory bank.

On his return to the main cipher room Bulganin was waiting, nursing a steaming mug of black coffee laced with vodka between his hands. He jumped up on the cipher officer's arrival, spilling some of the liquid over the floor.

'Well? Have you cracked it?'

'Not completely, but look here.' Petrov held up a sheet of paper in his hand. 'It is indeed an old code, Comrade Major' – he handed him a computer readout sheet – 'and according to the initial scientific analysis it was also transmitted on obsolete Soviet equipment. We can tell by the timing and strength of the signal.' He moved to the major's side and pointed to the sheet with a shaky index finger. 'See there. That's the recipient's name. He's the only person with the means to decode this message fully, and I don't need to remind you that Omega status is the highest there is. It is no test or training exercise, Comrade Major, but it is still a real puzzle. The equipment's obsolete. Do you recognize the name of this recipient? I've never heard of him before.'

Major Bulganin began to turn his head slowly from one side to the other; it seemed as though he was attempting to shake the thought from his mind but lacked the energy. He spoke softly, the words forced through a dry throat and mouth.

'I know the name.' He turned slowly to face the wall-mounted photograph of the Soviet President and Chairman of the Central Committee; a shiver went down his spine. 'But the man to whom this message is addressed died years ago!' He turned again to face the confused cipher officer. 'Major-General Boris Kurakin was the head of our organization. He died in 1972!'

Both men looked in astonishment at each other.

'*Da?*'

'Lieutenant-General Mikhailov?' The caller was nervous and hesitant. 'This is Major Vassili Bulganin from Section Six, Communications Centre, Fifth Department.'

'What is it?' The voice was cold and clinical.

'Something that I must bring to your personal and immediate attention, Comrade General.' Bulganin gulped before continuing. 'I have just received an Omega signal.'

'Follow procedure and be in my office by ten.' The voice never faltered; there was no sign of emotion. Before Bulganin could reply the line went dead. He replaced the receiver just as the first droplets of sweat trickled down his high forehead.

Lieutenant-General Alexei Vladimirovich Mikhailov was 1st Deputy Chief of the Glavnoye Razvedyvatelnoye Upravleniye. The man was an icon to those who knew him inside Soviet Military Intelligence. Bulganin had never had the opportunity even to speak to the icon before and he was glad of the anonymity up to now; he had seen too many of his fellow-officers stick their necks out and find themselves headless inside days. For Bulganin there could be no choice; standing procedure was specific in regard to the handling of Omega information. All signals traffic so classified had to be forwarded directly to the serving 1st Deputy Chief of the GRU. It had been a standard procedure as far back as Bulganin could remember and, although he had served in Section Six for many years, he had never received an Omega signal and to his certain knowledge neither had any of his comrades; it was unheard of. But, then, any outside discussion on such matters would spell immediate arrest and the inevitable consequences of breaching the GRU code.

In his Kalininski Street office Alexei Vladimirovich Mikhailov sat back and thought about the call he had just taken. Deputy Mikhailov was indeed a powerful man. He had his own supply of 'personal illegals', Russian agents who had been 'introduced' into other countries outside the USSR over a period of years – perhaps even as much as three decades. These 'illegals' appeared as normal and ordinary citizens in their chosen countries of residence, shrouded in a veil of respectability and seemingly more native than the natives. Mikhailov not only controlled the training of all 'illegals' but also had direct authority over all six GRU directorates. His singular mission was intelligence-gathering, and the lengths to which he could go knew no bounds. He was directly responsible to Colonel-General Viktor Nikolayevich Grechko, the GRU chief, and whilst the old and ailing Grechko had his own 'personal illegals' he was in the main an administrative functionary and adviser to the Soviet Defence Minister and Chief of the General Staff. The real power lay with Mikhailov, that was the way he liked it; it was also the way he had devised.

Ninety minutes later

Mikhailov set aside the file, closing the cover and signing it on the front cover just as the burly major was shown into his third-floor office by the female orderly. Bulganin was clean-shaven and had changed into his best uniform. He marched smartly to the centre of the floor, directly in front of the desk, before saluting.

The general scratched the side of his face as he stared up at the GRU major with the discoloured drinker's nose and cheeks. He straightened his tie and eased back into the leather chair, looking like a London stockbroker in his dark blue Savile Row pin-striped suit, set against an immaculate white shirt and blue silk Paisley tie pinned in place by a small gold tiepin just above the line of his waistcoat. Bulganin was somewhat taken back; he was aware of only some of the advantages of being one of the Nomenklatura in Soviet society – thousands of Soviet citizens who acquired the privilege of clothing, food and other luxuries unavailable to the average man or woman. Even in such times of famine and starvation inside the Soviet Union these things were still accepted; the system saw to it. The nearest Bulganin had come to seeing such style was browsing through a foreign fashion magazine.

'Major Bulganin reporting as ordered, Comrade Lieutenant-General.' He tried his best to hide his nervousness but became aware of his booming voice echoing around the large office. He had to impress; he just had to. It was not often that a middle-aged army major got the opportunity to appear personally in front of an officer such as Mikhailov. This was his chance, perhaps his last and only one. The general stared down at the file tucked under the major's left arm and then slowly returned his gaze to the man's face.

'Show me.' Mikhailov spoke almost in a whisper.

Bulganin found himself physically stooping forward to hear. He set the file on the desk and stepped back again, careful not to outdistance himself in case he missed his master's voice. The fifty-two-year-old general took a solid silver letter-opener and slit the side of the brown envelope stapled to the inside leaf of the file, checking its seals before removing another folded envelope from inside. Similar to the first, it was also sealed and stamped, and in addition showed the date and the time this had been done.

Again, but with a slight increase of speed this time, he cut open the envelope and removed the two pages from inside. The first was a computer readout depicting the coded message as it had been originally received at Moscow Centre. The computer had automatically printed the time of reception directly underneath. Mikhailov quickly flipped over to the second page. In accordance with procedure it was a typed résumé of Bulganin's actions and further included his own assessment of the matter. The report was scant, although it had clearly been embellished with a view towards impressing him. Mikhailov's narrow eyes visibly widened when he read the recipient's name.

'Who typed this?' Mikhailov kept his eyes on the report.

'I . . . I did, Comrade General.'

'I hope so . . . for your sake. Now, apart from you, you say in your report that only a Captain Petrov knows anything about this.'

'That is correct, Comrade General, he is the cipher officer who took the encoded transmission.'

'Comrade Major, why did you have the cipher officer interrogate the main computer retrieval system to try to decode

17

this signal?' The general looked up now, his dark beady eyes removing the last vestige of confidence from the burly major.

'I know, Comrade General. I know that it is not procedure to involve oneself at my level with an Omega signal. However, neither the cipher officer nor myself believed the transmission to be authentic. From the coding order the cipher officer felt it appropriate to obtain some technical data from the computer bank. The information we obtained indicated the message to have been transmitted on an obsolete transmitter. We – or, rather, I – believed it was a training exercise.'

'Very well.' Mikhailov eased back again, straightening his waistcoat. 'Just how far did you go in trying to decipher the message?'

'I . . . I know verification is not my job, Comrade General; but, as I said, the computer analysis indicated the transmitter to be very old and obsolete. Neither one of us had any experience of receiving such a signal before, although I came across something quite similar on a training exercise years ago.' Bulganin stole Petrov's opinion, hoping to convey his own efficiency. Suddenly he began to sweat again, hoping his sham would not be discovered; the general was not a man to mess with. Mikhailov raised an eyebrow and studied the major for a few moments.

'You have done well, comrade, to bring this to my attention so quickly. I will not forget your diligence in this, either.'

Bulganin gave a slight smile.

'You will, however, observe strict silence on the matter.'

'But of course, Comrade General.' The smile vanished; Bulganin's face was signifying a stern complicity with his master's statement. 'I have already instructed Captain Petrov on this very issue and reminded him of his duties.'

'And no copy of this report or computer readout exists?'

'None. Everything, including the computer interrogation data, was fed into Omega section the instant I realized the status of the Field Radio Signal. The primary memory banks of the main computer were wiped, and I have even incinerated the typewriter ribbon I used to compile my report.'

'Excellent.' Mikhailov arose and rounded his desk. 'I will not forget, Bulganin.' Much to the major's astonishment the general shook his hand.

Seconds later he was walking down the corridor away from the general's office. There was nothing he could do to keep from mumbling four words. 'He shook my hand.'

ARCHIVE DEPARTMENT, SECURITY SECTION, GRU HEADQUARTERS, MOSCOW

Mikhailov spent the afternoon in Omega section of GRU headquarters. It was a windowless room, scanned twice daily for bugging devices. The only authorized users were the present 1st Deputy Chief and the head of the 2nd Chief Directorate, the official and innocuous-sounding title of the GRU. To gain access Mikhailov had to place the palm of his right hand on an illuminated wall-panel set next to the access-door. It took the computerized security system five seconds to scan and permit access. Even then he still had to use a key, along with another key carried by the permanent GRU guard stationed outside the door.

Once alone inside the small room he had sixty seconds to engage the computer console and type in his personal code. Failing this, the computer would automatically shut down and the alarm systems would snap into action. He had only ever used the facility once before, on a matter of research and verification; owing to recent changes in policy only a small number of matters were now classified under Omega. The room contained a small computer terminal and console linked to the 'brain' sealed five floors below in the lower basement area of Kalininski Street. Mikhailov sat down on the swivel stool and began to type at the keyboard. The authorization signal flashed continually on the VDU. He had to pass five separate 'gates' before gaining entry. Finally he came down to the last two. He typed in just one word. 'Potemkin.'

The computer took exactly one second to respond once he punched the 'enter' button.

'7–5–9–2–3–1–4–6–8–0.' The numbers flashed up, burning a

clear green pattern across the screen. All he now had to do was punch in his response in the correct order.

'7–2–1–6–3–8.' He hit the 'enter' button again. Instantly the screen flashed up the heading title.

'Omega.'

He was in – into the most sensitive information-retrieval system in Soviet Military Intelligence; but, even so, there were limits on his viewing material. He took the papers from his pocket and typed in the code as it had been received at Moscow Centre. Omega would have already received the information and other data forwarded automatically by Bulganin earlier, but for security reasons it would be stored in a separate section. Nevertheless he still had to verify the area he wished to interrogate, and thus avert any possibility of a computer 'virus' being introduced or any outside interference with the information on store. Mikhailov could never have been prepared for what was to happen next. As he paused to light a cigarette the VDU began to flash. His mouth widened, almost dropping the cigarette.

OPUS 49 – FILE CLEANED – AUTHORIZATION: SORAYA

'What in hell's name is this!' gasped Mikhailov.

Someone had wiped all the information off the computer; there was absolutely no way of decoding the message apart from interrogating the main computer facility at Moscow Centre and taking pot luck as to the result.

OFFICERS' QUARTERS 5TH DEPARTMENT, GRU, MOSCOW
That evening

'He shook my hand, I'm telling you!' Bulganin slammed his glass down on to the table. The other five officers seated around him began to laugh again. Another GRU major, some fifteen years his junior, was next to speak.

'Come off it, Vassili! Mikhailov never shakes hands, he's a *General Govno*! He hasn't the emotion in his body even to smile!' A roar erupted in the corner of the officers' recreation-room set in the basement of the Department building.

'And what the hell would you know! You're a piss artist, Arkady! Not even wet behind the ears yet! I . . . I'm a . . .' The consumption of the alcohol was just about too much for Bulganin; he had been drinking heavily for three hours already. What had started as his private celebration of achieving what he felt was to be his final recognition had slowly developed into a drinking and boasting bout with his fellow GRU officers.

Laughter exploded anew as Bulganin reached over for his drink and failed to get the vodka to his lips, spilling everything down the front of his unbuttoned tunic and shirt.

Unobtrusively another young GRU officer sat alone in a far corner of the officers' rest-room busily reading a copy of *Pravda*. He never stared but he missed nothing. Lieutenant Viktor Romanov always kept himself aloof from his fellow-officers. He didn't much care for the solitude; but his masters did, and as the personal aide to the chief of the 2nd Chief Directorate, Colonel-General Grechko, he was not a popular type anyway. Naturally the other GRU officers distrusted him; in Romanov's position he could easily get access to any of their personal files, and there were those who believed he actually went a little further, offering his own opinion to the colonel-general about his comrades.

Bulganin struggled unsteadily to his feet and snatched one of the other officers' drinks from the table.

'I'm telling you all! He did! He did!' he blubbered. 'And! And I tell you more!' He was shouting now, his voice booming over the noise of the other drunken men. 'He said he wouldn't forget, either!'

Another roar of laughter broke out; some of the officers were almost doubled over, several hooting uncontrollably. One man across the table from Bulganin muttered something; instantly the burly major snarled across at the man.

'You'll see! You'll all see when Vassili Bulganin moves on to higher and better than the likes of you!'

The laughter and cries continued. No one was any longer paying attention to Bulganin, and it was just as well for their sake.

'How many of you bastards ever had an Omega signal? Eh?' continued Bulganin.

The copy of *Pravda* was moved aside now. Romanov watched the group carefully. They had been laughing and shouting amongst themselves so loudly that no one had heard the last statement; he was certain of that much.

Bulganin threw back the vodka; in one single motion he collapsed backwards, crashing into his chair and tumbling on to the floor. Romanov sat on as several of the other officers helped the semi-conscious Bulganin to his feet before dragging him off to his quarters. At least he could be sure that the drunk would not speak again that night.

LONDONDERRY
Easter Sunday

The main Easter Parade was on the nationalist west side of the city, split in half by the wide River Foyle, which also acted as the main dividing-line between the Protestant and Catholic sections of the city's war-weary community. The republican parade was held traditionally in the Bogside and Creggan areas, culminating in the gathering at the main republican plot in the city cemetery which overlooked the nationalist Bogside and Brandywell areas.

They say it all started on 7 December 1688 when thirteen of the city's apprentices locked the city gates in the face of the Catholic forces of James II. It was to mark the beginning of Ireland's most famous and painful siege. Everywhere throughout Ireland, England, Scotland, and Wales, all heads were turned towards Londonderry, for in its collapse or relief lay the future of Ireland. It was not until 28 July 1689 that the siege was lifted after reinforcements of the British Navy broke through the boom set across the River Foyle, which for so long had prevented the relief-ships from sailing upstream from Lough Foyle. Perhaps it was the level of deprivation that the city's population had to endure throughout that siege which left an indelible mark of hatred in the hearts of later generations, or it may be that the open conflict between Catholic and Protestant was fuelled by more recent circumstances. But, whatever the reason, Londonderry has since remained a barometer for trouble in Ulster and its divided community, a magnification of the continued distrust brought about by ignorance and by design. Unknown to all, another barometric reading was about to be taken.

Far on the adjacent east bank of the River Foyle, soldiers of the 1st Royal Anglian Regiment took up position in the nationalist Gobnascale area, the sole Catholic enclave on the east side of the city. The housing estate was a mixed area in the beginning, but like many beginnings the end-product was different. The estate had begun its metamorphosis almost before the mortar was dry. Slowly, but surely, through intimidation, violence, and pressure, the indigenous population evolved into what was widely known as a 'hard republican area' or, as graphically depicted by one loyalist politician, 'a scab on the Waterside landscape'.

The dangers of the area were heightened at times of nationalist celebration and remembrance. So it was that the local police chief had directed a detachment of soldiers to dominate the vantage-points in the hill-top housing estate, ensuring no disruption or demonstration on the main thoroughfares below, specifically the Craigavon Bridge and Spencer Road area.

The first six 'bricks' (the Army term given to four soldiers on foot) had taken up positions overlooking the bridge and Strabane Old Road at 1100 hours that morning. It was a long stretch for the soldiers, new to this unfamiliar area and many on their first 'tour' in Ulster. Although the regiment had served in the very same area only four years previously, the drop-out rate in the lower ranks meant that, apart from the NCOs, very few of the younger soldiers had ever experienced Ulster, let alone Londonderry. The main republican parade on the west bank was not due to commence until 1400 hours, but it had been determined essential that each of the four-man 'bricks' maintain maximum vantage over both the areas where they were situated and the arterial routes below well before the parade started.

The military operation that morning had worked like

23

clockwork. Each 'brick' had quickly settled into its predetermined position, making full use of all available cover and in turn covering each other. Upon the establishment of the observation-posts, the Gobnascale Estate, akin to other areas on the adjacent west bank, became saturated with additional foot and mobile patrols by soldiers from the battalion's support company. The observation posts could not operate independently and without fear of reprisal whilst the patrols of Support Company guarded their rear.

In the operations room at Ebrington Barracks on the east side of the Foyle, a young lieutenant watched the transmission from the 'Heli-Teli', on the television monitor hurriedly set up alongside video equipment at the end of the long operations room. The lieutenant, fresh from his platoon commander's battle course at Warminster, stared at the centre screen and began to study more closely the formation of the main republican parade which had already formed up and was now led by three flute bands and a colour party consisting of five young girls clad in black berets, sunglasses, and black dresses and carrying the various provincial flags of Ireland, not least the Irish tricolour. The hovering helicopter swayed in the strong wind blowing across the headland from Lough Swilly, only a few short miles on the other side of the border with Donegal. There was a brief shuddering of the image as the pilot gently manipulated the controls of the Gazelle helicopter to compensate for the changing wind-direction. Momentarily the picture went out of focus as the signals technician in the helicopter's rear compartment adjusted the zoom lens on the powerful camera.

The young second lieutenant was joined by a tall man in a grey tweed jacket. The silver-haired man, in his late forties, ignored the young officer and bent across the signalman seated in front of the television monitor mumbling something in his ear. It was out of the lieutenant's hearing, but he watched as the signaller began to speak into the microphone on his headset.

'The place is becoming increasingly crowded!' The young officer raised his voice above the background noise of the other signallers busy at their posts. The comment received no reply from the man with the silver hair, who continued to stoop over the signals corporal as he tried again to raise a response from the helicopter. The lieutenant moved closer and pointed a stiffened finger into the man's ribs, backing up the action in a raised voice. 'I say, would you care to tell me who you are and what your business is here?'

'Are you speaking to me?' The man spoke slowly and with a strong Belfast accent.

'I'm in charge here. Who are you?' demanded the officer firmly. 'I want to see some identification.' He clicked his fingers, emphasizing the point. It was a mistake.

'Piss off, sonny. Why, you're still wet behind the ears.' The man's voice displayed no anger; he was stating a fact. It served to add fuel to the younger man's fire.

Just at that moment a hand was placed on the officer's left shoulder. He glanced aside to see the regimental CO. The colonel guided him away from the television monitor, then once they were out of earshot he spoke.

'His name's McCormick and he's Special Branch.' The colonel spoke in a fatherly tone; he could see his young officer was livid. 'Detective Inspector McCormick has been here much longer than us, and he'll be here well after we're gone. In short we need him. I know you may not wish to cultivate his friendship, but we need to keep up a rapport. To be blunt, none of us can afford to cross the man. Do you understand?'

'Yes, sir, I understand.' The lieutenant forced a smile; it was hollow, but it was what the 'Old Man' expected of his YOs, and having been with the infantry regiment for just over seven months he didn't want to put a foot wrong.

'Good,' replied the colonel. 'Just keep out of his way and let him be. Remember, this sort of thing is his show, not ours.' He patted the lieutenant on the arm and left the ops room. The lieutenant reluctantly moved back towards the Ulster policeman. The detective spoke without turning round.

'Lieutenant? Just where the hell are your men at the cemetery located?'

'On the periphery of the cemetery, just over the walls.' The young officer swallowed his remaining pride.

'Over the walls? You mean, on the bloody outside?' snapped

McCormick, now turned to face him, an eyebrow raised in dismay.

'Yes. The local parish priest told us that any interference inside the cemetery would result in trouble at the parade.' He saw resentment in McCormick's eyes and qualified the statement. 'It was ratified by your local chief superintendent at Strand Road RUC station.'

McCormick's face broke into a smile for the first time. 'Trouble, you say! Look, son, there'll be trouble in any case. Just watch that bloody TV screen.' McCormick pointed towards the television and returned to watching the monitor.

The officer cleared his throat before continuing. 'If trouble does flare up, we should be able to direct our teams into the cemetery with pinpoint accuracy, by co-ordinating our actions using the surveillance apparatus you see before you. Actually we have three separate snatch squads just waiting for the word to move— '

'Snatch squads,' interrupted McCormick, turning his head around, 'are all very well, but when you've got women and children involved – and I would estimate about forty per cent of the parade to be just that – the question of rushing in does not arise.'

Before the lieutenant could reply the signals corporal broke into the conversation with urgency.

'Something's up, sir!'

Both men turned their attention again to the television screen. The parade had now entered the cemetery and stopped. The crowd was beginning to swarm into a circle. The corporal hurriedly switched the headset microphone on to the main speaker relay.

'Hello, Eagle 124. This is Zero. Over.'

A voice crackled into the speaker. 'Hello, Zero. This is Eagle 124. A lot of activity below us. Umbrellas being raised to obscure our view. I can see at least two men with masks. I am zooming in now. Over.'

Out on the ground, Support Company's commanding officer, Major Stevenson, directed his Land-Rover into the Strabane Old Road from the Gobnascale Estate. He was watching two youths standing at a nearby corner when he picked up the helicopter's radio transmission on the 'X-Ray' set.

'Hear that, chaps? The bastards are putting up a show!' the major addressed his men. 'Pull up, driver.'

The other three members of his Land-Rover patrol immediately jerked with interest. The driver pulled to a halt at a gap in the rows of mundane terraced houses fronting on to the Strabane Old Road. The two soldiers standing at the rear of the open Land-Rover alighted and took cover on opposite sides of the road. Stevenson fixed his attention on the helicopter now hovering a thousand feet above the city cemetery. From just across the Creggan Bridge two further and much larger birds soared into view and began to descend on the hovering Gazelle. The young major was now standing on the seat to get a better view.

'Look, it's the QRF.' The driver's face broke into a broad smile. 'That'll put the wind up them, sir. The bastards will probably think it's the SAS!'

Back in the ops room McCormick was engrossed as the TV image began to zoom in and three masked men dressed in olive-green combat-jackets gathered partly under a sea of umbrellas. An area of some fifteen feet was hurriedly cleared in front of them by the organizers, one of whom was clearly Seamus Maguire, who had been credited with a catalogue of terror. A fourth man, also masked, wearing a military-style jacket, appeared in the open area of the cemetery. The camera took in the three masked men coming to attention; the sophisticated boom microphone was already picking up their commands, which were shouted in Gaelic by the fourth individual.

Suddenly Maguire stepped forward and spoke into the ear of one of the masked men who immediately looked skywards at the Pumas thundering in from across the Creggan Heights, rotor blades beating incessantly as they began tightly to circle the cemetery just above the ceiling of the hovering Gazelle. On a further command the three men simultaneously produced hand-guns and moved position slightly. The crowd applauded.

'See that!' cried the young lieutenant.

'Yes,' replied McCormick in a droll fashion. 'And there's not a thing we can do about it, and those bastards down there know it!'

The camera shot included a number of journalists and photographers, all facilitated to the front row by the Sinn Fein organizers. As the cameras clicked and the flashbulbs exploded, the order was given and the three masked youths cocked and raised their pistols skywards at a forward angle. On a further command the guns cracked into life. The television picture shuddered and went out of focus.

'My God! I think they've hit the chopper!' cried the lieutenant.

The corporal pressed his 'send' button immediately. 'Hello, Eagle 124. This is Zero. Over.'

The reply came slowly. 'Hello, Zero. This is Eagle 124. Everything OK! Repeat OK! The pilot thought the gunshots were a bit too close and took us up a couple of hundred feet.' The observer was obviously flustered. 'Sorry about the picture. How are you receiving it now? Over.'

The lieutenant gave a visible sigh of relief just as the colonel rejoined them. The picture on the television screen had steadied, and the firing party had just concluded their third and final volley. They watched as the order was given for the gunmen to disperse to a loud ovation by the entire gathering. McCormick continued to stare at the monitor. Seamus Maguire had never taken his eye off the Gazelle the whole time.

'What's that man staring at!' snapped the lieutenant. 'It's as if he knows he's on camera. Who is he?'

'He's Seamus Maguire and of course he bloody well knows! Didn't he get the firing party to change position and fire higher than usual, right above the chopper!' McCormick snarled as he stood up and moved back from the bank of screens.

The young subaltern interrupted. 'If we get the go-ahead, we can try to move in once we have the lowdown on their direction of travel with the guns.'

McCormick smiled. 'You've a lot to learn, son.' He turned and walked out of the operations room, pulling the door shut behind him with a vengeance.

'He's quite right of course,' acknowledged the colonel. The subaltern's face reddened. The colonel patted him on the shoulder and addressed the signals operator. 'Corporal, tell the Pumas to withdraw and also pass that order to the snatch teams on the periphery of the cemetery.'

As they continued to stare at the monitors, the cluster of umbrellas began to develop into a sea blotting out all vision from overhead. After a few minutes the umbrellas went down. There was no trace of the gunmen. Seamus Maguire continued to stare into the camera's lens, smiling now. The procession slowly began to pick up momentum again and moved the final hundred yards to Derry's republican plot for the IRA's fallen heroes. A small wooden platform had been hurriedly erected beside the plot, and it was from there that Seamus Maguire began to address the rally through a battery-operated loud-hailer.

The colonel stood back from the television screen. 'Well, that's the show almost over for the day.'

'Yes, sir,' nodded the lieutenant. 'They've had their little show, and I imagine we'll now have it all over the Monday morning papers. Some publicity stunt.'

The colonel cradled his left elbow in the palm of his right hand as he crossed slowly to the far end of the ops room. He began to flex his outstretched left hand – a nervous action; something troubled him, but he could not decide whether it weighed on the side of Seamus Maguire or of Jimmy McCormick.

He had known little of the detective inspector except what he had been told by the local police superintendent. He knew McCormick had served over twelve years in the city, all of which was in Special Branch; he had quite a reputation for knowing just about everything there was to know. The IRA had tried to kill him twice in that time. There had been a bomb under his car when it was parked at his house in the Waterside area. The RUC had moved McCormick overnight, along with his wife and five children, into a new house in Limavady, but McCormick insisted on continuing to work in Londonderry. Then more recently the IRA had shot up his car when he went to meet a contact from the Bogside. McCormick had escaped with only a graze, but the contact's tortured body was later found dumped on the Letterkenny Road. That should have been enough to get him transferred to another county; but McCormick got results, so everyone turned a blind eye to sense and let him get on with the job. The colonel detested McCormick's manners but respected his advice, as did anyone with any wit. He stopped beside a police constable who was monitoring the Police Radio Network for the area.

'Constable, are you monitoring the Police Channel on the Waterside?'

'Yes, sir,' replied the constable, pointing to a wall map with his Biro. 'This area at Gobnascale was saturated as directed, and we have plenty of patrols monitoring the other possible flashpoints through the east side of the city.'

Just as he was about to elaborate, his radio console crackled. 'November Delta Zero from Zero 37.'

The policeman responded quickly: 'Zero 37. Send. Over.'

The radio crackled again. 'Roger, Zero. Sorry for the delay. We've just been stoned from the edge of Gobnascale Estate in Chapel Road. Can you ask our "friends" to give immediate back-up? Possibly forty to fifty youths, some of them masked, have just run back into "the Gob" across the waste ground.'

Before the policeman had responded his Army counterpart beside him was already issuing instructions to Support Company's CO, who quickly redirected his ground forces in the estate in an effort to cut off the mob. Major Stevenson knew exactly what to expect. He knew the dangers of indefinite static positions for both the police and the Army; this was a no-win situation. After a period of initial baiting, the gunman and petrol-bomber would step in. Now the baiting had begun, the only thing in their favour was the time of day. When night fell it would be a different matter entirely, but by then he would withdraw from the area and initiate a containment action.

The open-backed Land-Rovers spilled into the side-streets of the estate, on towards the flashpoint area. Stevenson's Land-Rover led the way and swept on to the waste ground after he caught sight of some of the youths in the back gardens of the houses on the rise above. On seeing the Land-Rover the youths immediately scattered between the houses and into the next street. The major relayed the information to the residue of his patrols now filtering through the estate towards him. It was the last command he gave. The Land-Rover was still in motion as the bullet crashed into his skull, driving directly between the eyes, exploding the cranium. The driver was instantly saturated in his CO's blood and tissue. In sheer panic he stalled the engine, and the vehicle shuddered to a halt on the waste ground.

The major's body had now slumped backwards in the seat, what remained of his face pointing skywards, his remaining eye motionless, mouth ajar, the back and one side of his head and neck missing. The two soldiers in the rear of the Land-Rover dived for cover and began to run from the vehicle towards the safety of some nearby derelict houses. The Army driver continued to sit there shaking, glued to his seat by shock, muscles locked rigid by fear.

The area was sealed within minutes, and the men of Support Company were on every street corner covering every road in and out of the area with one common wish: to get even. The Puma helicopters were still airborne and now swept in low from across the city, landing simultaneously in the playground of the nearby primary school. Each Puma unloaded its cargo of twelve men from the regiment's Quick Reaction Force. It took the police and the Army over thirty minutes to locate where the firing-point had been. The attic of the disused house was some 450 metres from the Land-Rover, which was now draped in olive-green groundsheets to shield Major Stevenson's body from the curious onlookers now packed tightly at the windows of the nearby houses. The police were now in charge of the murder scene, and a cordon had been established close to Chapel Road.

At the cordon, Jimmy McCormick was met by the local detective chief inspector from CID. Frank Murray was a small man and, although his bald head and wiry build gave the impression of the proverbial nine-stone weakling, he was physically fit for his fifty-nine years.

'Hello, Jimmy. One dead; their CO, a Major Stevenson,' Murray said grimly.

'I knew him,' nodded McCormick. 'What the hell happened?'

'Single shot from the attic window of a derelict on the rise. We just found the firing-point. Come on and we'll take a look together. They've found something very curious indeed. My men are already there,' replied the DCI. 'I'll fill you in on the details on the way.'

The attic was located in the end house of a derelict terrace block. The place was already swarming with soldiers, two with Labrador sniffer dogs on leads. Both policemen made their way inside the doorway and along the narrow litter-strewn hallway to the bottom of a steep wooden staircase. The place stank of damp and of years of abuse and neglect. Murray covered his nose with a handkerchief as he hurriedly ascended to the first floor. They were met by the colonel, who was standing with his adjutant directly under the open trap-door at the landing.

'Hello, gentlemen.' The colonel shone a torch up through the open attic trap-door. 'The sniper fired from up there.' At that a face appeared through the opening. A young detective constable peered out.

'Is that you, Chief? Come on, I'll give you a hand up.'

Once both policemen got up into the tiny attic roof-space and out of earshot of the soldiers, McCormick began to speak. 'Where's this empty casing, then?'

The young detective flashed his torch into the corner. At the junction of one of the roof-beams and a ceiling joist lay the shiny brass cartridge-case.

'I'll get it.' McCormick took the torch and went across the attic, careful to keep to the joists. He picked up the cartridge-casing on the end of his Biro and examined it.

'Unusual type. What do you think, Jimmy?' asked the chief inspector. 'Look at the markings. I wonder what it means.'

McCormick failed to answer. He was staring out of the open roof-light towards the waste ground and the stationary Land-Rover covered in the now flapping groundsheets as the wind began to pick up once again.

A short time later Murray and McCormick left the attic just as the scenes-of-crime officers arrived. Both detectives approached the Land-Rover as a police photographer was packing away his cameras and equipment. McCormick pulled back the first groundsheet and looked across the windscreen and over the front passenger-seat. He took in what remained of the white and bloody face of the major and carefully studied the fatal wound.

'Some mess,' the chief inspector commented. 'His head's almost blown clean off.'

'A hell of a shot,' replied McCormick as he let down the sheet again.

'I haven't seen anything like it in my life,' the other man responded.

'Right between the eyes,' continued McCormick as if ignoring the man's words. 'At five hundred yards. A hell of a shot, that was; but why only one shot? There were three others, at least, in this jeep, and they weren't going anywhere fast. It's not the way they operate. Why stop at only wasting one?' He replaced the groundsheet and turned towards Murray. 'He could have killed at least two more before they hit cover, and what about the driver? You said he apparently froze in his seat for some time after the shooting. That made him a sitting bloody duck for several minutes?'

The DCI looked around the scene. 'Maybe the sniper only had the one clear shot. Maybe the gun jammed or he was told only to fire the once to avoid a quick location of his position. Maybe he panicked. Maybe— '

He was cut short in mid-sentence.

'Maybe my arse!' McCormick snapped. 'Call a spade a spade, Frank! The boyo who took out the gallant major there took out a moving target at almost a third of a mile. Don't tell me he wasn't prepared, didn't think, panicked, or anything else! He did what he wanted to and no bloody more. The killer knew exactly what he was doing.'

The senior detective made no reply; his colleague was right.

McCormick continued: 'Where's the rest of the patrol?'

'Over at the ICP. Come on, and I'll show you,' replied Murray.

Both men began to walk slowly towards the incident control point, a group of three armoured personnel-carriers situated near by on the Strabane Old Road. They found all three soldiers sitting in the back of the second vehicle solemnly drinking coffee, but the driver was still in a state of shock, his mind still transfixed in another place. They quickly interviewed the assembled trio and then moved aside. McCormick began to speak.

'You know, Frank, the bastards tried to kill me on a number of occasions, and that never frightened me, but this shooting does.'

'Look, Jimmy, I want all the stops pulled out on this one. Get your boys on to it straight away while the trail's still warm. Use TCG – anything. If you need support to get what you need, I'll start making calls to Belfast.'

'Frank old son, I haven't seen you this excited since your last pay rise,' grinned McCormick.

'Let's say I'm just as worried about this one as you are. Pull out the stops. Get me a name.'

The post-mortem was carried out at Altnagelvin Hospital the following morning. McCormick arrived in time to meet the colonel coming out of the theatre door. There was a sorrowful look on the man's face as he forced a smile of recognition to the Special Branch officer.

'I had to identify him to the pathologist,' he said softly. 'Have you any leads?'

'Sorry, Colonel, nothing yet; but it's early days. We'll get them; you have my promise on that.' McCormick patted him on the shoulder. Already the Special Branch man was getting the wrong vibrations from the street; his sources all seemed to dry up at once. Try as he did, over the next weeks he faced an impenetrable and frustrating wall of silence.

GOVERNMENT COMMUNICATIONS HEADQUARTERS, CHELTENHAM
Monday, 27 April

The head of 'H' Division hurried to the departmental meeting in the main boardroom. As usual he was in a last-minute rush. He joined around a dozen of his peers from the other departmental sections for the 10 a.m. meeting. The group was already chattering away and drinking coffee when he arrived. Charlie Younger was followed closely into the boardroom by Antonia

Travis, the head of GCHQ's Operations and Requirements Department.

'Morning, Charlie.' Travis was in her usual relaxed and cheerful mood.

'Oh! Morning, Antonia. Didn't see you there.' Younger ran a hand through his long, tousled hair. 'Nearly closed the door in your face!'

'That's some file you've got there,' continued Travis, referring to the bundle of crumpled papers tucked under Younger's arm.

'You haven't heard the half of it,' replied Younger. 'Just wait until it's my turn to give in a report.' He raised both eyebrows.

Antonia Travis smiled. 'Something to look forward to and keep me awake!'

Charlie Younger watched her take the chair at the end of the boardroom table. She always wore her auburn hair in the same fashion, short and neat. Antonia Travis was strictly a creature of habit, always wearing the same style of immaculate clothing; a dark business-suit, usually navy, with the hemline never too far off the knee. It was a stark contrast to the casually dressed ensemble now seated around the conference-table. Standards of attire at GCHQ were never a point of issue; the staff found their own level, more than often casual clothing and jeans. Charlie Younger was no exception; his faded blue jeans were as much a part of him as his long dishevelled hair.

Whilst she undoubtedly possessed one of the best figures in GCHQ Cheltenham, Antonia Travis seemed to do her level best to hide the fact, concealing herself under drab uniform-style clothing offset only by her pretty face concealed behind a thick black-rimmed pair of spectacles reminiscent of the 1960s. With forty-two-year-old Travis it appeared that time had ground to a halt, and indeed she seemed relatively content with her spinster image. If she was having an affair with anything, it was with her work; with her, promotion was akin to a sexual climax.

Charlie Younger had long convinced himself that there was a sensuous and passionate woman beneath the façade ready to explode when the right button was touched. It was his fantasy.

Nothing sick or degenerate; he just believed that he understood her better than the rest, had a much deeper sympathy with the woman behind the bureaucrat image. He had to admit to a certain physical attraction; maybe it was the older woman syndrome – she was old enough to be his mother at a push. She was a woman in a man's world, doing a man's job better than any of her predecessors.

Antonia Travis was one of the favourite runners for the post of director when Sir Peter Churchman retired in two years' time. If she succeeded, she would be the first woman to hold the post, history would be made; but she had a lot of enemies in GCHQ, mainly jealous male colleagues who took exception to her professionalism and obvious ability. Charlie Younger was one of the few who liked her; he reckoned he could relate to her, she had a human side not many realized or wanted to realize. Perhaps it was the way she enforced her opinion, the authoritarian never too far beneath the surface of her pale make-up.

As Antonia Travis sat down at the head of the table her eyes met Younger's gaze. He flushed instantly. Did she recognize something? Maybe she actually guessed what he had been thinking! He looked away in embarrassment and began leafing through the files before him; then the meeting got quickly under way, and after a full hour Younger was finally asked to give his weekly review. He rambled through the usual weekly routine, highlighting the specific points he wanted to make, skimming over others. He left the most unusual piece of information to last.

'Part of "H" Division's job is general search and analysis of satellite traffic, and that leads me on to a report we got from the listening-post at Morwenstow. It was a message sent to GRU Communications Headquarters in Moscow, and sent from somewhere in Southern Ireland early this month.'

For once everyone was attentive. Younger opened the file in front of him.

'Our analysts say the transmission originated from an old type of Soviet transmitter using a VHF channel on 131 megahertz. It was a single-burst message lasting just over one second.'

'How do you know it's an old type of transmitter, Charlie?' queried Travis.

'The length of the burst, the weakness of the signal, and the airwaves used. It's very similar to something we came across before, back in 1975.'

'What was that?' continued Travis.

'We caught a Soviet agent with a "transceiver". It was an adapted Sony tape recorder on which the KGB agent could receive his information and prepare for transmission all sorts of lengthy reports. A "burst" of twelve seconds could easily contain up to fifteen minutes of information.'

'So this "burst"-type transceiver was used from somewhere in Southern Ireland. Can you be more precise?' asked Andrew Hogg. He was the head of 'J' Division with a responsibility for Special SIGINT (Signals Intelligence Section); he also had a profound dislike for Younger.

Charlie Younger shook his head. 'Now that we know it exists and also the wavelength of the broadcasts, I can tie in our other listening stations at Cricklade and London. Combined with Morwenstow we should be able to get a fix if we get another transmission.'

'What about the message? Can we crack the code?' Antonia Travis sat forward in her chair.

'The code is in a five-digit grouping. We haven't come across anything similar for several years. I honestly think we'll need to get a reverse transmission from Moscow or another transmission from the source before our IBM-10 can have a stab at it.' Younger was referring to the sophisticated IBM data-processing facility at Cheltenham.

'Of course we don't know for certain that this is a receiver as well as a transmitter, do we?' Travis was looking around the boardroom for input.

'Sounds like some student prank to me,' Andrew Hogg interjected. His animosity towards Younger was a well-established fact; an opportunity to embarrass Younger in public could not be missed. 'It also sounds like you're blowing this out of all proportion, Charlie.'

'Look! We don't know, and if we can't be sure we have a responsibility to investigate.'

'I don't know.' Hogg scratched his chin. 'We wouldn't be handling it your way in SIGINT.' He looked over at Ben Horwood from General SIGINT. The man nodded his head; they were closing ranks. Travis decided to intervene before things got nasty.

'All right, Charlie, just supposing this isn't some cheap hoax, and taking your concern on board, I suggest that to be on the safe side you liaise with both SIGINT divisions on this.' She looked directly at Hogg and Horwood. Both men agreed with reluctance; they knew better than to cross her.

Ten minutes later the meeting closed. Antonia Travis took Younger aside just as he was about to leave.

'Charlie, stay behind, will you?'

When the last person left she shut the door. 'This animosity between you and Hogg – when's it all going to stop?'

'Antonia, that idiot has been on my back for the last six months. How should I know?'

'I want it stopped. Shake hands. Bury the hatchet. I don't care what it takes but I want this thing ended. Now.' She raised her voice a fraction.

Younger nodded thoughtfully. Then she lightened her tone. 'Now, what about this Soviet FRS? Could it be similar to the hoax pulled by the Cambridge University graduates two years ago?'

'You mean the signals we picked up, supposedly from an alien spacecraft?' His face broke into a grin as he remembered what had nearly become a public embarrassment in the daily tabloids. Five science students had devised a wild scheme to embarrass everyone at GCHQ. It has all started as a prank on one of their friends who had graduated and had gone into GCHQ to train as a computer analyst. The idiot had inadvertently given his old friends the idea himself, and after they had got out of him some of the more obscure frequencies they began 'communicating' with the establishment, knowing that the information would end up on their chum's lap automatically. It did, so did MI5 and Special Branch, the end-result being a dressing-down by the University Vice-Chancellor and one job vacancy in the computer science section at GCHQ.

'Should we really be in such a hurry to discount the hoax theory?' she continued.

'Why not? That's what we're here for, isn't it?'

'It's something you shouldn't lose sight of, Charlie.' She could sense he was becoming annoyed.

'Antonia, I have a hunch on this one. It's big; I feel it in my bones.'

'Just don't forget you have other pending duties.' She picked up her case and smiled.

'Tell that to Hogg and Horwood!' he grinned back.

She shook her head and left. 'Charlie? Don't ever apply for the Diplomatic Corps, will you?' She was still smiling as she closed the door behind her.

RUC HEADQUARTERS, BELFAST
Friday, 8 May

Almost three weeks elapsed before the pathologist's report and the preliminary crime report both arrived on the desk of the Assistant Chief Constable for Crime at RUC headquarters in Belfast. Sam Nelson studied the documents closely. They were amongst a mass of papers placed on his desk that day, no different from any other reports except in one area; that Sam Nelson had a personal interest in the murder of Major A. J. Stevenson. He did not know the man, but he knew the circumstances; the *modus operandi* jumped at him from the page, especially after he had studied the pathologist's report for the second time. He pressed the desk-top intercom.

'Sally? Get me Doctor Garreth Russell at the Department of Pathology, and when I finish with his call have Stanley Davies from the Data Reference Centre standing by on the line.'

He clicked off the intercom and continued to study the preliminary crime report. It was signed by the detective chief inspector attached to Strand Road station in Londonderry. Experience told Sam Nelson he could rely on the man's judgement, but a sixth sense told him something else entirely. He glanced at the attached Special Branch report on the incident. It was scant, not the usual form for this sort of incident; the information was clearly not coming through from their usual sources. Why? He glanced down at the scrawled signature at the bottom of the page. If Jimmy McCormick wasn't getting the proper vibes, no one in the 'Maiden City' would. Before the thoughts could sting his memory further the telephone burst into life. He lifted the receiver hesitantly.

'Nelson,' he grunted.

'Hello, Sam, it's Garreth here. What can I do for you?'

'Look, sorry for bothering you. It's this report of yours on the Stevenson thing. Just one question.'

'Shoot.' There was a light sense of laughter in the tone. 'I don't mean that literally, old son. Sorry!'

Sam Nelson was becoming agitated; he wanted answers clarified, and his old friend's flippancy was testing his patience. Above all else Sam Nelson wanted to be proved wrong.

'Garreth, you mentioned the explosive impact of the bullet. Are you suggesting some sort of a "dumdum" effect?'

'Looks that way. It was the effect of a high-velocity bullet striking the target, in this case the poor soldier's head. Ordinarily when a bullet passes through a body three things happen. First of all a cavity occurs; and this will probably pulsate, thus damaging the surrounding tissue. Second, blood leaks into the tissue surrounding the wound canal; and, thirdly, a proper wound-cavity is created, much smaller than the first temporary one. The diameter of the canal will be larger at the beginning and smaller at the end, and all this is directly attributable to the sort of energy that is initially transferred to the surrounding tissue. In this instance the energy had nowhere to dissipate inside the skull, therefore the cranium exploded – in this case the head was almost blown to smithereens! If the penetration had been to another part of the body, ordinarily it would still have been what we term an "explosive wound", but possibly not fatal; but I might add that with a .30 cartridge the damage would have been phenomenal in any case. I can't be sure until the lab report comes back, but I'd make an educated guess and say this was no normal bullet; at minimum an extra charge was used.'

'So it could have been a "dumdum"?' Nelson stood up.

'Yep, quite sure. No metal fragments found in the tissue yet, but the damage speaks for itself. In fact I hear your forensic boys are scratching their heads over the cartridge-casing they found.'

Sam Nelson was taken unawares. This was new information.

'What about the cartridge?'

'It's got some sort of number on it apparently.'

'Look, thanks for all your help. I'll be in touch.' He quickly hung up and moved to the window. The telephone burred into life again. This time it was Inspector Stanley Davies from the Weapons and Explosives Research Centre at Sprucefield, Lisburn.

'Stanley, have you got the report on the Derry shooting on Easter Sunday?' Sam Nelson's heart raced.

'I have, sir. We've also got all the evidence from the scene. So far we've had no comparison with any of our existing records. I'm afraid the bullet disintegrated. We don't even have a fragment.'

'That's OK. I understand that,' responded the ACC. 'What about the cartridge-casing? What does it reveal?'

'We're checking that at the moment sir. It's probably been fired from a Garand, or that sort of weapon – a bit unusual on the streets of Ulster nowadays.'

'What makes you plump for a Garand rifle?' snapped Sam Nelson.

'The striation marks on the casing; they're caused by the ejector mechanism when the empty casing is released under propulsion by the energy of the gas— '

'All right! All right!' Sam Nelson was more than annoyed at the forensic lectures; he wanted facts not explanations. 'You said the bullet was destroyed. What about this number on the casing? Can you make any comparison with any cartridge-casings on record?'

'I'm sure we may, sir, but I really doubt if we have anything of this calibre. As I said, it's not the run-of-the-mill stuff. Frankly I've never seen anything like it before, especially this number that's been stamped on the brass cartridge-casing.'

Sam Nelson did not want to comment further on the telephone.

'Try 1971 and 1972. Your records go back that far, I assume?' The voice was that of a reprimand, and the inspector knew it.

'Oh, yes, sir. Yes, they do. We didn't exist as a department then, records were a bit haphazard – scattered, if you know what I mean – but we do have them somewhere here.' Davies looked despondently at the racks of files on the facing wall of his large office, then he thought momentarily of the piles of old papers locked away in the basement below. Suddenly he was regretful at having used the term 'a bit haphazard'.

'Well, get to work and research your files, Inspector!' Sam Nelson fought hard to control his temper. 'I want to know if a comparison exists and I want to know today! Do you understand?'

'Yes, sir! I'll get on to it right away. Good morning, sir.' Stanley Davies was unaware if his boss had picked up the latter half of his reply or any of it at all; the line was already dead.

That same afternoon

Stanley Davies was shown into the ACC's office at 3.10 that afternoon. He wore a worried look. With thirty-five years' service he could do without this hassle. For once he reckoned his wife was right and that he should retire after all. After the young secretary left the two men alone Sam Nelson was first to speak.

'Sit down there, Stanley, and take the weight off your feet.' He beckoned the grossly overweight inspector to a nearby armchair. 'Don't mind my abruptness this morning.'

Davies was visibly surprised. 'No, sir . . . That's all right . . . I understand.' He was embarrassed now. 'I got what you wanted. You were quite right. That's why I came over personally.' He handed over a sheet of graph paper depicting the information. 'It's a link chart. Your rifle from the Easter Sunday shooting is a Garand, a .30 M1 rifle. That is indisputable according to our people; and, as you can see, it has a hell of a history. Just how did you know?'

Sam Nelson failed to look up; his head was lowered and his eyes tightly shut. 'Eighteen incidents, eighteen murders, and all the same gunman, eh?'

The words took Davies by surprise. 'Well, we can hardly be sure of that, sir. You know these guns move about quite freely; there could have been a number of triggermen involved.'

'No!' interrupted Sam Nelson, his eyes flashing towards the inspector. 'One man! Only one man. The same MO each time: one shot, always to the head, always at a considerable distance, impossible distances, and he never missed. But always just one shot, except for the last job in 1972.'

'You sound as if you were there, sir?' enquired Davies.

'I was, Stanley, I was,' replied Nelson, closing his eyes again.

'So you know who he is, then?' retorted Davies excitedly.

'Knew!' Nelson smiled ironically. 'Past tense. The man I knew was killed in 1972 – at least, I thought he was until now. The circumstances of Easter Sunday were him to a T, and now it looks like nineteen murders. If I'm not mistaken, the number stamped on the cartridge-case is nineteen and it's in roman numerals, too. I'm right, aren't I?'

'Yes,' the inspector said slowly.

'It's him. It has to be!' Nelson pounded the desk with his fist.

'Well, it should be easy enough to check if he did die all those years ago. A funeral – there had to be a funeral. A post-mortem perhaps— '

Davies was cut short.

'He was shot! Supposedly killed by the Army during a street-battle in the Falls area. The body was slipped away during the ensuing riots, but we did have him lying on the pavement at one stage after the Paras shot him; then they were beaten back by a barrage of petrol-bombs and gunfire. When the soldiers regained control in the area he was gone without a trace.'

'Who was he, sir?'

'An American. The funny thing is his name was Garand, too!'

Antonia Travis was coming to the end of a tedious day. All she longed for now was a quick run home and a long hot bath. She had just taken another Paracodol tablet from the bottle she constantly kept in the top drawer of her office desk when there was a knock at the door. It was Charlie Younger, his eyes filled with an excitement she hadn't witnessed since watching her neighbour's three-year-old daughter opening Christmas presents.

'Have you got a minute, Antonia?'

'Do I have any choice?' She feigned a slight smile.

'You don't still have that headache, do you?'

'Does it show that much?'

'Nope!' he grinned. 'Your secretary told me on the way in.'

'Sit down, Charlie.' She sighed, rubbing a hand across her left temple. 'And, please, whatever it is, make it quick.'

'There it is.' He set down a sheet in front of her. 'Another message from Rip Van Winkle.' It was the code name given to the open file on the original Soviet Field Radio Signal received in April. Because of the obvious age of the equipment being used, Charlie Younger had decided on the code name after overhearing a joke by one of the monitoring operators who declared the sender had been in hibernation.

'Rip Van Winkle? Ah! The code name you've given to the old Soviet transmitter you were talking about. When was it? The end of March?'

'It was Good Friday actually.'

Antonia Travis opened the file and examined the latest short-burst transmission. She scanned the rows of numbers, comparing the configuration to the first.

570214	665290	071089
699523	291354	319447
109420	918830	782711
848106	096433	229884

'Can we crack it, Charlie?'

'It's already been in the IBM mainframe for a short time this morning. Nothing so far. But I'm booked in for four hours this evening. The comprehensive analysis of both messages gives us a better chance.'

'Overtime, Charlie?'

'Antonia, it's important, I know it is.' He frowned.

'I've witnessed your hunches before,' she smirked.

'I know I'm right. I feel it.'

'Need any help?' She examined his brief report.

'It wouldn't do any harm to see what Maryland says about this. They might well have something on their files that this can link up to.'

'I'll put it through tomorrow, but for now I'd rather keep it in-house if you don't mind.'

'That's OK, but there's just one thing. Andrew Hogg's raising a stink that I'm interfering in his work. I'm afraid I cut into his time on the mainframe this morning.'

'Not again! I thought I told you to smooth the waters with him.'

'How the hell can you smooth the waters with a forty-year-old hippie who takes his lunch in the men's room!'

'Aw! He isn't still doing that, is he?' She handed him back the file.

'Every day. He goes into the toilets and stands next to the washbasins and eats his sandwiches and watches himself in the mirror at the same time!'

'Has anyone tried to speak to him about it?'

'Sure, but look at him. *You* try speaking to him; he's like some hairy bull in a china shop! I'm telling you, Antonia, the man's sick.'

'Just think what the press would do if they ever got hold of that one!' She rubbed her temple; the pain was worsening.

'Look, I'll let you get home. You *are* going home, aren't you?'

'If you get out of my office, I just might.' She forced another smile.

Charlie Younger smiled back and went over to the door. 'By the way, I told Hogg and Horwood that you'd already authorized my overtime.'

'Get out, Charlie!' She slammed the desk drawer closed, immediately regretful at having done so as the noise echoed in her head.

TEWKESBURY
Four hours later

She was dozing in front of the television when the telephone on the table next to her armchair burred into life. Antonia Travis wearily turned down the sound with the remote control before lifting the telephone receiver.

'Hello?' she yawned.

'Antonia? It's Charlie here! I've got to come and see you.'

'See me?' She looked across at the wall clock. It was just after 11 p.m. 'Charlie, do you have any idea what time it is?'

'Look, I'm really sorry, Antonia. I wouldn't trouble you under any other circumstances, but I don't think this can wait.'

'It can't wait until tomorrow?' She sat up slightly.

'No. I'll only take up a few minutes. I can be at your place in less than twenty minutes. Please, Antonia?' There was a pleading tone in his voice.

'All right, but if you aren't here by half-past you can forget it. I was wanting an early night for once.'

The line went dead. Charlie Younger wasn't wasting a precious second. He knew better than to say any more on an open telephone line, but even the excitement of his voice could have been construed as a security breach by 'R' Section at GCHQ. It was not policy to discuss anything outside the confines of Cheltenham or a similar establishment. Everyone was only too aware of the ease with which electronic eavesdropping could obtain results.

Precisely on cue Charlie Younger pulled up on his Norton motorcycle just outside the stone cottage. Like many at GCHQ, he was a little eccentric but, after all, listening to the tedious Russian airwaves for endless boring hours was bound to put a strain on anyone. Younger pulled off his helmet and unzipped the top of his leather jacket as he walked up the short driveway. An elderly lady out walking her Jack Russell terrier gave him a disdainful glance as she hurried past, moving her cane over to her free hand just in case. Younger smiled at the woman as she went past. She ignored him, increasing her step. He could understand the woman's anxiety; he hardly appeared the pillar of the establishment in his faded jeans and black leather motorcycle-jacket, not forgetting the frizzed lengthy hairstyle and half-beard. Antonia Travis opened the door as he walked the final steps to the cottage.

'That was timely!' He smiled.

'The noise of that contraption of yours has probably awakened the dead!'

'Betsy you mean! Sorry, but my Jensen's in the garage getting the silver hubcaps replaced with gold ones!'

'Inside, and make it quick!' she ordered.

Younger went into the bright, pleasant lounge, sitting down beside the television.

'Coffee?' she asked drily.

'No, thanks, this is strictly business. I'll be out of your way inside a few minutes.' He set his helmet aside.

'Well, then, spit it out.' She flopped on to the sofa facing him.

'I've cracked it! Or at least part of it!'

'Go on.'

'Both transmissions are from someone calling himself Bloodstone.'

'Never heard the name before.'

'But you've heard of the recipient.' A smile on his face now.

'Have I?'

'Opus.'

'General Boris Kurakin, the head of the GRU!' She was excited now and sat up slightly.

'The *late* General Kurakin,' he corrected her.

'What about the messages?'

'I'm still working on them. Variable code-sequences – has to be for some sort of code-book or code-set that the sender has access to. No one could remember the variables.'

'So let me get this straight, Charlie. You have two messages

47

to date, both addressed to a man who's been dead for . . . how long?'

'Since 1972. I checked it with Research Division before leaving.'

'And this Bloodstone – we have no information on him?'

Younger shook his head.

'And what fix did you get on this second message?'

'Kent.' Younger handed over a sheet of paper containing the details.

'And the first signal was from Ireland. Right?' Antonia Travis scanned the paper.

'Yes,' Younger replied, unable to conceal his bewilderment.

'Well, Charlie, you're obviously here to decide the next step, so have you any bright ideas of your own? With these variable codes, it appears that even the IBM may not succeed.'

'We're going to have to involve Fort Meade,' he conceded.

'Charlie, what about all this being a hoax? I know we spoke about it before, but not at any great length. I don't want to involve the National Security Agency in a wild-goose chase; things are sensitive enough at the moment.'

Younger got out of his seat. It wasn't often he got annoyed about anything, but he was now. 'Look, I know we're on to something. It stinks! I've racked my brain trying to understand why the Russians are doing this; and, apart from this being a very unusual intelligence operation, there is only one other explanation.'

'What?' She was more than curious.

'Something's gone wrong. Perhaps a "sleeper" has been activated inadvertently. I don't know. All I know is it stinks.'

'Very well.' She nodded her agreement. 'I'll go and see Colonel Holbeck tomorrow.'

'Thank you.' There was an audible sigh. He pulled out a file from under his jacket and set it in her lap. 'There's just one more thing.'

'Charlie, please! My head!' Travis turned aside; the possible permutations of his blatant breach of security filled her mind.

'I need an authorization for our Moscow station to monitor specifically for these signals into the KGB's Lubyanka Communications Centre.'

'All right, it's authorized,' she agreed in frustration. 'Now, Charlie, leave me your papers and go on home!'

'Thanks.' He smiled and left immediately.

She watched the noisy old motorcycle disappear up the road before returning to the lounge and picking up the intelligence file. Perhaps she would stay up a while after all.

GOVERNMENT COMMUNICATIONS HEADQUARTERS, CHELTENHAM
Friday, 29 May

Antonia Travis did not often become excited about anything. She felt it undermined her authority and position. If nothing else, her male counterparts could never accuse her of being emotional or hot-headed. But she was excited now. Charlie Younger had done his homework as always, and she knew she could depend on his judgement; he had a habit of backing hunches at GCHQ and backing the right horse. She felt certain Younger could have made a fortune at a racetrack. Like the majority in his field at GCHQ, Younger had a university background; an MSc in electronics, taken at Cardiff University.

It was not a prerequisite for each applicant for GCHQ's hallowed sanctum to have a discipline in science; others such as Travis herself were gifted linguists, and amongst the other employees at the Government's listening station the variety of qualifications was almost endless. The discipline mattered little to the GCHQ selection board. What they looked for stretched far beyond the norm; they were recruiting not just intelligent and inquisitive minds but a form of 'responsible silence', an attitude towards security that would ensure continuity.

Travis dressed hurriedly that next morning, choosing a demure black skirt and grey silk blouse, finally easing into the matching black jacket as she flicked through the file on the breakfast-table. She knew there was only one avenue now, straight to the desk of her MI5 counterpart in Curzon Street. She arrived in the office just ahead of her normal time, placing the telephone call just after 9 a.m. using the rather sophisticated scrambler that had been nicknamed 'Fido' by using an acronym of its official and secret title. She rang the six-figure number; it was in fact an extension, all part of a complex communications network that linked no less than seventeen separate government establishments throughout Britain, including Whitehall and Downing Street. Naturally Travis was not privy to all the classified numbers, only to those she was entitled to, and that included Frazer Holbeck, the MI5 liaison officer for GCHQ.

'Holbeck.' The voice sounded hollow, a hint of electronic synthesization.

Travis moved closer to the desk-mounted two-way speaker attached to her telephone. It allowed her to work freely as she conversed; now it seemed like a bad idea – the voice sounded as if it was coming all the way from the moon. She turned the sound up.

'Frazer, this is Antonia Travis.'

'Antonia! My darling Antonia!' The voice was louder now; she realized the man at the other end was using a contraption similar to her own and had been standing away from the speaker initially. Now the voice blasted into her ears. She turned the sound down, wincing slightly. 'My dear girl, you have cheered me up on a rather dull and damp morning. How the devil are you? I haven't laid eyes on you in yonks!' She chuckled. Holbeck was just the same as always, a bit of a character and a renowned flirt, but everyone loved him; he had that sort of radiant character.

'Frazer, I haven't time to go gallivanting around London these days. I've given you the offer of some home cooking before, but you turned me down. Remember?'

A laugh. 'That's me told off. Now, how can I help you, my dear?'

'I need half an hour of your time – today if possible.'

'My, my. Now, let me see.' There was a short silence. 'I can fit you in around noon. How does that sound?'

'That's fine. I'll leave now.' She checked her watch.

'And perhaps a bite to eat afterwards?' The enquiring tone carried a hint of his Scottish accent.

'That's fine, too.'

'Good! Then it's settled. I'll see you at twelve. *Au revoir*!' And he was gone.

Travis switched off the machine. There was always a hint of theatrics about Holbeck; he was a rather larger-than-life character, not the normal sort of person that she associated with the intelligence services, yet she knew that to be where he was had to prove the existence of a darker and even sinister side of his character. She shook her head and began packing her attaché case.

DUBLIN
Fifty minutes later

The black Mercedes limousine travelled steadily at forty miles per hour along the broad thoroughfare through Phoenix Park. It was a brilliant morning, sunshine bursting through the tall trees shrouding the roadway in deep shadows. Michael Muldoon sat alone in the rear of the limousine, surrounded by an array of documents hurriedly prepared by his private secretary the previous evening. As always the window was wound down; Michael Muldoon liked his fresh air even if his two police bodyguards did not. He ran a hand gently through his thick white hair, pushing the waves round from his forehead and adjusting the gold-rimmed spectacles fully on to the bridge of his nose.

The fifteen-minute journey from his Dublin town house to the Irish cabinet rooms would give him the opportunity to catch up on the tedious agenda for the 10 a.m. meeting. He glanced at his watch before returning to the papers; it was almost 9.50. The two detectives from the Garda's Anti-Terrorist Squad sat silently in the front of the car, the driver maintaining a steady regulation pace as his colleague enjoyed the pleasant scenery. The Uzi sub-machine-gun nestling on his knees seemed almost redundant.

Suddenly blood splashed over the rear windscreen, almost obliterating the driver's mirrored view. The startled police driver jerked the steering-wheel, and the car lurched towards the opposite side of the road as he punched his right foot into the brake pedal. The other detective shot forward, uninhibited by a seat belt; his head smacked into the padded bodywork beside the front windscreen. Stunned, he was about to rebuke the driver when he read the horror on his face and turned towards the rear seat. Michael Muldoon, the revered Irish Justice Minister, lay sprawled across the light-tan leather-upholstery, his gold-rimmed spectacles angled obscurely to his face. The glass was missing from inside the left rim. His left eye had disappeared; in its place a black hole lay gaping to the bone. The powerful bullet had erupted the skull as it cut a path through the brain. Muldoon's features and gaping mouth only enhanced the aura of surprise emitted by his remaining glazed eye as it stared upwards.

Standard procedure directed the two policemen to speed out of the ambush area, but the urgency to escape the horror made the police driver flee the vehicle now lying at rest across the roadway. He stumbled out brandishing a Smith & Wesson .357 Magnum revolver. There was no visible target. Apart from the wind rustling through the trees and the distant rumble from a jet airliner high above the city, the silence was absolute, almost unearthly. No birds sang; there was only the constant rush of the wind through the trees. The policeman glanced at the side of the Mercedes; the reinforced glass panel in the nearside rear door had been turned down as always by the Minister for Justice. The assassin had known his routine and had used the open window to full advantage. The shot had obviously come from the left and probably slightly forward from their cruising position. He surveyed the empty parkland again from behind the revolver's sights. Far in the distance an old woman was walking her little dog along a small pathway, apparently oblivious to all the excitement. He called out to her; the old woman continued hobbling along, supported by a walking-stick.

'Probably deaf!' panted the policeman before joining his colleague who was already in the process of summoning assistance by way of the car's VHF radio set.

The old woman followed the pathway towards the children's playground and carpark. Once well out of sight, her hobble was replaced by sharper, quicker movements as she hurried towards the awaiting Renault car, its engine still running.

Lieutenant-General Alexei Mikhailov wasted no time in taking action. Following the original message coded to 'Opus 49' he had a special communications team set up to monitor the frequency that had been used. He had almost forgotten about it until the second message arrived. Now he had no option. He could no longer keep this to himself. His superior, Colonel-General Grechko, would have to be told. It was against his principles to tell Grechko too much, but this was now more than a puzzle; someone in the United Kingdom was communicating with them and using the highest-classification coding they held. What's more, the sender knew of the existence of an 'Omega' file, a file that was now wiped clean off the computer memory bank.

The sixty-four-year-old Ukrainian colonel-general and chief of the 2nd Chief Directorate sat behind his Louis XV walnut desk popping yet another pill and sipping mineral water. The old general's stomach ulcer was legendary throughout the Defence Ministry, but so were the guile and ingenuity that kept him at the top. Ever since the Soviet President had come to power he had insisted that the head of Soviet Military Intelligence accompany the Defence Minister to each Thursday meeting of the Politburo. Not everyone was sure why, but Grechko understood. He was there to counter any excessive behaviour by the present chairman of the KGB, General Grigory Glazkov, a man detested and distrusted by even his own organization.

Grechko did not really mind being 'pig in the middle', as the elderly Defence Minister and Chief of Staff, Marshal Malik, viewed it. Grechko rather saw the matter as being one of power and control. He was only too acutely aware of the KGB's attempts to veto the GRU and take control of it and whilst most of the time the two organizations worked much in tandem he understood just how important it was to be able to balance one off against the other.

Even though the Soviet President had gutted scores of senior army and air force officers since coming to power, using the case of Mathias Rust and the landing of his little aircraft in Red Square as the main excuse, he had always recognized the importance of the GRU acting as a stabilizer for the all-powerful secret police. Grechko was not content in his position, but content to know that while the present regime was in power Soviet Military Intelligence would remain autonomous although still answerable to the Defence Minister and Chief of the General Staff.

'Are you telling me that nothing exists in Omega, comrade?' Grechko eyed his junior carefully.

'Nothing. Not a scrap of information. Even the information fed into Omega this morning was automatically wiped,' replied Mikhailov.

'Impossible!' growled the senior general. 'And these messages? You can't decode them!'

'No, but I checked with the back-up facility. One of the computer controllers came up with the authority for the erasure of the information.'

'Who?'

'Your predecessor, Major-General Kurakin.'

'But he's been dead since 1972!' Grechko rubbed his portly stomach. It was starting to grumble again; he would have to feed himself on some bread or dried biscuits if the pain of the ulcer was to be stemmed. 'Alexei Vladimirovich, can you authenticate the transmission?' Grechko's eyes narrowed.

'Not at this time. But my instinct tells me that there is no deception.'

'You say that the initial interrogation of the main computer carried out by the cipher officer indicated that the transmission originated from somewhere inside the United Kingdom. You still believe that?'

'I had it checked again using personnel attached to Omega section. The result was still the same; our electronic analysis indicated the United Kingdom, possibly somewhere south of London.'

'Cheltenham! What about GCHQ involvement in this?' Grechko patted the desk-top, impatient for answers he was not to get.

'I cannot rule that out.'

'And, if not, we can in any case safely assume that the British have picked up the signal just as we have?'

'*Da*.' Mikhailov conceded the point.

'Incredible. A voice from the past!' Grechko rubbed his stomach again.

'Comrade Colonel-General, for the first time in my entire career I am lost for what action we should take next apart from waiting for a possible third transmission. Then perhaps our mainframe computer at Moscow Centre will be able to use comparative analysis with possible success.'

'You say the originator and terminator of the Omega file are defined as Kurakin?'

'*Da*.' He terminated the file on the twentieth of December 1972.'

Grechko stared at the papers on his desk. 'But it says here that General Boris Kurakin died following a seizure during a Politburo meeting on the eighteenth of December 1972; that was two days before the Omega file was removed according to what you found.'

Mikhailov was angry with himself at having failed to recognize the most obvious thing on the whole file. How could he have been so stupid? But it wasn't stupidity; it was exhaustion. He had been pounding his brain cells all night, only grabbing two hours' rest before the meeting with Grechko.

'I apologize, Comrade General. I can only beg your forgiveness for the oversight.'

'If you'd get some sleep and delegate a little more, comrade, you would soon be on top of the job!'

It was a rebuke, but not with any offence intended. Grechko was a kindly old man; a ruthless professional he might be, but to his fellow senior officers he appeared at least a humanitarian in part.

'Now, let us consider something else. Leonid Ilyich Vlasov was his deputy in 1972; he held the post until shortly after Kurakin's death. He and I jockeyed for this desk, and he retired when I beat him to the winning-post.' Grechko patted the desk, a legacy from his predecessor, like most of the other furnishings in the office suite. If little else, his predecessor had had taste. 'Vlasov lives in his dacha in Podolsk. He will know something about all this.' Grechko pressed a button on his desk-top intercom. 'Viktor, get me the address and telephone number of Lieutenant-General Leonid Ilyich Vlasov, retired; you will find it is listed in Personnel Section.'

'At once, Comrade General.'

Grechko turned again to Mikhailov. 'You will find it's only just over an hour by road.'

'I will leave this afternoon.'

Grechko stood and moved slowly over to the window overlooking the giant courtyard below. 'Alexei Vladimirovich, there is another matter upon which I must caution you.'

'Caution me?' Mikhailov straightened his pin-striped suit, a nervous reaction; his fastidiousness about his appearance was his only vice, and whilst he enjoyed revelling in the air of authority that surrounded his position his stylish clothing had become almost a camouflage for his own insecurity.

'You have a security problem,' Grechko continued. Mikhailov felt his heart skip a beat. 'I am told that a certain Major Bulganin was mouthing off about this affair to some of his comrades the day after he reported to your office, comrade.' He turned towards his second-in-command raising a hand as if understanding the rising panic he felt. 'I do not think that we have anything to worry about at this time. I have taken the wise precaution of arresting him along with the cipher officer – a Captain Petrov, I believe. It would be wise to have this comrade questioned closely about his breach of code.'

'Definitely.' Mikhailov's eyes narrowed. He kept visualizing the burly major; the dog would pay dearly for his foolishness.

'Alexei Vladimirovich, we cannot afford any leak of information; and, although we do not yet know how important these radio transmissions are, it is nevertheless Omega classification. So, apart from it being deemed important perhaps at one time many years ago, it would never do even now if our KGB counterparts got to hear of a classified leak at that level. To quote the English, who you yourself so often emulate, the KGB would score more than a few "Brownie points" if this was raised at a meeting of the Central Committee.'

'Bulganin will be interrogated. I will personally deal with him upon my return to Moscow.'

'I think you'll find the commandant at Noginsk Prison may be a little ahead of you in that respect, comrade.' Grechko was stern-faced.

A knock on the double doors was followed by Lieutenant Viktor Romanov's entrance. The young GRU officer, ever resplendent in his tailored uniform, handed Grechko a sheet of paper. 'The address you required, Comrade General.'

'Give it to Comrade Mikhailov and then patch me through to the dacha,' replied Grechko.

The young officer complied and hurriedly left for his desk outside.

'By the way, it was young Romanov there who discovered that Bulganin was violating regulations. He was in a drunken stupor and mouthing off to five other GRU comrades in the officers' quarters at Moscow Centre the night after he reported the first signal to you.'

'Then, we have much to thank him for,' mooted Mikhailov, although his feelings towards young Romanov ran contrary to his words. He did not like being shown up, and this young officer had made him look a fool. He would keep an eye on the young man in future.

Grechko lifted an envelope from his desk. 'This is a report from Romanov. The one saving factor, if there is one, is that apart from young Romanov none of the others present heard Bulganin mention Omega. You will find his report enlightening, I think.'

There was a smirk on Grechko's face. Without opening the envelope Mikhailov felt certain he had been the subject of some ridicule. Yes, Bulganin would suffer beyond his wildest nightmares.

The blue telephone burred once.

'That will be all, comrade. I shall tell the old buzzard to expect you at Podolsk later today.' Grechko's face was without emotion; an icy gaze followed Mikhailov to the door. As he left the room he overheard the colonel-general speaking on the telephone.

'Leonid Ilyich, my old and dearest friend! And how has life in the countryside been treating you?'

Mikhailov glanced back as he closed the door. Grechko's

wrinkled face was now illuminated by a broad smile. He was living up to his reputation of being all things to all men. He had more faces than an icosahedron.

Mikhailov walked back to his office and confronted his bodyguard and personal driver, a burly man with the features of an ape.

'Kapitsa, get me the GRU commandant at Noginsk Prison – immediately.'

MI5 HEADQUARTERS, CURZON STREET, LONDON

She arrived slightly early for the appointment but wasn't kept waiting; the secretary showed her into Holbeck's office immediately. She had only been in the office once before and that had been almost three years ago. Travis glanced around. It was strange just how the memory played tricks on one. She had always imagined the office to be much gloomier, she had remembered the mahogany wall-panelling to be oppressive, but there was a brightness about the place now; perhaps it was the bright yellow curtains at the high opaque window or a change of contract carpeting, or perhaps the last day had been even wetter than today? She cast aside the thought.

Frazer Holbeck was seated behind his desk watching the BBC national news on a portable television placed on a sidetable next to the window. He seemed hardly to notice her presence. She studied his profile. He was developing a third chin, and his shirt seemed to be more stretched than tightfitting; even his fat arms seemed to fill the sleeves to burstingpoint; his bright red-and-orange spotted braces clearly the most 'racy' thing about him. As always Holbeck was wearing one of his bow-ties, a yellow pattern, well set off by the crisp white shirt.

The sixty-year-old former Grenadier Guards officer would have passed for just another overweight City businessman or simply an overweight government bureaucrat filling in his remaining time until pension day. But there was nothing laid-back about Holbeck; he was one of the smartest brains that Five possessed and had an exemplary track record. Suddenly he seemed to catch her movement out of the corner of his eye and spun around in the swivel chair.

'Antonia!' He jumped up, shoving back the chair with his legs, and moved across to greet her. He was tall, well over six feet; the height seemed exaggerated with the extra poundage he now carried. 'My dear girl, how nice to see you again.' He touched her shoulder, kissing her obligingly on the cheek. She reciprocated. Kissing was a standard practice with Holbeck – everyone knew that; it was just pure affection with him. Perhaps that was one of the reasons he was so loved by all, so trusted. He was the only section head in Five to have been known to bring his PA a fresh flower for her desk each morning. It was a standard joke in Curzon Street that the day Frazer Holbeck failed to bring his secretary a flower was the day the ravens would leave the Tower of London.

'Please, sit down, my dear.' Holbeck pulled over a chair and set it in front of his desk.

'Thanks for seeing me so promptly.' She smiled.

'How could I refuse the most beautiful woman in GCHQ? Ann's bringing in some coffee, or perhaps you won't so close to lunch?'

'Coffee sounds fine to me. It was a tiring drive on the way here; I never realized the traffic could be so bad in the mornings.'

'Bad? It's always bad, my dear; and getting worse, I'd say. Now, tell me, how is good old Cheltenham? I hope the men aren't being too sexist?'

'I'm holding my own.' She smiled as the door opened and Holbeck's young personal assistant brought in a trayful of coffee and biscuits. She set it down on the desk and quietly disappeared again.

'Thank you, Ann,' he acknowledged just as she left the room. 'A fine girl that; she keeps me full of coffee and bikkies – one of my weaknesses, you know.' He looked down and shook his head as he examined his rounded and protruding stomach. 'I'm starting to feel like Falstaff! I was into amateur dramatics in a big way at Eton and Cambridge, you know.'

'That would not surprise me in the least, Frazer.'

He laughed. 'When did thou last see thy knees!' He patted his paunch affectionately and began to pour the coffee. 'Shall I be mum?'

She nodded, set her attaché case aside and eased back in the chair.

'I know this wonderful little fish restaurant in Covent Garden. I've taken the liberty of booking us a table for luncheon. Is that OK?' He smiled.

'Do you ever think of anything but your stomach?'

He handed her the coffee, staring down at her crossed legs. 'Not often.' He sighed.

'Flirt!' she admonished.

Holbeck sat down behind the desk. 'Actually it's my birthday today, and it's not every day I get the chance of taking a beautiful woman out to luncheon.'

'So, if I hadn't turned up, you would have dined alone?'

'Well, actually' – he lowered the tone of his voice – 'I had intended to ask Ann out there, so let's not say too much about it.'

'Happy birthday.' She sipped the hot coffee.

'Thank you, my dear.' A smug look on his face.

'Typical! How on earth can anyone take you seriously?'

'I have my serious side, too.' The eyebrows were raised now.

Antonia Travis set her cup and saucer back on to the tray. 'Can I be serious?' The worried look on her face announced the end of the humour. 'I want you to look at these.' She opened the case and handed over the partly decoded transcripts of the messages.

'Naturally I've seen the first.' He scanned the papers. 'The preliminary report on it with the intelligence evaluation passed through here just over a week ago.'

'I didn't know about any PR being forwarded to you!' Travis was surprised, though not completely – people at GCHQ were always jumping out of place and forgetting about line management – but the bigger problem was the danger of an incorrect evaluation, blowing it out of all proportion. It did nothing for the department's image and undoubtedly damaged its credibility.

'It was someone from your department, Antonia. Who was it now? I can't remember . . . Hold on a second.' He pressed the intercom switch. 'Ann? Be a sweetie and call up the blue file for the incoming report-sheets from GCHQ. I'm after a report on a Field Radio Signal; it came in just before last week.'

'I think I know the one.' The intercom was turned off.

'Now, what can you tell me about these?' He clapped his hands together.

'The location for the second signal has been pinned down to the Home Counties. Our scanners nearly missed the first transmission. It was from further west, north-west; but just as a precaution we looked out for a further transmission. It's from a short-burst capable transmitter.'

'The first signal you say came from the west? How far west?'

'Ireland, or perhaps a ship anchored in close to shore.'

'Ireland? Now, that *is* interesting! North or south?'

'Definitely south.'

'Go on.' Holbeck was hooked now.

'On the second occasion our scanners led Special Branch to a disused farm in Kent – of all places. The place was gone over with a fine-tooth comb, absolutely nothing found.'

'So the sender knows we have the ability to get a fix on him.' He looked at the reports. 'You reckon this is Soviet equipment being used, but could it be a prank, some sort of student mischief?'

'No.'

'Antonia, if I remember correctly, the file I was sent regarding this first Irish transmission contained an opinion that it was just a hoax.'

Travis was inwardly cursing. Could Charlie Younger have been so stupid as to send in a half-cocked report? There was a knock on the door. This time Ann carried in a blue-coloured folder and handed it to Holbeck. He signed a form clipped to the outer file-cover and handed it back to the PA who removed the coffee-tray as she left.

'Damned red tape,' he muttered as he broke the seal on the cover. 'These days you've got to sign for everything. I'm not being crude, Antonia, but it would surprise me none to have to sign for the loo paper around here in future.'

'Don't start me. I heard last night about one of our people who eats his lunch in the gents' toilet at GCHQ.'

'Andrew Hogg, Special SIGINT.'

'How did you know that?' she retorted.

'That?' He looked up and smiled. 'No, no, he's the one who filed the report. Here it is.' He passed across the file, and she read intently. It was plagiarism of the highest order. Hogg had picked Charlie Younger's brains and set it all down on paper, crediting it to himself. Of course he had gone off on a tangent, and the report meant very little, but it sounded good, it read well. 'Can't understand why you never saw this. There must be a copy at Cheltenham.'

Of course there is, thought Travis, buried obscurely in some file so as to avoid her attention. She would have Andrew Hogg's genitals on a plate for this. If there was any perception of her as a toothless tiger before now, the sceptics were in for a sharp reminder.

'If I told you Hogg was the one who ate his lunch in the toilets, would you understand?'

'I see.' Holbeck ended on a high note. 'Antonia, I get the feeling that this isn't why you've come all this way to see me.'

'One of our people, a young section head in my department called Charlie Younger, has come up with a partial breakdown of the code used in these transmissions. So far we've had very little except a few words.' She handed across a further sheet of paper.'

' "Bloodstone", "Fandango", "Exhibition". This is new to me, except for this "Fandango". That sounds familiar.'

'It should be, Frazer. It's the code name given to Major-General Boris Kurakin back in the late sixties and early seventies.'

'The deceased head of Soviet Military Intelligence. I remember him of course. Quite a character. Met him when he was over here in London once. Unlike any Russian I've ever met. He was quite class-conscious, you know, mad about antiques and flowers, too, if I recall. Boris Kurakin. Well, well.' Holbeck stood up. 'You think this is the real McCoy, don't you?' He frowned and re-examined the information before him.

'Yes, I do.'

'Antonia, I am perhaps something like Job's Comforter, but surely all this means is that someone has got hold of a Russian code-book and an old transmitter set.'

'We've thought about that. Charlie Younger doesn't think so. I'm inclined to believe him.'

'Who is this Younger chap anyway? Is he any good?'

'He's the youngest divisional head in GCHQ's history. A real whiz-kid in my books, and he has a knack of backing the right horse.'

'H'm. I wish I had.' Holbeck cleared his throat. 'The last time I was at the Cheltenham Gold Cup I lost a few hundred quid.' He shook his head, running a hand through the long strands of grey hair that had fallen across one eye. 'Look, what do you want me to do, Antonia?'

'I need access to the Main Computer Bank of the National Security Agency at Fort Meade.'

'The Cray-8!' Another bushy eyebrow was raised. 'The Americans are very loath to allow us any access to the NSA computer. Time costs money, as they say over there.'

'I don't want them to interrogate the computer for us. All I need is to see if their signals records can draw a match to these Field Radio Signals.'

'I see your point. It wouldn't be the first time the Americans have failed to let us have information; and, if this Kurakin thing was so important, they could well have kept it to themselves. I can hardly blame them with all the infiltration trouble we had in the sixties. All right, Antonia; it's a worthwhile try at least. I'll patch it through this afternoon. Now, let me take you to lunch.' He took back the file and gathered up all the papers, locking them in the office safe set against the wall behind him. 'You know, if it wasn't my birthday, I'd have scolded you for bringing these documents to me personally. What would have happened if, God forbid, you'd had an accident or something?' He was scolding her in the nicest sort of way. Security was his job, and he was right: she'd taken a chance bringing the papers out of GCHQ. Travis blushed.

What would Holbeck have said if he'd known that the papers had been in her house all night!

'Don't be hard on me or I'll not sing you "Happy Birthday".' She removed her black-rimmed spectacles. It was amazing how a beautiful face could be concealed behind such things. Frazer Holbeck was indeed going to enjoy his luncheon date.

After a rather extended meal stretching to just after three o'clock, Holbeck bade farewell to Travis just outside Covent Garden and watched as she walked off towards Bow Street. She really was quite beautiful, intelligent, and also available. It had taken every ounce of his courage not to ask her out again socially, and he knew she would have gone; that hurt even more. Yes, he was almost twenty years her senior; yes, he was a confirmed bachelor; but that didn't mean he could not enjoy a relationship, especially with a woman such as Antonia Travis. She had class; she was not the snobby hollow type of woman that Holbeck associated with the Army wives he had endured at the officers' mess during his days in the Guards. The woman had a natural elegance, a poise; he could really enjoy seeing much more of her. Of course he knew why she always kept herself aloof; but, then, it didn't pay to pry. He tutted to himself and walked off in the opposite direction. He had work to do. Ten minutes later Holbeck walked into the shopping arcade. He checked his wrist-watch; it was already almost three-thirty.

'My my, how time flies when one's having fun,' he mumbled to himself, attracting a peculiar look from a woman passerby as he entered the shop. The elderly female assistant in the flower shop was just a little taken back to see him come in.

'Colonel Holbeck! My goodness, I haven't seen you in the shop in the afternoon in all the time I've been here.'

'Now, Mrs B.' He raised a finger. 'Tut tut! You forget; on Mother's birthday last February I called in after lunch.'

She smiled. 'But I was off then, Colonel. Remember, I had that operation on the veins in my legs.' The elderly lady motioned to the thick surgical stockings, the swollen varicose veins still visible below the right knee. But, then, he already knew all that; Frazer Holbeck never made mistakes unless he wanted to.

'I'd like some roses, please, red and white, a mixture of around a dozen.'

'Oh, you are very thoughtful, Colonel. I just wish my sons were half as generous. They never give their old mum a thought any more.'

'Jimmy still working in Billingsgate Market?'

'Yes, he's only time for that old stall of his.' She began picking the flowers from the bucket in the window. 'And that bike of his. You know, he's motorbike mad, he is.'

'I can imagine, Mrs B, I can imagine. And what about William?'

She turned. Her face couldn't hide her worry. 'William's doing well; he's got promotion now, and him only in the Army these eighteen months. I got a letter last week; he tells me he's a lance-corporal now. But I'm awful worried for him.'

'How is that?' Holbeck's concern was quite convincing.

'His regiment's going to Northern Ireland next month.'

'I can understand your apprehension, Mrs B, but from what you've told me of William he's a sensible, level-headed young man. He's going far; Ireland should hold no fears for him. On the contrary, he'll come out of it with glowing colours.'

'Oh, I do hope so, Colonel, I do hope so. But look at that terrible thing in Dublin just this morning; it does nothing to calm you.'

'Indeed, Mrs B, indeed.' Holbeck nodded in agreement.

His concern seemed to calm the old woman. She went back to gathering up the very best she could find; nothing was too much trouble when Colonel Holbeck called. She turned to him after a few moments, her hands dripping and clutching an impressive bunch of red and white roses. 'Are these all right, sir?'

'Excellent. As usual you have impeccable taste, Mrs B.'

The woman reddened under the flattery from her favourite customer. Just as always he made her feel like she was someone; he always had time for that little extra word, and it clearly meant a great deal to the old woman.

'Mrs B, could I possibly presume and have the use of your phone while you wrap those for me?'

'Certainly, Colonel. You know where it is – just behind the

counter inside that doorway with those beads dangling across it.'

Holbeck smiled at the description and moved behind the counter as the woman proceeded to prepare the wrapping and a suitable ribbon and bow. He moved in behind the lines of threaded beads. He dialled the London number; it rang twice before the answering machine clicked in. There was no introduction, just a series of bleeps followed by a longer tone.

'Number five at seven tonight,' he said softly, before hanging up.

The afternoon was hectic for Frazer Holbeck. The difficulty he had faxing through the GCHQ information on the 'Gemini' file, as it was now code-named inside Five, was quite unbelievable. The direct computer link-up between Britain and NSA, Maryland, was always a busy communications channel. It was an almost daily occurrence for MI6, the FBI, or even the CIA to jump on the bandwagon and use the ultra-secure communications link for their own purposes.

'Sir, I'll have a window for your transmission in under five minutes,' a young girl called over to Holbeck from a computer terminal at the far end of the room.

'Excellent.' Holbeck scanned his report again. The 'Gemini' code name read easier than its official title 'RC 271940/92/PBX'. Anyway, the Americans preferred code names, or so it seemed to Holbeck; he put it down to their taste for adventure. All the information had been typed on to a special NSP form which was faxed straight to the NSA Computer Intelligence Section in Fort George G. Meade, Maryland. Holbeck cringed at the layout of the pink form; even after the uniformity of twenty years' service in the 1st Battalion Grenadier Guards he could never get used to standardized procedures. Filling in the blank areas on a questionnaire-styled form and having to answer twenty-eight sections fully, most of which were irrelevant anyway, seemed to stifle one's imagination.

'Can you imagine Wilfred Owen writing "Dulce et Decorum Est" on a postage stamp!'

The girl at the computer looked across with a bewildered expression on her face. He handed over the four-page report.

'The eccentric ramblings of a middle-aged man, but with the

best possible motive!' Holbeck smiled, raising his hand like a second-rate Shakespearian actor grasping for the remaining line. 'To save the English language from extinction.'

The girl blushed.

'Mock me if you will, my dear, but ten years from now these damned Europeans will have us away, the average Englishman will be coffee-coloured and Muhammadan! Just wait and see if I'm wrong!'

She laughed. 'Colonel Holbeck, you really are too much.'

He bowed and, taking her hand, kissed it gently. 'I will take that the only way I know how, my dear, as a compliment.'

'This will be transmitted immediately, if you allow me, sir!' She laughed again as he turned and walked towards the door.

'And the original – you will see that it goes back into the proper file, I presume?' A slight frown on his forehead.

'We always do, sir.' Holbeck winked at her before leaving. The girl was still laughing and turned towards her female supervisor, working at the other side of the computer room. 'He's so sweet, isn't he?'

The older woman looked up from her paperwork and nodded.

PODOLSK, NEAR MOSCOW
At the same moment

The journey had taken longer than expected.

Even using the central reserved lanes through the Moscow streets the city traffic had begun to build up by mid-afternoon. Mikhailov sat alone in the back of the black Zil sedan reading the personnel file of Lieutenant-General Vlasov, retired. It was an interesting file. The general's military life spanned from the 1930s when he had started his Army career as an eighteen-year-old artillery officer.

Like most files he knew that undoubtedly the best parts were not on paper, for reasons of security, but he could not fail to be impressed with some of the citations and awards the old man had received. He stared at the black and white photograph of the general; obviously taken some twenty years before, it showed a sixty-year-old face, a stern gaze from above ruddy cheeks and white thinning hair waving back from a receding hairline. The photograph had been taken only the year before Vlasov's retirement; it was the face of a healthy and determined officer with a path still to tread. This man was not contemplating an early retirement – he had another eight or ten years' service left – so why did he leave so hurriedly after his superior died, and what hadn't Grechko told him? The man had been the direct successor of Kurakin in 1972, and yet he claimed no knowledge of 'Opus 49'.

Mikhailov closed the file and set it back in his attaché case. He removed the other file he had quietly procured from Personnel. Opening the cover he stared down at another photograph: the face of Viktor Nikolayevich Grechko. He studied the file for about forty minutes. There was absolutely nothing to help him; parts of the personnel record had been replaced or removed; someone had doctored the record, and recently, judging by the quality and age of the paper. Finally he removed the envelope containing the report from Lieutenant Romanov and began to read about the loud-mouthed Bulganin and then Bulganin's original report. By the time he was finished there would be more than a typewriter ribbon incinerated.

The dacha was set in hundreds of acres of dense woodland surrounding a small lake near Podolsk. The main road to the place was the only access. To get there it was necessary to pass through a permanent KGB checkpoint at the interconnecting junction with the highway on the edge of the forest. There was nothing unusual about this arrangement: the service road connected into thirty private dachas, the private domain of a few of the Soviet élite, the Nomenklatura. Vlasov was only one of many in residence, some living as he did permanently by the lakeside, whereas others, not yet retired, still commuted on a weekend basis from their Moscow apartments. The uniformed KGB guards with their blue flashings patrolled the perimeter of the estate solely to keep the ordinary Soviet citizens from straying on to the private playground of the Nomenklatura.

Of course Mikhailov was under no illusions; this protective guard could readily be turned into a prison guard inside minutes. Even with his rank and position, he would have to take care in this place. The Zil sedan rolled off the highway bumping over the uneven camber at the junction and on towards the barrier just fifty metres beyond at the first line of fir trees. As is the norm with the GRU both passenger and driver were in plain clothes, but even before the car halted it was clear to the KGB guards from the number-plates and type of vehicle that it was government property. Kapitsa halted and rolled down his window, showing his GRU plastic-covered identity-card to a young KGB lieutenant. The officer took the card and examined it closely and then returned it to the driver before going to the back passenger-door. Mikhailov opened the window using the automatic switch set in the door panel. He held up his identity-card for the officer to view. The KGB man reached in to take it, and Mikhailov snatched it back, leaving the officer awkwardly bent over into the interior of the sedan.

'I am Lieutenant-General Mikhailov, 1st Deputy Chief of the 2nd Chief Directorate, and I am not in the habit of handing over GRU identification to anyone.' His voice was soft and controlled; it startled the young KGB officer.

'Comrade General!' The KGB lieutenant stood back and smartly saluted. 'I have orders to examine the identification of every comrade entering here. I apologize, but I must insist on personally examining your identity-card.' He looked down nervously at the GRU general.

'I see,' Mikhailov continued in his usual quiet tone. He nodded to Kapitsa.

'I will also need to know . . . ' the KGB lieutenant continued just as the Zil's engine roared up and it sped on through the checkpoint. The lieutenant was left open-mouthed, muttering the final words, 'where you are going to' – all to the amusement of the other soldiers beside the barrier. '*Pogannyi Pes!*' he snapped before returning to the white-painted wooden hut set beside the control-point. He toyed with the idea of informing his superiors but decided against it; he would be in trouble no matter what he said.

The gravel road was only wide enough for one vehicle. Every hundred metres or so a small area had been cleared beside the road to allow oncoming traffic to pull aside. The forest stretched for miles, although most of the dachas were situated in a small fifty-acre area bordering the lake. Towards the end, the road began to drop following the contours of the land; through the trees Mikhailov could just make out the lake's blue sparkling surface. The driver slowed the sedan, veering right at a small signpost indicating number 17. The driveway was slightly narrower than the service road; it continued on in a downhill fashion, winding through the trees and then widening out as it met a small wooden bridge spanning a narrow fast-flowing river which washed into the lake. The car bumped across the uneven timber surface of the narrow short bridge.

The dacha lay just ahead. It had a natural appearance, giving the impression of an old-style log cabin, yet the aesthetic quality had probably been more accidental than deliberate, saving the State the additional cost of cleaning and preparing the timber. The dacha was set in the centre of a two-acre green paddock; several geese ran across the gravel area at the front of the house as the Zil arced around beside the entrance-porch. Mikhailov waited for Kapitsa to alight first and open his door.

He stood admiring the dacha for several seconds. The house was built on stilts some five feet up from the ground surface, although beneath the shadows of the veranda he could see the stone wall of the basement recessed some ten feet from the open steps. The place had almost a Tyrolean air; the pitched roof ran from the veranda towards the rear of the dacha, the roof splaying out on both sides supported by timber beams running horizontally into the exterior lines of the house. The redwood-panelled walls served to highlight the white-painted windows and flower-boxes. Mikhailov could easily have obtained a dacha such as this for himself, but it was beneath him. What he wanted the State could not afford – yet. He was almost at the top step when the white panelled door opened. An old man in Soviet Army sergeant's tunic and trousers greeted him.

'Comrade General Mikhailov?' He brought his heels to attention, shoving out his chest like a cockerel. The general nodded. 'Comrade General Vlasov is awaiting you.' He opened the door further, stepping aside.

Mikhailov assessed the man to be in his sixties, well past

normal retirement age for someone of his rank. He paused inside in the wide hall while the Army sergeant with the shaven head shut the door. The entrance was bright and cheerful, and several Bukhara rugs hung around the walls. He noticed he was standing on a faded Chinese rug, more typical of the region of northern China with deeper and heavy colours. The place had charm.

'This way, Comrade General.' The sergeant bowed slightly and extended an arm towards the open doorway to the left. Mikhailov followed on into the main living-room. It was a large and ample room, although its size seemed diminished by the volume of furnishings and wall-coverings squeezed into it. An old man sat with his back partly turned, facing an open log fire. Mikhailov felt the heat hit his face the moment he entered the room. He waited as the sergeant crossed the large room and approached his master. From behind a winged library-chair a coloured rug shifted slightly and then was draped to either side of the chair. The sergeant mumbled something to the old man and then returned to Mikhailov.

'The general will see you now, comrade.' There was a detachment in the man's voice; he obviously had no fear of status or rank, but neither did Mikhailov gauge any contempt in the man's attitude. 'I will be in my own quarters at the rear if you should need me; the toggle bell beside the fireplace can be used to summon me.'

Mikhailov watched him leave before approaching the old man. Apart from anything else in the room, the one surprise he got was finding the mannequin positioned in a corner next to the fireplace, dressed in full general's uniform with gold braiding and epaulettes, and sporting four rows of no less than twenty-seven campaign and general service medals on the left breast with the Order of Lenin pinned directly above. The uniform was of an old pattern and faded, presumably worn by Vlasov during his latter service. It was clear to him that for the old man, as for many others in his position, the past was all that was left. The entire room was something of a personal museum, cluttered to the brim with memorabilia that stretched across four or five decades.

Even the coffee-table beside the old man's library-chair did not go unscathed; on it sat an old, faded, and split-edged photograph now safely encased in a gilt and glass frame. It seemed to mark the beginning of a fine career, a young artillery officer being decorated by Joseph Stalin. The proud eyes of the young officer clearly belonged to the old man, but now they were set into a cavernous bony face with withered skin, discoloured and stretched across the high cheekbones and sharp nose like a taut canvas tent. The old man stared up, his proud eyes reddened and strained owing to his refusal to wear spectacles.

'Comrade General Mikhailov, I presume?' The old man stared up at him. 'You will forgive an old man for not rising. My legs no longer respond.'

The words were sharp and clear. Mikhailov breathed a sigh of relief. No matter what the illness was that had crippled the man's body, nothing had impaired his brain.

'Thank you for seeing me, Comrade General.' He stressed the old man's title, hoping to solicit his confidence rather than demonstrate any respect. The only thing Mikhailov respected nowadays was his own intention to rise to power, as far and as quickly as could be accomplished. The cost was an irrelevance.

'Comrade General Grechko told me of your impending visit, but I hope that you are not here to bestow further false platitudes similar to those lavished on me by him!'

Mikhailov afforded himself a smile. 'I am nothing like General Grechko, comrade.'

'Good.' The old man tilted his head slightly as if curiously inspecting Mikhailov from another angle. 'Comrade, what is it that keeps me from my bed?'

'Can we speak outside?'

'Outside!' The old man's voice was querulous; then he seemed to understand and lowered his tone. 'Do you know it is beginning to rain?' Mikhailov nodded. 'And it is cold?' Another nod. Vlasov sighed. 'Help get me into that contraption.' He waved across to a folded wheelchair next to the mannequin. 'Ring for Popov.'

It was the first time Mikhailov had heard the man's name, but as he pulled the toggle bell beside the fireplace he remembered. In Vlasov's file a Popov was mentioned. The man had been Vlasov's valet and GRU bodyguard in the fifties and sixties; he had been decorated for saving the old general's life in Paris during 1968 when the 1st Deputy Chief of the GRU had been compromised by a certain section of MI6 during the defection operation of a British agent. Popov had clearly been allowed to remain in personal service with the old general after his retirement. The door opened, and Popov walked in; even at sixty-nine years of age and carrying extra poundage on his stomach and chest he walked as straight as a die, his back ramrod straight, his shoulders broad and muscular. He passed by Mikhailov as if he was not there and proceeded to extend the folded chair. Then, setting the wheelchair beside the library-chair, he carefully lifted the old general with apparent ease.

'It is raining, Comrade General.' He almost genuflected as he spoke to the old man.

'My hat, Yuri – and my mohair coat, I think.'

Popov left silently. Mikhailov was busy studying the row upon row of old photographs that covered all the walls of the room. There were shots of Vlasov taken throughout his life and in various places around the world. Several were obviously taken in London, another in New York; at least three had been in the presence of Nikita Khrushchev, one showing the two men playing a game of cards on the outer deck of a passenger-cruiser.

'Who won?' asked Mikhailov as he continued inspecting the photograph which seemed to be the centre of the photographic collection.

'I did, of course. Nikita was never very good at winning.'

'When was it taken?'

'On our way to New York, a delegation to the United nations. It was shortly before the Cuba impasse.'

Mikhailov turned, catching sight of the ivory chess set on a small table behind a long sofa. The chess pieces had been sculpted partly in the form of the imperial Russian cavalry and infantry with the Romanovs in full dress representing the King and Queen, while black depicted the German Kaiser and the imperial German army.

'Did Comrade Khrushchev play chess?'

'Not to my knowledge. At least, not with me.' There was an impatience in the old man's tone.

The conversation ceased upon Popov's return. He helped the old man into his black mohair coat and hat before wheeling him towards the door. Outside, at the side of the high veranda, a wooden ramp had been constructed running back and parallel to the side-wall. Popov carefully directed the chair down the five-foot incline and then stopped.

'Yuri, you return inside. The comrade general and I have business to attend to.'

Popov bowed briefly and returned up the ramp without question.

'Do you mind pushing me, comrade?'

'Of course not,' replied Mikhailov, looking around to see where they should go.

'Follow over to where that path leads off into the trees. It goes down to the lakeside; I go there sometimes to feed the ducks.'

Mikhailov began to push the chair across the uneven gravel and stony surface. Kapita was about to alight from the sedan and follow behind until Mikhailov waved him back.

'I see you have a bodyguard just as I do.'

So that was Popov's other purpose; apart from being servant, butler, and valet to the old man, he doubled as a minder. Mikhailov could readily understand why.

'A necessary precaution in these troubled days, comrade.'

'Popov has been with me since just after Stalingrad. We fought through the campaign together side by side. I can't say just how many times he saved my life!'

'I didn't realize he had been with you that long.'

'Popov? *Da*. He is a good man, as hard as nails; even now he could successfully arm-wrestle men twenty years his junior.'

'You are indeed fortunate to have such a bodyguard.'

'Popov is not just a bodyguard; he is my companion, my friend. He might only wear the uniform of an Army sergeant but he is much more. You know, he could have been an officer himself before the end of the war; he turned down the privilege more than three times, if I remember correctly. Even Beria wanted him for his secret police. The trouble he had staying with me is unmentionable.'

Mikhailov was getting more interested by the second. Here was a man who had personal knowledge of the dreaded Beria and who had met Stalin. He was almost regretful when the old man changed the subject to the purpose of his visit.

'But, comrade, you did not come to listen to me reminisce and you did not bring me out in the rain and away from listening walls for nothing.'

'No.' They were on the small path now half-way down towards the lake shore. Mikhailov cocked an ear. A peacock was calling out from somewhere near, the sound carried by the still waters. 'Do my ears deceive me?'

'You mean the peacock? No, one of my comrade neighbours has several; it is quite usual for them to call out to each other at this time of the evening. By the way, I must compliment you on insisting on us leaving the dacha; it is amazing just how an old man lets his security lapse.'

'When was the last time the dacha was swept for bugging devices?'

'Each week Popov arranges for one of the engineers from our organization to call, although it really is quite unnecessary. I discuss nothing with anyone nowadays, and whilst Popov is my confidant he does not possess the security clearance that would be necessary for me to do so.' He paused a moment, slightly breathless. 'Talking of clearances, what clearance-level do you hold, comrade?'

'I have Omega clearance, just as you, comrade; but, then, you will know that.'

The old man afforded himself the luxury of a smile. 'Of course, the 1st Deputy Chief of the 2nd Chief Directorate has always been privileged to such information. Tell me, comrade, is it still the same people who have Omega status?'

'Just Comrade Grechko and myself.'

'H'm. That is wise. In my day it was only one. It is a heavy burden on one individual.'

'Especially after one dies,' Mikhailov said slowly.

'Ah! So now we come to the purpose of your visit!' The old man chuckled. 'Now, tell me, what is so important that I have

75

to get wrapped up and be pushed along a bumpy path when I should be taking my tea?'

'Comrade Kurakin.'

'*Da. Da.* As you probably know, I was his deputy for over ten years.'

'I studied your personnel file on the journey here.'

The old general couldn't see the dark eyes of his visitor walking behind him. He knew himself to be at a disadvantage; if he saw Mikhailov's face, he could at least perhaps anticipate the questions. His mind raced. Was this an interrogation? Had someone had him set up, or was he going to be the scapegoat for something that had now gone wrong? These things happened. He had been an expert manipulator himself in his heyday, using the same tactics to full advantage; it was the only way to live at the top of the profession.

'My file? Now, did you find anything interesting, comrade?' he continued.

'It was more the lack of information that I found interesting.'

Vlasov laughed. 'Stop over there.' He pointed to a wooden bench set beside the gravel path just as it opened on to the lake shoreline and the gentle lapping water. A small open rowing-boat was moored against a flimsy-looking little pier, the oars sticking out over the gunwales.

'Popov likes to fish. The lake was restocked after the Minister for Mining took over a dacha on the south shore. Apparently his main hobby is fishing, so his friend, who is the Minister for Agriculture, had the lake restocked with salmon and trout several years ago – full-sized fish! Can you imagine the look on the faces of the people standing in the Moscow queues outside the empty shops if they got to hear of such a thing! No wonder we all need a KGB guard around this place. And now I'm told we have food riots in Kuybyshev.'

'*Da.* And Kirov!' Mikhailov sat down next to the wheelchair and removed a gold cigarette-case from his pocket, setting his attaché case beside him on the bench. 'We live in hard times, comrade.' He offered one of the Dunhill cigarettes to the old man.

'Comrade, if I took one of those English cigarettes it would be the end of me; my heart and lungs are almost at the end of the road anyhow.'

'Do you object if I . . . ?'

'Just blow the smoke in the opposite direction.' The old man grinned, showing his remaining yellowed teeth. 'The doctors had me stop smoking after my first heart-attack nine years ago, but even the smell of tobacco still attracts me. If it hadn't been for Popov's diligence, I would have continued smoking and been dead a long time ago.'

'Then, we both have much to thank Sergeant Popov for.'

'Have we?' The old man raised an eyebrow.

'What can you tell me about Opus 49?'

Even though it was in the back of his mind, Vlasov was not prepared for it, he couldn't hide being startled. 'Why?' he asked nervously.

'Boris Kurakin died on the eighteenth of December 1972. Two days after his death, using his authority, someone removed all record of the operation from our computers. There is no trace in the files any more and, as you said earlier, when you were Deputy only one person had Omega access, and that fell to you the moment Kurakin died. You removed all the information under the heading "Opus 49" and, furthermore, instead of using your own pass code you deliberately used Kurakin's. I need to know why.'

'You still have not told me why you need to know.'

'Two months ago Moscow Centre received a Field Radio Signal using a code related to the Opus 49 operation.'

'Origin?'

'The United Kingdom.'

'I find that impossible to believe! Everything, absolutely everything was terminated on that operation; all operatives and equipment were . . . eradicated.'

Mikhailov opened the attaché case and handed over Bulganin's report and the original encoded radio transmission. Vlasov leafed through the two pages, studying the comments carefully. 'So your people believe this to have been sent on perhaps the original transmitter?'

'Our electronic interrogation ability is now supposedly the

most sophisticated in existence; our computers can analyse and identify anything they receive.'

'Opus 49 was indeed terminated in 1972. I personally supervised the clean-up.'

'Why?'

Vlasov hesitated and glanced away towards the lake.

'I said, why?' There was an ominous threat in the words.

'I cannot see what good it will do you, Mikhailov. The operation never got off to a good start. I am quite sure that this radio transmission is just some sort of hoax.'

'Comrade, your opinion does not interest me, but your knowledge does. Now, you will answer my question. Why?' Mikhailov lit the cigarette but never took his eyes off the old man. Vlasov felt fear rise within himself for the first time since retiring.

'If necessary, we can continue our conversation at Noginsk Prison.'

'You wouldn't dare. You do not have the authority!' Vlasov's hands were shaking; he clasped them together on his knees.

'You know I do,' Mikhailov said softly.

Vlasov's will collapsed. He knew Mikhailov was right. He might have been able to forestall his 'visit' to the military prison, but the journey would be inevitable; friendship had its limitations.

'I knew nothing about it until I took over after Kurakin's seizure at the Politburo meeting. I got the message from the Defence Minister and reported directly to his office. I was to take charge of the GRU until it was decided who would be the next chief.'

'Go on.' Mikhailov removed a small Sony tape recorder from his coat and switched it on, setting it on the old man's lap.

'Is that absolutely necessary, comrade?'

'Here or somewhere less pleasant – it's up to you,' replied Mikhailov drily.

Vlasov gritted his teeth, regretful at not being a few years younger. He would have taught this man a painful lesson in manners.

'Well?'

'I assumed command, and part of my immediate responsibility was to oversee Omega-classified operations. Of course I knew Omega existed as a section of our intelligence bank, but I never expected anything like Opus 49.' He paused, his voice quavering slightly.

'What was Opus 49?' insisted Mikhailov.

'You mean you do not know?' The reality dawned on Vlasov. He continued uneasily. 'The destruction of NATO, the assassination of certain "targets", and the USSR being forced to take offensive military action in Europe.'

'Invasion?' Mikhailov's eyes widened. He hoped the tape recorder was getting all this.

'Ultimately and without warning the Soviet Union would have been forced to invade West Germany, and as . . .' The old man hesitated.

'As?' urged Mikhailov.

'As far as we could – the North Sea, the English Channel.'

'And how would this come about? Who sanctioned it?'

'I don't know the answer to the first part, but it seems Krushchev gave the idea to Kurakin inadvertently.'

'Did Chairman Khrushchev know about this?'

'No. At least, I don't think so.' Vlasov was choosing his words carefully, too carefully for Mikhailov's liking; he was hiding something.

'Did you discuss this discovery with anyone?'

'No!' He was excited now. Mikhailov had hit a sensitive chord. 'I couldn't. I was in charge. Just me! I had to destroy everything and abort the operation. Who in the Politburo would have believed I was uninvolved?'

'And who will believe you now, comrade?' Mikhailov stood up.

'I don't understand.' Vlasov's voice quivered again.

'Don't think this Opus 49 will go away, Comrade General. In matters such as these you are still answerable to the Politburo, especially now this has happened.'

'I knew nothing.' Vlasov glared up, his proud eyes fighting for survival.

'No, comrade, you knew something. A man such as you would have taken out insurance to safeguard an eventuality such as now.'

Vlasov's head flopped forward. He was beaten and he knew it.

'I want it,' continued Mikhailov.

'You already have it,' whispered Vlasov. 'In the Archive Section at your headquarters, Green Section, the inactive files, number KS 759161; it's an almost complete dossier on Opus 49.'

'Almost complete?' Mikhailov constrained himself from jumping with joy.

'As much as I could retrieve. The operation was almost two years old. Kurakin was an eccentric; much of the operation was contained in his head. He had strange tastes, too; fanatical about Chopin – that's clearly where he got the code name "Opus" from – and crazy about roses. He used the international horticultural conventions as a cover to travel worldwide; he even code-named the agents after roses.'

'And this file in Green Section – how can you be sure it is still there?' asked Mikhailov cautiously.

'It's there, General.' Vlasov was solemn. 'Will I be left alone now?'

'I will try my best, comrade.'

'Is it out of your hands?' Vlasov looked up despondently.

'Not yet.' Mikhailov lifted his tape recorder and switched it off. 'I'll return you to the house.'

'I think I'll stay here for a while.' Vlasov stared out across the water ignoring the farewell and fading footsteps of his unwelcome visitor. Was his insurance policy still valid? he wondered.

Three hours later

Popov left the dacha just after 9 p.m. General Vlasov was already asleep, exhausted after the afternoon meeting. The ex-soldier headed straight down the path towards the lake. Five metres from the small jetty the man stepped out from the shadows and stood directly in his path. Popov hesitated momentarily and then approached the man.

'What did they talk about?' asked the man in the brown raincoat.

'It's none of your business,' snapped the old soldier, his eyes fixed. 'Just give this to Comrade Rozhkov without delay.'

The man took the sealed envelope and left again, weaving through the trees and keeping away from the open shoreline. Popov carried on to the small rowing-boat and started preparing for an hour's fishing before dusk. Unknown to his invalid master, Popov had indeed succumbed to Beria's demands all those years ago. The old soldier had been a KGB informer for over four decades.

KGB HEADQUARTERS, MOSCOW
The same evening

Two hours later the man in the brown raincoat was getting out of a car inside the Lubyanka headquarters of the KGB. He went immediately to the second-floor office of Colonel Yosif Nikolayevich Rozhkov, head of Domestic Intelligence. The man reported directly to Rozhkov's assistant in an outer office. The woman assistant took the letter into the colonel's office. The KGB policeman stood watching through the partly open door as the diminutive Rozhkov got up from behind his desk and took the letter. He spoke to someone. It was then that the KGB policeman realized that the colonel was not alone; he was addressing someone on the other side of the room. The KGB man's eyes opened wide when he saw the other man come into view. The Soviet President's profile and mannerisms were unmistakable. The Soviet leader liked to keep his finger on the pulse; more than anyone in Moscow could imagine.

GRU HEADQUARTERS, MOSCOW
Midnight

Mikhailov threw down the faded green file marked 'KS 759161' with the word 'Inactive' overstamped across the cover in black lettering. Grechko looked up, his thick eyebrows flexed.

'Opus 49. It's all there in the file,' Mikhailov snapped.

'Vlasov wiped the computer, but kept it all on file! Why?' Grechko was puzzled.

'Insurance. He believed no one would believe his innocence, so to avoid charges of complicity arising at a later date he took precautions. He placed this file in our archive section. It was as safe as anywhere, right under our noses, yet there was no cross-reference anywhere in the system; it simply vanished amidst the sea of documents that we have stored away. It was brilliantly simple, Comrade General.' Mikhailov stood back; a smile crossed his pale features.

'Alexei Vladimirovich, you have succeeded beyond my wildest expectations. This is far more than I could ever have hoped for.' Grechko patted the file. 'Tell me about Opus 49.'

Mikhailov held the colonel-general's attention for over thirty minutes.

'So, this file we have here, it gives us a key to the codes?'

'*Da*. We are indeed fortunate that Vlasov was so meticulous.' Mikhailov handed across the decoded messages, attaching a short précis of both the killings in Londonderry and Dublin.

'This is preposterous! Someone is killing predetermined targets but passing on the information to us before carrying out their actions! Why? It makes no sense! This file here – does it state who the targets are supposed to be and why?'

'No, those details were all inside Kurakin's head; they died with him.'

'But why didn't Vlasov confide in someone? I was his fellow-officer; he could have depended upon me.' Grechko frowned.

'Vlasov imagined that after Kurakin's death at the Politburo meeting he would be the next chief of the 2nd Chief Directorate. He saw his promotion prospects dissolving in flames; no one would have believed that Kurakin had acted on his own.

The new chairman of the Central Committee had strong ideas of his own, and as a "new order" emerged in the Politburo Vlasov retired.'

'By a "new order", I assume you mean me?'

'Comrade General, I mean no offence. It was the way Vlasov perceived his situation.' Mikhailov was embarrassed; he had been so engrossed in relaying the historical events that he had forgotten the part played by Grechko. Mikhailov changed tack immediately. 'The question is now what we do about all of this.'

'It could still be some clever trap by the British or Americans to embarrass us at this time, especially with the food riots in our major cities. It could be devastating.' Grechko popped two more capsules and began crunching down on them.

'I have thought about nothing else, Comrade General, but I believe we have a responsibility to look into this,' urged Mikhailov.

'I do not agree.' Grechko pointed a chubby finger at the cassette recorder and green file on his desk. 'First, we get rid of that lot, and then we forget we've ever heard about Opus 49.'

'But . . . !' Mikhailov stopped as the door swung open. Romanov rushed in.

'Comrade Colonel-General! From the Communications Centre, extremely urgent, under Omega.'

Grechko snatched the envelope and jumped out of his chair. Romanov left immediately. By the time Grechko had scanned the pages contained in the inner envelope his face was ashen.

'What is it?'

'Another signal from this Opus contact!' He tossed it across to his 1st Deputy. 'Use the codes you've found and translate the signal.'

Mikhailov grabbed the green file and coded message and rushed into the adjoining office. It took him almost ten minutes before he returned. 'We have to take action now.' He handed the note pad to Grechko. The GRU chief reluctantly read the decoded message.

OPERATION NOW BACK ON SCHEDULE, EVERYTHING IN ORDER,
INTEND TO PROCEED AS PLANNED TO NEXT TARGET.
BLOODSTONE

'Now we have no choice,' Grechko replied, crumpling the
note pad in his burly hands.

NOGINSK MILITARY PRISON,
EASTERN OUTSKIRTS OF MOSCOW
Sunday, 31 May

It was early morning, and the sunlight had already begun to
dance its sad path around the damp grey walls of the tiny
basement cell. It surprised the cell's sole occupant that the light
managed to penetrate the two-inch-thick glass and wire of the
little high-level window encased in thick steel rods embedded
at four-inch intervals across the face of the tiny opening.

Sergei Petrov rubbed his weary eyes. He had long since
ignored the filth of his hands, just as he had become accus-
tomed to the stench of his tortured body. He sat huddled on
the barren wooden bed-frame, his only form of comfort and
warmth coming from the torn and rotten blanket they had
finally supplied after his repeated requests. He watched,
intrigued, as the sunlight cascaded gently into his abode of
several months, or was it longer? For the drugs and interrogations had long since deprived him of any sense of time. His
mind clicked over the images slowly. He tried again to remember the events since that day in the communications centre of
the GRU, but everything was cloudy now.

He, a trusted captain in the military intelligence organization,
a senior cipher officer of unswerving loyalty, had been accused
of treason. He rubbed his eyes again and stared at the light
pattern on the dank wall. What had he been thinking about?
His mind seemed numb. He could not understand if it was the
perpetual tiredness or the damp chill now entering into his
bones that slowed his mental process. Perhaps they had

destroyed his brain cells with the constant drugs, the electric shocks and the countless beatings which almost always resulted in his collapse into unconsciousness. Of course he had heard of these things before, he had even witnessed the similar treatment of others in his early Army days, but these others had been traitors. He was no traitor, but could he convince them? It seemed to Sergei Petrov that someone with a grudge had told lies about him; perhaps they had broken under torture and picked his name at random, for he knew that such things could easily happen. But for weeks now they had left him alone; that was almost worse than the pain, the waiting for what was to happen next and the faint hope of some official apology and release.

His thoughts were distracted by the sound of heavy feet outside the steel-lined door. He heard the guard fumbling with the keys before the door rattled, clunked, and swung open to reveal the bulky form of two military prison guards. Instantly his blanket was pulled from around him to reveal his withered and filthy form reduced by undernourishment and broken by the constant ill-treatment. He was dragged unceremoniously from the cell and made to stand barefoot in front of a further two guards. They were new; he hadn't seen them before. Both guards stared coldly at Petrov, now shivering more with fear than with cold, although his vest and trousers were in any case inadequate protection against the morning's chill air.

After the first two guards had completed relocking the cell door he was marched down the long arched and whitewashed corridor which ran the full length of the main prison-block. This day was different – he had already decided that – and his feeling was confirmed when he was marched left and upwards towards the prison courtyard rather than by the usual route to the offices of his resident inquisitors. The twenty-eight stone steps to the open gate and daylight seemed to take for ever. He had almost convinced himself that they had finally realized their mistake and he was going home when, at the top of the stair-case, he took in the sight of the firing squad. Eight soldiers lined up twelve paces from a stone wall.

It was a sick joke! Another form of mental torture! Petrov could not believe them to be serious. He was frog-marched into the small courtyard. An officer stood just ahead. As he passed by the officer he tried to stop, but was caught firmly from behind. Before he could utter a word a rifle-butt was thudded viciously into his kidneys. His already feeble legs gave way, and the guards began to drag him. Surprisingly he could no longer find the energy to shout or scream; the injection they had given him the previous night was still affecting him. Who had betrayed him? Sergei Petrov had long convinced himself that the coarse, ignorant Major Bulganin from the GRU communications centre was behind it. Had not the man turned on him the day before his arrest?

As he neared the line of the firing squad, he was dragged past the open coffins. There were two of them, one already full, another empty. Out of curiosity his eyes fixed on the empty coffin, the place where he would spend eternity. It was only fleetingly that he caught the pale twisted features of the other coffin's occupant. It was Bulganin! The man he had constantly blamed and cursed for his incarceration. His eyes never left the two rough wood coffins, even as they handcuffed him to the vertical wooden post set in its concrete bed only inches from the pitted wall-face.

There was no formal reading of a charge, no death-sentence proclamation, no last cigarette, and it was on that final irrelevant thought that Sergei Petrov closed his eyes and tried to shut his ears to the army officer's orders and the crashing of the rifle-breeches as eight AK47 assault-rifles were loaded and directed to bear on his grubby vest. Suddenly he felt his body shoved back into the wooden post then rising slightly upwards. No sensation except that sudden force. He opened his eyes momentarily; his head had already slumped forward incontrollably. He could see his vest now, a hanging mass of red, tissue and entrails protruding through the torn garment, but still no feeling of pain. The brain had already begun to cease functioning; his eyes now began quickly to glaze over. Sergei Petrov was already a memory.

LONDONDERRY
Wednesday, 3 June, three days later

The side-door of the green transit van rolled back, and the man jumped out, snapping it shut before walking across the parking-area at the back of the houses. Another car was parked just over a hundred yards away, close to the main road; the driver, a young woman, lit a cigarette. It was the 'all clear' signal. McCormick walked on, approaching the maisonette from the rear. The area was run-down and dilapidated; the rows of narrow gardens segmented by a cluster of overgrown hedges, high wooden fencing and broken concrete-block walls. McCormick brushed against the whitewashed wall just as he entered the kitchen; he cursed, dusting the marks off his jacket as he went through into the lounge. It was a grubby place, smelling of sour milk and the stench of uncleanliness associated normally with farmyard animals. McCormick raised a handkerchief to his nose, more to block out the smell momentarily than to help his cold.

A man stood at the far side of the room, next to the patched-up sofa; he was watching the street outside through the discoloured net curtains.

'Who picked this place?' snapped McCormick, his voice a little muffled by the handkerchief.

The man, in his early twenties, turned towards him, a surprised look on his face. 'You did, Boss.'

'Me?' McCormick mumbled something to himself. Then he addressed the younger man again. 'Where is he?'

'Upstairs. He felt sick.'

'Sick! I'll be sick if I don't get outa here! Get him down.'

The man disappeared. McCormick examined the room with the torn wallpaper and wrinkled carpet which was faded and frayed. Judging by the feeble attempt made at laying the carpet, this room hadn't been its first home. McCormick thought about the absentee owners who had cleared out a week before, just one step ahead of the rent man, the debt-collectors, and the law. He hated using such places for his 'meets' as he called them, but it was a good choice for a 'one-off'; nothing would be traced back to Special Branch if something went wrong. Inside another ten minutes the house would be empty again, the vacant property of the Northern Ireland Housing Executive.

The creaking staircase alerted him; then moments later the door opened, the man walked in just ahead of the other policeman. He was in his early thirties, balding with a ruddy complexion and a boozer's stomach which protruded so far that it entirely obliterated the waistband of his blue jeans. He was wearing a black anorak which seemed two sizes too small for his stocky six-foot frame. He nervously looked around the room as he rubbed the stubble on his chin. McCormick could see that he was sweating and very frightened.

'I'd trouble getting here.' The man opened up the conversation with a dry voice.

McCormick recognized and understood the tout's fear; he played on it a little. 'What have you got?'

The fat man moved to the centre of the floor, wiping his sweaty brow with the back of his sleeve. 'I said I'd trouble getting here. I think . . . I *know* they suspect something.'

McCormick turned from the window and eyed the man carefully. 'I didn't get you here to discuss your horoscope.'

The man began to shake, turning towards the fireplace and gripping it with both hands. McCormick motioned for the other policeman to go into the rear kitchen.

'Jesus! God help us! What am I going to do?' the man cried, trying to blot out all the nasty things that were entering his mind, and what might be awaiting him upon his return across the river to the Bogside.

'You're imagining things. Just what makes you think that they know?'

The man dropped his head as if trying to gain some inner strength. 'There was a meeting last night. I was excluded. I didn't find out about it until this morning.'

'So?' replied McCormick.

The man spun from the fireplace; tears filled his raging eyes. 'So this morning when I got up they were watching me! I went to the shop for the paper and some milk after I dropped the kids off to school. They were there!'

'Who was watching you?' McCormick's deadpan expression gave away nothing.

'Some guys; they've been brought in, maybe from Strabane, and there's others from the area.'

'Names?'

'I didn't fucking hang about to ask them, did I?'

McCormick sat down on one of the sofa arms. 'Sounds to me like your imagination, son.'

'One of the ones watching me was my own brother-in-law!'

'There you have it; it *is* your imagination,' McCormick replied coolly. 'Don't you think I'd have heard if something was going down?'

'Oh ay! You've got ears all right, but I know what I saw!'

'You know what I think? I think you've been on the booze again.'

'I was told! All right?' cried the man.

'Now, that is more interesting,' McCormick said drolly. 'Who told you?'

'The brother-in-law.'

'But a second ago you said he was one of the ones watching you.'

McCormick pulled out a cigarette. The man looked as if he could do with one himself, but there was no hope of him being offered one by McCormick.

'He had to make it look good, didn't he?' The man glared at the policeman.

'Well, then,' continued McCormick, 'how did you shake off your tail?'

'When I left the corner shop I saw them watching, then I knew the brother-in-law was serious when he rang up last night and told me.'

'Go on.'

'They'd no reason to be there; they'd no business in the area. I knew what they were up to. I've done the same myself in the past.' The frightened man took a deep breath and went back beside the fireplace. 'I headed for the Brandywell, as if I was going to the mate's house. I passed a Brit foot patrol. I was so feared I nearly asked them to take me in then and there. It was then I struck lucky. The Brits stopped the bastards tailing me.' He turned, a smile on his face. 'They fucking "P" checked them there on the pavement. It gave me an opener to get away.'

'To run away, you mean?'

The man became angry again. 'I didn't run. I laid low for a while, that's all.'

'Where?'

'In Chapel.'

'Well, you're here now, so get on with it.' McCormick blew some smoke into the air, coughing a little as the cigarette began to irritate his lungs. 'What's the story behind the Easter Sunday shoot? You said you had something for me.'

The man hesitated.

'Well?'

'It was a funny one,' he said in a subdued tone.

'Not so funny for the boyo who got wasted,' replied McCormick.

'Look, I don't mean that,' retorted the man, clearly eager to please now. 'It was from the top. No one knew about it in advance. Normally I'd have supplied the weapon, but not in this case. Even the Gobnascale boys weren't included in it.'

'There was a bit of stone-throwing by some kids just before the shooting.'

'There's always stone-throwing in the "Gob". Sure they were told to, but that's all.'

'Who gave the order?' It was clear that the stone-throwing had been used as a ruse to attract the soldiers on to the waste ground. Whoever had given the orders to the youths knew what would happen.

'Big Seamus.' The man referred to Seamus Maguire, the commandant of the Provisionals' Derry Brigade.

'But he was across the river in the cemetery at the time of the killing.'

'But he was in Gobnascale that morning.' The man wiped a bead of sweat from his cheek.

'OK. So the gun was brought in from outside. What can you tell me about the triggerman?' McCormick coughed again. He threw the unfinished cigarette into the open hearth.

'Rumour has it someone came up from Dublin.' The man spoke hurriedly.

'Dublin?' McCormick tried not to look surprised. 'Any name?'

'I heard Maguire mention the name Liam. Nothing else.'

'When?'

'A phone call from Dublin. He referred to the caller as Liam.'

McCormick's left eyebrow rose, indicating his disbelief.

'Look, it's the only Dublin connection Maguire's had for over three months. It's all I know.'

'There appears to be a lot you don't know, or maybe you're just not saying.' McCormick was now standing, hands thrust deep into his coat pockets.

'The day after, on the Monday, I was out drinking. I over-heard something. Maguire was doing the mouthing. Normally he doesn't say much, but he seemed to be celebrating; he'd been drinking steady for a few hours.'

'Get to the point, will you!' snapped McCormick.

'He said something about the shooting being a sorta test.'

McCormick looked outside towards the street. 'Right, here's what we'll do. I want you to go back home.'

'Fuck off!' cried the man. The other policeman re-emerged from the kitchen; McCormick gestured for him to back off. 'I'm a dead man if I go back there.' He moved forward, a clenched fist raised in defiance. McCormick removed his right hand from his coat pocket; he was holding a Walther PPK 9 mm pistol.

'What's going on?' shouted the man. He watched as the policeman pointed the gun at his head, clicking off the safety catch as he took aim. The man backed off against the fireplace, almost losing his footing as he stumbled against the hearth.

'I don't give a toss what you think,' replied McCormick. 'You either do as I tell you or you'll not even get a chance to face your mates.'

'I can't go back,' pleaded the man.

'Listen to me. I want you to leave here now and go straight home. It should take about forty minutes on foot. When you get to the house go upstairs and stay in the bedroom. Shortly afterwards your home is going to be raided and then you're going to be nicked under Section 11, understood?'

'No, I fucking don't!' cried the man, despite his fear of the gun still pointed at him. 'I'm a dead man if I go back. Why can't you take me into protective custody right here and now?'

McCormick dropped his aim, but still held the gun at his side. 'Because you're good for another while yet. I want to know more about Maguire's part in this Easter Sunday business, and you're the boyo to find out.'

'But I told you they're on to me!' He was evidently close to tears.

'Look, when you're inside, banged up for seven days, I'll create a little diversion for Maguire and his pals. By the time you come out they'll be off galloping down the wrong bloody track and you'll be no longer under any suspicion.'

'How?' asked the man incredulously. McCormick cocked his head to one side. The tout should have known better than to ask him. 'You sure this'll work?'

'We've got too much money invested in you for it not to work. Don't worry, you'll come out of this and maybe a little richer, too, if you come up with the goods.' McCormick placed his left arm around the man's shoulder as he pocketed his gun again and then led him towards the front door. He took out a twenty-pound note and stuck it into the man's jacket pocket. 'There, buy yourself some sweeties on the way home. I'll be seeing you later once you're scooped.'

The man didn't answer as he was let out of the front door. He stood on the step wondering. He was just about to turn to McCormick when he heard the door shut. He was alone again.

The younger policeman came into the lounge again. 'He's running scared.'

'So would I be if I was in his shoes,' replied McCormick as he lit up another cigarette. 'Let's get out of this shit-hole.'

The two policemen left the house and returned to the transit van where McCormick met another of his men.

'He's on his way home. Have you alerted TCG?'

'Everything's ready. An Army team's been standing by for the last two hours at Fort George. The surveillance teams will give them the nod when it's time to move in.'

'All right, but I want the Army arrest-team mobile and closer to the area. I don't want any fuck-ups. These bastards mean business.'

'Right, Boss,' replied the other man as he began to relay instructions back by radio.

But, unknown to any of them, the IRA had been hijacking vehicles all afternoon inside the Bogside and Brandywell. The tout passed across the bridge into the west side of the city and back into the Bogside on schedule. Just after he entered the area the first hijacked vehicles were left on the flyover next to the nationalist area. The Special Branch surveillance operation was completely disrupted. Inside five minutes eight suspect vehicles had been left on every route into the Bogside and Brandywell areas.

Unaware, the tout turned the corner into his street, empty except for three small children playing next to the old gas-works perimeter wall. He went in by the front door. The first thing that struck him was the absence of his own children and his wife. He called out; there was no reply. He moved into the parlour; it was empty and the coal fire was almost out. He picked up the electricity bill still sitting unopened on the mantelpiece. He opened the envelope and turned to go into the kitchen when he met them standing at the kitchen door. There were two of them; he recognized the smaller one as one of his watchers. The taller one had a handgun, a large .45 revolver. He was the first to speak.

'You've to come with us. Somebody wants to see you.'

He was just about to make a dash for the hallway and the open street when a third man appeared at the other door. All he could hope for now was the immediate arrival of the Army and the police. He was led out to a car. Seconds later he was being bundled inside. He tried to push up against them when they forced him on to the floor of the taxi.

'Come on, we want no fuss,' advised the taller man with the gun.

He complied. What was the point? he thought. What was the bloody point any more? His thoughts mingled with a prayer as the rug was pulled down over his head. He wondered if he'd ever see daylight again, or even if he really wanted to. What would his family say? Had he been betrayed by Special Branch, or were the boys just too clever after all? Where were McCormick's people anyway?

The taxi pulled away. He felt the gears snap up position as it sped out from the street. Where was his wife now? Did she know? His mind was a muddle of thoughts; it was strange the things you suddenly remember when you were about to meet your Maker, when you didn't know if the next thought or breath would be the last. But he wasn't that fortunate; he was to suffer horribly for over ten hours before they'd finished with him as they extracted every last ounce of information he possessed. If he'd had the strength or the fingers left to do it, he'd have blown his own brains out in the end.

LOS ANGELES
Wednesday, 10 June

The old man emerged from the German bakery on Los Angeles's prestigious Fairfax Boulevard. Just as his wife had directed, the brown carrier-bag was full of warm bread rolls. In the other hand he gingerly carried a small pastry-box so as not to upset the fresh cream contents; otherwise the evening's bridge-party would get off to a bad start, and that's just what he didn't need, especially with his wife's nagging temper.

Before leaving the sidewalk he checked the brass clock set high above the bakery's façade. It was only 4.20 p.m.; he had plenty of time before collecting his wife from the hairdresser's. If he hurried, he could just about make it across town and spend some time with the boys, his old colleagues at the Highway Patrol station. He could almost smell the hot coffee that would be awaiting him in the patrol sergeant's office as he began to cross the street towards his station-wagon.

He was half-way across when he heard the sound from his left side. Glancing up, he was just able to make out the large Volvo estate car as it swerved directly towards him where he stood on the central reservation. The last thing the old man saw was the heavy bumper and front grille as he was first bashed sideways on to the bonnet and then slammed into the windscreen. The racing Volvo carried his body the full length of the block before swerving across oncoming traffic, depositing the old man in the path of a delivery-truck which, unable to stop in time, dragged the body some yards down the road.

It took ten seconds from initial impact to the Volvo's disappearance around the corner – hardly enough time for the few pedestrians in the vicinity to realize what had happened, never mind get the correct colour of the Volvo or for that matter the false registration-plates. Inside another fifteen minutes the Volvo was lying at the bottom of a deep canal. By that time Charles Lincoln Tucker had already been pronounced dead on arrival at the ambulance station, the victim of just another crazy hit-and-run driver.

MOSCOW
Minutes later

It was almost 3 a.m. when the uniformed orderly entered the bedroom. The air smelt faintly of stale tobacco even though the top window had been open all night. He crossed the darkened room bathed partly in the beam of bright fluorescent light stretching outwards from the open doorway. Before he had reached the bed the small table-lamp was flicked on. The stout orderly was startled and glanced briefly into the bleary eyes of his master. The man eased back the blankets and sheet revealing a lean and muscular torso. Pale blue eyes focused quickly on the middle-aged orderly.

'My apologies, Comrade Lieutenant-Colonel, but my orders are that you should dress immediately. A car is waiting outside for you.'

The awakened man continued to stare as the little corporal nervously offered him a buff-coloured envelope in a shaky hand. The envelope was accepted, and the little man returned to the sanctuary of the doorway. He knew too well the temper of the beast he had awakened and had no intention of annoying him further; but, alas, he did have one last duty to perform.

He turned, his head lowered slightly so as to avoid his master's eyes.

'Comrade Lieutenant-Colonel, can I tell them you'll be down presently?'

He dared a single glance upwards and met the stern gaze. There was no need to ask such a stupid question. Did they not all serve with the same fervour? Was it not their life's existence to serve? The corporal squirmed with embarrassment at the silence and began to fumble for the door-handle.

When the door closed the man examined the buff-coloured envelope more closely. It was addressed simply enough: 'Lieutenant-Colonel Nikolai Andreyevich Ivanov'; and in red lettering in the right-hand corner: 'Personal – To be delivered by hand.' He opened the envelope slowly, pausing to light a cigarette from the open case on the bedside table. On examining the envelope's contents his tired eyes lit up. The urge to smoke abated, and he flung back the bedclothes setting the cigarette and letter aside. After checking his watch he crossed quickly to the adjoining bathroom – a luxury not afforded to many in military service, even with the rank of lieutenant-colonel in the GRU.

Within ten minutes he was washed, shaved, and dressed and climbing into his best uniform. He slipped the letter into a pocket of his greatcoat before hurriedly leaving the room, pausing only to snatch his new cap from the coat-rack next to the doorway. The journey through the Moscow suburbs took twenty minutes. The two men in the front of the black Zil limousine remained silent as their rear passenger lit his second cigarette of the day. The Zil travelled swiftly in the central lane along Leninskii Prospekt, down Kutuzovskii and on to Gorkii Street. After travelling the length of Ogareva Street it finally turned into Kalininski Street, a quiet cobblestoned street lined with old lime trees which served partly to obscure the headquarters of the GRU.

By the time they entered the gates of the main complex, light was beginning to settle and the dawn's rays were fighting for control over the gloomy sadness of this part of the city. Moscow, like so many Soviet cities, was becoming a battleground for the discontented. Every day another calamity seemed to befall the capital city. Food riots and demonstrations were almost a daily occurrence now. Even *Pravda* was describing the situation as 'the third horseman of the Apocalypse'; there had been no need for the second horseman of war – the Soviet system had done it all for them. The open outer gates were unguarded but under the constant surveillance of three infra-red cameras mounted around the entrance.

The staff-car passed slowly through into an arched tunnel leading to a second gateway; it was halted by two guards dressed in Soviet Army uniform and brandishing folded AK47 rifles strapped across their chests. Slowly the giant metal outer doors closed, obliterating the struggling sun's rays. The tunnel was a dismal place, poorly illuminated by four old wall-lamps which emitted a dull yellow glow from behind encrusted glass covers. The driver spoke briefly, and the heavy wooden gateway in front of them began rolling aside automatically. The staff-car slowly passed through and swung right across the central courtyard, its enormity exaggerated by the emptiness.

The Zil pulled up sharply on the wet cobblestones beside an unmarked doorway at a far corner. The sharp application of the brakes made the wheels screech, the noise echoing around the four-storey grey stone walls. Ivanov had already stubbed out a further cigarette in the door-mounted ashtray; now he alighted from the car, staring around the walls of the courtyard. All the windows were blacked out, except for the top floor which was bricked up in stark contrast to the dark grey stone walls. He had been in the place only twice before, and on each occasion had been very wary of the invitation. He saw no reason to change his attitude at this stage.

'Do you have orders to wait for me?' Ivanov snapped, looking at the driver as he adjusted his coat collar.

The driver and front-seat passenger looked quickly at one another.

'No, Comrade Colonel, we have no such orders.' The driver seemed almost surprised at being asked.

Ivanov straightened himself and nodded. The car sped off, circling around the wet courtyard. Ivanov stood and pondered over his situation. He was obviously not leaving this place in a hurry or returning to his quarters directly. He braced himself for what lay ahead, taking a deep breath of fresh air before going inside.

After another five minutes he had passed through three separate security checks and endless corridors, and was now being ushered into a lift by a sour-faced female orderly in military uniform. The lift was slow, and his ascent seemed to take for ever until quite unexpectedly the lift jolted to a halt and the doors slowly folded back. He emerged into a drab windowless hallway where he was met by yet another expressionless face: a soldier sat behind a metal desk pushed tightly against the side-wall of the eight-foot-wide corridor.

'Your authority, please, Comrade Lieutenant-Colonel.' The soldier was dressed in civilian clothing, a red identity-card and pass clipped to his lapel. He extended a hand and took the letter and identification-papers, briefly checking them before rising from his chair to return the documents along with a red-coloured pass similar to his own. 'Just follow the corridor and turn left through the doorway, then keep going until you can go no further. Please wear the pass, Comrade Colonel.'

Ivanov took the papers without response, clipping the pass on the lapel of his greatcoat. On turning left and through the glazed double doors he found the corridor facing him to be fully carpeted – luxury by comparison to what he had seen. It led directly to a large room which appeared to serve as a reception-area; the double doors leading from the corridor had been removed. As he walked down the corridor he could see a young Army officer sitting behind a desk at the bottom of the long room. The place had an air of opulence, and so it should, for these were the offices and private quarters of the head of Soviet Military Intelligence, Colonel-General Viktor Nikolayevich Grechko.

Ivanov mused over his apprehension. Why should he worry? He no longer had a career to consider; at the age of forty-five, the rank of lieutenant-colonel in the GRU was as much as he might hope for. He approached the young lieutenant, immaculately turned out in gleaming boots and crisply pleated uniform. It made Ivanov feel slightly inferior; he wondered if the hurriedly donned uniform beneath his greatcoat could stand the comparison. The young officer strode to greet him.

'Comrade Lieutenant-Colonel, thank you for coming so promptly. I am Lieutenant Romanov, aide to Colonel-General Grechko. May I have your letter, please?'

Ivanov returned the letter which, to his amusement, was quickly fed into an electrically operated shredding machine beside the desk. He watched as Romanov confidently lifted the telephone; he imagined him to be one of the 'protected species', probably under the protection and sponsorship of Colonel-General Grechko himself. He smiled briefly at the young officer, who seemed to read Ivanov's mind entirely and wilted under his gaze. The lieutenant looked away towards some papers on his desk, then he cleared his throat, placing his left palm across the receiver and glanced back at Ivanov.

'Please take a seat by the window. You shall be attended to directly.' But Ivanov had already turned and was crossing the large room to the row of armchairs set around a low coffee-table. Then Romanov began to speak in muffled tones, and it certainly was not to order coffee. Ivanov pulled off his great-coat and set it on one of the chairs beside him. It was time for another cigarette.

Grechko switched off the intercom and opened the bulky file in front of him. The inside cover bore a photograph; he studied the man's features carefully. He prided himself on knowing a man's character just by studying his face; it was always there, in the eyes, the most betraying feature.

'That is the complete file on him.' Lieutenant-General Alexei Vladimirovich Mikhailov spoke from his armchair angled beside the open coal fire. He ran the poker through the burning embers before continuing. 'He is the only one I trust.'

The head of the GRU was silent. He had moved his eyes away from the photograph and was flicking through the file for the résumé of the man's last operation. He found it in the yellow section, the last three pages. It was an outline of the man's activities in Afghanistan. Ivanov had been working in Afghanistan for almost a year before the Red Army came roaring down the National Route 2 from the north and began dropping its airborne brigades into Bagram and Kabul. The man had stayed on in an advisory capacity because of his extensive knowledge of CIA operations in the region and had later taken full charge of the Spetsnaz operations against the resistance groups in the hills and mountains. Ivanov had achieved much, co-ordinating the special force action against the Afghan rebels; he should have received his country's highest accolade, but instead they had quietly sent him home. Since then he had served in an administrative capacity, little more than a glorified clerk.

Grechko lifted the sealed envelope out and tore it open; it was the result of an internal disciplinary hearing on the lieutenant-colonel. He raised an eyebrow and stared at Mikhailov.

'This man should be dead.'

'I saved him for an occasion just such as this.'

'You went against the ruling of a military court!' snapped Grechko. Mikhailov remained silent and stared back into the glowing fire.

'Alexei, you take too many risks. One day it will be one too many!' Grechko admonished him. 'This file tells me absolutely nothing about the man. Tell me all about this Ivanov. Not the sort of rubbish I can read on his file – tell me what you know about him.'

'Lieutenant-Colonel Nikolai Andreyevich Ivanov was born of all places in the Daghestan Mountains in Georgia; his father was a local doctor, mother a schoolteacher. They had a fairly spartan existence even with their positions, and young Nikolai was their only child. He was exactly four years old when both his parents were killed in an avalanche. Their entire village was wiped out; over one hundred died. The only reason the child survived was because he was staying for a few days with some family friends in a town further down the valley. The child had no other relatives except for an uncle and aunt on his father's side who lived in Moscow. He went there in 1951. His uncle was Professor Vladimir Ivanov; he worked at Moscow University teaching science. And then we have the strangest thing. His wife had been born and bred in the United States. She, too, was a scientist. They met in Paris just before the war, apparently at some world conference. It was love at first sight; then they came to Moscow just before the outbreak of war.'

'And these relations – are they still alive?'

'No, but the best has yet to come.' Mikhailov paused. 'Ivanov's uncle was a close friend of Beria.'

'The devil of the Narodny Kommissariat Vnutrennikh Del!' Grechko referred to the NKVD, the forerunner of the KGB.

'Precisely. That is how the eminent professor was able to travel so freely around Europe and bring his American bride back home to Mother Russia. One can only assume that Professor Ivanov was working for or with the NKVD; and we are not quite sure about this, but it appears Beria met the young Ivanov just days after his arrival in Moscow. It was at a private dinner party in the professor's house. Beria threw down a challenge to Ivanov's aunt to transform the frightened and sickly looking youngster, to teach him to speak just as an American youngster would.'

'But why?' Grechko was puzzled.

'It was an experiment. Whether or not Beria was trying it elsewhere we can't be certain.'

'Go on.' Grechko was intense.

'The woman took up the challenge. It took much longer than she anticipated, but by the time Ivanov had reached six years of age he spoke and sounded like a child from Boston.'

'Incredible! So you think that Comrade Beria had a sinister motive in this affair?'

'Probably, but he never had an opportunity to do anything. A couple of months after young Ivanov's sixth birthday he was himself tried and shot, only a short time after Stalin's death in 1953.'

'And then?'

'Whether out of interest or by design the American woman kept up young Nikolai's American studies. By the age of ten he could write and work fluently in the language; and with his unique gift for recall, as the Americans would say, he was "streets ahead" of anyone his own age.'

'And the uncle?'

'Less than a year after the boy's tenth birthday Ivanov's uncle died from leukaemia. His aunt was going to return to her native Boston, but the KGB would not permit it. She created quite a stink. Her husband was a close friend of the then Leningrad party boss, Valeri Polyansky.'

'Now our Minister of Internal Affairs! She was indeed well connected. Yet you say she still did not succeed in obtaining permission?' Grechko frowned.

'By that time her husband's work at the university research establishment was far too delicate to allow any possibility of her even accidentally knowing and passing on any information to the Americans. It was harsh, but it made sense. They were both scientists after all; it seemed therefore natural that husband and wife would have discussed certain technical aspects of the work they had both trained to do.'

'What sort of work was Professor Ivanov employed on at the university?'

'Rocket propulsion.'

'Then the KGB refusal is understandable. And the woman – what happened to her?'

'Apparently suicide. It was two years later, and after she had exhausted every avenue to return home. By that time Ivanov had already begun schooling at a military academy in Moscow.'

'Her death must have had a great effect on him.'

'If it did, it never showed. He continued at the academy; it was a boarding establishment in any case, and he had been away from his aunt's house in Moscow for two years. At the most, he only ever saw her twice a year.'

'And then he joined the officer corps of the Red Army.'

'It was a natural progression from the academy. Then early on in his career he came to my attention. It was during a military exercise in East Germany when I met him and discovered his unique ability to speak just as an American. It was incredible; even after all those years he hadn't forgotten. After that it was a matter of recruitment into the GRU and then the training centre for the "illegals". Two years later he was living and working in the United States.'

'But I see from his file he did not stay there.' Grechko sat back.

'He established a number of aliases there, capable models for use at a future time; he established bank accounts and developed several profiles. At that time we had no specific job for him other than to settle into his new roles. Then in 1983 one of our people at the United Nations became something of an embarrassment. The bureaucrat slipped his KGB pursuers and tried to make contact with the FBI but was unable to do so initially and ended up in hiding. The KGB resident in New York asked our own resident there for assistance. He discussed the matter with me. The matter was of the gravest importance, and reluctantly I agreed, and Ivanov was activated. The traitor finally managed to give himself up into protective custody with the FBI. Inside forty-eight hours Ivanov had executed him. In and out of a Philadelphia police station and right under the noses of the FBI and the CIA.'

'Impressive.' Grechko rubbed his hands together. 'So why do you think he's so perfect for this operation? It's in the United Kingdom after all.'

'Cover is not a problem for him, even in Great Britain. I've taken the liberty of seeing to that already. But, to answer your question more fully, he's simply the best we have. He will carry out his orders to the letter, and he has an independence of mind that will be vitally necessary if he is to reach the bottom of the mess.'

'I never much trusted the Georgian sense of independence.'

'I trust Ivanov. Also, we need a man who is expendable from the outset. Ivanov has no family or loved ones back here, nothing to connect us to him if something should go wrong.'

Grechko flicked through the personnel file and updated report. 'I just hope for your sake that he's as good as you profess.'

'He is.'

'But there can be no room for half-measures,' insisted Grechko, 'and no room for returning failures.'

'There is always the furnace.' Mikhailov made a reference to one of the more favoured GRU methods of disposing of its own traitors. It was the sword of Damocles that hung over the head of every GRU officer. 'A terrible waste of one of our best "illegals", but I know him. Ivanov will complete the mission without question. See him, Comrade General. Judge for yourself.'

'You will take the responsibility for his failure; you know that.' Grechko leaned across the desk.

'My life depends on his success; that goes without saying, Comrade General.' Mikhailov's face was unflinching; if he was frightened, Grechko couldn't see it.

Outside, the telephone on Romanov's desk burred; he responded quickly and replaced the receiver.

'You can go in, Comrade Lieutenant-Colonel.' He gestured towards the blue-painted double doors at the far side of the room.

Ivanov rose slowly, adjusting his tunic and cap before dusting off some cigarette ash from his sleeve. He walked smartly to the doors, knocking once. Before entering he glanced sideways at Romanov; the young lieutenant was studying him like some zoo animal. He went in and saw that the chief of the GRU was not alone. Mikhailov was now standing beside a wall map of Europe. He had served under Mikhailov before, but since the Afghanistan conflict the general had avoided him; like so many others, he was *persona non grata*.

Mikhailov nodded slightly and smiled briefly at him. Ivanov ignored him. The much older Colonel-General Grechko, head of the GRU, was seated squarely behind an ornate Louis XV walnut desk. Ivanov had seen the style of furniture before on his frequent 'field trips' in the West and certainly inside the Kremlin, but he was nevertheless stunned to find such extravagance here in the GRU's Moscow headquarters. General Grechko, a fat ruddy-faced Ukrainian, was first to speak.

'Nikolai Andreyevich Ivanov.' Grechko nodded. 'Be seated.'

Ivanov saluted smartly before sitting on the lone chair set in the centre of the floor.

'Take off your cap and be at ease, Nikolai Andreyevich.' The general spoke almost with a certain concern, or at least it appeared that way to Ivanov. He had only spoken to Grechko on one previous occasion, during a medal ceremony in 1980. He was a virtual stranger to the man, yet the address was cordial. Normally he would have been addressed by his rank; this was almost the voice of friendship. Ivanov smiled, relieved that he had not been summoned from his obscurity to face some terrible retribution. Mikhailov was next to speak.

'You have been summoned here with some urgency. A crisis has arisen outside the Soviet Union, but with phenomenal implications for the GRU and potentially disastrous consequences for the Soviet people.'

What's worse than food riots and Soviet soldiers killing rioters in the Moscow streets? thought Ivanov.

'We need one man to carry out a task of the greatest complexity and sensitivity. That man must be you, Nikolai Andreyevich. I know you well, and you have been chosen only after the most careful consideration.' He glanced towards Grechko before continuing. There was no objection. 'It is agreed that within the GRU you are the officer most likely to carry out this mission successfully.'

Ivanov nodded gently; he was trying to determine the true meaning of the last comment. Was he being told he was expendable? Of course, he had accepted that a long time ago; but something else had changed, something was different about all this.

'Normally the task to which we refer would come within the sphere of the KGB,' Mikhailov continued, 'but, for reasons that will be revealed later, the entire affair must be kept entirely within this organization, if it is not to have fatal implications. Do you get my meaning?'

'I understand,' replied Ivanov coolly.

'Good!' Mikhailov slapped his hands together and looked again at Grechko. The old general nodded his agreement. 'You are immediately transferred from the Tenth Directorate and are hereby attached to my own Personal Illegals Directorate.' Mikhailov moved closer to Grechko's desk and removing a file he began to scan the first page. 'Later this week you will leave the Soviet Union. Of course you will have a cover story and the next four days to learn all about it and your mission. Think you can handle it?'

Ivanov smiled. He knew they would assume his answer. '*Da*, Comrade Lieutenant-General.'

'The identity I am talking about will be your main cover story, but naturally you will not assume that role until your final destination.'

The head of the GRU raised his hand, drawing his 1st Deputy to a halt.

'Colonel, the particulars of your mission will come later. I have only one final thing to say to you. This mission will have no back-up. You will be entirely on your own once you reach your final destination.'

'I understand,' retorted Ivanov drily. 'May I ask where on the North American continent I am destined for?'

'Not America,' replied Grechko. 'Great Britain.'

'But I specialized in North American affairs; I was an "illegal" there. To assume a safe identity I would need to use an existing American cover-story! Preferably one of my own profiles.'

Grechko smiled, but it was no longer warm and friendly. 'And you will, Nikolai Andreyevich. A true red-blooded American indeed, and a member of the CIA as well!' He began to chuckle to himself. 'You never know, Alexei, the Americans may even put him on their payroll!'

Mikhailov reluctantly joined in the amusement, unlike Ivanov, who was now rubbing at the pale six-inch scar which ran from behind his left ear towards his shoulderblade. The high neckline of his tunic was beginning to irritate him, a nervous sign. He was being unavoidably guided into an extremely dangerous situation, and there wasn't a thing he could do about it. As the two GRU officers finally left the room Grechko made a parting comment.

'One word to you both. Take it as a final warning. The KGB have no knowledge of this matter. It must remain just so; any interference, any suspicion would spell death to everyone in this room.'

'I shall not fail you, Comrade General.' Ivanov saluted.

The chief of Soviet Military Intelligence eased back in his leather chair. '*Da. Da.* I'm inclined to believe you.' A frown fell across his broad face.

As they walked away from the carpeted corridor Ivanov was first to break the ice.

'Just what the hell's this all about? I am ignored for years and left to rot in a stinking office and then I am supposed to save your hides.'

Mikhailov raised an eyebrow. 'Have you learnt nothing, Kolia? After all these years? You haven't changed at all. Still as impudent as ever!'

'But much wiser,' replied Ivanov, 'and still alive.'

Mikhailov patted him heavily on the back. 'It is good to have you working with me once again, my friend.'

Ivanov kept silent as they continued their laborious passage through the complex. He thought back to the days when he served under Mikhailov whilst in the United States and with Spetsnaz, the commando arm of the Soviet forces. A highly trained élite force, Spetsnaz units are capable of the most rigorous physical and battlefield feats. Ivanov had joined Spetsnaz as a young lieutenant, originally selected from the infantry, and to this day he retained the same military uniform; only the insignia had changed. He had been picked for stardom. Someone had been impressed with him; that someone was Mikhailov, then himself a lieutenant-colonel with the GRU and in charge of the 'illegals training centre'.

At that time Ivanov knew very little about the GRU except that it existed as a very top secret military intelligence organization. His new career development as an 'illegal' was meteoric, and his further indoctrination and lengthy training in the GRU were the cream on the cake. On top of being a highly trained assassin and saboteur he had then spent years training and learning all of the ways and means of intelligence-gathering, specializing in the United States. He had excelled in all but diplomacy; his high IQ and quick temper had got the better of common sense and placed him in conflict with his superiors on several occasions, and then there was Afghanistan. It had cost him dearly. He was a fallen angel, and everyone knew it; even Mikhailov could no longer help.

Ivanov's job in the 10th Directorate was mundane and laborious. In many ways he had been reduced to being a glorified filing clerk. He hated them all now, especially Mikhailov, and now the bastard needed him! Neither man spoke until finally they were inside Mikhailov's office suite on the third floor. The lieutenant-general studied his former protégé as he settled into a low settee set along one wall.

'You have kept yourself fit, I see.' Mikhailov got no reply

but continued: 'Good! It is good to see a man maintain peak physical condition, especially after the way they have treated you.'

The last statement stirred something in Ivanov. '*They* treated me! You could have stopped it, and you know it!'

'No. With the things you did I was powerless. You were lucky not to be thrown to the dogs altogether, strung up to some gallows or shot to death in a nameless prison-yard! Speaking of which – and I tell you this against my oath – two men have already died for knowing less than you about this operation and they were both serving members of our organization, and were very much in favour at the time.'

Ivanov looked up. 'We are now killing our own people because of a security leak?' He was not startled, just sickened. It had happened before on a number of occasions; undoubtedly it could happen again.

'No, they died because they just had knowledge, a little knowledge of a certain occurrence in the West.'

'So what becomes of me, Comrade Lieutenant-General? When do I perish – upon my return to Mother Russia?' His sarcasm frustrated Mikhailov.

'I only tell you this to reiterate the importance of you achieving success, Kolia. Failure can mean only one thing. General Grechko may seem a jovial old fool to some, but he was certainly not jesting when he made those parting remarks.' He smiled. 'What I now tell you is under Omega classification, understood?'

'Understood,' nodded Ivanov, removing his cap.

'In April our central cipher people received a split-second burst-type transmission from a transmitter somewhere in Great Britain. The cipher clerks were, to say the least, puzzled, as were our own GRU officers in the dissemination centre. The coding crystals used and indeed the Class IIX transmitter are well out of date and no longer in use by us; they have not been used in at least fifteen years. The coded message emanated from a source we had long since believed to be nonexistent and on equipment long since destroyed!'

'You mean one of our agents has supposedly continued on a mission, after all this time?'

'Precisely. But now the completion of that mission could have the most disastrous consequences – a mission, my dear Kolia, that should have never been sanctioned in the first place, but in the heady days of the sixties it seemed very proper indeed!'

Ivanov was speechless.

'The operation was called Opus 49, and it was all initiated by Colonel-General Boris Kurakin, chief of the GRU under Chairman Khrushchev. Khrushchev apparently gave Kurakin the idea in a speech he made to the Politburo expressing his feelings about the NATO alliance. He told the meeting, which also included Kurakin, that the Soviet Union must stop at nothing in turning Europe against the United States and vice versa. He even quoted history to back up his point. Whether or not the chairman knew of Kurakin's plan will never be known. Then in the early sixties Kurakin saw a unique opportunity to capitalize on the seeming confusion and weak feeling in the West. People were out in the street, singing about love and handing out flowers. The United States had committed itself to a war in South-East Asia that its politicians wouldn't let it win. The western hemisphere was in utter confusion, and the time seemed ripe for insurrection and international terrorism, deliberate chaos on the grandest scale ever imagined.'

'So Kurakin sent in his agents to the West.' Ivanov lit a cigarette.

'He didn't need to, Kolia. His plan was to use "sleepers", strategically placed years before, and create mayhem in the West through a series of assassinations. The sleepers were activated in 1965; by 1968 they were fully active. There were four "activates" in all. They were all really only pawns; no one except Kurakin and a small group of selected officers knew what lay behind the operation. The job of the "sleepers" was purely to activate and direct as ordered by Moscow. The important point, Kolia, is that no one in the Central Committee of the KGB had any idea Opus 49 existed. There was no GRU liaison with their KGB counterparts, no authorization from the General Secretary or the Politburo; it was a totally clandestine operation. I imagine that if the operation had been an unlimited success Kurakin would have revealed its existence in due course, realizing his own ambition to rise within the Politburo; but then he died, right in the middle of the operation.'

'What killed him?'

'Apparently a brain seizure, a clot of some sort; he took it while attending a Politburo meeting alongside the Defence Minister. Following his death Kurakin's 1st Deputy assumed temporary command of the GRU as was his duty. He entered Kurakin's office just two hours after receiving the news of his death. He had one duty to perform above all others. Each GRU chief has a data file, contained in a special safe in his office. In accordance with orders the officer assuming charge must open that safe and take charge of its secrets immediately.' The general sighed.

'Inside, apart from the sort of files the Deputy had expected to find, he discovered a letter addressed to himself. It was Kurakin's confession, disclosing the existence of Opus 49. All the information was contained under Omega classification, but little was on computer record. Kurakin was old-fashioned. He didn't trust machines; nearly everything about the operation was contained in a sealed file in the Archive Section of GRU headquarters.

'The Deputy was an intelligent officer; he made Opus 49 his absolute priority. An hour later he emerged from the Archive Section knowing what he must do, and fast. As Deputy to Kurakin no one was going to believe that he was uninvolved in the affair even with Kurakin's letter. He could also see the repercussions for Soviet Military Intelligence if the KGB gained knowledge of the operation. In a desperate act he sanctioned the killing of all four "sleepers" and the "activates", including the three-man team of officers that had co-ordinated the operation from a secret GRU dacha in Tula.

'By 7 p.m. that evening an élite killer squad was dispatched to the dacha, the three GRU officers personally ordered by the 1st Deputy to dispatch one word to the "sleepers" using the Moscow World Radio Service. It was sent during a horticultural programme during that same night. The word was "Dieback". There was nothing untoward in using the word. "Dieback" is a disorder of roses. The solution is to cut out and destroy, and that is exactly what the "sleepers" had to do to their "activates".

'After the message was dispatched everything was eradicated – code-books, records, and equipment. Everything, including the three officers, was destroyed; grenades were exploded inside the dacha killing and destroying everything inside. Afterwards the place was razed to the ground. Every scrap of evidence disappeared.

'Then the GRU *rezidenti*, whether legal or illegal, in London, Washington, Cape Town, and Bonn were given instructions to meet the "sleepers".' Mikhailov stood up and breathed in deeply before continuing. 'Kolia, they all thought they were coming home, a long and lonely job well done; instead each kept a date with his executioner.'

'What about their radio equipment?' asked Ivanov.

'On hearing "Dieback" the "sleepers" were to have terminated their individual operations; that included destroying their equipment and code-books and anything else that might incriminate themselves.'

'So they were all killed?'

'Three "sleepers" met with their executioners; but the fourth, code-named Bloodstone, had already been killed by the British Army in Ireland.'

'Have we confirmation that he died?' Ivanov's mind raced ahead.

'*Da*. He was in the Provisional IRA; he was killed after trying to crash a car through a British Army checkpoint in Belfast.'

'And his "activate"?'

'Supposedly killed the night before by the British Army. Shot during a gun-battle.'

'So who is sending these signals? You think it could be this Bloodstone?'

'That is what you must find out, and fast. Not only is the person sending signals; he's perhaps killing again!' Mikhailov continued. 'In 1972 the 1st Deputy had a very unsavoury task, especially closing the operation under a veil of the tightest secrecy. The saddest part about the whole episode was that Opus 49 was shaping up; it was a success.'

'But apparently not everyone involved was silenced,' Ivanov interrupted.

Mikhailov nodded. 'As I said, we can definitely discount the "sleepers" in South America, the Horn or Africa, and in West Germany, and they had each evidenced the demise of their "activates"; that was double-checked and confirmed. Nor was there anything tangible to connect them to the Soviet Union. "Dieback" worked like a well-oiled clock except for events over-running us in Northern Ireland. But it would have been a normal procedure for the "sleeper" to have destroyed his equipment immediately after hearing the code-word through the Moscow World Radio Service. Even if he hadn't done so, the transmitter and codes would have been well hidden in a deep hide, not somewhere that would have allowed their detection; and, even if the codes had been located, without the specific knowledge known only to each "sleeper" transmission would have been impossible. Yet we have already received these messages supposedly from Bloodstone.' He handed Ivanov a sheet of computer-printed information.

Ivanov read the messages. He was intrigued, especially when he read the report which followed. Someone was telling Moscow in advance who they were killing!

'Kurakin's 1st Deputy had done his job well in discreetly winding up the clandestine operation; but he needed insurance, something that would safeguard him in the event of a leak at some future date, something that would exonerate him and show that he had no complicity in Opus 49. He prepared his own file on the operation, stating what steps he had taken to safeguard and protect the international good standing of the Soviet Union. Thankfully he had the wisdom to include all of the code-words used in the operation. From those codes we have decoded the Field Radio Signals you now hold in your hand.' He handed Ivanov a further sheet of paper. The Russian intelligence officer read it carefully.

'This is a report from our scientists stating the type and form of the equipment. It is a one-way transmitter, probably contained inside a tape recorder and using domestic power or heavy-duty batteries. It would probably be linked to an aerial and a booster relay. It gives you little to go on, Kolia, but it is all we have. Our electronics experts tell me that the second and third signals originated from somewhere in southern England, just south of London; the first was from Ireland.'

'So this Bloodstone must still be alive?'

'His name was McGoldrick. We have very little on him now; it's all contained in this file.' Mikhailov passed across the file to Ivanov, who immediately began to leaf through it.

'This message? Why tell us what he is about to do? Why warn us of his intention? If you say the British killed him, then could this not all be a trap?'

'That's why you are here, Kolia.'

'Then, surely, if we know where he is going to strike in advance we can arrange to intercept him. Just as he told you in this!' Ivanov held up the computer readout and crumpled it in his large hand. 'It sounds like a trick instigated by the British Secret Intelligence Service or the security services.'

'A possibility. But our greatest concern is over Opus 49. If any information leaked on this, it would drive a wedge between us and the KGB so deep that nothing short of a thermonuclear device would remove it. Even our present leadership could be jeopardized; there would be a clampdown by the conservatives. The Soviet Union would enter another cold repressionist phase.'

'It looks to me as if they've collapsed already. Our economy is in ruins.'

'Kolia, out there on the street you have a certain entitlement to say what you think, but not in here!' Mikhailov snapped.

Ivanov changed tack.

'Perhaps the "sleeper" allowed the "activate" access to the codes and equipment?' He lit up another cigarette.

'We just don't know, Kolia.'

'Do we know where this killer is going to go next?'

'The "sleepers" got their directions through the Moscow World Radio Service. They would each receive signals allowing them to complete the codes they already possessed. Let me show you.' Mikhailov stood up and lifted a book off his desk. 'Think of this not as a textbook but rather as a code-book.' Then he lifted a small notepad from next to the telephone. 'Think of this as a digital reference, something that was pre-prepared here in Moscow before the mission began. Each "sleeper" would listen at set times to the radio broadcast. A word would be mentioned that would alert each one of them individually. It would be a different word for each; there would be no way that if an enemy government arrested one of the four they would ever be able to track down the messages being sent to the other three. After the signal word, the "sleeper" would then record the remainder of the radio broadcast. Depending on the day of the month the broadcast was made, the "sleeper" would use a certain section of his digital code-book. In sequence every tenth word or something similar would be a part of the signal he was to receive. At the end of it all each "sleeper" would then know his next target. Believe it or not, the coding format was all to do with different types of roses; it was ingenious if not rather supercilious of Kurakin. Apparently Kurakin's main pastime was rose-growing. Using his hobby and expertise as a front to travel freely throughout the western hemisphere he was therefore able to monitor his "sleepers" without them even knowing it.'

'What safety features were adopted?'

Mikhailov smiled. Ivanov was missing nothing. 'The message would tell the "sleeper" what was required of him next, but there was an added safety feature. He would need to refer to this book, a second edition of *The Western Intellectual Tradition*, and using the same message he would be able to find a page to which, following a set procedure already committed to memory, he would cross-refer what he had been told. If certain references did not add up, he would not proceed but await a further signal.'

'Would whoever is sending these signals need to know about this book?'

'No. It was only used for authentication purposes; the safety feature only worked one way.' Mikhailov reddened slightly. 'Find out what is going on, Kolia. You may be correct; it could be a trick by the British or even the Americans. You have to locate whoever is doing this. If we have a rogue agent out there, you must stop him. Kill him, Kolia! Kill him quickly!' Mikhailov jumped to his feet. 'Come, Kolia, we have much to do, and I have a team waiting to brief you.'

What Ivanov learnt astounded even him; the stupidity of his

forebears was unbelievable. He had just four days to prepare. He spent the first two days gorging all the information that his mind could take. He had of course been used to such procedures in the past; his memory-retention was tried and tested; he could scan a page of information inside seconds and be able to repeat it word-perfect a week later. His natural ability had been developed so he could recall codes and binary sequences from years past. He was perfect for the job. No need for notes; everything would be stored inside his brain.

Ivanov studied the files and additional research material supplied by Mikhailov, but something was troubling him; something wasn't right. He re-examined everything again and still he got the same feeling, but there was no tangible evidence to substantiate his gut feeling. It was just before three in the afternoon when he strolled out of the Kalininski Street gates for the first time in over forty-eight hours. He walked to the end of the tree-lined street. The Moscow traffic was brisk as usual. Getting out was much easier than he imagined. The two-man briefing team trusted him; they were both too busy tucking into a late lunch of Plov and garlic bread to notice he'd vanished. He headed up Ogareva Street, disappearing into the crowds of Muscovites.

Eight hours later he stepped out of the bar on to the pavement. Outside the Moscow evening had darkened into night. Ivanov checked his watch; it was already after eleven o'clock. He crossed the street and headed down towards the next junction. Kutuzovskii Prospekt was quite crowded; by their appearance the crowds were mainly tourists out for a stroll after the ballet. Their western fashions were in stark contrast to the two men standing just beyond the next junction on the opposite side of the road. Ivanov smiled; he wondered just how long it would take for them to catch up with him.

He turned right at the junction and had only walked a short distance when the black Zil sedan pulled up alongside. He stopped just as the back door opened and Mikhailov stepped out, dressed in evening dress, a camel mohair coat draped across his rounded and narrow shoulders.

'Walk,' he said softly, gesturing for Ivanov to move down the street towards the quieter area away from the constant procession of pedestrians. As they walked slowly along the pavement the Zil maintained a steady pace just a few metres behind. Ivanov didn't need to check on the two men he'd seen moments earlier; they were now walking in tandem on the opposite pavement.

'Nikolai Andreyevich, you have done some idiotic things in the past, but I can tell you that was the most stupid I have encountered.' Mikhailov still kept his voice subdued, but the anger was now clearly evident. 'Tell me why you did it.'

'I got a little bored with your briefing,' Ivanov said casually as he lit another cigarette. 'I had some thinking to do.'

'You know, if the KGB don't kill you, some day those things will.' Mikhailov breathed in deeply.

'Haven't you forgotten to mention the GRU?'

'It wouldn't be the first time a traitor has been shoved alive into a furnace.' There was a definite venom in the tone now.

'I'm no traitor!' Ivanov was angry. 'But both of us know that if I return to Moscow I'll be dead anyway.'

Mikhailov looked across at him. There was something about Ivanov that frightened even the GRU general. He felt suddenly vulnerable. Just how quickly could the two baboons across the street come to his aid? How speedily could Kapitsa, his body-guard, get off a shot from the pistol he always carried on his lap when driving the Zil?

'I remember well the cine film you showed me when I was being recruited into the organization,' continued Ivanov. 'I often wondered just who that poor unfortunate comrade really was. Perhaps some dissident who had become just too much trouble.' Ivanov was referring to the film record that had been made of the execution of a disaffected GRU major years before. After a secret military trial he had been brought to the boiler room of a certain military establishment and there, in full view of his fellows, he had been strapped on to a stretcher and then slowly lowered screaming through the open furnace-door and into the raging flames. The only saving grace had been the omission of a soundtrack. The film was shown to all GRU officer recruits. It was supposedly the ultimate horror that would befall any traitors. There could be no mercy given under the code of the organization.

'No one is suggesting that you are a traitor . . . yet. I still insist on knowing why you left Kalininski Street.' Clearly Mikhailov had made up his mind about him already; otherwise he would by now have been inside the Zil and *en route* to a military prison.

'The way this is shaping up, I'm a dead man no matter what happens.'

'Nikolai Andreyevich Ivanov a sceptic? Preposterous!' Mikhailov laughed mockingly.

'Comrade General, don't ever mock me.' Ivanov glared at the man.

'You mock yourself. You're a fool. I offer you an opportunity for redemption, and now you threaten to blow it all away.'

'*Yob Tvoyu Mat!*' Ivanov stopped and faced the general.

Mikhailov almost went for his gun in the snug-fitting shoulder-holster under his dinner-jacket but flexed back on sight of the two elderly tourists approaching them.

'No one has ever spoken to me like that! No one!' he growled.

'Think of it as experience.' Ivanov smiled back; the general was ready to explode.

'Excuse me? Do you gentlemen speak any English?' The deep Texan drawl was clearly evident. Mikhailov stared at the old man in the wide-checked cream and blue sports jacket and almost matching cap. He was sporting the latest Olympus camera around his neck on a broad red, white, and blue strap. His tubby little wife stood back a few paces, leaning against a wall and rubbing one of her feet. Before Mikhailov could gather his senses Ivanov answered.

'Sure I do. How can I help?' Ivanov played the part he knew best.

'Hey, you're American! Hear that, honey? These guys are from the States! Isn't that great!' he called over to his little wife, who smiled over at Ivanov, although from the lines on her wrinkled face it was forced; evidently she was in some pain. The American turned again to Ivanov.

'You sound like you're from the east somewhere.' Mikhailov inwardly cringed; if only the old man knew just how far east, he wouldn't have asked.

'Boston. Born and bred.' Ivanov shook the man's hand.

'J. D. Murphy's the name. This here is Lucielle, my wife.' He turned again to the woman; she was desperately trying to replace the shoe on her swollen foot and having little success. 'We're from Fairfield; it's just south a piece from Dallas.'

'Can't say I've been there, but I've heard of it all right.' Ivanov smiled.

Lucielle hobbled the short distance over, her heel protruding from the white toeless shoe. From the swelling around her ankles and legs Ivanov correctly diagnosed her to have arthritis.

'JD, I just can't go no further. Call a cab or something.' She smiled nervously at the two strangers. Mikhailov stepped back, trying to avoid any involvement in the affair.

'Hush up, honey. I'm trying to find out!' It was clear that JD was the boss. 'We're doing the world, visiting over twenty different countries. This is our fourteenth, I think.'

'And the way my feet hurt it seems like I walked it!' shouted Lucielle from just behind him. 'Hurry up, will ya?' she urged her husband.

'Lucielle's got arthritis,' continued the man. His wife fired him a look that could have stopped a tank in its tracks; it was clearly a touchy subject and definitely not to be discussed with two strangers on a Moscow street. 'Look, Mr . . . Look, the point is we're lost. We went to the ballet tonight and decided to take a stroll afterwards.

'Now I can't even find where I am on this damned map, and with all this unrest over here we're kinda worried for our safety.' He showed Ivanov a crumpled street-map giving all the main thoroughfares and tourist sights in Moscow. Ivanov looked at it.

'I'm not surprised. This only gives the main streets; side-streets such as this one aren't included. Look, you're here.' He pointed to the centre of a yellow block with grey lines depicting the various streets running across it.

'Holy shit! We're miles away from the Intourist hotel; we

must have been walking round in a circle for the last hour.' He showed it to his wife, who seemed little interested.

She grunted through clenched teeth: 'Get me home!'

Ivanov looked across at Mikhailov; the general's face had reddened, and he was gritting his teeth. Ivanov grinned at him, stubbing his cigarette out on the pavement. 'Look, I've an idea. Mr Rublev here is a Russian businessman who I'm over here dealing with. That car back there is his.' He pointed back towards the awaiting Zil. 'I'm sure that he wouldn't mind his driver giving you both a lift back.'

Mikhailov's eyes widened as Ivanov then addressed him in Russian. He couldn't chance arguing even in his native language. After Mikhailov's meagre protest Ivanov moved closer and whispered: 'Shall I tell the nice lady and man about the bulge under your left armpit?'

The GRU general stepped aside, conceding game, set, and match. He waved up the Zil and spoke to his open-mouthed driver, Kapitsa.

'This is real neighbourly of you, buddy. We sure won't forget it,' the elderly American sounded out, looking across to the Russian general who was still speaking to Kapitsa. 'You sure we ain't putting your friend here to any trouble? He looks as if he's all dressed up for a state banquet at the Kremlin.'

'The nearest my friend here will ever get to the Kremlin will be on a guided tour.' Ivanov's eyes widened; the GRU driver's eyes narrowed. Ivanov knew enough about Kapitsa to know the man couldn't be trusted any more than a green mamba. He had been Mikhailov's henchman for nearly ten years. Ostensibly assigned as his driver and orderly, the man travelled almost everywhere outside GRU headquarters with the lieutenant-general. Kapitsa was nothing more than a brutal, sadistic killer. Ivanov had witnessed his handiwork before. It was not enough just to carry out an execution; he enjoyed drawing it out. The two elderly Americans stepped into the back of the Zil, luxurious by Russian standards; it was even equipped with a mobile telephone as well as the VHF radio communications system installed next to the driver.

'Hey!' The Texan put his head out of the open rear window. 'If you're ever in Freestone County, Texas, you make sure you go to Fairfield, ya hear! I might be retired now, but you can bet your bottom dollar that the ex-Fire Chief of Fairfield will give you the warmest welcome of your life!'

'You bet!' the woman called across from the other side of the rear seat.

The American handed over a card. 'That's our address, so don't forget now, ya hear?'

'I hear.' Ivanov shook the man's hand once again and turned to Kapitsa, addressing him in Russian. 'Drive on, pig!'

The man smirked. 'You will keep,' he said flatly.

'Just get these nice people back to their hotel like a good little lapdog.' Ivanov stepped back. The American couple were too engrossed in examining the car telephone set in the middle of the front panel before them to have heard the conversation even if they had understood the language. Little did they know that what they were looking at connected the vehicle directly to the Vertushka, the official title of the Kremlin telephone system. Ivanov stood on the pavement watching as the Zil pulled away.

'You ever do that again and you are finished.' Mikhailov waved at the two men on the other side of the street to join them.

'So you mean I am not?' Ivanov pulled another cigarette out of his pocket.

'Perhaps. If you do exactly as you are told for a change.'

GRU HEADQUARTERS, MOSCOW

Colonel-General Viktor Nikolayevich Grechko sat in the front row of the small lecture theatre watching the CBS newsreel that was being transmitted live from Dublin through the CBS news network across the United States. The broadcast had been scanned by a Soviet telecommunications satellite and transmitted directly to Kalininski Street. Grechko deplored the unnecessary use of the satellites, but he had to see for himself what was happening outside the Soviet Union. He could no longer rely on the reports from his GRU *rezidenti* at the various embassies; drastic situations often required drastic remedies, and he was taking no one's opinion for granted, including official news agencies.

The young American female reporter pictured on the giant screen was vitriolic in her condemnation of the Irish Justice Minister's murder. The man had been a good staunch ally of the United States and one of the masterminds behind the Anglo-Irish Agreement; before becoming Minister for Justice he had secured literally billions of dollars in aid packages from the United States government. The International Fund for Ireland was now being brought into question. The Provisional IRA had denied responsibility for the murder in Phoenix Park, so had the Ulster Volunteer Force, and now a newspaper article in one of the British tabloids was suggesting that a professional hitman was involved and that millions of dollars had gone missing, presumably into the pockets of the IRA.

'Whatever the outcome,' continued the reporter, 'the allegations in the wake of Michael Muldoon's death two weeks ago, whether they be fictitious or not, have sparked off a blazing row between the Irish and British governments which it is feared will now involve our own government. The IRA have categorically denied any involvement in the killing and are said to be carrying out their own investigation. They have declined to make any comment on the *Daily News* report yesterday about having creamed off over eighty million dollars from the aid scheme set up five years ago by Mr Muldoon in conjunction with the British government. The Irish police are remaining tight-lipped about the killing which took place here in Dublin, but an unofficial source has said to this reporter that he believed the bullet that killed Mr Muldoon was in fact an explosive bullet, which detonated like a small warhead when it hit the Justice Minister. If this is to be believed, then it is a move away from the type of attack usually attributed to the IRA which may well give some credence to their statement last night. This is Jackie Drew for CBS News, Dublin.'

Ivanov and Mikhailov came in just as the broadcast ended and the lights in the lecture theatre were turned back on. Grechko never looked at Ivanov and kept staring directly at the blank screen.

'Colonel, you are a stupid *Ublyudok*. Comrade General Mikhailov has told me everything about your brief interlude from the briefing this afternoon. I had my doubts about you from the very start. I am not usually wrong, Ivanov. In my position I cannot afford to be.' He turned to Ivanov, his eyes like thunder. 'Death would be too good for the likes of you, Colonel, and your dying wouldn't undo anything you have done. I have to make the decision about whether or not to proceed with this operation. If it has any chance of success, the KGB must not suspect anything out of the ordinary. As you are aware, they have a file on all of us, including you, Ivanov. They will be sure to know about your little episode cruising the bars of downtown Moscow. They will be sure to check on you and where you are destined. When they see you are heading west every KGB operative in Europe will be ordered to monitor your movements.'

'If they do, I can lose them, Comrade General.' Ivanov really didn't care any more.

'You might!' Grechko jumped out of his chair. 'I have listened to Comrade Mikhailov pleading your case over and over for the last two hours. I am told there is no one else more suitable for this mission. I find that unbelievable, but I am forced into a situation where I have no choice any more!' Grechko breathed deeply as he tried to regain his self-control. 'Get out!' he screamed.

Ivanov walked out of the lecture theatre slowly. Grechko turned to his 1st Deputy and said in a low tone: 'Perhaps you are right. Ivanov will need watching very carefully.' He sat down again. 'You said you had something in mind?'

'Contrary to what we said before about Ivanov acting alone, I think we should use Mogul as a back-up and a little insurance.' Mikhailov sat next to him.

'Mogul! I should have guessed as much. Well done, Alexei; an excellent choice! We have been doing rather well from him recently. I read a report from him just last week.'

'He is very highly placed, as you know. I was reticent to use him for fear of compromise but, as you said yourself, drastic situations require drastic measures.'

'Will Mogul really do as he's told?'

'Absolutely. He often used one of our other agents.'

'You mean Wolverine?'

'Wolverine is also very well placed to help us with these Field Radio Signals; it would be of great benefit.'

'Wolverine does not know the identity of Mogul. We could lose them both if compromised.' Grechko rubbed his weary eyes.

'I think I know a way around that,' replied Mikhailov.

'All right, initiate.' Grechko stood up to leave. He had missed another night's sleep; he would have to get to bed now even for just a few hours. Mikhailov stood up beside him.

'Wolverine and Ivanov could well outlive their usefulness when this is all over,' continued Mikhailov.

'We are all expendable, Alexei.' Grechko eyed his 1st Deputy closely. 'All of us! Can we rely on Mogul to do the job?'

Mikhailov nodded in response.

'Good morning, Alexei Vladimirovich. I leave "the factory" in your capable hands whilst I sleep the next two hours.' He turned and slowly walked out rubbing his stomach. 'Contact me only in the direst emergency.'

Mikhailov lit one of his English cigarettes and sat back in the chair just vacated by Grechko. Some day, he thought, this will all be mine. Some day sooner than anyone can imagine.

The remainder of the briefing was with Mikhailov personally. Ivanov was whisked away during the early hours of the morning to one of the GRU dachas on the edge of Moscow. Kapitsa kept his eyes on the road, although he was finding it difficult with Ivanov constantly grinning like a Cheshire cat into the rear-view mirror.

Mikhailov leant over and pushed a button on the small control-panel next to the car telephone. A glazed screen whirred upward from the central section sealing the rear section.

'Kolia, stop grinning like that. Kapitsa's concentration-level is poor enough without you goading him.' Mikhailov opened his cigarette-case and offered a cigarette to Ivanov. 'Benson and Hedges.' Ivanov accepted the cigarette. 'Kolia, I wanted this opportunity for a quiet chat before we continue. You mean much to me; we've had our ups and downs, but who doesn't?'

'Is this to do with my loyalty?'

'Kolia, if your loyalty was in question, I would have fed you to Kapitsa by now.' Mikhailov drew on his cigarette. 'I want to warn you. Apart from the KGB being a threat to you, it may be that your main threat could come from Grechko.'

'Elaborate.' If Ivanov was worried, it never showed.

'You could become a liability. In fact, as you said earlier, you will be a liability no matter how this mission ends. It may not be wise for you to return here – at least, until I tell you. You understand what I'm saying, Kolia?'

'*Da*,' Ivanov answered quietly.

'But things have a way of changing, Kolia. Trust me and only me. You have your method for contacting me if necessary. Use it as a last resort and only in case of extreme emergency. We may have only one opportunity to communicate, so don't blow it.'

'I hope I'm not going to become one of your pawns.' Ivanov tried not to sigh.

'Kolia, if you are a pawn, then you are an "established pawn"; you are as important in all of this as me, perhaps even more. I told you before that some day you would have to pay me for saving you after Afghanistan, did I not?'

The Zil turned into the drive leading up to the dacha. Ivanov stubbed out the cigarette, glad that the final cat-and-mouse encounter was now over. He did not trust Mikhailov for a second, yet the man was all he had. His mind wandered back to his vulnerable childhood. Had it ever been any different? School, the Komsomol, the army academy – throughout it all he had been manipulated; the only time he'd really felt freedom was when he'd lived in the United States as an American, and alone.

The dacha was a large white-brick house sitting in its own grounds, remote and inaccessible. The place was well guarded and had clearly been used by the GRU before.

The next twelve hours were hectic. Mikhailov went over everything; Ivanov digested every scrap of information they had on Bloodstone, the 'sleeper' who had settled in Ireland. Of all four agents chosen by General Kurakin, Bloodstone seemed the most suspect. Born in Belfast in 1921, Bloodstone had joined the Royal Navy in 1940 and had served with GCHQ at Bletchley Park in Buckinghamshire as a top-secret linguist and interpreter. He had been finally turned during a student study-trip to Belgrade in 1950 and later 'trained' for a period at Moscow University. The 'activate' he had selected to do his dirty work was a disaffected American ex-serviceman called Harry Garand. Ivanov ran down the list of mayhem Garand had been responsible for in Northern Ireland. It had been as much a testing exercise by Bloodstone as anything else, although the serious effect on the British commitment to Ulster suited Moscow's purpose. Dublin and London were at each other's throat, daily and publicly. Ivanov set the intelligence file aside and went outside on to the veranda. It was already late afternoon; the sun was starting to fall rapidly from the sky. In the distance he could see the movement of the uniformed guards at the edge of the forest clearing next to the access road.

'The general said you were not to go outside.'

Ivanov turned to his left. Kapitsa, the ape-like captain who accompanied Mikhailov everywhere, was sitting in a chair next to the wall of the house. The Moldavian-born GRU captain was the epitome of everything Ivanov detested in the Soviet system: pompous and stupid, but above all vicious. Ivanov ignored the man and walked on down the steps and on to the lawn in front.

'I am addressing you, comrade!' continued Kapitsa.

Ivanov kept on walking. The burly thirty-year-old captain hurriedly followed, determined to goad him into a fight. 'I told the general you were past it; now it's confirmed.'

Ivanov stopped and slowly turned. 'Kapitsa, what do you want?'

'You!' growled Kapitsa, pulling off his leather jacket and shoulder-holster. 'I've heard much about you, now I want to see for myself!'

Ivanov remained calm. The secret of physically engaging an opponent is to maintain a 'controlled aggression', never to lose sight of your objective. An angry man is no use, his energy wasted quickly and usually unnecessarily. He smiled at Kapitsa, and the GRU captain flew into a burning rage; he had waited too long for this, and all semblance of control left in an instant. He surged forward, lunging at Ivanov who side-stepped. But it was not enough; the lunge was a feint. Kapitsa went into a half-roll, his left heel slamming into Ivanov's stomach. Ivanov fell back but quickly regained his balance, blocking off his mind to the pain.

The younger man had the advantage of fifteen years' youth and therefore stamina. Ivanov could not afford a drawn-out fight; it had to end quickly. Swiftly Kapitsa followed through in a crouched position, right arm raised and bent, his open hand held in line to his face. He moved in again, his left forearm extended and ready to block off any defence by Ivanov. Kapitsa jabbed out with his left foot, smashing into Ivanov's leg just below the knee. A sharp pain shot up Ivanov's leg as he stumbled backwards. Kapitsa hit out again and again with his left foot, striking mercilessly at Ivanov's legs; he was forcing Ivanov back towards the veranda. Ivanov gritted his teeth against the pain. So far he'd been lucky. None of the blows had broken any bones, but his luck was fast running out. Once against the veranda he'd have lost his manoeuvrability and been cornered like a rat.

Kapitsa was becoming confident now; he jabbed again and spun to the left, lifting his right foot into Ivanov's face. Using both hands, Ivanov snatched his foot only inches in front of his face and with all the strength left in his right leg he kicked up into Kapitsa's groin. A scream was followed by a shrill cry as Kapitsa's foot was twisted upwards to the point of dislocating his ankle joint. Ivanov pushed him away, and the GRU captain tumbled on to the ground; but amazingly Kapitsa got up again and came right at him.

Ivanov recognized the stance instantly; it was one of the attack sequences taught to all Spetsnaz recruits. Kapitsa was going in for the kill! This was no longer horseplay or a test of strength or ability. Kapitsa lunged the last two metres and brought his right hand up under Ivanov's chin, attempting to crush the windpipe. Ivanov blocked the attack by crossing his two arms at the wrist and pivoting his body to the right. Kapitsa went forward and down on his weakened ankle. Just as he was about to deliver a blow with his left arm a knee was driven

hard into his kidneys. He collapsed like a pack of cards. Ivanov
was over him. Instantly Kapitsa's head was locked firmly in a
vice grip. The man ceased to struggle immediately; it was all
over. He knew the terrible moment had come. Ivanov's right
hand was gripping his jawbone firmly; one single movement or
pressure and he was dead. Ivanov looked up. Mikhailov was
now standing on the veranda just above him, a smile on his
face.

'I see you haven't lost your touch, Kolia.'

Ivanov glared at the general; he had jeopardized a life just
to satisfy his own curiosity. He looked down at Kapitsa; the
man's terrified eyes were bulging.

'Live, Kapitsa, and remember the lesson,' Ivanov whispered,
releasing his grip. He let the man slump to the ground and
then walked up to Mikhailov. 'Perhaps I should kill *you*, comrade?' he whispered.

'But you have a great deal to thank me for, Kolia! Who
saved you in Afghanistan? I did. Who is giving you a second
chance now? I am. But you can't blame me being curious
enough to see if you are still the man you were.'

'Well, I'm not! And I've nothing to feel grateful for,' snarled
Ivanov.

'Kolia, you're lucky still to be alive.'

'Alive! Festering in a clerical job is living?'

'You killed a Soviet Army officer,' retorted the general.

'I stopped an animal killing defenceless women and children!'
Ivanov passed into the dacha. Mikhailov turned his attention
to his hapless assistant still sprawled on the ground before him.

'For pity's sake, Kapitsa! Stop lying there like some wet rag.'
He walked down off the veranda and past the GRU captain,
paying him no further attention. Kapitsa raised his head just
high enough to see his master walk away towards the forest.

'Bastard,' he hissed through gritted teeth.

Ivanov went to his bedroom, ripping off his sweat-stained
shirt before lying down on the bed. He lay there staring at the
ceiling. It wasn't hard to think back to that dreadful time in
Afghanistan; the incident haunted him daily. Sometimes the
memory clouds over on certain matters, but Ivanov was unable
to have that satisfaction. A cursed gift was how his aunt had

described it; a schoolmaster had put it into proper perspective, informing the nine-year-old that he possessed a wondrous ability: a photographic memory. When was the last time he had slept properly? When was the last time he had awakened without the nightmare memory entering his dreams?

It had been a freezing cold morning when the four helicopter gunships had flown in ahead of the transport helicopters carrying the Spetsnaz groups. Each of the troop-carrying Mi-8 Hip helicopters could carry twenty-six combat troops and all their equipment, but on this occasion the two helicopters carried only a half-load; they wanted prisoners back at Kabul. The Spetsnaz operations around Kantiwar Pass had not been going well. Now they had evidence that Americans were assisting the rebels in training and supplying equipment, especially surface-to-air missiles. And that was how Ivanov ended up being sent to Kabul even before the invasion; if any Americans were captured, the GRU wanted him to handle the interrogation ahead of the KGB. But now Soviet satellite surveillance confirmed what had already been reported to him from GRU agents on the Pakistani border: the Americans were operating in safety across the border, west of Peshawar.

To cut the continual boredom he had now taken to joining the early-morning airborne reconnaissance patrols of Frontal Aviation. Of course it was strictly against operational orders – there was too much at stake if he were lost or were captured by the rebels, especially with his specific knowledge of CIA operations in the region – but who with any seniority over himself would take the trouble of rising at three o'clock in the freezing morning and risk the danger of venturing into the mountains? Ivanov had hitched a lift in an Mi-24 Hind attack helicopter, taking a seat in the cramped confines of the forward gunnery position. He sat directly forward and under the pilot, a young Army Frontal Aviation major called Yazov. He had befriended the twenty-seven-year-old pilot during the first week of arriving at Kabul. The young officer was much like himself, independent and forward-thinking, unlike the stereotype of his comrades; he also had a sense of humour and a craving for excitement. He needed to, for the helicopter force at Kabul airbase had taken the brunt of the mujahedin offensive. The tribesmen were quick learners and fearless. If an Afghan could hit a target at a mile with an antiquated muzzle-loading musket, what could he not do with a Sidewinder missile? The young Soviet helicopter pilots had their combat techniques down to a fine art. They had no choice; only the quickest learners survived here. It was nothing anyone could teach them at aviation school; it was a knack, an imperative sixth sense.

Ivanov studied the terrain around him. Although he had the multi-barrel nose-gun at his fingertips, there was little need as the Hind was flying along a cleared vector with four Hinds already circling high above the target area. The Hind soared up the mountainside barely keeping clear of the craggy rock-face. Ivanov was impressed; the young major kept the helicopter at a steady one hundred and twenty miles per hour, keeping within a hundred feet of the mountainside, following it with an ease that was hard to understand – one flick of the wrist at the wrong moment, and the rotorblades would crunch into the rock-face in less than a second. As the Hind neared the top of the hillside Yazov veered to the left, increasing speed down into a wide valley. Far in the distance Ivanov could see two of the other Mi-24 Hinds circling in opposite directions one above the other. Every few seconds flares would shoot out from the sides of the attack helicopters, a normal precaution against heat-seeking SAM missiles.

Yazov's voice crackled in Ivanov's helmet earphones. 'Time to deploy, I think.'

Ivanov didn't quite know what the man meant until he saw the bright light streaming forward from the underside of his helicopter. He looked to his right; another flare was streaming sideways, the blue smoke-trail from the magnesium flare quickly dissipating in the thin atmosphere. Yazov kept changing direction and height; it was unwise to travel in the same direction for too long, even following a cleared vector. It would not have been the first time that the mujahedin had climbed out of a hole in the rocks and shot a rocket into a helicopter's exhaust-tailpipe.

Already the soldiers on the ground were making ready to leave. The operational order had been clear. It was an intelligence-gathering exercise; only selected prisoners would be airlifted back down to Kabul for interrogation, but the scorch-ed-earth policy would be followed to the letter. Every house and building had to be levelled, every farm animal killed, and the remaining villages and their personal possessions ordered, through an Afghan Army interpreter, to move down into the valleys below where the Soviet forces could control them more easily. Ivanov lifted the visor of his helmet and studied the scene below. All the mud and wooden farm buildings to the far side were either ablaze or had been blasted into smoulder-ing rubble. The area around the clustered single-storey struc-tures was blackened and pockmarked, obviously during the aerial attack by the other attack helicopters earlier on. Yazov banked to the right; his eagle eyesight had picked up some-thing.

'Comrade Colonel? What do you make of that down there?'

Ivanov didn't need to turn his head; it was staring him directly in the face, just three hundred metres away. Previously shielded by a small rise in the terrain, but now clearly visible, stood the remainder of the village, a total of forty-two old men and women and children. The women and children were all standing in line along the edge of a precipice overlooking a thousand-foot-deep gorge. The old men and older boys had their hands on their heads and were bunched together sitting in a circle further away from the edge. As the Hind slowed into a hover three of the Spetsnaz commandos began moving some of the women at one end of the line even closer to the edge.

'Land,' snapped Ivanov.

'But, Comrade Colonel, we are not supposed even to be here!' protested Yazov.

'Now!' demanded Ivanov.

Yazov couldn't see his passenger's face but he could feel his wrath. Landing was suddenly a lot easier to accomplish. Ivanov watched as the Mi-24 Hind gunship dropped the final distance to the ground. The soldiers were now prodding the terrified women with their AK47 rifles. Just before the Hind set down in a cleared area some two hundred metres from the villagers the shooting began. A soldier stepped away from the circle of old men and boys, his rifle levelled at chest height, clearly ordering the three soldiers back from the precipice. He glanced around towards the Hind, shielding his eyes from the flying dirt as the downdraught from the propellers blew up a small dust-storm.

Yazov was busy watching the ground come up to meet them just as a woman holding a baby was blown off her feet by the soldier's automatic fire. She disappeared over the edge of the abyss like some rag doll. Another woman standing next to her, and clutching her small daughter to her waist, was next. She gasped and backed in abject horror as the other woman disappeared. A bullet smashed into her shoulder, throwing her sideways. She slipped backwards; the child, covered in her mother's blood, was still gripping tightly on to her long dress as they both followed the first woman out over the edge. Their sickening screams could be heard echoing even above the noise of the helicopter as both mother and child plunged the final seconds to eternity.

Ivanov was out of the forward hatch even before the aircraft touched down properly. He raced towards the lone soldier, pulling off his helmet and dumping it aside as he increased his pace across the last few metres. The other soldiers stood aside as the same soldier lifted his AK47 to shoulder height to aim a further shot at an old woman who stood next in line beside a petite and undernourished infant. Ivanov launched himself forward, transferring his weight on to his left leg, and with a swinging movement slammed his right foot into the soldier's lower back. The man groaned, and his shot went wide as he catapulted forward on to the ground. Ivanov was on his feet before the Spetsnaz soldier could recover. The man sprawled on the ground, winded and momentarily confused. As he tried to raise himself from the dusty earth Ivanov pounced, straddling the man's flexed back, a knee between his shoulderblades and locking his neck in a death grip. The soldier tried to pick up his rifle.

'Touch it and I will kill you,' Ivanov whispered in his ear.

Several of the other soldiers moved forward threateningly. All they could see was a man wearing the uniform of a junior-ranking Frontal Aviation flier threatening their platoon captain.

A voice thundered in everyone's ears; most of the villagers cowered in abject fear as it resounded, echoing off the hillside.

'Attention, comrades!' It was Yazov using the powerful loud-speaker system attached to the belly of the Hind. Normally used for propaganda purposes and giving orders to the Afghan villagers on the ground, it was now being put to good use at last – at least, that was how young Yazov viewed it anyway. 'My brave comrades!' continued Yazov mockingly. 'I have at my disposal such an array of armaments that makes your pla-toon weapons seem like toys. Any further approach towards my comrade there and I will be forced to demonstrate the wrath of the Mi-24.'

Yazov had already identified Ivanov's victim, an Airborne officer with more than just a vicious streak. The man deserved a broken neck, but for now Yazov had to extricate his friend. 'I think I should tell you all that my comrade out there in the flying-suit is Comrade Lieutenant-Colonel Nikolai Andreyevich Ivanov attached to General Staff Headquarters at Kabul. Any attempt – no matter how slight – against my comrade will force me to kill you all.' The last word echoed around the nearby hills. Ivanov could hear the pitch of the Hind's engine change. Yazov was ready for an instant take-off; and, given the circum-stances, Ivanov couldn't blame him.

'Now, Comrade Captain, I suggest that you take your men and report back to Kabul,' Ivanov told the officer. 'I will be making a full report of this affair to General Staff Head-quarters.' The officer was gasping for breath, his face twisted and bent. There was nothing he could do; he had been pinned down by an expert, unable to twist free or even use his combat knife at his side. 'No more killing! Do you understand me?' The officer cocked his head slightly up to one side, his mouth open, his eyes filled with hatred. Ivanov tightened slightly, then released his grip. The man coughed and spluttered.

'What the hell do you think you're doing?' he demanded.

'I am Lieutenant-Colonel Nikolai Andreyevich Ivanov of the GRU. I am ordering you, Comrade Captain, to let the women and children go. If you really need these old men and boys for questioning, take them, but leave the others alone.'

'I . . . have my orders.' The man massaged his throat as

Ivanov fully released him, then he pulled away and stood up, obviously embarrassed at his humiliation in front of his platoon.

'Stuff your orders! You know nothing! These are Afghan tribespeople. You will never get them to talk using force or intimidation; they've had centuries of it. They're hardened beyond your imagination, Captain.'

Ivanov had already noted the red epaulette-flashes of the officer protruding from under the green-webbing shoulder-harness that supported the ammunition-pouches and field-rations strapped around his waist. The captain pulled his bush-hat back on after dusting it on his leg.

'Is that all, comrade?' he snarled. A soldier standing beside the huddled group of old men and boys raised his Kalashnikov rifle towards Ivanov's back.

'No!' yelled the captain over the helicopter noise. Ivanov glanced across as the man dropped his aim. As the soldier approached Ivanov could see he was a sergeant, a hard-faced man, seemingly in his early thirties.

'Come with me, Comrade Colonel!' The sergeant made no attempt to hide his resentment. 'I want to show you something.'

Ivanov followed the sergeant across the village to an Mi-8 Hip transport-helicopter which was sitting in what had been the village square. The aircraft was being guarded by three further soldiers; the two aircrew were busy working at the tail section of the aircraft.

'A minor repair. We will be ready for lift-off in minutes, which is more than can be said for this,' the sergeant said as he pulled open the sliding door at the side of the helicopter. A tarpaulin was draped across something on the floor. He reached in and pulled back the green canvas sheet revealing two badly decomposed bodies, clearly European.

'That is what's left of two of our men who went missing up here last week after one of the supply convoys was attacked.' Ivanov stared at the blackened and puffed faces protruding from underneath the sheet. 'The uniforms had been stripped of them, and they'd been castrated some time before dying.'

'Where were they found?' asked Ivanov.

'In a dried-up river-bed half a kilometre from this village.'

Ivanov stretched over and covered them up; the smell and

133

the flies were almost too much for him. Ivanov remained silent and walked back towards Yazov's Hind. The captain was still standing beside the women and children, cradling his rifle across his forearm.

'No more killing!' Ivanov shouted across to him. He felt like saying something else, but how could anything justify killing women and children?

'These bastards know what happened! They did it!' The captain was screaming now and began waving the AK47 around him with one hand. 'Look at them! Not an able-bodied man in sight! They're all mujahedin! Their young menfolk are up there in the hills with the rebels.'

'We don't make war on women and children!' Ivanov stopped and looked at the captain before turning towards the Hind.

He had only taken a few steps when the shooting started. He swung around, keeping low in a crouch. The captain was spraying the remaining Afghan women and children at the edge of the cliff. Most were blown apart and out into the abyss; others tried to run as the Soviet officer pulled off the brown metal magazine from the AK47, slammed home another thirty-round replacement and crashed the rifle mechanism forward ready to continue firing. Instinctively Ivanov had already drawn the 9 mm Makarov pistol from his holster.

'No!' he shouted once again to the captain, but the man ignored him.

As the officer aimed towards the women and children running up the hillside towards the cover of the rocks Ivanov fired. The single shot hit the captain behind the right ear, killing him instantly. He fell to the ground, the Kalashnikov blasting harmlessly into the dirt beside him. All the other soldiers were too shocked to react immediately. Ivanov simply turned and continued walking back towards Yazov's helicopter. One of the young soldiers standing guard beside the circle of prisoners decided to even the score and pointed his rifle at Ivanov's back.

'Halt!' yelled the platoon sergeant. 'Put away your gun! That's an order, Tamarov!'

The nineteen-year-old soldier dropped his aim, very much to Yazov's relief as he prepared to blast the young soldier into a few thousand separate unrecognizable pieces of meat. The sergeant took charge of the situation, ordering the release of the men and boys and an immediate withdrawal from the village. Nothing could be done for a few women and children that had been injured; their injuries were far too serious and beyond treatment other than pain relief by the platoon medic. As the Hind lifted clear from the village Ivanov studied the devastation they had left behind. Twenty-seven women and children had been slaughtered, a village destroyed along with the livestock, and nobody gave a damn; it was just another village and another operation. But he cared; suddenly, for the first time in his life, Nikolai Andreyevich Ivanov cared about something.

The general commanding the Kabul Airborne Division and Spetsnaz operations had wanted his head, and there was no shortage of volunteers from within the division to form the firing squad. If it had not been for Mikhailov's intercession, Ivanov would have been tried by a military court and then executed. In military terms, within the Soviet Union the GRU is omnipotent, and this saved the lieutenant-colonel.

Since then Ivanov had been kept in relative obscurity as a glorified filing clerk. Mikhailov had told him shortly after saving him from the firing squad that he would one day expect repayment. That day was now.

The door-hinge squeaked, and Ivanov looked over to see Mikhailov standing at the open door.

'Come, Kolia, it is time you went to work again.' The soft low voice was in contrast to the battle sounds that had moments before raged in Ivanov's mind.

Ivanov sat up. 'You mean it's time I started trimming back some roses, don't you?'

Both men stood there for several seconds; then, as if by some telepathy, a smile appeared on their faces simultaneously.

The next day, Monday, 15 June

Ivanov went over the information for the last time.

'This Mogul – how well do you trust him?'

'I've been his controller for nearly twenty years. You get to know a man in that time.'

'Who recruited him?' Ivanov knew he had no right to expect answers to any of his questions, but he was entering the unknown in less than five hours; once he set foot on that Aeroflot jet he'd be truly on his own.

'I did. I was attached to our London embassy at the time.'

'And he's reliable?'

'Very. We've fed him a few "dummies" over the years; he's always come through. As clean as a whistle, as the British say.'

'Motivation?' Ivanov studied the man's photograph in the file.

'The best kind – a mixture of resentment against the establishment and desire for financial benefit.'

'What pressure can we exert?'

'Mogul will do exactly as he's told.'

'But by whom – you or me?' Ivanov studied the general carefully. Mikhailov stared on impassively. 'Can he kill?' continued Ivanov.

'He was in the British Army for long enough; served in Korea and Malaya. I've never asked him, but I'd say he's killed before.'

'How do you contact him?'

'Through our resident in London.'

'So the GRU resident knows Mogul's identity?'

'No. Apart from Grechko and myself, you are the only other person to know his identity. It goes without saying that when this affair is over you extricate yourself without any compromise to Mogul.'

'And what if he *is* compromised?'

'I will take care of that, Kolia. You just do your job.'

Ivanov dropped the file back on to Mikhailov's desk and started for the door, but paused. 'I presume that Mogul will be told I'm in charge?'

'Naturally.' Mikhailov watched Ivanov leave the office. Whatever happened, Ivanov was a dead man.

Ivanov was to travel first from Sheremetyevo Airport to Oslo, ostensibly as a minor member of a trade delegation. On the assumption of a further identity he was to travel on to Schiphol Airport outside Amsterdam, and then finally to London Heathrow. Once in the United Kingdom he was to assume his final cover. It came as no surprise that the means of escape was left open to him alone; 'by whatever means he could find' had been the term used – no contact with the Soviet embassy, no assistance from any source except Mogul.

His prospects of return were indeed minuscule; of that much he was sure. But Ivanov no longer cared; this new venture gave his existence some meaning, something that he had missed for many years. It was 5 p.m. by the time he had completed his hurried briefing. The cover was easier than anticipated. The team had done their homework, and the main cover-story ran closely to a profile he had developed and used himself in the past. He had showered and changed. Just as he was finally checking through his briefcase and travel documents Mikhailov entered the room.

'Kolia! We've got trouble!' The frightened features of the general were obvious. 'Another transmission has been received at the Central Cipher Centre. Thankfully my people intercepted and translated the text themselves.' He handed a sheet of paper to Ivanov. 'It's the location of the agent's next proposed target, but it doesn't say when. If the last transmission is anything to go by, it will be within the next week.' Ivanov studied the message; it read:

> TO OPUS 49
> HUNGARIAN MILITARY ATTACHÉ, LONDON.
> COMPLETION IMMINENT – SITUATION NORMAL.
> BLOODSTONE

'When Bloodstone strikes I'll be waiting. I wonder just which idiot chose this target; it seems almost obscure.'

'Obscure, yes, but, well, who knows?' shrugged Mikhailov. 'I think it would be better if you caused the assassin to abort; much safer really. I am going to research our archives and try to predict the next targets in advance. We must have the answer. Now, come, or you'll miss your flight. I have a car awaiting you downstairs.' He smiled and patted Ivanov on the shoulder. 'And be nice to Kapitsa. He's rather sore at present, and I don't just mean his pride!' Mikhailov smiled, but not at his own attempt at humour. Ivanov had been taken in by the fake message just as Grechko had an hour before. The last time you did that to me was just before I parachuted into Cambodia, thought Ivanov. If his South-East Asian experiences were anything to go by, it was a thought not to be relished.

The journey to Sheremetyevo Airport took fifty minutes, and he took the time to give the situation the benefit of a final assessment. He would do what was necessary. Ivanov was cunning, intelligent; but, above all, given the slightest opportunity, he would blend back into anonymity with ease. He stared to the left as the Lada turned into the sweeping access road to the airport terminal, but in his heart something told him he would never see it again. The Lada drew to a halt outside the main entrance. Kapitsa had remained silent throughout the journey; now he stared at his passenger. The smile on his face said it all for Ivanov. Kapitsa knew the GRU colonel was a dead man.

'Keep up the practice, Kapitsa.' Ivanov stepped out of the car with his single bag, a small case. 'Try one of the Moscow girls' schools next time; they're more your level.'

The GRU captain bared his teeth and immediately snapped the Lada into gear. The car screamed off down the service road.

Ivanov had now donned the identity of a Russian businessman, but with only a short lifespan. He wondered if his own would be any longer.

OSLO

The British Airways 747 jet airliner touched down at Oslo International Airport. In accordance with international agreements the airliner was escorted to the southern side of the main terminal-block. Ivanov watched from his window-seat as the plane was prepared for disembarkation. It was raining heavily. He wondered how much brighter it would be once he reached London; or in fact if he ever would reach London, for he had already noticed the watcher five rows behind – KGB without a doubt. But why hadn't they stopped him at Moscow airport? Why follow him half-way across Europe? There could be only one answer; to obtain proof of the complicity of his GRU masters. Once they obtained that, the old hostility between Soviet Military Intelligence and the KGB would ensure his quick demise.

Ivanov passed through Customs without difficulty, and as agreed he was met by his first contact, a junior GRU officer based in the city. After a delay of twenty-four hours he was returned to the airport, carrying another assumed identity. He had been given assurances by Soviet intelligence operators based in Oslo that his tail had been 'dealt with', but that did nothing to allay Ivanov's fears.

SCHIPHOL AIRPORT, AMSTERDAM
Next morning, Tuesday, 16 June

Ivanov passed through Dutch Customs with relative ease. Like all Russian visitors he was video-taped and photographed secretly by the Dutch authorities. He proceeded through Passport Control, calling himself Vladimir Fokin, a junior delegate of the Soviet Agricultural Delegation and a specialist in plant machinery. After claiming his baggage Ivanov moved out of the Customs area and into the large arrivals suite. The KGB watcher was close on his tail as he strolled towards the information desk. Just before he reached it a dark-haired man, seemingly in his forties and obviously overnourished, stood in his path.

'Comrade Fokin?' The man spoke in Russian.

'*Da?*' replied Ivanov, taking the time to glance at the man's bulging waistcoat and tightly fitting suit; hardly enough room to conceal a gun, but perhaps a knife.

'I am Shipkov, from the Agricultural Delegation based at our embassy here. I have been sent to collect you. There's been a hitch.'

Ivanov nodded. There was nothing in the plan about this; he was to transfer alone. If this was a trap, he would have to make his killing-ground away from the airport. As they crossed the main lobby towards the escalator exit and carpark below,

Ivanov saw his watcher being met by two further men. All three stood, staring as he followed the fat man on to the moving staircase and slowly descended out of sight. After leaving the main airport complex the fat man indicated towards the short-stay carpark.

'I think we'd better get a move on before those buffoons catch up with us!' The man calling himself Shipkov rubbed his lips with the back of one hand after speaking, as if he was getting hungry already.

The man led him through a basement carpark area, an ideal killing-ground. They walked over to a Toyota estate car parked alongside a concrete pillar. Shipkov's shaky hands trying to open the door-lock gave away his loss of nerve; the keys fell to the ground, and the fat man hurriedly picked them up again. Ivanov had already satisfied himself they were alone, and the car didn't present a problem. Even the KGB wouldn't risk an explosion here. As Shipkov tried to place the key in the door-lock Ivanov pushed him gently aside and completed the task for him.

'I'll drive,' he said quietly in English. The fat man kept quiet.

As they left the airport service road and headed east along the main highway the fat man finally plucked up the courage to speak, rambling on in Russian.

'I'm very sorry, Comrade Fokin. Those KGB bastards have been breathing down my neck for the last two days! They're making life hell for every GRU operative at the embassy. Nothing's said! They're too careful for that. Just the constant watching, following; always there when you don't want them.'

'Speak in English, damn it!' The man nodded nervously. Ivanov decided to accept him for the moment. 'How long have you been in the GRU?'

The man seemed puzzled by such a question.

'Ten years altogether, but this is my first posting outside our country. I'm afraid I'm not very good at all this subterfuge.'

'Then, what the hell *are* you good at?' snapped Ivanov.

'Communications. I'm a communications assistant, that's all. I can assure you it was not my choice to be here with all this fuss going on.'

'Then whose choice was it?' demanded Ivanov, rechecking

his rear-view mirror. As expected, they had a tail. The red Ford saloon that had been behind them at the carpark's tollgate was still there, maintaining a cruising speed of fifty-five miles per hour. It would never do if the local police pulled them up for exceeding the speed limit. Ivanov began to accelerate gently, taking the Toyota up to sixty-five, and held the speed steady. He glanced across at the fat man, who was sweating badly. A trickle passed down from the hairline above his temple and disappeared into the fat folds of his neck.

'I asked you a question, Shipkov, or whatever the hell your name is. Who sent you?'

'The resident. But I was not to tell you that, comrade.' The man fidgeted in his seat and put his right hand inside his jacket.

Instantly Ivanov smacked him on the side of the head with an elbow jab. The man groaned and slumped sideways against the door, stunned but not unconscious. Ivanov checked again. The red Ford was still behind; the driver had increased speed and was still pacing him. He quickly tugged at the fat man's jacket; there was no weapon, just a single sheet of paper tucked into the pocket. Shipkov was starting to sound all right; stupid but clean. Ivanov unfolded the paper and read the message carefully. It was from Moscow without any doubt. He remembered the codings from his hurried briefing the previous day, but there was no way he was decoding anything with the KGB tail and a suspect front-seat passenger. Ivanov shoved the paper into his coat pocket and quickly turned his attention to Shipkov.

'Can you hear me, Shipkov?' Ivanov tapped him gently on the cheek with the back of his hand.

'*Da!* . . . Why? . . . Why did you do that to me?' Shipkov was almost in tears.

'Because I don't know you, you did not introduce yourself properly, or use any standard form of password in introduction! Because you've obviously let those monkeys behind us follow you around incessantly! Because you're either a blithering idiot or a very clever KGB assassin!'

The man forced himself upright, rubbing his tender face. 'No! No! I am a loyal GRU officer! I am not used to all of this! I'm a backroom type. Give me a computer terminal or a radio – that's my job! But put me into this situation and I'm all feet! I swear it! I swear it! The resident had no one else he could use!' Ivanov could smell the man's fear. 'I . . . I don't even know who you really are. All I was told was to look for the name Fokin and to give you that paper you have there and then try to lose our KGB tail.'

'And the GRU resident? Why did he not do it himself?'

'He is being too closely watched; the KGB are with him all the time.'

'And after I got this message – what else?' demanded Ivanov.

The man screwed up his face in puzzlement. 'That's what I asked, too. I was just told to get you out of town, head in any direction and try to lose the KGB tail. I was told you would know what to do.' The realization grew on Shipkov's face. 'You . . . you don't know what to do, do you . . . We've been set up, haven't we?'

'Tell me, are you always this clever, Shipkov?' Ivanov kept his eyes on the red Ford. It was still there, approximately a quarter of a mile back on the almost empty highway. 'My guess is if you'd any brains you'd be deadly dangerous!' grinned Ivanov.

The fat Russian began to rub his forehead with a yellow handkerchief.

'What are we going to do? What do the KGB want?'

'I think you'd better tell me all that's been happening at your embassy over the last few days. Just when exactly did this obvious hostility between the KGB and the GRU arise?'

The next fifteen minutes were taken up with Shipkov talking non-stop. Before he'd finished two things were very obvious. The operation was no secret – far from it – and he and Shipkov were going to be eliminated, seemingly with GRU approval!

They took the road south towards Utrecht. At a service station just north of the town Ivanov pulled the Toyota into the forecourt and around the back, following the sign for the automatic carwash. As agreed, Shipkov stayed in the car whilst it went through the wash.

Ivanov took off, hiding in the adjacent vehicle-maintenance yard. He didn't have long to wait. The Ford pulled up in the yard ten metres behind the carwash. Both cars were obscured from the roadway, which was as much to Ivanov's advantage as theirs.

The two KGB agents alighted, leaving their car engine running. Obscured by the jet-stream carwash, they could only just see the Toyota estate car through the haze of foam and steaming water. One of the agents pulled a 9 mm Makarov pistol from beneath his brown business-suit and moved to the side of the carwash, mounting a raised concrete area just above the Toyota. The other man kept his hands deep inside his three-quarter-length jacket, maintaining a covering position half-way between the Ford and the carwash.

The first KGB agent levelled the Makarov and fired twice down into the front of the Toyota. Behind them the Ford's engine was revved up instantly. The second KGB man turned just in time to hear the screeching tyres and see the Ford accelerate directly into him. There was no time to draw his compact Skorpion machine-pistol before the car smacked into his legs, forcing him forward with a thud on to the car bonnet. The Ford swerved towards the right-hand side of the carwash, tossing the KGB agent aside. It then hit a metal guide-rail before mounting the raised concrete area beside the carwash.

The first man had been more reactive than his colleague, blasting an uneven pattern across the windscreen of the accelerating Ford. Ivanov was already crouching across the passenger seat, bracing himself, instinctively keeping the Ford on course as it slammed into the Russian, squeezing him against a metal support of the carwash housing before skidding to a halt. Steam began to rise from underneath the buckled bonnet as Ivanov jumped out of the Ford and wrenched the pistol from the unconscious man's hand.

He fired a shot into the back of the Russian's head, then began to move towards the still form of the other KGB agent lying in the middle of the open yard. He fired twice again. The man's body lifted off the wet concrete in response to the impact. The carwash now began to stop automatically; the spraying water had finally ceased. Ivanov jumped down and opened the driver's door. Apart from the shattered door-window the car was intact.

'It's all over. You can come out now.'

Shipkov eased himself up from the floor behind the front seats. 'Are you sure?' he mumbled.

Ivanov pulled a rug from the rear seat and placed it over the wet driver's seat before climbing in. Without further comment he pulled out and back on to the motorway towards the airport. Shipkov remained in the rear as the Toyota sped north and then west at the first junction off the E25 route.

'You nearly had us killed there.' Shipkov was still shaking. 'How am I to explain all this – the killings, I mean?'

Ivanov didn't reply, and he snapped the car down from overdrive into fourth gear as if indicating his annoyance at such stupid questions. He looked in the mirror; there was no tail, but Shipkov had turned completely white and could not stop himself shaking.

'Get a hold of yourself, Shipkov! This operation was supposed to be a secret, and now it looks as if everyone and his grandmother knows more about it than I do. The only suggestion I have for you is to get the hell back to Amsterdam and plead for the immediate protection of your GRU resident!' He studied the man again. There was something not quite right; Shipkov was trying to make a decision, and it was obviously terrifying him.

'Get into the front,' continued Ivanov.

The fat man immediately scrambled across between the two seats, and it was then that Ivanov saw it. Shipkov had a stiletto-bladed flick-knife taped to his left leg, the handle and folded blade partly protruding from between his sock and his trouser turn-up. Shipkov strained to get into the seat. Ivanov did nothing. Shipkov would wait until they got back to the carpark at Schiphol Airport. Ivanov parked well away from the carpark entrance, pulling up into a vacant space between two other cars. As he applied the handbrake Shipkov bent down as if to tie his left shoe-lace. Ivanov snatched him by the hair, forcing his head into the dashboard in front and then backwards, wedging the fat man down between the two front seats.

'Touch the knife and you are dead,' he whispered into Shipkov's bleeding face. Two fingers were already positioned at the side of Shipkov's neck beside the main artery. 'A single pressure and you'll be dead in less than two seconds.' Shipkov stayed still. 'Who are you?

'I told you already!' cried the man. Ivanov pressed the side of the man's neck – not enough to kill, just adequate to register his threat.

'Honest!' exclaimed Shipkov, suddenly overcome with dizziness from the lack of adequate blood-supply to the brain.

'But you have orders to kill me, too, don't you?' insisted Ivanov.

'Yes, yes, but only if you were compromised and the KGB caught up with us!' pleaded the man. 'I wasn't going to do it, really!'

'You are bad liar, Shipkov, and thankfully a worse assassin. Who gave you the order to kill me?'

He fell silent again. Ivanov squeezed his neck tighter.

'The GRU resident at the embassy. It was sanctioned by Moscow Centre. Grechko, I think!' Shipkov had said too much; he was doomed either way, and he knew it.

'And that was all?' continued Ivanov. Shipkov tried with difficulty to nod in approval. 'Goodbye . . . comrade,' whispered Ivanov.

With the increase in pressure Shipkov blacked out immediately. He was dead seconds later. Ivanov cleaned his fingerprints from the Makarov and dumped it on Shipkov's lap. Leaving the car, he covered the body loosely with the car rug. After removing his luggage from the boot, he finally wiped clean all the areas that he had touched. It was not perfect, but it would all hamper the investigation and add to the confusion. After checking his wrist-watch he headed for the airport terminal; he would just be in time to meet the next connection for London.

Ivanov was relieved to have made it back to the airport undetected. He waited until airborne before using the privacy of the toilet located in the rear of the British Airways airbus. It took almost seven minutes to decode Mikhailov's message, and reading it did nothing to relieve his anxiety.

YOU ARE BETRAYED — CONTACT ME — M

He quickly tore up the paper, flushing it down the toilet. He couldn't trust Mikhailov, either; the man had sent him this

145

message in one hand, yet Shipkov had a knife ready in the other! He would have to lie low for the moment and damn the consequences.

MINISTRY OF DEFENCE HEADQUARTERS, MOSCOW
Thursday, 18 June, two days later

Marshal Andrei Leonidovich Malik sat behind his desk studying the documents that had been set before him. Never in his entire career had he read of such a mess. He looked at least ten years younger than his sixty-five years, but the stress of the last few hours was beginning to tell on him: black rings now encircled both eyes; his hardened features had visibly paled, and to his visitor the frown on his forehead looked as if it would remain indented there for life. As the Defence Minister of the Soviet Union, Malik had automatic control over and responsibility for Soviet Military Intelligence. Malik preferred to call it a vicarious liability; in other words, if something went down that the Politburo did not agree with, so did the sixty-five-year-old Minister, just like a stone.

Malik felt as defenceless as a newborn chick in a rat-infested coop; he was due to attend the extraordinary meeting of the Politburo in less than an hour, and now he knew why. The chairman of the KGB, Igor Glazkov, couldn't apparently wait another four days until the scheduled Monday-morning meeting. He looked at his uninvited visitor, the head of the GRU, Colonel-General Viktor Grechko, who sat nervously fidgeting in the seat in front of him. The Military Intelligence boss of the Soviet armed forces was just as frightened as he was.

'Grechko, I can't decide whether you are just a *General Govno* or simply the stupid *Ublyudok* I've always taken you for!'

'Comrade Marshal! I only found out about this myself just days ago after our communications centre started to receive the additional signals from the West.'

'But you had several choices! You could have simply ignored

the affair and reported the matter through proper channels. You could have used one of your British or Irish agents to sort out the matter. But now you have deliberately involved us personally. You sanction a clandestine operation involving one of your own personal illegals!'

'Ivanov is one of Mikhailov's protégés!'

'So what?' Malik screwed up his face even further. 'You have compromised me! You know as well as I do that Glazkov has been trying to destroy the GRU's autonomy for the last two years. Now you've played right into his hands!' He paused to recover his composure, but it was little use. 'Get in contact with this Colonel Ivanov and get him back!'

'At once, Comrade Marshal.' Grechko took his leave, glad to avoid further time with the raging old bull.

The power struggle between the KGB and the GRU had been going on for decades; even as far back as 1938 attempts were being made to have Soviet Military Intelligence come in under the banner of the NKVD, the forerunner of the KGB. There were always obvious advantages at having two separate organizations, and apart from the dozen or so practical reasons it served the Soviet leadership well to have each intelligence organization reporting separately to the Politburo.

Everyone remembered the story of Nikolai Yezhov, the head of the secret police who also became head of Military Intelligence. On 29 July 1938 the GRU chief Berzin had been executed by Stalin. By the morning of 30 July Stalin realized he no longer held the trump card. He had no one to compare Yezhov to; he had become autonomous. Thus Yezhov also became a liability, quickly following to a similar fate and a certain date with the firing squad.

THE KREMLIN, MOSCOW
Fifty minutes later

The morning meeting of the Politburo got under way at ten o'clock precisely. Instead of the usual attendance of twenty-four for a normal full meeting, only eight of the Moscow-based members arrived for the special closed session. Seven had been summoned to attend, the eighth had been ordered. The Minister for Defence, Marshal Andrei Malik, sat where he had been told to, at the bottom end of the zigzag table where normally each of the Politburo members sat diagonally opposite one another, all partially angled towards the chairman, seated as always at the head of the long table.

The Soviet President entered after everyone had filed through from the outer chamber beside the Secretariat Offices. A general silence now fell throughout the room. The President looked around the small gathering. They were all there, the real powerbase in the Soviet Union: to his left General Igor Glazkov, the fifty-five-year-old chairman of the KGB, seated next to Anatoly Bishovets, the Kamchatka-born Minister for Agriculture and also the youngest Politburo member at fifty-one. Further down the table, and alone as always, sat Nikolai Broshin, the ever-brooding seventy-nine-year-old Foreign Minister. To the right side were seated Peter Suzlov, the President's personal appointee to the Politburo as the newly created Minister for Food, then the Minister for Economic Development and Planning, Yuri Shalimov. Next sat the giant form of a former Leningrad party boss General Valeri Polyansky, the man in charge of the Ministry for Internal Affairs, and finally the Minister for Mining, Alexander Konstantinov.

The President, who also held the office of the chairman, never took his eyes off the Defence Minister as he spoke.

'Comrades, thank you for coming at such short notice, but I fear a matter of the gravest nature has arisen.' The silence turned into a deathly hush. 'I will let Chairman Glazkov explain.'

The chairman of the KGB sat forward; he epitomized everything the Western media described or categorized as a 'Kremlin Hawk'. Just like the rest of them Glazkov had fought hard and long for his position, but there was a burning malignancy within him; he had more than once attempted to usurp the Soviet crown for himself, and although rightly regarded with distrust by his comrades he was too powerful to usurp completely. Glazkov was also a careful man, far too devious ever to be challenged and defeated; even at fifty-five years of age he found it hard to dampen his insatiable appetite for power and wait that little longer. Wherever the Politburo found trouble the newly appointed chairman of the KGB could be guaranteed to be involved.

'Thank you, Comrade President.' Glazkov sounded almost conciliatory. 'Comrades, nearly three weeks ago the Irish Justice Minister, Michael Muldoon, was assassinated. Overpowering evidence has since reached the KGB revealing that this murder may well be related to actions of our fellow comrade citizens here in the Union of Soviet Socialist Republics.'

At the bottom of the long table Andrei Malik moved nervously in his leather seat.

'It is my grave duty,' continued Glazkov, 'to inform you, comrades, of an international infringement of irremissible proportions involving elements of the 2nd Chief Directorate, active in an offensive operation in the territory of both the United Kingdom and Ireland.' He looked down damningly towards the Defence Minister.

'I am aware of nothing!' snapped Malik. He knew full well that whatever he said was wrong. An admission would have condemned him outright, and ignorance could never be an excuse inside the Politburo. Accountability was their life-blood.

Glazkov turned towards the sixty-five-year-old Defence Minister, a condescending tone in his voice.

'Comrade Marshal, are you aware that one of your own "illegals" involved in the matter to which I have referred has already killed two KGB officers in the Netherlands just two days ago?'

'Why? Should I be?' Malik tried to turn the emphasis of the argument around. He was a past master of dialogue, but now it was dawning on him that he might be simply past tense. The younger chairman of the KGB sat forward. Malik was taking the bait.

'Sent there by you *en route* to the United Kingdom, so I am told.'

'Preposterous!' snarled Malik. The rows of campaign medals on the left breast of his dark tunic visibly shook as his voice thundered across the conference room. There was a collective look of surprise from everyone around the table, everyone with the exception of the President and one other. Minister Polyansky's face was hard and angry. He stared directly at the KGB chairman; he could read the bastard like a book.

'Comrade Chairman.' Malik directed his words now to the President but was careful to lower his tone substantially; he was not finished yet, not by a long chalk. 'I, as you can see, am totally unaware of these ridiculous accusations. I must be permitted to consult with the chief of the 2nd Chief Directorate without delay.'

'I understand, comrade.' The President's face was stern. 'Comrade Glazkov, have you a written report encompassing the facts to which you refer?'

Glazkov set his attaché case on the table and opened it slowly. Marshal Malik never took his eyes off him; it did not go unnoticed that the chairman of the KGB didn't even possess the courage to look the Defence Minister straight in the eye. Glazkov pulled out the file copies and set them on the table before him. One of the Politburo secretaries came to his side and, without a word spoken, began passing round the eight copies, each one numbered and marked with the name of each recipient.

'Comrade President, comrades, please read and digest. These files are coded "Omega"; they must be read only here in this room and then returned to me at the end of our discussion.'

The President already knew something of the content, divulged to him minutes before the meeting by Glazkov, so had the advantage of being one step ahead of the others. Malik snatched his copy from the secretary just as the President spoke again.

'Comrades, I would suggest a short recess for us to study the information submitted by Comrade Glazkov. I will go to my office next door and reconvene in fifteen minutes.' There was a general nod of approval from the others. The Soviet President looked down the table at his Defence Minister. 'Comrade Marshal, I would suggest that you have General Grechko available in this building ready to join us at a moment's notice.'

Andrei Malik looked up from his copy of the file and nodded as he rose to join the others now standing as the President moved to leave the room. He was followed out by one of the other Politburo members, his Minister for Food, Peter Suzlov. The tall and lean academic had been brought out of retirement to help formulate a long-term strategy for the Soviet Union's food supplies. As Minister for Food and Supplies the retired economist took the brunt of the national anger at the constant food shortages and near-starvation level now facing millions throughout Soviet society, especially those living in the cities.

Of course Suzlov realized the job ran severe personal risks, but at his age he had little concern for his future. He was happy to act as a buffer for his long-standing friend but, more important, the position would allow him to be a constant and close confidant. For that reason none of the other Politburo members trusted him. He turned, looking back at their long and drawn faces as he shut the adjoining door to the President's office suite. This was not the main office suite used by the Soviet leader, but the temporary accommodation he always used for the lengthy recess periods during Politburo meetings, which now often carried on well into the night. It was a sign of the times. No one in the Politburo needed to be reminded of Lenin's doctrine on personal sacrifice; if one didn't rise to the occasion, there were rows upon rows of vultures waiting in the wings, ready to fill the gap.

The Soviet President slammed his copy of the KGB file down on his desk as Minister Suzlov sat down on one of the two facing green-leather settees and began to leaf through his own copy. Both men had been briefed by the KGB chairman before the meeting. Matters of state security could never be raised inside a Politburo meeting unless the chairman had full knowledge beforehand. It all stemmed from an incident years before when Leonid Brezhnev was once grossly embarrassed during a full Politburo session when a delicate matter of internal security was raised openly in front of the non-Muscovite members. The meeting had ended in a total uproar and had to be finally adjourned while members from Lithuania and Estonia were physically restrained from attacking a Red Army major-general.

'So!' began Suzlov. 'Just what is our hawkish comrade chairman of the KGB after?'

'A full and embarrassing investigation,' replied the Soviet President in a calm voice.

'And fixed in advance!' snapped Suzlov. 'Inside a week he will have taken over the GRU; then it's only a matter of time before . . .' He paused, his voice fading away on the last words.

'Before it's me, you mean,' replied the President.

'Mikhail, it stands to reason. The implications of what Glazkov has tossed at us are potentially disastrous for you! I see this purely as a power struggle; he's found a weakness in Military Intelligence and he's out to exploit it to full advantage.'

The President remained silent.

'Imagine what it means if the KGB takes over full control of the GRU.'

'Total autonomy. Complete power in one person.'

'Mikhail.' Suzlov set his file aside and leant forward, removing his gold-rimmed spectacles. 'Balance will no longer exist. The counterweight of the 2nd Chief Directorate gone for ever!'

'And there's the worldwide implications to consider.' The President raised his hands as if holding a giant invisible atlas before him.

'Forget the worldwide implications. Mikhail! It's you Glazkov is after! Malik is just the means to get him there. With Military Intelligence under his portfolio he will automatically be the most powerful man in the USSR! You, the President, will fade by comparison.'

'I think your cynicism makes you paint too bleak a picture, Peter. I have more faith in human nature than perhaps you have, my friend.'

'And I am much older.'

'Do you have a suggestion? You always have had in the past.'

Peter Suzlov stretched back on the leather settee. 'Up to now you have been seen by the generals as more of an enemy to the Red Army than NATO itself. I cannot see you getting any valid support from that quarter. On the other hand, you have been effectively reducing the powers and overall authority of the KGB.'

'So I have placed myself on an island.'

'There's always the Ministry for Internal Affairs.' Suzlov

spoke softly as he began rubbing the lenses of his spectacles on a pocket handkerchief.

'The MVD? You may have something. Polyansky's totally hostile towards Glazkov.'

'So we can rely on Polyansky's automatic support when we go back inside. He will do anything to upset Glazkov's plans. Glazkov and Malik will have to abstain because they are both part of the issue. That leaves five including me.'

The Soviet leader began pacing the floor. 'Broshin has always stood by me; he'll have seen what's happening. And Konstantinov will do as he's told.'

'That leaves Bishovets and Shalimov. Both are beginning to lean towards Glazkov's camp.'

'I've noticed,' agreed the President.

'The vote could tie, but you can handle that with your own veto.' Suzlov replaced his thick-lensed spectacles. It was almost humorous to watch his tired reddened eyes magnify to twice the size behind the thick lenses; it gave him the aura of a man in a constant state of alarm. But there was absolutely nothing that could surprise Peter Suzlov. He had seen it all before; he had survived the Stalinist purges when as a young man he had pitted his formidable intellect against the NKVD.

Even Beria himself had failed to get the young university professor. Peter Berngardovich Suzlov was entirely outside Beria's league. Stalin's Secret Police chief and leading executioner had to content himself with some of Suzlov's friends and distant family. Stripped of his academic title and position in Moscow, Suzlov found himself working beside peasants in eastern Siberia; but unlike millions of others he had survived and was reinstated back into Moscow in 1954, less than a year after Stalin's death. He certainly was not giving up fighting now.

The meeting resumed; the room again fell silent as the secretaries attending the conference left. Once the door had closed the chairman began.

'Comrades, I have considered Chairman Glazkov's report very carefully. I see us needing much more information before we can debate this issue further.'

'Comrade Chairman, I must protest!' Glazkov did nothing to

153

hide his contempt; he was almost rising out of his seat. 'The longer this clandestine operation, sanctioned by the GRU, is allowed to continue, the closer the Soviet Union is drawn to the brink of something we cannot handle.'

The President wisely ignored the KGB chairman's remarks and addressed the entire gathering. 'Comrades, as you all heard at last week's Politburo meeting, we are close to a further breakthrough with the United States on NATO. The American President has already indicated openly his administration's intention to take all United States forces out of NATO. I must tell you that I am expecting a further communiqué direct from Washington within the hour. As you will understand, I will need an urgent briefing with the Defence Minister and Chiefs of Staff.'

Malik looked up in astonishment; he was being saved – at least, for the present.

'I suggest that we delay taking a vote on this issue and adjourn until nine o'clock this evening.' There was a general consensus. 'Comrade Glazkov, may I suggest that you meet privately with Marshal Malik and General Grechko later today, and be ready to give the Politburo a fuller report this evening?'

Glazkov nodded his approval; it was the most painful voluntary movement that his neck muscles had ever made. Suzlov followed the President out again and into the adjoining offices. He studied the Soviet leader carefully before speaking.

'And *are* you expecting a communiqué from Washington?'

The President smiled. 'I might be; then, again, who knows what these Americans might decide?'

The two men returned to the main presidential office suite at the far side of the Kremlin, overlooking the river. Neither spoke a word further until they were inside the electronic safety-shield of the office suite. All KGB surveillance on the General Secretary's private quarters had ceased some time before, and the ground rules had been changing ever since. The most recent development had been after a confidential meeting with some Soviet scientists. There would be no directional microphones picking up his every utterance, KGB influence and authority were being steadily stripped away to an acceptable level; but now perhaps all that hung in the balance. They deliberated over coffee.

'We are going to have to find out for ourselves,' continued Suzlov.

'Can you arrange it, Peter?' The leader poured himself another cup of black coffee.

'I can arrange most things.' The older man rubbed the grey stubble on his chin.

'Listen, old friend, I must know what is behind this. You saw Malik at that meeting; he was almost coming apart at the seams. You've known him longer than I have. What do you think?'

'Malik is not a man to excite easily. Whatever Glazkov has up his sleeve is terrifying him.'

'Get me Malik here in this office, then get me a face-to-face meeting with the head of the GRU. I want this issue tied up before Glazkov gets the bit between his teeth.'

Two hours later Marshal Andrei Leonidovich Malik was standing in front of the President's desk. He saluted smartly.

'Comrade Marshal, I hope for your sake that you've got a good explanation for all of this.' The President's tone sounded almost threatening.

The sixty-five-year-old soldier's face went white. He doubted very much if his President would believe a single word he was about to utter.

GRU HEADQUARTERS, MOSCOW
Two and a half hours later

Grechko had spoken to the Soviet President on a number of occasions at general meetings since his appointment but never in private. As ordered by Malik, he had kept himself unavailable for the meeting with Glazkov that afternoon. Malik had wisely decided to handle the KGB chief on his own for the moment. It was a shock to Grechko when the Kremlin call was patched through to Kalininski Street. The Soviet President was on his way to see him personally!

Never before in the history of the Soviet Union had the most powerful figure in the Kremlin taken to social calls; but, then, this would be no social call for Grechko. He watched from the third-floor window as the three Zils pulled across the courtyard; he had only minutes now before the arrival of the Soviet President in his office. Mikhailov came in just moments ahead of the President.

'Thank God you're here!' Grechko was sweating. He popped another two capsules into his mouth to ease the indigestion and his ulcers.

'God? That is the first time I have ever heard you say His name aloud.'

'Perhaps it is about time I started to believe in something more than myself, comrade!' Grechko stewed over the thought; he had little time before the door opened and the Soviet leader walked smartly in ahead of his entourage. He had already discarded his hat and raincoat and signalled for his protectors to leave them alone.

'Comrade President.' Grechko came to attention, but did not salute because he wore no cap. Mikhailov stood rigidly to attention in full uniform, saluting smartly. The President looked across at him briefly before staring back at the GRU chief.

'Colonel-General Grechko, you know why I am here, so let us waste no time, shall we?'

'I know, Comrade President.'

The President sat down heavily in one of the armchairs in front of the Louis XV desk. 'I want to know everything, warts and all.'

And he did. Over the next two hours he listened intently to what both army officers had to say, only intervening where necessary to clarify the veracity of the issues raised in Glazkov's report to the Politburo. At the end of the meeting he simply stood and nodded to Grechko, turning once he reached the double doors.

'General Grechko, henceforth on this issue you will answer to me only; no one else unless I authorize you to do so.'

'As you say, Comrade President.' Grechko was in no position to argue.

After the Soviet President left Grechko walked across the floor and slammed the door closed.

'How?' demanded Grechko. 'How did the KGB know about Opus 49 and Ivanov? Eh?' Mikhailov kept silent. 'There is only one explanation: your brilliant Ivanov is a traitor!'

'I don't believe that, Comrade General,' replied Mikhailov nervously.

'Don't be a *Govno*!' Grechko yelled, and then rounded his desk reaching for his medicines; his ulcers burned now, even more than his head. 'This is your fault, Mikhailov, yours alone.' He fired two capsules into his mouth. 'You decided on Ivanov; you also knew of his intemperate nature and the damned implications!' He sat down to help the pain in his stomach subside. Mikhailov stood in front of the desk, biting his tongue. How long would he have to continue suffering this old fool, he wondered.

'Ivanov's finished anyway. His killing of those two KGB officials in the Netherlands cannot go unpunished,' sighed Grechko.

'He's done more than that.' Mikhailov pulled out a folded sheet of paper from the inside pocket of his uniform jacket and set it unfolded before Grechko. 'I didn't think it appropriate to tell the President quite everything.'

Grechko scanned the two-paragraph report on Shipkov's death. 'He's gone crazy!' he exclaimed. 'But what the hell was this Shipkov doing there?' He glared up distrustingly at Mikhailov.

'After Ivanov left for Oslo I took some precautionary measures. I found that the KGB had tailed him to Holland. Yes, he dispensed with two of their field-agents from Department Five; but, if he had to, there was good reason. I took the liberty of sending a message to our station *rezident* in Amsterdam. It was to kill Ivanov if he was compromised in any way, thus covering our tracks in just such an instance as occurred. It seems clear Shipkov tried and failed.'

'So! Now we have Colonel Ivanov, an embarrassment to us, a security breach, and now alerted to the fact we are trying to kill him!' Grechko loosened his tie and sipped some mineral water.

'No, Comrade General, he just thinks it's you that tried to kill him,' Mikhailov said matter-of-factly.

Grechko spat out his water, almost choking. 'Ah! Me?' he shouted.

'I took the liberty of using your authority for Shipkov; that way, if the precautionary action of eliminating Ivanov failed, and he found out about the authorization, Ivanov would in all likelihood still trust me. That way I could get to him myself.'

'I don't care what the President wants. I want Ivanov dead. Is that clear?' insisted Grechko.

'I still think Ivanov should be allowed to explain his actions. There's got to be a reasonable explanation for all this.' Mikhailov played out his part well.

'No! No! No!' screamed Grechko. He was shaking, and he was pounding his antique desk now. 'Kill him! Kill him!'

Mikhailov kept his usual composure. 'Then, I will have to make arrangements to go to England personally. Ivanov, as I said, will trust no one else.'

'I don't give a shit! I want this *Ublyudok* dead, and I don't care what it takes!' Grechko reached for his tablets and capsules again and waved for Mikhailov to leave. As Mikhailov reached the door Grechko spoke one last time. 'Alesha?' Mikhailov stopped and turned. 'I do not want to see you again until this thing is over, understood?'

Mikhailov nodded. 'Completely, Comrade General.'

He left the office. If Romanov had been there to notice, he might just have detected the faintest glimmer of a smile on Mikhailov's face. Contrary to what Grechko imagined, things were going exceptionally well – for the 1st Deputy.

THE PRESIDENTIAL SUITE, THE KREMLIN, MOSCOW
4 p.m.

Peter Suzlov had hurried back from the Politburo secretariat. The President was sitting solemnly at his desk in the presidential office.

'It is worse than we could ever have imagined, Peter.'

'Tell me.' The older man sat down facing the Soviet president.

'It appears that in '68 the GRU, with possibly Khrushchev's approval, instigated a very nasty operation called Opus 49.'

The President paused, grinding his teeth as he contemplated his next words.

'It goes back even further . . . Opus 49 was the original brainchild of no less a person than Stalin himself.'

'I listened to part of the meeting between Malik and Glazkov; the KGB have got hold of the name of this Opus 49 operation, too,' said Suzlov.

'Well, it seems – at least, according to the GRU – that someone in the West has decided to resume Opus 49. They confirmed this subject's involvement in the death of some British Army officer and also of the Irish cabinet minister in Dublin.'

'It wouldn't be that they're lying?' Suzlov frowned.

'I don't think so. The GRU are now involved in this, too; they sent in one of their men, a Colonel Ivanov, to stop whoever is doing this. They also say that one of their agents inside the British security service has seen evidence that the British have also intercepted the radio signals sent to the GRU in Moscow.'

'Can the British decode the messages?'

'They are working on it; apparently they have passed it over to the Americans for assistance. Their man in the security service is trying to keep British Intelligence out of it, but they can give no guarantees.' The President sighed.

'So it is possible the British could get to this "subject", as you call him, before we do?'

'But there's more. This operation was an attempt to usurp and disturb Western influence in the early seventies. This subject they call Bloodstone was one of only four agents recruited by us. Bloodstone operated from Ireland; there were others in Germany, South Africa, and South America. They now think that before they abandoned the operation in 1972 the CIA already knew about the South American agent, perhaps even to the extent of having information on his Field Radio Signals relayed to our trawlers in the South Atlantic.'

'So the Americans could offer the British corroborative evidence! This could jeopardize everything you've striven for!' Suzlov stood up.

'At the minimum it will sway international opinion against me.'

'Mikhail! At minimum it will hurl you from office; you'll be lucky to live out your days in some dacha in Siberia!'

'Grechko's 1st Deputy is a man called Mikhailov.'

'I know him. I wouldn't trust him too far,' cautioned Suzlov.

'I trust none of them, Peter, but he thinks that Ivanov might just clean this up for us, and he may have a valid point.'

'This is worse than ever I imagined!' Suzlov removed his glasses and began rubbing his tired eyes.

'Mikhailov wants to follow Ivanov and meet up with him. If he can't clear up the matter, then he feels Ivanov must be liquidated.'

'You mean murdered, don't you?' retorted Suzlov.

'He knows too much, Peter. If he falls into the wrong hands, then we really are compromised; but I don't say I approve of killing, either.'

'And if he returns home he falls into KGB hands, right?'

'Da,' the President responded sadly.

'This Ivanov – does he really stand a chance? It all sounds so hopeless.' Suzlov shook his head.

'I've asked for his file to be brought to me. I think it's time I learnt something about the man our future rests with.'

THE KREMLIN, MOSCOW
9 p.m.

The adjourned Politburo session got off on schedule. Glazkov was sitting in his usual place at the left-hand side of the table, along with Bishovets and Konstantinov.

'Comrades.' The Soviet President opened the meeting. 'Since this morning's session I have had the opportunity to speak to Marshal Malik and make my own enquiries into this. Chairman Glazkov's allegations are indeed serious. Anything that can affect our present political course must be deemed serious. I am indeed satisfied that our Minister for Defence is in fact to blame. However, I think it only fair and proper for a tribunal to be established to look into all the available evidence.'

There was a murmur of approval from Shalimov and Polyansky.

'I now instruct you, Comrade Marshal, to terminate this operation immediately, pending a full tribunal hearing in closed session.'

Malik looked up from his seat at the bottom of the long table and nodded in confirmation.

'Comrade President, I must register my protest. This is now a matter of state security, and therefore the KGB must be allowed to take immediate steps to ascertain the exact facts.' Glazkov spoke up.

There it was. The challenge had been laid down. Glazkov was playing his cards much earlier than even Suzlov had anticipated.

'I agree, comrade.' The words startled the KGB chairman; he was expecting at least a fight. 'But how can we?' continued the President.

Glazkov was stunned. No one, but no one challenged the KGB; and that included general secretaries and presidents.

'I don't follow you,' he spluttered.

'Your report states that two murders have been committed. Foreign soil or not, if one of our citizens has committed murder and indeed murder against two of his fellow-citizens, then he will be subject to the full rigours of the Soviet judicial system.'

'But the perpetrator is a serving Soviet Military Intelligence officer! The law does not enter into it. This is now a matter of national security; certain strict guidelines have been established to handle such an occurrence . . .' He was flagged down by Suzlov.

'Comrades, let us consider this extremely carefully and not be hasty with our anger at two of our most loyal citizens being slain in such a fashion. The Defence Minister has now been given instructions to cancel this operation, whatever it might in fact be. But, comrades, the law is the law. Upon it we must all stand accountable; it is a fundamental of our society, any society. Comrade Marshal Malik assured me earlier that he has already issued instructions for this Army officer to return immediately to Soviet territory. He will be placed in military custody and then face the rigours of an investigative tribunal in accordance with military regulations, but only after he faces a tribunal as agreed by this Politburo, with full and wide-ranging powers over all matters pertaining thereto.'

'Ridiculous!' snarled Glazkov from across the table. 'You can give us no guarantee that this murderer will return, and I for one will not call off my men. If this operation continues further, it may well jeopardize any peace initiative our general secretary has mentioned earlier today.'

'No one is asking you to call off a hunt for this man, but I have been assured that he will be instructed to return of his own volition,' continued Suzlov.

'You seem to have made many enquiries for a minister in charge of food and supplies.' The implication was obvious.

'Just like you, comrade, I like to know all my facts before acting.'

'Comrades!' interceded the leader. 'I suggest that we establish from this table a tribunal of three to investigate all matters pertaining to this issue, with unlimited scope to examine every avenue fully. I further recommend that this tribunal can and should have the authority to make recommendations as a result of its findings and that this Politburo holds itself in reserve to accept those recommendations without equivocation or reservation. The law will be applied to any individual found in infringement of any offence under our military or civilian judicial code, and that will include those deemed equally guilty by their own negligence.' He paused. There was no further response. 'I will now ask for a vote. All those in favour of my proposal will acknowledge.'

The Soviet President eyed the group carefully. It was risky, for having tabled the motion he could no longer use his precious casting vote.

Suzlov was first to raise his right arm, followed by Broshin the Foreign Minister; General Valeri Polyansky, the sixty-two-year-old Minister for Internal Affairs, was next. The President looked across towards Konstantinov sitting next to Bishovets and Glazkov. The Minister for Mining had sided with the KGB. It didn't absolutely surprise him more than it worried him. Glazkov had something on the old Leningrad party chief; Konstantinov was never one to go against the vote, he would do anything for an easy passage.

It all hung on Yuri Shalimov, the fifty-eight-year-old Minister for Economic Development and Planning. The Soviet leader looked down at him; the man was sweating and staring down at the table in front of him.

'Yuri?' he urged. Shalimov glanced up and then across towards Glazkov. The KGB chairman stared directly in front as if oblivious to the proceedings around him. 'Yuri, are you unwell?' continued the President.

'I . . .' The man was seemingly struggling with himself; it seemed as if some inner battle raged in his mind. His eyes flashed again towards Glazkov and back again to the Soviet supremo. His left hand seemed to tremble, then it moved, just an infinitesimal distance from the highly polished wooden surface of the conference-table. Then it was in the air, not high, but high enough.

The President nodded. 'Thank you, comrade.' He looked around again; no one else moved. 'I carry the vote four to two, comrades.' He tapped the wooden plaque on the table with a small hammer hewn out of a solid piece of mahogany.

Glazkov was already glaring down the table at Yuri Shalimov. It seemed to the General Secretary that the Minister for Economic Development and Planning was almost about to crack at the seams. After another full hour of fairly meaningless discussion they decided to appoint Bishovets, Polyansky, and Shalimov on to the tribunal. Suzlov and the General Secretary breathed deeply. Round one had gone their way.

STOPHAM, WEST SUSSEX
Next afternoon, 19 June

The afternoon sun glistened on the almost still surface-water. The warmth from the high sun and the rising damp from the morning's rainfall gave fuel to the flies and insects fighting for indeterminable positions in the immediate inches above the river's sparkling surface. Steep grassy banks tipped slowly into the line of the thick reeds that surrounded the riverside, almost obscuring the definition of the river-bank as the light current wended its way, almost imperceptibly, downstream.

It amazed Alec Martin how calm the river could be, in utter contrast to the days following periods of heavy rainfall when the gentle meandering river was transformed into a raging torrent. Fishing never used to interest Alec Martin, but in surviving the frustration and boredom of retirement it had become an obsession. It was no longer just a release from his humdrum lifestyle. It was not that he no longer loved his wife and daughter; he just found himself unable to cope with the constant close contact with them, although in his daughter's case it was certainly eased by her university studies in Dublin.

His job had been his life, but that was all in the past. He had been fishing for several hours when he heard someone approaching and glanced behind. His daughter, Julia, was slowly strolling towards him with a stranger. It was only when Alec Martin squinted his eyes that he focused properly on the pair. The man was no stranger after all.

'Sam Nelson! Well, I'll be damned!' Alec Martin smiled, setting his rod to one side and rising from the canvas groundsheet.

Sam Nelson's face broke into a smile. 'You old fool! Just what do you think you'll catch sitting there?'

'None of your sarcasm, Assistant Chief Constable!' continued Martin as he burst into laughter, grabbing his old understudy's hand.

They shook hands warmly and exchanged greetings whilst Julia Martin took her leave, promising to return later with some tea and scones. Her comments were hardly acknowledged by the pair, now fully engrossed in each other's presence. The exchange of gossip, update of information and general items of interest soon abated, and Alec Martin began to give his attention to the limp fishing-line and bobbing float. Sam Nelson sat down on the bank beside his old pal, relaxing his weary body for the first time in twenty-four hours.

'What's troubling you, Sam? You didn't come all this way from Belfast for nothing. Well?' Alec Martin turned his attention to his float now drifting towards the far side of the river.

'Does my anxiety show that much?' replied the assistant chief constable as he unbuttoned his collar and pulled his tie apart.

'Afraid so, old chap,' smiled Martin.

'All right! You win, Alec, but I was wanting to lead into this gradually.' Nelson looked over at a curlew taking flight from amidst the copse to the right. 'Remember when you were a DCI on secondment to us from the Metropolitan Police in the early seventies? You arrived in Springfield Road in Belfast during the latter part of 1971, and I was appointed as your detective sergeant.'

'How the hell can I forget! It was the most hair-raising period of my life, Sam!' laughed Martin, but beneath his exuberant façade he felt an inward concern at the expression on his old chum's face. 'What's the matter?'

'Garand,' replied Nelson.

Martin screwed up his face, adjusting his gold-rimmed spectacles with his free hand. 'But he's dead and buried.'

Nelson stared directly at his old friend. 'Is he? Did we ever find a body?'

'No, of course not. But everything stopped after that night he was caught up in the shoot-out with the Army. It was back in 1972, wasn't it?'

Nelson nodded. 'Did you hear the news three weeks ago about the Irish Minister for Justice, Michael Muldoon?' Nelson stood up and stretched his long legs.

'I read about it in the papers. He was shot dead by a sniper in Dublin if I recall . . .' Alec Martin jumped to his feet, throwing his fishing-line aside. 'Now, wait a minute, Sam! Hold on! Harry Garand is dead. I know it! I tracked him long enough, didn't I? And for that matter so did you.'

It was just then that they were both interrupted by Julia

bearing a tray full of scones covered in thick cream and strawberry jam, along with a large silver teapot, cups, and saucers. They both fell silent. Sam Nelson took the tray gratefully; except for a snack on the plane, he had not eaten in over seven hours.

'Julia, thank you very much. You've grown quite a bit since I saw you last. When was it – 1981?'

'No, it was 1983; it was when you were passing through on your way to Cornwall for a family holiday.' The slender girl smiled; her penetrating blue eyes struck Sam Nelson as almost out of place. He imagined that every young man in the neighbourhood must be knocking at her door.

He was stunned by her precision.

'Yes, I think you're right; it was. I had the caravan with me if I remember.'

'That's right: a cream-colour Campus model, four-berth with double glazing, if I recall correctly.' She smiled again.

'You amaze me, young lady!' Sam Nelson did nothing to hide his feelings. 'She'd make a hell of a copper, wouldn't she, Alec?' Nelson looked over at Martin.

Alec Martin found the humour too difficult to handle. He took the tray from his old friend. 'Julia, Mr Nelson has come a long way to see me. Perhaps later at dinner, eh?'

Julia got the message and nodded curtly. Sam Nelson watched her walk back towards the house. She was wearing a pair of tight blue jeans which revealed the curvature of her hips perfectly; he could only imagine what lay beneath her floppy jumper. For a moment he found himself wishing he was thirty years younger.

'Let's have some of this,' continued Martin. Nelson turned his attention back again.

'Where's your wife?' continued Nelson.

Alec Martin had already begun to consume one of the scones. 'Norma's at a charity meeting in Horsham. She'll be back later.'

Sam Nelson sat down again and slowly sipped some tea, his lips registering the pain upon contact with the steaming liquid; he was so tired, and his mind so preoccupied, he'd forgotten to put milk in his cup.

'Ouch!' He set the cup aside. 'Alec, this killing in Dublin of the Justice Minister was not the first. Can you recall the fatal shooting of an Army officer in Londonderry on Easter Sunday last?'

'Only too vividly. I remember the chill running up my back when I saw the television news. It's funny, but ever since being in Ulster anything to do with the place always attracts my attention.' He looked towards the troubled Ulsterman. 'Sam, I think you'd better tell Uncle Alec all about it.' He patted Nelson on the knee.

Sam Nelson summed up both incidents, the reports he had received and the difficulties encountered in the intelligence field after the Londonderry incident. Alec Martin listened intently. He knew that his friend had to be wrong, but something in his subconscious disturbed him. Then Sam Nelson came to the point of his visit.

'And now to why I'm here, Alec. I need to go through it all again, from start to finish. Not the sort of things that are put in a crime file; I need to mull the whole thing over with someone else who was there – someone like you, Alec.'

Martin looked up at the dark clouds now obliterating the sun. 'Looks like rain. Why don't we go inside? You'll be staying the night of course.' He stood up, packing away his fishing gear.

'Sorry, I can't, Alec. This thing in Dublin is very serious. When I finish here I've got to fly back to Belfast for another meeting with the Chief Constable.'

'Well, at least you'll stay to dinner,' insisted Martin. 'Even your blasted Chief Constable can wait that long, eh?'

Sam Nelson was in no position to argue. 'Just a light supper. We've a lot to go over. That is, if you can remember it all?'

'Oh, I remember all right.' Alec Martin frowned. How could he forget? The murder investigation still haunted him to this day. 'Just how far back do you want to go, then?' Martin asked as they strolled towards the house.

'As far as you can, Alec,' replied Nelson wearily.

'It all goes back to Vietnam in 1967, I suppose . . .'

From within the copse that edged the lawn several branches moved slightly as the watcher tried to get a better view of the two men as they neared the house. Both were out of earshot now, but from their intense conversation on the river-bank the purpose was very clear. The leaves moved back into their natural position once again; the watcher had vanished into the thicket beyond.

Both men settled down in the rear drawing-room overlooking the lawns and river beyond. As the afternoon wore on Martin closed the french windows against the chill evening air. Every word was being recorded by the watcher. The laser directional microphone was trained on the glass doors, using the window as a modulator, with the glass carrying the vibrations of the conversation. Their discussion was interrupted only for a short time while they joined Norma Martin and Julia for some chicken salad. Sam Nelson found it difficult to talk casually to both women. He was desperate to get on with his conversation with Martin; it was something that did not go unnoticed. Afterwards the two men returned to the drawing-room alone, and Norma prepared a further meal for Nelson's police chauffeur.

While her mother chatted with the police driver Julia Martin excused herself and headed out in her little Mini Metro car. She went to St Louise's Convent School at Mayfield. It was her old boarding school and a second home to her. Apart from her parents, the only other person with any meaning in her life was Sister Marianne who acted as librarian at the convent school. The old nun had shared a close relationship with Julia ever since she was a child. Cold and severe with other children, she seemed to melt at the sight of Julia. At times she had been like a regimental sergeant-major, hard and severe, but as time passed Julia grew to love as well as fear the nun. It was more than respect, more than she understood; God's wrath seemed to be endemic in the woman.

Julia crossed the courtyard. She had always gone to see Sister Marianne faithfully each week when she was at home and not away studying at Trinity College, Dublin. She always made a point of calling to see the old woman immediately on her return visits to Stopham; to do otherwise was as close to a mortal sin as one dared. As she approached the cloisters she remembered how for two months before the Christmas exams she had stayed on in Dublin to catch up on her studies and thus missed visiting the convent. Perhaps it had all been a needless exercise for one so intelligent, but she felt nevertheless that she had to make up for the time spent on other, less academic pursuits; it was her penance, but guilt tore at her soul. The old nun had castigated her terribly when she returned home that Christmas.

'You've broken faith with me!' the old nun had cried. 'When you left this convent school you promised me in front of your dear parents to come and see me each month, and for eight weeks I haven't seen sight or sound of you.'

Julia cast the echoes of the nun's thick Irish accent aside as she noticed the pale yellow light shining from between the cloistered arches, a warm glow emanating from the uncurtained windows of the convent library. She knocked on the door and quietly stepped inside.

'Is that you, Julia?' a voice croaked from behind the high shelves of books that stretched the full length of the room away from where Julia stood.

'Yes, Sister Marianne, of course it's me. Who else would it be?'

The old nun rounded one of the tall bookcases next to a small reading-table. She peered at the girl with piercing eyes that shone out from a craggy, scarred, and wizened face, the paleness of which seemed magnified by its setting, surrounded by the starched white frame of the head-dress and black habit. The girl rushed over to the old nun and hugged her tightly. Sister Marianne displayed no emotion, nor did she reciprocate the gesture, her hands remaining at her side.

'I have that book you were wanting,' she said without emotion.

'A lot's been happening at home, Sister. We had a visitor today, an assistant chief constable from Northern Ireland no less.' The girl was childlike in the presence of the old nun; her aura of womanhood had vanished, all she wanted was to please the old woman.

'Come and sit down,' Sister Marianne replied, her twisted face stern as always. 'You can tell me all about it before we have some tea.'

There was a chilliness in the girl's eyes as she followed the old nun towards the table and chairs next to the cold stone wall.

It was after 9 p.m. by the time Julia returned to her parents' cottage. The unmarked white Ford Granada police car was still sitting in the gravel driveway. The police driver momentarily stirred from his slumber as Julia garaged her car and strode into the house. She looked over at him. He sat up and smiled; she ignored him completely. Passing into the kitchen, she could hear the muffled tones of her father coming from the drawing-room. She hesitated before switching on the kettle, pausing to pick up the conversation through the closed hatchway cut into the party wall between the lounge and the kitchen.

'You're home early, dear.'

The words startled her. Norma Martin was standing in the kitchen doorway, knitting in one hand and an empty tea-cup in the other. Julia flushed slightly. 'Oh, Mother, you took me by surprise. I was just about to make some coffee. I could hear Daddy's friend still talking to him next door. I didn't know whether to interrupt them or not.'

'I'd leave them. You know how your father is.'

'Care to join me?' Julia faintly smiled.

'An excellent idea, Julia.' Norma Martin lifted two mugs out of a cupboard. 'How was Sister Marianne?'

'She sends her love as usual.' Julia looked away, fearful of her mother noticing the worried look on her face.

Next door Alec Martin sat back heavily in the large sofa, tapping his pipe into the ashtray at his side; it was a nervous habit he simply couldn't lose. It seemed to Nelson that his old friend had aged considerably in the last few hours. He moved across the floor and glanced outside through the french windows on to the massive lawns and beyond towards the river, now shrouded in the enveloping darkness. Outside the window small insects and moths danced in the light from the carriage lamps mounted on the ornate patio. He checked his watch; it was time to leave already.

'Alec, you'll have to forgive me if I take my leave now.' He smiled, trying to dampen the rising feeling of despondency.

'Do you not think you're taking this thing too personally?'

Alec Martin stared at the fire of logs and coal now roaring steadily in the tall rustic brick fireplace.

'Alec, it's started all over again. The last time eighteen soldiers and policemen died, and now already in less than eight weeks two more people are dead; but this time it's different. It's him all right, but his targets are not just soldiers or policemen cut down in the line of duty; now it's more political, and Dublin was the proof of what I say. I'm sure Easter Sunday was just a trial run.'

'Think you can nail him?' Alec Martin stood up, straightening his maroon waistcoat, and watched as Nelson picked up his overcoat and briefcase.

'I believe so. Our intelligence nowadays is excellent. But the thing that's troubling me is that he knows you, Alec. It was through your efforts that Garand was finally tracked down and shot. He has a score to settle with you.'

'You think that after all this bloody time he'll try to kill me?' Martin began to light up his pipe again.

'Don't discount it. Your name might not be in *Who's Who*, but you're not exactly hard to find, either,' Nelson said drily.

'Sam, there is one thing you don't know about.' Martin began to puff quickly on the pipe. 'Garand was betrayed.'

Nelson almost exploded. 'What! Why wasn't I informed of this before? Damn it, Alec! This could be our first real break. Who was it?'

'It was the IRA. The Provos, to be precise.'

The words took some seconds to sink in before Nelson could reply in a more subdued tone. 'The very people he was working for? I don't understand.'

'No, neither do I, Sam. Perhaps it was some personal vendetta, some jealousy, some doubt about his allegiance. Let's be frank. Those terrorists are afraid of their own shadows at times, and Garand was a Protestant married to a Catholic and living on the Falls Road.'

'Well, I suppose I should say thank you for telling me after all this time!' Nelson shook his head in disbelief. 'Why didn't you tell me this before?'

'I didn't know then. Intelligence only filtered through months later, after the investigation had ended. By that time you had been transferred to another division and Norma and I were packing up to go back to London. I suppose it didn't seem to matter with Garand supposedly dead; the information was put into a Branch file and the cover was closed.'

'At least it's something to work on. I'll see what Special Branch can make of it.'

'Sam, be honest. You've really no idea what you're hunting, so be bloody careful.' Alec Martin crossed the room and placed a hand on the shoulder of his old pal. 'You take this thing too personally and it just might come looking for you.'

'I'll be in touch, Alec, but do yourself a favour and take some precautions around this place, just in case. I will keep you informed of any developments and all that, but do me just one favour. If any more stunning pieces of information happen to pop into your mind, I want to hear about it first! Understood?'

'Understood.'

Sam Nelson decided against disturbing Norma Martin and Julia; he was now trying to pace himself to reach Gatwick in time for the last scheduled flight to Belfast. The waiting white Granada, courtesy of the Metropolitan Police motor-pool, was standing in the middle of the red gravel turning-circle at the front of the rambling nineteenth-century cottage. The police driver was stretched out and dozing in the front seat. Sam Nelson took the final opportunity to speak to Martin.

'This really is a splendid place, Alec. I'm sure it must have cost a fortune.'

'As a matter of fact it did; but, after living for almost forty years in London, Norma and I decided to put everything into getting this place, our retirement paradise. Mind you, we bought the place some twelve years ago, and the prices were modest in comparison to now. Norma loved it for a number of reasons and, then, of course, Julia was of school age and it was handy for us to send her privately to a convent school at Mayfield. In fact the child loved it so much she later went as a weekly boarder. Of course, by then I had retired, and after spending the last few years commuting to London or staying overnight at New Scotland Yard I was glad of the opportunity to be at home.'

Suddenly Alec Martin was aware of Nelson's irritation at his rambling; the man was obviously impatient to be on his way.

'Sorry, Sam, you've a plane to catch and here's me repeating my life story to you for the umpteenth time!' He forced a smile.

'I just wish my visit had been more cordial. I've hardly said a word to Norma all evening. You will give her my apologies?' Nelson frowned as he opened the car's rear door.

'Look, don't keep your Chief Constable from his bed!' Martin smiled.

They shook hands briefly before Nelson climbed into the rear of the Granada. The driver was already awake and had straightened himself up after being aroused by the sound of voices.

'To Gatwick Airport, sir?' He looked at Nelson through the interior mirror as the engine charged into life.

'And don't spare the horses, will you?' He winked.

The young driver from the Metropolitan Police motor-pool smiled. 'You'll be there in a jiffy, sir.'

The car pulled away from the forecourt, crackling over the uneven gravel. Alec Martin watched as it sped out of sight up the long winding driveway and on to the adjoining country road beyond the trees. He had an uneasy feeling, as if someone was watching him. He shrugged his shoulders at the stupidity of the idea before re-entering the house.

Stopham is a tranquil place, set off the main arterial routes in West Sussex just beside the River Arun. The peculiarity of the place, if there is any, is that the village is served by only one road – one way in and one way out. The Granada sped down the narrow road towards the Stopham bridge. Erected around 1423, it spans the River Arun, and is mounted on piers segmented by seven low-level archways. Owing to the narrowness of the bridge structure, traffic is controlled automatically by lights at both approaches, allowing traffic to flow one way only at a time.

As the Granada approached the bridge the traffic-lights changed to green, and the young driver dropped the car into third gear, slowing slightly as the car lifted on to the small incline leading upwards on to the bridge surface. Forming part of the Norman structure, a series of 'refuges' were built beside the main bridge-path. Extending out over the side of the bridge, they afforded sanctuary to any pedestrians trapped on the bridge in the face of approaching traffic.

As the Granada passed the first refuge the driver thought he saw some movement from beside the low parapet wall. He was about to register his thoughts to his back-seat passenger when he saw the car directly ahead. The vehicle seemed to take no heed of their presence and bounced up the incline on to the first stage of the bridge, effectively blocking their path. With the car headlights on full main beam the police driver was almost blinded.

'What the hell's that idiot think he's doing?' the policeman growled, averting his eyes as he quickly applied the brakes, bringing the Granada to a halt on the middle of the bridge. To his relief the other car also stopped. He waited for its stupid driver to reverse, but nothing happened. 'Now what's he think he's at!' exclaimed the policeman. Sam Nelson's Ulster experiences made him more acutely aware of the inherent dangers of being pinned down in such a position; tense seconds ticked away as Nelson assessed the situation.

'Reverse up! Pull off the bridge!' he demanded, easing forward to have a closer examination of the obstruction ahead. It was the last voluntary movement he ever made. The rear windscreen shattered to the clatter of automatic fire as the AK47 assault-rifle emptied into the saloon car. Sam Nelson thudded forward between the front seats, slumping to one side on the floor behind the driver's seat.

The police driver, only grazed on the left shoulder during the initial burst of gunfire, tried to get out of the car, his right hand fumbling for the door release-catch. Only after he had unsuccessfully tugged at the catch several times did he remember having earlier engaged the vehicle's central locking system. His distorted face was still pushed tight against the window when there was a sudden movement just outside the car. He threw himself across the front seats, sheltering his head with both hands. Then he heard a clunking sound and the sound of someone running away.

He lay there, unbelieving, as his ears picked up the roar of the obstructing car's engine as it quickly reversed off the bridge, headlights arcing away from the stricken Granada. Moments later, as the headlights finally disappeared, the policeman sat up and looked into the rear of the car. The assistant chief constable's face was spasmodically convulsing, but the stillness of his gaze was unmistakable. The young driver breathed a sigh of relief at his good fortune and flicked off the central locking-switch, opening the door just as the delayed fuse ignited the Russian hand-grenade which had been tossed in through the broken rear window on to the floor beside Nelson's body. The explosion tore the car apart; hot shrapnel ignited the car's fuel-tank, turning the vehicle into an inferno moments later.

Eight hours later, 20 June

Alex Martin sat forward, his head cupped in both hands. His tranquil world had been violently shattered in a single day. The local constabulary had finally left him alone, although they had insisted on leaving an armed police guard at the cottage for the time being. Now, approaching dawn, he was preparing to swig back yet another neat whisky. The answers were inside his head; he knew that much. He had to remember, but could he? Alec Martin painfully thought back to the start of it all, all those years ago to 1969 . . .

PART TWO

THE BEGINNING

NORTHERN IRELAND 1969

When the British Army first arrived in Northern Ireland they were hailed as the protectors and saviours of the Catholic community, especially in the cities of Belfast and Londonderry. It was in the cities that the street violence and terror had been at their worst. Streets and families were moved overnight, taking what possessions they could readily muster by cart, lorry, even in some instances in overladen prams, containing only the smallest, most valuable, and sacred of their possessions. Some made it with the clothes they stood up in, others were not so lucky. Houses were being set ablaze by roving crowds from the Protestant areas.

In Belfast the Protestant mobs poured down from the Shankill and Woodvale into the adjoining Catholic Springfield, Falls, and Cliftonville areas. But the worst trouble was in the confused hinterland between the Shankill and Falls: an area where Protestants and Catholics had lived in quiet tolerance of one another for decades, only to be lifted from their religious complacency by the half-drunk Protestant gangs, hell-bent on stamping out the rising nationalism then being voiced so loudly by Catholic politicians and the Civil Rights Movement. There were widespread allegations that Protestant rioters were being assisted by the Royal Ulster Constabulary's infamous 'B' Specials, and in some instances the allegations went deeper to include the equipping of Protestant gangs by the police. There were also reports of beatings and shootings by the part-time and full-time mobilized 'B-men', as they vented their wrath on the Catholic population.

Many accounts exist of the numbers killed and injured that year, but no one can ever be certain just how many perished in the vast upheaval of communities, as overnight the population of north-west Belfast was transformed and re-formed. Cupar Street ran from the Springfield Road in a semicircle on to the Lower Falls Road. It was in the shadow of Clonard Monastery that Mary Malloy had brought her newly wed American husband to live. She had met Harry Garand in London where at the age of sixteen she had been sent to work as a maid in a down-market guest-house. Mary had earned just enough to send home some money each month to her impoverished family. Yes, the money was paltry; but it was necessary, and she stuck out the long hours, working a tedious seven-day week to send home the pittance that kept her widowed mother and five younger brothers and sisters from starvation.

It was during the summer of 1968 that she had met Garand. She was attracted to the American immediately. She had first seen him standing in the foyer of the London guest-house, clutching a canvas grip, dressed immaculately in the uniform of the United States Marine Corps; his black hair, cropped short, only seemed to emphasize the rugged but handsome features of the soldier's face. She had never seen anything quite as impressive as the Marine sergeant with his muscular six-foot-two-inch frame outlined in the tailored uniform. Their eyes had met instantly when the young Marine sergeant came in from the street. Mary had glanced up from dusting the reception-counter and caught his smile. That moment had seemed like minutes. In her three years' service in the guest-house no one had ever looked at her in quite that way. Yes, many times she had recognized the lustful attention of admirers, but the American's smile hit her like the sight of land to a shipwrecked mariner. She was now nineteen and since leaving Belfast in 1965 she had only travelled home twice: once at Christmas in 1966; and then in September 1967, and that was for the funeral of her mother's only remaining brother. It had been a bad time. Mary could no longer hide her feelings of loneliness and had pleaded with her mother to be allowed to stay; but both of them quickly realized the necessity of Mary's income, especially with the extra money she was now earning from odd jobs. What had become Mary's darkest secret had also become her heaviest chain of conscience; she could almost see the rust marks of her shackles when she undressed after each night of prostitution in the Piccadilly area. Mary found she could earn more in one night than in a fortnight as a maid, but she needed the front of respectability the guest-house offered. Besides, if she left, questions would soon be asked back in Belfast. She detested her method of additional income and shut out the horrible realities of life from her mind as she counted the rising bank balance in her new Lloyds account.

Mary had been introduced to the world of vice by another maid at the guest-house called Susan Eccles, a young girl who had originally run away from a bullying father in Sheffield. Susan was four years older than Mary; slightly overweight for her height, she was nevertheless able to transform herself from a dull-looking linen-maid into a dazzling redhead for her night-time pursuits. In her stiletto-heeled patent shoes, red leather mini-skirt, and matching jacket she was stunningly sensual. Mary could not decide what she liked most about the older girl. Perhaps it was her sharp humour, or indeed her shameless philosophy of life. It was not until she finally agreed to accompany Susan one evening that she realized Susan's game was not just to flirt with the boys she met and enjoy a 'good time'! Disgusted, Mary had left the Regent Palace Hotel piano bar that evening, fighting back the tears until she was safely back in her dull attic bedroom.

Then, two weeks later, her brother Anthony had sent her a letter, telling of the Protestant landlord's increase in the rent for the squat-like family home, and how her mother had collapsed with exhaustion while doing chores for some old lady on the Cliftonville Road; and Mary finally decided to join Susan on the streets and lose her virginity. Her dark secret had remained safe for over a year, but now with the arrival of Marine Sergeant Harry Garand and his undeniable advances Mary could hardly comprehend how to keep that sordid side of her life a secret any longer. She wanted him more than anything in the world, but how?

Garand had been staying at the hotel for just two days and, although they only exchanged conversation briefly as she served him breakfast and dinner, those brief moments became more intense each time. She was drawn to him as if by some magnetic force. On the third day he invited her out for the evening. She hesitated; it was a management rule for the staff not to fraternize with guests, and she knew the manager, a Liverpudlian called Connors, had no mercy. A month earlier Susan Eccles had been unceremoniously sacked after having been seen leaving a guest's bedroom at four o'clock in the morning.

Mary agreed to meet Harry that evening at the end of the street. It was taking a chance, but she had already decided that being caught did not seem to matter any more. Suddenly she was aware of a new sensation, an excitement she had never before experienced. They met, as arranged, just after seven that evening. Garand was out of uniform, dressed in a grey suit, and as always he was immaculate. Although it was not evident at the start, Harry wore a leg-brace. Initially Mary had just imagined him to be recovering from a broken leg or some other injury. It was much later that she realized the seriousness of his disability.

After the show, a rather poorly done Agatha Christie play, they strolled for a time along the brightly lit streets towards Piccadilly. Mary Malloy hadn't felt as close to anyone in her life. Suddenly she got a terrible sick feeling in her stomach as she saw the two figures walking towards them. Mary immediately identified Susan Eccles. The young woman was clearly drunk, judging from the way she clutched the arm of her uniformed British sailor who seemed preoccupied with peering down the front of the low-cut dress. As they neared, Mary clutched Harry's hand tighter and moved closer to him, burying her head in his shoulder. The American responded, putting his bulky arm around her and holding her closely, as he guided her towards the roadside and away from the staggering couple. Just as they were about to pass, something stirred in Susan and through her drunken haze she recognized Mary.

'Well! Hello, Mary luv, what ya doing on this patch, then?' What started in a slur ended in a shout.

Mary pretended not to hear and continued on past, still clutching close to Harry.

'What's wrong, pet! Cat bit yer tongue?' continued Susan unabashed. She was now pulling away from the arms of her drunken sailor. 'Don't tell me I'm no longer good enough for Mary Malloy! Didn't I teach you every trick with a dick you know? You little slut! Don't walk away from me!'

Mary shut her eyes, trying to blank out the nightmare. Suddenly to her horror Harry Garand stopped in his tracks. He released her from his grip; but, instead of the coldness she anticipated, she was somehow being comforted by a soothing voice. 'Take a stroll on down the sidewalk, honey. I'll handle this.'

She hesitated briefly before being gently guided on her way by a firm hand. She took a few steps before unavoidably stopping and turning around. The sailor had now grabbed Susan Eccles by the arm and was trying to keep her back, but Susan was having nothing to do with the interference and swung her shoulder-bag directly into his face. He staggered back, releasing his grip on Susan and also on the bottle of gin he had clutched in his other hand; it smashed on to the pavement.

'What the hell is it with you, luv?' yelled Susan. 'Always thought you were too good for the streets, didn't you? Or maybe you're frightened I'll take this big hunk of yours and show him what a good time really is!' She rotated her hips.

Mary cringed. She wanted the pavement to open and envelop her. Anything, but anything would be better than this. Already heads were turning on the far side of the street, but it wasn't them she really cared about. She had suddenly become aware of her real concern at losing Harry Garand. Susan Eccles had already begun to stagger towards Mary.

'Why don't you leave the lady alone?' Harry insisted.

'Lady? Don't make me laugh!' cried Susan. Harry Garand instantly blocked her path.

'Get outa my road, you Yankee bastard!'

Suddenly Susan's anger was redirected towards the American. She saw the look in his eye, a combination of pity and revulsion. She just wasn't good enough for him. Susan's blood boiled. She swung at him with the heavily laden shoulder-bag. Harry easily blocked the swinging weapon, ripping it from her fingers. The bag fell on to the pavement, bursting open on impact. Susan's purse and the instruments of her trade lay scattered all around.

'You bastard!' she screamed at him. 'I'll kill you!' She went at him again, this time with clawed hands. Harry simply side-stepped, and the woman fell to the ground, bursting into tears. A small crowd began to gather across the street.

It was all too much for her sailor companion; he was witnessing his night of ecstasy dissolve into the gutter. He came forward, a heavy brute of a man in his forties, with a fury in his eyes.

'You Yanks! All the same, aren't you? Come over here and think you can do what you like! Well, Yank, I'm going to teach you a lesson you'll never forget!' He pulled up his sleeves and threw away his cap. Then he moved, lunging forward and swinging widely with a left hook. Garand flexed his neck, avoiding the blow by a mere inch. As the sailor tried to regain his balance he felt a sharp jab in the ribs. The sailor doubled over; only pure determination still kept him on his feet. Harry had no war with him, hurting the man further would have been stupid, yet he had to be sure the fight was over. He looked back at Mary now standing some yards away; she was shivering with fear. He was about to forget the sailor and take her in his arms when her eyes warned him. Even before she shouted the warning to him he had identified the danger.

The sailor had pulled a flick-knife from inside his sock. The blade had already snapped open and was coming up towards Garand's stomach. Harry Garand didn't mess around. He moved to the sailor's right, taking his now extended arm by the wrist in a vice-like grip, twisting the man's arm downwards, quickly bringing up his left hand and smashing into the man's straightened elbow; the joint cracked instantly. The sailor gave a high-pitched cry, dropping the knife on to the pavement. Then Garand slammed his knee into the sailor's right side. It took the wind out of his sails completely. The burly sailor went down like a sackful of potatoes. The man writhed in agony on the pavement as Garand spoke in a low voice.

'Listen, pal, if you can hear me stay on the ground. I don't want to hurt you any more, and I'm not going to tell you again. Understood?'

The man managed to nod once as he lay sprawled out. Susan Eccles rushed over to the sailor's side wailing like some banshee, or so it seemed to Mary. Harry Garand went over to Mary, pulling her away from the Soho street and the small gathering of onlookers. 'It's all over, so why don't you folks go home?' he yelled across. Mary felt the strength in his grip as he guided her around the street-corner away from the gaping faces. Once past Piccadilly they kept on walking in silence, yet he hadn't discarded her. Why? Mary was petrified to say anything. Her secret was out, but she didn't want to lose him.

She tried in her mind to prepare some sort of statement for him, but nothing seemed to sound right. Then he hailed a black cab. Immediately she anticipated the brush-off. As the cab pulled into the side of the road Garand pulled open the back door and guided her in. She tried to turn and speak, to say something, but much to her amazement he followed her into the cab, giving the driver instructions to go to an Italian restaurant in Hoxton. Throughout the journey there was still nothing said. At one of the sets of traffic-lights the taxi drew to a halt behind several other cars. Mary couldn't take it any more; she moved for the door and almost had it open before strong hands silently pulled her back. The driver looked back through the glass panel aware of what had happened.

'It's OK,' replied Garand.

The driver nodded hesitantly, carefully watching the couple in his mirror before turning right and dropping them outside the corner restaurant. Mary recognized the place but had never been inside before. Her escort obviously had. Garand paid the driver and guided Mary inside. It was on two levels; part of the restaurant was set in a converted basement-area, a wooden staircase leading down from just beside the main foyer-area. The main restaurant appeared to be at street-level. Mary looked around. The place was packed; a small queue had begun to gather near them around the reception-area. She was about to talk Garand into going back outside when a young swarthy looking waiter with a smiling face approached them.

'Mr Harry! What a delight to see you three nights running!' He shook the American's hand and then turned his attention towards Mary, dressed in her grey maxi-coat open down the front, revealing her yellow patterned mini-dress and knee length patent boots. She was sensational. The young waiter's eyes lit up instantly.

'And you are not alone, I see,' the waiter continued.

'Carlo, let me introduce you to Miss Malloy.'

'Delighted.' Carlo continued smiling; Mary smiled back, nervously looking up at her escort to gauge his reaction. There was nothing.

'As you can see, Harry, we are fully booked; but, if you and your charming lady-friend wish, we have a small cocktail-bar on the next floor up.' The waiter signalled towards a further narrow staircase at the far end of the main restaurant. 'It's small but it's private.' Another grin.

'We'll take it,' replied Garand. Carlo nodded and guided them past the queue and past the tightly set tables to another staircase set against a rear wall. They followed him up the steep staircase to the first floor. The cocktail-bar was a small affair which could only accommodate around ten or twelve people, Mary imagined. It was also empty. She cringed at the thought of giving an explanation. Carlo disappeared around a small bar-counter set against one wall. Finally Garand looked at her. 'Who was she?' He stared directly into Mary's eyes; there was no point in lying.

'She worked at the hotel up until last month, then she got the sack for playing about with one of the guests. Mr Connors is very strict about that, you know.' Her voice quivered as she spoke.

Carlo interrupted, setting down two stemmed glasses and a bottle of Chianti.

'Compliments of Carlo. Enjoy. Enjoy!' Then he was gone again back down the rickety staircase.

'Maybe I should go, too.' Mary lifted her handbag from the floor beside her chair and stood up.

'Sit down.' His voice was almost soothing. She'd never heard a Colorado accent before; it was a bit like being at the pictures.

'Every time I hear your voice I half-close my eyes and imagine John Wayne.' She fought back the tears.

'Sit down,' he repeated. She did. 'Now, tell me all about this Connors guy. He sounds a real mean piece of work. I've seen him in action, at the hotel reception the other day; he smacked one of the maids across the face.' He smiled. 'Funny, but when I thought of you I nearly got involved myself.'

Mary looked down at the table. He began to pour the red wine into her glass.

'Connors picks on all the girls; he's a real bully. He also has a peculiar sense of values, one for himself and another for the rest of us.' She took the glass unsteadily in her right hand, drinking deeply. Garand watched her closely. 'He doesn't miss an opportunity to make a few extra bob by cheating the hotel-owners and the guests if he gets the opportunity. Take a piece of advice if you will: don't leave any money lying around in your hotel room. Connors checks each and every room once a guest leaves the key back in reception. Terry – he's the recep-tionist – tells him when the coast is clear.'

'I've seen him. That's the two-hundred-fifty-pound ape that hangs around the foyer, right?'

'I don't know how many pounds, but he's heavy, ay. Terry's an ex-boxer. He's Connors's unofficial minder, if you know what I mean.' She looked up at him for a split second but averted her eyes once she discovered he was staring at her.

'I see,' he said softly.

'I doubt it. Connors, for example, takes a real delight in catching any of the girls misbehaving yet he'd screw the pants off a statue if he'd the opportunity.' She was shaking now.

'Here, take some more wine.' He filled her glass up almost to the brim. 'So that's what happened to the girl we met back there on the street.'

Mary nodded, taking another drink. 'She was one of the ones Connors didn't get into his bed. That was why, when he found her having been with one of the guests in the hotel he gave her the boot; but not until after he'd kicked her about a bit.' Another slug. 'Even refused her two weeks' back pay. One minute she was in the hotel and the next she was lying face down in a back entry, dumped amidst the rubbish-bins.'

'It sounds to me like the only rubbish around your hotel is Connors.'

'So, what am I?' There was an angry tone now; the nervous-ness and apprehension had vanished. 'What type of low-life filth does that make me?' They stared at each other for several moments before Garand broke the ice.

'I think I love you, Mary Malloy.' His voice was muted.

She was embarrassed. Was he playing with her? Why would anyone want her, shop-soiled and used? But what if he did mean it? What if someone really cared about her? Her eyes danced; she could hardly hide her excitement.

'You hardly know me, and I don't know a thing about you. For all I might know, you're married or something!' She was extremely serious now, frowning as she spoke. To Harry Garand she seemed like a lost child. Carlo suddenly appeared at the top of the staircase.

'I see the waiter coming. Let's eat in peace and talk later, Mary Malloy.' He squeezed her hand tightly. Her frown blossomed into a smile once more. And talk they did, walking in Hyde Park until sunrise.

She learnt his full name to be Harold Carl Garand. He was twenty-seven years old, a native of Denver, Colorado, and he had joined the army under Lyndon B. Johnson's conscription programme. South-East Asia had seemed more inviting than the prospects he faced after an orphanage upbringing on the wrong side of the tracks. He had no interest in high school and flunked his graduation. Yes, his conscription-card had been a godsend, for only three days previously the local sheriff had scooped him for being drunk and disorderly, not to mention attempted grand theft of an automobile. The kindly old sheriff had waived a prosecution after the intervention of the orphanage director, especially on hearing of Harry's imminent call-up.

After the drafting procedure was complete Harry had gone on to do well in basic training; the orphanage upbringing helped him cope with the rigours of a regimented army life. After the United States Marine Corps' 'boot camp' he began training in earnest once inside his division, and began specializing in reconnaissance operations; then his natural marksmanship secured him a place on an extended sniper course. Vietnam beckoned. He quickly received promotion and on his first tour of duty in South-East Asia found his forte in the murderous jungles of Vietnam.

He told her of the more amusing aspects of the rookie GIs meandering through the forests with high-band transistor radios taped to their helmets and blaring so loudly that they couldn't hear an order if they ever received one, which was seldom. Of the vast numbers of conscripts who turned to smoking hash and harder drugs just to relieve the fear and boredom. Of the patrols who, direct from Uncle Sam's backyard, went out for the first time all bushy-tailed, knowledgeable, inevitably getting lost, sometimes for days and then frequently ending up shooting at their own side or sometimes even the tail end of their own patrol as they kept going round in circles.

After telling her of his promotion and his third tour, Harry finally told her of his injury which had occurred during a Vietcong mortar attack on a forward army post he had only been airlifted into three days previously. That was almost six months ago yet the memory burnt as vividly as the pain in his right leg. It was during the night-long offensive that he had received shrapnel wounds to the right leg and foot, having previously fought his way back through the VC lines in the faint hope of getting airlifted out of the Forward Base Camp established on Hill 427. Because of the lack of proper immediate treatment and the fact that the remnants of the hundred-strong command-post lay marooned in their shell-torn wire and earth dugouts on top of Hill 427 for a further two days, his wounds became terribly infected.

Finally help had arrived in the form of Cobra helicopter gun-ships and converted Dakota aeroplanes fitted with high-powered multi-barrel machine-guns on each side of the aircraft fuselage, firing thousands of bullets a minute. The aerial action was completed with saturation napalm bombing, temporarily 'sanitizing' the surrounding jungle just before a fleet of Bell helicopters soared in from the east to airlift the remaining nineteen survivors of Hill 427. He was a sergeant then, with his first platoon command, having lost his young lieutenant during the first few hours of fighting. Even with the injuries he had continued to extract the best from his war-weary group. It wasn't bravery, he said; it was a determination to survive.

Although having made a reasonable recovery, the lack of medical attention had resulted in permanent damage to the right foot which a month later was amputated from just above the ankle. The doctors at Saigon had told him he was lucky – he could have lost the leg to the knee even or worse – but what could have been worse than leaving the only thing he loved: army life? They awarded him the Silver Star, presented during a ceremony in Saigon by the visiting Vice-President. In the citation little was mentioned of the fact that eighty-one Marines had perished during the battle; and it saddened him, for the medal on his chest was theirs. They had fought like dogs, hand to hand, and when the ammunition began to run low they used their bayonets, hands, stolen enemy weapons, anything they could find; but amazingly there had been no unit citation forthcoming, nothing of the countless reports of heroism Garand had himself reported.

Disillusioned as he was, he had fought to stay on in the army; he owed the dead that much. He tried for an instructor's post at Fort Lauderdale but failed. It was another blow to him when he was sent to West Germany for further treatment, pending discharge in another few months. Now he was on holiday in London, taking a break on transit back to the States and trying to decide what to do with the rest of his life. But now it was her turn.

Mary began slowly, telling him of her upbringing in the poverty-stricken area of the Falls Road in Belfast. He had of course heard of the place and of the IRA, but little else. She told him of the government which ruled her country from a place called Stormont, of the imbalance of the system that privileged few and the poverty which struck both Protestants and Catholics alike, and of how few were wise enough to see that and those that were wise enough to keep their mouth shut. But Mary painted another picture of a prospect Harry Garand had about given up on: a home of his own.

She continued to tell him of her mother's plight after her father had been killed during a fall from an insecure ladder at Mackies Foundry in the Springfield Road. Apart from the shipyard it was the biggest employer in Belfast, but unlike the shipyard it took in employees from both sides of the community. Because of the importance of the manufacturing giant, no one was prepared to rock the boat and there was no compensation for her mother; just a tiny cardboard box with his personal belongings brought down to Cupar Street by the Protestant foreman and a month later a coroner's report stating simply 'Accidental Death'.

The foreman was a kindly family man called Billy Reid. He did not need to be a genius to realize the serious implications of life without a breadwinner for the Malloy family. The foreman had organized a whip-round at the foundry that same day, much to the noted displeasure of the management who were more concerned with the legal implications of a civil suit by the widow. But they had little to fear; few in the lower working classes had ever heard of such a thing, and Mrs Malloy's mind only stretched to God and her children, nothing more, for that was what the Church had taught her. The whip-round amounted to £108, a colossal sum at that time. It was enough to bury her father, but even the local parish priest, Father O'Neill, resented the intrusion of the Protestant Reid.

After the funeral was over the only regular visitor Mrs Malloy ever had was Billy Reid, a burly man of fifty years, himself a father of six children. Mary imagined he felt a sort of kindred spirit existed between himself and the Malloys that seemed to span any religious divide. Every Friday pay-night, without fail, he always stopped off on his way home with his small rucksack full of fresh fruit and the odd bar of Cadbury's chocolate for each of the children; and before he continued on to the Shankill Road he always placed a five-pound note in the palm of her mother's hand. She was later to find out that it was a weekly collection raised from her father's closest workmates. Without it they couldn't have survived as a family, even with her mother now out working, doing cleaning jobs wherever she could find them and accepting whatever pay was offered, which usually amounted to coppers.

Then, when she was sixteen, Mary got herself a job in London through the assistance of Father O'Neill, who had written a letter to one of his cousins in the hope of getting Mary employment. The priest's cousin was Frank Connors, the new manager of the Berkeley Guest House, near London's West End. So that was how she started in London, keeping a step ahead of Connors' lecherous advances which preoccupied her time both on and off duty. She would have left the job right away; but she didn't even have the money for her return fare, and her mother had already borrowed heavily to pay for her journey in the first place. The loan had to be paid back somehow, and that gave Mary no options. Garand watched her closely as she hedged his questions and paused, feigning tiredness and carefully phrasing her replies.

He did not want to rush her, but she was becoming hesitant and nervous again. Harry Garand was uncertain of many things, but one thing was sure: he was going to Belfast and he was going to marry this girl, if she would have him. She counted the chimes of Big Ben.

'Oh, goodness, it's gone six o'clock. We'll have to get back right away. I'm supposed to start at five-thirty sharp!'

Garand laughed at her concern, but at that moment Mary didn't share the humour. It was twenty-five minutes to seven when the taxi pulled up outside the hotel. Mary quickly darted around to the side-entrance reserved for service staff, while Harry finished paying the taxi-driver and picked up a morning paper from the stand in the foyer. Terry was already at the reception-desk; he eyed Garand cautiously as he handed him his key. Garand took the key from the rough-looking, heavily built man with the clear appearance of an ex-boxer who had had one fight too many.

It was while he waited for the lift that he heard the yelling. It was the voice of a man, a man with a peculiar accent. Then it hit him; it reminded him of one of the Beatles. Harry pressed the lift button again. The shouting continued, much clearer now, coming from the nearby open door leading to the kitchen area.

'You little whore! That's what you are! You tramp!'

Then he heard a girl scream, and something inside him began to erupt. Garand hobbled quickly towards the open doorway. A brightly lit white-painted corridor lay beyond. Harry walked on when he heard the same man's voice again; it was coming from somewhere at the back of the hotel.

'Hey, you can't go down there!' shouted Terry.

Garand ignored the man and continued on.

'You're finished here! Pack your bags and crawl back to Belfast, you Irish slut!' The voice was louder now.

Garand stopped at the first doorway on his right; it led into the manager's office. He saw the burly figure of Frank Connors standing beside his desk, from behind which he could hear a girl sobbing. Connors was staring down at the girl unaware of the intrusion.

'Nobody's good enough for you! Not even me! And you stay out all night with a cripple!' he yelled.

'That's enough!' Garand snapped as he banged the door fully open and into a filing-cabinet. He could see Mary's black handbag lying on the floor in front of the panelled desk.

Connors turned in astonishment, but reacted swiftly. 'Who . . . ? How the hell did you get in here? Guests just aren't allowed! Get out!' he demanded.

Harry closed the door behind him and limped heavily across the floor towards the desk, shoving Connors aside in the process. Mary was lying curled up against the side of the desk, almost in a foetal position, her face held in both hands, yellow dress torn in several places and her tights laddered. Blood was oozing from a graze on her left knee where she had fallen. Garand took her hands in his and helped Mary to stand up. Blood was also oozing from her bottom lip. He quickly produced a handkerchief from his jacket pocket.

'Here, use this, honey.' He touched her gently. 'Now, do you think you can make it to your room to pack?'

'Pack? She's sacked! Fired!' snapped Connors, making sure he stood out of reach by the wall. Mary ignored the remark and nodded to Garand.

'I'm going to see *you* fired, mister.' Garand's voice was cold.

Connors moved towards the door, blocking Mary, a wild look in his eye. 'You'll do nothing! Neither of you is going anywhere.' He partly opened the door and yelled: 'Terry! Get in here! Now!' The hefty night-porter was at the door immediately, having followed Garand down the corridor. Connors perked up, no longer afraid of the crippled soldier.

'There's a customer here who's been too nosey. I think he needs a lesson before he leaves.'

'Let the girl go. Your call's with me.' Garand's face was like stone.

Connors began to smirk. 'Suit yourself.' He glared at Mary. 'Get out, slut!' She still held on tightly to Garand.

'No, I won't leave you,' she pleaded.

He smiled down at her. 'Suit yourself, honey. I'm sorta short-tempered now. Probably couldn't wait until you left anyhow!' He moved her towards a corner beside the desk. 'Stay here.' He smiled down at her.

'What about the jacket, big man? Not want to take it off?' smirked Connors, now full of confidence.

'Oh, I shouldn't think it'll take all that!' replied Garand. He was no longer smiling as he turned to face them.

Terry moved forward first and struck out with his right foot to kick the American in the groin. Garand grabbed the man's foot and ankle in both hands. There was a loud crack and a scream as the man fell to the floor, his face contorted in pain. Connors was already forward, swinging wildly with a metal coat-stand, but he found himself being thrust backwards into the filing-cabinets as the stand was ripped from his hands. The Liverpudlian, now close to the door, made his final mistake and, instead of beating a hasty retreat, swung at Garand with his right fist. He could not understand what happened next; it was all so fast.

Before Connors could determine whether his punch had landed or missed he felt a jagging pain; hard knuckles jabbed his right side. He crumpled under the excruciating pain. Before he touched the floor a knee smashed into his face. All he could feel was a sudden nausea, mixed with pain, then everything went black. Frank Connors lay unconscious on the floor with a fractured nose and three cracked ribs. Despite a broken ankle Terry had crawled to the other side of the room, making sure he avoided further injury. Garand turned towards Mary as he fixed his tie, examining the other man. 'When does the boat for Belfast leave, honey?' He smiled at her.

'Whenever you're ready,' she blubbered, running around the desk and throwing herself into his arms.

Harry Garand spent the remainder of his three-week fur-lough in Northern Ireland staying in the cramped accommo-

dation of a guest house in the Falls Road. He appeared genuinely excited about the prospect of staying in Belfast. It was an
excitement Mary could not share, but by then she had already
committed herself to sharing his life, wherever that was to be.
Their meeting with Father O'Neill was cool enough; he had
obviously made his own enquiries with Connors as to why Mary
had returned so suddenly from London. It was with reluctance
that he finally agreed to marry them, insisting on knowing every
aspect of Harry's past; but the wedding would have to wait
until the American was finally discharged. Secretly, Father
O'Neill was hoping the delay would dampen Mary's determination; he had already received a letter from Connors which
had more than coloured his perception. He was certain that
the American would quickly forget about the girl once he was
home, but the priest could not have been more wrong. For the
first time in his life Harry Garand had the real prospect of a
family, of belonging.

Harry Garand returned to the United States and sought his
ticket out of the army; but it took longer than expected, and
it seemed that after his long fight to stay in the Marines they
were now reluctant to let him go. Before discharge he was
required to return to Fort Lauderdale for a further period of
waiting and medical treatment. After three long months Harry
Garand was finally returned to civilian life and given an air
ticket for any destination inside the United States. He used the
travel warrant for the first leg of his trip to New York's Ken-
nedy Airport. He sent a telegram to Belfast before boarding
the first available flight to Dublin Airport.

The message was addressed to 'The future Mrs Harry
Garand' and said simply: 'I'm coming home. I've done my
time.'

He arrived at Belfast's Great Victoria Street railway station
on the 11 a.m. Dublin-to-Belfast Express. He was both surprised and delighted to see the lone figure of Mary awaiting
him. Since the arrival of his telegram the previous day she had
checked the flight list of every incoming flight from New York
to Dublin and anticipated his arrival by train – although she
tried to convince him for a moment that her presence was
solely due to ESP. They got married within three weeks of the

banns being read and made house in Cupar Street at the Falls Road end.

Garand paid cash for the small terraced house, using a portion of his considerable savings accrued over the years of army service. He had no trade or qualifications for work other than a willingness to try anything and, although intelligent, he could not get the most menial of clerical jobs in the city. Billy Reid, who had been invited, along with his wife, to the small wedding at Clonard Chapel, soon got to hear of the young couple's plight from Mary's mother and arranged an interview for Harry at Mackies Foundry.

It was a manual labouring job, mainly sweeping-up and general maintenance. The word back to Reid was that the job was as good as Harry's, except for a simple interview. The young manager who interviewed Garand took a different view upon noticing his slight limp. After they had determined the nature of the disability, Garand was politely shown the door. Harry Garand had expected as much, but Mary was heartbroken; even a labourer's job would have brought in something on top of his meagre army disablement pension. After some considerable thought she approached Billy Reid again; she knew she could trust him wholeheartedly.

Finally Reid agreed to approach his brother, a welder in the predominantly Protestant Harland & Wolff shipyard. There were a few vacancies in the yard; he knew that for certain. Dirty jobs, but well-enough paid. To Harry's amazement he got a job inside two weeks, of all things driving a fork-lift truck. He soon became well respected in the firm and after the management got to know a bit about his background and war record he was offered a supervisor's job with an additional £10 a week. Things were beginning to look up, and Garand was already openly expressing his desire to start a family. Mary had been too concerned over her now ailing mother and ensuring her youngest brother and sister got started in life ever to consider a family of her own. The only thing that had grieved Garand since their return to Belfast was how Mary had become more involved with her family than with him. Perhaps it was the haste of their relationship, perhaps it was tradition; he just hoped it would sort itself out in time, and it did with Mary's unplanned pregnancy and delivery nine months later.

With the arrival of a baby girl in November Mary's hands were full. At last they were a proper family. But their world began to collapse completely when street violence flared following several marches organized by the newly formed Civil Rights Association, mainly supported by well-meaning university students and left-wing socialists. It was like a spark from a tinderbox on dry firewood. Ulster began to smoulder; and then suddenly, as if by command, it seemed as if the whole province was on fire. The trouble flared first in Derry and then spread into other areas. Both Catholics and Protestants fled their homes to avoid bloodshed.

Sporadic shooting took place in the Lower Falls area of Belfast. Each night it seemed to be getting closer and closer to the Garand house in Cupar Street. Garand was no stranger to battle and he knew what to expect, but Mary was different; she had been through enough. A chill ran down his spine that evening when Mary failed to come back from visiting her mother's house, so he went in search of her. It was during his arduous journey through the mainly blacked-out streets that he noticed the two figures running across the road towards him from the entry. They couldn't see him in the pitch darkness, he was sure of that, but he could see them clearly in the light emitted from the only remaining gas-light by the corner of Leeson Street.

He moved cautiously into a doorway as the two men ran past, one wearing heavy boots announcing his presence like a fog-horn on a still sea, the other panting heavily. Garand stood watching whilst both men stopped at the corner, peering down another street. Then one of the men produced a Thompson sub-machine-gun from underneath his coat. Suddenly both men were caught in the beam of a strong searchlight; a clatter of gunfire was directed up the street. Garand could see the intermittent tracer rounds splashing off the walls around the two men. Neither had the training or sense to move out of the light; both seemed to freeze. Another burst of gunfire ripped into the man with the Thompson and he was hurled backwards out of the light and towards Harry's position, the gun still clutched tightly in his dying hands. The other man finally responded and dived for the cover of the street-corner. He fell and then clambered for the cover afforded by the first doorway, but to his surprise found it occupied. Harry grabbed the man by the shoulders.

'Holy Mary! Mother of God!' The young man's heart almost stopped.

'Take it easy! I'm just taking shelter the same as you,' replied Harry in a quiet tone.

After a few moments the young man regained enough composure to speak. 'I don't know who ya are, mister, but we'd better get the hell outa here, for them ones there will kill us for sure!' The bright searchlight began to move; in the next street a heavy engine could be heard revving up. The man fought to pull away from Harry, but the American's grip was too strong.

'For God's sake! C'mon, will ya?' pleaded the young man, adrenalin pumping through his veins and perspiration now trickling from under his cap and down one side of his face.

'If I get you out of this, where do we go to?'

'Follow me down the road. There's a house not far off. It runs on to the back of Leeson Street; we'll be safe there.'

Garand stepped into the road and picked up the Thompson sub-machine-gun from the dead man's hands. He looked over at the frightened young man. 'Stay there and don't move,' he whispered, but with a commanding tone. The words seemed almost unnecessary; the youngster was fixed to the spot with fear.

Garand moved stealthily towards the corner. The Shorland armoured car was less than one hundred yards away; it was moving slowly up the middle of the riot-torn street. The spotlight slowly arced along the first-floor windows of the tiny terraced houses searching for any movement from inside. Except for the heavy drone of the engine, the stillness of the night was uncanny. The five armed 'B' Special Constables who had followed on foot behind the armoured car now stood further back towards the bottom of the street, huddled in a group. He could see at least two of the men sharing a cigarette while the others huddled around their apparent leader while getting their instructions under the light of a flickering gas street-lamp oblivious to the stupidity of their situation.

The Thompson felt heavy in his hands. Garand had only ever fired a Thompson sub-machine-gun once before, and that was at an Army gun club. It had been a collector's item, heavy, cumbersome, even beautiful with its inlaid silver details, but wildly inaccurate in any but the most experienced of hands. He knew that out of a short burst only the first and possibly second bullets would be on target at a distance of fifty yards, and that was also dependent on the accurate adjustment of the gun's sights. After that the gun would list off to the right. He smiled at his predicament; if he faltered, the Browning machine-gun mounted on top of the armoured car would disintegrate both him and the street around him.

Leaning tightly against the corner of the wall for support, Harry took careful aim, cocking and preparing the gun. He held his breath as he aligned the sights on to the search-light. His heart raced as he gently squeezed on the oily trigger; like most of the weapon it was still smeared with the manufacturer's grease. The two-second burst broke the stillness of the air, blanking out the noise of the armoured car's engine. The lamp shattered, and Harry could hear the screaming. The policeman who had stood partly out of the top hatch manipulating the lamp had taken a .45 slug through the right hand. Harry fired a second burst above the heads of the group of policemen further down the street. He stood no chance of hitting them, but panic soared as they dived for the cover of the gutter and doorways. As Garand disappeared around the corner he could hear the shouts above the screams as someone tried to instil order in the group.

'C'mon! C'mon!' panted the young man as he beckoned Garand to follow him down the street.

Garand stopped. 'What about him?' He looked at the distorted face of the other gunman where he lay sprawled on the road, overcoat covered in dark stains.

'C'mon, will you? He's nothing in this life now! Save yourself, mister!'

The young man turned and began to run. Garand didn't hesitate, but moved quickly after him. Even with the artificial foot he still could maintain a reasonable pace over short distances. Although Garand had familiarized himself with all the side-streets, the speed at which the man moved indicated a knowledge that only came from a lifetime in the area. The young man stopped outside a green-painted door in the middle of a row of terrace houses several streets away. He gave a single knock, and the door swung open immediately; it was dark inside, and Garand was aware of the presence of a young woman as he squeezed past into the narrow hallway.

They moved straight through the house out to the backyard and through a back door, across the alley and into the rear of another house. Again in the darkness, Harry fumbled, banging into a bin in the open yard, almost losing his balance. Once inside the house the door closed behind him, and the kitchen light was turned on by an old woman. Garand saw the young man clearly for the first time; he was no more than nineteen. He was standing beside another, older man whom he took to be the old woman's husband. Both men went into the living-room and although the room remained unlit both were bathed in the light from the kitchen.

'Who the hell's this?' snapped the older man, pointing towards Garand.

'No time to explain now! First hide the gun and we'll leave by the front,' panted the man.

'No time, eh?' replied the older man as he scowled at Garand. 'And you bring a stranger into my house! Where's Liam?'

'Dead!' blurted the young man. 'He's dead!' Then he turned towards Garand. 'See him there? Well, he's a friend, right! So take that gun and do your job. We've lost enough for one night!' Garand could see the tears come into the young man's eyes as he spoke. Trying to keep his temper, he reminded the American of some of his raw recruits on Hill 427. The old woman moved towards him. 'I'll be having that,' she whispered, taking the sub-machine-gun in both hands. Garand had no opportunity to argue as the younger man beckoned for him to follow.

'C'mon, you! You stay with me,' he insisted.

The old man stepped aside as Garand followed through the house and back outside on to the pavement.

'Where to now?' Garand asked.

'We'll head for the Falls. We're well enough away now.'

'If we're stopped, what do I call you?' continued Garand.

'Sean. And you?' snapped the young man.

'Call me Harry.'

Within five minutes both of them were sitting in the back room of a dingy damp-smelling Victorian terrace house. From the wall-mounted gas-light Harry studied the room. It had a high ceiling from which hung an array of clothes all draped over a wooden trellis which operated on a pulley system and on to a small brass handle screwed into the wooden surround of a high curtained window.

Another man came into the room and stood whispering to Sean. He was in his early fifties, with a shock of white hair, tall and lean with the look of a hungry cat. From behind steel-rimmed spectacles his blue eyes stood out from his drawn face like organ stops. He surveyed Harry from head to toe before drawing Sean out into the hallway. Garand sat back waiting for the inevitable questions. He did not have long to wait. The white-haired man came back into the room followed by Sean.

'Just what's your game, then?' he snapped.

'It depends on who's asking, doesn't it?' replied Garand.

'Listen, you are talking to the IRA, and we do the asking – understand?'

Garand looked over at the door. Sean was now nervously holding a .45 Webley revolver in both hands.

'For God's sake, he saved my life!' pleaded Sean. 'If it weren't for him, *I* might have got it, too. Hell, ya should have seen him! He was brill!'

'You speak to me of admiration after the death of Liam?' retorted the taller man with a clear air of authority.

'Look, I don't know who you are,' interceded Garand, 'and I don't want to know, either, but for the record my name is Harry Garand and I live at 26 Cupar Street, I'm married to a local girl and I keep myself to myself just as she taught me to from the moment I came here. I did your man a favour tonight.

'Let's say I'd have done the same for anybody in the same mess.'

'You're American?' asked the white-haired man, adjusting his spectacles.

'Yes.'

'Cupar Street? Yes, I've heard about you. You married the Malloy girl!'

'Well, then, there's no problem, is there?' smiled Garand.

'I'm afraid there is. You know a lot about us and, although we're very grateful, you have to understand our nervousness on the matter.' The man moved in front of Garand and extended his hand. 'The name's "Peter" to you, and this one here's called "Sean". Now we need to know all about you. You've got nothing to fear just so long as you tell us the truth.'

Garand nodded. 'Any chance of some coffee?'

A smile broke on the man's face. 'I think we can do with something a little stronger.' He turned to the young man. 'Don't you think so, Sean?' Sean was now trembling, the shock of the episode was catching up on him quickly. 'Put that bloody gun away before you blow your balls off and get us a bottle in here.' Peter took the gun from him and nodded for him to leave. 'I don't think I'll be needing this.' He set the gun aside; a smile broke over his drawn features.

They sat there until daybreak. It was clear that Peter was totally intrigued by Garand's background, and from the exchange of stories Sean could see a developing affinity between the two men. It was 6 a.m. when a rap came to the front door. Garand could hear the bolts being released and the door creak open. A shaft of strong sunlight illuminated the hall; there was some mumbled conversation followed by the door slamming shut. The young man reappeared at the living-room door again.

'It's all clear. The area is dead quiet. The peelers have been withdrawn to their stations.' Sean spoke with bravado now.

'Just as well for them, too. There'll be hell to pay when word of Liam's death gets out.' Peter nodded and looked at Garand. 'Your wife will be wondering where you are. She's sure to be worried.'

Garand stood up. 'I'll be off, then.' He extended his hand to Peter, who rose to bid him farewell.

'I'll not forget you for what you did for young Sean here.'

'It was nothing,' smiled Garand. 'I'd do the same again. Call it self-preservation if you like.'

'Sean here will show you out,' the man replied.

Garand smiled and left the room for the bright sunlight. There was a chill in the air; he pulled up his collar against the cold wind. After bolting the door Sean joined the white-haired man standing in the back room.

'A good man that, for a Yank,' Sean said shakily. The shock of Liam's death was still with him.

'Too good to be wasted in the shipyard, Sean.' Peter McGoldrick spoke with conviction.

'I'll make us some tea, then, shall I?' whispered Sean as he slipped away into the grubby little kitchen. The noise of the kettle filling up drowned out McGoldrick's next words.

'It's about time Harry Garand went to war again,' he said quietly as he looked at the Webley revolver on the table.

It took Garand fifteen minutes to walk to Bernadette Malloy's house. Mary Garand's relief at seeing her husband safe and well was over-ridden by her anxiety which unleashed a volley of angry comments. Harry took it all in his stride, and it was not until Mary's anger dissolved into tears that he attempted a reconciliation. Mrs Malloy produced a tray of tea and toast in the front parlour where Mary was now sitting on the sofa, cradling the nine-month-old bundle on her lap, her head tilted on to Harry's shoulder. After a few minutes they were found by Anthony, Mary's sixteen-year-old younger brother; he stood barefoot and dressed in a pair of old trousers held up by a single brace. He wiped his hands on his vest before taking a mug of tea meant for Mary, then he sat by the window peering into the deserted street.

'A hell of a morning after a night like last, eh?' He turned to Harry, smirking. 'Where the hell were ya? I was lookin' for ya, and for that matter so was half the bloody street!' There was no annoyance in his voice. Garand sensed a certain bravado.

'I got caught up in Cupar Street when I went out to look for

Mary. I took cover in a house and waited until daybreak when the shooting died down . . . Seemed like the sensible thing to do.'

Anthony saluted him with the mug. '*Slante*,' he said loudly.

The salute surprised Garand, but he smiled back and then stared down at his wife and infant daughter wondering just how long he could protect them from the reality of the situation.

The IRA, depleted by years of apathy, had disintegrated in the fifties and had almost disappeared, but now they had attempted to regroup and many were flocking to their ranks, seeing them as the sole protectors of the Catholic population. McGoldrick's task was to scour Belfast for guns. The 'arsenal' left over from the fifties had either vanished or was so out of date or beyond restoration it was deemed useless. Sympathizers in Eire were scouring the country for weapons and money especially in the wake of massive sympathy that now swept the twenty-six counties, but time and the lack of organization were against him as he fought to amalgamate the remnants of resistance throughout the North into a cohesive force.

Violence flared continually for the remainder of that summer. Shooting and systematic burning and looting became more widespread. McGoldrick had begun to attempt to regroup the old IRA. Many of its rank and file from the fifties campaign were well past their prime, and those that weren't had no means to carry out their aims. The reality was that the only guns on the Falls at the outset of the trouble were a .45 Thompson sub-machine-gun, a rusty old Webley revolver and a few rounds of ammunition.

Each morning Harry Garand slipped out of his tiny terraced house and walked to the shipyard. Each morning he passed by the aftermath of the previous night's violence. Upturned burnt-out cars, smouldering houses and shops, roadways littered with old furniture, bricks, broken and uprooted paving stones and broken glass everywhere. Each morning it appeared to be encroaching further towards his home. He wondered just how long they had before having to flee in the middle of the night, just as so many others had done. He thought of the people affected the most, always the so-called lower working class.

Just where did they go? Just where would it end? But yet the Stormont government seemed to do nothing.

On 3 August the police armoured cars began to break down the makeshift barriers raised in Belfast and Londonderry. In the days that followed the situation became uncontrollable. By 11 and 12 August serious rioting broke out again in Londonderry. It was finally clear that the RUC could no longer contain the violence. On 14 August, British troops marched on to the streets of the Falls and Ardoyne areas of Belfast following the eventual intervention of British Labour politicians and the whistle-stop visit to Ulster by James Callaghan and his entourage. The British Army had arrived on Ulster's streets.

The Army General Officer Commanding at that time was Lieutenant-General Sir Ian Freeland. He gave a number of press conferences, reiterating each time the supremacy of the Army in its peace-keeping role. On 19 August, Freeland took control of the 'B' Specials. By 22 August the Specials had been ordered to disarm. The soldiers were cheered as the saviours of the Catholic minority beleaguered by the months of violence and burning; but, in Sir Ian Freeland's own words, the honeymoon period would not last. By 10 September over seven thousand soldiers had arrived in the province. Then on 28 September a 'peace wall' was erected by the Royal Engineers separating the Falls and Shankill areas; simultaneously traffic curfews were imposed throughout the troubled riot-torn areas of Belfast.

Peter McGoldrick was at his busiest now; it was the job he had been trained for, the job he had waited too long to do, reorganizing the IRA and ensuring its split into both the Officials and the Provisionals. But that was only one portion of his mission. He had already decided that Harry Garand was the other.

Following appeals by Ulster's Prime Minister James Chichester Clark, some of the illegal barricades were removed; then on 10 October 1969 the Government announced the disbandment of the 'B' Specials. Inside twenty-four hours British troops turned on the Protestants of the Shankill Road using CS gas; sixty-nine people were arrested. The rioting and shooting were swiftly followed by the Army's announcement that they would shoot back at snipers.

McGoldrick travelled between Belfast and the 'Maiden City' of Londonderry over the next months, working diligently behind the scenes, keeping the momentum going. Through Mary's brother Anthony and Sean Flynn, he was keeping a watchful eye on Garand. Little by little the American was being manipulated towards McGoldrick. By the time McGoldrick was ready, Harry Garand would be straining at the leash. McGoldrick pushed on, manipulated and expanding his field of influence; he knew better than most that to achieve his aims the violence had to increase.

On 9 February 1971 the first British soldier was killed as a direct result of the violence on Ulster's streets. He died amidst a bomb and gun attack. Two days later three more soldiers were set up and shot dead by an IRA gang in Belfast. Ulster began to percolate and boil. The Prime Minister was forced into resignation and replaced by Brian Faulkner. The killings continued; a bombing campaign ensued. To McGoldrick the republican casualties were irrelevant in every detail but one: they produced martyrs, and martyrs produced volunteers.

Peter McGoldrick got exactly what he wanted on 9 August 1971 when the Prime Minister of Northern Ireland sanctioned the introduction of internment without trial. The principle was simple, and in theory it made good sense. In order to quell the increasing violence and resurgence of the IRA activity in Northern Ireland the main suspects would be arrested and interrogated. Some would be released again, but a number would be detained for an indefinite period, thus allowing the situation to normalize again. One of the biggest catalysts to the rise of terrorism took its effect. Three thousand were arrested by the police and the Army, taken from their beds, from the very streets they were walking on or from their place of work, and put in such establishments as Girdwood Park Army camp off the Antrim Road in Belfast, or Palace Barracks at Holywood just outside the city limits. In other areas of the province similar places were utilized, and overnight they began to fill with men and boys – placed in silence, forced to sit for days on end staring at blank walls, taken periodically for brief interrogation by Special Branch and Military Intelligence, sometimes with reason, other times completely without.

In Palace Barracks the interrogation methods were magnified somewhat. Soldiers, specifically members of the Parachute Regiment, having the fresh experience of Aden in their hearts, used the methods of noise and sleep deprivation to their biggest potential. Undoubtedly results were obtained and real intelligence gathered before a halt was called to these methods. But irreparable damage had occurred, not just to the credibility of the forces of law and order, but also to the poor unfortunates innocently caught up in the practices of torture . . .

It all started for Harry Garand at 4 a.m. on 9 August when he and Mary were awakened by the crashing of the front door. He jumped quickly from the bed, leaving the calliper still resting against the corner of the small bedroom. He hopped on one leg to the first-floor landing. The crashing and banging had now stopped, giving way to the thud of feet and rush of figures into the narrow darkened hallway below. He heard the voices now, Scottish voices, and the flash of torches as the first soldiers into the hallway stumbled over the pram as they fought to find the light-switch.

Garand was completely dumbfounded; his imagination raced trying to determine what was going on. He hopped back to the bedroom and pulled on a pair of briefs before being illuminated in the hall light. Mary Garand was sitting up in the bed, her eyes wide with terror. He started to say something to her just as they rushed in. The floor trembled under the feet of so many. There was no opportunity even to speak as the baton-wielding soldiers in flak-jackets charged into the bedroom. The first two grabbed him by the arms and began trailing him out. He could have struggled but he knew it would only make things worse; there were another four soldiers already lined along the upstairs landing. Garand turned towards Mary as she lay huddled beneath the bedclothes, trembling in fear.

'Get that bastard outa here!' demanded a fat-faced NCO.

Before Garand could speak he was being pushed and hauled along the landing, past the baby's room. The child was crying by now – not that it mattered to any of the uninvited guests. He stumbled at the turn before descending the staircase. The soldier in front raced three steps at a time towards the hallway below, yanking the American sharply by the wrist. While Garand could move fast on just one leg, it was just too much for him; his left leg buckled, and he fell into the burly man and then banged into the banisters, tumbling head first towards the bottom. Garand lay still, sprawled out at the bottom of the staircase; it was taking him every ounce of effort not to retaliate. He raised his head enough to see the shattered front door lying partly on one hinge and broken inwards against the wall. Suddenly he was grabbed by the hair and pulled sharply down the hall. Another soldier had him by the left arm now. His only instinct was to fight; then he thought again of what they might do in retaliation to Mary, and he held back as they dragged him from the terraced house.

It was when he'd been dragged to the doorway he heard her scream. It all flashed before him: Connors, Mary lying sprawled behind the desk. Another scream, this time louder; a sickening terrified sound. Harry Garand reacted; he lashed out with his right hand, gripping the broken door firmly. He ignored the grip on his hair and yanked the other soldier down with his left arm. The soldier lost his balance, falling back into his companion who immediately lost his grip on Garand's scalp. Garand spun around on his back, slicing it on the broken glass around the shattered doorway. He kicked out, smashing his bare heel into one of the soldiers' faces. The young man reeled backwards. Garand slammed the edge of his hand into the side of the second soldier's neck, rendering him semi-conscious. A third soldier standing on the road rushed at him with the butt of his rifle. Garand had already propped himself into a crouched position; as the soldier bore down he deflected the blow with his left forearm and, using the man's own weight, lifted him head over heels with his left foot, sending him crashing into the hallway. Another sickening cry came from upstairs. Garand held on to the SLR and was just about to slam the soldier's face with the wooden butt when the crashing sound of the guns being cocked made him stop.

'Drop the gun!' demanded a voice from behind.

He had no choice. Some things never die, including the instinct of an ex-soldier, especially one seasoned in combat.

He's trained subconsciously to count the number of shots he fires; it's not healthy to need to change a magazine at the wrong moment. He's also trained instinctively to tune into the sounds of the battlefield. Garand estimated three soldiers covering him. He set the rifle beside the soldier he had just toppled. The man immediately grabbed his rifle and jumped up. He smiled at his three pals that stood in the doorway.

'Thanks, fellas,' he said, panting. Then he slammed the rifle-muzzle into Garand's solar plexus. Garand fell to his knees. A rifle-butt smacked into the side of his head just as he heard Mary scream again.

When Garand came round he focused on the child's pram at the kerbside outside his house, broken and upturned. Just like me, thought Harry as he fought to determine what was happening. He was lying on the road outside; at least five soldiers stood over him. Then he was forced up into the rear of the armoured personnel carrier and made to lie face down on the steel floor; every muscle and bone seemed to hurt, his face was throbbing and his left eye was almost closed. He lay there for several seconds before his clothes, false boot and the attached leg-calliper were tossed on top of him.

'Right! Get the fuck out of here, laddie,' snapped the Scots NCO as he climbed into the high front passenger door beside the driver.

Garand managed to look up at him; it was the very same corporal who had ordered him down the stairs of his own home. Then he remembered Mary and the child. His wife had been screaming! He tried to get up. A metal toe-cap dug into his side. He blacked out instantly.

The Saracen armoured vehicle rumbled into life and roared slowly down the street. When Garand came round again he kept still to avoid further punishment. Through the open rear door and between the bulky shapes of the soldiers Garand could see at least one other Army vehicle closely behind them – a covered Bedford lorry by the look of it. They all came to an abrupt halt at the end of the next street. Immediately the NCO in the front passenger seat spoke. Garand was kept face down with several feet on his back, the muzzle of a rifle stuck into the nape of his neck for good measure.

'Right lads, it's number six, the blue door over there. Get moving!'

All the soldiers pulled out except for the driver and another who remained in the back with Garand. He slowly pulled the shirt and trousers around beside him and began clipping the boot and brace on to his leg. Garand heard the banging again; with considerable pain he glanced around through the open rear doors. He could just see them in the glow from the corner gas-light; two of the soldiers were smashing in the front door of one of the houses. Garand watched the lock mechanism give way and the door part company with the side-frame. Then they all rushed in, the corporal standing by the door patting each one on the shoulder as he rushed past; it reminded Garand of the aircraft dispatcher checking the numbers of jumpers at the open tailgate of an aircraft during an airborne drop. The soldier in the back noticed Garand's interest; he leant over and stuck the muzzle of his rifle into Garand's back again.

'Keep your eyes to the front, Mick!'

He'd never been called that before; even through the pain it almost amused him. Garand took the opportunity to ask a question.

'What's going on? Where are you taking me?'

The young driver turned and thrust a large baton in front of Harry's face. 'Keep it shut, bastard, if ya know what's good for you!' The driver smirked and prodded him on the chin. Garand's head jolted slightly; he bit down his anger.

It was obvious that they revelled in their behaviour. He would do as he was told. Before another minute passed a frail-looking man, seemingly in his sixties, was presented at the rear doors of the 'pig'. He wore only a pair of trousers and a vest. Garand was forced to sit up behind the driver, then the man was hauled into the vehicle beside him and the remaining soldiers piled in. Garand didn't know the man, although he recognized his face; he was just someone he had seen in passing, usually on the way to work but never to speak to. What did he have in common with this old man? What was happening to him? Them? Where were they going? The last question was answered first.

The journey to Girdwood Park Army camp was uneventful,

but all he could think about was Mary screaming and the baby yelling. What had the bastards done to her? Was she all right? Where were she and the child now? Finally he managed to squeeze into his trousers but not into the shirt. The fifteen-minute journey ended when they were hauled from the 'pig' and trailed into a prefabricated wooden building. Both he and the old man then had their hands bound behind their backs with plastic handcuffs. They were in fact white plastic strips with one-way tighteners. Garand had used them himself on VC prisoners; he also knew the tricks. He flexed his wrist muscles as the soldiers tightened the cuffs up to the point of cutting off his circulation.

They put him first into a brightly lit room; it had three desks, pushed together into a long row behind which sat two soldiers, one of whom was a captain. The other Garand recognized as having the rank of staff sergeant. Both men wore the insignia of the Black Watch. Harry relaxed his wrist muscles, allowing him some relief from the tight cuffs. The staff sergeant then whispered into the officer's ear; the young captain nodded in agreement.

'Name?' shouted the staff sergeant in a broad Glasgow accent.

Garand remained silent.

'Name?' he continued.

The corporal leading the arrest teams got embarrassed and spoke up.

'Garand, Harry.'

'Age?' continued the staff sergeant, without looking up.

'What the hell's going on?' demanded Garand.

The staff sergeant set his pencil on the notebook in front of him. 'If you know what's good for you, laddie, you'll answer the question. Now, what's your age?'

'Thirty.' Garand had no fear, but what was the use in arguing?

'Occupation? What's your occupation?' continued the staff sergeant.

'Supervisor in the Belfast shipyard.'

The staff sergeant continued without looking up. 'All right, your number is twenty-eight. Remember that. Right, Corporal, take him away and bring in the next one.'

Garand pulled at his two escorts. 'Hey! Wait a minute! Just what the hell's going on? God damn it! I've got injuries from your monkeys here! I want to know about my wife and kid! I've answered your questions. You answer mine!'

The young officer interceded, displaying an obvious boredom for the entire proceedings. 'You are arrested, Garand, on suspicion of being a terrorist.' He spoke with a clipped English accent.

'I don't give a fuck about your suspicions! On whose word? That's what I want to know!' Garand pulled at the plastic handcuffs that now bound both hands behind his back; the corporal yanked at them, tightening the cuffs even further. Garand winced. 'Look at me! Look what your goons have done!'

'You are in no position to say anything, Garand!' shouted the officer. 'I am informed you assaulted my men when they called at your house. What do you expect? Sympathy?'

'Your men are shit, just like you.'

'Garand, let me make it clear that you face charges of assault and also of illegal possession of a firearm with intent to endanger life. You are lucky my men didn't shoot you; they had a right to.' The captain looked towards the staff sergeant, who nodded in confirmation. 'Now, take him out! We've had enough of his type for one night.'

'I want to see my wife, damn it!' Then they grabbed him.

Garand fought to stay in the room, but it was no use; with one on each arm and another pulling on his hair he was going just where they wanted him. He tried to shout back, but several blows to his stomach with a baton put paid to his utterance. Outside the room he was given yet another beating before being dumped in a windowless room and forced on to a chair. It was one of four chairs in the room, one facing each wall. He sat there, hands still bound, shirtless and shivering in the chill of the morning air now entering through the open door.

Garand found himself now in the company of two RUC men in their bottle-green uniforms. The army corporal leading the arrest entered the room and pointed towards him.

'A tricky one, is this laddie; he tried to rough up a couple of my lads when we went to pick him up.' Garand glared at him. The corporal spat in his face and walked out amidst the policemen's laughter.

Garand felt the spittle trickle down his cheek. The door slammed shut behind him, then the two policemen began whispering. Garand continued to stare at the whitewashed walls, fighting off the pain especially from his swollen hands. It was not long before the remaining seats were filled with more suspects all wheeled in off the streets. One was an old man, sobbing continuously. Garand listened as one of the policemen spoke softly to him. From what he heard, the old man had been on his way home from his work as a nightwatchman when a passing army unit sprang on him, snatching him into the back of their Bedford lorry. He sounded pitiful. Garand reckoned he would admit to anything they wanted him to. The other two prisoners stayed silent; from then on no one else spoke. After another hour one of the policemen tapped Garand on the shoulder.

'Are your hands sore, mate?' Garand stared at him. The middle-aged policeman actually looked concerned; it surprised him. 'Your hands – they're going purple; those cuffs look too tight.'

'That's affirmative,' grunted Garand, returning his gaze to the wall in front.

He wasn't expecting any favours, but the policeman produced a penknife and began to cut slowly through the plastic handcuffs. It took him some time before he had finally cut them off. Garand's wrists had become so swollen that cutting into the flesh was inevitable. Garand never acknowledged the pain of the razor-sharp blade. He was not going to acknowledge anything to these people; he had decided that some time before. He was examining the knife-cuts to his wrists and rubbing his hands when the door opened and another uniformed policeman walked in.

'Prisoner 28.'

Garand was tapped on the shoulder. He stood up slowly and with extreme difficulty; apart from the beating he had taken to the head and face, they had laid into his kidneys and stomach with their rifles and batons. As he limped from the room he noticed for the first time that a white card displaying a number was pinned to the back of each chair. Number 28 was now vacant. He smiled, imagining the bastards' faces if they all switched cards. Who could tell who was who? Then he found out how they did it. Outside in the corridor he was placed against a wall and given a card to hold up in front of his chest. A flashbulb exploded, then another. Afterwards he was led to a medical room where a medic somewhat roughly treated his injuries. Half an hour later he was brought into an interview-room further down the corridor.

The grilling by the two Special Branch detectives was constant. Garand would not participate until the officers confirmed his wife and child's safety. Only then did he decide to play their game. They never used force, which surprised him, but the pressure was on nevertheless. He had question after question to answer, but all he wanted was just to convince them of his innocence. He answered everything as best he knew how. He had experience of interrogation techniques in the Marines; he knew what the bastards were doing all right. Maybe he was stupid to play on, but he was innocent; they just had to believe that. Hadn't they? During the interviews they were in reality building up a picture of Harry Garand, and with that picture they would highlight weaknesses they could perhaps use against him. It was a bit like knowing that you hated spiders but were too frightened to tell in case they put you in a room full of the crawly creatures, or a fear of snakes and then being dangled inches over a snake-pit. It was the beginning of many such interrogations, or 'chats' as the RUC put it. But they knew their art well. You were that bored with being kept alone that when interviewed you'd talk for hours about absolutely anything, given the chance. That thought stayed in his mind in the hours that followed.

Four days passed, and the pattern never faltered: six hours' sleep, the remaining eighteen on a chair staring at a wall except for the time you were being interviewed or needed to attend to the call of nature. On the fifth day everything changed. It was 10.30 p.m., although time was only approximate to Harry at that stage; devoid of a watch or clock, he had already set in his mind a rough time based on the schedule of each day's events: two hours per interview, six-hour breaks, back on the chair again, fifteen minutes to eat what they gave you each morning and again each evening. It all fell into a pattern; he wondered if his interrogators knew that, or maybe they wanted him to become like a laboratory-trained rat. But now he knew that was no longer the case; instead of going directly to the interview-room they took him outside. They snapped on hand-cuffs again – metal ones this time and to the front.

Then the police handed him over to two soldiers. Neither man wore any head-dress, but both men wore the combat-smock of the Parachute Regiment. Garand recognized the pat-terned jump-smock instantly; it was not unlike that used by the US Marines. He was dragged around to the rear of the build-ing. He heard the swishing of the rotorblades and gradual ear-piercing shrill of the Wessex helicopter's engine before he actu-ally rounded the corner and saw it. The transport helicopter was being started up.

'Where are you taking me?' quizzed Garand. No reply. The noise of the aircraft now overtook everything else.

Garand was ushered quickly up into the belly of the aircraft, yanked in through a side-door and forced on to the reverberat-ing floor. As the soldiers climbed aboard Garand confirmed his deduction about the soldiers when he noticed one to have the blue-and-white winged shoulder-flash of the Parachute Regi-ment; then another three paratroopers climbed aboard, all armed with SLRs. The bird began to lift. Garand could feel the transformation of energy as the helicopter frame shuddered and twisted under the strain; even before the aircrew man slam-med the side-door shut, they had started on him. The soldier behind him pulled his hair until Garand was tight against the webbed netting draped against the far side of the craft. Another soldier, fair-haired with a thick Mexican moustache, began the 'softening up', first with face-slaps and then with the odd body-punch. Garand saw no point in messing with them. He imagined they just wanted their little bit of fun *en route*.

Then the black hood was pulled over his head and a draw-string tightened on his throat from the side. He was now breathing deeply – not totally for breath, but also for what he anticipated was going to happen next. The punching increased to both his injured head and his torso. He began to lash out instinctively, but without the sense of sound, with everything drowned in the noise of the helicopter's engine, he was at their mercy. Finally, semi-conscious, he felt the wind on his body, but it was no use struggling; they had already edged him to the open side-hatch. The wind drew the hood tightly round his features. Suddenly his feet were dangling outside the helicopter; he was being held only by the strong grip of the soldiers as two of them grasped his forearms. The helicopter suddenly surged; Garand's senses no longer registered the fact. He was expecting the worst. A voice then yelled into his right ear.

'We're out over Belfast Lough, and there's an ebb tide, so when you go over the side your body will wash out to sea! Understand?' There was no response. The soldier continued. 'Now we're at a height of one thousand feet, so you know what that means!' Garand got another punch to the ribs; this time adrenalin compensated for the pain. 'This is your last chance to admit you're a fucking IRA man! It's up to you! Just nod! Nod!' shouted another voice from his left.

'Well?' yelled the voice from the right. 'What's it to be? The water or the fucking truth?'

Harry Garand was no longer inside the hood now tightened around his neck. His mind had long since transposed to Hill 427 and the killing – the smell of the place, the acrid stench, the pain, the lost friends, the failures, the struggles of a war that just hadn't stopped at ripping his leg apart. The trauma remained deep inside him, but now it was dancing in front of his eyes, triggered for him by people he didn't know. He remained silent.

'I didn't hear you!' cried the soldier to the left, his voice failing to pierce into Garand's vivid picture-show.

Harry Garand had a choice to make; duck from the incoming mortar-fire and seek refuge in the nearest bomb-crater or take it face-on. He was no longer dangling from a helicopter a thousand feet up. He was in the jungle of Vietnam now. Everything seemed to be happening in reverse. Something was dragging him away from the hill now, back and down into the murky jungle, the deadly jungle.

The Recon Patrol were moving along the river-course on the

final approach to their Fire Support Base when suddenly the night sky lit up a bright orange as the thunderous applause of the mortar-fire announced the beginning of the VC attack on Hill 427. Marine Sergeant Harry Garand froze fast in the waist-high river-water. He was riding 'point' on the eight-man reconnaissance patrol, now tired and weary after nearly four days in the jungle. Guzman, Apollo, and Ripcord held fast just metres behind. Jamie Lee was the second-in-command; he held the rear area, almost forty metres behind the rest along with the remaining three 'grunts'.

Slowly they all eased back in against the river-bank, avoiding the illuminations as the attack heightened with additional cannon-fire. The sky ahead was now being lit up by parachute flares as the defenders of Hill 427 tried desperately to determine what was happening. The white flares now bathed everything in an emerald green. Jamie Lee began to move forward past Ripcord and then Apollo. A tumultuous thunder rang inside their ears.

'What the fuck!' blurted Apollo.

Jamie Lee quickly raised a dripping wet hand to the Marine's mouth. It was enough. Apollo didn't need reminding: sound travelled a considerable distance across water, and now this area just had to be crawling with Gooks. The big Negro looked down at the short Mississippi-born corporal. Jamie Lee gave the man one of his 'looks'; it was enough for any of them. The hardened little Marine corporal only had to glare at them in a certain manner and every one of them kowtowed. That's what made the little soldier so indispensable to Garand; he needed another guaranteed pair of eyes for this sort of job, someone who could think and act the way he did, someone who would ensure that everyone who could would get back safely no matter what. Now 'what' had happened; their worst fears over the last two days had been realized.

They'd been into the Recon Patrol just two days when they happened on the first evidence: an ammunition-dump had been set up just ten kilometres west of the hilltop base. The next day they followed the trail of some VC to a camp set close to a village in the northern sector. The VC were busy making wooden coffins by the hundred! That was the final evidence they needed; no self-respecting VC would go into battle *en masse* without the sure knowledge of his or her final resting-place. It was macabre and hard to take in, but it was neverthe-less a cold fact. Not that any further evidence was necessary. They had their absolute corroborating evidence several hours later when, under the cover of darkness, groups of VC and even North Vietnamese Regulars began to mass in battalion strength. The base was about to be hit and, to make matters worse, they had been unable to raise anyone by radio for over thirty-six hours.

They had been running ever since, dodging trouble, trying to keep just one step ahead of the enemy, but now they were trapped. Their only access route to the base was blocked, and now it was being pounded with 81 mm mortar fire, backed up with 75 mm recoilless-rifle fire and several 130 mm field-guns. Jamie Lee moved on again, careful not to ripple the water too much as he fought against the current. He passed Guzman, the oldest man in the team. The veteran of three tours in Vietnam lay in close to the river-bank, almost totally concealed in the reeds; only the whites of his eyes flickered as the Southerner pushed on past to the 'point'.

He reached Garand seconds later. The sergeant was also down in the reeds, surveying the area dead ahead. Jamie Lee said nothing and waited for his boss to make the first move. Slowly Garand raised three fingers, then he pointed forward. Jamie Lee tried to adjust his eyes to see what Garand was pointing to. It was hard with the Technicolor display being played out almost overhead. Then he saw them: three Vietcong dressed in their usual black apparel, two on the river-bank just forty metres ahead and another one in the water fairly close to the bank. Another white flash suddenly lit up the sky anew; this time a multitude of explosions followed, tracer rounds screeched skywards. The VC had just hit the main arsenal at the First Support Base.

'Jesus!' groaned Jamie Lee. 'We can't go back. There's a VC column heading right this way.'

'Then we move on. Our only chance is to reach the hill and get airlifted outa this shit,' whispered Garand. 'Otherwise we're the sandwich-filler.'

'What about those Gooks ahead there?'

'It's white-knuckle time,' replied Garand, slipping off his webbing equipment and passing his M1 rifle across to Jamie Lee. 'Give me two minutes. Start counting the second I go under. Don't shoot unless you have to.' He eyed the trio ahead busily unaware of any hostile presence as they continued laying the anti-personnel mines on the river-bed, then he turned finally to his second-in-command. 'If I don't make it, blast your way through. Don't stop for nothing. Make for the emergency entrance on the east flank of the base.'

There was no need for a response from the corporal. Garand unsheathed his fighting-knife, putting the matt black blade between his teeth, then he vanished under the rolling water. 'One . . . two . . . three . . .' Jamie Lee began the count in silence. He watched with baited breath, motioning for Ripcord and Apollo to move up alongside. Without needing to be told, Guzman was moving back to the others to prepare them for the move forward. They all waited impatiently. Jamie Lee found himself sweating even though he was now chest-high in the cold water. 'Ninety-seven . . . ninety-eight.' He was starting to become worried now. Had their sergeant got himself trapped in something? The Gooks were forever throwing barbed wire into the river. Maybe he'd been swept on downstream; the water was flowing out pretty fast from the river-bank. He slung Garand's rifle over one shoulder and began to aim his own towards the three figures. He was counting the final twenty seconds now and into single figures: 'Seven . . . six . . . five . . . four . . .' He hadn't made it!

Suddenly the water erupted next to the VC laying the mines. Like some giant sea-serpent, Garand came up behind him. Instantly the knife sank into the back of the man's neck as a giant hand clasped around his mouth and hauled him under. The other two VC on the river-bank had been too busy priming the mines to notice what had taken place. Garand lurched forward. There were only ten feet between him and the bank, but he was already fatigued after the swim and the current was against him, shoving him sideways. Miraculously he made it just as one of the VC crouched over the mines turned around and spotted him only a few feet away. Garand almost hesitated.

Up to now the young girl's face had been concealed behind the soft khaki hat. Her eyes widened on seeing the Marine so close; she let out a cry just as she was pulled forward on to the knife point. The knife sank in just under her second rib; Garand twisted the eight-inch blade as he pulled her on to himself. She was barely two inches from his face, her eyes a mixture of fear and surprise; he thought the sixteen-year-old almost pursed her lips before blood spurted out from one side of her mouth. He cast her aside easily; her light body immediately started floating off downstream. But he had wasted too much time already.

Her companion had now grabbed his MAT-49 sub-machine-gun from his side and was raising it in the soldier's direction. Garand was still in the water, and with the slippery bank he stood no chance of scaling it let alone covering the eight feet to where the young man sat crouched. He brought the knife up quickly, clutching it by the blade-end. The knife left his hand just as the shots rang out. It sank three inches into the man's throat, just above the collarbone, as the 5.56 mm bullets also tore into the man's left arm and side throwing him sideways.

Jamie Lee dropped his aim and rushed forward through the swollen river-water. The rest of the team followed quickly now. There was no longer any need for concealment; inside minutes the entire area would be crawling with the enemy. They reached Garand; he had been covering their advance with the dead man's sub-machine-gun.

'You OK, Boss?' asked Jamie Lee, puffing and almost out of breath.

'I was until you broadcast us all over the fucking place!' Garand was furious.

'Sorry, Boss, I thought he had you.' The man's concerned look melted the Marine sergeant's anger.

'Let's move it!' he growled, taking off at speed down a nearby trail leading into the dense undergrowth.

The team followed, first Apollo, then Ripcord. Jamie Lee waited on the bank as Guzman led the other three upstream. They were only a few metres off when the third man, carrying the squad's M60 machine-gun, triggered off one of the underwater Soviet-made mines. The water exploded and the man screamed almost simultaneously; then he was gone, washed downstream by the floodwater. The 'Tail-End Charlie' had just about gathered his senses when the machine-gun opened up from across the river. The first burst cut up the water before him. The Marine tried to react and get to cover just as the second burst got him in the chest; he went under instantly. Guzman opened up, as did Jamie Lee. The VC ceased firing and had to take cover.

'Move it!' cried Guzman at the remaining Marine.

The nineteen-year-old youngster was carrying the squad's radio in a back-pack. The extra weight was inhibiting him; he used every ounce of his God-given strength as he battled against the current. He passed Guzman and had just about made it to where Jamie Lee lay prone on the bank and was climbing out when a Soviet RPG-7 grenade exploded in the earth-bank directly under Jamie Lee's position. The courageous little corporal was killed instantly, decapitated by the blast. The youngster took the force of the blast on his left side. Burning shrapnel tore off his arm and most of the side of his face; he was tossed back into the water.

Guzman cried out in anger and opened up with automatic fire towards the far side of the river, killing the VC with the rocket-launcher; then he turned towards the machine-gun position and blasted away the remainder of his ammunition before clambering out of the river. He swiftly cast off the empty maga-zine and snapped on another as he lay on his back gasping for air. He heard the sound to his left and rolled over ready to fire when Harry Garand came bursting out from the under-growth, now brandishing his own rifle, and landed heavily at his side.

'What about the rest?'

'They're gone, man,' panted Guzman.

Garand closed his eyes for a second. 'Jamie Lee.'

'He's upstream. An RPG took his fucking head off, man!' Guzman was almost out of control with anger.

'You OK?'

'Yeah,' sighed Guzman.

'OK, Guz, stick with me. Apollo and Ripcord are half a K from here.'

Both Marines crawled back until safely into the cover afforded by the dense jungle; then they ran. They were fortunate – the first section was mainly on the level; then the ground began to rise before them. Guzman was fit, but Garand had the edge of seven years on his side and kept up a punishing pace. Thankfully the ground dropped once again; the trees were becoming more widely spaced owing to the rock outcrops on the hillside. The trail began to level off again and sweep through the undergrowth. Garand cleared the fallen log, leaping nearly ten feet across on the far side. After landing he realized what he'd just missed; he pivoted round, raising his left arm to wave Guzman back, but it was too late. The other Marine had already followed on, but he was tiring now and couldn't make the distance Garand had. He landed on the foliage, then everything gave way. His leg crashed through the light bamboo framework concealed underneath the twigs and foliage. He gave out an agonizing cry. Garand rushed back.

Guzman had fallen into a punji stake trap. It was a two-foot-deep pit, three feet across and about four feet in length. Stakes made from lengths of sharpened bamboo, hardened by heating over a fire, had been set vertically in the base of the pit. Guzman had landed heavily, and two separate bamboo stakes had pierced straight through his boot and foot, one at the bridge of the foot and another just at his toes.

'Jesus help me!' he cried, dropping to one knee as he tried to wrench the foot free. But it was worse than he could ever have anticipated. The booby-trap had been refined. Additional stakes had been set into the walls of the pit angled down diagonally towards the base; one of these stakes had also penetrated his heel, and a further one closer to the surface was threatening to go into his calf if he attempted to extract his foot further. Garand examined the situation; he could see it was hopeless. Guzman was by now writhing in agony, partly supporting himself against the fallen tree-trunk. He forced himself to try to move the leg; it only made matters worse. 'It's no good! Go on, leave me!' he insisted.

Garand ignored him and pulled out his knife and started to cut away some of the stakes at the back of the Marine's leg; but cutting through the hardened bamboo was going to take time that they couldn't afford. Guzman gripped him by the arm, the pain on his face only too evident.

'They can't be far behind. Get outa here while you still got a chance.'

Garand continued cutting at the bamboo. Already he could hear the VC shouting to one another; they were only on the other side of the small ridge and would be coming straight over the top any minute. Guzman ripped off his dogtags and forced them into Garand's hand. 'Here, take them and get the fuck outa here. I've got these!' He winced at the rising pain. Garand stared at the two grenades in Guzman's other hand.

'OK,' he replied softly. He knew there was no point in his best friend being taken alive; with his sort of wound he'd be dead in no time from the infection. The voices were becoming louder; already Garand could see more than six figures scurrying around on the ridge-line.

'Thanks.' Guzman forced a smile as he bade farewell.

Garand patted him on the shoulder and ran on ahead, pausing to wait further on down the trail. Amazingly Guzman was still smiling at him, a fixed expression on his face. He cursed. There wasn't a damn thing he could do; there were too many to fight, even it he had had Ripcord and Apollo with him. They were coming over the ridge like ants now, dozens of them in their 'black pyjamas' and soft hats, pouring down through the trees shouting garbled messages to each other in high-pitched voices.

The voices heightened; some of the leading ones had spotted Guzman lying there on the trail like some stuck pig. Garand kept under cover and watched helplessly as they descended the final distance to his friend. Guzman kept his back to them, staying crouched over as if gripped in agony. There was little he needed to act out. The pins had already been pulled on both grenades; he had one wedged under his free leg and the other under his right armpit. The first VC jumped across the log to one side of the pit, prodding and teasing the American with a bayoneted AK47 rifle. Inside seconds four others arrived, including an officer. They could see Guzman wasn't going anywhere, nor was he any threat; his M16 was lying where it had fallen, well out of reach.

It was when Guzman was told to put his hands on his head that the fun started. He complied, still grinning at them as the grenade fell from under his right arm, fully primed, the precious seconds ticking away. One of them yelled, and they scattered in every direction, but it was too late: Guzman had already shifted his body weight enough to prime the second grenade moments earlier. The two explosions lifted Guzman out of the pit, killing him instantly along with three of the Vietcong and severely injuring the other two. It was the blinding white flash of the explosions that stayed with Harry Garand as he sat dangling out from the side of the helicopter. All he wanted now was to run, to escape from the nightmare . . .

With a sudden wrench he was free of both soldiers and sailing through the air. He tried to count the seconds to death, but never got started. Almost immediately upon tugging himself free he had landed abruptly on the concrete beneath the hovering craft. He had only fallen six feet, but it was enough to jar his spine and hip as his callipered leg took the full brunt of the impact. He lay there under the helicopter's downdraught uncaring. He was no longer lucid. He writhed on the concrete more in frustration than in reaction to the torture. He pulled and tore at the hood; it was tied tightly at the side. Then suddenly it became his real terror. He tore at it again and again, breaking two fingernails as he clawed to find the seam. The soldiers watched from the hovering helicopter as the writhing figure on the concrete below kept clawing at the black hood. The spectacle was interrupted when Harry was finally pulled away by some other soldiers on the ground. He was still trying to undo the suffocating hood and near to fainting when someone realized his anxiety and cut the sash cord. He began breathing deeply immediately the hood was loosened and then retched violently, much to their amusement.

Harry Garand was now in Palace Barracks, Holywood. Within minutes he was rushed into a large white room, and the hood was finally removed. Made to stand against the wall, he was gradually stripped of everything except his underpants and leg-calliper. Afterwards he was mercilessly beaten again by two further soldiers wielding heavy wooden batons the size of baseball bats; but they were more expert than the others, inflicting maximum pain without damage to any vital organs. By the time they'd finished there wasn't a part of his body that didn't ache. He was left on the floor for another ten minutes before someone removed the handcuffs and he was forced to stand naked with both hands outstretched against the white wall; then they hooded him once more. This time it was quite loose with no drawstring, so large that it fell about his shoulders making everything totally black. Standing still for another hour, he could periodically hear other men being brought into the room. Sometimes without any fuss, more often with an accompanying beating.

At one stage he turned his head to the right in reaction to one man's cries. It was then that he knew he was not alone as a truncheon was prodded sharply into his lower back. When the row of six suspects, all naked and hooded, were in position and facing the wall, the six accompanying soldiers adjusted their ear-defenders; then the signal was given to the next room to commence playing the tape-recording.

Over two giant wall-mounted speakers a strange hissing noise was emitted. It reminded Garand of the static on a television or radio set, but then the volume increased; not an unpleasant sound initially, but as the minutes dragged into hours the noise became unbearable to the hooded subjects. Thoughts washed from their minds as the 'white noise', as it became known later, flowed through their heads crushing everything in its path. It gave Garand a headache, added to the fact that he now had cramp from leaning against the cold wall and balancing his weight precariously on his only good leg. Above the noise he thought he heard someone cry out. It seemed like a child's cry, but from an adult throat.

Very soon, as if capitulating their will in unison, each of the hooded prisoners fell and was led out. Finally only Garand remained, but after another hour he slowly fell in towards the wall and his knees began to buckle as he slithered on to the floor. There was no punishment this time, and he was trailed out of the room. He felt the coldness of the air almost immediately; it revived him slightly before he was dropped on to the wet tarmac. He tried getting up, but there was little use; his body no longer responded. Then they turned a high-pressure hose on him, showering him with freezing cold water. His body moved under the force of the stream, and he began to crawl, only to be hosed up against a wall. There he sat huddled until they had finally done with him. Afterwards he was trailed inside and dumped in a room, and only when he heard the door lock behind him did he pull the hood off. He was in a barren cell, no window, the grey walls in contrast with a bright red door.

'Don't go to sleep! Stay awake, if you know what's good for you!' a soldier yelled through a small inspection-panel in the door.

When the panel shut again Garand could hear it once more. The 'white noise' was back again, the sound coming from the ventilator grille in the ceiling. It was as before, tolerable at first but steadily increasing. He clutched his ears, but the noise just penetrated through his hands. Harry Garand lay shivering, huddled on the cold floor for twelve more hours. The door opened again, and a green Army-issue boiler-suit and plimsolls were thrown beside him.

'Get dressed, 28,' insisted a voice. Garand did not look round. 'Come on, will you? I haven't got all day, you know.'

Harry glanced around and stared up at the man. He was older than the other ones: grey hair, balding, with sideburns and a bushy moustache. The man was dressed in civilian clothes, bell-bottom trousers and a pink shirt and tie. An empty shoulder-holster dangled under his left arm. There was a kindness in the man's eyes that was unlike anything Garand had experienced up to now. He felt new hope, but discarded the thought immediately; that's exactly what they want, a false sense of security, he reasoned.

'C'mon, 28, we haven't all day.' The soldier had a broad Yorkshire accent.

Garand dressed quickly and was then taken from the cell down a long corridor and up a flight of concrete steps, past a series of heavily draped windows. He could just catch glimpses of daylight as he passed up the stone steps. The interview-room was modern and bright; the single chair in the room sat beside a metal table in the centre of the floor. The window was closed by metal shutters sealed in the middle by a heavy padlock.

There was another, younger, man present, also in civilian

clothing, a smart navy three-piece suit, white shirt and maroon tie. He smiled instantly, beckoning Garand to sit down, and within seconds he had ordered food for the prisoner. A tray carrying a large plateful of bacon, eggs, fried bread, and beans was ushered into the room. Garand ate without waiting for permission, and both men watched in silence as he devoured the food and then washed it down with a mug of piping-hot sweet tea before finally sitting back from the table and facing the two men. The man in the navy suit spoke first; he had an Ulster accent. The other man in the pink shirt leant back against the wall.

'Good! I like to see a man who enjoys his food.' He grinned at Garand. 'I'm a police officer. You can call me Sam. This gentleman beside me is from Army Intelligence. I must apologize for your treatment – not of our design, truly.' The man appeared to mean the apology, though appearances could be deceptive. This new twist did not surprise Garand, who continued to remain silent.

'We've a few questions to ask you, and I would advise you to consider each one carefully.'

There appeared some hidden threat in the 'advise' bit.

Garand snapped back: 'I'm an American citizen. I demand to see my ambassador!'

The Ulsterman moved closer to the table. 'Sorry, mate, no ambassador in Northern Ireland; but there is a consul. I'll see what I can do, but for your own sake I would earnestly ask you to consider this other gentleman's questions.' He raised a hand, beckoning the soldier forward.

Then the questions started; they were simple enough, almost childlike.

'Do you know anyone in the IRA?'

'Do you know what the IRA stands for?'

'Is any member of your family in the IRA?'

'Do you or any member of your family support the cause?'

'Do you not feel a threat being a Prod and living on the Falls Road?'

The questions all seemed so trivial, but he answered; he no longer had any will to fight them. Why should he? He was innocent! The interview ended after almost an hour. The policeman spoke as he was about to be led back to his cell.

'It's been very nice talking to you, Harry. Next time you must tell me all about Vietnam; it must have been hell.' He nodded towards Garand's leg. It was the first of many interviews Garand would have with the thirty-year-old policeman who called himself Sam. Garand found himself smiling back. He had rather warmed to the man; Sam had a sincerity, if nothing else.

'Just get me the American consul,' grinned Garand.

But they didn't. After several days and the dictation of his life's history Harry was moved along with three other men to Belfast Harbour where they were unloaded on the quayside to board the rusting hull of HMS *Maidstone*. The old ship was now used as a temporary prison to house the 'internees'. Garand found himself now in the charge of the Royal Military Police. The 'Red Caps' were all over the ship; it was truly a prison. From the main deck they were led in line through the maze of corridors and steep stairways down into the hull, and finally to a small room where an MP sergeant addressed them.

'Right, lads, clothing has been left for each of you by your relations. Each of you find your box and get out of those dungarees.' He gritted his teeth. 'Right, Make it snappy. We haven't all day!'

The four men undressed, discarding their soiled boiler-suits and putting on their own clothes. Garand found he had been left a thick grey pullover, jeans, and white T-shirt. He pulled on the clothes with a renewed vigour. He was in touch with the outside world again. Mary had probably packed these clothes herself; for a moment he believed he could smell her perfume off the woollen sweater. Finally they were led into the bowels of the ship, down steep grey metal steps almost steep enough to be ladders, it seemed, then in and out of the vessel's bulkhead sections. They ended up outside a small grey metal door which opened inwards. To each side of the door stood a further MP, each one carrying a handgun in a webbing holster to one side and a baton in a white pouch at the other side.

The small group entered the room. It was the forward section of the ship. The area was full of perhaps thirty other men and boys, some of whom looked bewildered. They were mostly sitting in the chairs pushed against the metal bulkhead, some choosing to stand instead in quiet huddled groups. Everyone in the room stared at the new arrivals. Some showed glances of suspicion, others just blankly looked on.

'There's room over here.' A voice came from his left. Garand turned and looked at the man. He hadn't seen him in over a year, but how could he ever forget him? Peter McGoldrick smiled up and moved down the bench a little. Garand wedged in between McGoldrick and another man.

Garand glanced down at the wrinkled paperback on Peter McGoldrick's lap, entitled *The Western Intellectual Tradition*.

'The name's McGoldrick.' He spoke in a low tone.

Garand replied quietly: 'I'll not ask you what brought you to a place like this.'

McGoldrick perked up, his blue eyes widening noticeably. 'And what about you? You look as if a tram has hit you.'

Garand smirked. 'It appears your nationality or religion doesn't matter if you live on the Falls Road.'

McGoldrick nodded. 'The rumour has it that they've scooped over three thousand since the morning of the internment.' He looked around at the others in the room. 'I wonder where the other two thousand nine hundred and sixty-odd are now.'

Garand looked at him in astonishment. 'That's a hell of a lot of people! What I'm worried about is my wife and kid back home.'

'Knowing the resilience of the average Catholic, they'll muddle through all right,' McGoldrick continued in his quiet tones, his voice deep, almost imperceptible to Garand's ears at times. Then he closed his eyes and leant back, his head resting against the cold bulkhead. The conversation continued in dribs and drabs, interrupted by the MPs bringing them in food and refreshments at regular intervals. Garand found himself discovering that McGoldrick was also from the Ardoyne area of West Belfast.

McGoldrick didn't say too much about himself, just enough to keep the flow of conversation from drying up. Buckets were then provided in a corner of the room behind a wooden screen for the men to relieve themselves. It was becoming clear they were expected to stay here for a while. As night fell Garand could see the moonlight enter through the tiny portholes. They were mostly asleep now, huddled in the Army blankets in groups around the floor. Garand couldn't sleep; he kept thinking of Mary and the baby.

'You awake?' whispered McGoldrick. Garand nodded. 'Hey, wouldn't it be fun if one of the younger lads managed to squeeze out through one of the portholes and jump ship, so to speak?' continued McGoldrick. 'You see, this is only a transit section for the Brits. I reckon they haven't thought it through properly. It could be done.'

Garand thought McGoldrick was humouring him until he met his eyes in the light of the single wall-light in the room. 'You don't think it possible, then?' continued McGoldrick in his usual soft tone.

Garand puckered his lips and blew a kiss absently into thin air. 'Yeah, it could be done, but I think some dieting might be necessary first. Those portholes must be only ten inches wide.'

'Twelve inches, to be precise, and if someone screwed off parts of that brass surround – who knows?' smiled McGoldrick. He got up and quietly tiptoed across the floor, returning with another prisoner, a dark curly-haired young man who squatted down directly in front of Garand. He looked at Garand through bleary eyes.

'This here's Liam Heggarty. He's a wiry sort of critter, don't you think?' smiled McGoldrick.

Garand looked at the boy. 'What weight are you, son?'

'Eight stone,' replied the boy.

McGoldrick stared at him. 'Narrow bone-structure . . .' He rubbed his chin, now sprouting two weeks' full growth owing to the unavailability of razors. 'Think you could lose another few pounds, son?' He smiled.

The youth looked bemused. He screwed his face up in response. 'What for?'

'For the cause,' continued McGoldrick, patting him on the shoulder. 'Now, there's a good lad. Get on back to your mates over there and say nothing. And, by the way, avoid the steak and kidney pudding at supper-time.'

He was still smiling as the boy stood up. He touched Liam's leg just before he moved away.

'Hey, son, I forgot to ask you if you could swim.'

The youth looked back, eyes wide. McGoldrick almost burst out laughing as the boy tiptoed away. He was still smiling as he turned to Garand.

'Now, that would be something, wouldn't it?'

Garand burst into laughter. It was a temporary release from the nightmare. He spent the rest of the sleepless night talking to McGoldrick about himself and his family. The night wore on painfully slowly. Although emptied and cleaned at regular intervals, the waste-buckets had begun to fill through the night; the smell was putrid. By breakfast-time the men were all restless, like a pack of hungry dogs, hungry for liberty and fresh air.

The announcement by the little MP sergeant was warmly greeted. They were all to be moved into hastily prepared bunks on the deck below. As they all eventually filed out at midday each man gave his name and number to the guard at the door, who then ticked off the name, checking each face against his wad of Polaroid photographs. As Garand filed out in front of McGoldrick, he was stopped by the sergeant after revealing his name.

'Garand? You come with me, please.'

The respect and politeness was unnatural. Garand glanced at McGoldrick, who smiled at him as he was shown to the 'head' and given washing and shaving materials. After he had shaved off the stubble and washed under supervision, he was handcuffed to an MP corporal and led to the main deck. Without explanation he was brought down the steep grey-painted gangway and off the ship. The same policeman in the navy suit who had interviewed him at Palace Barracks was standing beside a dark blue Cortina saloon.

'We meet again, Harry,' smiled Sam Nelson. He looked at the military policeman. 'You can undo the handcuffs now.'

The corporal obliged and returned up the gangway without comment. The policeman opened a rear door of the car.

'Get in. You're going home, Harry.'

Garand hesitated before climbing in beside another plain-clothes policeman. The door closed, and Nelson joined the police driver in the front. As the car drew away from the dock Garand stared back at the grey rusting wartime ship towering high over the quayside. His heart was with McGoldrick and the rest of them; they had a common bond now. Then his thoughts were interrupted by Sam Nelson.

'First, we take you to the American consulate in Belfast, and there you'll meet your wife.'

Garand stared at him. The policeman seemed to understand his new worry.

'It's OK. We're not deporting you – can't anyway while you remain married to a British citizen.'

'Irish,' Garand retorted. 'After this I don't think she's anything in common with the British.' He looked out from the window again; they were passing through the main exit from the docks into Corporation Street. Sam Nelson continued to watch Garand. The American had changed; and he wasn't the only one to notice a difference.

Mary saw something similar when, after the commotion of the diplomatic handover and welcome home, she tried to talk to him. He was different now, unemotional, no longer communicative or responsive to her conversation or affection. Part of him seemed dead. He would not talk of his ordeal in any way, except to keep reassuring himself that the soldiers hadn't harmed her during the ordeal of internment night. Mary reassured him, careful to avoid the subject when possible; she knew he could never handle the real truth of that terrible night. Despite her interest and concern about what had happened to him during his incarceration, Harry Garand just kept shrugging off the questions with whimsical replies, quick to change the subject of conversation, or at other times he simply ignored her. He did not sleep much, either; he sat for hours downstairs, mostly remaining in darkness. She would find him in the mornings, still sitting in the armchair, chin down on his chest, staring down at the floor. Much of his behaviour she tolerated, telling herself that in time he would heal, but now he even ignored the child; he no longer took the little girl on his knee, playing with her as before.

Mary tried different methods of approach. She got the local

doctor and even Father O'Neill to see him, but nothing seemed to get through to him. He no longer wanted to work – not that he could return to Harland & Wolff since his services had been dispensed with after the news of his arrest and internment; they had already convicted him out of hand. The management had said it was in the interest of his own safety, especially with some of his Protestant workmates having uttered veiled threats to his safety if he ever returned. No, the management made it clear they hadn't bowed to pressure, but the fact was that they were not going to budge; people did not get interned without good reason, they said. He was unclean now, not to be associated with any more, his severance pay posted by recorded delivery to the house.

Through Mary's aunt, Garand got an appointment with a shirt factory in the Springfield Road. He was offered a job as a packer at just over half the salary he had had in the shipyard, but beggars couldn't be choosers. The work was hot and sticky; most of the employees were female, employed as stitchers. Garand found it hard to keep going. He was on his feet constantly; the right leg was beginning to ache, especially where the calliper cut into the flesh just below the knee. Two weeks passed uneventfully; then during a lunch-break one of the van-drivers came bursting into the tea-room.

'Hey! I've just heard the news! There's been an escape! Seven prisoners escaped from the *Maidstone*. They squeezed through a tiny porthole the size of a penny, and straight into the water. It's all over the lunch-time news. The Brits are screaming! Hell slap it up them for thinking they could keep some Irish Paddies on an old rusty boat!'

The small mixed group of men and women all laughed. This sort of incident crossed the political or religious divide; everybody admired spirit, even in the case of an internee.

'Any names?' cried one of the women over the laughter.

The van-driver shouted over noise. 'Some eighteen-year-old called Heggarty; that's all I heard so far.'

Garand's eyes lit up. He thought of McGoldrick sitting on board *Maidstone* laughing his head off. There would be the inevitable witch-hunt on board the ship, and he felt sure this would just add to McGoldrick's amusement.

Garand arrived home as usual at 5.30 that evening. Mary had his dinner in the oven. He helped himself to the meat pie and potatoes smothered in the thick gravy, and had just finished settling down by the fireside when a young man called at the door asking for Garand. Mary kept him at the doorstep and summoned Garand to her side. Harry's eyes brightened at the sight of Liam Heggarty.

'I was told ta give ya this.' Garand took the small white envelope and was about to show the boy inside but he had already begun to run up the narrow street. He stepped out on to the pavement to see him disappear round the corner like a whippet set loose on a hare. He opened the envelope and studied the note. Mary moved to his side.

'What is it?' she asked.

He crumpled it into a ball as if it was irrelevant. 'Oh, nothing much. Just some guy wanting a favour, honey.' He turned to her. 'That's all. Nothing to it.'

He shoved the note inside his trouser pocket and guided her back into the hallway, closing the door tightly shut. The late news that evening confirmed the name of the other escapees. The list included a Peter McGoldrick, a fifty-year-old republican from Ardoyne. Garand tried to hide his humour from Mary, but she was too astute.

'You know this McGoldrick?' Her eyes narrowed.

'Nope. Can't say I do. What about turning in? I'm dead beat.' He stretched his arms and yawned.

She was pressing his trousers the next morning when she found the note, still in the same pocket. She smoothed it in front of her on the ironing-board. It was printed in block capitals.

HELLO, YANK,
JUST TO SAY I'M OUTSIDE AGAIN AND KICKING! OWING TO
CIRCUMSTANCES BEYOND MY CONTROL I CANNOT CALL
PERSONALLY TO SEE YOU, BUT I WOULD APPRECIATE A
MEETING ASAP. IF YOU CAN FIND THE TIME CALL TOMORROW
NIGHT AT THE HARP BAR BESIDE CLONARD CINEMA. I THINK
YOU MAY FIND IT IS TO OUR MUTUAL BENEFIT (8 P.M.).
MCG

She read it again and again. The meeting was for that night. Why hadn't he said anything? Then her heart almost stopped. 'McG' was McGoldrick; it had to be. Mary decided not to broach the subject, and awaited his reaction as the clock neared the hour that evening.

'I've got to go out.' He spoke almost absently.

'Where?' she responded. He sensed the crackle of nervousness in her tone. He kept silent and crossed the room, lifting the navy donkey jacket off the sofa. 'I said where?' she continued. 'You never go out!'

Garand kissed her on the forehead; it was one of the first conscious acts of affection he had shown since returning home.

'I've a message to do, as your old Uncle Barney would say.' He smiled and turned towards the door. 'I shouldn't be too long, honey, but don't wait up just in case.' Then he was gone, and in her heart she knew what it was about – especially the reference he had made to old Uncle Barney, an IRA veteran of the twenties. The IRA was calling him – and he was answering.

The old pub stood on the corner of Clonard Street. It had suffered the ravages of time and now war. The Protestants had tried to burn it down, and the IRA had booby-trapped a car just outside the place, but only a fraction of the home-made explosive had detonated. It had been meant to kill members of an Army patrol lured into the area by stone-throwing youths, but the only thing they killed was the bar trade. The fat barman watched Garand enter the public bar. Although Garand enjoyed a drink, he never ventured into this sort of establishment unless in the company of old Uncle Barney.

The old rascal relished such places, full of stories and old memories, but now it seemed cold, alien to Garand. He followed the length of the bar towards the frosted-glass door marked 'Snug Bar'. Two elderly men sat huddled by the bar-counter, deep in muffled conversation; neither took any interest as Garand limped past. On opening the door of the snug he saw McGoldrick sitting at the end of a bench seat.

'Hello, Harry. I knew you'd come.' He smiled. 'Close the door and sit yourself down..'

'So you made it too.' Garand obliged, accepting the awaiting bottle of Guinness covered by the upturned glass tumbler.

'The deck below had portholes three inches wider than the one we were looking at! It's good to see you, Harry. I mean it.' McGoldrick adjusted his steel-rimmed spectacles. 'Got over the time inside yet?' he continued.

'You never get over it,' replied Garand, sitting forward now. 'Look, are you not taking a hell of a risk being here? You haven't been out two days and you're still hanging around Belfast. I would have been half-way to Cork by now.'

'You'd a bad time back there,' said McGoldrick, quietly changing the subject. 'They gave you the "special treatment" at Palace Barracks. Not everybody got that. Only a few, thank God.'

'You seem to know a lot of what happened to me.' Garand glared at him. 'A lot of which I didn't tell you!'

'Relax, Harry. I'm on your side. I just did a bit of checking, that's all.' McGoldrick leant forward.

'And whose side is that?'

'The side of the people. They want us now, you see. August the ninth did it for us, much more than all the campaigning in the world.'

'The IRA?' interrupted Garand.

'The Provisionals,' replied McGoldrick in a whispered voice. 'What do you want with me?'

'To kill.' He paused, letting the words register. 'You're part of a rare breed, Harry. You have military experience and you've got the guts for it!' He reached over, touching Garand's arm. 'You're a marked man, Harry. Do you think the bastards will forget you now you're out? Don't think it all stopped when the American government put pressure on them to release you.'

Garand eased back against the wooden panelling of the seat. 'I don't know. At one time, immediately after being released, I'd have said yes, but now I'm not so sure any more.'

'Don't tell me your nerve has gone, Harry boy.' McGoldrick's face was unsmiling.

'Don't patronize me!' Garand slammed the glass down, tipping the half-empty Guinness-bottle on to the table, spilling the remaining contents everywhere. He ignored the liquid dripping off the table on to his trouser leg. 'You're full of shit, McGoldrick!'

McGoldrick changed tack. 'I didn't go through the sort of treatment they gave you, thankfully. Neither did very many others. I can only imagine what it must have been like.'

'No!' Garand became conscious of his raised voice only when the barman peeped around the corner to be immediately signalled away by McGoldrick. 'All right, asshole, you can imagine. So what? Bullshit! You expect me to lay my life on the line for piss-all!'

McGoldrick raised his hand in a gesture of peace. 'No, not for nothing. Setting aside "the cause", I'm giving you the opportunity to get your own back on the bastards, and of course we'll pay you – handsomely. Per head, if you like!'

Garand stared at him in disgust. 'Think you've enough in your little piggy bank to keep up with me? No, I'll tell you! Period! I don't need any of this! I'm Mr Ordinary, a regular guy working to exist. I admit to sharing sympathy for your "cause" as you put it, but that's where it stops, understand?'

'Oh, yes, I understand all right!' McGoldrick appeared upset now. 'The romantic notion of our colonial brothers. That's just great! You let the Brits walk over you, but don't think they'll leave you or your family alone. Special Branch have you on record. The Brits probably have your photograph circulated in the bad guys' gazette. For now they're satisfied with stopping you in the street to check you out, but don't think it'll stop there. Sooner or later they'll have another crack at you, and it'll not be just you that'll be suffering! Think of your family. Think on that a while!'

Garand pushed the table aside and stood up. 'You've had your talk, McGoldrick, and that's that. I don't fully know your game-plan but, then, I'm not in the football team, and I won't be! Period!'

McGoldrick reached across and grabbed Garand by the arm. 'You wounded a policeman that night 'cause you had to. You can do it again, Harry. We need you!'

Garand was half-expecting the comment, yet he was still a little stunned. He had just about cleared his mind of the night in the Lower Falls when he had saved the fumbling IRA volunteer Sean Flynn from certain death when he unleashed the ancient Thompson at the police armoured car.

'That was self-defence!' he retorted.

McGoldrick smiled. 'Don't worry. Your wee secret's safe with Peter McGoldrick.' He broke into a laugh. 'Hey, this isn't the Harry I came to know!'

Garand was quick to snap back: 'You don't know me, McGoldrick. We shared a room for a while nothing more! You've got the wrong guy for the job, and I advise you strongly to forget me!' Garand pulled open the door. 'I'll see you around.'

'Oh, you'll see me again, Harry. You can be sure of it,' smiled McGoldrick.

Ten minutes after Garand had stormed out of the pub, McGoldrick was joined in the snug by two other men.

'He didn't bite; but, then, I expected as much.' He looked into his unfinished pint of Guinness. 'He'll need a bit of coaxing to play along – some Brit trouble, if you know what I mean.' He swallowed the remains of the pint, then he eased back in the seat. There was a satisfaction in his manner. 'He'll come around, you'll see.'

Over the next fortnight Garand found himself being stopped more frequently when out on the street. He was always body-searched each time, sometimes quite roughly. Mary never spoke of how she felt, but she, too, had been the subject of a 'P' check and body-search in the middle of the street. Even the baby was 'frisked' as she was lifted from the pram. It was perverse, but not as perverse as the night Mary walked home from visiting old Uncle Barney, admitted to the Royal Victoria Hospital with a major heart-attack. She was delighted to see her favourite uncle in such high spirits; he seemed oblivious to his critical condition. All taped and wired up to the bedside monitors, he seemed almost trussed up like a turkey. It had only been discovered a month before that the old man was suffering from angina, but after a few drinks too many one night followed by some rough handling by an Army foot patrol on the Falls Road he had finally collapsed on the doorstep of his house. He had been found half an hour later by a neighbour setting out the milk-bottles. He was lucky to be alive, but time was running out for him.

She left hospital with a tightness in her own chest. Uncle Barney was dying, and after looking at the thick lip and black eye on the eighty-seven-year-old man's face it was clear to Mary the part the Army had had to play in his present predicament. Her mother had always said the booze would kill Barney. Little had they known. Mary tried to cheer herself up, humming a Simon and Garfunkel song to herself, but her mood floundered when she rounded the street-corner and was confronted by an Army foot patrol near Broadway on the Falls Road. They started with the usual questioning, but then after searching through her handbag one of the soldiers went to search her physically. She objected, demanded a female searcher; it was her right.

Finally the impasse was broken when she was slapped about the face several times. They meant business. Mary was beginning to wonder if perhaps these were the ones who had put her own uncle in hospital. Her mouth bled, and her right ear was burning with the force of the assault, but she was angry, remembering only too well that terrible night in August when the door had come crashing in on her home. The soldier moved in again; she no longer objected, there was no option. He began slowly at first, feeling her outer garments. Then he unzipped the anorak, tugging to release the bottom clip; his hands were inside and on her jumper instantly.

The other soldiers began to smirk; one giggled. She closed her eyes as he slowly felt around her back, moving his face in close and staring hungrily down at her breasts; then he stepped back and reached forward, grasping and squeezing both breasts. She cringed as his nails dug through the light wool and flimsy bra. Then his hands moved on to her hips and down the outer seams of her jeans. She knew what to expect next, but she refused to show any sign of fear.

He was crouching now; his hands moved slowly up the inside of both legs, past the knees and along the thighs. Then she felt him, squeezing and tugging again. She pulled away, unable to restrain herself, and ran, fast and furiously. The soldiers didn't follow; they were all too busy laughing and whistling after her.

She ran and ran with no direction in mind except to get as far away from them as possible. Finally she stopped, almost falling as she ran into the darkened alley, bursting into a torrent of tears. Only one word echoed forth: 'Why?' She screamed out over and over again, but no one answered.

Mary took some time to calm down before going into the house. Garand, much to her relief, was sleeping, stretched out across the sofa, his feet touching the side of the hearth. She didn't tell her husband about the incident immediately, but by next morning Harry Garand realized something was wrong; then, after a short interlude, the dam burst. At midday, when the family received the news of Uncle Barney's demise, Mary began crying unreservedly and unashamedly. By the time she had revealed the full nature of what had really happened on 9 August they were both crying. As they held each other in their arms Harry Garand's face hardened. He remembered McGoldrick's words: 'Sooner or later they'll have another crack . . . it'll not be just you that'll be suffering . . . Think of your family.'

The next day Garand returned to the Harp Bar and left a message with the barman. That evening he was met by Liam Heggarty and taken to a house in Whiterock. It amused Garand to think how Heggarty managed to walk around West Belfast almost unrestricted and yet he was number one on the wanted list after the *Maidstone* escape. There was no messing around this time. McGoldrick was struck by Garand's forcefulness.

'Why the change of heart?' he asked.

'The bastards raped my wife,' Garand said coldly.

'I'm sorry,' replied McGoldrick in genuine sympathy.

'Fuck the apology!' barked Garand. 'OK, so you were right and I'm a sucker. A guy can take so much pushing around, but when it comes to his family he hasn't any choice.'

'In many ways I can sympathize, Harry. I was a bit like you once. Did you know that back in the forties I quit university after fighting like a dog to get there and instead I joined up? Ay, the Royal Navy no less. I trained as a radio operator but I had a gift with linguistics, you see; at that time I could speak three other languages fluently, and that included German.'

McGoldrick allowed himself a smile. 'By the end of the war I could speak another three languages on top of that again.'

'I don't get your drift.'

'I gave up my studies of my own volition. There was no conscription in the North of Ireland. I could even have gone south to the neutral territory of Eire. But I didn't. I joined up. I wanted to fight. King and Country, and all that shit. Religion never entered into it in those days. Then, after my war, after five long wasted years, I applied for a scholarship to Oxford or Cambridge. I was amply qualified, and there was even a special entrance scheme for ex-servicemen. I didn't even feature. You know what my commanding officer said to me when I was being demobbed? "You can go back home, McGoldrick, and start planting potatoes again." Oh, it was meant as a joke, but a joke with a sting. Everyone thought it was funny – everyone, that is, but me!

'I was no more use to them, just like thousands of others, a second-class citizen in his service greatcoat which he was supposed to have been thankful to keep. All that and a five-bob demob-suit that would have been too big for a man twice my size. I came back here to nothing. The Unionists at Stormont put the boot in place all right. Just like the rest I was back home, discharge papers in one hand and a letter for the dole queue in the other. There was a girl; but there was no point in even thinking about marriage when I couldn't get a job, never mind a house! I had to move back with my widowed mother and five brothers and sisters living in a two-up-two-down terraced hovel that leaked in winter and stank from the broken drains in the summer. I was home! Now can you understand what's made me what I am?'

Garand simply nodded; words were insufficient.

'At first . . . at first I was just a political agitator. I'm a Marxist and proud of it. I organized labour marches, and then later, much later, the armed struggle. And why not? I was a no-hoper, Harry, just like you unless you get off your arse and act now!'

'McGoldrick! I'm here now, so let's get it over, shall we?'

'All right. You're in. But understand clearly what I'm about to say. Any breath about what we've discussed or about what you're involved in, to anyone, including Mary, and you're a dead man. It's no offence to you, Harry. It's the rule; break it and there's no apology afterwards, no second chance.'

'Accepted.'

'And there's another thing. No matter what, I choose the targets. It doesn't matter how stupid it might seem at the time; but it's up to me, and you don't question it. OK?'

'We'll see.'

'Harry, there's no "seeing" about it. If you are really going to hurt the Brits, it'll have to be as I say; otherwise Harry Garand may as well piss into the wind for all the good it'll do.'

'What can you offer me?'

'Guns are at a premium, Harry. The split from the "Stickies" messed us up, and frankly the Brits have been pretty lucky in their searches recently. They found two of our hides, and we lost eighteen rifles, some handguns and ammo.'

'Listen, McGoldrick, either you've got something or you haven't. If not, then stop wasting my time. Maybe I should go to the Official IRA after all!'

'Steady up, Yank! Steady!' He smiled. 'How would you fancy a wee holiday in Greece, all expenses paid, eh?'

McGoldrick explained that they had already arranged for Garand to go with one of their men to Greece and meet one of their new suppliers. It had also been agreed with the supplier that Harry would be facilitated there to train without inter-ference well away from the watchful eyes both north and south of the Irish border. So it was that Harry Garand set off the following week with only the feeblest of excuses to his wife and teamed up with McGoldrick's man. They travelled separately as arranged. Harry took the train to Dublin and then on to Rosslare where he took the ferry to Le Havre and then on to Paris. From there he flew direct to Athens where he made contact with McGoldrick's man, and then it was a hazardous seven-hour car-journey through the Greek Peloponnese until they arrived at the coastal town of Kalamata.

Garand was quite happy with his companion. McGoldrick had teamed him up with a dummy! The dumb man went by the name of Michael. The only communication between the two was either hurriedly written on a piece of paper or con-veyed by gesticulation, but his silent partner knew exactly what he was doing; he'd obviously been there before. Garand was unimpressed with the supplier, a fat little Greek called Goukas. He ran an import-export business from a side-street office in Kalamata. After the dumb man communicated with the Greek in sign language, Garand was shown into a back office. Goukas locked the door once both men were inside. The Greek then tried to palm Garand off with some discarded rifles left over from the Second World War. Harry Garand's blood began to boil. He hadn't quit his job and come all this way for nothing; he could have picked up better in a scrapyard.

'Listen, you little shit! And listen good! I want to see all the M1 rifles that you've got stashed away.'

'But you have seen all that I have,' replied the Greek, throwing up his chubby arms. Garand hobbled towards Goukas. The man could see this stranger meant business; it unsettled him. He had only been doing business with the Irishman for just under a year, and all transactions so far had been politely completed, but this crippled American was different. He frightened Goukas.

'Look! I want all the M1s that you've got, and I want them by tonight. Then I'll tell you what I need.' Garand slammed one of the old rifles back on to the table.

'OK! OK!' cried the Greek.

Goukas was speechless after what Garand did later that evening. The American stripped the selection of over twenty rifles and began selecting only the best components for the construction of just one rifle. Goukas satisfied himself with the thought that he could patch up all the remaining parts again and sell the reconstructed weapons to some inexperienced middle-man at a later time.

'You do reloads, don't you?' questioned Garand.

'Why, yes, but the ammunition I have for the M1 is in mint condition.'

'Mister, you just do as I say and we'll get on fine. Here, take this.' He handed the Greek a scrap of paper. 'Make me up six cartridges to that specification for tomorrow morning.'

Goukas examined the paper; his eyes widened. He excused himself and went off to his office. What Garand eventually had before him on the workbench at the rear of Goukas's import-export offices was a .30 calibre M1 rifle, gas-operated with an eight-round internal box-feed magazine. The heavy wooden butt was mauled and scratched, but there was not even a tiny speck of rust on any of the working parts. Garand picked it up. It was heavy – around 9½ lb – and fairly bulky. He examined the sights and pulled back the cocking mechanism to reveal the breech. The rifle, a bastardization of six different rifles, was in mint condition.

'So what do you think of the Garand?' quizzed Goukas as he joined both Garand and Michael in the rear store.

Michael stared briefly at Garand and then at the rifle. He had never realized that the M1 rifle was more commonly referred to as a 'Garand', named after its designer. The dumb man's face lit up as he thought of the American using a gun bearing his own name; he felt sure it was a good omen.

'She'll do. I'll see you tomorrow. Just make the ammunition that I want and also get me a suitable telescopic sight.' Garand's face was stern. Goukas nodded obligingly.

After the Greek had left again Michael scribbled on his notepad and tapped Garand on the shoulder. The note read 'Garand'. Garand looked up from the workbench. Michael motioned to the rifle and then to Garand. The American smiled. 'You've got it in one, pal. Call it poetic licence if you like!'

Michael smiled for the first time since Harry Garand had met him.

Early next morning

Although it's possible to strike a fair-sized target at a thousand yards and even beyond, it usually requires a series of shots to get on target, with each shot being individually calculated to consider the prevailing conditions at that moment in time. It requires the eye and hand of an expert; nothing less will do. For example, wind variation can affect the placement of a shot at that distance by as much as five feet, even with a marksman.

A good marksman can achieve a head shot on a first-shot basis up to four hundred yards but only under reasonable conditions; to go beyond would be, at the very least, risky. However, a body shot is possible up to seven hundred yards using the same practice of targeting on a first-shot basis. But Harry Garand was not just good; he was magnificent.

He had been a top US Marine Corps marksman, he was his division champion; they came no better qualified. The following morning Goukas brought Garand and Michael some distance southwards along the coast to an old disused quarry between the main coast road and the rocky shoreline. The place was totally desolate apart from a few mountain goats scattered here and there. Part of the quarry floor had developed into a small lake extending now across the entire width of the quarry until it met the sheer limestone walls on either side. Garand stood staring across to where the rock rose out of the water again on the far side. A Nubian goat bleated loudly across the lake upon realizing it was no longer alone.

'How did the goat get over there?' asked Garand.

'Probably fell from that ledge up there.' Goukas pointed to a tiny path cut into the rock on the far side of the quarry; it stopped at a small jagged outcrop of rock just twenty feet above where the goat stood.

The path had obviously crumbled away, and the goat had probably fallen the rest of the distance on to the quarry floor. It was trapped; there was no way out. Goukas had procured a Yugoslavian-manufactured telescopic sight. Garand took the scope and examined it closely. The magnification was suitable and, better still, Goukas had mounted it ready for attachment to the rifle. Garand took a small screwdriver from his shirt pocket and began fixing the sight into position. He would naturally leave the fine adjustments to later.

'Where's the ammo?' he asked coolly.

Michael watched intently as Goukas reached into his bag and produced two fifty-round boxes of .30 rifle ammunition, setting them on a granite rock beside the American.

'And the "specials"?'

Goukas produced a small box from his jacket pocket and handed it across carefully. Garand glanced around the place.

The quarry was about six acres in size, surrounded on four sides by two-hundred-foot towering white limestone walls. Behind them lay the only entrance to the place, down a winding path that led from the top of the quarry face. The path had once been the service road for all the equipment and heavy vehicles, but now after years of attrition it had been eroded into a narrow path, only safe for the most sure-footed. Their car had been left on the access road above, well concealed beside an olive grove back towards the main coast road.

Garand took the Zeiss field-glasses from Michael and focused on the far side again. He calculated the distance to be around seven hundred yards, then he found what he needed: a small outcrop with some vegetation growing over it. It was the perfect target, the size of a man's head. He wasted no more time; the sooner they were finished and away the better. He loaded the first eight-cartridge clip. Pulling the rifle's operating-rod to the rear, he pressed the clip down on top of the magazine-follower; it was caught instantly by the clip-latch. Removing his right thumb from the line of the bolt Harry let go the cocking handle, which automatically ran forward under the compression of the powerful spring. He slammed it home with the heel of his hand for good measure. The rifle was ready, a cartridge already in the breech mechanism.

Michael watched, intrigued by the speed and familiarity of the American. It was as if he had been born with the gun in his hands. Harry Garand slipped his finger forward from the trigger-guard and flicked the safety-catch to the rear.

'Safety first. You should always remember that, Michael.' He grinned across at the Irishman, who began smiling and nodding his head several times; the excitement was getting to him.

Garand lay down beside the granite rock, supporting one shoulder and the rifle against it for good measure. He quickly adjusted the rifle's leather strap and twisted it tightly around his left shoulder and forearm. It was a favoured sniper's trick, steadying the rifle, even in the very worst conditions. He studied his 'target' through the Yugoslavian sight; it was obviously old, not much younger than the rifle, but the enhanced imagery was even superior to field glasses. Goukas had done well after all. He flicked off the safety and held his breath, firing instantly.

'Crack!' The ear-piercing sound echoed and died away. He was yards off to the right, nearly hitting the goat, which was now scampering away behind some rocks.

'Sorry, Mr Goat,' he whispered, taking the screwdriver to the telescopic sight.

'Crack!' The second shot went to the left and slightly high. A small dust-cloud formed around the disintegrating rock, the sound echoing longer this time. Getting in closer to the target was becoming harder now; the slightest movement left or right could place the shot a world away from the target. Goukas was already becoming impatient; he had never experienced any trouble with his customers before, and he normally did not get this involved with his clientele, but the hurried production of the 'special' ammunition required his presence – and at a hundred dollars a cartridge with the potential of a large order how could he refuse? It took Garand another two clips of ammunition to zero the rifle, but even then he still was not satisfied. The range for a head shot was in excess of what he would have preferred, but if he could do it at this distance there would be no stopping him on the streets of Belfast. Goukas looked across at the target through the Zeiss field-glasses.

'You are doing fine, but the noise is a giveaway. What about using a silencer? I have some in supply that might do.'

'No silencer. It's unnecessary with the ammunition you manufactured for me.' Goukas couldn't understand and simply shrugged his rounded shoulders. 'But I could use a flash-guard. Could you get me one?'

'I can supply anything, and what I can't get I make, eh!' Goukas chuckled. His whole body seemed to shake every time he laughed; it was as if all the body fat had become loose at one time. He turned away, casting an arm in the air as he walked the short distance over to Michael.

'This American of yours, I think to myself he is cuckoo! A Garand bullet will penetrate the armour shell of a light tank or any armoured car that I know exists. Who the hell needs more power than that?'

His answer came swiftly. 'Crack!' But their eyes never regis-

tered the sound; the explosion at the other end of the quarry
was instantaneous and echoed back in a raging thunder 'Boom!'
Goukas turned in shock. Even he had not expected such devastation. Michael jumped for joy like an excited child, waving his
hands in the air as he rushed over to Garand.

'It's the sound of the devil! Oh my God! What have I done?'
cried Goukas, still consumed with disbelief.

The far end of the quarry was a massive cloud of white dust.
Goukas couldn't see clearly the damage caused to the rock-
face, but the size of the cloud spoke for itself. Garand had
specified a reload using a heavier grain of powder. The bullet-
head had also been drilled and then filled with nitroglycerine,
the top then sealed with wax. Not only was the bullet now a
dumdum; it was also highly explosive. On impact its force
would be extended out instead of allowing the bullet to travel
on further. If Garand now fired the rifle at an armoured car
using a special load, the bullet would no longer penetrate but
instead would explode on impact and in that particular case be
harmless, but on a human skull the effect would be totally
devastating. Goukas looked through the field-glasses. The dust
was beginning to blow to one side. The rock-outcrop had vanished; now there was a two-metre-wide crater cut in the rock-
face. Garand stood up and wiped the sweat from his forehead.
Goukas walked over to meet him.

'Goukas, make me fifty more like that one, and I want each
of the "specials" numbered consecutively.'

'Number them?' The Greek screwed up his face.

'Stamp a number on to the side of each shell-casing. Use
roman numerals. You know how to count in roman, don't
you?' Garand smiled and picked up the rifle. Michael busied
himself gathering all the empty cartridge-casings along with the
remaining ammunition. He stooped down to pick up a casing
that had fallen beside where Goukas now stood. The Greek's
smiling face finally turned into fury; he shoved the Irishman
aside.

'You Yankee! You are insulting as well as being ignorant!'
Goukas was unused to disrespect; in the private arms trade he
was somewhat of a revered character.

'Think what you like, just so long as you get me what I

want.' Garand brushed past the Greek and helped Michael to his feet.

'You are so brave with your rifle, eh? Very brave! But have you the guts to kill? That is what I want to know! Have you the guts? Eh?'

Suddenly Harry Garand was on the turn, spinning and bringing up his rifle level with the Greek's chest as he fell on to his right knee. Goukas let out a cry as he stared down the rifle-muzzle. He dived to the ground.

'Crack! Boom!' Goukas squirmed on the stony ground. He hadn't been hit; he was still alive. He glanced over at the American; Garand was still targeting the rifle over to the other side of the quarry. Goukas wriggled around, still fearful of rising too far off the ground. Across the small lake the rocks around where the goat had taken shelter were blood-red, smeared and splattered. The goat had been blasted into fragments.

'Fifty!' Garand was on his feet again. 'And each one numbered consecutively!'

Goukas lay there watching the American hobble back up the path followed by his Irish lap-dog. It would take another five minutes for Goukas to regain his usual composure. The American would get exactly what he wanted.

Within a week Harry Garand was back in Belfast minus the rifle. He kept a low profile as directed by McGoldrick. Mary had no questions for him; she knew his game, and it was indeed better not to know, only try to make the best of whatever time they had together before Harry Garand began limping towards the gallows. She could never blame him for taking action. If it had not been for the child, she would have done the same, she imagined. She would back him, no matter what.

Five weeks later

Word came to him a month later; the rifle and ancillary equipment had just come north from Dublin. They had his 'hits' well planned out. As agreed, McGoldrick's people organized his arrival to and safe departure from each chosen firing-point where the rifle awaited him. After the single shot he left immediately, as did the 'Garand', carried out in separate hands. From then on the only time he handled the weapon was for a few minutes just before each 'shoot' and always with rubber surgical gloves and a balaclava face-mask and combat jacket, thus avoiding the discovery of firearms residue in the event of him being arrested afterwards and subjected to swabbing by the police forensic experts. After each killing the gloves, balaclava and combat jacket were immediately taken away by another party, separate to the removal of the rifle. McGoldrick had the procedure down to a fine art.

By January 1972 Harry Garand had accounted for eleven soldiers and two policemen. The military had by then given him a nickname: 'One-Shot Charlie'. It was soon to catch on. Even the newspapers began to recognize his trademark – always a difficult shot, always at an unbelievable distance, and always to the head; but they only knew half the story. The rest had been suppressed by an official news-blackout – nothing short of issuing a 'D' Notice. He was becoming a cult figure. No soldier, walking or driving around the streets of Belfast, was immune. He was in a league of his own, unknown to anyone outside a small cell of people hand-picked by McGoldrick. The killings became the centre of everyone's imagination. Rumours flew around Belfast of a Dutchman helping the IRA; others said he was an ex-Legionnaire with a hatred for the British; another story was that of a disaffected former British soldier gunning for profit; but no one even suspected the calliper-aided disabled man who now hobbled with the aid of a walking-stick. Garand played the fool well, a cripple with no nerve left, no will to fight, a broken figure, yet all the time he was hobbling the streets searching out new targets and weaknesses in the procedures and practices adopted by what he now called the 'occupying forces'.

Alec Martin was brought into Springfield Road station in that month. He had the onerous task of collating all information on the 'One-Shot Charlie' killings as they were now known. It was not uncommon for the mainland police forces to send over CID personnel during the early seventies to help the depleted resources of the RUC; even members of the Army's Special Investigation Branch, the Royal Military Police version of civilian CID, were drafted into every CID office in Belfast and Londonderry. The files were vast, mainly comprising irrelevant stuff; but Alec Martin, then a detective chief inspector with the Metropolitan Police, had to wade through the lot just in the slimmest hope of detecting a trace or lead of any description.

He was given an assistant, a local RUC detective sergeant from Special Branch called Sam Nelson. It didn't take any genius to tell Martin that this younger man was undoubtedly going places and destined for greater things. Martin was delighted to have him on the staff; with his SB clearance Nelson could access information Martin didn't even know about. There was a need for a concentrated and dedicated approach to the investigation if anybody stood a chance of finding a lead on the killer, and Alec Martin was determined to succeed at whatever cost. On confronting the mountain of files he reminded himself of the old story of the obituary for a retired architect which stated he was found lying dead over some old plans whilst trying to get some new ideas. He desperately needed new facts, and on top of everything else his wife was being difficult.

Norma Martin hadn't much warmed to the idea of her husband's secondment to the Royal Ulster Constabulary. She would have warmed even less if she'd known he had volunteered. Then there was the publicity, the public announcement in the papers and on television about New Scotland Yard sending across some of its top detectives to assist the overstretched Ulster CID. She initially would not even countenance the idea of accompanying her husband, but then the following week she discovered the duration of his secondment. He would be away for at least six months, and the prospect of him being allowed home to London on a regular basis was small. She had a choice: become a vegetable in their North London house or move. But she loved the house; it had been her parents' home, and she and Alec had moved in after her father died in 1960.

It was a large Georgian terrace house, massive rooms with high ceilings, the place filled to the brim with a heavy mixture of antiques and out-of-date furniture; but it was home. She even missed the house when they holidayed each year. How would she cope for six months? And who would look after the place? After Norma's ailing mother died in 1965 she and Alec took the opportunity to strip out the entire house, but were careful not to disturb any of the ornate mouldings or detail. Now the place had style, the Adam fireplaces were shown off to their very best, the place echoed a careful balance of old and new, there was no longer any clutter. Her second question was answered first. One of Alec's senior officers was in the process of moving house and was very glad of the opportunity to lease the house for six months. The man was perfect; both he and his wife were close to retiring age, and she knew them well. The house and contents would be in safe hands. The RUC had also found the Martins a detached house in Lisburn just ten miles outside Belfast. It was safe enough and quiet. The house was owned by a police inspector who was now on an extended course at the National Police College at Bramshill. The man's family had accompanied him on his posting, and the house was available and fully furnished. The Martins fitted the bill perfectly.

Norma Martin finally gave in and joined her husband. It was a pleasant enough house in a middle-class estate just on the edge of the market-town of Lisburn but within easy walking distance of the shopping-centre and also easy travelling distance of Belfast city centre; but that was one place Norma Martin had vowed to avoid. The indiscriminate bombing campaign had grown in intensity, and the death rate had risen sharply over the last months; she was determined not to become yet another Ulster statistic. Whilst she had been introduced to many of the RUC wives who lived in the area, she still found herself unable to communicate. It was not that she felt any different from them; she just didn't want to hear about their fears and trepidation. It was enough to be living in Northern Ireland without being drawn into it.

Her isolation perplexed Alec Martin to such an extent that he asked his assistant Sam Nelson if his young wife could help. A dinner party was arranged at Nelson's house in Bangor, County Down. It was an unqualified success; the two women hit it off instantly and became almost inseparable afterwards. The weeks ran into months, and Norma Martin found herself enjoying herself for the first time in years.

It was a cold night. Alec Martin returned home, as always

careful to vary his route and mindful of that car in his rearview mirror. It was late; Norma Martin had gone to bed. He tiptoed upstairs and undressed in the bathroom so as not to disturb her; then he crept into the unlit bedroom, setting his gun on the bedside table as usual. He still couldn't get used to carrying the Walther PPK 9mm pistol, or be sure he could use it if his life depended upon it. He was no soldier; he was a London peeler. Even the guns they carried in the Metropolitan Flying Squad made him cringe. Would there come a day when all British policemen would be armed? God forbid, he thought. Then in the darkness it all seemed to come together; the future. This was the future: an armed British police force unless murderers like this 'One-Shot Charlie' were stopped in their tracks. He eased between the sheets, and she stirred.

'What time is it?' Her voice was clear and alert; it rather surprised him.

'You're awake! Sorry if I disturbed you.' He kissed her on the forehead as she moved closer against him. 'It's half-past twelve.'

'What sort of time is that to come creeping home into a pregnant woman's bedroom?'

Martin had just fully eased down into the warm bed and closed his eyes when her words smacked him on the face. In an instant he was sitting up, fumbling for the switch on the bedside table-lamp and knocking the pistol on to the floor in the process. The light went on, and Alec Martin stared down at his wife, her face beaming and radiant.

'Pregnant?'

She nodded, her tear-filled eyes saying everything. 'We've waited twelve years for it, and it finally has to happen in Northern Ireland.' He hugged her. They held each other for several seconds. 'I told Jane Nelson. I hope you don't mind. I just had to tell someone after seeing the doctor. She reckons it's the change in the drinking water over here.'

Alec Martin moved back slightly, his head gently motioning sideways. All the worries and fears of the investigation lifted instantly. 'Let's celebrate!'

'At nearly one in the morning!' She pretended to scold him.

'Just kiss me instead, but be careful – I'm fragile!' She laughed and he did, popping off the light again.

Two months later

The days turned into weeks as the two policemen sifted through the available information and evidence on each incident, cross-referencing at every opportunity, until finally their cluttered office displayed a 'link chart' which spanned an entire wall. From top to bottom they had listed, in chronological order, all the different murders, and running along the top from left to right they had again listed the various component factors pertinent to each incident.

The first column showed the location and time, the next day of the week, the third included the prevailing weather conditions, the fourth mentioned the approximate distance and angle of trajectory the sniper had used and so on until a total of eleven columns were listed, but most were only partly completed. In most cases the FP, or firing-point, of the sniper could not even be definitely ascertained, and the only entry in column ten entitled 'Return Fire' indicated two shots discharged by a soldier in reaction to one incident, and if the truth had really been known the soldier had only panicked, discharging his rifle harmlessly in the air whilst bound in the grip of fear. They both knew that, if they were to stand any possible hope of catching him, at least another two dozen areas of comparison had to be drawn, but there just wasn't the information.

Alec Martin petitioned the Assistant Chief Constable for Crime at Brooklyn, the RUC's Belfast headquarters, and additional detectives were drafted in to help, but every lead drew a blank; it was as if the sniper didn't exist, except to appear every so often to kill again. He was like a ghost. They had to predict his next move, get ahead of him and lead him into a trap. The murder inquiry had also been further hampered in recent months by the 'no-go' areas set up in Belfast. Barricades had been erected throughout West Belfast; complete communities came under the direct control of the paramilitaries; the police and the Army seemed powerless. Armed terrorists paraded openly at the barricades flaunting themselves in front of television and news cameras, brandishing their fire-arms. Operation Motorman earlier in the year had ended the 'no-go' areas, but now there was no public assistance for the police; now it was up to Martin and Nelson to get the bastard.

By now Martin followed a routine of staying behind in the office each night until early into the following morning, sitting for hours alone, occasionally referring to the enlarged Belfast street-map depicting the west and north sides of the city. On it he had each incident's location marked with a red cross from which he had drawn a fine black line depicting the direction of fire on to the target. Also, where possible, he included the firing-point. Most of the lines were pure guesswork. The mur-derer picked his ground very carefully: always two, perhaps three clear vantage-points to choose from, but often he had dozens of permutations. Martin absently puffed at his pipe. It had long since gone out, but he seemed not to notice.

Sam Nelson had been to Army HQNI to cross-refer state-ments with the SIB. On returning to the station he joined his boss with some fresh coffee. It was already close on 1 a.m.; they had both been at it since early the previous morning, and after another hectic day Nelson was just about shattered. Only stubbornness kept Alec Martin going. He was looking for something; he didn't know what it was, he just hoped he'd recognize it when it popped up.

'You know, Sam, we're tackling this the wrong way.' He took a mug of coffee from his assistant.

'Lateral thinking, Boss,' replied Nelson.

'What?' Martin stared at the younger man, but then realized he was sending him up.

'Sorry, Boss, I meant from another angle. You're right of course, but I can't honestly see it.' He moved from the apology towards agreement.

He thought highly of his English boss; he was learning a lot from Martin's vast experience. The man had proved himself over a lifetime on the London streets, and had more guile and cunning than any villain he had ever met. Nelson thought of the thin dividing-line between the criminal and his 'tracker'; at times there seemed little difference in the way they thought or, for that matter, operated.

'Sam, let's get on to our Army friends in Intelligence, see if they can compile a list of all male persons in the indigenous population. I want to cover the entire area of West Belfast. I'm looking for any person who would have had any sort of military training, and while they're at it I want a list of possible "runners" who'd help a killer like this and see if your "Branch" people can come up with any more suggestions for a master-mind behind this. There's got to be. I just feel it.'

The return from the combined Army resources arrived on Martin's table the following afternoon; it revealed three hundred names of likely candidates, but this was reduced somewhat by age and physical infirmity. Harry Garand's name was dropped from the list on the first check, although Sam Nelson gave him more than just a passing thought. He remembered clearly his long chats with Garand in Holywood Barracks in August 1971, but the American was a cripple and at that time Nelson was sure he wasn't involved. Eventually they had fifty-six possibles; all that remained was to find a connection between each man and the Provisionals and of course the known terrorist quartermasters for each area. To Martin's disgust they drew a blank again.

Suddenly the investigation was violently interrupted by a further killing. This time it was a young second lieutenant from the 1st Royal Regiment of Wales. He had been fatally wounded as his Land-Rover cornered into Flax Street in the north of Belfast.

They both rushed to the scene. The local CID and other police were already engaged in the preliminary investigation. The headless body had been taken off to the Royal Victoria Hospital. Alec Martin surveyed the situation. The local Army commander had the area saturated with his men, they were securing the complete area including the roof-tops. The single shot had come from somewhere up Flax Street, but that was all anyone knew. With the target on the move at the time of the shooting and the vehicle taking some distance to stop owing to the confusion and panic of the young driver, exactitude did not exist.

Later in the evening, whilst one of the Army patrols was walking through the old linen mill, making a final sweep of the third floor, an eagle-eyed lance-corporal spotted a shiny brass cartridge. It glistened back at him from where it lay wedged in a deep crevice in the pitted timber floor. He carefully eased open the window beside his discovery; it was a perfect 'bird's-eye view' of the junction where the shooting had taken place. Police forensic experts swamped the building in no time at all; but, alas, there was no other clue, just the casing apparently left behind in the gunman's rush out. Martin and Nelson left Flax Street like spent lovers, having failed to climax after the exhilarating preamble.

As they travelled back to Springfield Road in the police car Nelson was first to speak.

'We'll give it another go in daylight. Something might turn up.'

'Nope. Not a chance in hell,' replied Martin. 'We were damned lucky even to find that cartridge-casing; it's not his normal form.' He studied the brass casing now in the plastic bag in his hand. They passed along Alliance Avenue and were suddenly confronted with the yellow flashing lights and red tail-lights of an Army Land-Rover at a checkpoint.

'What's going on here, I wonder?' questioned Nelson.

'A sealant operation. I didn't tell you before, but I left instructions with the Army that the next time something like this happened they should seal every road leading into and out of West Belfast, and keep up the operation for at least six hours. The object is to check and log every damned person entering or leaving the area.'

They were stopped at the side of the road. The two cars in front had already been waved through. A young soldier carrying a red torch approached the driver's side. Alec Martin was in the process of showing him his warrant card when Nelson glanced out of the side-window. He watched the man in the shadows being frisked on the pavement by the other members of the Army patrol. There was something familiar about him. It was only when the man was allowed to pass through the narrow opening between another Army Land-Rover mounted broadside on the pavement and the gable wall of a house that he saw that the man limped, supported by a stick. Martin put the car into gear and began to move off.

'Take it easy going through the checkpoint,' snapped Nelson. 'I want to get a good look at that man on the pavement.'

As they drew level Nelson saw him more clearly under the glow of a street-light. He recognized Harry Garand immediately. His mind began to tingle as if knowing he was being watched. Garand tilted his head and glanced over, meeting Nelson's eyes; he stared at him coldly.

'What is it?' queried Martin.

'I don't know yet,' replied Nelson. 'Drive on.'

Martin slipped the car down into second gear and accelerated off towards Springfield Road.

Harry Garand watched the car vanish into the distance; he felt under threat for the first time since accepting his 'commission', as McGoldrick had put it. He would have to be extra careful in future; he knew his ex-interrogator had recognized him, but would he make the connection?

The following morning Alec Martin arrived at the office to find Nelson standing in front of the wall-mounted Belfast street-map. Another red mark had already been placed on the map at the junction of Flax Street and Crumlin Road. Sam Nelson was ruling a fine pen line depicting the trajectory of the shot. Martin took advantage of the situation to kindle some conversation.

'You're doing me out of a job, lad.'

'I'm impatient – afraid I can't help it,' muttered Nelson. He moved back from the wall clutching a ruler and pen in both hands. 'There, it's done.' He turned to Martin. 'I'll leave the wallchart to you, shall I?'

Martin smiled. There was a strangeness in Nelson's eyes. He no longer emanated any despondency; from somewhere he had found a new energy, perhaps even inspiration.

'Oh, I almost forgot.' Nelson grinned, as he turned and flicked open a manila file on the desk-top, and pulled out an enlarged photograph of Harry Garand, blown up from a photograph taken at Thiepval Barracks in 1971. He carefully lifted the black and white photograph and pinned it on the display-board beside the street-map. 'That'll do for starters.'

'It will?' mused Martin. 'Would you mind explaining?'

Nelson turned. He was no longer smiling. 'I've a nose for things, and I think I developed it more from working with you.' He stared at his boss. 'He's the one I saw last night in Alliance Avenue.' He picked up the list from the table. 'This is the list of names the Army came up with initially. Remember? We excluded all the aged, disabled or sick.' Nelson's attitude became tense. 'I've been bloody thick!' he roared, banging the list on the table. 'I should have checked that list out more thoroughly. I knew that man when he was scooped following internment. I even had many a long chat with him. He told me about his Vietnam experience. I even felt sorry for him and recommended his release before the bloody American consul became involved.' He glared at the wallchart and pointed a finger at the list of names. 'He's on that flaming list! There, in black and white, and we excluded him because he's got a game leg; but it's him, I feel it in my bones! That stare he gave me last night told me. He remembers and he knows I'm on to him. His eyes, Boss. It was his eyes that betrayed him!'

Martin was speechless.

'I'll get right on it. I'll collate everything we've got,' continued Nelson, looking at his watch. 'Give me until this evening. I should have it all by then.'

Martin began turning his head from side to side. 'No, Sam. For the moment, just get me a list of his associates and sightings from Army Intelligence, but remember to play this low-key; I don't want any Army twit to start hassling him on the street.'

Nelson had moved to the door. He turned with a grin on his face.

'Here's me going off to get his details, and I haven't even told you his name. It's Garand, Harry Garand, 26 Cupar Street.'

Four days later

He was picked up during an early-morning swoop. It was nothing like the first time; the Army and the Military Police knocked on his door just a little after 5 a.m. Harry Garand answered the door; he'd been half-expecting as much, but not with such consideration. The Garands were all kept in the small

259

living-room while the house was meticulously searched, but it was unnecessary. The house was 'clean'; but, then, they were only going through the motions. It was him they'd really come for.

Martin took the decision to allow Sam Nelson to handle the first interviews, hoping that the earlier rapport he'd established with the American could be developed, gaining the prisoner's confidence and hopefully his admission. But the man Nelson had interviewed after the internment was totally gone now. In his place a restless and hungry animal had reared from dormancy and now lurked barely hidden under Garand's cool exterior. Martin watched from the sidelines, collating all the necessary back-up information necessary for Nelson to pursue his technique of interviewing, but the young Special Branch sergeant was getting absolutely nowhere. The only response he got was aggressive, at times just short of physical violence. Finally, after two days of getting nowhere, Alec Martin decided to have a go. He started just after lunch, hoping the subject would have tired a little after his morning session with Nelson.

'My name's DCI Martin,' he said, sitting down opposite the American.

'English?' replied Garand coldly.

'Cigarette?' answered Martin, shoving an unopened packet across the table along with some matches.

'Bribery?'

'Call it a gesture,' smiled Martin.

'What do you want?' continued Garand, ignoring the cigarettes.

'I want "One-Shot Charlie" to stop what he's doing.'

'You're wasting time. Your buddy over there's been on about it for the last two days.' Garand glanced across at Nelson, who was standing next to the interview-room door.

'It has to stop.' Martin's tone almost sounded like advice.

'I've heard about this guy. The papers called him that name.' Garand lifted the cigarettes and began to open the packet. 'They say he's killed over two dozen so far.'

'Fourteen,' replied Martin.

'There it is, then. Speculation as usual. You just can't trust anyone, can you?' He grinned as he popped a cigarette into the side of his mouth.

Martin pointed to a thick folder on the table. 'That's you in there. Everything I never wanted to know about you; but I do – and you know what? You fit the bill perfectly.'

'Like shit,' snapped Garand as he lit the cigarette, tossing the match on to the floor. He inhaled deeply and then blew the smoke across into Martin's face. 'Sure it's a big file you have there, but can you prove it?'

'Oh, I will.' Martin shot forward, leaning across the table. 'You're finished, one way or the other.'

'That sounds like a threat.' He sucked on the cigarette again. 'Let me guess. It's white-knuckle time, right?' Then that same grin again. After all the months of frustration it was almost enough to put Martin completely over the edge.

'It's a promise!' he growled.

'I think you're all hot air, mister.'

'We'll see about that, shall we?' Martin held back; he couldn't afford to let the bastard get the better of him again.

Then the interview started in earnest. Garand had a barrage of questions thrown at him. Sometimes he answered; other times he remained silent or simply grinned back across the table. The table was becoming like a physical barrier to Martin now. It seemed that he was getting so close; at times the American seemed almost to want to answer, then the glimmer of hope vanished again behind his veil of hatred and aggression. The session wore on, taking more out of the policeman than out of the prisoner; but that was the way it was. The onus was always on the side of the interviewer to keep up the pressure; if the rhythm was affected, it was all lost, and that's exactly what happened. It was just after 8 p.m. They'd taken a break for forty minutes just after 6 p.m., and Martin was just getting into the swing of it again, changing tack and concentrating on Garand's wife and her possible knowledge of the murders, when he triggered off something.

Garand flicked the half-smoked cigarette across the table, barely missing Martin's right eye. The Englishman almost lost control. To Nelson it seemed that both men were locked into combat like two stags, antlers locked. The fight was to the end.

'I want to see a lawyer!' demanded Garand.

'There's no US constitutional rights here! You'll answer me one way or the other, you bastard!'

'Now, that's the second time you've said that!' grinned Garand. It infuriated the detective even further.

Martin suddenly lunged across, grabbing the American by his jacket lapels; the last months of waiting and painstaking search had amounted to nothing. All his hopes were now fading fast. Sam Nelson tried to intercede, but before he moved forward Alec Martin was getting cast aside like a rag doll. Garand swung his left arm in a clockwise motion, bringing his forearm and elbow down on to the Englishman's arms. Martin was nearly tossed out of his seat. Garand was now holding him by the throat and had already raised his right hand, the index and middle fingers extended within inches of the detective's eyes.

'No!' shouted Nelson. Instantly a uniformed RUC constable burst in from the corridor. At the very last moment Garand held back, but kept his hold on the Englishman, his right hand still ready to strike. 'Give it up, Harry!' pleaded Nelson, but the American no longer heard him.

Alec Martin was shaken. He stared up into the man's eyes; for a moment he imagined he was staring at pure evil. The hatred was indescribable. He was only now starting to realize the American's real impact; for the first time he really understood fear. Somehow Garand surpassed the very worst Martin had ever come across.

'You'll keep,' Garand said slowly. Martin couldn't let him get away with it; he had to retort.

'You don't have the bottle!' he snapped back. Garand simply raised an eyebrow and stared at his two fingers still just inches in front of Martin's face. A slight smirk formed as he finally let the Englishman go. Alec Martin gasped for breath. Just as Garand was releasing him he'd exerted further pressure to the man's throat, just enough to get his message across. Then it hit Martin like an express train; the American could have killed him at any time over the last seconds by simply crushing his windpipe.

'Get him out of here,' Nelson told the uniformed officer.

Garand stood to leave the room. Alec Martin jumped up

from the table, sending his chair flying into the wall behind. He was furious. He took in a deep breath, almost gagging as he spoke.

'You're dead meat!' he croaked. 'One way . . . or the other I'll have you. That is a fact!'

'We'll see.' Garand had that stupid grin back again as he walked out of the room. He was still grinning when he was shown outside the gates of Springfield Road RUC station.

Sam Nelson returned to the interview-room. His boss was still sitting there. The door was ajar. He knocked before entering. 'Can I come in?'

'Is he away?'

'I showed him to the gates myself after he'd had his property returned,' replied Nelson. 'The bastard was still grinning when he left.'

'If I have my way, he won't be grinning for very much longer.' Martin buttoned up his shirt collar and adjusted his tie. 'There's more than one way to skin that cat.'

'What do we do now?'

'Get me the Army Intelligence files on all the known Provos in West Belfast. I want to see the ORBATs, especially for their second battalion in Turf Lodge.' Martin stood up and left the room.

Sam Nelson picked up the intelligence and briefing file on Harry Garand. It was just then he noticed the letters scrawled after Garand's name in angry black ink: RIP.

Four days later

Harry Garand was sitting at home staring into the fire when the call to the front door aroused him. His leg hurt from all the walking he had had to do. He moved slowly to the door, opening it with one hand as he braced his weight against the wall with the other. Liam Heggarty smiled up at him.

'Can I come in?'

Garand pulled the door fully open, and the youth passed quickly up the hallway and into the living-room. When Garand entered the room Liam was standing beside the fire rubbing his hands; they were white at the knuckles and appeared blue with the cold.

'Good. We're alone. There's nobody else in the house, is there?'

Harry shook his head.

'Expecting anyone, are you?'

'Cut the crap, kid. You know you shouldn't be here. What do you want?' Garand was in great pain now; he wanted to reach for the bottle of painkillers sitting on the fireplace behind Liam, but it would show a weakness he was not prepared to reveal.

'I've a message for you. Yer to meet with the man this afternoon at that address.' Liam hesitantly handed him a piece of paper.

Garand examined the message before setting it on the roaring fire.

'You'll remember it, will you?' questioned the youth. He seemed genuinely concerned that Garand might forget.

'I'll remember,' said Garand. Then he heard the noise at the front door. It was Mary with the child; she couldn't get in past the latch and was calling up the hall. Liam left silently by the backyard and disappeared down the alley as Garand let her in. Her suspicions were aroused immediately.

'What's going on?' she demanded, also upset at having to stand in the cold for an extra few seconds. She pushed past him, leaving the child still fast asleep in the buggy in the living-room. Garand stared at her tiny face and rosy cheeks shining out from beneath the warm woollen clothes; he was so proud of her. He followed Mary into the kitchen. She stared at the back door as she filled the kettle and then looked out of the window above the sink. The footmarks were evident on the light layer of snow outside.

'Who was here?' she asked, turning to set the kettle on the gas ring.

'Oh, just a friend,' he replied, standing in the open doorway and leaning against the door-frame.

'Why all the secrecy?' she persisted, the concerned look on her face melting into anger. 'Why? Don't you think I don't know what's going on?' She was loud now. He glanced around.

The child stirred. He shut the kitchen door. 'What's wrong? Frightened the child there might hear her da's a murderer? And for the bloody cause!'

'Keep it down, honey!' He tried to calm the situation and attempted to take her in his arms, but she shrugged him away.

'Don't touch me, Harry, or as God's my witness . . . !' Mary's voice was much lower, but the anger had intensified. 'Just tell me, when's it going to end? Eh?' She closed her eyes, her head turning away towards the brightness from the window. Snowflakes now thickly filled the air. 'I know, I know we agreed for you to help them after what happened, but God! I never thought it would be like this. Living each day waiting for you to come home, not knowing where you are or what you've been up to, picking up snippets the next day from the wireless, or if I'm really lucky a snippet or two from the women at the shops . . . Harry, killing's one thing, but they're using you! Don't you see that?' She turned towards him, her eyes filled with tears. He took her in his arms, and she didn't reject him this time. 'I don't want to lose you,' Mary blubbered into his chest. 'I don't want that.' The child in the living-room was beginning to awaken.

McGoldrick was delighted to see Harry. Michael was present, standing by the door like some protective giant gargoyle. Garand liked him. Perhaps it was because he could not speak; there were too many people in this world with just too much to say for themselves, Harry reckoned.

'Thanks for coming. Sit down.' McGoldrick smiled, indicating for Harry to sit beside him on the small sofa. 'That was a fine job you did last week. You did well.' He passed over a piece of paper to Harry. It was a counterfoil from a building society. It was marked clearly with a deposit of a thousand pounds. 'Put it in myself for you just this morning. It must be a tidy sum you've got in your account, eh?'

Garand screwed the paper into a ball and tossed it into the cinders of the tired fire. 'I don't do it for the money,' he replied. The paper turned colour slowly, bursting into flames after several seconds.

'But it all helps, doesn't it?' McGoldrick smiled.

'You're taking a chance, McGoldrick. Personal service to the building society, and now a meeting only a few days after the job. You're breaking your own rules, aren't you?'

McGoldrick removed his steel-rimmed glasses and began to wipe them with the end of his scarf. 'Something's come up. We want you to do another job very quickly, and it's big.'

'How big?' Garand glared across at 'Quiet Michael', as McGoldrick had dubbed him; his face was stone-like.

'We want to draw the Brits into a real pitched gun-battle at an area verging on to the Shankill Road. I want you to take out two, maybe three of them in one go.'

'And that's it? What's so big in that?' Harry returned his eyes to McGoldrick. 'There must be more to it.'

'Oh, there is.' He returned Garand's glare and replaced the spectacles tightly against the bridge of his sharp nose, his reddened cheeks touching the underside of the rims. 'But you leave the rest to me. By the time I'm finished with the Brits they will be razing the Shankill to the ground.' His blue eyes pierced into Harry's heart.

'You've never asked me to take out more than one before.' Garand wondered at what else McGoldrick had in store.

'I said this was to be special, Harry. We want it to seem like a war's exploded on the Shankill.' McGoldrick's eyes widened.

Harry shrugged his shoulders. 'OK. Whatever you say. I'll go for three, maybe four if my luck's in.'

It was more than McGoldrick could have wished for.

'OK. But there's one thing I need you to do. Can you put in lots of shots, not just the usual one per target – make the bullets dance off the walls and streets? I want the Brits to think the Second World War's coming to Belfast.'

Garand could not understand it; there were easier ways of doing it. 'Sure, but if you want that sort of action you could use a couple of your own gunmen instead of me; it's not my style. What you want is a general-purpose machine-gun or a couple of SMGs.'

'But I trust you, Harry. I trust you to do the job right.' McGoldrick turned his head from side to side. 'The quality nowadays, Harry, it just isn't there any more. Maybe it's our own fault in part, setting kids on the streets armed with bravado instead of zeroed Armalites.' There was an amused tone in his voice.

Garand laughed. McGoldrick joined him, but 'Quiet Michael' never flinched.

Garand returned home. He was limping very badly now; the stick, once used as a disguise more than anything, was now almost a necessary item. The cold weather was beginning to cut into his bones. The only time he cast the stick aside was on a job, but his slowness was increasing his risk of capture. He thought of the previous week and having used the heavy rifle as a virtual crutch as he hobbled fast across the enclosed courtyard at the back of the Flax Street Mill, making his escape into the adjoining tumbledown weaving-house. He kept thinking about it as he crossed the Falls Road through the troughs of slush and grey-coloured water; the steady flow of traffic slowly passed as he stood in the middle of the road.

Then from amidst the line of traffic an Army Land-Rover approached; it was open at the top and stopped several feet from him, creating a break in the traffic. He nodded curtly to the drenched and heavily clad soldiers. The Army driver and soldier in the front seat watched him carefully edge across the remainder of the road, then for some reason the other two soldiers occupying the rear of the Land-Rover joined in their colleagues' stare. *They're watching me! They're on to me! They're watching my every move!* His mind raced; panic nearly overtook him. Just then the Land-Rover went on, followed slowly by a similar vehicle. Garand stood on the pavement watching them drive on down the Falls Road towards Broadway. The snow was falling steadily again, but it didn't seem like Christmas was two weeks away.

Two days later

The snow had melted from the Belfast streets, the ground and atmosphere were cold and damp. The blackness of the night air only enhanced the soldiers' depression as they moved stealthily along Agnes Street in Belfast's Shankill area, avoiding the street-lights and open spaces as always. They crossed a junction, running one at a time across the road, returning to the security of the shadows once again. Each time one darted across at least two other members of the eight-man patrol covered their colleague's progress, surveying the area through the night sights mounted on top of their rifles. This enabled them to make some use of the darkened backstreets, and through the light-intensification systems everything was visible to them.

This was Protestant territory and, although the soldiers took some reassurance from that fact, the possibility of an attack being mounted by terrorists was not to be dismissed. They remembered well their pre-patrol briefing. 'React and be on the alert at all times and in all areas and you have the best chance of survival,' the company sergeant-major had roared. 'The terrorist plays on your weaknesses. Give him an opening and he's into you. Show him a tight patrol and he'll back off.' The CSM was of course quite right – statistics showed him that – but neither he nor the patrol had banked on Harry Garand. They could put on whatever sort of show they liked; it was all the same to him.

A car screeched to a halt at a nearby junction. The last two soldiers on each side of the road, acting as 'Tail-End Charlies', had both been walking slowly backwards at the time. One fell to his knee, rifle raised to aim. The other took refuge in a doorway, bracing himself hard against the brickwork protrusion. He raised his night sight instantly, examining the car's interior. Just a single driver, and the man appeared to be lost, unaware of the soldiers' presence some thirty feet away. He peered out of the open window at the street-signs before turning left and driving slowly in the opposite direction. A dog barked as someone fumbled with a metal bin-lid somewhere near by. The night sounds of any city, mused the soldier with the IWS; if he closed his eyes, it would almost seem like his home town of Huddersfield. He stepped out from the doorway whistling briefly to his partner on the other side of the road. The soldier glanced over from between the parked cars before rising again to full height.

Just as he began to step back, adjusting the webbing strap dangling from his rifle and attached to his right wrist, the first boom of the Garand rifle rang out. The other soldier from the doorway watched in disbelief as his mate's head split from his body. Blood, tissue, and bone flew out from directly behind his head as he spun towards the pavement, crashing into the side of one of the parked cars. The soldier in the doorway hadn't time to give a signal, dive for cover, or complete any other action, conscious or otherwise, before the second shot broke into the reverberating echo of the first. He didn't hear it, already being thrown back into the doorway; with sledge-hammer force, a bullet had just penetrated his head behind his left ear. Everything seemed to slow down now; no noise, no feeling, nothing. He slumped to the ground.

The remaining six soldiers were by now well under cover. They reacted as trained, the patrol commander screaming a situation report into the Pye radio-set microphone protruding from beneath his flak-jacket. The others were already making ready their rifles; the air was filled with a new sound as each man crashed the slide of his rifle, feeding a 7.62 mm round into the breech of his SLR. Two of the soldiers moved up the street slowly towards their prostrate mates. Then the Garand exploded again, showering bullets on to the street around them. Because of the situation Garand had chosen to use ordinary cartridges. He began emptying the rifle-clip. The bullets frag-mented on impact, sparking against the asphalt surface and ricocheting into the lines of parked cars. Garand changed the ammunition-clip swiftly and emptied it aimlessly up the street from his vantage-point at the first-floor window above the corner shop.

He was three hundred yards away. They had no chance of hitting him unless with a lucky shot and, judging by their reac-tion under fire, it would have had to be damned lucky; but nevertheless he didn't like this action of disclosing his position – it went against the grain and his common sense. He emptied the second clip and reloaded the final one, this time using his 'special' cartridges. He took careful aim, and zeroed in on a soldier lying under a parked Bedford van. He fired once, taking the soldier in the crown of his head.

'Boom!' The bullet exploded under the vehicle; the van's petrol-tank immediately exploded, engulfing the dead soldier and surrounding area in a sheet of brilliant flame. It lit up the entire street like Bonfire Night. A further soldier, scorched by the flames, leapt from his hiding-place on the adjacent side of the road. He ran into the road screaming, his combat jacket sleeve and flak jacket already on fire. The flames had blinded him, his hair was singed, and his face was already scorched by the searing heat. The next shot also found its target, the bullet entering between the soldier's fingers which now covered his twisted face. His head exploded; what was left, crumpled like a pack of cards, dissolved on to the ground, still burning. A second explosion occurred as the petrol in the van's fuel-pipeline and carburettor ignited. It was virtually ignored by the patrol commander, busily feeding in the position of the firing-point to his base.

Garand stepped back from the window and moved out of the old storeroom. There was no time to lift any of the cartridge-casings from the floor of the darkened room and, anyway, there were far too many of them. He had already spent too long at the scene, far too long. As he rumbled down the back staircase he heard the clatter of the return fire; the soldiers were panicking. He met Michael at the bottom of the staircase and passed him the rifle. Garand moved with a renewed speed; the leg no longer hurt. Adrenalin now flowed steadily through his bloodstream. He moved into the backyard and followed the alleyway just as he had been told. He ran on, stumbling over a dustbin set out too far from a crumbling back-yard door. He picked himself up, turning right through the maze of back alleys; then he fell again, a sharp pain in his right leg this time. He ran on, almost hopping as he strove to put distance between himself and Agnes Street. He was out of breath now, pulling at the balaclava; it was off as he rounded the corner. 'Turn right,' McGoldrick had said, 'then across the main road and you're back home again into Catholic ground.' He kept on running down the dark alleyways. His mind raced back to Vietnam. Why did it always have to be the same? In the darkness the picture-show began to take form before his very eyes . . .

He was back on the trail, watching Guzman blowing himself and the Gooks to smithereens. He was running now; a new energy surged through him as he caught up with Ripcord and

Apollo waiting in the gully. No one asked any questions; all they did was run as fast as their legs could take them. They kept to the dried-up river-bed. The river had been diverted months before by US Army engineers in a vain attempt to irrigate some farming land for the local villagers and help avoid the yearly flooding that accompanied each rainy season.

Like everything else in the region, it had been a complete waste of time; the VC had killed every male in the village because of what they saw as complicity with the enemy. The women and children had been driven north for 'rehabilitation'. Now the village was dead, and very soon the three Marines would be, too, if they didn't reach one of the entrance-points into the Fire Support Base. Of course that worked on the premise that the base hadn't yet been overrun; but, then, they didn't have too many alternatives left. Garand led them up out of the river-bed into the trees. They were now on the east flank of the hill. The bombardment had started to ease up, the prelude to an attack. They took a brief rest in the cover of the trees.

'Guz?' panted Ripcord.

Garand shook his head as he rested his back against a tree.

'How come we ain't seen Charlie for the last K?' asked Apollo. The giant Negro pulled off his helmet and ran a camouflage scarf across his shaven head to dry up the sweat.

'They've pulled back. My guess is they've tried already and are regrouping over there somewhere.' Garand pointed into the pitch-black jungle they had just emerged from. Now and then the jungle sparkled into life as another white parachute flare was fired off from the base. The rain was now falling in torrents; in many ways it was to their advantage, blocking out any sound they made and reducing visibility, but it also created problems.

'But that don't mean they've left no one behind between us and home,' said Ripcord.

'One sure thing. We can't stay here.' Garand rose into a crouch. 'I'll lead. Rip, you keep me in sight. Apollo, you take the rear.'

'Just what I like, man,' grinned the large Negro, displaying his pearl-white teeth. 'I just loves a bit of asswork!'

'Just keep your mouth shut. Charlie could see your teeth a

mile off,' replied Garand. Both men smiled as they prepared to follow their leader.

They pushed on, slowly now, fearful of ambush. The terrain was becoming quite steep, and the going was difficult, due mainly to the water now running down the hillside and turning everything into mud. Finally the ground began to level off somewhat; there was still an uphill gradient but it was mild by comparison. Garand fell to one knee, keeping perfectly still; so did Ripcord, just ten metres behind. He looked around for Apollo, but he wasn't in sight. Then Garand motioned for Ripcord to come up beside him. The Marine complied, taking care not to rush it.

'Charlie's got an OP up ahead. My guess is they're directing down the mortar-fire on the base.'

'How come the base hasn't picked up their presence?' Ripcord was referring to the surveillance equipment in use at the base, some of which could pick out a man at five thousand metres.

'Weather isn't helping. Besides, we don't know what state the base is in,' whispered Garand. Both men looked on past the tree-line towards the Fire Support Base; at least a dozen fires were raging out of control, but the perimeter was still intact. 'Have you a blue flare?' continued Garand. The Marine pulled a metal-cased flare out of a pouch at his side just as Apollo caught up with them. The look on the ex-footballer's face told them to expect the worst.

'We're just ahead of a fucking VC battalion, man. I ain't seen nothing like it since they made *The Ten Commandments*!'

'What time have we?' snapped Garand.

'Two minutes outside,' panted Apollo.

'Let's move it, people,' replied Garand.

'I just hope to hell those guys in there see a blue flare through all of this shit,' groaned Ripcord.

There was no time for anything but to rush the VC observation-post. Garand surged forward with Ripcord at his side. Apollo held back a second and then followed, after discarding his backpack full of medical supplies. Four Vietcong were lying down, well concealed in a ditch they had cleared out just five metres from the edge of the cleared area that surrounded the base. With the noise of the heavy rain they didn't hear the Americans coming until they were on top of them. Garand shot two of them with an automatic burst from his M16.

The VC radio operator turned just as Ripcord was at the edge of the ditch. He shot the VC through the head with a three-shot burst from his rifle; the little man almost cartwheeled backwards. The fourth man, seemingly an officer by the way he wore the Sam Browne belt over his 'black pyjama' top, drew his Chinese-made pistol and fired as Ripcord came down on him. The bullet grazed the Marine on the shoulder as he closed in, sticking the VC with the short bayonet clipped to the underside of his M16 rifle. The man screamed, his face horribly contorted, as the bayonet jabbed into his stomach. Ripcord then fired into him, sending the man backwards off the end of the bayonet. Apollo had by now caught up with them.

The blue smoke rose into the air despite the heavy downpour. They waited a few seconds for the bright blue smoke and fizzling flare to be identified by their comrades. There was no return signal from the base, but they couldn't wait.

'I hear them coming!' cried Apollo, looking back through the trees.

They were running again, as fast as their legs could carry them, weaving out across the cleared 'killing zone' towards the 'east gate', as it was called. It was a small opening in the wire perimeter used as a secondary entrance or escape exit in the event of the base being overrun. They knew full well that after the attack started the main entrance to the Fire Support Base would be sealed and mined. The 'killing zone' had lived up to its name: they raced and skipped over dozens of black-clad bodies left after the failure of the first wave of the attack. The ground beside Apollo was churned up further as an enemy machine-gun opened up from somewhere to their right. Garand was in the middle, just ahead of the other two, weaving and ducking as the hot lead filled the air all around them. The bullets zinged past as they closed on the final hundred metres to the 'gate'. They could already see some of their buddies busy pulling back the wire just below the sandbagged fence-line in readiness for their arrival. Tracer rounds whizzed over their heads from the heavy machine-guns at the base perimeter, cutting up the jungle behind them.

A bugle sounded, then a black wave descended from the jungle like a plague of locusts, ready to destroy everything in its path. The base's remaining 105 mm howitzers and 81 mm mortars erupted; the ground behind the running Marines shuddered and lifted into the air. Several of the mortars were used to provide overhead illumination for the defenders, but it also highlighted the running trio. Ripcord was shot through both legs just twenty metres from the outer perimeter defence-line. He fell forward heavily, landing face down in the mud next to a dead Vietcong. He cried out, and Garand turned in his tracks, diving to his aid. He lifted him over his left shoulder and began the final run in. Apollo made it in ahead, running in past the two Marines who were holding the triple-dannert barbed wire apart. He was careful to follow a young officer who showed him on through the secondary line and safely past the camouflaged Claymore mines and trip-flares that were laid all around the perimeter of the base. Garand reached the wire several seconds later. The vigorous response put up by the defenders had crushed yet another attack-wave; the VC were being forced back into the trees for cover.

Once inside Garand was helped by a medic to carry his friend to the nearest bunker. They laid Ripcord out across some ammunition-boxes. He was dead; shot in the side of the head as he was being carried the final steps to safety. Then the enemy mortaring commenced once again, this time backed up by artillery-fire. The first salvo destroyed what was left of the communications centre and administration area. The second salvo included a direct hit on the command post where Apollo had just been taken by the young second lieutenant. No one survived.

That was the way it was for days. The Vietcong had pushed forward in a new offensive, and owing to the weather and battle conditions Hill 427 was not getting any assistance from anyone. The helicopter gunships were grounded indefinitely at the rear, and the two other Fire Support Bases that 427 depended on for mutual support had already been overrun. Harry Garand fought on with barely a handful of survivors.

Despite terrible shrapnel injuries to his leg he held them together, retreating to the inner bunker-line as the perimeter was finally overrun. Now Jamie Lee, Guzman, Ripcord, and Apollo were all before him, urging him on, crying out to him. But was it encouragement or a warning . . . ?

He came to the end of the alley and without stopping pushed on across the road. It was a foolish move but, then, he'd never felt this vulnerable before. Then it hit him. It was that look he had got from McGoldrick on their last meeting. The bastard had set him up! Permutations clouded his mind again mixed with more abstract images of Vietnam. It all merged into one as he neared the pavement on the far side of the darkened alleyway. His heart stopped – or, at least, it felt that way – as out of the shadow of the alley, directly in front of him, appeared the soldier with the red beret and cap badge of the Parachute Regiment. From the tough blackened face peered two of the blackest eyes Garand had ever seen.

He was still hobbling towards the soldier unable to stop quickly because of the momentum of the swinging callipered leg. His eyes widened as he watched helplessly as the soldier raised his rifle, as if in slow motion. There were only a few feet between them now. The soldier's finger took up the trigger pressure. Harry took in a gulp of air just as the 7.62 mm bullet went through his chest. It ripped open the green combat-jacket, filling it both front and back with darkened wet patches. He was falling back now. The pain of the injury would not register; his eyes caught the gable walls as he landed heavily on the ground. His mind seemed to go blank. There was a strange comfort in it all; it all seemed so natural. The soldier was joined by the rest of his patrol. One of the Paras pulled the balaclava from Harry's pocket. A full Garand clip fell on to the ground beside him.

'Got him! We got the bastard!' He spat at Garand before sinking his boot into Garand's side. Harry Garand never moved.

'Better get an ambulance, Corp,' replied the soldier who had shot him.

'Fuck the ambulance!' the Corporal replied, reluctantly

radioing back to his ops room, knowing that the arrival of an ambulance would be a natural progression now.

Inside seconds the soldiers were inundated with petrol-bombs hurled by a crowd of youngsters from down the road. The bombardment was getting dangerously close, and the young Para corporal was about to give the order to return the assault with rifle-fire when his mind was made up for him. 'Crack! Crack! Crack!' The soldiers dug further into their cover, one falling over behind Garand's bleeding body. 'Boom!' A blast-bomb exploded yards from them. Then the automatic rifle-fire continued. Two, maybe three gunmen from two separate points, the corporal estimated. Slowly they were forced across the road and into the adjacent alley from where Harry Garand had appeared. One soldier was hit in the ankle as he tried to drag Garand across the road. He was removed to safety by two of the other soldiers as the corporal laid down covering fire, emptying the SLR magazine in the direction of the fiercest attack. The mob, nearly two hundred strong, surged forward from the lower end of the road.

'Where the hell have they come from?' the corporal yelled, snapping on a fresh magazine before spraying another six rounds over the heads of the mob.

The crowd faltered, and then a further flash of gunfire came from within their swollen ranks. Brick and mortar chipped from over the corporal's head as he turned and ran after his mates. Harry Garand was left lying in the road. One of the soldiers had already thrown the injured soldier over his broad shoulders and was running in a stooped position. Another carried the injured man's rifle. The four-man patrol raced along the alley-way, not knowing their direction and just following their instincts. Two more petrol-bombs exploded dangerously close behind them, and the corporal and another soldier spun around opening fire.

They were no longer playing, and three youths to the front of the mob fell immediately. Again there was another burst of automatic gunfire, but the bullets went wide and above the soldiers' heads. The two Paras fired in unison, and the gunman to the fore of the crowd was hit twice in both the face and the shoulder; the safety of hiding amidst the crowd no longer applied. The mob dispersed when further shots found several more targets. One young man dropped a petrol-bomb only feet from where he stood; he and several others were badly burnt and jumped backwards in terror. The mob was no longer surging into the entry, but retreating in pandemonium, leaving their dead and wounded behind.

The Army had an extremely tense and difficult task that night. As rightly predicted by McGoldrick some of the patrols rushing to the original scene encountered the local residents of the Shankill. Feelings were high but pushed beyond boiling-point when a passer-by on the Shankill was allegedly shot dead by the Army. Of course the soldiers on the ground at the time knew nothing of it and a further IRA gunman had already made good his escape into the Falls. But the people of the Shankill were incensed; an old pensioner out walking his dog had been killed by an over-reactive soldier. For two nights and a day hell reigned on both the Shankill and Falls Roads.

The following morning during a temporary lull in the rioting, Martin and Nelson stood over the pool of dried blood at the foot of the alley and the smeared marks where Garand had been dragged over the road by the soldiers. Some time during the night Harry Garand or the body of Harry Garand had been secretly taken out of the area. That was the question that would nag Martin for weeks after: Which was it – body or body and soul? Martin and Nelson tried in vain to follow up their leads. Mary Garand and the child had already left Cupar Street; the house was deserted and almost stripped of all the furnishings.

Two days later McGoldrick and Michael were caught up in a shoot-out at an Army road-block in the Andersonstown area of Belfast. Michael was killed instantly, but McGoldrick steered the stolen car through the road-block despite stopping a bullet in the back. It was much to McGoldrick's regret that he had not died outright, for owing to the military saturation of West Belfast he was forced to lie low in a safe house in the Twin-brooke Estate. Denied hospitalization, and with the minimum of medical aid, he lasted six excruciating hours before giving up the ghost.

Martin and Nelson persisted in their enquiries, saw local priests and doctors amongst their other contact, but the 'One-

Shot Charlie' killings had nevertheless stopped. That seemed the only compensation for their tedious investigation. Finally, after months of negative results, news of Mary Garand and the child finally arrived at Martin's office following a fire at a hostel in Dublin. St Clement's Hostel for women and children run by the Sisters of Mercy had been destroyed by fire on 19 February 1973. The old Victorian building had been gutted, thirty-seven women and children had perished in the blaze, and the list included a Mary Garand and an infant named Patricia Garand. The fire had been so intense that bodies had just disintegrated.

Nelson checked the report and followed it up; a counterpart in the Garda in Dublin meticulously checked every detail of the tragic incident. Alec Martin's questions were quickly answered. No, there was neither a man seen before the fire nor any body discovered in the ashes that fitted Harry Garand's description. Yes, Mary Garand and her child had been seen in the heart of the building only seconds before the fire broke out. And finally, yes, it was a tragic accident, a gas leak, confirmed to be 'without any malice aforethought' as the Garda detective superintendent aptly put it.

Throughout the following months, even for years after, Alec Martin had still retained doubts; but the killings never repeated themselves, and he eventually concluded the file to be closed. But now Garand had returned to him, awakening his doubts and fears all over again. Martin shook himself and stood up from the armchair, rubbing his cold arms as he stared into the rising dawn light. He was retired now; he wanted no part of it. Why should he? Yet his old friend had been killed only a few miles from his home. He was involved whether he wanted it or not!

PART THREE

THE HUNT

LONDON
Sunday, 21 June

Frazer Holbeck reluctantly kept the appointment as directed. He drew up outside the warehouse near King George V Dock on the River Thames and parked the MG beside a wooden hoarding. The place was deserted and quiet. A recent fall of rain had allowed the street-lights to bounce and shimmer their reflection across the uneven road-surface. He checked his Rolex; it was just past 3 a.m. He was late, but what did that matter? If the rendezvous was as important as they said, his contact would wait.

As he crossed the street he felt the cold outline of the .38 Smith & Wesson Bodyguard revolver in the right-hand pocket of his overcoat. He'd obtained the two-inch-barrelled airweight version years before as his insurance; he'd also been thankful that it had never been fired, but he would use it if he had to. If Holbeck had retained one fascination upon leaving the Guards, it was for firearms; he knew them inside out, especially small arms. The five-shot hammerless revolver was perfect for him; it could be rapidly fired single-handed without difficulty, and there were no tell-tale cartridge-casings left lying around.

He went down the dark, partly lit side-alley and found the door. It was open just as he had been told. Inside the place was pitch-black; he took just a few steps, and the metal fire-door slammed shut behind him. He froze.

'Mogul?' a voice with an American accent whispered behind him.

'Thor?' replied Holbeck.

A torch was switched on, illuminating the Englishman's back. 'Turn around slowly, hands out of pockets.'

Holbeck obliged, slowly drawing his right hand from the

revolver and raising both arms to either side before turning to face the bright torchlight.

'Do you mind, old chap, it's bad enough suffering from night myopia without having to look at that.' He smiled nervously.

Ivanov set the torch on top of some empty crates and stepped forward. Both men were now visible in the light-beam.

'Ah! That's much better. Any more of that and I'd have been seeing spots before my eyes for the rest of the night.' Holbeck smiled. 'You know me of course.'

'Yep.'

Holbeck glanced around nervously into the darkness of the damp fetid warehouse. 'I assume that we are alone?'

'Just you and me.'

'And you are Mr Tucker.' Holbeck smiled again. 'So, Tucker, I am to give you all the assistance I can.'

'That's the general picture.'

'Where in the dickens have you been? I've been waiting to meet you every night for the last three days.'

'Things haven't quite gone exactly to plan,' replied Ivanov coldly.

'Care to explain?' Holbeck was getting nervous again.

'Nope. Now, can we go?'

'My sports car is outside. May I suggest we get out of this seedy place?'

'My sentiments exactly,' said Ivanov. 'My luggage is still at Euston Station.'

'We'll pick it up in the morning. Tell me, why is it you people have to be so dramatic anyway? I can't see anything wrong with meeting for morning tea at the Café Royal, can you?' He smiled and thrust both hands back into his coat pockets.

'Just as long as that gun stays in your pocket, we'll get along fine.'

Ivanov moved aside, picking up the torch before following the Englishman out to the car.

On the way back Holbeck was careful to ensure that they were not being followed. Holbeck took him to a flat he used in Chelsea, just overlooking the River Thames and Battersea Park beyond. It was one of the more favoured of the locations he had scattered around the country. They entered the apartment just a little after 4 a.m.

'This will be yours for the time being.' He handed Ivanov a set of keys. 'There's an intruder alarm set to British Standard 4737; it works on the principle of low-pressure sodium lighting fitted with photo cells, and it's linked to a private security company that I have dealings with. They're far more reliable than the local police and far more discreet. I'm also notified the moment the alarm is triggered here. I'll go over the details of how it works later.'

Ivanov studied the small Israeli-made device mounted high into the corner of the lounge. He'd seen them before, of course; it was part of his profession to get in and out of situations undetected. He followed Holbeck through the spacious three-bedroomed apartment; the place was immaculately furnished, modern but tasteful.

'Personally I hate modernism in furniture. I tried in the past to get a healthy balance of traditional and modern but never succeeded, so I reverted to surrounding myself with the traditional style. I'm not quite sure just what that says about me.' Holbeck grinned.

Ivanov raised an eyebrow.

'This place is just to impress. I had one of these interior designer poofs do it up for me a couple of years back. It's not bad but really not my cup of tea.'

'Holbeck, can we just get down to business? I didn't come all this way to hear a lot of crap.'

'My goodness!' Holbeck pretended to be upset. 'Do they teach you no manners back home?'

'When was this place swept last?'

Holbeck went to a wall-cabinet next to some bookshelves and opened one of the drawers, removing a brown leather attaché case. He set in on the dining-table next to the Russian and flicked it open. 'It's the very latest in electronic detection. It can even detect someone trying to use a directional microphone as well as sweeping somewhere for the normal sort of "bugs" one finds. And it's portable; power-supply nickel cadmium batteries, rechargeable by this.' He pointed to a small lead and three-pin plug in the corner of the case. 'I was told you'd be familiar with it.'

'I am.'

'Excellent. The apartment was swept by me no more than two hours ago, so don't worry yourself.' He switched on the machine; apart from one small hand-held component the entire case was the housing for the device. After five seconds a white light began to flash at the top left corner next to a series of push-button controls. 'There we are – clear! Nothing in this room or any of the adjoining rooms, and no directional microphone in use. If ever the red light is displayed instead of the white, then you know you've a problem. Use the hand-held device to sweep each room, and if nothing shows, then you've got a problem from outside. To jam a directional microphone simply hit this switch next to the red light; it will engage the microphone and give you a clear signal in under one second.'

Ivanov went and sat down. Holbeck was more than disappointed at the Russian's lack of interest in his toy.

'Tell me everything you know about this affair.'

'You probably know more than me, old boy, but I'll gladly fill you in. Since getting my instructions from Moscow I've been doing some research through our own files on this thing. The first killing was, as you know, in Northern Ireland, an Army captain; the second was the Irish Justice Minister in Dublin – awfully nice chap, knew him well.' Holbeck tutted. 'Forensic reports on both murders are compatible; also a cartridge-casing was left at both scenes, each one stamped with consecutive numbering using Roman numerals.'

'Someone wants to be noticed.'

'Obviously. Now, the Ulster shooting was being investigated in part by the Royal Ulster Constabulary's Assistant Chief Constable for Crime, a man called Nelson. He was murdered the evening before yesterday when visiting a retired ex-colleague in West Sussex.'

'Can his killing be linked into the other two?'

'Not forensically, but clearly there's a link. He was killed by what appears to have been at least two terrorists, using AK47s and Soviet-made grenades. So far the Sussex Special Branch and New Scotland Yard have drawn a blank. The RUC are naturally eager to get those responsible but, again, they have also come up with nothing – not even a murmur in the Indian camps.' Holbeck grinned.

'This ex-policeman that Nelson went to see – who is he and what's he got to do with this?'

'He's called Alec Martin. He was seconded to the RUC during 1971 and 1972. Sam Nelson was his assistant during that period. They investigated what we still call the "One-Shot Charlie Killings". During that period a sniper was active on the streets of Belfast. He was good; in fact he was bloody brilliant!' Holbeck seemed to praise the fact. 'During a fourteen-month period eighteen soldiers and RUC men were killed by this sniper. No one knew who he was. There were rumours of a former French Legionnaire; my department even spent some time across in France checking through Foreign Legion records. Someone even thought they'd traced the likely suspect to the Deuxième Régiment Étranger de Parachutistes.' Holbeck paused, savouring his perfect French. 'It turned out the man had died two years before in a prison in Bordeaux. Other opinions varied; some viewed the sniper as a former British soldier, either Irish or with Irish republican sympathies, and, of course, there were rumours that he was in fact an American. The last turned out to be correct.'

'So you know who he is?'

'*Was*, dear boy. He got caught one night in a shoot-out with some Red Berets who proved too much even for him. Mind you, he shot up a patrol just beforehand.'

'Who was he?'

'Harry Garand, a former United States Marine Sergeant, married to an Irish girl from Belfast. He'd been living right under everybody's nose the whole time. The body-count was so high that they even had to slap a "D" Notice on it at one stage. If the British public had got to hear how bad it was, there wouldn't have been any need for a "Troops Out" movement; the Army would have been withdrawn from Ulster inside weeks, and that was the educated opinion at the time.'

'Nelson died just after visiting this man Martin, didn't he?'

'Only two miles away from the house in Stopham. I can anticipate your next question, Tucker. Yes, they obviously thought Martin had told him something; but, then, why spare Martin? The Sussex police are of the opinion that the killing was simply a terrorist attack and purely a coincidence, but they don't know about this.' He returned to the cabinet and unlocked another drawer, removing a red plastic file which he handed over to Ivanov. 'These are copies of some of the documents that Nelson was carrying at the time of his murder. Thankfully the originals he carried were destroyed in the fire after his car exploded, but my department managed to obtain these from the RUC. I can't suppress them much longer, and sooner or later they'll become public knowledge to both the British and Irish police.'

Ivanov opened the file, reading the first document. It was a report from the Northern Ireland Forensic Science Laboratory in Belfast dated 1972.

'Study the file for yourself, but you'll see a clear forensic link between the "One-Shot Charlie" killings and that of the Army officer and the Irish minister. The same rifle, and the same cartridges, the numbers running consecutively. Whoever is doing this knew exactly where to follow on. Tell me. Just why is Moscow so interested in these killings?'

'I suppose you'll have to know some time. Garand was being used by one of our sleepers, an Irishman called McGoldrick, code-named Bloodstone.'

'My God!' Holbeck was aghast.

Ivanov left the file aside. 'How sure are you this Garand is dead?'

'That, my dear boy, is up to you to find out. Even I have my limitations, but I can be of some assistance to you.' He handed over an envelope. 'Inside you'll find a CIA identification-card in the name of Harvey Tucker. There's also a list of contact numbers for me; destroy it after you memorize it. I also happen to know Alex Martin. He liaised with MI5 during the late seventies over some London criminals who went up for hire by the KGB; we became great friends, so I can get you an invitation to meet him.'

'Why not do it yourself?'

'My dear chap, I want to keep out of this as much as possible. I fully intend to live on here after this affair has blown over. If I stick my nose into it too far, I'd be liable to get it chopped off.'

'So Mikhailov told me.'

'Good old Alexei! How is he?'

'Just the same.'

Holbeck lifted his coat and checked his Rolex. 'Look I'm going to have to dash for now. You'll find everything else you need in that black cabinet over there. I'll get back to you later today by telephone. By the way, one thing Moscow doesn't yet know: GCHQ have tracked the three Field Radio Signals you received.' Ivanov's eyes narrowed. 'Don't be too concerned; everything they get has to come to me. I'm going to arrange to introduce you to one of their department heads – a woman called Antonia Travis. She'll be invaluable to us.'

'Why introduce us? You can handle that side of things.'

'Tucker, the woman works for me. She doesn't know who I am, but she still works for me.'

'Wolverine?'

'Exactly. I can instigate a procedure whereby she will report everything directly to me. She will believe it to be a top-secret CIA–MI5 operation. That's where you come in. I also want you to get her confidence, see if she is telling me everything. Frankly I've had my suspicions for some time now.'

'Holbeck, this sucks!' The glare on Ivanov's face unsettled the Englishman.

'Look, she'll get an instruction from Mogul telling her to co-operate with us. She's not working for any British intelligence agency. That leaves us with the Americans to consider. If she thinks she is being compromised, she'll likely tell you before her CIA controller.'

Ivanov was on his feet, his face raging with anger. 'Holbeck! If Moscow had known about the mess you're in, they wouldn't have touched you with a bargepole!'

'Tucker, you help me and I'll help you. There are things about Moscow that you just don't know. If you want to return there a hero – or, for that matter, at all – just make sure that you cover my back during your stay here.' He donned his coat. 'By the way, I've taken the liberty of arranging luncheon for us at L'Escargot. It's a little restaurant I frequent in Greek Street in Soho. Ask any cabbie and he'll take you there.'

'That is an unnecessary risk.'

'Tucker, I find that the more obvious one is the less likely it is to draw attention to oneself, and I do have a purpose in all of this: to get you and Miss Travis off to a good start. By the way, the other set of keys in the fruit-bowl on the table is for the red Ford Sierra saloon sitting in the private carpark outside. Toodle pip!' He smiled and was gone.

Ivanov cursed aloud. He had never depended on anyone when he had lived in America; it was just him and the system. He could trust himself, rely on his own judgement; but Holbeck's character was reminiscent of a Russian doll, and just how many layers did Moscow know about? He examined the apartment for himself; the fridge and freezer were crammed with enough food to last him several months.

In the cabinet he found a 7.65 mm HSc Mauser pistol, a box containing a hundred rounds of hollow-point ammunition, and an Israeli-made silencer. The gun was not new but in mint condition. Ivanov lost no time in stripping down the mechanism and used the cleaning kit Holbeck had left him. Then he checked the Mossad-style silencer, making sure that the screw threads were compatible with the Mauser; it made the gun heavy and cumbersome, and he set it back on the table. Then he played with the gun. To the uninitiated this might have seemed an immature action, but to the professional it was imperative. The logic was painfully simple: a man who didn't know a gun couldn't fire it. In combat there was no time for hesitation; it was purely reflex action and training. The training, once implemented, stayed for ever; it was the reflexes that usually got people killed. Forgetting to remove a safety-catch, failing to grip the gun correctly and snatching off the first shot – it all had to be practised until the gun was literally an extension of the body.

Ivanov practised over and over again, dry-firing the gun and getting used to its feel. Holbeck had also left him a Bianchi shoulder-holster, but it was unnecessary; there was only one position to carry a handgun – at the base of the spine, tucked securely into the belted waistband. He practised continually, taking on an imaginary target from behind. The draw was simple; instead of having to turn around, he fired from behind, drawing the Mauser with his right hand and at the same time twisting his torso to the left, bringing up his left forearm and elbow to protect his chest profile. The Mauser would be fired from waist-level using a sense of direction only perfected after patient years of practice.

The gun held eight rounds in the magazine, another in the breech if preferred, but a man such as Ivanov didn't need such fire-power. He loaded the magazine with seven rounds, loading one into the breech and setting the safety-catch. The prospect of stoppages was reduced by less strain on the magazine-spring, and the gun would be carried at all times henceforth with the safety-catch off. For back-up Ivanov loaded a second magazine with another six rounds. The heavy silencer would also have to be carried separately. Ivanov hated the thing. Apart from slowing up the bullet, it limited his actions; but it might come in useful.

Finally he got some rest and tried not to think of the mess he'd walked into. Now he knew Mikhailov was also lying through his teeth. Holbeck had only mentioned three transmissions; nothing about the Hungarian attaché. It could only mean one thing; he wanted Ivanov off on a wild-goose chase! Who the hell could he trust? An Englishman with more faces than a fifty-pence piece? Mikhailov, who'd kill his own mother if he hadn't already? Grechko? The GRU chief hated him! No, he wasn't going to sleep, no matter how he tried.

GREEK STREET, SOHO, LONDON
Lunchtime

The main restaurant was upstairs. Ivanov arrived a little after one o'clock and was shown across the crowded restaurant by a young waiter. Holbeck was already waiting with Travis at the corner table set slightly further away from the main dining-area.

'Ah! Tucker my dear chap.' Holbeck was the perfect host,

rising to greet the Russian like a long-lost brother. They shook hands, and Ivanov looked down at the woman. She was immaculately dressed in a purple and navy two-piece suit and white silk blouse. 'May I have the honour to present Miss Antonia Travis, one of the most beautiful women I know?' continued Holbeck.

Ivanov studied her as he took her hand. She really was quite good-looking, although somewhat scholarly in appearance because of the heavy black-rimmed spectacles and severe clothing, more suited to a much older woman.

'Pleased to meet you, Miss Travis. I've heard a great deal about you.'

'All good, I hope.' She smiled back.

'Naturally. Colonel Holbeck sings your praises all the time.'

'Less of the official title, old chap. It's all chaps together here, don't you know? Sit yourself down and sample the wine with us; I really can recommend it.' Holbeck patted Ivanov on the back.

The meal was the most enjoyable Ivanov had tasted in years. He found himself enjoying not only the food, but the company as well. Antonia Travis proved to be quite a witty and interesting lady, and Ivanov was drawn to her almost instantly. After the meal Holbeck ordered a taxi and took them to St James's Park.

'I always say that a good luncheon should be walked off afterwards. Does wonders for the digestive system, you know.'

The rain had stopped, although it was still quite overcast. They walked down towards the lake. Travis walked between the two men, her hands thrust deeply into the pockets of her cream raincoat.

'Frazer, just why are we here of all places?' she asked.

'As I told you just before lunch, Tucker here is with the CIA. Before I go any further, Antonia, I should warn you that what I am about to say is absolutely top secret. The CIA have it under a Nová classification.'

Antonia allowed herself a short whistle. 'They come no higher.' She looked over at Ivanov.

'Antonia, these Field Radio Signals you gave to Colonel Hol-

beck could have serious implications for us at the Agency.'
Ivanov took up the theme.

'I don't understand.'

'Well, as you know, the transmitter is old. We reckon from
the information sent Stateside over the wire that it might be as
much as thirty years out of date.'

'That much?' She couldn't help but raise an eyebrow.

'What's more is that the guy who was using the transmitter
and same code all that time ago was an American working for
the GRU. We reckoned he was dead, but now it looks as
though he's maybe still alive. The fact is we've got to find him
and fast.'

'Can I ask why?'

'Sure you can. You remember the Irish Justice Minister
killed in Dublin? Well, he killed him.'

'How can you be sure?'

'Because, dear girl, the second radio signal you gave me told
Moscow all about the killing before it happened!' Holbeck took
the reins.

'Before! So you've cracked the code?' She looked back at
Ivanov.

'Parts of it, Antonia. We've been able to patch it up to
something similar we've had on our mainframe for some time.
This killer was not alone; there were others in various places
all over the free world.'

'What can I do I haven't done already?' she continued.

Holbeck took her by the arm. 'Antonia, I don't know just
how to tell you this, but your department has a security breach.
Now, we don't know how far up the line it goes, but we are
certain of one thing: someone in your department is passing
information to Moscow.'

'My God!'

'We don't know what Moscow's up to, stirring up all these
ghosts from the past,' continued Ivanov, 'but you can see why
we've got to be one step ahead of them and catch whoever's
doing this without the spy in GCHQ giving them advance
warning.'

'Yes, I understand all that, but something troubles me about
all this. Why give anyone an advance warning of what you're

about to do? The Russians are bound to know that our scanners can pick up the signals easily; the point was proved by the location chosen to send the second transmission.'

'Antonia' – Holbeck clicked the point of his umbrella sharply on to the path – 'we don't have an answer for everything. If we had, we wouldn't be here. Will you agree to assist in this?'

'Of course. What do you want me to do?'

'Act as normal, give no suspicion to anyone. Whatever you do, do not discuss this conversation with anyone, and that includes Sir Peter Churchman.'

'I can't even disclose this to the director of GCHQ?'

'No one, Antonia. We don't know how far this all goes. Now, what you must do is notify us immediately another of these short-burst transmissions comes through. Let me know instantly, night or day. I will have a team standing by to go to the location of the transmission. I also need a copy of the transmission immediately, my eyes only. Tucker here will hopefully be able to decipher most of it.'

'What about this mole?' Antonia Travis started to feel another of her headaches coming on.

'I have people watching your personnel. Hopefully at the same time we will uncover the miscreant!' Holbeck attacked the last word with venom.

Travis halted. 'You can depend on me.'

'I know, my dear.' Holbeck kissed her on the cheek. 'I'll see you later, Tucker. See this gorgeous lady safely home for me, there's a good chap.' Then he turned on his heels, heading towards the Mall.

'Mind if I tag along with you for a while?' he asked.

'Why not?' She took his arm. 'Do you have a first priority?' she asked enquiringly.

'Dig into history, I suppose.'

'Do you know much about the origins of this transmitter?'

'Some. It was used by a Soviet sleeper in Ireland during the early seventies. In a roundabout way the matter was investigated by the police. Of course they didn't know what they were getting into at the time, but I think that's where I should start.'

'So you're off to the Emerald Isle?'

'Not exactly. The policeman who investigated the case is now retired and living in Sussex.'

'Your line of work must be very exciting.' She looked up at him, a mischievous look in her eye.

'Not really. At least, not until I went into this Soho restaurant today and met this broad. She really was something.' He smiled down at her as she playfully swung her handbag towards him. Stopham would wait a while longer.

CHELSEA, LONDON
Next morning, 22 June

The telephone rang just after two in the morning. Ivanov was alert instantly as the answering machine clicked on. He rose from the bed and went into the lounge just as Holbeck's voice cut into the machine.

'Tucker, if you're there, lift the receiver now.' There was the sound of panic in his voice. Ivanov tapped a switch disconnecting the recording device and speaker and lifted the receiver.

'What is it?'

'We have to meet, now! Right now. I'm coming over straight away.'

'Is that wise?'

'Wisdom is something I haven't time for at the moment, dear boy.'

Half an hour later Frazer Holbeck was letting himself into the apartment. Ivanov met him in the lounge.

'Sweep the place.' He was sweating and out of breath from running up the staircase.

'I did just five minutes ago. Your little black box over there is engaged.' Ivanov nodded towards the brown leather attaché case sitting open on a side-table.

'There's been another transmission.' He handed over a fax copy of the encoded message to the Russian.

'How did you get this?'

'The London embassy GRU *rezident* delivered it personally.

293

I watched him do it just over an hour ago. Can you decode it?'

'I should be able to. Wait here.' Ivanov went back into one of the bedrooms, locking the door. Holbeck didn't think much of the Russian's behaviour, but there was little he could say. Shrugging his shoulders, he threw off the double-breasted overcoat and the hat and went into the kitchen to make some coffee. Ivanov re-emerged after almost ten minutes. His face said it all.

'Good heavens! What on earth is it this time?'

'It's the next target.' Ivanov handed a sheet of paper across to Holbeck.

The Englishman's eyes widened considerably. 'The Prime Minister!'

'Where is he at present?' asked Ivanov clinically.

'I don't believe it.' Holbeck was numbed. 'GCHQ were to tell me of any further messages. I've heard nothing.'

'I said where is the Prime Minister at present?' Ivanov went over to the cabinet and lifted out a box of ammunition and the Israeli silencer.

'In Number 10, I suppose.'

'Don't suppose. Check it out,' snapped Ivanov. 'And while you're at it figure out my best way of getting in and out of there tonight!'

'Nobody can nowadays.'

'*I* can. Just do as I ask.' Ivanov turned and went back to his bedroom to get ready. Holbeck followed him.

'It's totally impossible, I tell you. The PM's residence is impregnable; there's no way into it. Even if a bomb got past the security and into the front lobby, it wouldn't matter; the entire lobby's reinforced to take the blast.' Holbeck fiddled with his bow-tie, something he always did when he was nervous. 'Anyhow, why do you want to get to the PM?'

'One sure way of putting off an attack is to have one,' replied Ivanov. 'What about the back?' He began to strip off his shirt.

'The entire rear is now covered with dozens of electronic alarms and sensors. You couldn't even fire a shot through those reinforced windows.'

'Where does the Prime Minister sleep?'

'In his apartment, up on the second floor.'

'What about fire exits?' continued Ivanov, changing into a navy polo-neck sweater.

'Look, old chap, there's no chance. I've even reviewed the security measures in the past myself; it can't be done.'

'What about the roof?' Ivanov wasn't being put off.

'Even the lining of the roofing structure has been reinforced to protect the place from mortar or rocket attacks.' Holbeck went back into the lounge; it was time for a stiff drink.

'What's the procedure when a threat is imminent? In the case of attack where does the Prime Minister go?' shouted Ivanov after him.

'The basement. There's a private lift. There's even access to a special bunker in case of an imminent nuclear attack.'

Moments later Ivanov joined him in the lounge. 'It has to be done tonight.'

'I'll confirm the PM's whereabouts.' Holbeck took a slug of neat whisky and then placed a telephone call to Curzon Street. He got his answer a minute later from the night duty officer. He set the receiver back again and slowly poured himself another drink.

'Well?' asked Ivanov, a hint of impatience in his tone.

'She's in Number 10 all right,' he said slowly. 'Look, it might be nothing, but I've just thought of something. Perhaps there is a way inside after all.'

'How?' asked Ivanov, lifting up his pistol and screwing on the silencer.

'A door. It's on the first floor, connects the Chancellor's office at Number 11 with Number 10.'

'And is it electronically protected?'

'Yes, but I know the combination for the locking mechanism; it hasn't been changed in over a year.'

'Convenient,' nodded Ivanov.

'Bloody stupid, come to think of it!' Holbeck frowned, more than a little annoyed with himself.

'Can you get me into Number 11?'

'Now, that is possible; there's a separate entrance into it that we can use.'

The news of the burglary at 10 Downing Street took the media and public quite by surprise even with the government statement giving an assurance that the Prime Minister was not in residence. It was an official lie. The security system was said to make the Prime Minister's offices impregnable; but, nevertheless, the occurrence had placed the security services in some obvious embarrassment. The official version told of a burglary at the rear of Number 10, nothing stolen, the thieves having escaped empty-handed, only a window smashed. The truth would have been unmentionable.

Two MI5 agents engaged on security duty had been slightly wounded by gunfire during an apparent attempt on the Prime Minister's life as she lay asleep on the second floor of the building. The would-be assassin had uttered some comment with a thick Irish brogue, before knocking out one of the wounded agents. The episode was put down to Irish republican extremists, and a red alert echoed throughout inner government circles. Apart from the Cabinet only the Leader of the Opposition had been taken into confidence.

The port authorities throughout the country were automatically placed on a full alert; the excuse was the interception of dangerous drugs. The Prime Minister's itinerary was modified and curtailed. Ivanov lay back in his Bayswater apartment. His little sortie into Downing Street had been successful; reluctantly MI5 had grabbed at the Irish connection, and the Prime Minister would – for the time being, at any rate – no longer carry out any public engagements. A press release would later explain such a restriction as being the result of the PM's mild ill-health. Garand, or whoever he was, could no longer fulfil his mission to kill the British Prime Minister – at least, for the moment. Ivanov slept lightly on that note.

GOVERNMENT COMMUNICATIONS HEADQUARTERS, CHELTENHAM

22 June

Antonia Travis emerged from the co-ordination meeting just after 11 a.m. It was a normal Monday morning, and the meeting had run just a little over schedule. She'd noticed Charlie Younger to be absent; he'd sent his deputy along as stand-in. There was nothing unusual in that but, mulling over what Holbeck and Tucker had told her the previous day, his absence could be quite significant. Her concern heightened when she walked into her office to find Younger waiting for her.

'Charlie! What a surprise. I was expecting you at the meeting. What happened?'

'This happened.' He handed over a blue file-cover containing a few sheets. 'There's been another transmission.'

'When?'

'At 23:16 hours last night.'

'Damn you, Charlie! Why has it taken twelve hours for me to be informed?'

'Andrew Hogg was duty officer last night. He sat on it. Maybe he spent the whole night in the toilets. What do I know?' Younger was agitated at being scolded, especially by someone he thought of as a friend.

'That's a surprise! After the rush he made to send that report to MI5 I'd have thought he would have done overtime on this one!'

'Look, I'm sorry, Antonia. I only got this thing just after eight this morning; I've been working flat out.'

'I'm sure you have.' She sighed and leafed through the file.

'The procedures you set up went ahead anyway. After the Field Radio Signal was identified our computer automatically set in motion a Special Branch follow-up. I'm told Special Branch officers were at the scene inside twelve minutes.'

'That was quick! Where was it?' She leafed through the pages. 'Horse Guards Parade! That's next to Downing Street!'

'You haven't heard the news, have you?' Younger turned his head. 'Number 10 was burgled last night.' He let the news sink in. 'I've only been able to decode some of the signal, but it would seem to relate to the Prime Minister.'

Another sigh. She eased into her chair. 'Charlie, who else knows about your decoding?'

'Just the two of us.'

'Keep it that way. There's something I've got to do. See me again around five and keep trying to get the rest of that code, will you?'

'Sure. By the way I think I've an idea about those code-words "Bloodstone" and "Fandango": they're names of different types of rose.'

'Very interesting,' she nodded as he turned to go. 'And, Charlie, find out what really happened to Hogg last night and discreetly.'

'I am your obedient servant, O gracious one.' Younger did his best Pakistani imitation, bowing and saluting from the forehead three times.

'Charlie, get out of here!' Travis smiled, she was her usual self again, almost.

All telephone traffic to and from GCHQ goes through a listening service. What that means is that each call is analysed and also recorded indefinitely. She rang Curzon Street, choosing her words carefully.

'Holbeck.'

'Frazer, it's Antonia Travis.'

'Antonia my dearest girl!' He sounded as if he hadn't seen her for months. Of course that was the impression he wanted to portray.

'I'd like to see you, please.'

'Of course, my dear. Anything to oblige. When would suit?'

'Immediately.'

'I've a long-standing engagement at Sandhurst this afternoon. I'll not be back in London until this evening.'

'Look, I'm sending you a facsimile on the Alpha system. You should have it in a few minutes. Study it and I'll see you tonight.'

'You sound like you're a busy girl, Antonia, too busy to be coming up to town. Tell you what. I'm only visiting an old chum at Sandhurst; I'll be through quite early. I'll see you at your home if that's all right.'

'You know where I live?' She couldn't hide her puzzlement.

'Of course I do. You've invited me often enough for all those home-cooked meals, remember?'

'Stupid of me. What time?'

'The earliest I could make it would be just before seven.'

'I'll see you then.' Travis hung up. What would Mogul think if he found out about Holbeck at her house?

TEWKESBURY
That night

Frazer Holbeck arrived on schedule and was greeted warmly at the door. The smell of the roast lamb did more than distract him a little.

'H'm, something smells good.' He handed her a bunch of flowers. 'Mother always said never to call empty-handed.' He kissed her on the cheek and was shown into the lounge. Jasper, the cat, had been banished outdoors and the dinner-table had been set.

'Some sherry?'

'I'd prefer a brandy if you have it.' He settled into one of the armchairs. 'I went over what you sent me. It's very interesting, but why the delay in sending it?'

'It seems that GCHQ had a breakdown in communications, but the automatic signal went through to liaison. Special Branch were on to it quite fast.'

'Not fast enough. Two of our people got themselves shot up inside Number 10.'

'Killed?' She almost dropped the brandy glass.

'No, they were fortunate. Of course the department clamped a "D" Notice over it. The PM was in residence at the time; no doubt about it being an assassination attempt.'

'Do you know who's responsible?'

'Irish terrorists by the sound of it.'

'It always goes back to Ireland.' She gave him his drink.

'What's happening with you?'

'I've put Charlie Younger on to the thing full-time; he's getting some pretty interesting results.'

'Really!' Holbeck sipped his brandy and then changed the subject. Something was going to have to be done about Younger.

CHELTENHAM
Late the following night, 23 June

The old Norton motorcycle was Charlie Younger's passion, 250cc of power, completely rebuilt over a period of five months. He'd loved bikes ever since he was a teenager. It stemmed from a rebellious nature. His parents were both set against motorbikes; it made the determined teenager even more eager to get one. That was the start of it; but an act of defiance had now become an obsession.

It seemed strange to everyone that somebody as outward-going and anti-establishment as him would have ended up in a place such as GCHQ, and he wouldn't have considered it in a million years if he hadn't been approached. But the carrot had been dangled. He had just qualified with a Master's degree in electronics, and like hundreds of others just like him he'd thought the world was his oyster. It was more than a shock when the job invitations failed to flood in. When a substantial salary and the opportunity to play with one of the country's largest mainframe computers landed on his lap he snatched it up.

The frustration of working in a place such as GCHQ was vented daily on the old Norton. Younger could push the motorcycle to the limit, pitching on the bends almost to the point of no return. In his youth he'd always been struck by the colour photographs he'd seen of Mike Halewood racing in the Isle of Man TT, especially the shot of Halewood skimming barely a hair's breadth from the road-surface as he rounded a bend at one hundred and twenty miles per hour. Now he was doing it for himself, along the country roads just north of Cheltenham.

He knew them off by heart, and the one good thing was that the police never came along this way, especially after midnight; he could let rip. For a few minutes now *he* was Mike Halewood.

Just as he came out of the downhill bend he saw the black Ford Transit van. He toed the gears and eased back on both brakes. The van was parked at the roadside, oblivious as he approached down the winding country road. He was still travelling at just slightly over seventy miles per hour and began to pull right to overtake; he still had plenty of distance and room, and apart from the van the road was empty. He was almost level with the van's tail-light when it pulled out, directly across his path. Younger's experience was pushed to the limit. There was no choice in it; he couldn't afford an emergency stop at the speed he was travelling. He banked to the right, steering the bike towards the hard shoulder, and twisted hard on the accelerator. He could have made it if the van had levelled back on to the left; but it just kept going, pulling directly across the road as if in the process of a three-point turn.

There wasn't even time to scream as Younger stared his fate directly in the face. He hit the brakes, the bike skidded and pitched slightly to the left, then he impacted. The front wheel smashed into the low grassy banking. His mind raced. He anticipated one of two things now; the second happened. Bike and rider took off skywards. Angled up by the incline, the bike smashed through the hawthorn hedge and into the air; the 250cc engine almost exploded its pistons as it whined to an almost deafening pitch. The motion had pitched the bike high into the air over the field; it was now turning over in a backwards somersault. Younger tried to let go, but it was all too fast; he impacted first, his back taking most of the brunt. The Norton smashed down on top of him, crushing his pelvis and stomach. His left leg was caught up in the gyrating rear wheel; the spokes ripped through his leather trousers, tearing his kneecap completely out of its socket. The bike bounced again, and the handlebars came smashing down on to his face and head this time. The helmet split under the pressure as part of the rubber-covered handle smashed through the visor and took half of Younger's face off.

The bike went up and over him as he finally lay sprawled half on one side. He was aware of the engine still whirring loudly. Something had jammed the accelerator cable. Then it stopped. The silence was unbearable; so was the pain. He couldn't think of a part of his body that didn't hurt. Amazingly he was still conscious, but he was going into shock fast. He tried to move. Nothing worked; his spinal cord was severed in three places. He was lying with his head facing down the slope towards a small drainage-ditch that ran behind the hedge just parallel with the road. His body was twisted like a half-wrung towel, his legs twisted and wrapped into each other; if he could have seen his feet, he would have realized that the left foot was now twisted completely backwards, the leather boot still in place but now ripped and twisted, too. What remained of his left arm was trapped under the weight of his body, and his right arm now flapped uselessly across his chest; for some reason the arm kept twitching like some dying fish on a river-bank. He heard the man approaching across the field behind him and then stopping beside him.

'Dear, dear. What a mess you are.' The man's voice was cultivated and concerned.

Younger tried to speak, but nothing happened; the left half of his mouth was ripped open. Holbeck walked around and knelt down to have a closer look at him. From the bright sticky orange blood now oozing through Younger's remaining teeth he could see that time was running out for the twenty-six-year-old.

'What a pity it all is. What a waste of a life.'

Younger imagined he could just see the hint of a smile on the man's face as he stood up again and left. He was being left alone to die; but there was no panic, just a feeling of hopelessness.

An hour later Mogul returned the black Transit to the hire company's depot. There would be no need to destroy it. The company wouldn't even be aware it had been used that night.

STOPHAM, WEST SUSSEX
Thursday, 25 June, 10 a.m.

The telephone rang continuously for nearly two minutes before
Alec Martin tried to answer it. He stood in the garden fiddling
with the radio telephone, desperately trying to get the thing to
respond. It was no use. 'Newfangled and space age' – that was
how he had described it to Norma when she arrived home with
the bloody thing! He had threatened to sell all his British Telecom shares in disgust at the intrusion on his sedate lifestyle.
Finally, much to the amusement of the onlooking police guard,
Martin threw the thing on to the patio table before hurrying
inside and using the ordinary telephone on the side-table in the
drawing-room.

'Hello! Yes, what is it?' he grunted.

There was a pause before the caller spoke. 'Hello, Alec, this
is Frazer Holbeck. How are you, dear chap?' Holbeck had
detected the annoyance in the tone immediately. 'I hope I
didn't disturb you.'

Alec Martin hadn't heard from the man since before his
retirement. On his last major investigation just before retirement Colonel Holbeck had been assigned by Curzon Street to
liaise with Martin's murder squad following a terrorist bombing
outrage in London in 1980. Despite Martin's natural apprehension of working with MI5, he had nevertheless struck up a
friendship with Holbeck; but friendships do not often transcend
retirement, and Holbeck had been no exception to the rule.

'Hello, Frazer. Nice to hear from you. It must be at least
ten years, I'd reckon, so I don't assume this to be merely a
social call. Am I right?'

'Alec, you old dog! You never were one for beating around
the proverbial bush! And indeed you are quite right. We just
received a signal from our American counterparts. One of their
men has been assigned to interview you. He's called Tucker.
Look, old chap, I know it's a bit short notice, but I'm afraid
he'll be coming to see you later today – if it's not too incon-
venient, that is. I can assure you it's all a straightforward for-
mality really; he just wants some background on that terrible

thing that happened down your way a few days ago.' There was silence on the line. 'Is that OK, Alec?'

Martin hesitated. 'Sure. All right. I don't understand, but I'll be in all afternoon in any case.'

'Thanks, Alec. Perhaps we can meet imminently for some luncheon. My treat, of course!'

'Now, would this be social or just a follow-up on the Yank's activities?' Alec Martin was irritated by the man's casual presumption after ten years of silence.

'Well, cheerio, old chap,' Holbeck replied drily.

Alec Martin set the receiver down. As he did so, he glanced down at his muddy wellington boots and then looked behind. 'Oh hell!' he roared, cringing at the sight of the muddy trail he had created right across the carpet from the direction of the open patio windows. Suddenly his mind was thrown from the impending visit to where his wife kept the carpet shampoo and Hoover. 'Oh well! A wash and a good blow-dry should do it!'

On her return from the convent school Julia found him on both knees with a hairdrier, trying desperately to dry out the patches he had scrubbed clean. After she burst into laughter and he hurriedly explained his stupidity Julia sent him to the kitchen to help her mother make some tea while she covered up the rest of the damage. As she was tidying up the last vestige of mud from underneath the telephone-table she glanced over and caught sight of the note-pad and the hurried scribble: 'Tucker – this afternoon. Holbeck, Curzon Street.' After staring at the note-pad for several more seconds she returned to finishing the cleaning-up.

It was almost 3 p.m. The doorbell rang once. Norma Martin answered slowly. The arthritis that had developed throughout her body over the last few years had slowed all her movements. She had contemplated a hip-replacement operation the previous year, but had not gone through with it. It was at times like this that the slowness of her movement made her more than just regretful at having declined the operation. Over the last years she had quietly committed herself to the voluntary work with a handicapped centre at the nearby town of Horsham. She was busier now than ever. The operation could wait that little longer; it could always wait.

On opening the solid panelled door she gazed at the man standing outside the glazed vestibule-door. He was a tall, fair-haired, handsome man, seemingly in his late forties. Norma Martin opened the outer door.

'Good afternoon. Mrs Martin, I assume?' The American accent was obvious, not strong or heavy, but there nevertheless. He had a pleasant smile.

She smiled back. 'Yes?'

'My name is Tucker. I believe your husband is expecting me.'

Before she could speak Alec Martin was at her side, eyeing the stranger with a certain curiosity that only a lifetime's police work could instil. 'I'm Alec Martin. I take it you're Mr Tucker?'

Ivanov smiled and extended his right hand. 'Harvey Tucker. Just call me Harv.'

Martin accepted the handshake and showed the man into the rear lounge. Once alone Ivanov produced an identity card for Martin. It didn't take an expert to read a CIA identity card.

'I don't want to take up too much of your time, Mr Martin.'

Alec Martin smiled and crossed the room, reopening the door and calling to his wife. He returned seconds later, shutting the door once again. 'Tea is on the way, Mr Tucker – I mean Harv. I do nothing on an empty stomach!'

Ivanov was standing by the french windows rubbing the scar on his neck. 'Beautiful view, just beautiful.' He turned and faced Martin again.

'Yes, it is. The idyllic cottage in the country, so to speak.' Alec Martin sat on the edge of the sofa. 'But, then, you haven't come here to talk about the setting, have you?'

'You're quite right, I haven't. Last week you were visited by your late friend Sam Nelson. Colonel Holbeck suggested that I see you on the same subject.'

'What's the CIA's interest in a ghost?' Martin frowned. For the first time in years he noticed his hands shaking.

'Well, you know how it is. Governments helping governments and so forth. I got roped in because of a report from the RUC via our consulate office in Belfast concerning one of our citizens bumping off people in the Emerald Isle.' Ivanov sat back in an armchair and crossed his long legs. It seemed that he was there to stay, or so it appeared. Martin found that his annoyance at this intrusion into his retirement no longer mattered; he didn't know how to help, but if he could bring Sam Nelson's murderers to justice he'd see it through.

'I do hope you are talking in the past tense! I believe the American of whom you speak has been dead for several years; and, while you're at it, call him by his name. It's Harry Garand, if you've forgotten.'

'I haven't forgotten, Mr Martin, but there have been the recent killings in Ireland.'

'Look, the recent shootings only bear a resemblance to Harry Garand's form, nothing more. I should know! Yes, the same gun was used, but so what? What does that prove? I'm afraid that you've had a wasted time coming down here.'

'I'd like you to see this.' Ivanov pulled out a folded sheet of paper from his pocket and passed it to Martin.

Martin took it and fumbled for his reading-glasses. Even at his age he was embarrassed at his dependency on such things. 'Blasted glasses,' he muttered, trying to get them on with one hand. After adjusting the reading-glasses he examined the paper. It was a report; the heading read: 'Northern Ireland Forensic Science Laboratory.' He read on; it was a ballistics report from a senior scientific officer at the Belfast laboratory. He scanned it quickly and then more slowly, evaluating the content closely. Finally he removed the spectacles and stared at Ivanov.

'I didn't know! This puts a completely different light on the matter.' He slowly handed the paper back to the Russian. 'All the time Sam Nelson sat in that very same chair you're now in, he knew it was Garand!'

'So you agree that it's him?' pressed Ivanov.

'According to the forensic report you've just shown me, it has to be him, for who else could have known about the way he made the "home loads" for that bloody rifle he used? Why didn't Nelson tell me about this?'

'I don't know. Maybe he didn't want to get you too excited.' Ivanov looked at him closely. 'You investigated the killings back in 1972. You know his style. That's something no one else can tell me. That's why I need your help. So you're sure it's him?'

Martin raised his right hand to his forehead, partly shielding his eyes. 'From what you've just shown me, yes.' His thoughts were disrupted by the knock at the lounge door. By the time Norma Martin brought in a trolley of tea and cakes and then left, Alec Martin had gathered his thoughts and continued. 'But so much doesn't make sense. The time-span for one thing. The evidence surrounding his apparent death is another. It could just be that someone is imitating his style, using the same rifle, and bullets already doctored – even all those years ago.'

Ivanov rose, shaking his head. 'I'm sorry to disappoint you. The bullet-casing found at each incident was doctored and reloaded with a more potent explosive mixture just as they were all those years ago, and I've had the casings checked and counter-checked. Although they are recent reloads they are made in exactly the same fashion as before and on the same apparatus.'

'What about someone out there just copying his style?'

'Yep, OK, but how could that person know the exact load Garand used?'

'Perhaps they obtained a few original cartridges along with the rifle. It would be easy for someone to analyse their contents,' continued Martin.

'Or unless he actually is alive,' continued Ivanov.

Something bothered Martin about this stranger in his home. He cast off the doubts and gave him a résumé of what he had told Nelson. They chatted on for over two more hours, passing opinions, but more often humour. Martin noted that his visitor had a distinct way of disarming a person; his quick-witted humour transcended the seriousness of their subject matter. After some further tea, followed by drinks, Martin showed Ivanov to the front door. As they walked to the car Julia drove the Mini Metro into the large turning-circle at the front of the house. She waved at one of the uniformed police guards and then briefly at the two men before steering the little car into the empty garage.

'My daughter Julia,' commented Martin.

Ivanov watched as she left the garage and strolled slowly

towards the open front door. She was wearing a blouse and long skirt with open-toed leather sandals. It hardly did her any justice. She ran a hand absently through her short hair and glanced across for a second look at the Russian. She reminded Ivanov of a wild cat stealthily hunting in search of prey. He smiled across at her. She didn't respond and went on inside the house.

'Attractive girl.' He glanced at Martin, who had noted his attention. Ivanov decided hastily to revert to the area of paternal instincts. 'You must be very proud of her.'

Martin smile. 'And very protective. Mind you, she has a brain of her own, working hard at Trinity College, Dublin, at present doing Classics.'

The girl hesitated just inside the vestibule and glanced back at Ivanov. He could almost feel her stripping him with her eyes. It was pleasantly unsettling.

'Well, I'm off. In case you remember anything else, you can ring me at this number.' Ivanov passed a plain card bearing a London telephone number. 'If I'm not there, you can leave a message on the answering machine.' He climbed into the Ford Sierra and roared the engine into life.

Martin stood beside the open driver's door. 'Just what are you going to do?'

'I'm going to find the son of a bitch! What else?' Ivanov replied as he closed the door and spun the wheels. The car disappeared up the narrow tree-clad driveway towards the main road.

That night Alec Martin kept by himself in the rear lounge. He sat back heavily in the large sofa, tapping his pipe into the ashtray beside him. He glanced outside through the french windows towards the river-bank, now shrouded in the enveloping darkness. Just outside the windows small insects swarmed in the light from the carriage lamp mounted on the low patio wall; several spiders had already been busy spinning their traps. He was deep in thought, and began staring towards the fireplace, into the licking flames. One of the logs broke and rekindled the dull fire.

Suddenly Martin thought he could see the eyes staring out from amidst the dancing flames, the eyes of an adversary, a killer's eyes, the eyes of the rabid dog he knew as Harry Garand. He sat there, fixed, unable to move from the sofa, thinking over all the events once again, trying desperately to decide if the hunted had returned from the grave to become the hunter once again. He sat on, mind transfixed, until suddenly the noise from the french windows interrupted his trance-like state. He looked up. A figure was standing just outside the windows. For one awful moment he could see the hunter's eyes! There was no mistake about it! Martin jumped to his feet, knocking the ashtray on to the floor.

'Dad! Are you all right?'

Alec Martin wiped his eyes with both hands and focused again. Julia Martin came in from the patio, locking both french windows tightly shut behind her.

'Lord, it's you, Julia. I'm sorry, I must have dozed off or something.' Martin tried to hide his inner fear and began picking up the ash with his shaking hands.

'It's really not your day, is it, Daddy?' She crossed the room after switching on the wall-lights beside the windows, and knelt down beside him. 'First you get mud on the carpet and now tobacco ash. Leave this to me and go on inside to Mummy. She's in the front lounge; she'll be wondering about you sitting here all alone.' She smiled at him; there was no doubt in his mind that she could wrap him around her little finger any time she wanted to, and she knew it! He kissed her on the forehead and stood up, helping Julia to her feet.

'You're a terrible young lady. You have a way with me every time.' Martin began to smile again.

She leant over and kissed him on the cheek. 'Go on in there and let me tidy up!' she scolded lightly.

He obliged without argument, but paused at the hall door to look back. She was busy sweeping up the remnants of ash on the thick-pile carpet. Julia glanced around and saw him standing there. 'Will you go on? I'll make supper since you missed dinner earlier.'

It was only then that he realized he had forgotten dinner whilst so engrossed in the conversation with Tucker. He smiled at her and left.

He felt hungry, but just as quickly the notion left him as the eyes in the flames came back to him again. There seemed no escaping them. The third degree that he received from his wife was as good as he would have expected from any of his old CID colleagues, and she did not miss a point, subtle, but penetrating and always with the loaded questions. The more he side-stepped, the more Norma Martin persisted; there was no escaping the inevitable.

He tried steering his wife on to the subject of their forthcoming visit to Buckingham Palace. The invitation from the Lord Chamberlain had been in recognition of Norma's services with the centre for the handicapped in Horsham. Only the previous week she had received the gold-embossed invitation card to attend the garden-party in the grounds of Buckingham Palace. It had been their topic of conversation for days now, but on this occasion Norma Martin was not going to be distracted.

'Look, Alec, isn't it bad enough that some Irish terrorists just happen to pick this spot to kill a senior RUC officer and also one of our oldest friends? Now you tell me you are visited by some representative from the United States government and again it's about the same thing apparently. I think it's high time you told me what is going on.'

He capitulated, nodding in agreement. 'Do you remember back in 1971 and 1972 when I was seconded to the RUC and ended up investigating a whole series of killings involving an American ex-serviceman?'

'Of course. We almost divorced over it, didn't we? Me pregnant and living alone while you lived twenty-three out of twenty-four hours in a police station. I wished month after month of my life away in a rented house and without a soul to talk to except Sam's wife!' She glared at him. 'Is that what this is all about?'

'They think that he's still alive, Norma – and killing again.'

'Oh my God!' She put her hands to her face. 'You mean he killed Sam Nelson?' He didn't reply; then Norma Martin's eyes widened in horror. 'Don't tell me that he's after you now! Is he?'

'I honestly don't know, dear.' Suddenly he felt a chill on his back. He turned to see the door open and Julia pushing the trolley into the room. 'But I think it's high time you and Julia took a holiday away from here. Your sister in Glamorgan hasn't seen you in months. She's always inviting you.' Martin patted his wife on the arm. 'Don't you worry about a thing, dear.'

Norma Martin nodded. 'Yes, I think you're right. The break's probably a good idea, but I can't stop worrying.'

'Worry about what?' enquired Julia.

Martin spun around, taken unawares. 'Nothing, young lady, nothing at all. Just your mother thought I was rejoining the force again and forfeiting my pension rights.' He smiled, and both women began to laugh, albeit nervously.

TWENTY MILES NORTH-WEST OF LIMASSOL, CYPRUS
Twelve hours later

George had moved his Autumn Harvest team out of North Africa – the terrorist entry into Britain would be easier from Cyprus. François Debré and the Greek, Nikos Papadopoulos, were putting the group through its final preparations. The assorted terrorists had finally gelled into a cohesive fighting unit; even George's cynicism lifted.

Out of an original one hundred selected terrorists from eight different terrorist organizations only a mere two dozen had passed all the training and tests. They were fit but above all they were ready, ready to kill. The Greek hurried across the small training-camp towards the ruined church which now served as George's quarters. He climbed the steps and went in past the two guards. George and François were both sitting at a table eating melon.

'Nikos! Come in and sit down.' George beckoned. The sturdy little Greek complied. George eyed him carefully. 'Nikos, it's good to have you here on the team. Your experience is invaluable.'

'I just did my job, nothing more.' The thirty-nine-year-old veteran was not given to emotion or compliments.

'Rubbish!' continued George. 'You took a bunch of soft-stomached amateurs and moulded them into steel.'

'We also killed forty-two in the process.' Nikos was still smarting over the Arab's insistence that training had to be as realistic as they could make it. As a result the hundred carefully chosen young men and women were subjected to pure hell for months on end. It was akin to gladiators fighting in the arena, and George only wanted the best; the rest were fodder along the way. Nikos reduced the impact of the merciless training, weeding out those he knew for sure would never make it; he felt he owed it to them. Of course it was going against George's wishes, but he had considered the consequences carefully; for the moment George needed him, so he was safe – at least for now.

'Forty-two is not a high price when we consider our goal.'

'And what *is* our goal?' asked Nikos. Up to that moment the Greek had been kept in the dark. Of course he had an idea. Every one of the hundred chosen had to speak fluent English; the job was either in North America or in the British Isles.

George stood up and checked the door. The guards were busy smoking outside and well out of earshot. 'It's in England. A NATO summit conference scheduled for the seventh of July. François here devised the initial plan himself.'

The Greek stared across at Debré. The Frenchman looked across at the Arab.

'In eleven days?' he retorted. Nikos remained as calm and collected as always; he just did what he was told and without question.

'Is something troubling you, François?'

'*Oui.*'

'Now, what exactly would that be?' George placed his foot on one of the chairs next to the table and leant forward. From the look on the Arab's face Debré knew not to push much further, yet he had to know what had changed, what the Arab hadn't yet told them.

'You said back in Libya that my plan was changed. You said we now go for "gold", not "silver". That is what you said.'

'So?' replied George.

'Autumn Harvest was my idea, my plan; it doesn't need any refinement!'

'When you joined our élite little band you took an oath to obey; that includes you not sticking your nose into something that doesn't concern you!'

'It concerns me!' shouted the Frenchman. To his utter amazement the Arab began to laugh, displaying his yellowed and twisted teeth.

'Yes, my friend, it does indeed concern you.' He continued laughing and moved around beside the Frenchman, patting him on the shoulder.

'Don't patronize me!' insisted Debré. But he wasn't.

A razor-sharp blade flicked open against Debré's neck just below his right ear. George had him by the hair; the Frenchman's head was yanked sharply backwards. Before he could utter a single word the edge of the four-inch blade was pressing against his skin.

'George! Let him go!' protested the Greek. The Arab ignored the appeal.

'Well? Do you still want to know?' he whispered into Debré's ear. The Frenchman could smell his foul breath, then he felt the pain as the Arab slid the sharp blade against his skin. It wouldn't take much to slice Debré's artery and he knew it.

'Non,' he replied.

The knife-blade cut a little deeper; blood began to trickle from the wound. Debré flinched. 'Please!'

'I still think you need a lesson, my friend, something everyone can see,' whispered George. Debré's eyes widened. He moved the knife up underneath the man's earlobe. The Frenchman froze, anticipating the very worst.

'But for the moment I need you. For the moment.' George pulled back.

Debré quickly applied his handkerchief to the wound, using it as a pressure bandage; thankfully it was not a deep cut.

'The arrangements have been made. The first batch of our people leave tomorrow,' continued George as if nothing had happened. 'Nikos, you are to go with them.' The Greek stared impassively at him.

George pointed towards Debré with the point of his

flickknife. 'You go with the last batch. I want this place swept clean before we leave. No evidence. Nothing.' The Frenchman said nothing in response.

'I go early next week to confirm the operational arrangements with our masters. If everything is ratified, then there is no turning back.' He smiled again. It reminded François Debré of a carnivorous animal.

He detested the Lebanese terrorist leader. At that moment all he wanted was to kill him; but if they could strike a severe blow for the International Revolutionary Movement, then it was all worthwhile – he'd tolerate the Arab a little longer.

'It is anticipated that all the heads of state and their Defence Ministers will be at the conference on July the seventh. Comrades, we take them all. Everyone dies.' He grinned again. 'Everyone without exception.'

Debré looked over at Nikos Papadopoulos. The hardened little former Greek Marines officer came as close to smiling as he'd ever see again.

UNITED STATES EMBASSY, GROSVENOR SQUARE, LONDON
Friday, 26 June

Alec Martin had, through the nature of his latter working years, made a number of acquaintances in the intelligence community, and his contacts were not just confined to MI5 and MI6. The telephone burred twice before being answered.

'Burger,' a deep voice responded.

'Frank. It's Alec Martin.'

There was a long pause before the deep voice exploded in recognition.

'Alec Martin! Well, well, well. I thought they'd put you out to pasture long ago!'

'They have, Frank, but may I add it was all of my own choosing?'

'Your choosing! Alec Martin volunteer for retirement? I

don't believe you, pal! I always said you'd fester once you left New Scotland Yard.' The FBI London Station chief chuckled.

'That's just it, Frank. I was festering in the job. Suddenly one cold morning I woke up and found my only daughter had almost grown up and I'd missed it all. It's a long story, so I won't bore you.'

'Well, old buddy, it's great to hear from you. Now, after all this time you haven't buzzed me just to discuss your domestic life, have you?'

'Frank, I need a favour. I had a visitor to my house; he calls himself Harvey Tucker, said he was from your . . . embassy – worked for your other "firm" specifically, if you get my drift?'

'Sure, I get it. I can check it out, but why?' Burger was perplexed. 'Are you in trouble, Alec?'

Martin forced himself to hide the nervousness his response echoed. 'No, for heaven's sake. All I want is a confirmation on this chap. He was sent to me following an introduction by Curzon Street.'

Unsatisfied, Burger relented. 'OK, pal, but if MI5 cleared him I don't see that you've got a problem. Give me your telephone number and I'll get back to you later.'

It was much later when the telephone rang again at Rose Cottage. Alec Martin had anticipated the call and took it in the quiet sanctuary of his study.

'Hello, Alec. It's Frank Burger.'

'Thanks for getting back so quick.' Alec Martin sat forward in his leather buttoned chair.

'Look, I did what you asked. There is a Harvey Tucker with the Agency's London office.'

Martin smiled with relief. 'Thanks, Frank, I owe you one.'

'Wait up there, fella! That's not all,' continued Burger. 'You'll have to wait some time if you need to see him. Apparently his old man was killed in some automobile accident in LA. He had to fly back to the States on a compassionate furlough and is still over there.'

Alec Martin paused and swallowed against his drying throat.

'Are you still there, Alec?'

'Yes,' blurted Martin. 'Look, thanks, Frank. I may need to speak to you again soon. I'll be in touch. Keep it low!'

Burger laughed and bade him farewell. Afterwards he sat back in his third-floor office overlooking Upper Brook Street at the side of the United States embassy in Grosvenor Square. Martin's tone had been nervous, and his request for information had been tainted with that same note. He shrugged it off and went back to work.

STOPHAM, WEST SUSSEX

Next morning, 27 June

Early the next morning Norma Martin and Julia left as arranged to visit Norma's sister in Wales. Martin was relieved that they would be out of the way for at least a full week. Norma took him to one side of the car out of Julia's hearing.

'You be careful. I can't see why you aren't coming, too.'

Alec Martin smiled. 'I've too much to do around here. Anyway, the local police said they'd want to be seeing me again next week, and I've still got the police guard here.'

'Alec, it's not healthy for you to stay here alone and brood. Come with us,' she pleaded.

'Look, darling, I'll be OK; and, anyway, I'll be joining you next week in London for this garden-party thing.' He smiled and squeezed her hand gently.

'I love you.' She hugged him tightly.

'I know you do.' He held her in his arms, briefly shutting his eyes. 'I'll give you a ring in a day or so.'

She stood back from him and nodded. He walked her towards the car and opened the passenger door, peering in towards Julia sitting impatiently behind the steering-wheel. 'Look after your mother for me.'

'I will,' she replied, blowing him a kiss. 'Oh! Daddy, don't forget the garden-party. I left the car-window stickers and the instructions they sent us on the mantelpiece in your study. We can't get the car parked at the Mall without them.' She smiled.

'Where's the invitation card?' he replied.

Norma Martin prodded him gently on the shoulder. He turned to her, and she patted her handbag. 'In here, darling. I'm taking it to Wales to show my sister.'

'You vain thing!' he grinned back at her.

'Well, it's not every day one gets asked to afternoon tea with the Queen!' She was naturally very proud of the invitation.

'Even if there just happens to be another four thousand people invited as well!' laughed Julia, leaning across the front seat of the Mini Metro.

'Look, dear, we'll probably be back in good time. Of course, we may even go directly to London and meet you there at the Hilton as discussed.'

'And do some shopping perhaps?' he goaded her gently.

She kissed him on the lips and eased into the car, the stiffness in her joints blatantly obvious. 'Now, dear, you'll not forget the car stickers in case we do go on directly, will you? They're on the mantelpiece in your study.'

'Of course!' He smiled. 'Now, how the hell could I forget the things when you've both reminded me inside the last minute and you've talked about nothing else all bloody month!'

Norma Martin placed a finger on his lips and frowned. 'No foul language, please!'

He smiled back at her. Then he looked at his daughter. 'Julia, once you get your mother settled at Aunty Margaret's you'll need to pay attention to that summer course-work you've to do for university.'

'I will! I will!' she exclaimed, blowing him another kiss.

Then they were off. With a tooting of the car horn the Mini Metro disappeared round the bend in the tree-clad driveway. Alec Martin stood there wondering if he'd ever seen them again, but he allayed his concern with the knowledge that they were at least travelling to safety. As he turned to re-enter Rose Cottage the sights of the hunting-rifle zoomed on to the back of his head. He slammed the red door behind him, temporarily obliterating the watcher's view.

The local police superintendent was surprised at the request. He had anticipated keeping an armed police presence at Rose Cottage until Criminal Intelligence could tie down the whereabouts of the terrorists responsible for Nelson's murder. Until they were sure the terrorists were either out of the country or arrested, the Chief Constable for Sussex was taking no chances.

'I must protest, Mr Martin. It's in your own interests to have our men present at your home. I can assure you— '

'No!' Alec Martin shouted down the telephone line. 'You can't give me any assurances, Superintendent. Now, you listen to me! I insist that you remove your men immediately. My wife and daughter have already left to stay with relations in Wales, and I intend to follow later tonight. There is absolutely no need for all this police presence. Whilst I am grateful that you have my interests at heart, I feel sure that your boys could be better employed elsewhere. I am in no danger, I assure you.'

There was a pause. 'Well, if you insist, Mr Martin, I can't keep my men there without your authority; but I must ask you to confirm your request in writing and give it to one of my men immediately before they leave your house.'

The bastard was covering his back without any doubt. It didn't surprise Alec Martin; he'd have done the same himself. 'Superintendent, will you relay the order to your men by radio?'

'Very well, Mr Martin. Good evening.'

Martin set the receiver down. He was already scribbling his request on the memo-pad. Within twenty minutes the two uniformed policemen left in their panda car. The sights of the hunting-rifle continued to train on the white police car until it vanished up the winding driveway towards the road. Alec Martin lifted the receiver and dialled the number Ivanov had given him; it was indeed an answering machine just as he had said. Following the message Martin opened the top drawer of his desk and took out the Walther PPK and magazine-clip containing six rounds. He had been permitted to hold on to it as a memento from his time in Ulster. He hoped he could still remember how to fire it.

It was 9 p.m. before Ivanov arrived at the cottage. It was already dark outside; the new moon had been obliterated by the dense storm-clouds coming in from the south-west. Alec Martin showed him into the study without comment.

'Sorry I took so long to get here, but I only got your call when I buzzed in to check on my answering machine.' Ivanov looked around the room carefully; it was cluttered and small. He set the brown attaché case on the desk and flicked the small switch set under the handle; any electronic eavesdropping devices either in or directed to the room were now rendered useless.

Alec Martin had already locked the Georgian panelled door. He slowly turned with the gun-barrel pointed directly at Ivanov. 'All right! Just who the hell are you?'

The Russian turned slowly. There was a smile on his face. 'I'm not with the CIA; but, then, you obviously already know that.' He gestured with his right hand.

'Keep your hands by your side!' Martin's gun-hand trembled slightly.

'Look, I'm not going to harm you. On the contrary, I want to help you.'

'Well, then, you can bloody well start by telling me your real name!' The Walther 9 mm pistol was steadier this time. Alec Martin was beginning to get more confidence in his position.

'My real name doesn't matter.'

'If you're not from the CIA, just where the hell are you from?'

'Moscow,' replied Ivanov in a matter-of-fact tone.

'Russian!' Martin swallowed deeply.

'Although I'd prefer it if you'd still just call me Tucker; it would make life a lot simpler, and I never did like the name Harv anyhow.'

'You're a bloody spy!' Martin snatched the hammer back on the gun.

Ivanov frowned. 'Look, may I sit down before you blow my balls off?'

'Be my bloody guest! Use the chair nearest the fireplace, but before you do I want your gun. I presume that you're armed, and don't deny it – just you say where it is, and I'll tell you how to dispose of it.'

The Russian smiled once again. 'It's at the base of my spine, tucked inside my belt. A Mauser semi-auto, if you must know.'

'Turn around slowly and lift up your jacket.'

Ivanov complied, pulling the brown cord jacket up around

his armpits. Martin saw the butt of the gun protrude just above the belt of his trousers.

'Stand perfectly still,' continued Martin.

Hesitantly he crossed the room and began to ease out the pistol with his free left hand. Suddenly, just as he retrieved the gun, Ivanov's left elbow came crashing into his chest. The Russian followed through with a pivoting action forcing Martin's arms to one side. Before Alec Martin knew what was happening a mighty right hand dropped into the side of his neck and he collapsed, sprawling on the floor. When Alec Martin came to he found himself propped up in the same armchair he had ordered the Russian into. His eyesight was blurred, and his chest and neck ached.

'I'm real sorry about having to hurt you, Alec.' The voice sounded almost surreal. In the haze that was now his vision he could just about focus on the source of the voice.

'You bastard!' He forced the words through clenched teeth.

Ivanov laughed. 'Come on! You were shaking that much you just might have killed me by accident.'

'I should have killed you the moment you came inside!' Martin winced in agony. 'Tell me. Your cover-story? The real Tucker returned to the United States because of the death of his elderly father. I take it your people had the poor old bastard killed to give you this opportunity and the cover?' Martin could see properly now and stared at the Russian's face. 'No, don't answer that. Your face tells all. You bastard!'

'If it means anything to you, I knew nothing about this until just yesterday. Yes, I was told the real Tucker would be called back to the States and I had a safe period of operation for two weeks; that was all. Alec, the people I work for are ruthless, quite beyond your imagination.'

'Balls!' cried Martin. He was thinking of Frazer Holbeck from MI5. Was he a Russian agent, too?

'Yep, I feel like I'm in a creek with alligators up to my balls.' Ivanov set the Walther pistol on the desk-top. 'Perhaps you will understand once I tell you the purpose of my visit here.'

'Yes, I'm curious to know what the infamous KGB is up to, especially now that I've experienced how you operate at first hand!'

'Not KGB. GRU, or to you Soviet Military Intelligence. And if it's any consolation to you the KGB want to liquidate me.'

Martin stared blankly at the Russian.

'Look, let's not waste time. I need your co-operation and, after what I'm about to tell you, you may just judge in my favour.'

'I doubt it!' grunted Martin.

'A long time ago, a decision was taken by a very senior officer in the GRU to instigate a clandestine operation. The chairman of the Central Committee, the KGB, and the remainder of the Politburo were kept in the dark. It was daring and highly dangerous, but this officer believed that because he had the blessing of the Party chairman in principle he was immune to criticism. The operation was thankfully discovered and stopped, but before any action could be taken against the main instigator he died suddenly, and that is where we thought the matter ended – at least, until now.'

'Look, you speak in riddles. Just where do I fit into all of this?'

'One of the main participants in the general's plan was Garand.'

'I don't believe you! He was American, an ex-GI. How the hell could he have been a Russian agent?'

'He wasn't, not knowingly. He didn't know what he was killing for; he thought it was just to get even with the British Army. He was recruited by one of our people masquerading under the guise and within the ranks of the Provisional IRA in Belfast. All Garand's killings were to an end, but we know little more. After the operation was discovered everyone connected with it was eradicated. Anyone who had any knowledge of the operation was permanently silenced, one way or the other, and it was therefore assumed that the matter was a closed file. At least, until now!' Ivanov paused for questions. Martin remained silent. 'Last month, as you know, a British Army officer was killed in Northern Ireland. A day or so earlier a signal was received by our Moscow communications people – we believe on the same transmitter that was used all those years ago by our agent operating inside the IRA. After that Moscow received a further transmission, again on the same equipment. The following day the Irish Justice Minister was murdered. A third message stated that the first killing was a test run and that the operation of 1969 was now back on course once again.'

'You mean that this killer actually told you in advance of what he was going to do? That's bloody preposterous! Why didn't anyone notify the Irish government and avert the killing?'

'Believe it or not, Alec, sometimes things can take a little time to happen, especially in Moscow.' Ivanov frowned.

'But you still haven't explained just how I fit into all of this.'

'You already are in all this. The RUC officer, Nelson, called on you and was then immediately killed only a few miles from here, and of course your house here has been under constant surveillance for some time now.'

'You're lying! The police have been guarding here for days. Why should I believe such a story?'

'Someone has been watching this house for days, and it's not the British security services and it's not the Americans; but, whoever they are, I can tell you they're damned good.'

Ivanov pointed to the attaché case. 'See that? It's a rather sophisticated jamming device, and it's turned on. Up to the moment I came in here every word spoken in this house was being picked up on a directional microphone by someone in the woods just above here. And they aren't amateurs, Alec; they're professionals.'

'But not good enough, if you spotted them, eh?' smirked Martin. 'OK! So let's say you've convinced me – which you bloody haven't! If your people know so much about the original operation in the early seventies, then you're bound to know the next move.'

'The matter was so sensitive that all traces of the original operation were eradicated. No record has been kept. No one really knows what the next step will be.'

'So you're in the dark, dependent on the next radio transmission from the killer.'

'From the radio transmission we know the immediacy of the next incident, but not where. Also, the radio equipment that is being used is not capable of reception; therefore there is no way of contacting the source, although our computers indicated that the last three messages came from somewhere here in England.'

'What was the fourth message?'

'You don't need to know, but suffice to say the assassin has been thwarted temporarily.'

'If you want my help, you'd better tell me!' Alec Martin was not going to be swayed. Ivanov decided to take a real chance.

'All right, it was to the effect that the British Prime Minister would be killed imminently. I have taken steps to thwart the plan.'

'My God!' Martin was starting to believe at least part of what the Russian had to say; he'd heard the news broadcast of the break-in at 10 Downing Street. 'So Garand is in England?'

'If it is Garand, but I don't think so. From what I've been told it seems fairly likely that he perished back in '72.'

'Maybe to you, but not to me!' Martin prodded his sore chest. 'I've a gut feeling, something I can't explain, but it's a feeling that has never let me down in the past and it won't let me down now.'

'So you'll help me?'

'What exactly do you expect me to help you with, and how?'

'The answer to all this lies with Garand. It has to; everything revolves around him, and I need a good detective like you to help me track him down before anybody else dies. No one knows him better than you, Alec.'

'Track him down and then what?'

'Then I kill him and whoever else is involved.'

'Is that your answer to everything?' shouted Martin.

Ivanov stood up. 'It's time I was off.' He glanced out of the window. 'It's just about dark enough for me to engage our watcher out there.'

'And kill him, too!' Martin felt helpless.

'That depends on him.' Ivanov turned towards the door.

'Killing – that's your only answer, isn't it?'

'Alec, we're not playing games. The guy out there is probably part of the murder gang that wiped out your pal Nelson.'

Martin suddenly realized Ivanov spoke sense. 'But you'll try to avoid killing him, won't you?'

Ivanov remained silent.

'Tell me just one thing, "comrade". Just what do you suspect the end game to have been all those years ago?'

'Thermonuclear war, with a view to Soviet expansionism throughout the northern hemisphere. To create a situation whereby the Soviet Union would be forced into an aggressive state of action and mobilize her forces on a first-strike basis.'

'You mean to manipulate your government into taking an aggressive war action?'

'And all without warning – no sabre-rattling, no indication of military action, nothing,' Ivanov said flatly.

'My God! That's horrific!' Martin was mortified.

'Yes, horrific, and now it all seems so probable once again. Only this time we fear the threat may well come from the West! Times have changed and, although the formula remains the same, the political atmosphere has changed. The matter is so volatile the GRU cannot even approach our own Russian politicians, let alone any foreign powers. All this has to be done with discretion, if that is possible after the intrusion of the KGB a few days ago.'

'The whole bloody thing sounds like a riddle to me.'

'Alec, think back to who was the Irish Justice Minister in 1972. He was called O'Malley, and also a strong advocate of trade with the Soviet Union, but before his appointment in 1971 he had been the Irish Foreign Minister and had even propagated the idea of the increased use of Irish ports by Russian ships. He was also the strong advocate of a permanent Russian trade mission based in Dublin. His killing at that time would have been viewed as an act against Soviet expansionism, a warning to the Kremlin by the Americans – and, after all, wasn't Garand an all-American boy?'

Martin stared at the floor in front of him. 'So Garand was being set up?'

'I don't know for sure, but will you as the only man now alive with first-hand information on Garand help me get him?' Ivanov began to screw the silencer on to his Mauser pistol.

'Tucker, I don't trust you, but I need to get to the bottom of this just as much as you.' He stared at the silenced gun. 'I'll help you, God help me.'

'Good. Now, listen carefully. When I leave here check your watch.'

'Why?' asked Martin.

'Show-time,' smiled Ivanov. 'After I leave wait precisely twenty minutes. Leave the house by the french windows at the back. When you get on to the patio light your pipe and take at least ten seconds to do it; that's important. Then stroll into the garden and down towards the river and stay there for another fifteen minutes before returning to the house by the same way you left. Once inside, pull the curtains and wait for me in the back lounge. Leave the patio door open.' He took the Walther pistol from the fireplace and handed it to the Englishman. 'Take this just in case.'

'What's to stop me shooting you here and now?'

'Because, old chap, you've given me your word to help and furthermore I've had your telephone tapped since my visit yesterday, so I frankly expected to walk into a trap anyway. If you'd wanted to kill me, you would have done so the second I arrived.'

Alec Martin remained silent and thanked God for his decision to talk Julia and his wife into going to Wales. He waited, silently counting away the minutes. At the time appointed Martin stepped on to the patio and after a few seconds pressed his gas lighter and slowly puffed at the pipe. The sudden glare from the lighter dazzled the watcher, and he pulled the starlight night scope from his eyes, cursing quietly. It had been his second night in the woods overlooking the thatched house, and he was beginning to detest the very sight of Rose Cottage. The starlight scope played out towards the strolling figure. Martin was heading down towards the river.

Unknown to the watcher, his viewfinder had already given him away, Ivanov had already picked up the greenish tint from the scope and was now silently circling around him like a fox, but the Russian's main concern was that a secondary or backup watcher could also be in the woodland. He circled him twice again before being entirely satisfied. He was now only five yards away from the figure who lay in a hide constructed cleverly in the thick undergrowth downhill from his position. Even the police search after Nelson's murder had failed to reveal its existence.

A rush was out of the question. Ivanov moved closer, covering the ground inch by inch. He was only seven feet away now and could see that the watcher was covered in an olive-green groundsheet. Although it was a dry evening, the watcher had kept up the plastic hood of the sheet for protection against the chill night air. It was his only amateurish act, for the hood reduced his chances of hearing, especially anything approaching from the rear. Ivanov watched as Martin re-entered the house, pausing at the french windows, bathed in the lounge light. The watcher visibly moved as the light caught his eyes again through the night scope.

Ivanov moved, cat-like, but the watcher had at the last moment heard enough to turn in a defensive position. He failed to pick up the hunting-rifle at his side and swiftly pulled a large fighting-knife from his belt. Ivanov stamped his left foot into the man's chest, and he stumbled backwards, downwards, crashing into the bushes and undergrowth below. The man groaned but was quickly on his feet again, the sign of a professional. He was still brandishing the knife, but now in a fighting position. He glared, forward and around, but his attacker had vanished.

The man moved back to where he had left the hunting-rifle, keeping the knife ready at waist-level, free arm extended to take whatever initial attack might be inflicted. He was still in his crouched fighting posture when he reached the rifle. Just as he reached out to lift the weapon the ground before him erupted. Before he could understand what had occurred he was on his back, pinned to the ground by his attacker. The watcher tried to cut Ivanov with the side of the blade, but as he raised his knife hand Ivanov twisted his wrist backwards, snapping the watcher's taut arm at the elbow with a blow from his foot. The man screamed before dropping the knife from between twitching fingers. He tried desperately to force himself off the ground, but Ivanov's flattened palm smacked squarely and upwards under his chin. There was an audible crack, and the watcher slumped back on to the broken and twisted foliage.

Martin jumped at the sound of the rattle at the french windows. He turned nervously, clutching the pistol, only to find Ivanov standing in the open doorway. Ivanov threw the telescopic infra-red night viewer, the directional microphone, and hunting-rifle on to the floor.

'Good Lord! He had all that?' Martin was appalled. 'Who is he? Who sent him?'

'Mid-Eastern by appearance and Soviet-trained by his behaviour. Probably PLO or some other Arab group, I suspect. Nothing to identify him except a French-made wrist-watch and a fairly new gold signet ring apparently purchased somewhere in Greece.' Ivanov locked the door behind him.

'But what did he say?' insisted Martin.

'Nothing. I'm afraid that I hit him too hard and his neck snapped. Third vertebra, I imagine.'

'You imagine? You imagine! Thank God you only decided to play with my neck and chest earlier, otherwise I might have ended up a bloody lump of mincemeat!' It appeared to Martin that it seemed almost irrelevant to the Russian that he had killed a man.

'I've removed the body and dumped it a discreet distance away from here.'

'What happens when his pals discover him missing?'

'We'll check that out in daylight. They will be forced to follow you when you leave in the morning, and then we spring our trap.'

'So what now?' Martin scratched his head.

'You tell me everything you know about this Harry Garand, and then you give me somewhere warm to lay down my weary head.' Ivanov smiled.

'There is one possibility that we shouldn't exclude; it's something that I've been mulling over in my head. If I recall correctly, the arms-supplier for Garand was a Greek.'

'It's a pity we can't get access to the police investigation files that you prepared in '72.' Ivanov frowned.

Martin smiled. 'On the contrary. Follow me, old chap!'

The two men went out of the room and entered a large utility room just off the kitchen area. Martin indicated a wooden trap-door set snugly between two large oak beams stretching across the full width of the ceiling. Martin was still smiling.

'My wife says she lived in fear of the ceiling collapsing with what I have stored up there.' He went to the garage and returned with a fragile-looking aluminium folding ladder.

Ivanov followed Martin into the roof-space. He entered a well-lit but dusty chamber which stretched the entire width of the house. The joists had been reinforced and covered with makeshift flooring comprised mainly of heavy blockboard. Rows of old tea-chests were stacked three high and set in line with every second joist, giving a two-foot-wide passage for access. Ivanov noted that most of the boxes were marked with white chalk.

First he noticed one marked '1962', then another labelled '1963–6 – June'. The next one read: '1966 (June) to end of 1967.' He smiled at Martin's fastidiousness. While he assumed it to be a prerequisite for his old job, it was a side of the man that he found almost amusing, especially when he considered the present mess in Martin's study.

'Each one of these boxes represents an area of my life, you know. Papers of the most important cases – a biographical record, if you like.' Martin couldn't hide his pride. 'I always had a notion that one day I'd write my memoirs from this lot of boring old crap!'

Ivanov nodded. He was impatient. 'What about 1972?'

Martin was annoyed at the man's persistence. 'You know, I don't bring just anyone up here. Now, come on over here,' he said almost resignedly. They had to squeeze to the far side of the roof-space, and there amidst the dust and cobwebs stood three tea-chests marked: '1971–2 – The One-Shot Killings.' There it was, one chest left aside for the biggest murder investigation of Martin's career.

'There she is. Shall we take it downstairs?'

Ivanov lifted the chest off the top row. It was a dead weight.

'Tell me, just what have you got inside besides details of this Greek? The Elgin Marbles?'

'Bloody funny! Bloody funny!' grunted Martin. 'But if you'd put your bloody back into it we'd be a lot closer to finding what we want!'

After trying hopelessly to negotiate the narrow walkways, they both decided against taking the entire box downstairs. It took Martin five minutes to check through the inventory of suspects and witnesses. After a further minute he was staring at a cream folder marked 'Intelligence Source Reports'.

'Should you have that?' asked Ivanov.

'What are you bloody going to do? Report me to the CIA?' snapped Martin.

Ivanov looked away and cast his eyes upwards in mock annoyance. He was beginning to understand Martin's sarcasm and wit – or was it just sarcastic wit? He hadn't really decided that one yet.

'Here it is!' exclaimed Martin. 'It was from Special Branch at Scotland Yard. They must have got it from MI5. The only name we had to go on originally – and that was from a source inside Ulster – was the name "Goukas", but to our delight we found Mr Goukas to be Kostas Goukas, a known international arms-dealer and -smuggler, living and operating from the southern Greek coast. Not in a big way, mark you, but enough for him to make a handsome profit without upsetting the applecart and coming to the attention of the Greek authorities. He was a professional, never soiling his hands on anything domestic or even remotely associated in an indirect fashion. A cute operator with the blessing of the CIA, apparently.' He looked at Ivanov and handed over the file.

Ivanov read aloud from the folder. 'Kostas Goukas. 23A Sidirodromikou Strathmou Street, Kalamata, Greece.'

'He must be the bastard who's making the new reloads for the rifle,' continued Martin.

'I think you had better tell me everything you told Nelson, don't you?' replied Ivanov.

'I thought you said you wanted to get some sleep. This could take hours!'

Ivanov looked at his watch. 'You have my full attention until 5 a.m. After that I'll have to split. I suppose there's no chance of some hot coffee?'

The Russian left just after 5 a.m. After driving up on to the country road he turned left and headed down past the other side of the woods. He travelled for a quarter of a mile until he reached a sharp right-hand bend in the road. He steered the car carefully into the bend. Suddenly a green Renault shot across his path from the opposite direction and into a narrow lane which ran directly on to the bend from the left-hand side. Ivanov hit the brakes, steadying the car just in time. He glanced back in his rear-view mirror. The Renault's brake-lights were illuminated. A black-clad figure jumped from the rear of the saloon car and disappeared down into the woods running beside the lane.

'Interesting,' muttered Ivanov. Once across Stopham Bridge he found the telephone-box at the crossroads. Alec Martin jumped when he heard the telephone ring. He hovered over the telephone. What if it was the terrorists? Who else knew he was at home?

'What the hell!' he snapped, lifting the receiver. A series of bleeps were followed by a voice.

'Thank God.'

'Tucker! Is that you?'

'Alec, listen to me and do exactly what I'm about to tell you.'

'What's wrong?' Martin began to sweat.

'There's been a hitch.'

'A hitch!' He was beginning to panic now.

'Well, not exactly a hitch. I'd say more like a change in plans.' Ivanov cringed at his poor use of words. 'Let me explain . . .'

Alec Martin did exactly as he'd been told and left by the patio doors carrying the fishing-rod and plastic tackle-box just as he always did around six-thirty each morning. There was a definite dampness in the air that late June morning, but the smell of the countryside and awakening bird life more than made up for the prospect of rain. Martin walked the length of the garden which gently swept down to the river-bank.

The distance was only two hundred metres yet it seemed the

longest walk he'd made in his life. Every step felt like his last. What if the man calling himself Tucker had failed? What if whoever was out there had already decided he should meet the same end as Sam Nelson? A cold shiver ran up his back. Could Garand really be out there, waiting? A twig cracked somewhere up in the copse to his right. He dared not glance yet it was difficult not to. Suddenly he had a compelling urge to take the Walther out of the tackle-box; it was hard to ignore. Another crack, followed by a rustling sound just ahead of him and to his right. He saw something move in the undergrowth out of the corner of his eyes. This was it! The thick undergrowth and heather at the edge of the manicured lawn moved again; a brown doe rabbit broke cover and raced for all it was worth across the lawn directly in front of him.

Alec Martin breathed a sigh of relief and tried not to show it. Then another horrible thought came to mind. What had spooked the rabbit? He tried not to think about it as he neared the bank. The river was flowing faster than normal owing to the heavy rainfall over the previous two days. He started to prepare the carbon spinning-rod. The massive pike had been devastating his fishing on the stretch for the last two weeks; over the last week he had been concentrating on trying to catch it. He had set aside his usual fly-rod and chosen the heavy-duty carbon rod; it was capable of landing a shark, but even so the fishing-line was still a problem. He'd chosen Drennan double-strength nylon as a spinner; it was half the thickness of a normal nylon line, and had a twenty-two-pound breaking strain. Finally he took the size-four gold-coloured Mepp from the tackle-box; it had a treble-barbed hook which would hold the toughest fish. Just as he was about to cast the line the figure appeared like a dark ghost just twenty metres away on the opposite river-bank.

'Jesus!' he cried out.

Martin couldn't believe his eyes as the black-clad figure with the black balaclava helmet materialized before him. Only seconds before he had looked across to the other side; it had only taken him moments to attach the new fly beside the treble hook. Now the man was there, facing him, but where had he come from? What was he going to do? The man slowly removed the balaclava. Martin felt a slight relief that it wasn't Garand. He was Middle Eastern by the looks of him – a trimmed black beard and tousled wavy black hair that was almost shoulder-length. He watched in shock as the man unzipped his black windcheater and drew out the handgun with the bulbous silencer.

'Oh my God!' groaned Martin. 'Tucker! Tucker! Where the hell are you? Tucker!' He was yelling now at the top of his voice.

Across the river the terrorist was raising his gun-hand to fire. Martin looked down at the open tackle-box at his feet; there was no time left to dive for the Walther inside. There was only seconds left now; the man was actually grinning at him. The bastard was about to kill him and he was grinning at him! Something snapped inside Alec Martin's head. He was no longer in fear; he was furious!

'You grinning bastard!' he yelled across, his clear cockney accent echoing loudly across the water.

In a single practised movement that he had completed dozens of times each day he flicked back on the carbon-fibre fishing-rod and cast it directly at the terrorist. The line flexed over and across; the terrorist hadn't even the eye to see it coming as he pressed on the trigger of the silenced pistol. The treble hook landed squarely on target; two of the large hooks sunk into the terrorist's neck, just barely an inch under the left ear.

Martin instinctively snapped back on the spinning-rod, and the nylon line went taut. The hooks cut deeper into the man's soft tissue. He screamed and staggered forward, trying desperately to grab hold of the line with his left hand. Martin pulled again, giving a little but taking more; it was like playing in the massive pike that he had hooked but lost the day before Sam Nelson was killed. Suddenly his anger renewed. This was probably one of the bastards that had killed his friend. A sod of grass just to the right of his feet lifted; he glanced down and then at his 'catch'. The terrorist's gun puffed again; a small cloud of white smoke drifted away from the gun-barrel. The bastard was shooting at him now!

'Game's over, you bastard!' Alec Martin played the rod again, easing back slightly. The terrorist took his only opportunity to try to wrap his left forearm around the heavy nylon line; he was already inches away from the river-bank and couldn't afford to give any more ground away. The line tightened again, the two barbed hooks dug even deeper; blood spurted out from the man's neck and he screamed, dropping the gun into the water.

'And now for you, sonny,' Martin grunted as he yanked expertly on the line. The man spun to the right and was immediately pulled off balance and into the river.

It was deep and fast-flowing; there was no opportunity to get a foothold. In any case he was being pulled by the current into the middle of the river, and every time he tried to get his breath the fishing-line was played just enough to pull him under again. Slowly the struggle abated; he was drowning and there wasn't a thing he could do. The only chance the terrorist had really was if he'd used his body weight to break the fishing-line, but now it was all too late. The line finally snapped just after the terrorist lost consciousness. Alec Martin watched as the man's half-submerged body was quickly rushed off downstream. He breathed deeply and wiped the sweat from his face as he flopped down beside the tackle-box, his legs feeling like jelly.

'Alec, did you call me?' Ivanov walked out from the copse just twenty paces upstream.

'Where the hell have you been?' demanded Martin, still unable to stand up.

'What happened?' asked Ivanov casually.

'Happened! What the hell do you think happened! Some prat across the river there decided to take a swim. He just dived into the water, didn't he?' Martin was almost bent double with the cramps in his stomach; the shock was beginning to set in.

'*Dove*. The word is *dove*,' smiled Ivanov as he neared the Englishman.

'Well, stuff you, you Russian bastard! Dived! Dove! What the hell does it matter? I've just killed another human being!'

'He was hardly what I'd have called a human being,' Ivanov replied casually. 'Look, I'm real sorry. I just couldn't flush the bastard out. I knew if you turned up as usual on the river-bank he'd be headstrong enough to come looking for revenge for his buddy back there.'

'You were supposed to bloody protect me!' yelled Martin.

'It looked to me that you didn't need any of my help,' Ivanov smiled.

'You mean you were standing there the whole bloody time!' Jelly legs or not, Alec Martin forced himself on to his feet. 'You crazy bastard!'

'If he'd got anywhere near you, I'd have wasted him for you.' Ivanov turned and walked back towards the house. 'By the way, that was some catch.'

Alec Martin was totally speechless. One half of him wanted to be sick; the other half wanted to crawl off somewhere and die.

By 9 a.m. Martin had regained his composure enough to carry on. Ivanov had left an hour before. Now he was alone again. He left the house as agreed and began to start the Ford Sierra Estate. The cold engine coughed into life, expunging the sounds of the river and the birds. He was tired, but the invigoration of doing something for the first time in years gave him new life; he was evening the score for Sam Nelson.

As he pulled away from the house and up the steep winding driveway new eyes watched with interest. After travelling only three miles along the road he noticed the green Renault 21 with its two passengers keeping a steady pace behind him at a distance of around two hundred metres. A chill travelled down his neck, and he began to sweat.

'I just hope you know what you're doing, you Russian bastard!' he muttered.

After several more miles he spotted the signpost that he had agreed on with Ivanov. He took the left fork and finally a right turn into a forest lane extending towards the middle of a hundred and fifty acres of dense woodland. The Renault hesitated at the entrance, and Martin was almost thanking God until he saw it begin to advance slowly along the stony track straight after him.

'Oh shit!' he exclaimed. As the followers rounded the first bend they heard a rumbling sound from their left. Through the trees the front-seat passenger caught sight of a giant mechanical digger on the side-track, caterpillar tracks crunching up the ground as it bore down on collision course with the passenger-side of the Renault.

'Step on it! It's a trap!' screamed the passenger. The driver slammed down the accelerator, and the back wheels slipped, spinning gravel in every direction. They had no sooner accelerated past the side-junction when the car headed towards the back of the abandoned Sierra Estate.

'Can you get around it?' screamed the passenger. The driver wasted no time replying and tried to force the Renault off the track, squeezing between the stationary Sierra and the nearest tree-line, but the wheels stuck in a shallow drainage-ditch and the car slid broadside. Neither man had time to jump clear before the digger spade crashed through the side of their car, shoving it firmly against the Sierra, which jerked violently against the impact.

A small fire began in the Renault's engine-compartment, and smoke started to engulf both car and occupants. The passenger was already unconscious, his feet hopelessly trapped in the tangled wreckage. The driver scrambled out through a shattered side window and on to the back of the Sierra Estate. Just as he reached what he imagined to be safety, firm arms came from behind and locked him in a stranglehold. He struggled momentarily, gasping for air, fainting after a further few seconds. When he came round he was lying in the woods, bound hand and foot.

'Who are you working for!' Ivanov spoke in a dangerously low tone. The terrorist remained silent.

'IRA or what!' continued Ivanov.

'Piss off!' groaned the man, still trying to focus his bleary eyes.

Ivanov produced the fighting-knife he had obtained from the dead watcher and stuck it sharply into the man's upper left arm muscle, cutting a two-inch wound. The man screamed and began writhing on the damp ground pulling at his bonds. Ivanov left the knife sticking into the arm as he grabbed the man's hair.

'Answer!'

'INLF!' cried the man. 'Please! Take it out.' The man's eyes pleaded with him.

'When you've answered some more questions. Now, what's this all about? Why are you watching Martin?'

The man became unresponsive again. Ivanov twisted the knife into the oozing wound. The terrorist screamed again. When he regained control he began to talk non-stop. Ivanov discovered him to be called O'Donnell and from a village called Dungiven, amidst Ulster's Sperrin Mountains. He was only twenty years old, yet already an officer in a terrorist cell of the Irish National Liberation Front, yet another splinter group formed from the Provisionals. He had, three months before, been given instructions to team up with members of the PLO in Libya, although he was no longer to take directions from Dublin.

Ivanov mused over the idea of the Arabs working alongside the INLF, but the man knew no names except that of a Lebanese terrorist called George and a Frenchman called François, but nothing else; the other terrorists in the mixed group used only numbers in place of names. But the young man had soon realized he was part of an important international operation. Using numbers was one thing; hiding French, Spanish, and German accents was altogether something else.

'Tucker!' Martin came into the clearing, running. He winced at the sight of the bleeding terrorist. 'We've got to get the hell out of here! A local farmer has just arrived with a fire engine from one of the villages near here. They're at the wrecked vehicles already! The local police are bound to follow.'

Ivanov nodded. 'Go to my car. I'll be there presently.'

'Is that bloody necessary?' Martin pointed to the knife protruding from the man's arm.

'He'll be staying here. Now, go.' Ivanov arose and guided Martin towards the trees.

'You make me sick!' snapped Martin.

'Wait at the car,' demanded Ivanov. The Englishman reluctantly left.

After Martin had disappeared, Ivanov returned to the terrorist, removing the knife from his arm. The man groaned again. Before he could speak the long knife was jammed upwards into the soft flesh under his chin, the knife-point penetrating into the base of the brain. Death was almost instantaneous. The man's body shuddered for a second and then went still. Once they had driven out of the forest Martin began to breathe a sigh of relief.

'OK, what did you find out?'

'I don't really know.' Ivanov frowned.

'Well, who is he – IRA or what?' snapped Martin.

'He was called O'Donnell. He was from some place called Dungiven; it's in Northern Ireland. Said he was with the Irish National Liberation Front, although he was recruited into something else that I don't quite understand. Tell me, what do you make of an Irish terrorist carrying a poison capsule to avoid capture and interrogation?'

'That's a new one for the Irish. I remember one time, though, years ago, some of the boys in MI5 telling me of a PLO man who used poison after being detained by Special Branch near Heathrow; but he was a courier, not a soldier.'

'Well, that's what puzzles me. He had this capsule in his pocket, a refined version of cyanide, standard issue to Soviet special forces on certain missions.' Ivanov dropped the capsule into Martin's lap.

'Are you saying he was one of your men?' Martin cringed at the sight of the yellow capsule and carefully set it in the car ashtray.

'No, he was an Irish terrorist, recruited into a multi-national terror group, comprising members of the PLO, the RAF, the Basques, the INLF, and the Provisionals. A mixed assortment, hand-picked from all over Europe and the Middle East, but trained as one fighting unit.'

'A what?' Martin was really confused now.

'A highly trained combat unit. Originally they started off with a hundred but now they're whittled down to thirty plus after a rigorous training programme in Libya.'

'Whittled down?' Martin was sweating; he loosened his tie.

'Killed during training.'

'Killed! Who trained them and why?'

'Two names; a Lebanese calling himself George; his second-in-command is a Frenchman called François. But the guy back there didn't know the mission's objective; only that it was vitally important. Important enough, it seems, to make each of the terrorist mother organizations redundant. He also said he wasn't selected for the final group; he wasn't good enough. He was being used as a back-up instead. He was relieved at that; apparently from the final sixty chosen to go on training only half survived the six-month course.'

'Bloody crazy!'

'Alec, he said something else, something he picked up by accident in Libya but he shouldn't have known. The groups was training for one job, to act as a small commando force, trained to such a pitch that it could easily dismiss any regular Army unit twice its size. The group was preparing to leave the terrorist camp in Libya just two weeks ago.'

'I think we'd better take this to the appropriate authorities. I have contacts in the intelligence community.' Martin was beginning to panic.

'Alec, I don't think so. Just what are you going to say anyway? At the moment we haven't even got a clear picture of the show. Anyway, who's going to believe that a GRU agent being pursued by the KGB is trying to stop a seemingly Soviet-orchestrated plot dating back to 1972? At the very least I would be hunted by the CIA and MI5 on top of the KGB, and don't imagine for a second that they'll forget about you. Alec, we need to track down this group; the connection with Garand is crucial.'

'So what do we do?' quizzed Martin.

'I suggest you go to Ireland and try to follow up any lead on Garand you can. Start with that old priest called O'Neill that you told me about; see if he's still living. And while you're at it pull in any old favours you still have with the Ulster police; see if you can find out more about the Easter Sunday shooting in Londonderry.'

'Oh great! I get all the hard jobs. Now, what have you arranged for yourself?'

'I'm going to Greece to pay this guy Goukas a visit.' Ivanov jotted down a number on the back of one of his cards and handed it to Martin.

'What's this?'

'If for some reason you can't get me at the Chelsea address, use that number.'

RUC HEADQUARTERS, BELFAST

The Chief Constable of the Royal Ulster Constabulary was surprised to received the telephone call from Alec Martin. He knew Martin from his secondment days and had met up with him at Sam Nelson's funeral. Although initially delighted to speak to his old acquaintance once again, his attitude soon changed once the true nature of Martin's intentions became clear.

'You want to go to Londonderry and speak to the policeman in charge of the Easter Sunday case? You must be joking, Alec! Why?'

'John, I think Sam Nelson was murdered because of his interest in the case. It was partly the reason why he came to see me just hours before he died.'

'I know why he went to see you; it was all mentioned in the copy of your statement sent to us by the Sussex police. But, Alec, don't you think our own men can investigate this themselves? I understand your anger, but I can assure you we are pulling out all the stops over here on this side of the Irish Sea.'

This conversation was not going the way Alec Martin had intended it. At this rate he would be lucky not to be warned off for interfering.

'Look, John, all I want is to speak to someone who investigated the shooting in Londonderry. Can that really do any harm? I might even be able to help your boys – who knows?'

'I doubt that.'

'It's worth a try, John.'

'But, Alec! You are no longer a serving policeman. You realize of course that if any of the officers with whom I put you in contact decided not to co-operate with you there's nothing I can do?'

'Yes, I understand that entirely.' A feeling of relief was

beginning to flow over Martin. 'So you'll help me?' The question was ignored.

'And another thing. I'll be keeping a close eye on you. I'll have to assign a man to stay with you the whole time you're over here in Northern Ireland. I want to see you here at Brooklyn before you go anywhere. I can't afford another killing on home soil.'

'Whatever you like, John. I've decided to fly over today or first thing in the morning. I can be in your office at nine o'clock sharp tomorrow morning.'

'I'll see what can be arranged, but I can't promise anything. Goodbye, Alec.' The line went dead. The Chief Constable was angry with him; not that it mattered any more.

LONDON
Several hours later

Ivanov met Holbeck back at the apartment. The Englishman was looking nervous and concerned; he had clearly been drinking.

'Where the hell have you been?' Holbeck demanded.

'Out.'

'Where's Martin?' continued Holbeck.

'He's safe.' Ivanov crossed the room and poured himself a gin.

'The reports have been flashing into my office all afternoon. Bodies are being picked up all over the Stopham area! Some bastard's just been fished out of a weir three miles downstream from Martin's place, and two more have been found in a forest in the same vicinity.' He was on his feet now.

'Only two? They've missed one.' Ivanov added some tonic water and saluted the Englishman.

'This isn't some bloody game!' cried Holbeck. 'It was supposed to be a quiet operation, an in-and-out job! Now, where's Martin?'

'Safe. I sent him packing to Ireland.' He checked his wristwatch. 'And I'm off to Greece in the morning.'

'Why?'

'I think I've found a possible contact, a black-market arms-dealer who lives in Kalamata.' He handed over a slip of paper. 'That's his details. Maybe you can run a check. You should have something on file.'

Holbeck examined the paper. 'What about Martin? Does he suspect anything?'

'He knows.' Ivanov took a drink. 'I had to take him into my confidence; it was the only way.'

'You told him!' Holbeck almost dropped his empty glass. 'Then, he knows about me.' His face reddened.

'He knew about you already. After your call he ran a check with the FBI London office, they let it slip about the real Tucker being Stateside.'

'Listen to me. Martin must be killed. There's no other way.'

'I need him.'

'Well, when you don't need him any more! Just make sure he doesn't talk.' Ivanov said nothing. 'There's something else. The county police are now looking for Martin. For the present they're being very quiet about it; I've even managed to suppress any media broadcast about the bodies. If he should get picked up— '

Ivanov raised a hand to halt him. 'I'll take care of it.'

Holbeck set his glass down and picked up his overcoat. 'By the way, Antonia Travis was looking for you. She's left two messages on the answering machine.'

Ivanov nodded. 'I'll keep in touch. I reckon Greece should take two days maximum.'

'Frankly, old chap, I'd rather you took two years. This may not be a very healthy place for you to return to.' Then he left.

Ivanov checked the answering machine. She'd left a London number for him to ring. He dialled the number, a little surprised at the speed with which it was answered.

'Hello?' Her voice was tense.

'Antonia, it's me.'

'Thank God! I must see you immediately,' she insisted.

He gave her the address. She was only five miles across the city, staying at a friend's house. She arrived in less than half an hour. The black taxi pulled up outside the apartment-block, she hurriedly paid the driver and rushed to the front door, a little frustrated by the delay in having to use the security intercom at the main entrance. He let her in immediately. Just as she disappeared from the brightly lit entrance hallway into the lift, Mikhailov emerged from the dark shadows of the carpark just facing the entrance.

Ivanov already had the door open for her as she emerged from the lift. As the door shut behind her Antonia Travis broke down, weeping uncontrollably. She had almost lost every vestige of self-control now. After calming her down he learnt about Charlie Younger's death. She was convinced it was no accident, but who and why? Was there really a 'mole' inside GCHQ, taking lethal steps to secure his survival? She kept harping back to Younger. To make matters worse, the police had been unable to contact his parents – out of the country on holiday; she had had to make the post-mortem identification. She cried steadily, but there was something else she wanted to tell him; she was hiding it, and not too skilfully.

'You know something? All my life I haven't needed anybody, a loner, but now . . . after seeing Charlie lying there I just don't know any more.' She fought to keep control. 'Sure, they'd cleaned him up, but it didn't hide too much. I know he was a bit crazy, but he was safe on that motorcycle of his; he treasured it!'

'What did the police say about the accident?' He stood up from beside her and drew the curtains.

'What do *they* know! "Speed was the contributory factor here" – that's all the chubby inspector could tell me at the mortuary.' She looked up at him, appealing to be believed. 'Look, I even told Frazer Holbeck about the great progress Charlie was making into these Russian-type Field Radio Signals; he agreed with me on the importance of what Charlie was accomplishing. He was making clear headway. Given a little more time – who knows?'

'When were you talking to Colonel Holbeck?'

'He was at my house for dinner the night before Charlie's . . . death.' She was still refusing to call it an accident.

'That's strange. He didn't tell me he was talking to you,' replied Ivanov.

'Probably slipped his mind,' she replied. 'I could use a drink.'

'Coming right up.' He fixed them both drinks.

Then they talked for several hours. Finally she fell asleep on the sofa – a combination of the alcohol and a reaction to off-loading some of her tension. He made her comfortable, setting her head carefully on to the cushions, and fetched a blanket from the bedroom. He turned down the lights and sat staring at her for ages; she was being used just like himself, both of them part of Mikhailov's carnival. Ivanov kept returning to Holbeck. Could he have caused Younger's death and, if so, for what purpose?

WINDSOR
9 p.m.

'Mother? I'm home.' Holbeck hung up his bowler hat and set the umbrella in the hatstand beside the door. He sniffed the air; he was sure he could smell tobacco smoke.

'Good evening, Colonel.' It was Lucy the housekeeper who also doubled as nurse for his blind and elderly mother.

'Evening, Lucy. Is Mother up?'

'Yes, sir, her ladyship is with the gentleman in the conservatory. I've just served them coffee.'

'What gentleman?' Holbeck was startled. No one visited the house without his express authority, let alone had coffee with Mother.

'Brigadier Forsythe-Jones. He gave me his card. He served with you in Korea, he said.'

'Ah, Forsythe-Jones, yes. You said he left a card?' Holbeck tried to smile, but he'd never heard of a Brigadier Forsythe-Jones in his life.

'It's over there on the hall table, sir. Shall I get something for you also, Colonel?'

'That would be nice, Lucy. Thank you.' Holbeck lifted the gilt-edged card. Lucy had got the name right; there was no mistaking it.

He considered getting a handgun from the study but

discarded the idea instantly. The man, whoever he was, was hardly a danger if he'd taken the trouble to leave his fingerprints and calling-card, never mind take tea with Mother. He went through the large drawing-room and towards the Victorian conservatory in the east wing. Mikhailov stood up as he walked in.

'There you are, Frazer my dear. An old friend of yours has popped in to see us.' The old lady croaked out her words.

'Really!' Holbeck's eyes widened.

'Frazer, you're looking exceptionally well,' smiled Mikhailov. 'The brigadier was telling me of some of your exploits in the battalion. You really are a sly one, my dear.' The old woman's voice was fragile and weak. 'He was telling me of some of your boyish antics at Sandhurst. I never knew you got into trouble for borrowing the adjutant's charger and racing up the steps of the Grand Entrance of the Old Building half-way through your training.'

'Mother, some things are better left untold. A boyish prank, as you say.' He glared at the Russian.

'Actually, Lady Holbeck, it was all taken in the best of humour; it'll hardly be the first or the last time a "Young Rupert" gets up to some high jinks!' Mikhailov laughed. The old woman joined in.

'Mother, I get the strong impression that you haven't taken your medicine this evening. Am I right?' Holbeck side-stepped the humour.

Just then Lucy walked in carrying a small tray. 'You are quite right, Colonel,' the maid chirped up, 'if you forgive me for interrupting, her ladyship wouldn't take it in case it made her drowsy, and she wouldn't leave the brigadier by himself.'

'Lucy, you little tittle-tattler!' The old woman scolded.

'Mother! Time for medication. Remember what the doctor said,' insisted Holbeck, motioning for Lucy to push the old lady out in her wheelchair. 'I'll be up to see you once you get settled into bed.' He leant over and kissed her, before taking Lucy's tray.

'Very well.' She reluctantly gave in. 'Nice to have met you, Brigadier. Do come again.'

The Russian took her hand and kissed it. 'The pleasure is all mine, your ladyship. I look forward to meeting you again.'

Over my dead body! thought Holbeck.

'Such a charming man,' she whispered to Lucy as she was wheeled away into the drawing-room.

Holbeck watched the glass doors to the drawing-room close. He turned on the Russian instantly.

'What the hell are you playing at?'

'I need your help, *old chap*,' Mikhailov said quietly, still using his clipped English voice and stressing the latter part.

'Not like this!' snapped Holbeck.

'I'm afraid you might not be able to stay on after this has blown over,' continued Mikhailov unabashed.

'It's that serious?' Holbeck's anger subsided as he flopped into the nearest chair; he was close to panic now.

'Yes.'

'What will Mother say?' replied Holbeck, his face buried in both hands. 'This will kill her, you know!' He almost groaned out the words.

'What's Tucker up to?'

'He's found the name of a possible lead to Bloodstone. This is it.' He handed over the piece of paper Ivanov had given him. 'He's a black-marketeer in guns.'

'Goukas, Kalamata.' Mikhailov examined the paper. 'When's he going to Greece?'

'Tomorrow morning. I don't know.' Holbeck was near to panic. 'Maybe he'll go tonight instead.'

'I hardly think so. He's entertaining Wolverine at present.' Mikhailov pocketed the piece of paper.

'Antonia at the apartment! Why?'

'I was hoping you'd be able to tell *me* that.'

'I've no idea. I introduced them just as you told me. I told him to cultivate the relationship as you said, but I didn't think they were that close.' Holbeck felt almost betrayed by the woman. 'I'll find out.'

'You'll do nothing of the sort. *I'll* handle this. Just as I'll handle this Greek issue. Now, what about this Martin character?'

'Tucker's sent him to Ireland.' Holbeck adjusted his shirt collar.

'You seem a trifle stressed, my friend,' continued Mikhailov.

'Martin knows Tucker works for Moscow. That means he knows I'm involved also,' blurted Holbeck.

'Martin can be eliminated. That is not a problem,' snapped the Russian. 'Perhaps there is a way you can stay after all, provided you do exactly as you are told.' Mikhailov waited several seconds for the words to hook his fish.

'Anything! Anything you say,' replied Holbeck, a tear forming in his eye.

LONDON
Monday, 29 June, early morning

Antonia Travis awoke to the chimes of the grandfather clock in the hallway. It was 6 a.m. She was momentarily startled by the surroundings, then she remembered despite the pounding in her head. She sat up slowly, pulling back the blanket and rubbing her weary eyes.

'I see you're up,' Ivanov said cheerily. He came in from the hallway carrying a silver tray containing toast, marmalade and a large pot of tea.

'Morning,' she whispered.

He set the tray next to her on the glass-topped coffee-table and then opened the curtains. The sun had already started its ascent over the London skyline, casting deep shadows across the Thames. Ivanov glanced below. For a split second he imagined his eyes were deceiving him. Kapitsa was standing next to a Range Rover at the far end of the carpark.

'Did you have to do that?' Antonia Travis shielded her eyes from the sunlight.

He turned and smiled at her, then he looked outside again. Kapitsa was gone. He had a plane to catch, and little time for conversation. Their exchange was brief as Ivanov prepared his overnight bag and got ready. He insisted on her coming with him in the taxi – at least, as far as her friend's house where she'd been the previous evening. The taxi waited while Ivanov joined her on the pavement outside the Victorian terrace. He wasn't quite sure if this was *bon voyage* or farewell.

'Antonia, I want you to promise me you'll take care of yourself while I'm away in Greece. Don't take any risks. Don't talk to anyone about your suspicions, and stay away from Holbeck.'

'Whatever for?' She frowned.

'The colonel might not be telling us everything. It's only a hunch. Just trust me.'

'I do.' She smiled. 'It's funny, I've only ever met you a couple of times yet I do trust you. I . . .' She hesitated as if forgetting her line. She leant forward on tiptoe and kissed him on the cheek. As she stepped back he removed her spectacles and took her in his arms and kissed her on the lips. They embraced, oblivious to time passing or passing pedestrians who had to circumnavigate the obstacle on their way to work.

The taxi-driver pumped his horn and leant out of his side-window. 'Look, mate, if you're wanting to make Gatwick Airport we'll have to step on it,' he said concernedly.

She stepped back from him and they looked into each other's eyes. He smiled. 'You'll be needing these.' He handed back the spectacles.

'Not really,' she answered softly. 'Sometimes I think I just hide behind them.' Her face lit up.

'Not any more,' he continued. 'Just take care until I get back. I'll call you.'

She kissed him again, this time hurriedly; then she rushed up the stone steps into the house and was gone.

RUC HEADQUARTERS, BELFAST

At 9 a.m. precisely, Alec Martin arrived at the outer gates of the RUC's headquarters situated in Knock Road. He was expected; an officer was awaiting his arrival and escorted him to the Chief Constable's office. Their meeting was brief but not sweet, the advice pointed and simple; he was being tolerated under sufferance. A detective sergeant had been detailed to escort him during his brief stay in the Province; no matter what happened he was catching the evening shuttle back to London.

They travelled in silence to the 'Maiden City'. The scenery across the Glenshane Pass was breathtaking, but it soon faded for Martin as they approached Dungiven. Martin recognized the name as being the home village of the terrorist Ivanov had interrogated. Twenty minutes later and they were at the outskirts of the divided city.

LONDONDERRY

The meeting was arranged for 1 p.m. at the Everglades Hotel on the east bank of the River Foyle. The sergeant took care of the hotel registration, and Martin followed him to a suite overlooking the gardens and river beyond. Lunch was served in the room while they waited. There was a knock on the door precisely on time; a tall silver-haired man with a Mexican-style moustache came in. After McCormick introduced himself and produced his warrant-card the detective sergeant left them alone. Martin surmised McCormick to be from Special Branch. Nothing was said. It was the man's attitude; it set him apart from other policemen. It was the abrasive hostility mingled with indifference. McCormick volunteered nothing, barely answering the questions put to him over the next twenty minutes.

'You said that you checked with your local sources and they knew nothing about the shooting?'

'Nothing,' replied McCormick.

'I was told that the Branch had Derry stitched up at present.' It was Martin's first comment on Special Branch; he was desperate for the man to open up more.

McCormick got out of his cane chair. 'Look, I was ordered to see you! I don't have to give a has-been who imagines himself to be Sherlock Holmes any access to my SB50s. I'm bound by the Official Secrets Act, so don't expect what you know I can't deliver!'

Marton stood up and stared out across the river.

'You've had a wasted journey!' continued McCormick. 'Believe me, if I knew something I'd have nailed the bastards myself before now.'

Martin tried to assess the statement. Was it the brush-off or was it sincerity? He turned towards McCormick. 'I appreciate you seeing me like this.'

They shook hands loosely, then McCormick left, pausing at the open door. 'I take it you'll be leaving now? You'll hardly be staying in the city, I mean?'

'I don't know,' replied Martin.

McCormick raised a finger towards him. 'Just don't go tramping over my patch!'

It was a threat. Martin took the bull by the horns. 'I'll do exactly as I please.'

McCormick moved back closer to him until barely inches separated the two men's faces. 'Piss off!' he growled. Alec Martin could smell the sour breath intermingled with a strong scent of garlic. He was not going to be bullied.

'Temper, temper . . .' He smiled back at the man's reddening face.

McCormick turned on his heels and left, slamming the door behind him.

'You ignorant bastard!' continued Martin.

The detective sergeant returned several minutes later. By his contrite attitude to Martin's request to view the scene of the crime it was obvious that Detective Inspector McCormick had spoken to him on his way out. Reluctantly he finally took Martin to the derelict house from which the gunman had staged the attack; at least, if nothing else, Martin had found out its location from McCormick. The sergeant waited outside while Martin ascended the rotting staircase towards the first floor. Then with some difficulty he scrambled into the open roof-space. With the aid of a pocket torch he scoured every inch of the place.

From the roof-light he examined the waste ground below where the Army vehicle would have been positioned at the time of the shooting. He ran his hands along the damaged tiles and rusty edge of the broken roof-light, cutting himself slightly on one finger. He could just peer out and downwards but no more. The gunman had to be at least six feet tall; from his files he recalled Harry Garand to be six feet two inches. Below him the figure moved silently up the rotting staircase, avoiding the weaker areas as he approached the first-floor landing. Martin was too engrossed in the view from the window to hear a sound. He was about to give up his search, turning towards the trap-door, when in the darkness he banged his shin against something.

'Shit!' He flashed the torch downwards. It was an orange-box; furthermore a protruding nail had plucked some threads from his new trousers. He cursed again, kicking the wooden box to one side. It still contained the blue-coloured packing-paper inside; some of it tumbled out on to the floor. Martin reached over and used some of the damp paper to wipe the blood from his dripping fingertip. Just as he reached the trap-door a voice boomed out: 'Now what do you think you're up to?'

Martin looked down, his eyes meeting a cold stare. 'My goodness, if it isn't DI McCormick!'

'I told you earlier that I don't like people tramping over my patch, so what is it? What can I do for you before you get yourself wasted by some equally inquisitive Provos?'

Martin climbed down, guided by McCormick as he stepped on to the shaky banisters below.

'They already know you're snooping up here, you know. This town's renowned for the original tom-tom drums, and they're beating right now. That's what brought me here, too.'

'I think you know something else about this. What is it?' Martin stared at the man.

McCormick hesitated. 'See you've cut your finger.'

'Look, stop mucking me about. I accept you have to keep confidences, but I need to know.'

McCormick looked around and down the staircase. 'I had a tout, a runner within the Provos. He got nobbled shortly after the Easter Sunday thing happened. He'd run his course. Frankly he was becoming a liability to all concerned, but he had the only information I could get on this thing. Now, he mentioned some outsiders being involved: a man called Liam, apparently from Dublin. The other thing that puzzled him was when he overheard in passing that the shooting was some kind of "test run", a sort of "trial run".'

'And I suppose there must be ten thousand people in Dublin who fit the description of this Liam?' groaned Martin.

'That's just it! No description; no nothing. We don't know a thing about him. And now I've no tout; he got himself a head-job over in Donegal last week.' McCormick had the image of the tout's tortured body lying on the mortuary slab still planted vividly in his brain. He gave Martin a handkerchief for his bleeding finger. 'Now, I suggest you high-tail it out of here pronto – before you get a head-job, too.'

As they reached the awaiting unmarked police car and embarrassed detective sergeant now surrounded by an eight-man military patrol, Martin pulled McCormick aside.

'A thought's just hit me. You said that roof-space was thoroughly checked by SOCO?'

'Of course it was.'

'I stumbled on an empty fruit-box; ripped my bloody trousers, too. I assume it was there at the time of the shooting?'

'Search me. These old houses are a playground for every kid in the area. Who knows how many of them have been through the place since the shooting?'

'But the paper inside that box was damp; it had to have been there for some time.'

'So what? What are you driving at?' McCormick was getting annoyed again.

'The sniper was either very tall – over six feet – or else he had to use that box to reach the sill of the roof-light; that makes him a lot smaller, maybe not more than five feet.'

'So what?' grinned McCormick. 'We've a lot of "wee men" around this bloody city, and all of them trying to act big boys!' The grin turned into a smile.

'It's just a thought, McCormick.' Martin climbed into the car. The sergeant wasted no time in speeding out of the republican estate, heading for the main Belfast Road.

McCormick stood watching the car disappear. 'Bloody English!' he grumbled.

ATHENS

The noon flight brought Ivanov to Athens at 5 p.m. Greek time. He used one of several false passports that had been supplied for him. Ivanov spent most of the three-hour flight dozing, trying to avoid needless conversation with an American lady in the adjoining seat. He kept his eyes tightly shut, hoping that the divorcee from New Jersey would turn her attentions towards someone else. She did. He made the 5.40 p.m. connection from Athens airport directly to Kalamata with just minutes to spare. Only carrying the minimum of hand-luggage, he was able to save time by squeezing through the crowds at the Athens Customs desk.

During the short thirty-minute flight from Athens, Ivanov took the opportunity to study some maps in the back of an Olympic Airways magazine. Kalamata was on the southern coastline of the Peloponnese, the peninsula set to the bottom of mainland Greece. Apart from that, his eyes wandered around the map, resting momentarily at the circle entitled Moscow. What was happening? Had there been any new developments? Alas, he would have to wait until getting back to London. Then there was Frazer Holbeck to consider. The man was a contradiction. He couldn't be trusted; he'd sell his soul if the devil didn't already possess it. Then there was Antonia Travis. There had been absolutely no need for Holbeck to introduce her to him. Why? And then there was his feeling for her – a kind of feeling that he had long since thought he'd lost for ever. The frustration of his blindness was overwhelming; for once on an operation he did not feel in control, and he had always relied on being two or three moves ahead of the enemy at all times. He was being dragged along; it was uncomfortable, if not unbearable.

KALAMATA, SOUTHERN GREECE

After landing at the joint civil and military airfield just outside Kalamata, Ivanov took a taxi into the town centre. It took a little searching before he found Sidirodromikou Strathmou Street. It was a pile of rubble. Over ninety per cent of all the buildings had been destroyed either partly or completely in Kalamata during a recent earthquake, and even after all this time the effects were still obvious; rebuilding was slow, for this was Greece and there was always tomorrow.

Some of the façades appeared quite normal from the outside; but on closer examination, through open shutters and cracked doorways, it was clear that many of the buildings had just collapsed within themselves. Before he was even aware of it, Ivanov was nervously rubbing the scar on his neck once again. He strolled towards the far end of the street and found a small café reopened amidst the destruction. A young man in a white apron joined him at his pavement table. Ivanov nodded to him.

'Glad to see someone's still in business!'

'What would you like, please?' The young man spoke clearly in English. His face broke into a wide grin, displaying two gold-capped teeth to one side of his mouth.

'Nescafé,' snapped Ivanov. 'And some information since you can speak English so well.' Ivanov pushed a torn fifty-dollar bill across the table to the wide-eyed young waiter. 'And you get the other half when I get my information.'

It took over an hour for the waiter to ascertain where Goukas had gone to. He rejoined Ivanov in a somewhat excited state. Goukas was still alive and now living at his shoreline taverna near Acroiliae, a fishing village some fourteen kilometres south of Kalamata.

To the waiter's clear delight he received the other half of the fifty-dollar bill for his service. After renting a car and finding a suitable hotel for an overnight stay, Ivanov drove directly to the taverna. It was not a grand affair by any standard. Like most buildings on the southern coastline it had a flat roof, and in the main appeared to be constructed of concrete blocks loosely skimmed with plaster and cement. Large cracks had appeared along one side of the building, clearly the result of the earthquake. There were a few people sitting around the small glass-topped tables which were located by the water's edge, just a few metres from the building.

Ivanov waited and watched from a safe distance. He saw the little fat balding man serving out several platters of grilled fish to some of the customers amidst a flurry of excitement as the young waiters hovered in the background, giving the little Greek a real air of importance, akin to some master chef preparing a *flambé* in the Café Royal in London. It just had to be Goukas. So as to avoid attention in the little village Ivanov headed back up the steep winding road and on to the main coast road to another taverna a little further back along the coastline.

BELFAST

Alec Martin thought over what he had learnt. He arrived back at the airport in time for the 7.15 p.m. shuttle to Heathrow. Bidding his driver goodbye he entered the airport terminal and, once satisfied the police were not watching him, he made straight for the Avis Car Hire desk. Twenty minutes later he was behind the wheel of a Datsun Bluebird saloon and heading towards the city of Belfast. The sights surprised him; the city had indeed been transformed over the years, but as he neared the Lower Falls and Clonard area strange reminiscences began to flood back through the mists of time. A street-corner, a pub now derelict, a street-sign – it was all coming back to him. He found Clonard Monastery without difficulty. Upon ringing the doorbell a young novice opened the tall oak panelled door. Martin was searching somewhat in the dark, hoping the man was still alive.

'May I speak to Father Thomas O'Neill, please?'

The nun seemed startled at the request. 'Old Father O'Neill, you mean?'

'That's right.' Martin smiled.

'Please come in. I'll see if he's receiving visitors at the present. Can I say who's calling, please?'

354

'My name's Alec Martin. The Father and I met many years ago.'

She closed the door and looked at the clock set high on the grey-painted wall.

'It's very late for him to see anyone, you know.' It was a rebuke; then she disappeared through a doorway at the end of the reception-hall, leaving Martin to stare at the dull surroundings. Minutes later she returned.

'The Father will see you but only just for a moment, Mr Martin. Please follow me.' The nun showed him to Father O'Neill's room. It was not much more than a large bedroom. To one side sat a single divan bed and free-standing wardrobe beside which stood a white handbasin and small mirrored cabinet above. At the other side of the room was an old man with a priest's collar, sitting back in an armchair beside a small table piled high with books. On top of the pile sat a large Bible embossed in gold. The old man's legs were wrapped tightly in a tartan rug, his slippered feet outstretched towards a small electric fire built into a mahogany-veneered surround covered with old photographs and personal items. The curtained window excluded the last remaining light of the evening. Now the only light came from a single bulb surrounded by a metal shade, suspended from the centre of the high ceiling. A wooden chair had been set beside the fireplace for the visitor. The nun crossed the room and switched off two bars of the electric fire, leaving only one still burning.

'I think the room's hot enough now, Father,' she shouted at the old man.

He raised a shaky hand in reply. As she passed Martin on the way out she stopped. 'You'll have to raise your voice. He's quite deaf, you know.'

Martin nodded and watched the nun leave before introducing himself to the old priest.

'My name is Alec Martin, Father. We met several years ago here in Belfast.' He extended his hand towards the priest.

'Can't shake hands . . . had a stroke . . . it affects my right side . . . little movement, you know.' The old priest stuttered out the words.

'I'm terribly sorry. I didn't know.' Martin was embarrassed.

355

'Sit yourself down, lad . . . What do they call you again?'

'Martin. Alec Martin.'

'English?'

'That's right, Father.'

The conversation continued for several minutes. He found the old man had retired as the parish priest for the area over ten years before. The old man was quite forthcoming. He had in fact been the eldest son of an RIC sergeant from Tipperary. He slowly related many stories to him until finally Martin wound him around to the reason for his visit.

'We met in 1972. I was a police officer with the Metropolitan Police, sent over here to help with some of the RUC investigations. That's why I've come to see you. It was during one of those investigations that I met you.'

'Really?' enquired the old man. 'And what was that?'

'The time all the soldiers were being killed by the sniper, mainly here in West Belfast. Do you remember?'

'No . . . I don't think I do . . . Wait, you were the one who came to me trying to find one of my parishioners, didn't you?' His tired eyes lit up at the recollection.

'That's right. He was called Harry Garand, and his wife Mary; and there was a young child, too.'

'I remember now all right. You feared Harry was dead, but his body had vanished, isn't that right?'

'Yes, that's right. I saw you several days after they had all disappeared. Did you ever hear from them after that?'

The old man stared at him for a few moments. Martin wondered if he had heard him. Then he spoke: 'Sure what would you be wanting to know that for after all these years?'

Martin began to tell him briefly of as much as he was able relating to the recent killings. It was clear from the response that the old priest had since been aware of Garand's involvement in the earlier killings. The American had become a form of cult figure on the Falls Road.

'His family, the woman and child . . . they perished shortly afterwards in that terrible fire in Dublin . . . a shocking business . . . you heard of the fire, didn't you?' Memories slipped back to the old priest.

'St Clement's Hostel, you mean?'

'That's right . . . I officiated at their burial meself, at the request of the Bishop of Dublin . . . I brought down to Dublin a bus-load of those that had known her . . . Oh, it was a sad, sad trip, that . . . I don't know what was worse, all them wailing women or the fact I couldn't nip off for a Guinness or two to quench me thirst.'

Martin did not know whether to laugh or remain solemn. The priest made the decision for him with his next utterance. 'You don't happen to have a wee dram on you, by any chance? . . . They don't allow me any more, you know.'

'I'm sorry,' replied Martin. Remembering about the hip-flask full of whisky that he kept in his coat pocket, he couldn't decide whether it was safe or not to let the old man have some.

'Pity.' The priest licked his lips.

'There was never any trace of the husband, then?'

The priest pulled out a red handkerchief from beneath his cassock and blew his nose. 'The husband, the American, that poor unfortunate, may the Lord forgive him for those terrible deeds . . . He must have been demented to do such things.' He wiped his nose again. 'They say it was what they did to him . . . following his arrest on internment night . . . that affected the balance of his mind, you see . . . and him a cripple and all . . . Of course he was born a Protestant, but that was a minor sin to those who knew him. He carried his disability with dignity . . . You're not a Protestant, are you?' The old priest looked as if he had just stumbled over his own words.

'No, I'm Catholic,' smiled Martin.

After that Father O'Neill's concentration appeared to slip. Martin stayed a while longer; he felt more than a little guilty at rushing off. The young novice returned with tea and biscuits at 9 p.m. From her look, Martin read the message clearly; it was time to go. He was hurriedly finishing off his tea when the old priest spoke again.

'Isn't it funny now – a Catholic priest requested to officiate at a Protestant's funeral?'

Alec Martin set his cup aside. 'Say that again, Father?'

'Oh, you mean about me officiating? Yes, I suppose it was strange that, but it was her request, Mary Garand's wish, and I couldn't deny that now, could I?'

Alec Martin couldn't believe his own ears. 'Where was he buried, Father?'

'Let me see now.' The old priest gazed away, as if digging into the depths of a lifetime's memories. 'Trim, it was. At the local Catholic cemetery there. Ay, Trim.'

'When did this take place?' Martin's head pounded.

'I think about . . . about a week or so after he'd been shot . . . At least, I think so . . . You know, the mind can play many tricks on you.'

'The body. Did you see the body?' insisted Martin.

The priest began to smile. 'Now, how can you have a funeral without a body?'

'Father, I can appreciate you saw a coffin, but perhaps it was closed?' He knelt down beside the old man.

'Yes, you're right; it was closed. It was an awful hurried affair, you see, attended only by his wife and that wee bundle of a child and a handful of others . . . It was a rotten day, I remember, pouring out of the heavens, gale-force winds . . . That coffin made a terrible splash in the waterlogged grave.' He smiled again. 'I'm surprised it didn't float up to the surface!'

'You said the Catholic cemetery at Trim, is that right?' continued Martin.

'The one at St Dorothea's Chapel, if I remember clearly . . . about a week or so after the shooting.'

'Why Trim?'

'A terrible business when the dead have to be buried away from the Six Counties in order to retain some of the decency and respect for the act of interment . . . I think it was the wife's decision to bury him there. She'd left the North, vowing never to return, poor creature.'

'Why were the wife and child never buried beside him at Trim?' Martin persisted, even after the nun had returned again to the room.

'You may take that up with the Bishop of Dublin. He decided on the burial arrangements for most of those poor homeless ones who died in the fire . . . You see, the fire was so intense they couldn't work out who half the bodies were, so a communal grave and headstone were more appropriate under the circumstances.'

'Thank you, Father.' Martin squeezed the old man's hand.

'And yer sure you haven't a wee dram on you?' the old priest whispered.

Alec Martin slipped out his small leather-covered hip-flask that his wife had bought him for his last birthday. He carried it with him everywhere; but the fact was he'd never used it or needed to, until now. He set the flask on the old priest's knee, careful to pull the rug to cover it. The old man's eyes lit up.

'God bless you, my son . . . I'll be saying a special one just for you tonight.'

Martin excused himself. His head still pounded, but now with new thoughts. How the hell had none of them ever discovered this before?

ACROILIAE FISHING VILLAGE, SOUTHERN GREECE
Tuesday, 30 June

He returned shortly after 1 a.m. The taverna had already closed, and he knew that Goukas lived above the restaurant in his first-floor apartment. The place was in darkness except for a dull light that shone out from inside the taverna. Ivanov crossed the square, careful to keep out of the moonlight and stay in the shadows of the buildings. He approached cautiously. There was no sign of life from the darkened first-floor living-quarters; perhaps Goukas was working late inside the taverna. He reached the plate-glass window next to the entrance; there was only the one way in. One of the double glass-fronted doors was open and swaying in the breeze now coming in off the sea. This could be a trap. Ivanov knelt down and peered inside. A single light bulb burnt from just above the bar counter; the place seemed empty. There was nothing else for it; he had to go in. He went in quietly, more than anticipating a trap now, but nothing happened. He moved slowly between the stacked tables and chairs which had been brought inside at closing-time and then towards the counter.

He saw the feet first, someone lying outstretched on the tiled floor. As he rounded the bar-counter he saw the pool of blood surrounding the boy's body. It was one of the two young waiters that had been helping Goukas earlier on; his throat had been cut. Ivanov picked up one of the heavy butcher's knives that hung on the wall next to the cooking-area and moved on towards the rear office and storage-area; it was pitch-dark. He turned on the light outside one of the offices, instantly illuminating the body of the other young waiter; he'd been similarly disposed of. The sixteen-year-old had been stripped to the waist and left sitting, slumped in a chair and drenched in his own blood. A thick pool of blood had spread out across the floor from where it had run down the legs of the wooden chair. His hands were bound behind him, and his neck had been slashed across, but he also bore a series of superficial slashes across his chest and stomach; he'd been tortured. He searched the rest of the ground floor; one of the offices had been ransacked, but there was no sign of Goukas.

The basement door was at the bottom of a small storage-area right at the rear of the premises. Ivanov peered down the steep stone steps that led to the wine-cellar; someone had left another light on down below. He descended slowly. The basement was quite large, stretching the entire length of the taverna. Five rows of wine-barrels piled three high segmented the room into four narrow passageways. Ivanov surveyed the place from the fourth step from the bottom; there was still no sign of Goukas. Then he heard the groan; it came from the far end of the room.

'Hello?' he sounded off, but there was no response.

He stayed in the passage next to the retaining wall where the first row of barrels had been piled up, keeping the fourteen-inch-bladed knife at the ready. As he neared the bottom of the room there was another groan, but fainter this time; it came from the left. At the end of the aisle of barrels to his left the room opened out into a work-area. Several long tables covered in wine-bottles stood in the centre of the floor; it was clearly the bottling-area. One of the large wine-barrels against the far wall had been opened. The front section, with the tap still attached, lay on the floor; the interior was a series of three shelves. It had clearly been someone's secret hiding-place.

Papers lay scattered around the floor below the mock wine-barrel. Ivanov picked some of them up; they were blank End User Certificates, necessary for the international transport of arms and explosives by licensed firearm-dealers – forgeries used by Goukas when he occasionally found it necessary.

Another groan. It was coming from an open doorway next to a pile of empty crates. He went over and shoved the heavy metal panelled door fully open. He had found Goukas. The little Greek was dangling from a meat-hook attached to one of the hanging-rails that stretched across the cold store. The hook had been inserted just under his left armpit, and he had been left dangling at an awkward angle only inches from the floor. He'd clearly lost a great deal of blood from the sight of his saturated clothing and the floor below him. A rat was feeding from the pool of blood; it scurried away as Ivanov entered the room. Goukas was barely conscious; his face had turned a grey colour, blood trickled from his mouth. Ivanov could see that the side of his lip had been cut. He lifted up the dying man by wrapping his arms around his torso and as gently as he could he eased him on to the floor, careful not to let the meat-hook dig further into him.

'What happened?' He patted the Greek's face. Goukas's eyes flickered open; he tried to speak. It was then Ivanov realized someone had cut out his tongue; a mixture of congealed and fresh blood vomited up through the man's mouth. 'Did they get what they were after?' continued Ivanov.

Goukas almost passed out. He gripped on to the Russian's arm with his right hand; from the weakness in his grip he had little time left. He managed to turn his head sideways once and then again.

'Where is it?' Ivanov persisted.

The man let go of his arm and unsteadily drew his arm back, only just managing to raise it towards several lamb carcasses hanging to one side. He convulsed; he tried to rise, getting his head nearly a foot off the ground; his eyes bulged from their darkened sockets; more blood, bright orange in tone, issued forth from his mouth. Then he went totally limp, dead in the Russian's arms. Ivanov eased him down. The rat scampered across the floor heading for the door, trailing something from its mouth; it was Goukas's tongue.

Ivanov didn't take long to find the clear plastic bag wedged inside the skinned carcass of the ewe lamb; it contained a cassette tape, some papers, and a photograph. Ivanov looked at the photo of Goukas talking to a much taller man in a denim suit. From the blurred imagery around the edges of the photograph it seemed that it had been taken with a telephoto lens. Ivanov didn't know it yet, but he was staring at the side-profile of 'George'. He cleared out fast. Just as he almost reached the ground-floor exit he heard the siren. Ivanov doused the light and headed outside, keeping in the shadow of the building as he sneaked round the rear. He had just managed to get out of sight when the police car skidded to a stop outside the taverna entrance. The two uniformed Greek policemen tore out of their saloon car and straight inside. Someone had tried to set him up.

He headed out of the tiny fishing village, taking one of the winding paths up to where he'd left his hired car, just off the main coast road which ran along the cliff-top. There was nothing for it now but a six-hour treacherous drive back to Athens through the mountains. When news of the killings became public it wouldn't take very long for the police to obtain his description from the waiter back in Kalamata – that was, if they didn't already have it from whoever had set him up.

LONDON
Tuesday, 30 June

Regardless of Ivanov's advice, Antonia Travis complied with the summons to Holbeck's Curzon Street office. She arrived just after 10 a.m. and was met by Holbeck's PA.

'Miss Travis! What a pleasant surprise.' The woman stood up to greet her.

'Morning, Ann. Afraid I'm a little late. Shall I go on through?'

'I'm so sorry, madam, but Colonel Holbeck's come down with the flu. His maid was on the telephone first thing this morning.'

'He said it was important we had a meeting,' replied Travis. 'I don't suppose you have any idea what it's about?'

'No, I'm sorry, madam,' smiled the woman as she arose from behind her desk. 'Can I get you a cup of tea? You look as if you could do with one.'

'Thanks, but no. I've a conference back in Cheltenham later this afternoon.'

'I did try to get you, but you'd already left your house,' the woman continued apologetically.

'I've been on the road since early this morning. Look, I'll go on. If the colonel rings in, have him call me at GCHQ.'

'Certainly, madam. Good morning.'

Antonia Travis left the Curzon Street building and walked straight to the carpark, but her Ford Escort wouldn't start. Even the carpark attendant couldn't help her. She used his office to summon the Automobile Association, but it was all going to take time – time she didn't have. She left the car keys with the reluctant attendant, agreeing to arrange for someone to pick up the car later on once the AA mechanic had attended to it. There was nothing else for it; Green Park Underground station was just down the road – she could get a connection to a main-line station and take the train back to Cheltenham.

The Tube station was crowded as usual, commuters jostling on the platform as the train approached. The overhead sign flickered: two minutes until the next arrival. She waited. Another train pulled in on the platform behind, a thunderous noise; then the train stopped, disgorging its passengers, some of whom came straight on to the platform beside her. A crowd of about one hundred and fifty had now gathered; she could feel the wind being forced up the tunnel towards her as the train approached, then a rumble, growing louder by the second. The sound increased considerably as the train made its final approach; the brakes screeched and squealed as the metal wheels bit into the tracks. A light now appeared from the tunnel, the rush of air lifted her short hair up from the side of her face.

She adjusted her black-rimmed spectacles and gripped her shoulder-bag a little more tightly as the people around her began to push and shove against her; she was almost standing on the white line that was painted along the edge of the platform. Suddenly she felt the rush. No, it wasn't the air from the tunnel; it was a rush of fear, inexplicable, except that she kept remembering Ivanov's advice. Images flashed of that old black and white movie she'd seen of the man being pushed off the Underground platform in front of the speeding train. She panicked; she had to get away, get back to the surface.

It was when she turned, shoving back against the bodies, that she saw him. Unlike everyone else on the platform, the dark-haired man with the pale scar over his right eye was watching her, not the incoming train. Kapitsa was standing almost behind her; an elderly Indian woman was the only obstacle between them. The GRU captain stared at her blankly; it terrified her. Travis pushed aside, almost falling on to the high-voltage lines in any case. Two young university students grabbed hold of her just in time, and she pushed in through the crowd towards the main exit. Kapitsa tried to follow, but the train heading for King's Cross had just about rumbled to a noisy halt; the train's automatic doors opened a second later, and people began to fight their way in and out. Kapitsa was caught up in the wave of communal movement; by the time he managed to follow, Antonia Travis had disappeared.

TRIM, COUNTY MEATH, REPUBLIC OF IRELAND
The same morning

It was amazing what a hundred pounds sterling in the hand of the groundsman of St Dorothea's did to loosen his attitude towards helping. Alec Martin established the location of the unmarked grave. It was relatively simple. After checking the approximate date of interment the groundsman conferred with the churchyard ledger and then a map of the cemetery layout.

There it was in area G2, number 36, under the name of Malloy, Mary Garand's maiden name.

It took the JCB digger just over five minutes to scoop the earth from above the coffin lying in the unmarked grave beside the oak tree. The tree's root system had grown across the area of the grave quite substantially over the years since the burial; it somewhat inhibited ready access. Finally the grave lay open; there four feet down lay the top of the coffin, bare except for a few remnants of dirt. The groundsman was obviously quite expert at his job of opening graves, manipulating the digger-scoop precisely, so as not to damage any of the coffins already buried. Martin stared into the grave; the groundsman jumped down from the digger to join him.

'Drop the scoop on to the coffin lid,' demanded Martin.

'What?' cried the man over the engine noise.

'Break the lid off that coffin!' insisted Martin.

'Mister, you paid me to open the grave, and that was it; you said nothing about any exhumation.' The man was indignant; he saw an opportunity to steal another fifty notes. Martin turned back, and climbed on to the digger, pushing the red lever forward. The scoop, hanging directly over the grave, was sent crashing into the hole. The groundsman dived for cover as the scoop slammed on to the coffin lid, splintering the rotten wood. Martin pulled the keys out of the digger's ignition before returning to the graveside. Now there was silence. The coffin lay split open. From beneath the teeth of the dormant mechanical shovel Martin could see only sand and the remnants of the rotting sandbags.

'Hey, you! You bloody fool! Give me them keys right now!' The groundsman pulled Martin by the shoulder before staring into the grave himself. His eyes widened. 'What the hell . . . !'

Martin slapped the keys into his hand. 'Here, fill up the hole.'

ATHENS
Several hours later

The civilized sights of Athens were in stark contrast to the southern Peloponnese. Ivanov took a taxi to the city centre, booking a room at the Olympic Palace Hotel in Filellinon Street. The air-conditioned bedroom was a welcome luxury after suffering the midday heat in the traffic-congested streets around the city. Ivanov managed to borrow a cassette tape recorder from the hotel management. He ran through the tape he'd obtained from the taverna; it ran for only just over four minutes, but by the time it had ended he knew there was little time left.

The Athens embassy of the Soviet Union is situated at 28 Nikoforou Litra Street. It is constantly monitored by the Greek security service, and every person entering or leaving the embassy is noted, just as every telephone communication is intercepted and recorded. The Russians had long since balanced the disadvantage of constant surveillance. Their unofficial activity was now centred well away from 28 Nikoforou Litra Street, and combined with sophisticated radio and laser communications facilities at the embassy they continued to keep at least one step ahead of their watchers.

There are set procedures in every capital in the world for a Soviet GRU agent to contact his *resident* at the Soviet consulate or embassy without ever having to go near the place. Athens was no exception. The practice is simple. The mode of contact is a 'one-time' method. It can never be used again for fear of compromise; therefore it is only used in the most essential and desperate of circumstances. Ivanov looked up the telephone-book and dialled the Athens number, using a kiosk several blocks away from his hotel. He dialled the number 672–5325, and then waited. After nearly a minute it was answered.

'Good afternoon,' a female voice said curtly in Russian.

'I am a Soviet citizen visiting here in Athens. I have lost my wallet. I think I left it in a taxi or perhaps a bar. Can you help me?' Ivanov kept to his mother language.

366

Hesitation, then the woman telephonist replied: 'If you will hold on, please, I will get someone to assist you.'

Ivanov already had his pad and pencil ready.

'Can I help you, comrade?' It was a man's voice this time, still in Russian; then, it had to be.

'I have lost my wallet. I think I left it in a taxi or perhaps a bar.'

'Yes, I think we can assist you, comrade. You should first report the loss to the police; you will find their number in the directory.' The man chose his words very carefully; he had to.

'Thank you, comrade. If I need any further assistance, I will ring again. Good day.'

'Good day, comrade,' the man replied casually.

The initial contact had been made. Ivanov checked his note pad to ensure he had all the words down perfectly. He had. He left the kiosk and headed for a café further up the street. His reasons were twofold; first, he could wait and see if the Greek authorities had traced the call and any of their security people turned up at the kiosk; second, he needed the opportunity to decipher the information contained in the man's statement. The words were first joined together without any gaps, then every fifth letter was converted to its numerical equivalent. After five minutes Ivanov was left holding the code name and telephone number of his secondary contact.

'Spyros – 321–0601.'

Ivanov waited a further ten minutes. No one showed up at the kiosk; so far at least he was in the clear. He moved on down the street and into a small piano-bar. There was a safety feature built into the contact procedure. Ivanov had only two windows daily when he could make further contact along the chain; the first was between 10 a.m. and 12 noon, the other was during the period 2 p.m. to 4 p.m. It was already 3.56 p.m. He dialled the number quickly, hoping that 'Spyros' didn't suffer from a lazy streak. The number rang for nearly two minutes. Ivanov watched the clock above the bar tick away towards the hour; he was just about to call it a day when the telephone was answered.

'Yes?' a man's voice said wearily in English. It seemed as if Ivanov was right; the man had been having a siesta.

'Spyros?'

'Yes.' The voice changed now; the man was alert and precise. The primary contact had been made.

'Are there any delays in the flight to Moscow today?' Ivanov followed the procedure to the letter.

'Maybe,' the man said casually. 'Ring 646–8103 today.'

Ivanov quickly hung up. To anyone listening in, the Athens telephone number just quoted was real, but it was not necessarily correct. The answer lay in the last word. 'Spyros' could have said one of three things – 'now', 'soon' or 'today'. Depending on the word given, certain amendments had then to be made to the last four digits. Even if a foreign intelligence agency had broken into the contact chain this far in, a computer interrogation of the number and possible permutations would result in literally a six-figure list of possible intercepts. It would take days to sort out. Ivanov only needed two hours at the most. Already 'Spyros' was cleaning up his apartment; his role in Athens had come to an end. In less than twenty-four hours he would be across the Albanian border; already 'Spyros' no longer existed.

The walk to the dentist's surgery on Vasilissis Sofias Street could have been accomplished inside ten minutes from the hotel, but Ivanov followed procedure. It took him over forty minutes of painstaking backtracking and deviation before he was satisfied that no one was following. Already it was approaching closing-time. He could ill afford to wait any longer; the danger of a delay until the following day was too great. He studied the entrance to the dentist's surgery from the news-stand across the busy road. Therein lay the real danger. The contact-point could have already been blown and, whilst his instructions from Moscow Centre had been specific on no contact apart from Mogul, he now knew that caution must be cast aside, regardless of the fact that someone had sanctioned Shipkov to kill him. His senses told him to stay away, but there was only one way to disprove his suspicions. He crossed the road and went into the building.

The dentist's offices were on the first floor, large and spacious. Ivanov introduced himself as Pierre Thibeau, a Canadian; gesticulating wildly, he explained to the young Greek receptionist about his severe toothache. He was sympathetically shown into a waiting-room fronting on to the street. There were only two patients before him; one was an elderly lady, well dressed and clutching firmly a red crocodile-skin handbag amidst a pair of chubby hands festooned with diamonds and gold; the other was a young Asian man with long straggly hair and thick-lensed spectacles who was preoccupied with holding the left side of his rather swollen face, cringing almost continuously. The man was seen first, and eventually after almost half an hour the woman was called. Ivanov took the opportunity to survey the place. From the large plate-glass window he could see the continuous flow of traffic and pedestrians below. The pavement across the road was somewhat constricted by the news-stand and a kiosk selling sweets and tobacco. As he stared down a young man in jeans and a white T-shirt arrived at the kiosk. He exchanged a few words with the woman behind the counter. Afterwards they changed places and she left carrying a large shopping-bag. After serving several customers the young man in the T-shirt allowed himself a glance up directly towards the dentist's surgery.

'Next, please.'

Ivanov turned to find the young female dentist standing smiling at the open door. After he was seated and had explained his supposed problem, she began her examination whilst her male assistant busily sterilized the instruments used on the previous patient. She was not pretty – plump with thick black hair that was tied back in a bun. She gave the impression of being middle-aged rather than a thirty-year-old. Her white coat was inches too long and two sizes too big, rolled up at the sleeves and draped over her rounded shoulders like a sack. After she removed the probe from his mouth he played his card.

'You are Anna Bassakaropolos, are you not?' He spoke in English.

'Yes, that is correct,' she answered back in English, and then stood back from him, a curious expression filling her round face.

'You were highly recommended by my friend. He studied with you, I believe.'

'And who might he be?' she replied again in English, her words stumbling out.

'Spyros.'

She smiled. 'Oh, yes. How is he? I have not seen him for three years now.'

'Fine. He still works in Rome. I saw him last on June the twelfth. He sends his warmest regards.' The contact had been made.

She studied Ivanov for several seconds. 'I think you have an abscess under that tooth. For the present all I can do is inject you with something to numb the pain. I can also give you a course of antibiotics to reduce the infection.'

He nodded.

She turned to the assistant, reverting to Greek. 'Kostas, you can pack up now; it's time to close anyway. I'll fix up the gentleman myself.'

The young man nodded and quickly left. The dentist returned to Ivanov.

'I will have to give you an injection into the gum beside that tooth.' Her voice was raised as if to carry through the glass door. She leant over him and continued to examine his mouth, speaking in a much softer tone. 'You are my twenty-fourth patient today.'

Ivanov nodded slowly; she had accepted the contact. She leant over, pretending to inject the gums. As she did so Ivanov slipped a folded sheet of paper into her hand. The woman stepped back. Ivanov clutched her wrist firmly; her face turned red.

'This injection? It will work immediately, will it not?'

'Of course.'

He let go, acknowledging the glare in her eyes. She hurriedly scribbled on the prescription-pad and tore out the top sheet, handing it to him. 'Take this to any pharmacist. One tablet each morning and evening for seven days. Then come back and I'll see what I can do with the tooth.'

He left without further conversation. Once in the hallway outside the surgery he glanced at the form. It said simply: 'Being watched.' There was only the one entrance; he had little choice but to brave the elements. The opposition was unknown except for the young man still present at the kiosk opposite. He passed on to the street slowly; there was no point in alerting them any more than was necessary. He headed west towards the parliament buildings and on through a labyrinth of narrow backstreets just off the main thoroughfare. It took some time before he could establish just how many were actually tailing him. There was a female dressed in jeans and a denim jacket behind him on the same side of the road, and further back on the far side a man in a light grey suit with his jacket thrown back over one shoulder. Ivanov turned right at the next junction. Two hundred metres further down the street a sign projected over the pavement from above a doorway. The red and yellow sign was in Japanese on one side and in English on the other; it read: 'Shogun Japanese Cuisine.' He paused as if to study the menu displayed in the window. He could see their reflection clearly in the glass. The girl began to cross the street diagonally away from him; the man in the grey suit entered a bookshop at the street-corner just up from him.

'Amateurs,' muttered Ivanov.

Once inside he ordered only tea. Quietly excusing himself, he strolled to the toilets. The small window opened directly into a rear yard, and within seconds he was through the narrow opening, across the service yard and out past an open gateway leading down a passageway on to another street. Instead of leaving the confines of the street and chancing a run-in with his watchers, Ivanov made a straight line into the rear entrance of an apartment store directly opposite. He passed through the store, finally arriving at another exit which he estimated now placed him two blocks away from his followers.

He glanced around momentarily as he swung the glass door open. There, only feet away amidst the store's sports section, was another watcher, a stocky young man who was visibly sweating. The blond-haired young man, in a red T-shirt and white trousers, rushed past Ivanov at the exit, squeezing past the shoppers in the process. Ivanov knew the ploy well; the watcher had professionally frisked him for a concealed weapon as he briefly passed by. The man now knew that Ivanov had no gun under his jacket, but that was all. It was a silly move, a move more out of panic than anything else; Ivanov could still possess a gun or knife concealed in at least four or five other places. Ivanov left the exit point and strolled back into the store, ostensibly to examine a row of tracksuits. The watcher had read the ploy and approached a uniformed security guard just outside the exit point. They both looked back into the store in his direction.

It was then that Ivanov found the gold cigarette-lighter in his jacket pocket. The watcher had been more clever than he had expected. It was perfectly simple: he was being set up for being a pickpocket, which, in turn, would involve the local police, then a passport seizure – the works. It would be only a matter of time before the inevitable happened. Ivanov paused briefly, igniting the lighter and setting it inside the pocket of one of the cotton tracksuits; immediately he began to move towards a further exit to his right which would place him at a street-corner in line with the junction of another street. The security guard and watcher re-entered the building in pursuit. Suddenly there was a scream, followed by another; someone else shrieked, another cried. Then the fire-alarm bells began to sound. By now smoke and flames bellowed from the sportswear department. The line of tracksuits was well ablaze, fanned by the ceiling ventilation system which had yet to be turned off. Ivanov passed easily into the street and headed south towards the area of his hotel.

The watcher charged into the street behind him and began to run directly towards him; he was clearly in peak physical condition and began gaining on him immediately. Ivanov ran down a staircase leading to a basement barber's shop. The watcher made his one and final mistake. On seeing the door to the barber's shop lying partly open he followed his target. An enclosed area is not the place to go when your opponent has already got the advantage of being there. The young man was descending the stone steps, turning half-way down as he neared the entrance door, when he was violently pulled downwards by the ankles. His legs went from under him; he thudded into the steps, taking the full force on his back and smacking his head on a side-rail. Powerful arms reached out from the shadows under the return staircase; there was no time for questions now. Clenched knuckles slammed into the man's larynx, snapping the bone. The young man hopelessly fought for breath and began to pull at his throat, writhing wildly. Ivanov quickly checked the struggling and dying man for identification. He found a wallet containing a Greek driving licence in the name of Lou Vergas. There was no other identification, but the watch on the man's left wrist told him what he wanted. He ascended the steps leaving the writhing man to die on the darkened staircase, quickly rejoining the milling crowds in the street above.

Meanwhile an hour later a delivery of pizzas was left at the service entrance of 28 Nikoforou Litra Street. The delivery boy left the invoice as directed by the manager of the pizzeria. The food was taken to the main kitchen and as instructed a junior GRU officer took the invoice directly to the second-floor office of the GRU *rezident* in Athens, Major Colonel Produkin. The colonel locked his door and pulled a loose-leaf pad on to his desk. He examined the invoice and began to write out the prices from left to right. When completed he used a cipher-book from his wall-safe to formulate the expression. Finally he sat staring at fifteen letters of the alphabet, none of which made any sense to him and rightly so. The encoded message was transmitted to Moscow Centre within the hour.

THE MEDITERRANEAN SEA
Tuesday, 30 June. 7 p.m. local time
Autumn Harvest: zero minus 150 hours

The three-hundred-and-twenty-foot luxury yacht was anchored some twenty miles north of Malta. Señor Juan P. Lopez sat in his wheelchair on the rear sun-deck watching the evening sunset. Right on schedule the red and white helicopter buzzed into view only fifty feet above the calm surface, a white light beaming out from its belly. The Aérospatiale Ecureuil helicopter banked up and circled the yacht slowly before easing into a steady landing position on the helicopter-deck situated to the rear of the yacht's elevated bridge. A lone crewman guided the pilot in safely as the old Spaniard was wheeled indoors by one of the attendants. He had just locked his wheelchair into position beside the large mahogany dining-table when the Arab was shown inside. The two men waited until the door closed before they greeted one another.

'Nice to see you again, my friend,' smiled the Spaniard.

'Señor,' replied George, bowing his head slightly as a mark of respect.

'It has been some time since we last met. I am sure much has happened to you.' Lopez removed his hat.

'Have you not received any messages?' The Arab stared in puzzlement.

'Of course I have, George, but your information was minimal. I want to hear all the details. Please sit down; we have much to discuss.'

The old Spaniard poured brandy from a crystal decanter. George inspected the room; it was entirely panelled in mahogany, the wood grain and panelling highlighted by numerous wall-lamps and spotlights sunk into the ceiling which in turn was covered entirely in cream-coloured hide. On the walls hung several Picassos and a Dali oil painting. In pride of place hung a photograph of King Juan Carlos shaking hands with one of his closest advisers; the man in the wheelchair smiled back at the king, the warmth of the greeting plainly evident.

'You move in high circles,' commented George.

'I assume you haven't had a return to religion.' Lopez handed a half-full brandy glass to his guest.

The Arab accepted the glass gratefully, ignoring the obvious insult.

'A toast. To Autumn Harvest,' continued the Spaniard, raising his glass.

'To Autumn Harvest,' replied the Arab, touching the glass with his own. They both drank deeply.

'Now to business, my friend. The training – it is all complete, is it not?' quizzed Lopez.

'Yes.' The Arab removed a videotape from his jacket pocket and set it in the middle of the table. 'For your edification, señor, a film of the final training scenes.'

The Spaniard frowned. 'You take chances yet again.'

'We all take chances,' retorted George. 'What about the supplies? Have they arrived yet?'

'They are already ashore, in the docks at Glasgow in Scotland, landed by a Spanish-registered cargo ship on the nineteenth – part of a consignment of car parts. Everything went through very smoothly; no hitches at all, including the explosives that we had sent via a tea shipment from India. And you – what about your men?'

'The first will begin to filter into Britain by tonight. Travelling alone or in groups of two or three, they should all be in the country by the weekend. Have you a date yet for the conference?'

'Yes, but owing to a change in their security arrangements the British are changing the venue from their Prime Minister's country residence at Chequers.'

The Arab set his glass aside. 'Then it can't go ahead.'

'On the contrary, we already knew their second option for the venue, and the new security arrangements they now have make the operation even easier.'

'Where is it?'

'Chevering Hall, East Sussex. I have all the maps and outlines of security-alarm systems awaiting your arrival in England. You will get them from your contact there.'

'Who is the contact?'

The Spaniard opened the briefcase beside him and handed the Arab a photograph.

'She's called Sister Marianne, a nun. She is a librarian at St Louise's Convent School at Mayfield, also in East Sussex, only twelve miles from your intended target.'

George stared at the broken scarred features and penetrating eyes of the old nun. 'What happened to this poor creature?'

The Spaniard tapped his silver engraved cane against one of the table legs. 'You might say it was self-inflicted!'

'And what of the other target?' asked George.

'Taken care of.' Lopez stared at the old nun's photograph. 'We'll leave that to Sister Marianne.'

The Arab raised his glass again. 'To the success of Autumn Harvest!'

'Likewise.' Lopez saluted with his glass. '*Y vaya con su dios.*'

The helicopter took off again and headed back for the Sicilian coastline just thirty-five miles away. Lopez prepared his coded report and then passed it to the ship's radio room; the chairman of the 1st Chief Directorate did not like to be kept waiting. While Señor Lopez was almost eighty years old, and had been a cripple since the Spanish Civil War, appearances could be deceptive. For the last twenty years he had held a senior position in the KGB's Executive Action Department, known inside the KGB as Department V. It was the highest position a non-Soviet could hold, and while Lopez only held the official rank of colonel he wielded formidable power. For two years now he had been under the direct control of Chairman Glazkov and with the help of 'George' he had followed the KGB chairman's plan to the letter. There was much Lopez did not understand, and he distrusted 'George' totally, but orders were orders, even if you were in the shadow of your own grave.

LONDON
Wednesday, 1 July
Autumn Harvest: zero minus 133 hours 30 minutes

Ivanov had gone straight to Athens International Airport and taken the first available flight out of the country, an Air France A-300 airbus to Charles de Gaulle Airport at Paris; from there he was able to get a direct flight back to London. He couldn't risk waiting for the next scheduled flight from Athens to London or even returning to the hotel. The gloves were off now; they wanted him out of the way permanently.

Ivanov spent the return flight checking through his briefcase. Goukas had given him some vital clues, but would he still have enough time to stop it happening?

He made straight for the safe house he had established just off the Bayswater Road during his first three days in England; it was his ace in the hole, and Holbeck's Chelsea address was no longer a safe option. After relaxing in a hot shower and changing into some fresh clothing he rang the Chelsea apartment using his code to check the answering machine. There was just one message; it was from Antonia Travis, and she sounded frightened. Ivanov was just about to lift the receiver to ring her when the telephone rang. It was Alec Martin, and he was in trouble.

'Thank God I found you!' Alec Martin sounded close to panic.

'What's up?'

'I just got back into Heathrow a couple of hours ago. I can't be sure, but I think I'm being followed.'

'Where are you now, Alec?'

'I'm in the Tate Gallery.'

'I know it. Stay there, and stay in a public place; they'll be less likely to try something with witnesses about.'

'Great! I stand here like some prize chicken while a bastard sticks an umbrella-point into my leg!'

'Is it raining?' Ivanov checked the London street-map. The gallery wasn't too far away; he could be there in minutes.

'Cut the wise-arse stuff and for God's sake help me. They've been on my tail ever since I got into Heathrow!'

'How many of them are there?'

'Two for sure, maybe three. How the hell do I know? Just get me out of here.'

'On my way. Stall a bit, then head for the entrance. Try not to go outside until I get there.'

'Just bloody hurry up, will you?' snapped Martin as he started counting the seconds away.

The Ford Sierra screeched up outside the Tate Gallery. Alec Martin timed the arrival perfectly; he was just pushing out through the glass doors when Ivanov arrived, but a party of schoolchildren were walking up the wide series of steps directly in Alec Martin's path.

'Damn,' grunted Ivanov as he watched the crowd of school-children impede Martin's exit.

The uniformed school outing was already beginning to file in past the civilian security guard standing at the entrance. Two men, both in their late twenties, shoved out past the children as they tried to catch up with the Englishman. Alec Martin glanced around and then began to run.

'Come on!' urged Ivanov, flinging the front passenger-door open.

Another man, slightly older than the other two men, burst out of a side-entrance and began shouting to his associates. He was also looking down towards Lambeth Bridge and began to speak at the same time. Ivanov realized what was happening instantly. The man was wearing what appeared to be a hearing aid; it was in fact part of a radio transmitter. He was speaking into a throat microphone concealed under his cravat and calling his back-up. The two fit-looking young men were gaining on Alec Martin. Game as he was, he was just no match for them. Some of the children suddenly began screaming as one of the men pulled out a snub-nosed revolver from under his jacket. Alec Martin was just reaching the pavement when the man aimed.

'Down!' shouted Ivanov.

Alec Martin didn't hesitate; he flung himself on to the pavement beside the open car door. Ivanov fired twice through the open passenger-door, hitting the gunman both times in the heart. His associate grabbed several of the screaming schoolgirls and began firing at the Ford Sierra. Martin tried to get up from the pavement and into the car.

'Stay down, Alec!' Ivanov gritted his teeth, quietly cursing in Russian as he aimed for the man's head.

The gunman went to fire again; as Ivanov anticipated, he revealed a target from the shoulder upwards. Ivanov fired, using both hands to steady his aim; the single shot was all he could afford. The second gunman's neck exploded in a sea of bright blood covering the hysterical schoolgirls as he was tossed backwards on to the steps.

'Get in!' urged Ivanov.

Alec Martin needed no second reminder. He had barely climbed into the Ford Sierra when the third man began firing with an Ingram sub-machine-gun. The side of the car was ripped asunder as Ivanov punched the accelerator; the car lifted off from the kerbside, wheels spinning over the asphalt surface as it raced out of the lay-by on to the road. Just ahead on the far side of the road a Peugeot saloon made an emergency stop.

'Stay down and brace yourself!' shouted Ivanov, pulling the Ford Sierra left into a side-street just as a further gunman in the rear of the Peugeot opened up with a burst of automatic fire. Alec Martin was no coward, but he couldn't help but cringe as the rear windscreen shattered in around him.

'Can't you drive a little faster?' he appealed to the Russian. The car banked right and then seconds later a sharp left down past Westminster Hospital. 'Just who the hell were those bastards?'

'Terrorists,' retorted Ivanov, looking behind. There was no tail; they had made it. 'The official sort.'

'What?'

'I'll tell you about it later.' Ivanov began to slow down a little.

'Let's find the nearest cop shop,' urged Martin.

'Can't do that. They're looking for you at the moment.' He dropped into second gear as he reached a corner. 'Something to do with all the bodies that keep on appearing in the vicinity of your house.'

'Talking of bodies, I think you'd better brace yourself! Garand's not dead. I found his grave; the coffin is full of sandbags.'

'And the Greek was making more explosive bullets for his rifle,' retorted Ivanov.

'Bloody brilliant! Then, what can we do?'

'Let's dump this car, and I'll tell you.'

After dumping the car into the river at the East India Docks, they walked for several miles before taking a taxi to the West End. Forty minutes later they arrived at the safe house in Albion Mews just off Bayswater Road. The apartment was on the third floor. Alec Martin went to the window and looked out towards the Georgian façade on the opposite side of the mews.

'What is this place? Why didn't we go back to the other apartment?'

'Too risky. Nobody knows about this place, and that includes Holbeck.'

'You don't trust him?'

'I don't trust anyone.'

'I could do with a drink!' grunted Martin.

'Do with that instead,' retorted Ivanov, tossing a large envelope in front of the Englishman.

Martin pulled out the contents.

Ivanov continued: 'It's a present from Goukas. By the way, somebody got to him before I did. I found him dangling from a meat-hook, with his tongue cut out; he died in my arms.'

Martin glared back at the Russian. 'Just what the hell have I got into?'

'What's more important is this.' He tossed across the cassette tape. 'It's part of a conversation between Goukas and the ugly mug in that photograph.'

Martin studied the photograph. 'George?' he asked, but in his heart he already knew the answer.

'Yep! It would appear that over recent years the Greek had taken out a little life insurance. Where possible he kept a record of his transactions and his transactors. Whoever left him to die on that meat-hook thought they'd got every incriminating bit of evidence he had, but they missed that lot.'

'But how the hell did they get to him before you?'

'Only three people knew I was going there: you, Holbeck, and a woman called Antonia Travis – she works at GCHQ. It's not you, so it's down to one or maybe both of them.' Ivanov threw off his coat. 'Tell me, when did you pick up the tail?'

'At Heathrow when I flew in from Dublin, it had to be.'

'Alec, Holbeck knew you were in Ireland.'

'I thought he was on your side!'

'I'm not ruling out anything for the moment. Study that and I'll tell you about the tape afterwards.'

Ivanov left the Englishman to digest the latest evidence; he went to one of the other rooms and dialled the number. It rang for over a minute before it was answered.

'Yes?' The woman was hesitant.

'Antonia, it's me.'

'Thank goodness. I've been trying to reach you for ages.' She sounded close to tears.

'I've just got back. What is it?'

'I think someone tried to kill me.' Her voice quivered.

'You *think*?' He was concerned, but he had to assess this clinically.

'Yesterday morning, Holbeck sent for me.' She was getting out the words in short bursts. 'When I got to his office he wasn't there. I left, but my car wouldn't start. I went to the nearest Tube station. I was standing at the edge of the platform waiting for the next train. When something made me turn around, and there he was.'

'Holbeck?'

'No. A man. It was the way he was looking right at me. If it hadn't been for a woman squeezing between us, I might have been . . .' She couldn't go on.

'Describe him.'

'I think in his thirties, with black hair; he had a scar across one eye. He tried to follow me, but I escaped in the crowds.'

Ivanov's face hardened. 'You're sure you couldn't have imagined all this?'

'Tucker, I had the Automobile Association send one of their mechanics out to my car. Someone had tampered with the distributor cap!'

'Have you spoken to Holbeck since?'

'No. He's still at his home; apparently he's down with the flu. I've stayed at home myself.'

'Antonia, I don't think you've anything to worry about, but stay inside; I'll get to you by tonight.'

'Thanks, Tucker, that's a load off my mind. I'll see you later.' As she hung up a blue BMW saloon drove past the end of her driveway. Kapitsa studied the house very carefully.

Ivanov returned to the lounge. Alec Martin had gone through the papers for a second time.

'According to these papers a large arms shipment was delivered to George just a year ago; part of that same shipment included three hundred cartridges for a Garand rifle. At George's specific request Goukas numbered and doctored precisely eight of the cartridges in exactly the same fashion as those recovered from the Garand killings in 1972. All the cartridge-casings recovered during the 1972 shootings were franked and numbered in chronological order. As that forensic report showed, the casings from Londonderry and Dublin were consecutively numbered to follow on from the 1972 killings.'

'So?' Ivanov was too concerned about Antonia to reason it out for himself.

'So I deduce, dear Watson, that our murderer still intends to kill at least six more people if he has any sense of poetry.'

'I have passed on a request to Moscow to get information on this George character. I should know soon enough.'

'Tell me, just who the hell were those bastards back there at the gallery?' Alec Martin loosened his tie.

'From an educated guess I'd say they were KGB; they were after me in Athens after they failed to fix me up for a murder rap.'

'What makes you so sure it's the KGB?'

'They used classic KGB tactics at the Tate Gallery. I'd say at a guess the KGB *resident* used his own henchmen based here in London. If they'd used their boys from Department Five, you would never have made it to the car. The other point to consider is that I was followed from outside my hotel in Athens and when I confronted the man following me he was wearing a Boljot wrist-watch. The odds against a Greek wearing a Russian wrist-watch like that are too high to ignore.'

'Where do these terrorists fit in? Just who's working for who?'

'That is the million-dollar question.'

'And Garand?' Martin felt nauseous just thinking about the American.

'That's the two-million-dollar question,' Ivanov sighed.

'What about the tape?' continued Martin.

'It's part of a conversation between Goukas and this son of a bitch called George. It relates to another arms shipment which was being sent to a wharf number three at Glasgow docks on the nineteenth. My guess is that the nineteenth means the nineteenth of June; in other words, last month.'

'Why last month?' questioned Martin.

'The young Irish terrorist I spoke to said it would all be over in a few days; he was no more specific than that.'

Martin looked at the date on his watch. 'Tucker, it's already July!'

'Precisely, old chap; we may be too late. That's why, with yet another dead end, we've got to clutch at this straw.'

'But we still don't know the target!'

'During the taped conversation, this George guy mouthed off a bit about bringing every Western government of the

NATO alliance to their knees; he sounded high on drugs or his own ego. Whatever they have planned it's big, real big!'

'Tucker, there's a NATO conference to be held in six days. I heard it on the news. It's at Chequers, I think.'

'That's it! It's got to be! Look, you've got to act fast. Check that wharf at Glasgow, alert whoever the hell you like at New Scotland Yard and make sure that conference is stopped.'

'What are you going to do?'

Ivanov frowned. 'I'm going to have to involve my people; that is, if I can. The repercussions for my government are too great.'

'But you said yourself you can't trust Holbeck.'

'Fuck Holbeck!' snapped Ivanov.

An hour later Alec Martin was making a call from a public telephone kiosk in Piccadilly. After waiting some time he was connected with the Metropolitan Police commander responsible for Special Branch. The man was an old friend and ex-colleague; of course he knew about the unofficial manhunt for Martin, but wisely he chose to listen rather than have the call traced. At the end of it he was very appreciative of the fact that every call to his office was automatically recorded on tape; his pencil would never have kept up with Martin's delivery.

LONDONDERRY
Autumn Harvest: zero minus 123 hours

The Bogside street was deserted except for two young children playing at the street-corner. Inside a mid-terrace house, borrowed just for the night, Seamus Maguire was warming his feet at the fireside while in the process of instructing his local PIRA company commander as to what further action he required.

'I'll come to the point. I've just had a phone call from Dublin. It's been seen that this Special Branch bastard called McCormick might just get too close to who did the shooting on Easter Sunday.'

The other man nodded. 'We've been watching. He's been speaking to that other tout of his. We're only passing on what we want him to find out, although he's been sniffing around just too much for my liking recently.'

'I thought he'd have got the message after his other tout got topped.' Maguire cleared his throat and spat into the fire. 'I know for a fact that McCormick hasn't done anything about his last two meetings with your man; he's keeping things to himself because he knows he's on to something big. It's time to take him out, and I want it done quick. Understood?'

The man nodded and left.

THURSDAY, 2 JULY
Autumn Harvest: zero minus 116 hours

It was 4 a.m. when the Army patrol was passing down the Letterkenny Road. The driver of the Land-Rover was the first to spot the Ford Granada parked at the lay-by, tail-lights still visible in the sunrise. It took the soldiers a few minutes to circle the car before closing in. The first sign of anything amiss was when the young corporal leading the patrol saw that the entire front windscreen of the Granada had been shattered. He drew closer, training his torch into the car's interior. There, amidst a blood-splattered interior, lay Detective Inspector McCormick and his tout sprawled together like spent lovers, their bodies drenched in blood, riddled almost beyond recognition.

TEWKESBURY
Autumn Harvest: zero minus 100 hours

Antonia Travis waited impatiently at her Tewkesbury home. It had just gone 8 p.m. One of the main enjoyments of working at GCHQ was the fact that she could live amidst Shakespeare country. It was the old England that she had dreamt of as a child, the sort of thing that postcards were made of. With the little inheritance she had obtained a few years ago she had left the house in Cheltenham and moved to the country town, investing in a small stone cottage set in a quarter of an acre just on the outskirts of the old town.

It was convenient, being only nine miles north-west of Cheltenham; and the cottage was also within easy walking distance of the town's shops, although she preferred to cycle everywhere when she was at home, carrying the groceries on the front of the old butcher's bicycle she had picked up at the auction in Banbury. One of the things she liked about the place was the casualness of everyone and the honesty. Milk could be left standing all day without threat of pilfering; even her post was left in a small red-painted box at the top of the driveway. The previous owner had told her the postbox had been used since before the First World War and there had never been as much as a single letter gone missing; it was that sort of place.

A noise alerted her. She turned towards the hall door that had just creaked; her heart raced until she saw the long white-haired cat walk over to where she sat curled up in the armchair and jump up on to her knees. 'Hello, Jasper. What have you been doing all day, eh? I've sort of neglected you, haven't I?'

The cat purred deeply, jumped, and ran out to the hall. It was Jasper's usual procedure; he didn't like to waste any time this close to feeding.

'You'll just have to wait a second.' She headed for the front door to let the cat out while she prepared his dinner. The cat cried as she unlocked the white panelled door. 'OK, wait a minute.' She pulled open the door, and Jasper ran on outside as she picked up the milk-bottles; and then she saw it, the manila envelope lying on the carpet behind the door. A letter delivered to the front door meant only one thing; it was from Mogul.

She picked it up. Jasper cried out for some of the milk. 'Shut up!' she shouted, slamming the door in his face. Returning to the lounge, she opened the unaddressed Jiffy bag and removed the cassette tape, quickly loaded the cassette into the hi-fi unit and turned it on. The distorted high-pitched voice started to come through the twin speakers. She'd often thought of getting the voice tape analysed to find the man's identity, but her true masters had forbidden it. In any case they knew who Mogul really was; what she thought didn't matter.

'This is Mogul. I have another little job for you, something right up your street. One of our adversaries is proving troublesome. You know him, so it should make it easier. His name is Tucker. That's right, the American. It might shock you to know that he's on to you; he knows what you are, and unless he's removed the consequences are inevitable. So far he hasn't confided in Holbeck and he hasn't reported the fact to Grosvenor Square. If he keeps digging, he could jeopardize everything. His death must be as public as possible; we want maximum embarrassment for the United States government. I suggest you kill him at Rose Cottage; with all the police attention there it should make headline news. Do it quickly.'

The tape ran on into static. Antonia Travis switched it off and lit the log fire. Fifteen minutes later she tossed the cassette into the burning logs and watched it melt away. What on earth was going on? She thought over what Holbeck and Tucker had said in St James's Park; the mole they were referring to might have been her, but how did Mogul know so soon what the American was thinking? Unless Mogul had him under surveillance; in which case she was also under surveillance.

But why had they always refused to tell her who Mogul was? Could it be that they were also protecting him? Then there was the business in the Underground station. Holbeck again; even Tucker distrusted him. Why had Holbeck been so secretive, pledging her to keep even the GCHQ director in the dark?

The man was a member of the Joint Intelligence Committee; there was no higher in the land. By comparison Frazer Holbeck was way down the ladder. She knew Peter Churchman as well as anyone could. After all, they had been lovers for a short period in 1980. She was not in the habit of having affairs with married men; but, then, orders were orders, and those orders had come directly from Mogul. There would have been no need to spy on Churchman if he'd already been a Russian agent. Just what was Holbeck really up to? If she had to kill Tucker, then it would wait; it was time to contact someone else now.

The doorbell rang. She looked outside through a chink in the lounge curtains. Ivanov was standing on the doorstep. Just how was she going to get through the night, knowing what she must do?

LONDON
Friday, 3 July. 7.12 a.m.
Autumn Harvest: zero minus 88 hours 48 minutes

Ivanov got back to London in the early hours of the morning. After catching a couple of hours' well-earned rest he headed out just before breakfast, leaving Alec Martin still asleep. He went directly to Euston Station and to the baggage-locker. He opened it extremely carefully; there was a brown leather and canvas sports-bag inside. Once in the gents' toilets Ivanov found a spare cubicle and began gingerly to open the bag using a sharp penknife. They had tried to kill him once already; he was still at risk, and certainly he was not going to be taken in by a booby-trap bomb. Opening the bag from the bottom, he made a three-inch gap in the canvas, easing his fingers inside. It was slow and laborious, but necessary. Finally, after some minutes, satisfied that it was clear, he opened the bottom completely and began to examine the contents. The sports clothing revealed nothing, but inside one of the training-shoes he found what he was looking for. It was a pink hotel laundry-tag marked 'Suite 101, Savoy Hotel'.

Alec Martin awakened to find Ivanov had left him a note saying he would be back later on. He watched the television as he prepared some coffee and toast, then he took the opportunity to ring his wife in Wales. He was relieved at hearing Julia's voice rather than his sister-in-law. While he was fond of the woman, she was a gossip; once on the line she'd be hard to put off.

'Daddy! Is that you? Where have you been? Mummy's been trying to get you for two days.'

'Hello, my pet. Look, I'm in a terrible rush. Is your mother there?'

Alec Martin looked at the television mounted on the kitchen worktop; the news broadcast was just starting.

'Sorry, Daddy, you've missed her. She and Aunty Margaret went out early. Shopping again! Confidentially I think Mummy's getting her new outfit for Tuesday's garden-party.' Julia laughed.

'Damn it! I'd almost forgotten about that. What date's that?' Martin reached across and began to pour some more coffee from the steaming pot. Behind him pictures of the news headlines flashed across the television screen.

'It's Tuesday the seventh,' continued Julia. 'Don't tell me you're starting to dote, Daddy dear?' Julia mocked him gently. 'Where have you been for the last few days? Mummy has been trying to reach you. You haven't got a girlfriend, have you?' He could hear the laughter in her tone.

'Don't be silly! Actually, I've been abroad, dear.'

There was a pause. She was silent; then she continued. 'You were abroad?'

'I was in Ireland. Look, it's a long story. I'll tell you about it when I see you on Thursday.'

'Thursday! Daddy! It's Tuesday!' she shouted into the telephone.

'Of course it is. Sorry, Julia; my head's in the clouds.' Martin rubbed his tired eyes, turning in time to focus on the photograph of the man flashed on to the television screen.

'You'll not forget to collect your morning suit on Monday, will you?' Silence. 'Daddy! Are you still there?' Still silence. McCormick's hardened features filled the television screen for another few seconds, then the scene flashed to a bullet-riddled car sitting in a roadside layby. Even with the sound turned down the essence of the report was obvious.

'Daddy? Daddy?' Julia continued.

'Yes! . . . Yes, dear, I'll not forget the suit. Tell your mother that I'll ring her from home this evening.' He rubbed his eyes.

'I love you, Daddy,' she whispered.

'And you, too, dear. Bye-bye.' Alec Martin set the receiver down again. His jacket was draped over the back of the chair next to him. He felt in the pocket and pulled out the Walther PPK. Ivanov was right; it was better to be ready.

Julia Martin sat alone in the house thinking about her father. He sounded very nervous, almost agitated. It was unlike him; he was always the epitome of calmness, his relaxed attitude was something she had always respected. But why had he been abroad? She lifted the receiver and dialled the STD code for Sussex and then the number for St Louise's Convent School. The direct telephone line in the school library by-passed the school switchboard.

'Yes?' the voice croaked at the other end of the telephone line.

'Sister Marianne, it's me.'

'Julia!' The old nun's voice lifted on hearing the girl's voice. 'Where are you, my dear – still in Wales?'

'Yes, Sister. I'm afraid so. Look, I have something you should know. You told me to tell you if anything unusual happened. Well, it has! Daddy was on the telephone just a few minutes ago. Apparently he's been over in Ireland.'

'Do you know exactly where, child?'

'I'm afraid he didn't tell me, but he's ringing Mummy tonight. I should find out then.'

'Good.' The nun drew out the word. 'When you've got news don't ring, come and see me directly.'

'Yes, Sister,' said the girl reverently.

LONDON
8.32 a.m.
Autumn Harvest: zero minus 87 hours 28 minutes

'Good morning, Mrs B.'

'It's you, Mr Holbeck, sir. How nice to see you. A foul morning, though.'

'Indeed, Mrs B. But we can't have it all our own way now, can we? Remember the flowers need water, too, you know.'

'You're so right, Mr Holbeck, just as always.' The old woman smiled. 'Now, is it your usual this morning?'

'No, I'm going to be different today. I'll have one of those pretty yellow carnations I see in the window over there.'

'With pleasure.' She picked out the best she could find as always. 'Dear me, I nearly forgot. Your mother rang up just after we opened at eight o'clock this morning. It would appear that you've left your keys at home. She was worried in case you'd be in a panic before reaching your office. A lovely woman she sounded, too; just like the Queen Mum, she was.'

'Damn!' It was the first occasion she had ever heard him curse. He patted his jacket pockets. 'And I left my pipe behind as well.'

'I am so sorry, Mr Holbeck.'

'Abstention for a day will do me no harm, Mrs B. No harm at all.'

'Quite right, sir.' She carefully wrapped the flower in a small Cellophane cover and handed it across the counter. 'Shall I put it on the account as usual?'

'Thank you and good morning, Mrs B.' He touched the brim of his bowler hat and walked briskly outside, raising his umbrella against the blowing rain. Things were coming apart somewhere, or so it seemed. Mrs B had just unwittingly given him an emergency contact directly from Mikhailov. He looked up at the hanging clock as he passed the jeweller's, bowing his head and tightening down his bowler hat against the increasing wind. He just had time to call before going to the office. At the next junction he found an empty phone-box, and fumbled in his breast pocket for the Telecom paycard. 'Bloody thing,' he muttered to himself as he tried to set it into the slot the right way round. 'Whatever happened to the good old red telephone-box and penny call-box? Yankee progress, that's what it is. We're all becoming bloody Yanks!' He punched in the number, but a strange voice answered.

'This is Gerald.'

'Mary here. We need to meet,' snapped the female voice.

'Impossible!'

'Apollo has authorized me.' The female used Mikhailov's field code name.

390

'I don't give a damn! It's not on.'

'Does Apple mean anything to you?'

It did. Holbeck's heart began to thump hard, almost painfully. It was the code-word he had never wanted to hear. He had been discovered! Someone was on to him! Who? Mikhailov had promised he'd be OK. His mind raced; it just did not seem possible.

'Are you still there?'

'Go on,' he answered slowly.

'The Strand Theatre, seven-thirty this evening. A ticket has been reserved for you.'

He hung up, and tried to act natural. He proceeded on towards Curzon Street. There was no visible tail; that was something. The rain fell heavier now. Quickly he moved across the road between two static lines of traffic. London's traffic problem was getting out of all proportion. Suddenly Holbeck wondered how much longer he would have to consider it at first hand. And then there was Mother to consider. The eighty-eight-year-old was almost blind and totally dependent on her only son. What would become of her?

'This will kill Mother!' he muttered, clearing the last line of traffic and stepping on to the pavement.

STRATFORD-UPON-AVON
Autumn Harvest: zero minus 86 hours

Antonia Travis took the morning off and made her arrangements. It was short notice for a meeting, but she just had to discuss the development with them. The meeting took place in a carpark backing on to the River Avon, just before 10 a.m.

'I cannot help you.' The man was firm and to the point.

'What are you saying?' insisted Travis.

'I have my orders. I cannot help you.'

'I don't care about your orders. I'm being told to kill a CIA agent. I'm also in the middle of a "mole" hunt inside GCHQ. It could get messy.'

'Antonia, things might be a little out of perspective to you.'

'I can't go through with this!' she pleaded.

'Is there anything else?' The curly-haired man checked his watch. 'I've got to be somewhere else shortly.'

Travis sank her head back against the headrest of her car seat. 'So that's it,' she sighed.

'Afraid so.' He opened the car door and climbed out. 'Look after yourself.' He smiled at her before shutting the door and walking to the other car. She watched the grey Audi drive away and sat in the empty carpark for another hour. She raced through the entire episode again and again. How could she not have things 'in perspective'?

SAVOY HOTEL, LONDON
11.30 a.m.
Autumn Harvest: zero minus 84 hours 30 minutes

Mikhailov opened the door of suite 101 slowly. Ivanov gave no hint of surprise as he entered. The hotel suite in one of London's top hotels lived up to his expectations. The blue and yellow wallpaper combined delicately with the matching furnishings and thick pale-blue carpet and Chinese rugs.

'You appreciate style,' said Ivanov.

Mikhailov turned on the television set and increased the volume. 'Just in case,' he replied in English, gesturing Ivanov towards a long settee placed in the centre of the large room. Before Ivanov sat down he checked each of the two adjoining bedrooms and the bathroom for unwelcome company. Mikhailov frowned.

'Kolia, I am alone. Surely you do not think ill of me?' the general said drily as he sat down on one side of the settee.

'You're hardly alone.'

'You mean Kapitsa,' smiled Mikhailov. 'He is becoming a trifle obvious, isn't he?'

'Especially in Tube stations.'

'I've been here for a full day awaiting your return.' The general ignored the comment.

'I've been busy,' replied Ivanov, still moving around the

room. He remained on his feet beside the television screen. 'What is it you want?'

'Grechko wants you to come back home with me immediately. After the episode in Holland it was agreed that I was probably the only person you would trust to meet with.'

'I don't trust anyone and, after Holland, especially you!' Ivanov raised his voice. Mikhailov gestured for him to lower his tone.

'An unfortunate mistake, Kolia. It was all Grechko's doing; he panicked, and he admits that now. All he wants is you back.'

'To tidy up the loose ends? Is that what I am now – a liability?'

'There's no doubt about it. If you come home alive, the KGB will be awaiting you with eager and open arms. Clenched fists maybe, but open arms anyway. I hardly think our organization can protect you from them at all.' He laughed. 'In fact I don't think it can even protect *me* from them.'

'Did you receive my message from Athens?'

Mikhailov nodded. 'Very interesting. A link-up of different terrorist groups for one job.'

'It's much bigger and heavier than we ever imagined. From what I've found out there's to be a strike on the NATO Summit Conference scheduled for July the seventh. I have all the details of their supplies, but just in case I'm too late to stop them by using the British we are going to have to do it ourselves. In any case, you cannot afford them to be taken alive, can you?'

Mikhailov nodded in agreement. 'From what you say, it sounds as though these terrorists are already in the country somewhere. I followed your scant message and had a satellite sweep of the Greek Cypriot mountains. There's no evidence of any terrorist camp; they obviously dismantled it some time ago. I think you had better tell me everything, Kolia.'

The two men discussed the situation for over an hour. Towards the end Mikhailov stood up.

'I have a contingency plan, Kolia. I think you'll like it; it's rather daring as a matter of fact!'

They talked on for another ten minutes before Mikhailov poured them each a vodka from the cocktail-cabinet.

'Not as strong as we might be used to, eh?' He handed Ivanov a glass. Ivanov set his on top of the television untouched.

'Come now, you don't think I'd poison you, Kolia?' Mikhailov drank his glass in one gulp. Ivanov handed him over his own glass. The Russian drank the second glass instantly.

'Just as well,' retorted Ivanov. 'If you had hesitated, I would have killed you.'

'Kolia, if you really must know, Grechko did send me here to kill you, but from what I've revealed to you here you can see that I've got other ideas in mind.' He laughed. 'Just remember one thing, my old friend: no matter how we come out of this, you must never return home. Get lost somewhere. Don't worry, I'll confuse the tracks for the KGB!' Mikhailov hugged Ivanov for the last time. 'Take care, my friend; I can only do so much. One thing: let Mogul and Wolverine help you in any way they can.'

'Mogul hasn't contacted me for days. I think he's frightened.'

'I'll see him, then. Do not worry.' He patted Ivanov warmly on the shoulder; the GRU colonel would have to live a little longer after all. Ivanov left immediately, waiting some time downstairs in the American Bar until he was sure that no one else was after him.

Ivanov arrived back at the safe house at around 2 p.m. Alec Martin was jumping around as if he'd ants in his pants.

'Where the hell have you been to this time?' Before Ivanov could reply Martin continued: 'Never mind! Never mind! Remember I told you about a Detective Inspector McCormick that I went to see in Northern Ireland?'

'Yes,' replied Ivanov, removing his jacket.

'Well, he's just been on the news headlines. Shot bloody dead! Found yesterday with some other person in his car!'

'The bastards don't waste time, do they? McCormick was obviously getting too close to whoever was involved in the Easter Sunday shooting,' continued Ivanov, lighting his first cigarette in days.

'But all McCormick could tell me was that someone called Liam was involved. Apparently he came up from Dublin.'

'Well,' Ivanov sucked deeply on the cigarette, 'maybe it's

time to go to Dublin and pay a visit to this St Clement's Hostel where Mary Garand is supposed to have died.'

'When are we going?' asked Martin.

'Alec, I'm going alone. I want you to stay here in the apartment. Don't go out and don't make any phone calls. I'll ring you when I get to the hotel tonight.' Ivanov recognized the anger building up inside Martin. 'You're needed here, Alec; it makes damn good sense. Anyway, if Garand is alive and kicking, he can identify you.'

'He's alive all right,' Alec Martin insisted.

LONDON
8 p.m.
Autumn Harvest: zero minus 76 hours

The theatre was still running a comedy called *Don't Sleep with Your Wife*, starring Frazer Holbeck's most favourite artiste. He sat alone in his aisle seat all through the first half. No contact; not even a glimmer. The curtain started to rise for the second half, and he began to settle down again to enjoy the humour. He was even beginning to relax enough to join with the rest of the audience, laughing aloud when the approach was made. A young woman passing up the aisle from one of the front rows stumbled just in front of him.

It was very realistic; even Holbeck was taken in just for a second. He helped the woman to her feet, and she thanked him. It was when he sat down he found the theatre programme lying on his seat. Leafing through the programme, he quickly found it; the name of a carpark scribbled on the inside of the back cover right across an advertisement for Smirnoff vodka. How appropriate, he thought. He waited until the end of the show and left, getting rid of the programme in a litter-bin at the main exit point.

He collected his MGB GT from its parking-space in Dean Street just a few streets away from the theatre and drove the three miles to the multi-storey carpark, taking his ticket from the automatic exchange and driving up to the second storey as directed. He sat in the sports car in the semi-darkness for over ten minutes smoking a cigar before the side window was eventually rapped. He rolled it down slowly; it was the young woman who had stumbled at his feet in the theatre.

'Well, well.' He smiled, looking her up and down. She was dressed in a tight-fitting brown leather mini-skirt and matching high-heeled knee-length boots which altogether lost their effect when matched against her black fishnet tights. Her black shiny plastic raincoat fluttered in the breeze blowing in through the windowless sides of the multi-storey carpark, revealing the young woman's yellow see-through blouse. It didn't need unbuttoning; she was braless. The very glimpse of her protruding and enlarged nipples seemed enough to assure an erection to an incontinent OAP.

'I see that you're liberated anyway,' Holbeck continued, smiling. He stared into her face; she was really quite pretty, even with the crude over-indulgence and misuse of facial rouge and bright red lipstick and cheap-looking blonde wig.

'Are you interested or not?' she asked almost indignantly in a broad Liverpudlian accent. He nodded his approval.

'A full job's fifty and a hand job's twenty. Something special costs extra.' She was chewing gum as she spoke, her mouth opening and closing like some fish.

'I'll take the extra.' He kept smiling. The woman walked slowly around the front of his car and climbed in the passenger side.

'Where to?' he asked, starting up the engine.

'The George Hotel. It's in Pentonville. I'll show you the way; just drive. The room's going to cost you another tenner an hour.'

'Another tenner it is, then.' He smiled, nervously now.

'Know which road to take?' She leant across, placing her left hand on his knee.

The smell of her sweet perfume aside, Holbeck hadn't dreamt of having anything as sensual next to him again in his life. She ran her hand up the inside of his thigh and then eased back in her seat, pulling on her safety belt. She was playing the part well. If he was being watched, they'd see it; if they were using DMS (Directional Microphones to the uninitiated), then the natural groan Holbeck had just emitted would clarify his liaison with the prostitute. The façade would hold well. The car-park was a place known to be frequented by streetwalkers; even if MI5 or Special Branch swooped in they would be able to prove absolutely nothing under the Official Secrets Act, and a charge of procuring would hardly be considered.

The drive to the hotel was quiet and uneventful; much to Holbeck's displeasure, so was the hotel room. It was a seedy place, the wallpaper barely hanging on the walls. He followed the young woman into the bathroom where she closed the door, turning on the shower and the handbasin taps. The noise of the water would nullify the finest of eavesdropping equipment.

'You can relax. Your apple hasn't quite ripened for picking yet.' The Liverpudlian was gone; she was now speaking with a clipped English accent.

'What the hell do you mean? The phone call!' growled Holbeck.

'We needed to see you urgently. I didn't say that you weren't in line for picking; I just said you were safe for the moment, but you'll need to act.' She pulled off the blonde curly wig, revealing her short black hair.

'So I am safe, then? No one's on to me?'

'No, not yet,' she agreed. 'You are going to have to kill someone.' Her voice was assertive.

'Who?'

'Thor.'

'But I have that in hand.'

'If you mean Wolverine, forget it! Wolverine didn't do it the first time you told her.'

He was a little stunned that they knew that; then, they knew most things already.

'Then she'll do it the second time,' he retorted.

'Perhaps.' She raised an eyebrow as if considering the matter.

'On whose orders?' he demanded.

'Apollo sent me. Thor must be liquidated immediately. Can I pass on your absolute assurance?'

'I want to see Apollo!' insisted Holbeck.

'Too late; he's left already,' she replied, pursing her red lips.

Holbeck wiped his forehead; he couldn't quite decide if it

was perspiration caused by the humidity in the bathroom or simply tension.

'Well?' she pursued.

'I'll take care of it straight away.'

'We think you might be losing your bottle.' She was pushing him now.

'I'll ignore that remark!' he growled.

She reached over and opened his trousers, slowly unzipping him. 'This is supposed to look real,' she whispered, 'and I can see no point in wasting a hot shower, do you?' Her hand was inside his trousers already. It was as much as Holbeck could do to pull off his red and orange braces. Little did he know of what the woman had yet to tell him, but she would wait just a little longer; no point in destroying the moment irrevocably. She had chosen correctly; his new instructions devastated the Englishman. Twenty minutes later she had left the hotel. Holbeck was left naked, still standing in the shower, unable to move. Had the water not cascaded down his face, the tears would have become noticeable. His world was coming apart after all. He would have to be strong about it; there was no other way. Both Thor and Wolverine had to perish.

DUBLIN

4 July. 10 a.m.
Autumn Harvest: zero minus 62 hours

Ivanov surveyed the St Clement's Hostel for Women and Children. From Martin's description of the terrible fire almost twenty years before, it was hard to imagine how such a tranquil setting could have been the grave for so many women and children. The River Liffey flowed to one side of the grounds whilst the remainder of the site was festooned with mature oak and cedar trees. Once inside the colonnaded façade it was clear to see that the interior structure had been completely rebuilt. From the original stonework erected in 1896 by the Sisters of Charity, the Victorian features gave way to a bright and spacious modern environment.

He was taken to the Sister Superior's office by a novice; inside the cream-coloured office he found a charming old nun called Sister Mary.

'Ah, Mr Tucker. I am so pleased to meet you. I got your telephone message late this afternoon. I think you were speaking to one of my novices. Please sit down.' The nun gestured to a wooden chair beside the large walnut desk. Her warm smile lit up the room. Ivanov settled, and after declining refreshments he came straight to the heart of the matter.

'Sister Mary, I'm a lawyer representing the estate of a James Malloy, the late brother of a woman who was apparently at this hostel at the time of the fire on February the nineteenth 1973. I'm trying to trace any of his remaining relatives. The woman's married name was Garand. Would it be at all possible for me to see a list of all those who died and also the survivors of the fire?'

'Yes, I can get you the information.' The old nun ran her fingers along the desk-top. 'In fact after your explanation on the telephone earlier I took the liberty of extracting from the files all the necessary information.' Sister Mary patted a white file at the side of her desk. 'But, first of all, I'm curious as to why you should want such information. Surely Dublin City Hall records would have sufficed?' She was not prepared for his reply.

'I think that the fire was used to conceal the disappearance of at least two people; and, if I'm right, all thirty-seven victims of your fire were possibly murdered.'

Sister Mary was shocked. The thought had never entered her head that the fire could have been a deliberate act of arson. She had reconciled herself to the matter being an act of God; the very thought of such a consideration was too horrible to comprehend. Nevertheless she retained her composure enough to question his hypothesis.

'Mr . . . Tucker, I was one of those who lived through the fire of seventy-three. You must understand that at that time, apart from the front entrance that you used on your arrival, most of the building was an old warren of corridors and rooms, mainly lined in wood, with the poorest of electrical and heating installation. According to the fire brigade's report submitted at the inquest, we were indeed fortunate that the building hadn't gone up in flames even sooner. If such a tragedy had occurred even a week prior to the fire, over twice as many souls could have perished.' She was shaking now, trembling with the recollection of the night-time horror that still haunted her dreams. 'You don't know how much I've thought and prayed about what happened. But I can assure you that no evidence of such a heinous act was even suspected, never mind hinted at during the inquest. All the reports were conclusive: a fire started in the kitchen towards the rear of the building and swept through the entire place within minutes. Most of the poor souls were asleep and overcome by the fumes and smoke in seconds. The rest is . . . academic.' A tear trickled down her cheek. 'I know you are wrong, Mr Tucker. You have to be!'

'I'm sorry, Sister. I don't mean to upset you. Just like you, I want to have the peace of mind that no mortal's hand was involved in this incident. I know it's a long shot, but I want to try anyway.'

'Very well.' She was angry now, pushing the white folder across the desk to him. 'You'll find in there two lists, one of all those who perished and another of those who survived; but if you want to trace any of the survivors you may find it difficult. Most of the addresses have naturally changed since then.'

'Thank you, Sister.' He took the folder.

'I do not want to appear rude, Mr Tucker, but would you please now go?'

Sister Mary fought to maintain her self-control. Ivanov stood and extended his hand to the nun. She was no longer looking at him, staring down at her desk. Ivanov lifted his coat and headed towards the door, opening it quietly. He turned to bid her goodbye, but the sight of the nun cancelled any intention he had. Already she was down on her knees at the side of the desk, praying and sobbing uncontrollably.

He left the building, crossing the forecourt to the hired Volvo saloon, which he had left reversed into the corner of the tree-lined car-park. There was a deathly silence about the place; not even the sound of a bird to break the silence. The wind picked up, a sound now, trees rustling and swaying to and fro in the breeze. Just as he was about to open the door a figure emerged from the shadows beside a large oak tree, only several paces away from his car.

Ivanov's training obliterated all other thought or action; he dropped the folder immediately and turned slightly to the right. A man dressed in a ski-mask and combat jacket was only inches away, brandishing a stiletto-bladed knife. Ivanov swung the door open into the man's path. The attacker reeled back, but swung round and upwards with the knife. The point pricked into the Russian's shoulder as he began to distance himself from his assailant. Ivanov had already designated his killing-ground; he was in the open now, no constricting features to his defence. The attacker had picked the ambush location well. Ivanov was initially trapped between the trees and the car; it would enhance his success considerably, but now his advantage was gone. As if reading the Russian's thoughts, the man lunged forward, kicking the car door shut. The attacker began to circle him slowly now, testing the reflexes of his opponent; it was obvious the man had professional training.

Ivanov had already ripped off his torn jacket and thrown it around his left forearm. The man moved in again, knife-point upwards, ready to cut into the centre and upper regions of his opponent; he was more cautious now, bringing up his left arm across his chest. The stance was almost classical; the Russian wondered just what Soviet school of instruction he had attended. Then the attacker lunged forward again, cutting upwards. Ivanov parried the blow with his jacketed left forearm; still the knife penetrated his skin, cutting a six-inch superficial wound just above the wrist. The attacker then made his mistake: instead of returning to his circling posture, just outside Ivanov's reach, he hastily decided to try for a quick kill and brought the knife back and in towards Ivanov's throat. The Russian moved sideways with uncanny speed, grabbing the man's outstretched arm at the wrist and twisting it to one side. Ivanov followed through with a vicious kick to the man's rib-cage, directly under the armpit, then he stamped on the man's leg just behind the knee. The man was on his knees instantly.

Ivanov then used his left arm to snap the man's right elbow. The attacker screamed. The stiletto dropped from the man's fingers. Now he was being twirled around into the rear of the

Volvo head-first, his head crunching into the tail-light, shattering the plastic. Ivanov pulled him back from the car; the man's ski-mask was now saturated in blood, his eyes almost closed. Then the attacker's eyes widened considerably as he realized what the Russian was going to do next; but before he could do anything his head was snapped around and upwards, instantly breaking his neck.

Ivanov looked around. There had been no witnesses. He quickly trailed the body to the side of the car and pulled off the man's ski-mask. He did not recognize the badly cut up face of Liam Heggarty. Then he searched the body; the man had been careless. There was an Irish driving licence in the name of Liam Campbell, with an address in Dublin. Was this the 'Liam' McCormick had told Martin about? Ivanov continued searching; he found an identity card indicating the man to be a medical orderly working at St Dominic's Men's Nursing Home in Percy Street, Dublin. After removing a bunch of keys from the combat jacket Ivanov quickly pulled the body into the bushes beyond the trees. He found his attacker's transport, an old Yamaha motorcycle, the crash helmet still strapped to the handlebars. A quick survey of the bike revealed nothing. Ivanov pushed it off the road down a small embankment. He hurried back to the car; his only lead was to go to the dead man's home address.

TRINITY COLLEGE, DUBLIN
3 p.m.
Autumn Harvest: zero minus 57 hours

The girl student answered the payphone in the draughty corridor; she reluctantly went off to fetch the recipient. Julia Martin appeared from the bathroom, dressed in a bathrobe with her wet hair bandaged in a yellow towel.

'Julia Martin,' she answered expectantly. To the old nun it sounded like she was expecting a suitor; she felt betrayed.

'Julia?' The nun's voice was stern and unyielding.

'Sister Marianne!'

'Listen, child. Listen very carefully to what I am about to say.' A pause, then she continued: 'I need you to do something very special.'

'Tell me.' The young woman was eager to please.

'I've just found out that the American you spoke of is now in Dublin.'

'Tucker?'

'Liam says he's staying at Boswell's Hotel in Molesworth Street.'

'I'm close to it!' replied Julia.

'I've been trying to contact Liam since this morning without success. In his absence I need you to do something.'

'Anything!' beseeched Julia. Her enthusiasm almost put the nun off.

One hour later
Autumn Harvest: zero minus 56 hours

Ivanov found that 66A Old Stanley Road was in the northern suburbs of Dublin City, only one mile from St Dominic's Nursing Home. Heggarty's home was an apartment on the ground floor. It was now 4 p.m. Ivanov parked the car towards the end of the street, but before leaving the vehicle he checked his left forearm; the sticking plaster and lint purchased at the roadside filling station had stemmed the flow of blood from the long gash, but the cut to his right shoulder stung badly. He walked back to the bottom of Old Stanley Road. The street was a Victorian terrace of sixty houses. From the outside it was clear that most of the terrace had been converted into flats and bedsits. He passed by a young couple out walking their dog, pausing to tie his shoe-lace just outside the steps leading up to number 6.

Everything was quiet. Ivanov took the opportunity to climb the short flight of steps and enter the open doorway; he found the blue door marked 6A at the darkened far end of the downstairs corridor, below the main staircase. From Heggarty's bunch of keys he selected the only Yale key that seemingly matched the name on the door-lock. The scratched and pitted door opened easily. The lights were out. Ivanov moved around the darkened interior cautiously, satisfying himself that he was alone. Then he pulled the curtains over another fraction and turned on the light. It was a small bedsit, and his suspicions had been right; the man had lived alone. He searched the apartment thoroughly. It was clean; if nothing else, his attacker had been careful.

Easing back on the bed, he took the white rolled-up folder from his inside jacket pocket, running down the list of the deceased; it was in alphabetical order. He found the names quickly: 'GARAND, Mary, DOB 4.5.49, Cupar Street, Belfast', followed by 'GARAND, Patricia, DOB 5.11.69, Cupar Street, Belfast'. He ran down the other list. There had been only ten survivors; as before, the list was in alphabetical order. Naturally there was no mention of any 'Garand' or 'Malloy', but under 'M', his eyes caught momentarily 'MARIANNE, Sister, DOB 14.2.38, Order of the Sisters of Mercy, County Louth'. Ivanov checked again; there were no male survivors, and the only two men that had perished were workers at the hostel and, as Martin had told him before, they were part of the handful of victims who could be identified by their dental records. Yet another blank. The only solution was now to go to his attacker's place of work, but that would have to wait until the following morning.

DUBLIN
6.30 p.m.
Autumn Harvest: zero minus 53 hours 30 minutes

He returned to Boswell's Hotel in Dublin's Molesworth Street and tended to the superficial wounds. He'd just finished his coffee when the bedside telephone burst into life. Ivanov hesitated – no one knew he was staying at the hotel – then he lifted the receiver slowly. 'Yes?'

'Mr Tucker? This is Julia Martin.' The voice was high-pitched, almost emotional.

'Julia!' Ivanov had never really spoken to the young woman before, yet from Alec Martin's ramblings it was as if he knew everything about her.

'My father told me you were staying at Boswell's. Can I see you – now?'

There it was: the first lie. Alec Martin had no idea where Ivanov was.

'Sure. Just where are you anyhow?'

Hesitation this time. 'I'm at the female halls of residence here at Trinity. I'm just over for a couple of days to do some research.' Too much offered; he was sure now that she was lying.

'OK, I'll meet you in the hotel lobby – when?'

'Ten minutes?' she asked nervously.

'See you then.' He listened as the line went dead, then he lay back on the bed. She was definitely lying, but why? What was she up to?

She was already standing in the hotel lobby when he came down the stairs. She was dressed in a green cotton jacket and matching mini-skirt with a white fluffy V-necked pullover. As he approached her she smiled, greeting him like some long-lost friend.

'Hi!' She sounded nervous, looking all around her like some terrified cat. 'Can we go somewhere?'

'What about the bar?' Ivanov smiled.

'I'd thought we could go out somewhere.'

'If it's all the same to you, Julia, I'm expecting a call from New York in about an hour. Let's go to the lounge bar.' He guided her across the lobby towards the bar. She never resisted, but he could see she did not want to stay. Once settled at a corner table, he continued: 'You don't look too happy. Have you someone to see?'

'No, it's just . . . Oh, nothing.' She grinned just as the young waiter approached.

After that she seemed to calm down and even joke with him. To his surprise she accepted his invitation to dinner. Ivanov was becoming more curious by the minute. The girl was evidently lying through her teeth. What did she want? He played for time as they went through to the dining-room. The conversation throughout dinner was quite stimulating. It was the first time that Ivanov had had the opportunity to talk with her. She was highly intelligent and extremely witty; but nevertheless she always seemed evasive, not that he had given her cause. He found himself physically attracted to her; he shook the idea from his mind. As they finished their drinks Ivanov watched an old priest at the corner table. The man had been dining with a woman and another man; as the evening progressed, their conversation had grown louder, helped by the copious amounts of alcohol that they had consumed before and during their meal.

'Are they annoying you?' she quizzed.

'No, not really.'

'Why don't we leave?' she continued, nervously fingering the strap of her black leather shoulder-bag.

'OK,' he replied, signing the restaurant bill before leaving the table.

At the reception area Julia headed for the lift instead of going into the main bar. Ivanov followed in silence. They stood alone in the lift. She stretched up and kissed him on the lips, and then stood back staring at him.

'Did that startle you?'

'Nope.' He kept a straight face. Suddenly the lift halted and the doors opened and they alighted on to the second floor. Ivanov led the way down the hall, opened the door to the bedroom; Julia stepped in, switching on the lights as she went, but careful to set the bag within easy reach. He closed the door and removed his jacket, setting it on the chair. She saw the bloodstains on his arm and shoulder.

'What happened?' She looked concerned.

'Cut myself shaving,' he replied, smiling back.

She walked over and slowly unbuttoned his shirt, examining the bandaged wounds briefly. 'I think you'll survive,' she beamed.

Ivanov watched as she crossed the room and took off her cotton jacket. She unzipped the matching green skirt and let it drop at her feet. Very slowly she lifted the fluffy white pullover, revealing fully the brief black silk knickers, then her flat stomach and finally her firm breasts. Julia climbed into the bed and stretched back on the pillow. Ivanov watched her as he removed the remainder of his clothing. He momentarily thought of Alec Martin and was tempted to tell her to get out, but he had to find out what she was about. He switched off the light and climbed in beside her, but before he could speak she was on top of him. Throughout the encounter she never spoke, acting akin to some pawing wild animal, arousing him in a way he'd almost forgotten. He lay there in the dark as she loved him; he wanted to say something, but somehow it seemed inappropriate. The ecstasy continued; he felt drained beyond belief, but somehow she kept urging him forward. She was insatiable; he tried several times to take a rest, but each time she forced him on and on. He felt her clawing at his back and buttocks, then she started biting his injured shoulder, before finally climaxing, crying out aloud. He had barely noticed, but during their love-making Julia had several times reached down towards the bag. He could never have imagined the inner torment she was experiencing.

Afterwards he lay beside her, rubbing her back as she lay on her stomach facing away from him. Suddenly without warning she arose. Ivanov reached over to touch her, but Julia shoved him aside.

'What's wrong?' he called out. She ignored him, grabbing up her clothes and heading for the bathroom, slamming the door. Ivanov reached for one of his cigarettes, but dropped the packet on the floor. As he bent over to pick them up he saw the Sterling .25 pocket-size pistol inside the half-open bag. He closed the top flap and lay back in the bed. He had just lit the cigarette when she emerged, leaving the bedroom without comment as she slammed the door closed. Ivanov switched on the lights and got up. He caught sight of himself in the wardrobe mirror; his torso was covered with long scratches to both the chest and the shoulders. A bite-mark had begun to bruise the skin just above his bandaged wound; his back was bleeding in several places.

Outside Julia ran from Molesworth Street; she didn't stop running until she'd reached one of the bridges spanning the River Liffey. The area was quiet except for a car passing on the far side of the bridge.

'No!' she screamed. 'I couldn't!' Then she broke down, crying and gripping on to the guard-rail for support. She removed the gun from her bag and stared down at it in the palm of her hand; her hand was shaking.

'To hell with you all!' she cursed through gritted teeth. Even her head was twitching from side to side. With her arm outstretched over the rail she turned her wrist slightly, dropping the gun into the water. Then she was sick, retching over the side of the guard-rail. 'To hell . . . ' she sobbed.

The following morning, Sunday, 5 July
Autumn Harvest: zero minus 40 hours

The next morning was even more peculiar for Ivanov, for it was as if nothing had happened the night before. Julia returned to the hotel and joined him for breakfast. She was polite, even reserved, making no mention of the previous night; the conversation was general and evasive. Finally, before they left the table, he put his hand across and touched her arm. She pulled back immediately; her eyes had a wild look about them.

'Don't touch me!' She spoke aloud. 'I can't stand anyone touching me!'

A few heads turned as Ivanov tried to calm the situation. Instead she just smiled at him.

'I must go, Mr Tucker.' She stood up and replaced her napkin on the table. 'Tell my father and mother I was asking after them, will you?'

Ivanov remained seated and speechless. He watched her leave the restaurant, turning the eye of every red-blooded male in the room in the process. One part of him urged him to follow the young woman, but time was quickly running out and there was much still to do.

He called early on the chief nursing officer in charge of St Dominic's Men's Nursing Home, introducing himself as Peter Campbell, a distant American cousin of Liam Campbell. The nursing officer, a middle-aged effeminate-sounding man called O'Leary, was keen to help.

'Oh! It's awfully nice to meet a relation of Liam's, a lovely young man; but I'm awful sorry, Mr Campbell – you see, Liam isn't due to start work here until tomorrow. He's off on annual leave at the moment – fishing, I think. Have you tried his flat? He only lives a short distance away, you know.'

Ivanov scratched his head. 'As a matter of fact I did, but he was obviously out. You don't happen to know where he goes to socially?'

The man laughed and touched Ivanov's wrist. 'Come with me.' Ivanov spotted a definite twinkle in the man's eye. He followed the swaggering little man as he walked down the long marble-floored hallway towards the rear of the nursing home. 'By the way, my name's Desmond, but you can call me Des; everybody else does.'

Ivanov smiled; he almost anticipated Des to have wanted to finish off the statement by saying '. . . if you give me a kiss!'

'This was once one of those "stately homes" you hear about,' continued Desmond. 'It lay in ruins for years after the Easter Rising and was then converted with Church money in the thirties – a lot of it raised in the United States, so I'm told.' Desmond seemed rather proud about that point. Ivanov wasn't really sure if the man said it to placate him personally or just to make an American visitor feel welcome.

'Tell me, Mr Campbell, does Liam have many relations in America?' You know how quiet a person he is; I can hardly get a word out of him. Come to think of it, I know nearly nothing at all about his private life.'

'No. Just a few cousins, like myself. Tell me – I've really forgotten – just how long has he worked here?'

O'Leary grunted. 'A lot longer than me, and I've been here twelve years. Now, would you credit that, eh?'

They turned a corner and headed through a series of fire-doors, finally emerging into a large ward subdivided on both sides into single cubicles, leaving a six-foot corridor running down the centre of the room.

'Please don't be alarmed by what you might see here, Mr Campbell. This is known as our "isolation ward". I know it sounds as if we're treating a bunch of cholera victims, but that's not the case. This is where our long-stay patients are kept. Most of them are suffering from senile-dementia and like conditions.'

They began to walk slowly past the glass-panelled cubicles. Ivanov stared at the pitiful sight of the elderly men, some asleep, one crying, another tossing continuously in his bed from side to side.

'You said you were going to show me where Liam spent his free time?' Ivanov was puzzled.

'And this is it!' O'Leary smiled. 'If you would excuse the expression and ignore the implication, Liam's always been a wee bit funny to some, but I like to call it dedication, although he's always declined any sort of job promotion.' He studied Ivanov, hoping he hadn't offended him.

'You mean he stays here in his free time?' Ivanov looked around him.

'Not quite. He stays with a friend of his, a very special friend.' O'Leary smiled and waved his fingers, beckoning Ivanov to follow. 'Come on, I'll show you.' At the end of the ward O'Leary knocked at a curtained glass-panelled door and entered the bottom cubicle. Ivanov could hear him speak to someone inside. 'Someone to see you. You've got a visitor.' He stepped outside again. 'Please come on in, Mr Campbell.'

Ivanov stood at the doorway. Seated in a wheelchair, his head flopped forward on to a side-mounted table which stretched across the front of the wheelchair, was the crouched figure of a grey-haired old man. O'Leary gently eased the man back into the chair and raised the man's head by the underside of his chin. Ivanov recalled the old Polaroid photograph Alec Martin had attached to his investigation file, but he didn't recognize the bloated face immediately. He glanced down to the man's feet; from underneath the long dressing-gown he could plainly see the man's right foot was missing. Then he stared back into the man's eyes, and it hit him hard; the eyes hadn't changed. It was Harry Garand! Alive!

'Mr Campbell, may I have the pleasure of introducing you to Harry Adams; he's one of our oldest patients here. I mean, in years of confinement rather than of age. He's also Liam's closest companion.' Ivanov crossed the floor. Harry Garand's eyes were blank, his mouth open and slobbering. 'Yes, Liam spends most of his time here with Mr Adams. Of course Harry can't respond, and I doubt if he even understands a single word we're saying, but Liam has a devotion for him that far outstretches any common practice. To some it may sound quite unhealthy for a man in his thirties to coop himself up in a place like this for sometimes up to twelve hours a day, but that's Liam for you!'

'Just how long has this patient been like this?'

O'Leary paused, letting Harry Garand's head droop gently sideways on to his shoulder. 'I'd say since he came to us some time in 1973, if my memory serves me correctly.'

Ivanov was stunned. O'Leary misread the Russian's facial expression.

'Look, why don't we leave Harry alone for now? It'll be his bed-time soon, and the other nurses will have to prepare him. Let's go to my office for a wee cup of coffee.'

Ivanov was hesitant to leave Garand, but reluctantly agreed so as not to arouse the man's suspicions. During coffee Ivanov pursued the question of Garand, pushing aside O'Leary's small talk about America.

'Tell me about the patient back there called Harry. What happened to him anyway? I see he's lost a leg.'

'Not the leg, the foot to just above the ankle.' O'Leary set his cup and saucer on the tray. 'Poor, poor man. Badly hurt, as you could see. The result of a road accident only a short time before he came here. Apparently the steering column of the car he was driving went right through his chest. You ought to see the scars he has – quite horrific.' O'Leary shuddered. 'Somewhere along the line he had the blood-supply to his brain interrupted and that has resulted in this vegetable-like state that you've just witnessed.'

'Is there any hope for him?'

'Mr Campbell, Harry's got permanent brain damage. He's been like that since I've known him; and, as I said earlier, I've been here twelve years.'

'You said Liam stays with him. Does the man not have any relatives or visitors of his own? Frankly, Mr O'Leary, I find it

411

rather unhealthy that my cousin should spend so much time looking after him.'

O'Leary was flustered at the implication. 'Mr Campbell, Liam's a dedicated charge nurse here. Whilst I have voiced my opinions as to him spending so much time with Harry, the patient's relatives are quite insistent that Liam can spend as much time with him as he wishes.'

Gold dust! Ivanov could hardly resist the temptation to jump out of his seat. 'What relations does Harry have?'

'Very few. Just a sister.'

'And she lives here in Dublin, too?'

'Alas, no, that's why she was so agreeable to Liam spending so much time with her brother.'

'She wasn't in the car crash as well?' Ivanov was trying desperately to keep on the subject without arousing Desmond O'Leary's suspicions.

'Thank God, no. Mind you, to look at her you'd think she had been.'

'What do you mean?'

'Her face, and God knows what else of her! She's got very bad facial scarring, the result of a fire many years back. A tragic family, if you ask me.' O'Leary sipped at his coffee.

Ivanov's brain was in overdrive. 'Where was the fire?'

'It was a big fire – in a Catholic hostel, too – just here in Dublin. I can't rightly remember the name of the place, but nearly forty people died; she was one of the few survivors. It was a long time ago.'

'That's just terrible. Miss Adams must have been quite lucky to survive at all.' Ivanov pushed the conversation on.

'Oh, I'm sorry, Mr Campbell. I'm afraid I've misled you.' He leant forward from his chair and placed a chubby hand on Ivanov's knee. 'She's a married woman!' O'Leary paused and then began to giggle. 'Forgive me, forgive me; it's my wee joke, you see. She's married all right, but to the Catholic Church. She's a nun; they call her Sister Marianne. She belongs to one of those teaching orders, you know: the Sisters of Mercy or something like that.'

Ivanov moved his legs; O'Leary was forced to retract his hand.

'Does she visit her brother very often?'

'She can't, Mr Campbell. The poor woman is very badly disabled herself and, to make matters more difficult, she now lives at a convent school somewhere in Sussex, so it's fairly difficult for her to visit here too frequently; but she manages the journey every few months.' He smiled again. 'But Liam makes up for it. You know, your cousin and Sister Marianne have become very close. When she visits here she spends much of her time with Liam.'

More alarm-bells began ringing in Ivanov's head. 'Look, Des, I've taken up far too much of your time already. When Liam returns perhaps you'd be good enough to get him to contact me. He knows where I'm staying.'

'Why, of course I will.' They walked to the front of the home and to the adjoining carpark. Ivanov was beginning to think that he wasn't going to get rid of the man. He was just about to unlock the Volvo when O'Leary dropped another bombshell.

'You know, you may just be getting invited to a wedding soon.'

Ivanov stopped, looking around in puzzlement.

O'Leary continued. 'Harry Adams's daughter. She visits Harry nearly every week; goes to Trinity College, Dublin. Her mother died in childbirth, poor thing. Well, as I was saying, she seems very friendly with Liam. In fact sometimes I think that may be the reason that Liam spends so much time with her father.'

'Surely she must be a lot younger than Liam if she's still at university?' Ivanov's eyes narrowed.

'Oh, she is indeed – and very attractive; she turns all the heads in here with that blonde hair of hers. In fact she was visiting here only yesterday.'

Ivanov smiled. 'What do you call her?'

O'Leary had to think for a moment. 'She's called Julia.'

Ivanov waved goodbye. 'Hope to see you again. Thanks for the tea.'

Ivanov stopped off at the halls of residence at Trinity College. From Julia's student friends he discovered that she had already packed and gone away two hours earlier. He cursed at his slowness to realize. Alec Martin would have to wait; he had much to do and little time left.

GRU HEADQUARTERS, MOSCOW
11 a.m. local time
Autumn Harvest: zero minus 40 hours

Mikhailov awaited his moment carefully. He found Grechko sitting as usual behind his French desk stuffing capsules and milk down his flabby throat.

'Come in! Come in! Tell me what is happening. This Ivanov, I presume he has been dealt with as I ordered?' Grechko set his glass of milk aside then began rubbing his stomach.

'He's dead.'

'That is good. And you, Alexei Vladimirovich, you got out of Britain without difficulty, I assume?'

'*Da*. But something's up. The British have changed their NATO conference to a place called Chevering Hall; they clearly know there's an increased possibility of an attack.'

'Good! That is good; then, these terrorists will not succeed.'

'I think that they might still try.'

'Nonsense! Anyway, the British are quite able to carry out their own security precautions.' Grechko sniffed deeply.

'But what if they aren't? I'd like to make sure.'

'Use Mogul, you mean?'

'I was thinking of Spetsnaz,' Mikhailov said quietly.

'Preposterous! You know, for a supposedly intelligent officer you can display some stupid traits. I don't want to hear any more! Understand?'

'I understand,' Mikhailov replied. 'But if something is going to happen at this Chevering Hall, then let us examine the killing-ground; it may be necessary to convince the Politburo.'

'*Da*. I like the idea. Can we get a flyover of one of the Red Bear satellites?'

'We can do better than that, Comrade General. We could make Viliuisk by air and watch the entire thing on "Realtime".'

'Excellent!' Grechko popped a further pill as he pulled on

414

his jacket covering his bulging shirt. 'Get me to Viliuisk.' Grechko was already pulling his overcoat off the stand.

Mikhailov lifted the receiver and began dialling. Of course he knew the military aircraft was already waiting, but didn't he have to play his part? Little did Grechko realize that Spetsnaz had already been tasked! All that was needed now was confirmation from Ivanov. When Mikhailov made his final play for power, the Viliuisk facility would be the feather in his cap; overnight he envisaged himself becoming the youngest Minister of Defence in the history of the Soviet Union.

LONDON
Autumn Harvest: zero minus 26 hours 30 minutes

Alec Martin gave his wife every assurance that he would be ready to join her at the Hilton Hotel in London, either on the evening of the sixth or instead on the following Tuesday morning. His left ear was beginning to ache; Norma had been on the telephone so long with him he reckoned his ear was about stuck to the receiver.

'Look, my dear, can we continue this tomorrow? I'll tell you everything when I see you, all right?' He looked at his watch; it was 9.30 p.m. She had been on the telephone for over an hour already, and the Russian had told him never to use the telephone in the safe house unless absolutely necessary.

'No! It is not all right, Alec. We've been terrified, worried sick, to think that your car was found by the police days ago and you had vanished. How do you think we all felt here?' She began to sob. Alec Martin could hear someone in the background; eventually Julia was able to wrestle the telephone from her mother and speak to him.

'Daddy? Mummy's too upset to talk further; perhaps you should leave it until the morning.'

'Thank you, young lady, at least, for saving your poor Aunt Margaret's telephone bill.'

She laughed. 'We'll hear from you tomorrow. I love you.'

'Just a minute, young lady. What are you still doing in

Wales? I thought you had to go to Trinity College for a summer course.'

'I did, but for just two days; I came back today. I have to get ready for Buckingham Palace on Tuesday, don't I? Daddy dear!' she laughed.

'Less of the cheek, young lady!' he rebuked in a soft tone. 'Tell me, did you see Mr Tucker? He went across to Dublin yesterday.'

Hesitation; then: 'No, Daddy, I didn't.'

'That's strange; he said he'd try to look you up for me. You were staying at the halls of residence, weren't you?'

'Yes, but he didn't call. I'm sure if he didn't contact me he had a very good reason.'

'All right, dear, speak to you tomorrow. Try to calm your mother down for me.' Martin scratched his forehead.

'I will,' sighed Julia. 'Good night, Daddy.' She rang off.

After Norma Martin went to bed Julia was back on the telephone; it was time to report.

ST LOUISE'S CONVENT SCHOOL, MAYFIELD, EAST SUSSEX
Monday, 6 July. 1 a.m.
Autumn Harvest: zero minus 23 hours

The car entered the grounds of St Louise's Convent School at around 1 a.m. It kept to the sweeping driveway that led to the rear of the school buildings, avoiding the area of the boarders' dormitory-block and the nuns' quarters. The car left immediately after dropping the man off. He pulled up the collar of his leather coat against the drizzling rain and headed into the school library from the rear, using the fire-exit door as he had been instructed. The old nun awaited him.

'You are on time.' She studied him.

'I'm always on time,' George grinned and moved out from the shadows. 'You are Sister Marianne?'

She nodded. 'Come with me.' She hobbled across the library towards the main door with the aid of a walking-stick. The

Arab followed her as she guided him out of the cloistered courtyard and past the chapel towards the ruins of the old abbey set in the grounds well away from the school. It was a moonless night. George wondered how the old nun could keep going without getting lost; she must have known the place like the back of her decrepit hand. After nearly ten minutes they came to the ruins of the original sixteenth-century abbey. Only the stone walls remained intact. She guided him to the side of one of the ruined walls and took a small torch from beneath her habit, shining the light towards a large crypt amidst an old overgrown graveyard set beside the abbey's perimeter wall.

'Down there,' she whispered and moved off. George followed on. The rusty gate at the top of the crypt steps was open. At the bottom of the steps there was another iron gate. Sister Marianne hobbled down, producing a large key with which she unlocked the padlock, removing the rusty chain. Most of the crypt was set underground; George saw that it contained at least twenty old coffins, all set in against the damp walls on shelves cut out of granite. The smell of decay was evident. Some of the coffins were very ornate, especially the early Victorian ones containing the last members of the Lancelyn family.

'All these names, they are the same.' George spoke in a deep voice.

'The Lancelyn family donated the land here for the abbey in the sixteenth century. You might say they have a sort of proprietary right to be here, I suppose.'

George stared at the old nun's scarred face in the torchlight; it would be as close as he'd ever come to witnessing a real-life horror picture, he imagined. In the centre of the crypt floor stood a stone altar with the sculptured features of a knight in armour, his legs crossed, a long sword extending the full length of his body from chiselled hands clasped over his chest. The old nun tapped the floor beside the altar three times with her stick. There was a rumbling sound and then the complete altar slid to one side revealing another series of steep steps, a dim light glowing up from the bottom.

'The abbey monks used this for a time as a refuge hundreds of years ago. I shall leave you now. Come to me tonight at eleven o'clock. Everything you need is down there.' She turned and hobbled back, reclosing the iron gates. George walked slowly down the narrow steep staircase; as he reached the bottom the altar above rolled back into place. Following a short tunnel he entered a large room. François Debré and Nikos Papadopoulos stood towards the front of the thirty men. Everyone was dressed in police uniform. Without exception they jumped to attention immediately.

'All present and correct, sir,' snapped Papadopoulos. George grinned, showing his yellowed teeth. Nothing could stop them now.

SHIELDHALL WHARF, GLASGOW
Autumn Harvest: zero minus 17 hours 45 minutes

The police search operation had been a hurried affair. Acting on information received from the National Drugs Intelligence Unit, the Glasgow City Police and Drugs Squad descended on number 3 wharf at Shieldhall at 6.15 precisely. There were five warehouses fronting on to the quay; all were deserted. The warehouses were entered simultaneously, locks snapped open and doors smashed, much to the disdain of the local harbourmaster. But the planned search revealed absolutely nothing. The sniffer dogs attached to the Drugs Squad were sent in first, but none of the handlers reported anything unusual in their dogs' response. A further manual search also turned up nothing.

After several hours of intricate searching the Assistant Chief Constable in charge was about to call off the operation when PC Burrows took his black Labrador bitch called Tinker out of the police van for some exercise. He was quite at a loss as to why his superiors had ordered him and his dog on the search, for Tinker was an explosives sniffer dog, used mainly on port and airport duties, but such was the panic that morning that anything or anyone even in the vicinity of central Glasgow was eligible for the dockside search. Tinker bounded off straight into the third shed, followed closely by her master. The search teams had already packed up and moved to another location. After the six-year-old Labrador had relieved herself, she waddled across the empty floor towards a pile of crates at the far end of the shed.

Burrows immediately identified the dog's interest as it began to whine and scratch at the bottom of one of the crates. The tedium of the morning lifted like a weight off the policeman's brain as he jogged over to the discarded crates, encouraging the dog on. Tinker began sniffing around the other crates left lying open by the police search team, but the dog kept coming back to the same crate. Burrows peered inside the crate; it was empty and as clean as a whistle. He was becoming slightly annoyed with the dog's stupid persistence until he saw the scratch marks on the dusty concrete floor. The crate had been moved at one stage, and whatever had been inside had to be really heavy to cause those marks; yet the stencilled notice on the outer crate casing read 'Tea – Product of India'. Burrows put his weight against the large crate and eased it over on to its side.

The dog yelped and barked excitedly; when Burrows looked down Tinker was standing by his side, tail wagging furiously. The dog was holding a piece of green greased paper in her mouth; the torn piece of paper had somehow fallen and become covered by the crate when it had been shoved some time earlier. Burrows took the paper and smelt it. Apart from the Arabic lettering along the margin, the smell of marzipan was unmistakable.

'What's going on, Constable? This shed's been cleared already!' A uniformed chief inspector with an angry look in his eyes stood at the open warehouse doors.

'Gelignite!' shouted Burrows indignantly. Tinker barked furiously in confirmation.

EASTERN SIBERIA
5.15 p.m. local time
Autumn Harvest: zero minus 16 hours 45 minutes

The Red Bear reconnaissance satellite maintained its orbital path just 175 kilometres above the earth's surface. At the Omega-classified satellite communications centre at Viliuisk the atmosphere in the intelligence room was electric. Colonel-General Viktor Nikolayevich Grechko no less had just landed by private jet at the Yakutsk airbase and was on his way to the top-secret establishment by helicopter.

The man in charge of the centre was a thirty-year-old scientific genius called Suvorov. He also held the rank of GRU colonel, although the rank was of little relevance to him or the GRU general technically in charge of the centre. Suvorov ran the show; what he said went without question, what he wanted he got. The sixty-one-year-old General Chernyavin was there as window-dressing, a glorified security guard with a garrison of six hundred to ensure Suvorov remained undisturbed. Even the KGB were unaware of the establishment's true capability. That was why staff selection was so important; there were only two ways out of Viliuisk – to another GRU posting or in a box.

The Hind swept down over the snowy terrain and across the four separate security zones that ringed the complex for over three miles in every direction. The pilot banked just past the main radio control centre and touched down on the landing-circle beside the administration building. Grechko was followed off the Hind by Mikhailov; both men hurriedly crunched across the snow to the main entrance. Suvorov and Chernyavin were waiting just inside the warm entrance-hall; even the normal Spetsnaz guards had been dispersed from the immediate area. The two men pushed inside the swing-doors. Suvorov's eyes widened; it was the first time he had seen both men out of uniform.

'Comrade General.' Chernyavin saluted. 'I trust you had a pleasant journey.'

'Chernyavin!' Grechko finished unbuttoning his heavy over-coat and passed it to a rather unimpressed Mikhailov along with his hat as he stepped forward to embrace his old friend. 'You have put on weight, my friend.'

'I am almost sixty-two, Comrade General,' smiled the man.

'And overdue for a peaceful retirement at a dacha beside the Black Sea. When this is all over I'll see that you get it, I promise.'

The man's eyes lit up.

Grechko turned towards the younger Suvorov. 'And you, young Comrade Suvorov, for you I will buy ten more satellites.'

'Four would be ample, Comrade General.' The scientist grinned.

Grechko placed an arm around the younger man's shoulders and walked off down the long corridor. Mikhailov handed the coat and hat to the still grinning Chernyavin. 'Your job, I think, comrade.' The old general's face dropped. Mikhailov was a different beast entirely; he let the deputy head of the GRU walk ahead. Chernyavin was old enough to be still religious; he'd say a prayer to St Peter. God protect them all if the bastard ever took over the reins completely.

The inspection of the mainly underground communications centre and intelligence facility took over half an hour. The whole time Suvorov was locked in conversation with Grechko, the questions were searching, especially in the intelligence-analysis room.

'Suvorov, you are absolutely sure the locking mechanism on the Red Bear will stop the Americans from seeing what is going on?'

'Absolutely. We have the most up-to-date information on their latest "Project 1010" Reconsat programme; we're five years ahead of them at least.'

'At least I have a valid argument for the Politburo if someone asks me to justify the billions of roubles you spend here each year,' grunted Grechko. 'Very well. I want to be kept informed; there is to be no delay.'

'No, Comrade General.'

'Very good!' Grechko smiled and patted the younger man on both shoulders. He pulled Chernyavin aside. 'Now, old friend, where do you keep the brandy?'

Suvorov returned to his office just beside the communications control centre. The complex was in fact quite small; apart from the billet for the six-hundred-strong security force and the staff quarters for eighty, it was the housing for the bare minimum of offices and facilities. Most of the complex was under the snow-covered landscape except for two electron-optical Deep Space Surveillance telescopes housed in camouflaged domes measuring just ten metres across and five metres high. The centre could monitor everything Suvorov wanted; with the addition of a simple computer program he could create 'ghost' satellites and play havoc with NORAD and NASA in seconds.

The jamming facility was only an off-shoot; like most technological breakthroughs it was discovered by accident, and by Suvorov himself. The principle was childishly simple; the satellites targeted at Viliuisk were given mirror images, similar to a recorded overlay. The discovery had obvious military implications – battalions, even armies, could vanish with the flick of a switch – but the discovery was only in its infancy; they had to walk before running. Suvorov had been forced into allowing his discovery to be used for real. He had warned of its shortcomings, also of its vulnerability; keeping his mouth shut hadn't been easy at all. Mikhailov came in to the office, his face stern as always; he terrified the scientist, and he knew it.

'Well, comrade, things are going well.'

'Comrade General.' Suvorov stood up, his mouth suddenly dry.

'I have just been looking over your centre. You have done well.'

'Thank you, comrade.'

'I presume that old idiot Chernyavin suspects nothing?'

'Nothing. He is not . . . technically minded. Computers terrify him.'

'But he knows you, comrade; you spend much time together. You haven't given him reason to suspect, I hope.'

'None. We play much chess together; there is little else to do sometimes.'

'Well, think of it as playing chess, Suvorov, and in "X-Ray Check".' Mikhailov's beady eyes closed a fraction. 'I want a mistake made. Your equipment is going to malfunction, and

422

the Americans are going to see exactly what is going on at Chevering Hall and the other places, too. Do not fail me.'

'I will do as you say.' The young scientist flopped into his chair just after the 1st Chief Deputy of the GRU left to join Grechko and Chernyavin. He was glad of having committed himself to another in advance of this day. It did not pay to serve one master, especially one such as Mikhailov.

LONDON
Autumn Harvest: zero minus 10 hours

The discovery at Glasgow was enough. The Special Branch chief went directly to the Metropolitan Police Commissioner's office before lunch; by 2 p.m. the Prime Minister's office had confirmed that the venue for the NATO summit conference due to commence in under twenty-four hours had been changed from Chequers to Chevering Hall in East Sussex. Frazer Holbeck got confirmation from his deputy director-general just after 2 p.m. It did not surprise him; and, frankly, in full consideration of what had been going on around him recently, he imagined nothing would ever surprise him again.

MI5 already had a contingency plan in operation to make quite sure that the venue was so changed. Now Holbeck could remain quiet in the background, happy in the knowledge that his intervention was no longer required. The earlier bogus information from the Middle East via AMAN, the Israeli military intelligence organization, along with the panic in Glasgow, would be sufficient for the venue to be changed to the more readily accessible Chevering Hall. He thought about Mikhailov; the Russian had known the venue would change all along.

'The bastard!' Holbeck grunted to himself.

EASTERN SIBERIA
1 a.m. local time
Autumn Harvest: zero minus 8 hours

General Grechko was well intoxicated by early morning. He and Chernyavin had cleared a full bottle of Napoleon brandy between them, washed down with several black coffees laced with vodka. They were now in the monitoring studio overlooking the main control room of the communications centre.

In the wide room below them they watched the several dozen white-coated technicians and scientists as they worked fastidiously at and around the banks of computer terminals and data processors which stretched across the room in three inverted semi-circular rows, turned inwards to face a massive computerized wallmap of the world based on a Plate Carrée Projection showing also each of the twenty-four time-zones. It spanned over fifteen metres and stood five metres high. To the right-hand side another screen depicted two revolving worlds: the bottom showed the planet movement in real time, the imperceptible changes impossible to witness with the naked eyes; the upper model was a computer project, simulating the programming of each satellite in the Red Bear programme.

The two drunken men watched as Suvorov joined his team in the communications nerve-centre below them. Grechko's eyes narrowed slightly as he watched Mikhailov hovering in the background beside the raised back row of computer terminals. It troubled him that his deputy was taking such a personal interest. Mikhailov was well known for his delegation of responsibility and distancing himself from those around him; this eager interest from the normally dour-faced but now smiling Mikhailov was unsettling.

The technicians were well into their fixed sequence, providing an inventory of each satellite's condition. The main wall-display was now illuminated, showing the tracking paths of each of the four Red Bear Spysats, the critical parameters being plotted several revolutions ahead. Suvorov moved about his domain like a prowling cat. This was his castle. Here he was king; all the Mikhailovs in the world were an irrelevance to him in here. They needed him, and that was that; no compromise or half-gestures, no countermanding his orders. Yes, here he was his *own* man.

'Well, Sasha?' Suvorov moved beside Budyenny, his forty-eight-year-old second-in-command. The physicist nodded without looking up from his VDU; he was rechecking the countdown procedure in preparation for the satellites' passage through a series of 'gates', essential for their preparation to receive the new targeting data.

'Everything is running perfectly, Nikolai. I'm ready to start the time sequence in under three minutes. We have confirmation on all four trajectories.'

'All right.' Suvorov patted his colleague's shoulder. 'I'll not crowd you, my friend. I'll leave you to it.'

Budyenny smiled and got on with his job. Initially he had been resentful of the younger man being brought in over his head; but as time progressed, so did his change of heart. Suvorov was indeed a genius, perhaps several decades ahead of his time. Budyenny felt almost sorry for his young boss; if it had been another country – or, for that matter, outside Mikhailov's iron-fist grip – Suvorov would have been hailed as another Einstein. Already in the field of astrophysics Suvorov had just about rewritten the book; yet, because of his work in the Omega top-secret establishment, the book would never reach the publisher's desk.

'Timing sequence, countdown beginning.' A female technician's voice broke the atmosphere in the control room, booming out through a series of wall-mounted speakers. Seconds later they began counting down the final minute.

'Sixty . . . fifty-nine . . . fifty-eight . . .'

Grechko began to pop another couple of capsules; the alcohol had done nothing for his stomach ulcers. He was beginning to pale and sweat.

'Are you all right, Viktor?' asked Chernyavin.

Grechko rubbed his stomach and loosened his tie. '*Da*. It is nothing I cannot handle. But, old friend, I wish I could say the same about him.' He nodded down towards Mikhailov; the 1st Deputy was almost standing on tiptoe trying to catch every detail of what was going on.

'Thirty-three . . . thirty-two . . .' The female voice continued over the sound system.

'He's like a spoilt little schoolboy with a new toy!' Chernyavin said mockingly.

'He's a dangerous little bastard! That's what he is,' snapped Grechko as he began to cough. He didn't know which was worse, the current burning pain in his intestines or the rattling cough which seemed to loosen every nut and bolt in his ailing and ageing body.

'Perhaps I am the lucky one, Viktor.' Chernyavin turned towards his friend. 'Maybe I'm stuck here, but at least I'm out of the Moscow rat race.'

'*Da,*' replied Grechko. It was about all he could manage to emit as he tried to control his breathing and the pain. Damn that bastard Mikhailov, he thought, for bringing him to such a place; even in summer it was cold.

'Five . . . four . . . three . . . two . . . one . . . contact!' The voice echoed across the communications room.

'Contact confirmed, ignition procedure on, Red Bear One activated.' It was Budyenny's voice now. 'Two activated.' A pause now. The tension began to mount. All the computer predictions meant nothing unless the four Spysats activated in perfect unison.

'Three and four activated!' continued Budyenny, his voice carrying his anxiety to everyone present.

Mikhailov rubbed his hands together and checked his watch: in less than three hours they'd be ready for a most spectacular show indeed. Above the earth, in low orbit, the Spysats' telemetry began to change; small explosive charges ignited to change each satellite's pitch and direction. Each satellite was now already well into a multitude of repetition sequences as the on-board computers chopped through their programs. Having already been repositioned several orbits earlier, the final adjustments were now being made; they were flying in line through space pitching in on a trajectory which would take all four satellites in over the United Kingdom at 51°20′ N and also directly over Chevering Hall. Each satellite had the ability to survey a fifty-kilometre track in any kind of weather. Suvorov had produced a system whereby during night or day the Red

426

Bear satellite's nuclear-powered telescopes and sensors could pick out a vehicle registration-plate if given the angle of approach. Now, with all four on continuous fly-over, they had a limited but extended viewing-window to see the target area. As the hour approached for Red Bear One to close into the final approach stage, Suvorov rejoined his colleague Budyenny.

'Sasha, I want to see the control list for all four birds,' he said calmly.

'Which section?' replied the scientist.

'Delta three,' continued Suvorov.

Budyenny typed in the command. Instantly a checklist of over four hundred items began to flash on the VDU. Suvorov leant across and smashed one of the arrow keys; the itemized checklist began to fly up the screen, disappearing at the top edge.

'Anything the matter, comrade?'

A chill went down Suvorov's spine; he paused in what he was doing and turned to Mikhailov standing right beside him.

'Nothing is the matter, Comrade General.'

'What are you doing?' Mikhailov was not being put off. He detected something; he wasn't quite sure what it was yet.

'My job, Comrade General.' Suvorov knew he sounded arrogant, but somehow he didn't care any more.

Mikhailov glanced over the young scientist towards the VDU. 'What is that?' he demanded.

As Suvorov was about to answer Mikhailov continued: 'You, Comrade Budyenny, you tell me!'

Budyenny was a little startled. 'It's a checklist for the satellite control system.'

'But surely everything is under control already, is it not?' Mikhailov's voice became loud. It was out of character for him; heads began to turn around the control room.

'Everything is under control,' insisted Budyenny.

'Then, why are you checking it again?' Mikhailov demanded in a threatening tone as he looked back at Suvorov.

'I thought the inquisition went out with Stalin!' retorted Suvorov. Had he seen himself, he might have remained silent. He was shaking with anger and an underlying feeling of guilt. Who was this stupid soldier to question the likes of him?

Mikhailov got a sudden urge to draw his pistol and shoot

the young man there and then, but he contented himself with prodding Suvorov sharply in the left shoulder with a jabbing finger.

'You little bastard! Don't you ever speak to me like that again!'

Suvorov was speechless, his anger rising like a volcano awakened from its dormancy.

'Comrade General?' Grechko's voice came across the Tannoy system which operated independently from the observation room overlooking the control centre. 'Comrade General Mikhailov, will you join me in the observation room?' A pause, then: 'Immediately, comrade.' Grechko was firm.

'I will deal with you later!' Mikhailov reverted to speaking in his normal low key. Yet the whispered words now seemed more menacing. He turned and walked out, leaving Suvorov standing red-faced and short of breath.

'Phew!' Budyenny gave a deep sigh of relief. 'Nikolai? Remind me not to let you stand too close to me in the future.'

'I hate him!' replied Suvorov.

'And doesn't he know it!' Budyenny said through clenched teeth. He patted his computer terminal. 'Now, what was it you were wanting?'

'Three-seven-one,' replied Suvorov, looking up at the glass-fronted observation room and catching Mikhailov's glare as he glanced down at him.

'Got it,' replied the scientist. He studied the information in puzzlement.

The VDU display flashed before him.

SPYSAT: RED BEAR ONE
SECTION: DELTA 3
LISTING: 371

10	—	1	CODE	—	ALLOCATION	(1–12)
7	—	2	CODE	—	DISPATCH	(1–12)
173.6	—	3	CODE	—	PROXIMITY	(1–300)
ON		4	CODE	—	LOCK-IN	
ON		5	CODE	—	ISOLATION	
ON		6	CODE	—	LINK-UP	
ON		7	CODE	—	COMMS SHIELD	

'What's this?' He really was startled now. 'I haven't seen this before.'

'It's a back-up for the primary lock-out control against hostile interrogation.'

'I didn't know about this!' continued Budyenny.

'I only reprogrammed it myself last week,' replied Suvorov, now staring down at the screen.

'Why?'

'Because I'm going to override the system and turn the shields off.'

'Are you crazy?' exclaimed Budyenny, trying not to draw attention to himself.

'No.' Suvorov studied the information before him. Codes 1 and 2 were as normal. Code 3 revealed the presence and proximity of a hostile satellite. It read 173.6 and began falling to 172 as he considered his options. The remaining codes related to the control of the 'mirror image' capacity each Spysat possessed to throw up artificial images to intruder satellites.

'What is that at 172?' Suvorov asked.

Budyenny tapped into another VDU beside him and gave the answer immediately.

'It's a NATO-4 Geostationary Combat.'

'All right.' Suvorov leant over. 'Trust me, Sash, and don't ask me any questions for now.' He began changing codes 4, 5, and 7, and then pressed the 'Enter' key. A small red light began to flash against each of the display codes. Budyenny covered his face with his hands.

'Please, Sasha, no scene here,' Suvorov whispered.

'No, I'll save it for my firing squad,' he groaned.

Suvorov ignored the remark, looking down to the row in front of him; the two technicians monitoring Red Bear One had not been alerted to the change in the satellite's disposition. Suvorov had overridden his own interrogation procedure. The satellite was no longer giving its 'mirror image', and its communications system was open to complete interrogation, but the technicians monitoring would see no change. Suvorov had reversed the mirror back in their faces! He hit another key, and Red Bear Three flashed up showing the same Delta 3 371 listing. Suvorov repeated himself; the red warning lights came on, and he gave a cursory glance over to the right. The monitors for Red Bear Three remained normal.

'Now, Sasha, act normal and relax. Everything is under control.' Suvorov smiled as he turned the VDU back to normal mode. The scientist remained silent, but he was not going to relax for the rest of the night.

Suvorov had relied on his knowledge of the existence and position of the American-built NATO-4 communications satellite. Apart from its normal use for transmitting and transposing high-level NATO traffic, it had the ability to interrogate automatically any hostile satellite that came within its reach, and all four Red Bear Spysats would do exactly that in sequence. He also knew that the NATO-4 would digest the information from each Red Bear satellite and run a comparative analysis; the existence of the 'mirror image' ability would be revealed, and he knew the Americans would act fast. Their own Landsats and Spysats would start following the Soviet satellites; the 'hot' and 'cold' imagery of Chevering Hall would be almost public knowledge inside both NATO and NORAD headquarters by morning.

Similarly, but more important to Suvorov, his Soviet counterparts in the Plesetsk Space Centre would also see what was happening. Viliuisk would become Kremlin knowledge. Regardless of what Chairman Glazkov had promised the young scientist, Suvorov had become the master of his own destiny for once. For once he was doing what he wished and all at a time when he could cause maximum damage to Mikhailov personally, whatever cover action Mikhailov had going in the United Kingdom. It took every ounce of willpower for Suvorov not to grin like the cat he was as he continued to move around his domain – a domain that would no longer be his prison.

LONDON AIR TRAFFIC CONTROL CENTRE, WEST DRAYTON

Monday, 6 July. 9.02 p.m.
Autumn Harvest: zero minus 2 hours 58 minutes

'LATCC, West Drayton, this is flight LOT 281 inbound from Warsaw. I have an emergency. Repeat, I have an emergency. We have . . .' Static broke up the airwaves, obliterating the remainder of the signal. Sam Fowler was one of the duty air traffic controllers at London Air Traffic Control Centre, based at West Drayton on the outskirts of London. Fowler had been monitoring the Polish Airways Ilyushin 62 airliner for some minutes as it travelled inbound for Gatwick across his sector area.

'State your emergency, LOT 281. This is LATCC, West Drayton. Are you declaring a Mayday? Over.' There was no response, just continued static. In his twenty-two years' service as an ATC, Sam Fowler had just about seen every emergency plan in operation, from mid-air collisions to hijacking. Whatever the problem, LOT 281 had no better help than Sam Fowler. He tried raising the aircraft again without success. Fowler turned to his chief sector controller, already standing behind him. The CSC had been independently assessing the situation for several minutes beforehand.

'Give me your evaluation, Sam.' The CSC exuded his usual calmness.

'A Polish airliner, flight LOT 281, inbound for Gatwick in Upper Romeo One. It was at thirty-one thousand feet and positioned fifty miles east of Clacton when I got the initial report, but now it's dropped to twelve thousand and still ten miles out. Cause of emergency unknown.'

'OK, Sam, I'll clear all other traffic out of the flight-path. You keep trying to raise them and let me know about any deviation in their direction immediately.'

After instigating the necessary back-up procedures the CSC returned to Fowler's side. The watch supervisor was already at the console checking all the other air traffic in Upper Romeo One.

'Fred, I presume that you've heard?' quizzed the CSC. Fred Bagley, the night watch supervisor, nodded.

Just then Fowler interrupted. 'Chief, it's a Mayday all right. I've regained an intermittent signal; it appears that three engines are out completely and one of the remaining two isn't stabilizing. Apparently something to do with oil pressure. They're still losing height, now down to five thousand and still dropping. Not enough to make Gatwick. We'll have to divert, but even then I still can't be sure if they'll understand my signal!'

The watch supervisor was already leading the CSC to one side. 'We've no choice. We'll have to keep her well away from London. It'll have to be Stansted. Southend couldn't cope with this bird, especially if there's a crash on emergency landing.'

'I'll get right on it.' The CSC turned towards the nearby back-up controller already tuned into Upper Romeo One.

All air traffic originating from Eastern Bloc countries is automatically monitored by an RAF unit attached to West Drayton. The Air Defence Surveillance Unit had been relaying all the information on LOT 281 by telephone and computer link to RAF Waddington since overhearing the original emergency signal. A Nimrod AEW Mark 3 jet, now circling high above the southern coastline, was placed on full alert. The Nimrod, part of the British NATO Airborne Warning System, had been following a number of inbound flights approaching across Belgium, France, and the Irish Sea.

Owing to the nationality and place of origin the Ilyushin jet was not only a civil emergency, but was now also treated as a threat to national security. As the Nimrod concentrated on the Polish airliner, the Ilyushin's course began to deviate considerably southwards. Number 11 (Fighter) Group of RAF Strike Command was now racing against the clock. Two Tornado Mark 3 interceptors from 56 Squadron were scrambled from RAF Wattisham. Within minutes the two fighters were airborne and screaming towards their target, the fighters' multi-mode Marconi radar systems responding rapidly, giving both pilots accurate directional information, closing distance, and estimated time to intercept. The two Tornadoes screamed towards the Ilyushin airliner at Mach 1, climbing to a service height of five thousand feet.

By now the airliner had begun to lose further height rapidly and was falling towards the lower limits of the radar scanners. Sam Fowler protested quietly to himself as he finally lost contact with LOT 281. The Nimrod, on the other hand, was still able to follow the airliner's flight-path, but from its distance and altitude it was not all-revealing; the close proximity of the Ilyushin to the undulating terrain began to cause interference with the radar image. At precisely five hundred feet the tail belly loading-doors to the airliner were opened from within the cargo-hold. The aircraft maintained a steady altitude, travelling just above stalling speed. Instantly twelve Spetsnaz commandos parachuted from the cargo-hold in a 'close stick' formation. After several seconds a warning signal in the airliner's cockpit told the replacement co-pilot that the hold was now empty of its human cargo, the loading-doors released automatically by computer. The pilot looked on in agitation as the GRU replacement co-pilot handed back full control of the aircraft to him. Only a minuscule blip registered for a split second on the Nimrod's electronic surveillance apparatus.

Obliterated against the terrain just south-west of Canterbury the landing went unnoticed. All twelve Russian commandos hit the ground inside seconds of leaving the aircraft, their black parachutes opening only vital moments before each soldier hit the ground at phenomenal speed. Even with the most rigorous training, the most experienced of jumpers could readily break his neck under such conditions, but inside seconds all the Spetsnaz commandos had landed safely and undetected on British soil.

By the time the Tornadoes had visual contact with the Ilyushin, the Polish captain had already informed West Drayton of an improvement in the aircraft's performance. The airliner had already begun to climb, albeit erratically, to a height of three thousand feet and was now in full communication with LATCC, West Drayton. Following the pilot's assurance of the improved engine performance, it was decided to allow the airliner to continue west towards Gatwick under the guidance and supervision of the RAF. Amazingly, throughout the entire incident the civilian passengers and other crew members had remained totally oblivious to the drama. The RAF alert was now reduced to normal status, and after shepherding the Ilyushin to Gatwick the Tornadoes steered off north-east towards their home base. Sam Fowler breathed a deep sigh of relief once he handed over control to Gatwick Tower.

The following morning's Civil Aviation Authority inspection of the Ilyushin 62 would reveal the explosion of a minor pump and hydraulic failure as the direct cause of the jet's combined engine failure. The precise cause of the explosion would be attributed to a heavy oil-leak from two servo pumps which in turn were ignited accidentally by the pilot's actions in the normal course of flying the aircraft. The difficulty in radio transmission would be attributed to a power failure and electrical overload, once again as an off-shoot of the engine difficulties. Of course the poor safety record and crash history of the Ilyushin 62 would go far towards allaying any ongoing suspicion by the British authorities.

The precision landing of the commandos had been co-ordinated by a present computer program fed into the airliner's autopilot by the GRU operative acting as co-pilot, the 'black box' flight-recorder having already been programmed with information and data corroborating the aircraft's 'symptoms'. The drop zone had been carefully and deliberately chosen, being an extremely flat and isolated farm area of Kent. At landing speeds of up to sixty miles per hour every care had to be taken to reduce risk. Landing from five hundred feet was hairy enough, but at night there were obvious complications. To enhance the survival rate each jumper wore night-vision goggles to aid landing techniques and also assist rapid regrouping once on the ground. In addition, each man had an audible paging device set into an earpiece fitted inside his protective headgear; even in pitch darkness and under a moonless sky the group could re-form in total silence.

Without a single word being uttered the group leader checked with the section leader who in turn signalled the safe landing and grouping of the entire unit. The black parachutes had already been gathered up and rolled into carrying pouches by each man. They would be dumped at a later time along with any ancillary material. Only three minutes had elapsed since their departure from the cargo hold, and the group had already begun to melt into the countryside, evaporating towards the pick-up point.

The largest of the nearby farm buildings was the old barn; built originally in the early 1950s, it had reluctantly stood the test of time and now with its new coating of red paint it at least looked as fine as it had been when originally built. At least for the next few months the old rust patches and patch-work repairs would be obliterated. The owner lived some eight miles away, and since the death of his brother the old farmer had leased out the two-hundred-acre holding on a yearly rental basis. The new company that leased the property had done little but comply with the legal requirements regarding the upkeep and repair of the old farm buildings. What did the old farmer care if some London-based company interested in potatoes and barley hadn't utilized the ground to its full advantage so long as they not only paid the rent but had offered to paint the old barn as well. The red barn was now a perfect landmark for both the commandos and the elements involved in the pick-up.

Once in the safety of the barn the soldiers rid themselves of the jump gear. Twelve men in British Army combat-smocks began to put on their sand-coloured berets; there was no mistaking the badge of the Special Air Service. From now on every man responded in perfect English. The individual accents were of second nature; in reality they each knew more about the British Army and their respective roles than the average serving British soldier. There could be no abort to their mission, no turning back now. They had a tense waiting period until the Royal Mail parcel-delivery van arrived at the farmyard and backed into the unit barn. Silently the Spetsnaz commandos climbed on board and huddled together in the rear compartment of the van. Within one hour they would reach their destination.

The telephone rang for almost a moment before Alec Martin answered. He had fallen asleep and was finding it difficult even to focus on the receiver let alone pick it up.

'Yes?' he growled, snatching at the wall-mounted telephone.

'Alec, it's me.' It was Ivanov.

'Where the hell are you?' Martin demanded, putting on his glasses to check the time.

'At Dublin Airport. I'm just about to board the last flight for Heathrow.' There was silence at the other end.

'Alec, are you there?'

'Of course I'm bloody here!' yawned Martin.

'Alec, I've some bad news. You were right. Garand is alive. I've seen him.' He allowed a few moments for the words to register, trying to prepare the Englishman for the worse to come. 'But he didn't do the recent killings. The man's now a vegetable, isolated in a Dublin nursing home.'

Martin's heart sank. 'Go on.'

'But I believe that Mary Garand is alive.'

'Where?'

'Remember you told me about the old nun that your daughter went to see all the time?'

'Sister Marianne.' Martin was now fully awake.

'Well, I'm pretty damned sure that it's her.'

'But she's twenty or thirty years older than Mary Garand!' protested Martin.

'You said she was badly scarred around the face. She was burnt, Alec, burnt in the fire in Dublin. Can you imagine how that would age somebody's appearance? She just replaced the real nun who died; it was a perfect opportunity for her to escape, an opportunity she created herself!'

'Oh my God! All those people,' gasped Martin.

'She'll stop at nothing.'

'Bloody hell! I have to warn Julia; she's in contact with her all the time.'

'Alec! Alec! Listen to me, will you? Is Julia adopted?'

'Why the hell do you ask that?' Martin's anger was almost out of control; all he could picture was the old woman diseasing his daughter's mind for all those years. Then slowly the reality started to dawn.

'She is, isn't she?'

'How in damnation did you know that?'

'Alec, where did you get Julia from when she was a baby?'

Alec Martin was panicking now; he was desperately trying to blot the dawning truth from his passive mind. The conscious side of his brain had already confirmed what he didn't want to be told.

'It was shortly after we came home from Northern Ireland. Norma had lost the baby; it was stillborn.' His heart felt heavy now.

'Alec, there's no easy way to say this, but Julia is Garand's daughter and that damned old nun is her real mother.'

'I . . .' Alec Martin was speechless.

'Look, I checked it out with the records offices in Dublin and Belfast. I also checked the convent and Catholic orphanage involved. I can show you the proof.'

The line went dead.

'Shit!' growled Ivanov. He burst out of the telephone-kiosk and raced across the open concourse of the departure lounge as the last call for boarding was announced; he hoped that he wasn't going to be too late.

Alec Martin finally found a taxi firm that was prepared to accept a fare all the way to East Sussex after almost an hour of frustration. He had to point out the directions to the bemused West Indian driver, remembering the route to Mayfield from the times when he returned Julia to the boarding department early each Monday morning. He thought back to the old days when life was simple, he had a devoted wife and a loving affectionate daughter; but now he was losing one of them, if he hadn't done so already. Just who did Mary Garand think she was? Julia was his child, his and Norma's; they'd nursed her through all those childhood illnesses, they'd encouraged her when she needed it, they'd been there, they loved her, and he was convinced that she loved them.

After negotiating a series of winding country roads, the taxi finally passed through the pillared entrance to the convent school grounds. He got the taxi to let him off at the carpark fronting on to the main school entrance. He knew where to find the old nun, just where she always was, in the library. Moving fast and out of breath, he ran through the cloistered courtyard until he reached the library situated at the side of the main school building and chapel in the older section of the institution.

A dim yellow light cut through the leaded windows beside the library door. Alec Martin no longer had any reason left; he knew what he was doing was absolutely crazy, but so was the thought of losing his only child. He paused outside the latched door and waited. There was no sound from within. From across the courtyard the school chapel bell began to toll for midnight mass. Martin checked his gun, keeping the Walther inside his jacket pocket, before opening the door. He burst into the library. It appeared deserted, yet he knew she had to be there.

'Mary Garand! You rotten whore! Come on out and face me!' He stood in the middle of the stone floor looking around at the rows of shelves which spanned out towards the rear of the library. He heard a noise, a shuffling sound. He spun around to find the disfigured nun hobbling out of the shadows, supported as always by her wooden stick.

'So there you are, Mary!' He almost pitied the pathetic sight of her scarred and wizened face, but then he thought of what she'd done. 'Where's Julia?'

'Gone.'

'What do you mean – *gone*?'

'Gone to London. Where else?'

'I should have guessed a long time ago. An Irish nun working so close to my home and then so involved with our daughter.'

'You mean *my* daughter surely.' Mary Garand afforded herself a slight smile. It hardly registered on the twisted face.

'Stop persecuting me! Just tell me what the hell you've done!'

'Done? I've done nothing. I only directed my daughter as I saw best.'

'Best for who?'

'You'll have to ask your Russian friend that.'

438

'So it was you who sent those coded messages to Moscow?'

'The transmitter and codes were those used by an old associate of my husband's. He was called McGoldrick. Remember him, do you?'

'McGoldrick was a Russian agent?'

'You catch on slowly for an apparently intelligent man.' She hobbled over to a side-table and eased her body slowly into the chair. She was in pain, as always, but he no longer pitied her.

'Tell me one thing. Did Garand know anything about the Soviet involvement in the matter?' His voice trembled now.

'No, of course not. None of us knew. None of us had any idea of McGoldrick's real role at the time. It was only after he was shot and dying, on the run from the police, that he confided in me while I nursed him through his last hours in Belfast. Of course McGoldrick wanted me to find and destroy his radio transmitter and codes before they fell into enemy hands, as he put it, but I had ideas of my own.'

'Go on.' He gripped the gun in his pocket tighter.

'After my husband was left a vegetable I became quite caught up in the struggle that he'd so bravely volunteered for. It took me a long time to pay you all back. You know, after we smuggled my husband out of the North he lay in a coma in a hospital in Dundalk for a long time; he almost died twice.'

Alec Martin was not interested. 'So when McGoldrick died you took over – is that what you're saying?'

'In a way.' She smiled. 'But it was my opinion that the Russians had to pay just as much as the British. That's why I used McGoldrick's old transmitter and codes to put the fear of God into those heartless animals in the Kremlin.' She laughed now. 'Obviously it was also likely that the British would pick up the signals I sent, and that would incriminate Moscow even further.'

'You didn't think this all up yourself. There had to be someone helping you.'

'I said you were intelligent.' She laughed. 'I could have done so much more, you know, but when one is limited, burdened with the responsibility of motherhood!' She laughed again.

'You old bitch, you palmed your only child off just to get at me? You really are sick!'

'No, not sick. It was all very well thought out. I had little choice, for after the fire in Dublin I was so badly injured I would have been of no use to the child anyway. Fortunately I was mistaken for poor Sister Marianne who perished in the fire. I lay in a Dublin hospital swathed in bandages for seventeen weeks. I pretended to have a lapse of memory and to have lost the power of speech. It was so easy to learn about the nun from the constant stream of visitors to my bedside. She had no family; the nuns that had been closest to her had all died in the fire. It was an identity that I was happy to adopt. You were having me hunted both north and south of the border; it was perfect for me.'

'And Julia – how did she escape the fire?'

The old nun grinned. 'She was never there. She was already living in England with some of my friends. Then through the adoption agency I manipulated you and your wife to adopt the child.'

Martin grimaced, closing his eyes, trying to blot out the very idea.

'As far as the child was concerned, I just had her drop her first name, Patricia, and use the second name, Julia.'

'So what about the fire – accident or design?' He fought back the urge to kill her there and then.

The old nun rubbed her scarred face and chuckled again. 'That would be telling; but I tell you this, Mr Martin. I have a better relationship with my child then you ever had.' She began to raise her voice. 'Or, for that matter, your own wife.'

'You're evil!' Alec Martin turned and walked towards the door. 'I'm going to see you put behind bars for the rest of your natural!' He was just reaching for the handle when he felt the force slam him in the back. He was thrown up against the door. Alec Martin pulled the Walther from his pocket, but it fell to the floor. He began to force himself to turn round, but slid towards the stone floor, one leg buckling under the other. Mary Garand was still sitting at the reading-table; she held a silenced Beretta pistol in her right hand. The barrel was still smoking gently.

'The end, I think.' She smiled.

Alec Martin fought the welling pain in his back; blood was already slowly entering his mouth.

'Just tell me . . . Why? For God's sake.' He began to cough on the blood.

'Tomorrow morning a NATO conference with the heads of all the Alliance countries will meet at Chevering Hall. They will meet for the last time.' She chuckled again. 'Since forming our little breakaway group from the Provisionals we've made powerful new allies, as you discovered. With the combination of all that we have planned, every major government throughout the northern hemisphere will be thrown into confusion. You might say it is derivative of what the Russians themselves had planned some decades ago, but a few refinements have been added.'

Alec Martin fought to keep conscious. 'Where . . . does Julia come into this?'

'Who do you think killed the soldier in Derry, and then the Irish Justice Minister?' She chuckled again. The coldness of her laugh added to the chill that Martin now felt. 'She is an even better shot than her father. He would have been proud of her.'

'I *am* proud of her.' Martin coughed painfully.

'But she's a murderess, Mr Martin! Do you remember the year before she went to university, the year of the extended summer camp in France? Well, she went to northern Spain to a terrorist training-camp instead, and she graduated with the fullest honours. She's truly Harry Garand's daughter! You and your stupid little wife were only vehicles; you were there to give her the right environment, the right start in life, and through the Catholic adoption agency I was able to keep full control on which school you sent her to. I moulded her, not you; never you.'

'Damn! You evil old whore!' Martin was now almost hoping that the insults would precipitate his termination. Another bullet would finish him off completely, ending the rising pain but also the anguish. He tried to crawl towards the coat-stand beside the doorway and pull himself up; he had nothing to lose. After struggling for several seconds the stand came crashing down on to the floor in front of him. Slowly he eased himself back against the stone wall.

'It's no good, Mr Martin. You're already a dead man. It's only a matter of time now.'

Martin stared down at the smeared blood that he had trailed behind him as he'd moved across the floor. The bitch was right. He wasn't even able to stretch over to the Walther lying beside the door.

'If you sit there perfectly still, you may be able to stretch it out for a while longer. Plenty of time to say an act of contrition.' She chuckled again.

PART FOUR

AUTUMN HARVEST

CHEVERING HALL, EAST SUSSEX
Midnight, 6 July
Autumn Harvest: zero hour

Chevering Hall is a massive Georgian mansion bequeathed to the nation by the last Earl when facing the end of his family line. The ninety-one-year-old earl had the relevant papers drawn up as he lay on his deathbed at Chevering. That was in 1952; it took almost ten years for the government bureaucrats to determine what to do with the thirty-five-bedroom house set in two thousand acres of woodland and pasture, including a twenty-acre lake and bordered to the north-east by over a mile stretch of the best salmon- and trout-fishing river in the county.

Many schemes were prepared at the time, all of which were dismissed by the Land Commission which had assumed guardianship of the property. Then time itself intervened; the Government found itself more and more reliant on a small group of facilities for the now ever-increasing international conferences it was required to host. Nowadays Chevering was used at least four or five times a year for major conferences and seminars; the revenue created by the management of the large majority of the estate acreage paid handsomely towards the upkeep of the old mansion and the multitude of farm buildings. The main house was set amidst an inner paddock of twelve acres of carefully manicured lawns that stretched out in every direction from the three-storey grey stone house. It was quite unique and indeed majestic. Each corner of the main house was built into semi-circular bays which protruded from the line of the building and stretched up to the roof parapet line.

The gravel parking-area at the main entrance had been crunching steadily all afternoon; cars arrived and left by the minute, bringing the secretaries and ministerial staff to the conference. The first VIPs arrived just before tea-time; the British

Prime Minister and the Defence Secretary arrived by car; less than an hour later the others began to fly in by helicopter. Inside three hours the heads of state of the fifteen member countries of the NATO alliance were all at Chevering Hall. The entire estate was buzzing with the tightest security ring ever mustered by the security services.

The SAS and security service had the job of maintaining the close security necessary for the five-day conference. They had ringed the house, creating an invisible screen of sensors and alarm systems, effectively sealing it off except for the single approach road. Some of the SAS were dressed in police uniforms so as to demilitarize their appearance. After the incident at 10 Downing Street, and in the light of the latest threat-status report, the Prime Minister had wisely insisted on minimizing the overt security; she was not going to be intimidated by some terrorists, nor were his guests. The conference was going to be difficult enough because of the new American President's stance without everyone consumed with feelings of doom and disaster. The command headquarters for the security operation was established in a rear annexe, well away from the hustle and bustle of the main house. The two SAS radio operators and their major were too busy to see the man come into the communications room initially.

'Good to see someone busy.'

The major turned around to see Frazer Holbeck standing at the door immaculate as always with a camel coat draped over his shoulders partly obscuring his dinner-suit.

'Holbeck's the name. Colonel Holbeck. I'm with Five.' Holbeck produced his identity. The Army officer examined it briefly.

'Colonel, my name's Major Chalmers, OC "B" Squadron, 22nd SAS.'

'I know, Major. I reviewed the security arrangements myself. What strength have you on the ground?'

'Thirty-two out at present, another twelve on permanent reserve just next door.' The officer became a little embarrassed.

Holbeck cocked an ear; he could just hear the men talking over the noise of the blaring television.

446

'Major, I suggest you call all your men in somewhere for another briefing.'

'Why, sir?' The officer was totally puzzled.

'We have some new information on a terrorist threat here at Chevering. With the information I now have we stand an excellent chance of taking the terrorists out – permanently.' Holbeck was as usual totally plausible and convincing.

'Afraid I can't bring them all in at once. You understand, of course.'

'Of course!' Holbeck smiled. 'May I suggest we use the groundsman's sheds. They're on the south side; it'll be a lot easier than bringing them back here.'

'It certainly would,' smiled the major, thankful for the advice. He turned to the corporal sitting next to where he stood.

'Corporal, get X-ray 2. Ask him to collect X-rays 7, 9, 12, 13 and 14 and move to' – he paused, studying the map – 'reference 189726 for SITREP, Status Urgent.'

Holbeck kept back, a smile on his face; seconds later he and the major were headed for the Range Rover parked outside.

'I'll tell you on the way, shall I?' continued Holbeck, his voice fading down the corridor as one of the SAS radio operators looked after the two men. The soldier didn't notice the briefcase left behind by the man in the dinner-suit.

It was 2 a.m. when the police vans approached the roadblock at the entrance to the two-thousand-acre estate. The policemen on guard duty were not alarmed, having already been informed of the impending arrival of additional manpower five minutes earlier. The call had been placed to their security hut using a direct telephone link from the main house at Chevering Hall. Unknown to anyone, all calls to and from the house had been diverted for the last ten minutes. The first police van pulled up at the barrier. The police driver flashed his warrant card. The police sergeant at the checkpoint noted the police superintendent in the front passenger-seat. He saluted him immediately. François Debré acknowledged the salute, speaking in perfect English.

'Hello, Sergeant. All quiet, I presume?'

'Yes, sir.' The sergeant smiled.

'Have you many men out in the grounds at the moment?' François Debré already knew the answer.

'Over eighty officers and men in the outer cordon. Then about twenty or thirty military types in the inner cordon, about a quarter of a mile from the main house, sir.'

Debré nodded, screwing up his lips slightly. 'SAS, I suppose?'

'Yes, sir. Did nobody brief you at Headquarters?' The sergeant was slightly puzzled.

The Frenchman grinned. 'Of course they did. The deputy chief constable gave me the briefing personally.' He began to frown. 'He also told me that only those necessary were to know of the SAS involvement. You could take a risk mouthing off about it.'

The police sergeant stepped backwards. 'Yes, sir.' He saluted again before ordering one of his party to raise the metal barrier. Debré ignored the salute as the police van accelerated through the checkpoint, followed immediately by a second van.

'Cheeky young bastard!' cursed the middle-aged sergeant as he strolled over to the barrier. He tried to save face with the young constable who had overheard his reprimand. 'Did you see that? He didn't even acknowledge my salute, the bastard.'

The young policeman grinned.

At the next barrier the SAS had already been informed by a similar bogus telephone call. Their closed-net transceivers were not tied into the house directly but to the annexe buildings situated at the rear of the main house where a command and control post had been established. Owing to bogus intelligence from the Middle East only days before, along with the present scare after the Glasgow search, coupled with the abortive attempt on the Prime Minister's life, the security services had been only too glad of the switch in locations, giving the Personal Security people a chance to review the safety and security arrangements at all of the Prime Minister's residences.

Although Chevering had always been a substitute site for the conference, the security arrangements had been nevertheless hurried, and gaps had been left in the overall security umbrella. Large gaps. The SAS checkpoint was far more thorough by comparison. The barrier and hut were the same as before but, apart from two soldiers standing either side of the metal barrier, no other soldiers could be seen; yet Debré knew that for the last five hundred yards the two Transit vans had been under constant scrutiny. The police vans halted.

'Yes?' snapped the soldier.

The terrorist leader had difficulty making out his camouflaged face; the green and dark-brown camouflage-cream was smeared professionally right across the soldier's face, making it look like some macabre extension of his camouflage-jacket.

Debré leant across. 'Superintendent Mackell and party. We're expected.'

'Don't care, mate. I want you all out, checked and searched – warrant cards, the lot.'

'But surely you must realize we are in a terrible rush. Just who are you anyway?'

'I'm Sergeant Dodds.' The camouflage-cream hid any facial expression the soldier may have possessed.

'Well, Sergeant, I'm a police superintendent and, apart from not appreciating being addressed as your "mate", I'm also unimpressed with your attitude!' Debré glared across at the soldier.

The soldier didn't flinch. 'I apologize about the form of address, Superintendent, but the rest still applies. It's everybody out.'

François grinned. 'Well, Sergeant, you'd better call in your men from around you and start checking.'

All the conversation had been relayed into the rear of the second van by open radio. Papadopoulos and another man had already alighted and were off the road into the trees beyond. As anticipated, the lights of the vehicles and the commotion had focused attention well away from them. This was an unrehearsed improvisation that had to work.

Suddenly the world erupted into hell. Both police vans were strafed with automatic gunfire without warning. A LAWS rocket was launched into the open rear of the second van, exploding instantly, killing everyone inside. The terrorists in the leading van began pouring out of the rear doors; already three lay dead inside. The first ones clear of the rear doors opened up with their Valmet M76 assault-rifles, laying down a murderous covering fire, but they were in a totally exposed

449

position with nowhere to hide. A female terrorist was next out of the rear doors, exploding smoke grenades to allow her comrades some cover; but before the grenades could take effect the young woman was shot through the temple. A grenade exploded amidst her escaped comrades, nullifying their covering fire. Before the others still trapped inside the back of the van could react, several more high-impact grenades were tossed in through the rear doors.

François Debré jumped away from the van, rolling down the slight camber from the road. He glanced up. The driver tried to follow him through the side-door. In the confusion following the explosion it was every man for himself. The terrorist driver had taken cover on the floor; protected from the impacting grenades, he then clambered across the passenger seat and was about to leap clear of the van's cab when Debré saw the man's chest explode outwards, ripped open by a burst of automatic gunfire from the other side of the van. The driver landed only two feet away from him, writhing like a beached fish. The Frenchman had already succumbed to the idea of failure. They had been betrayed; there was only escape left.

One by one the remaining wounded and maimed terrorists tried to make their bids for freedom. It was hopeless. Suddenly the second Transit van exploded anew as the fire spread to the fuel-tank; it only highlighted those terrorists still alive inside the first van. The van was racked with machine-gun fire from four separate positions.

Debré watched as years of preparation and months of painful training were washed away in his comrades' blood, literally inside seconds. He watched from the darkened roadside as the remaining four terrorists tried to leave the van, but were mowed down in a merciless crossfire of machine-guns. It absolutely amazed him how it all happened so quickly; it was all over in less than one minute! He slid further on down the bank into a small stream, waiting. No one followed; but, armed only with a silenced Soviet 9 mm Makarov pistol, Debré knew he was hardly a match for the SAS.

Far on the other side of the road, deep in the undergrowth, lay Nikos Papadopoulos and one of his men. The hardened little Greek was too much of a veteran to intercede. Someone tossed a hand-grenade into the front police van for good measure. The force of the explosion made the Greek duck; he knew they had to get out of the estate immediately, but for the moment it seemed impossible. When he thought it was safe to move he motioned to his companion and they slipped off into the thick woodland, away from the road-block.

They were more fortunate than Debré; both carried Valmet M76 assault-rifles and spare magazines, and the Greek was hoping that the police uniforms might just give them the advantage if met by an enemy patrol. They had moved across a ditch into the next tree-line when the ground before them opened up. A light machine-gun emptied into them. The Greek was cut down first, a line of bullets tearing his stomach apart. The other terrorist managed to fire a single shot into the trees before he took the full force of a second burst in the upper chest and head. Papadopoulos tried to get to his feet again. Pulling himself up on to his knees, he squatted, bent over his protruding intestines. He grabbed his Valmet rifle just before a third burst of gunfire hit him squarely in the chest. He was tossed backwards into the bushes, dead hands still clutching the rifle.

Debré had by now slipped slowly downstream. He ignored the shooting; distance was the object now. He had just imagined himself to be safe for the moment when a voice spoke.

'Stop right there!'

Debré froze.

'Drop the handgun,' continued the voice, stern and uncompromising. He complied, dropping the gun in the knee-high water.

'Now, hands on your head and turn about – slowly.'

On turning around he saw the SAS soldier standing on the other side of the river-bank, just above him. The soldier had a camouflage-netting which stretched down across his entire face; Debré had to look twice to see him properly. From the look of his muddy and saturated outfit he had been crawling through water for some time.

'Move it!' insisted his captor. The soldier was holding his semi-automatic rifle by the pistol grip with just one hand, the other arm dangling away from his side. He was not tall, but his muscular frame was evident even through the camouflage-jacket. After Debré placed both hands on his head he let his right hand slip gently back towards his neck. As the SAS man slid down the bank Debré struck. With a single action he unsheathed the throwing-knife strapped to the back of his neck and chucked it towards the soldier. He was just about to follow through, diving towards him, when the soldier fired a short burst from the rifle. The three bullets cut into Debré's left thigh. He screamed, falling into the stream face-down.

'You OK?' a voice rang out. It was the same sergeant who had stopped the terrorists at the checkpoint.

The young soldier looked up towards the bank, briefly nodded and looked down towards the knife stuck deeply into his left arm.

'You're a stupid bastard!' The sergeant reverted to Russian as he scrambled down beside the man and examined the wound. The Russian soldier gasped as his comrade wrenched the knife from his arm. Debré was writhing in the stream, crying out for help from the two Russians. The sergeant waded over and pulled him roughly to the river-bank. 'And you will do me nicely, Superintendent,' he continued.

Inside an hour the entire grounds of Chevering Hall were buzzing with military and police personnel. The occupants of the country mansion had awoken to the sound of the gunfire and explosions; the heads of state and their immediate staff had been assembled in the main banqueting hall by members of the security services and the Police VIP Protection Detail. The pyjama-clad group was in total disarray. The American President was first to try to bring calm to the gathering.

'Gentlemen, please! Let's cool it a little. I'm quite sure that, whatever the problem, the British have it all under control. Am I not correct, Prime Minister?' He addressed the British PM, looking for support rather than an answer. The Prime Minister was still dressed, having been working late on some cabinet papers.

'Of course we have, Mr President. Gentlemen, please let us remain calm while our security staff properly evaluate the matter.' She looked towards her private secretary, who turned and left the room accompanied by a plain-clothes policeman brandishing a Heckler & Koch machine-pistol.

The first SAS men were found in the 'operations room' in the annexe to Chevering Hall. Both were lying inside a cupboard unconscious, drugged and bound for good measure. Army and police helicopters were thick overhead by the time a search-party stumbled upon the groundsman's sheds towards the southern side of the estate. In the rear toolshed they found twenty-six SAS men lying unconscious, again tied hand and foot, mouths and eyes bound tightly with broad adhesive white plastic tape. Each man had been heavily drugged by means of an intravenous injection to the side of the neck. The other searchers had by that time already found the dead 'policemen' at the secondary checkpoint. It did not take long to establish that they were imposters; the local police HQ had by now confirmed that Superintendent Mackell and his party did not exist.

'But who killed them?' demanded the Prime Minister, standing beside the desk in the library.

The Chief Constable was dismayed. 'We don't know. The SAS contingent that was supposed to be at the inner checkpoint was found tied up and drugged on the outskirts of the estate. An Army medical team is there now trying to get just one of them into a semi-conscious condition, but until they do we just don't know what's happened!'

'Chief Constable, I want a full report on my desk by noon. I've to attend a garden-party at Buckingham Palace this afternoon, and no doubt Her Majesty will want to be fully informed.'

'Yes, Prime Minister.' The Chief Constable saluted and turned to leave the room.

'Chief Constable, there is one more thing.'

The policeman stopped at the door.

'For the moment, we think it would be most advisable not to panic the general public.' The Prime Minister looked towards his private secretary. 'Accordingly there must be no press disclosures of this matter.'

The Chief Constable nodded in approval. 'I'll make the arrangements for a "D" Notice in the morning, sir.'

'Chief Constable, it will be done now. Do I make myself clear?'

'Yes Prime Minister.' The Chief Constable left the library; he was used to the Home Office bullying him about, but this woman made him feel like a young probationer constable. He walked off, musing over the idea of voting next time for the Opposition.

ST LOUISE'S CONVENT SCHOOL, MAYFIELD, EAST SUSSEX
3 a.m. 7 July

Alec Martin was just about losing consciousness. He was sweating badly and also shivering uncontrollably when he heard the old nun speaking to someone. He imagined her to be speaking on the telephone; then he heard the man's guttural tone. He could just about lift his chin to see the nun standing further down the library talking to a man. It didn't register immediately, but slowly as if through some haze he made out the features of the man he had seen in one of Goukas's photographs. It was the Arab called George.

He tried to pick up the conversation but found himself listening to his own shallow breathing. They both looked over towards him. All Alec Martin wanted now was a hasty end. He'd already said his absent farewell to his wife; he'd even forgiven Julia for her part in the matter; and, if a dead man could leave a valid curse on anyone, his was all spent on the so-called 'Sister Marianne'.

They moved towards him.

'He's still alive,' commented the Arab, almost uninterested. 'Why didn't you finish him?'

The nun chuckled again. 'Why waste another bullet? This way he suffers just a little. He'll be a long time dead – isn't it fitting that he should at least have time to prepare for it? At least one act of contrition.'

The Arab failed to share the humour and checked his watch. 'They should be just about there by now.'

The nun moved closer to Martin and prodded him in the shoulder with her stick. 'Aren't you the sorry fool who couldn't leave well alone?'

Martin mustered all his strength. 'Just tell me . . . about . . . my daughter . . . What part does she play in this?'

'She's going to kill your Queen!'

'No!' The Arab grabbed her by the wrist. 'You have said too much already, old woman!'

She pulled away from him. 'Take your heathen hands off me!' She raised her stick towards the Arab.

'Getting involved with you was a mistake! I have always said so,' snapped George, his face in rage.

'Mistake! Without me you couldn't have made your plan work. Thanks to me and the radio messages I sent, the Russians are in a total state of confusion, and at the end of it they'll get the blame for what happens tonight. Even if the British realize that the Russian plans are years old and just rehashed, they'll still blame them in any case . . . You should thank me! I'm giving your people Europe on a plate!' She laughed. 'If there isn't a full-scale war in Europe before the end of the month, I'll be damned!'

'You are!' snarled the Arab. Mary Garand began to laugh again, mockingly. 'Just shut up, you old fool! I'm going to bring the car around to the back of the library. I suggest you finish him before we leave.' He pointed a finger at the Englishman before storming out towards the back entrance. Martin heard the rear fire-door slam; the noise jolted him awake again. He could see the nun lift the gun from the table and limp towards him. The energy was draining from his body; it would only be a matter of moments now before—

Crash! Glass from the window above Martin showered in. The nun was thrown back against the side of the centre row of bookshelves. A tiny hole had appeared in the centre of her forehead. Her body convulsed slightly before she fell against one of the reading-tables, knocking the table-lamp over in the process. Martin stared at Mary Garand's craggy scarred features; she was staring ahead, eyes fixed and empty. The door to his right-hand side creaked open. He no longer even had the ability to turn his head.

'Aw, shit! Alec!' Ivanov was kneeling in front of him. 'I told you to wait, pal.' He touched the Englishman on the arm. The blood smeared across the wall and the pool of blood on the floor around Martin told him what he feared.

'Tucker, listen . . . Chevering.'

Ivanov interrupted. 'Save your breath. I've already taken care of it.'

'But that's not all . . . Julia . . . Visit . . .'

The seldom-used fire-door creaked slightly. It was enough. Ivanov catapulted to the right behind the nearest bookshelves. The shot had already been aimed directly into his back. Martin took the bullet meant for Ivanov in his left eye. Ivanov paused to look at the Englishman, now lifeless, head slumped sharply to the left by the force of the impacting bullet; he felt angry for the first time since Afghanistan. There had been no sound of gunfire; his opponent was armed like himself with a silenced pistol. Ivanov extinguished the remaining ceiling light with a single shot from the silenced Mauser pistol. The darkness was his only advantage.

He listened for any sound. Silence reigned. Ivanov remained still, controlling his breathing, for he had long since learnt as a seasoned veteran that a frightened man's position and cover were more often than not disclosed by his own actions, especially heavy breathing and unnecessary movement, however slight. He lay still for a further few minutes. The library's wall-clock ticked away; the noise was almost overpowering his concentration now. His assailant would have to come at him from down one of the corridors between the four rows of bookshelves stretching down the room towards the rear fire-exit.

From the shot that had finished poor Alec he knew the gunman had been in the centre of the room beside the fire-door, which put him about fifteen metres away. The only light entering the library came through the broken window above Martin's body and from the high fanlights along the far side of the room. The fanlights opened directly above the cloister roof but the cloudy sky almost obliterated the moonlight. The wall mounted lamp outside the entrance-door sent a dim yellow glow in through the glassless window. It was to Ivanov's disadvantage to remain where he was, yet it was suicide to move

Suddenly there was a creak from the direction of the firing-point, similar to the previous noise he had heard; either his attacker was getting ready to make a quick escape or he was being very clever indeed.

Then the latch at the main entrance-door clicked sharply. Ivanov turned, still crouched low. The door swung open. Another nun dressed in a black raincoat stood in the open door-way; she was setting her umbrella down beside the door when she saw Martin's discarded gun lying on the floor.

Before she could reach the light-switch Ivanov heard the single puff; the nun groaned and crumpled on to the stone floor. The gunman had made a mistake; the nun's still body now blocked the door from closing.

Judging by the sound of the silencer, the gunman had moved forward into the library. Another puff, and the wooden shelving just above Ivanov's head splintered. He dived and rolled across the floor. Two more bullets hit the rows of books just above him. Ivanov trained his semi-automatic into a gap in the bookshelf. There was no sign of the attacker. He moved stealthily along the floor now. Suddenly he heard another noise. Amidst the pitch-black row of books just next to him someone had knocked a book on to the floor. Ivanov could hear the man's breathing now, hurried and panting; he was on the other side of the bookshelf, giving away his position. The attacker had been playing cat and mouse, shooting towards Ivanov's probable position and then using the vital seconds after each shot to change his own position. Ivanov knew that he couldn't place a clear shot from behind the shelves; he awaited his chance. The man began to move back towards the fire-exit.

Just as he drew level with an opening between the book-shelves Ivanov struck from his crouched position. Two 9 mm cartridges hit George's stomach, ripping upwards deep into the torso. He groaned and fell on to his back into the ray of light emitted from the open doorway. Ivanov waited. There was no movement from the man. He slowly moved to his side and pulled the man's gun from his twisted fingers; it was a silenced version of a Spanish Star BKM automatic. Ivanov checked the man's neck; there was still a faint pulse – only just. He recognized George instantly. The two shots had been on target and had caused a lot of damage; the man's breathing confirmed a fatal lung injury, and the other bullet had severed an artery. George was haemorrhaging internally. The Arab flickered his eyes, staring up at the ceiling.

'George, can you hear me?'

The Arab turned his head slightly to look at him. 'Ivanov.'

'You know me?' Ivanov moved closer. The man's breathing was completely erratic. 'How do you know me?' George stared at the ceiling again in silence. 'Tell me about Julia's visit.'

'Julia . . . ?' the Arab whispered, a trickle of blood appearing at the side of his mouth. Ivanov propped the man's head up to assist his speech and breathing. He grew paler by the second. Ivanov knew he had little time left to find out what he needed to know.

'Where's Julia going to?'

The Arab grinned at him. 'Fuck you!' He gritted his teeth against the rising pain, then his body began to spasm and jolt. Ivanov held him firmly until he became totally limp in his arms; he would answer nothing more.

Ivanov returned to Martin's body. Gently, almost reverently, he checked the jacket pockets until he found the bunch of keys. He felt bad about leaving him there, but he was out of choices. Alec Martin's head was a mess; the Arab's bullet had blasted out Martin's eye and blown half of the back of his head away. Ivanov stooped over and lifted one of the nuns' capes from the fallen coat-stand and draped it over Martin's body. Standing in silence, he then saluted the body. It was all he could think to do, nor could he understand why; it just seemed the very least respect to pay. In the open doorway lay the other nun, a novice, dressed in a cream smock under the open raincoat. She looked only eighteen or nineteen, no more than a child. The Arab had killed her instantly with one shot through the heart; the look of surprise on the girl's pretty face was pitiful. Ivanov eased part of the nun's head-garment across her face, moving the body gently into the library and then locking the main door from the inside.

'I'm getting too old for this,' he muttered.

Before leaving the library, Ivanov found the Uher 4000 tape

recorder in one of the bottom cupboards. The modified German tape recorder had been McGoldrick's original transmitter. He grabbed the loose wires and coiled aerial and bundled them together, along with McGoldrick's old code-book; the nun had indeed been careless. He left by the back, pulling the fire-exit door tightly closed behind him. Ivanov tossed the equipment into the boot of the hired Toyota Celica Coupé.

He thought of the innocent-looking young novice nun and then of another girl – entirely without innocence. Where was Julia Martin now, and what visit did Alec Martin mean? Just outside Haywards Heath he found a secluded river-bank, well overgrown with gorse bushes. The tape recorder and paraphernalia were well packed into plastic sheeting and again sealed into another bag to ensure the contents were watertight. Then it was buried some way down a disused fox-den partly dug out some time before by hunters. The prickly gorse bushes above and around would keep nosey eyes and hands away from the temporary hide. Ivanov cut back the short distance across the meadow to the car. It was beginning to dawn already.

WEST SUSSEX COAST

The Royal Mail parcel-delivery van entered the coastal town of Littlehampton close on 5 a.m. The local village bobby had just completed his third round of all the lock-ups, parking his police car in the lay by to swig back the final stewed remains of his vacuum flask, when the mail van passed him, turning off the main road into the grounds of the local yacht club. He hesitated for a minute, tempted to radio the information back to the police station, but curiosity had captivated him. The young constable put on his cap and started up the Ford Escort's engine. A forty-foot cabin cruiser was waiting alongside the narrow wooden jetty at the club.

The mail van slowed to a halt on the concrete landing, next to the jetty. Immediately the back doors burst open and twelve men in British Army uniform baled out. Debré, hooded and drugged, slept peacefully in the back of the mail van, a field-dressing already applied to his leg wounds.

'Wait!' snapped the young Spetsnaz major dressed in the British Army sergeant's smock, in English. 'Car headlights approaching from the road!'

No order was needed or given; each man took cover instantly behind the small parapet wall of the landing-area. The police car drew to a halt alongside the mail van; the back doors had already been shut again. The van-driver climbed out of his cab clutching a plastic lunch-box.

'Morning, mate,' smiled the van-driver as the young policeman climbed out of his navy-coloured Ford.

'Hello,' greeted the policeman. 'Can I ask you what you're doing here?'

The driver walked around the police car, stopping beside the constable. He held up the sandwich-box, chewing on some bread as he spoke. 'Tea-break – you know how it is. I've been on the road all night.'

The young policeman was undaunted. 'May I see inside your van?'

The driver tutted. 'Sorry, mate. Company rules and bonding seals. Can't be opened unless at a sorting office.'

The policeman walked to the back of the van followed by the driver. He looked at the rear doors. 'There's no seal on these doors, is there?'

The driver kept chewing on his sandwiches. 'Sure you won't have one? Tuna and mayonnaise.' He held out his lunch-box to him.

The young constable fired him a dirty look. 'I want to see inside the van. Now – if you don't mind.'

'OK, help yourself. Mind you, it's against the rules; you could end up with a complaint very quick.'

'I'll be the judge of that! Open the doors,' he demanded, now sure he was on to something.

'They're not locked.' The van-driver shrugged his shoulders.

The policeman had just convinced himself that the man was a lazy good-for-nothing lout when both doors swung open to meet him. He stood with mouth ajar, gazing with total disbelief at the camouflaged man in British Army uniform. The soldier was pointing an Enfield assault-rifle directly at his head. The constable never heard the sound of the other man coming from behind; a paralysing blow to his neck rendered him unconcious. Within five minutes the Spetsnaz group and their prisoner were well out to sea heading for their next rendezvous-point thirty miles south-west in the English Channel. By breakfast-time all twelve commandos were safely on board the Soviet oceanographic survey ship *Khariton Lapter II*. The cabin cruiser was by then approaching Alderney on the other side of the Channel.

Embarrassment ensued for the young policeman. He was aroused by his fellow-officers after being discovered in the rear of his police car still parked at the yacht club. He rubbed his bleary eyes and tried to sit up. The roar of laughter from his four pals was too much for him. One of the policemen opened the car's rear door and lifted out the half-full bottle of vodka from the seat beside him.

'Aw! Shut up, will you? What's happened to me?' He rubbed his aching neck and head, and then he stared down. His trousers were missing. The laughter and taunting increased until a few seconds later the sergeant arrived. Unlike his men, he could not see the funny side, and the young constable's explanation of how he was confronted by an armed soldier only added to the sergeant's annoyance. The young man hurt all over, so much so that he failed to notice the jag mark in his thigh. By the time he did, the drug had disappeared into his system without leaving a trace. If only the police sergeant had known how close he was to the real truth, he would have eaten his words. On returning to the police station he repeated the matter to his inspector.

'A mail van, he said, and a bloody soldier in full combat gear with a gun!' The sergeant was still angry.

'And a bottle of vodka and no trousers?' added the inspector sceptically.

'I suppose next he'll be telling us that the soldier was really a Russian who gave him the vodka as a parting gift!' continued the sergeant. 'You should have seen the flaming idiot! He still doesn't know what he's done with his trousers!' The sergeant's

stern features fell apart, and they both began to laugh uncontrollably.

TEWKESBURY

Antonia Travis was still overcome with grief and self-doubt;
she hadn't slept all night. She was not given to outward emotion, but something about Charlie Younger's death haunted her
every thought. Perhaps it was his age or, more, the way he
died. He was much more than just another colleague; he had
been a friend. Now she needed to talk to somebody, but she
had no one; her situation could never allow for that. Even the
phone call the previous night from the GCHQ director, Sir
Peter Churchman, had done nothing to console her; she was
unable to confide even partially in her ex-lover.

She looked at the clock; it was just after 5 a.m. She dialled
the London answering-service number, leaving the message for
Mogul.

Two hours later she got her reply. She lifted the telephone
and heard the tape recording switch on. It was the same chilling
voice as before; Mogul's voice.

'Carry out what you were asked to do and do it now. Go to
the postbox.'

The line went dead. Antonia Travis rushed outside and up
the small driveway to the wooden mailbox. A small white
envelope was sitting inside. She hurried back into the house
opening it quickly. It had been typed in block capitals and
printed out on a computer sheet.

TUCKER MUST BE ELIMINATED IMMEDIATELY. HE IS NOW AT
ROSE COTTAGE IN STOPHAM, WEST SUSSEX. GO NOW. THE MAP
WILL SHOW YOU EXACTLY WHERE. DO NOT DISAPPOINT ME
AGAIN.
MOGUL

She looked at the photocopied map showing Alec Martin's
house in Stopham, marked in a circle of red ink.

STOPHAM, WEST SUSSEX

Rose Cottage was deserted and, whilst it was an unhealthy risk going back to the place, there seemed little choice for Ivanov; he had to know more. An early-morning mist surrounded the cottage set in the tree-clad hollow on the banks of the River Arun. Ivanov left the Toyota Coupé at the gravel turning-circle beside the front door. He let himself in by the white latched door at the front of the house. It was quite pleasantly warm inside; Alec Martin had failed to turn off the central heating when he had rushed out the previous night. Ivanov walked around the house looking into every room, finally checking upstairs. He stood for a moment in front of the dressing-table in Julia's bedroom. From his haggard reflection he knew he could do with some sleep. Having gone without sleep for almost three days and nights was beginning to affect his mental state. It was only too easy for him to sit on the divan bed; it was even easier for him to lie back and immediately doze off.

The sunlight on his face aroused him instantly. He shook his sore head and glanced at his Rolex watch. It was already midday; he had slept for over six hours! The sun was shining into the room, having travelled around the southern side during the course of the morning. He found the bathroom and freshened up, using Martin's electric razor to clean up the stubble on his pale face. Luckily Martin took the same collar-size, and Ivanov selected a fresh shirt and tie to go with his fawn-coloured Italian suit. He failed to hear the car approach, but the banging car door aroused him immediately. He replaced his jacket and pulled the semi-automatic pistol from his belt; he had already removed the bulky silencer.

From the bedroom dormer window he could just see over the thatched roof-line to the gravel turning-circle below. The white car was partly obscured behind the Toyota, but he could not see anyone. Then the doorbell rang. He proceeded down the stairs cautiously; he had left the white latched door ajar. It was then that he saw the head and shoulders of Antonia Travis through the outer vestibule door. He replaced the Mauser in his waistband at the base of his spine. Slowly he moved the final steps, taking his time to look through the vestibule door as he moved along the hallway. Ivanov returned the woman's smile as he opened the door.

'Antonia! What a surprise. Please come in.' Ivanov opened the door wider and showed her inside. She was wearing a brown Norfolk herringbone jacket and beige moleskin trousers over a pair of ankle-length leather riding-boots. 'You look as if you've lost your horse.' He smiled. Antonia Travis reciprocated – only just. He showed her into the back lounge facing out on to the lawns and river. The early-afternoon sun filled the room with a brightness that almost cheered Ivanov up until he thought of Alec Martin. She walked across to the french windows and stood there. 'How did you know I was here?'

She turned slowly, a 9 mm Beretta pistol held firmly in her right hand.

'So that's what shoulder-bags are for,' smiled Ivanov, seemingly unmoved by the occurrence. 'I almost had a similar experience in Dublin.'

'I am sorry, Tucker. If there'd been any other way, I'd have taken it.'

'I'd like to know why,' he said calmly.

'Orders.'

'Orders from Mogul, I suppose.'

Her eyes widened. 'What do you know about Mogul?'

'I know who he is, and you don't.'

'I think it's time we levelled with each other, don't you?' She raised her voice before giving an audible sigh; she was being used just as she'd always expected.

They talked for over an hour. Ivanov was beginning to wonder just who he was supposed to be working for when the french windows opened.

'Greetings!' Frazer Holbeck stood in the opening, a hammerless .38 revolver in his hand. Thor and Wolverine were exactly where he wanted them.

'Mogul,' replied Travis, an angry look on her face.

'So you've talked, I see.' Holbeck smiled at her. He looked over at Ivanov standing beside the fireplace. 'No wise move with that gun you always carry at your back, if you don't mind. Otherwise . . . And I so despise violence.' Holbeck shuddered as if feeling a sudden chill. 'Goodness, as Mother said the other day, it's as if someone's walked over my grave.'

'And that might not just be as far away as you think, Holbeck,' retorted Ivanov.

'Oh! Dear, dear, dear. What have we here – complicity with the enemy? Wolverine and Thor together, eh?' Holbeck smiled.

'We established that nearly an hour ago, Frazer. Look, there's something you should know.' She went to move towards him.

'Back! Or I'll shoot. No funny business!' He waved the gun at her.

'Frazer! Listen to me. We're all pawns in a KGB trick. We have the proof!' she pleaded.

'No! You're the trick, Antonia, and I'm not falling for it any more. I fear an executive decision must be made in the field. You, my dear, are no longer of any use to me.'

'Just the way Charlie Younger was. I'm right, aren't I?' She was trying to control her anger, more than regretful at having replaced her gun in her shoulder-bag earlier.

'He was allowed to get too close. If you want to level blame, my dear, blame yourself; it was you who permitted the young man to delve so deeply.' He frowned.

'Ah!' She nodded her head mockingly. 'So everything's everyone ele's fault. How damned convenient for you, Frazer!' She stepped forward.

'No!' Ivanov shouted.

A shot rang out, and Antonia Travis smacked backwards into a wall-cabinet. Ivanov's single movement was swift and deadly. Even with his experienced and tested ability with a handgun, Holbeck was no match for the Russian. Ivanov pivoted partly to the right, drawing the Mauser behind his back just as practised. A single shot took the Englishman just under the knot of his bow-tie. His body jerked backwards into the french windows, smashing through on to the patio outside. He lay still, shrouded in glass and broken wood. He could no longer breathe; his windpipe had been completely severed by the bullet. Arterial blood was flowing steadily into his lungs and mouth. Ivanov watched Mogul's final moments until satisfied that a further bullet was unnecessary. He turned to Wolverine lying slumped against one of the chairs; she was alive.

'Can you hear me?' he whispered in her ear. Antonia Travis looked up, slowly raising her head. Ivanov saw the wound. She had been fortunate; the bullet had only injured her left arm.

'I'm all right! Just a tissue injury. I don't think anything's broken. But it stings like hell!' She grimaced as she began to feel the burning effects of her wound.

'Let's get out of here, pronto.' He helped her to a chair; she fell into his shoulder willingly. 'You know, I'd never have nailed the bastard without you moving like that. I owe you.'

'I'll bear that in mind.' It was then that she saw the car security pass for Buckingham Palace marked 'The Mall – Tuesday, 7 July 1992', with the words 'Buckingham Palace' clearly marked across the bottom. 'Tucker! It's the seventh!'

'Very good. At least the shock hasn't affected your memory!'

'Shut up!' she rebuked. 'The card on the mantelpiece – it's for Buckingham Palace today!'

Ivanov looked over. 'Julia!' he exclaimed. 'The little bitch!'

'From what you told me, she's going to kill again! Tucker, it's the royal family!'

'Can you find your own way outa here?' he snapped.

'Just hurry, quickly!' she pleaded. 'I'll be all right.' Her head flopped back on the chair; she was barely conscious. It was decision time, and he had a bitch of a decision to make. He cursed under his breath.

He was running to the car in less than a second, out through the broken patio doors, jumping over Holbeck's body and on towards the rented Toyota car. He opened the car door and jumped inside. The cold muzzle of the gun touched the nape of his neck.

'Don't move.' It was Kapitsa, standing beside the door. He had been hiding around the other side of the parked cars.

'Kapitsa.' Ivanov identified the voice without turning around. 'I thought you'd have been playing with all the big girls back in Moscow; it's so much more your style.'

'Shut your mouth and get out! Put your hands on the door first.'

Ivanov obliged, swivelling to the right, stepping awkwardly

from the low-seated car while clutching the top of the door. Kapitsa knew what he was doing; he snatched the Mauser from Ivanov's belt and tossed it on the gravel.

'You're forgetting about something, aren't you?' smiled Ivanov. Kapitsa said nothing. 'The woman's still inside. Aren't you frightened she'll come out here and slash your wrists witn her hairnet?'

'Move!' insisted the other Russian. 'Down towards the river, hands on head.'

Ivanov started to walk on to the grass, raising his hands as ordered.

'Why not kill me here, along with the woman?'

'She doesn't die,' replied Kapitsa, enjoying himself now.

'Why?' continued Ivanov.

'None of your business!' growled Kapitsa.

'Mikhailov's orders,' retorted Ivanov. 'You wouldn't have the brainpower to work that one out, would you?'

Kapitsa laughed. 'You'll do anything to give yourself another few seconds.'

'That's right, I'm wasting time – just as you're wasting time right now.'

'Shut up, I said!' Kapitsa prodded him sharply in the back with the gun.

'Just why do you think Mikhailov wants the woman alive? Think about it if you can,' Ivanov persisted. 'A domino effect. She's going to kill you after you kill me – can't you see it?'

'You forget one thing. I was watching what was going on inside that cottage. The woman was shot. Besides, you'd never guess the reason in a million years.'

A loud crack resounded. Ivanov pivoted low to the right, coming up beside the other Russian. Kapitsa had partly turned towards the cottage. Antonia Travis was standing on the patio supporting herself against a low stone wall. She was clutching her own gun, but barely had the strength to hold it after firing the first shot wide. Kapitsa knew there was a greater threat from Ivanov than from the woman. He turned again, determined to finish the job there and then. He spun back to the right, gun-hand partly out from the body. Ivanov grabbed his wrist and smashed his left hand, knuckle first, into his ribs.

Kapitsa involuntarily humped into the air, the force of the punch almost taking his feet off the ground. He was pulled forward, his right arm wrenched to the side and then snapped at the elbow. He screamed just as Ivanov stomped on the side of his head. The GRU captain blacked out just a moment before his neck was snapped under Ivanov's foot.

Ivanov rushed up the lawn. Antonia Travis was barely still on her feet.

'Did I get him?' She stumbled the words out.

'We got him,' he panted. 'Now, come on. You're coming with me.'

'No, I'll be fine now. Anyway, you haven't got the time.' She urged him to go.

He handed her the keys to the safe house. 'You remember where it is, don't you?'

Antonia Travis forced a smile. 'Come back to me.'

He ran back to the Toyota, grabbing his pistol as he jumped inside. As he shoved the car into gear he looked at the digital clock. There wasn't enough time left. 'There's got to be!' he shouted to himself, spinning the car round and sending gravel in every direction as he sped off towards the road.

BUCKINGHAM PALACE, LONDON

Each year Buckingham Palace is the venue for at least three or four garden-parties, each catering for up to four thousand guests, all specially selected for their services to the community and mostly on a confidential basis. Because of the very nature of the occasion it probably affords the least security than at any other time for the royal family.

The queue for the garden-party began to gather around 1.45 p.m. and by 2.30 the line of guests stretched around the palace perimeter from Queen's Gardens and well into Buckingham Gate. All those attending were invited guests for the first official royal garden-party of the year.

'I wish I knew where your father was,' sighed Norma Martin.

'Stop worrying, Mummy. He'll turn up,' replied Julia.

The women looked ahead of themselves in the queue. There were at least a couple of hundred people in front of them as they stood in line on the pavement outside the palace. Julia looked around; it was only two o'clock, and already another several hundred had gathered behind them. The security cordon was tight. All around them patrolling policemen kept on the move, some on horseback, others standing at intervals along Buckingham Gate which was sealed with metal barriers across the junction at Birdcage Walk and also down at Palace Street and Grosvenor Place. Constitution Hill was similarly closed at the junction with Wellington Arch. Only the Mall was open to traffic, facilitating the vehicles attending the royal engagement. A slight smirk filled Julia's face as she passed through the outer palace gates. They were in, and no one could do anything about it now.

Ivanov was already racing the Toyota towards London. From the road-map he had taken from Martin's study he plotted out the best route, estimating the distance to be around sixty-five miles. He checked the clock. It was 2.05. Choosing to stay on the A29, he by-passed Horsham, meeting the A24 at Kingsfold. Two miles north of Kingsfold he ran into the roadworks. The temporary traffic-lights were fixed at red, and there was a two-hundred-yard line of traffic in front of him. Impatiently he waited, keeping an eye on the time and on his fuel-gauge. He cursed at his stupidity; the fuel-tank was almost empty. The on-coming line of traffic dried up, and the lights changed. Slowly, like some Chinese dragon, the line of lorries and cars in front of him began to weave forward in and out of the narrow access across the railway bridge. The progress seemed to take for ever; then the lights changed to red again. A work-man halted an impatient lorry-driver thirty yards ahead of the Toyota; the queue of traffic drew to a halt. Ivanov looked again at the time. It was already 2.30.

'Shit!' he exclaimed.

Snapping the gear-stick into first, he pulled the car out of the queue and accelerated up the right-hand side of the road. From just over the humpback bridge he could see that the oncoming traffic was already on the move, advancing the short distance towards the bridge. Ten yards from the bridge the workman operating the mobile traffic-lights tried to wave him down. Ivanov shot past, mud and water splashing up from the uneven road-surface, covering the angry workman. The Bedford truck was already on the incline to the bridge and, although the driver had slowed up on seeing the Toyota approach, he was unable to do much else owing to the constriction on the bridge and the queue of traffic directly behind him.

At the last moment Ivanov pulled the Toyota out of the truck's path, on to the freshly laid tarmacadam covering the left side of the bridge. The row of plastic-cones were the first casualties, being tossed in every direction like skittles. The Toyota slid partially on the hot tar, leaving deep troughs in the side of the road as it bounced off the stone wall at the side of the bridge. Ivanov slowed down the gears again, and the car slithered across the road, sending a red and white wooden barrier into the side of the Bedford truck. There was just enough room between the giant orange road-roller and the white truck for the Toyota to squeeze through. With more chance than expertise Ivanov got the car through the gap, crashing into another barrier and the workmen's caravan on the other side of the bridge. The car banged off the caravan, and Ivanov fought to control the steering-wheel. A woman driver in a stationary Volkswagen on the other side of the road gasped, covering her eyes, at the sight of the advancing car. Ivanov raced by with barely inches to spare. If he was held up again, it would be too late to do anything.

The party was officially to start at 3 p.m. However, owing to slow passage of the guests through the hastily increased security cordon as ordered that morning by the Prime Minister, the royals were forced to wait inside the palace building until all the guests had been given access. The sun beat down on the milling crowd, now mostly segmented amidst the rear lawns by a series of ropes and wooden posts which formed corridors for each of the royals in attendance to follow, thus maximizing their contact with the guests. The residue of late guests was being ushered through the palace banqueting-rooms on to the rear patio area. Norma Martin was very depressed; even pleasure in her new yellow tailored dress suit could do nothing to diminish her concern at her husband's absence. She wiped away a tear from her eye and was comforted by Julia as they stood towards the front of the crowds at one of the rope barriers set in the palace gardens. Guests milled all around them.

'Cheer up, Mummy. I'm sure there's a very good reason why Daddy couldn't be here.' Julia patted her mother's arm, but her eyes were already fixed elsewhere.

'How could he do this? He knew how important this was to me.' She looked towards her daughter, anger turning suddenly to fear. 'You don't think something has happened to him? I mean, that he may have had an accident or something?' She was beginning to panic.

'No, of course not. We would have heard, and I did leave a message for him at the Hilton, didn't I? Perhaps I should go and have a look round for him just in case. Well?' Julia moved back slightly.

'That would be silly, dear. Your father can't get in now. Remember, I have the invitation-card here.' She touched her handbag.

'Silly of me. Forget it,' replied Julia irritably. She had to find some excuse to leave the woman; she would wait until the crowds began to gather.

They were both suddenly aware of the crowd's stillness. It was as if one might hear a pin drop on the short-cropped lawn. There, on the large rear terrace-area, entered the royal party. First walked Her Majesty Queen Elizabeth II, accompanied by the Duke of Edinburgh. Then, slightly to the rear, followed the Prince and Princess of Wales alongside the Princess Royal. On a signal, the band of the Welsh Fusiliers stuck up the national anthem. Norma Martin stiffened slightly to the strains of the music; she was immersed in the occasion, clutching the white guide-rope, staunchly securing her advantageous position on the edge of the central corridor route. If the royals never spoke to her, the close proximity would make up for her disappointment; even a smile would suffice. As the anthem ended and the crowd applauded, Norma Martin turned towards Julia. She had vanished; her pink and grey dress and distinctive hat were nowhere to be seen. All around Norma Martin a swirling sea of ladies in bright outfits and gentlemen in morning suits was now surging forward, pushing her tightly against the sagging guide-ropes. She looked on, unable to take her eyes away from the royal party now descending the steps into the gardens.

Julia was met at the top of the steps by a junior uniformed footman of the royal household. She followed in silence as the young Irishman led her down to the palace boiler rooms, directly underneath the enclosed swimming-pool.

Ivanov had a clear run past Epsom and on to the A3. It was already three o'clock. He raced through most of the built-up areas, jumping traffic-lights at one stage and mounting a pavement to get past a slower car. It was 3.40 p.m. when Ivanov raced up the Mall and on to the roundabout at Queen's Gardens. One of the policemen tried to stop him, without success. The speed of the saloon turned more than one onlooker's head as it swung sharp right, past the enclosed forecourt of Buckingham Palace and along Constitution Hill.

Two-thirds of the way down the road the Toyota veered to the left, bumping on to the pavement, directly across the path of several pedestrians, passing through the tree-line on to the grass verge at the side of the palace garden wall. Ivanov scraped the car tightly against the ten-foot brick wall before stopping. To the astonishment of the passers-by, the Russian climbed on the bonnet and then proceeded to jump on to the roof of the car.

Then he was gone, vaulting over the wall and barbed wire above, landing safely on the other side, safe in the seclusion of thick undergrowth and trees. Apart from a slight tear along the seam of his jacket sleeve he had entered the palace grounds safely. He adjusted the Mauser pistol in the waistband of his trousers before heading further into the grounds. Already alarm-bells were sounding inside the palace. In the central security control room, based at the Ambassadors Court annexe, the seismic sensors embedded at intervals along the inside of the perimeter walls had fed back a signal indicating probable intrusion.

'Alarm to the north perimeter wall, sir.' The female technician sat forward in her seat.

The police superintendent looked at the wall-panel depicting a detailed map of the palace gardens and security perimeter; a single red light was flashing alongside the perimeter wall on Constitution Hill.

'Probably a stray guest; it wouldn't surprise me at all. Probably having a pee!' he muttered, taking another swig of coffee.

'Usual procedure, sir?' continued the technician.

'Yes, of course,' replied the superintendent. He had a gut feeling that it was just going to be one of those days.

The police perimeter patrol was on the spot inside a couple of minutes, but already their uninvited guest was mingling with the thronging crowd. What the superintendent failed to do was unforgivable: no patrol was sent to check the external side of the wall. If they had, the abandoned car would have precipitated a full security alert; as it was, the conclusion that a stray guest had wandered too far was welcomed with only little reservation.

Ivanov held the torn area of his sleeve against his torso as he moved through the gathering, circumnavigating the main area of interest as he manoeuvred himself up past the rows of caterers' marquees containing table upon table of strawberries and cream. He had already examined the VIP enclosure towards the northern side of the gardens. It was fenced off from the main grouping of guests, and contained various foreign ambassadors, numerous titled individuals, and an assortment of political figures. It was clearly the ideal spot to kill, in entirety, all those attending members of the royal family.

From his glimpse through the crowds he could just make out the head of the Duke of Edinburgh, and further across a break in the crowd revealed the Prince and Princess of Wales busy in conversation with some of the guests. On across the lawn he could only see the heads turn and move in succession; Ivanov construed correctly that the object of greatest interest was the diminutive figure of Queen Elizabeth. He checked the ripped seam on his sleeve, casting a further eye around the gathering; he was thankful that his two-piece suit was not at all out of place, for whilst the majority of men wore morning dress a large number of the male guests had chosen lounge suits.

He moved back towards the VIP enclosure, where it seemed the royal family would eventually congregate. Ivanov began to pinpoint a probable sniper's vantage-point. His eyes moved up and across the rows of windows facing on to the gardens from the rear of the palace itself. Ivanov's heart began to race as he stared at the roof; on initially entering the grounds he had noticed two figures up there, which he had assumed to be police guards, possibly marksmen. They had been positioned at either end of the roof on the parapet-line, one man situated on the roof just behind the Queen's Gallery, another above the domestic offices which formed a partial third floor directly overlooking the gardens. Now there was only one man visible, and he was no longer moving. Ivanov tried to hide the urgency of his step as he moved around the crowds towards the rear of the palace, past the Queen's Gallery.

Near to the indoor swimming-pool he encountered a rope barrier, but thankfully with no security and also partly secluded by the rows of caterers' marquees. He passed under it and along the side-wall of the pool until he came to a green coloured wrought-iron gate and railing, the small brass plaque on the gate bearing the inscription 'Boiler Room – Strictly No Admittance'. Moving along the line of the railings, he could see that the steps below led down towards a basement. Heading past, in what appeared to be the direction of the kitchen, he encountered three women wheeling out the metal racks of additional food, destined for the marquees in the gardens. They were too intent on their own conversation to notice him immediately.

He jumped over the low railing to his left, falling some eight feet on to the bottom of the stone steps. Ivanov pushed tight against the wall, keeping in the shadows as the women steered their rattling trolleys past. No one had yet spotted him, and the absence of surveillance equipment in the immediate area was more than a relief to him. He approached the steel door at the bottom of the stone steps with caution: it was ajar. Ivanov drew the semi-automatic from his waistband and slowly pushed inside the open doorway.

The large boiler room was well lit; the massive boilers and generating equipment droned away continuously. Besides the strong smell of fuel oil, the heat was almost stifling. A conglomeration of equipment filled the room; lagged pipes ran in every direction – along the floor, up the walls and even overhead suspended by metal straps from the concrete ceiling. The initial scan of the room indicated it to be empty. Towards the far end he saw another door. He screwed the silencer on the gun, cautiously moving through the maze of pipes and machinery. Still there was no one to be found. Then, on nearing the door, he glimpsed the bodies of the two boilermen. Both lay on the tiled floor amidst a common pool of blood. With his worst fears now confirmed, he surged through the door and along a passageway.

High above, the palace's head butler stepped from the service lift on to the bedroom floor, which was in fact the second floor just above the principal floor containing the Queen's living-quarters. Following the blue-carpeted corridor towards the rear of the palace, he saw the open window leading on to the slightly pitched roof, easily identifiable by the fluttering net curtains. He frowned at the discovery; it was against his express instructions to leave open windows leading on to the roof, nor could he understand why the security alarm had not sounded, for only months previously a new security system had been installed and each window was now fitted with contact circuits, so that any unauthorized opening of any window would immediately spark off the entire palace alarm system.

Shuffling over to the sash window, he found the bottom fully opened; a plastic-covered wire extended from a magnet attached to the contact point on the raised window towards the other metal contact at the base of the window-frame. Despite his age and stiffened joints, the butler painfully negotiated the sash window, easing himself gently on to the roof. The uniformed policeman lay sprawled in the lead-lined guttering that ran parallel to the building's external wall.

The old butler moved closer; from his experiences during the Second World War he was no stranger to this sort of thing. The policeman had been shot through the base of the skull and at point-blank range, judging by the powder burns to the surrounding hair and tissue. The policeman's holster still contained the Smith & Wesson .38 Special revolver. Hesitantly the survivor of Dunkirk wrenched the gun free and moved on towards the rear of the building, but as he clambered over one of the roofing ridge-lines a tile to his left shattered. The butler turned partly to see a figure standing at the open window, a handgun supported on the window-frame and pointed directly at him.

Without hesitation he flung himself reluctantly over the ridge, sliding uncontrollably down the side on his stomach. The sudden relief of escaping the assassin's gun-sights was superseded by the horror of sliding off the roof-top altogether! His feet thudded into the guttering. The old man glanced around; he was indeed at the edge of the roof-line on the south-west elevation. After the two-foot-wide stream-gutter in which he stood, only a four-foot-high parapet wall separated him from a sheer sixty-foot drop, one slip backwards and that was it!

The service lift jumped slightly to a halt, then the doors opened automatically. Ivanov stepped out on to the thick pile royal-blue carpet. A young man in a servant's uniform was standing thirty feet further down the corridor beside the fluttering curtains leaning out of an open window. The lift doors clanged shut, the man's attention was immediately drawn in Ivanov's direction; the man spun sideways into a crouched position, at the same time raising a Beretta pistol with a fixed silencer. Ivanov was impressed; the man was no amateur. Before the man could pull the trigger the first bullet hit the terrorist in the right arm just above the elbow; the Beretta lurched violently in his grip. The gun puffed, two bullets ripped into the carpet beside Ivanov's feet. The terrorist desperately tried to change gun-hands, but a second shot slammed into his skull just above the right eyebrow, sending him backwards to the floor. Ivanov raced down the wide corridor and hastily climbed on to the roof, spotting the first policeman's body as he ran along the leaded gully set between the gentle pitches of the main roofing trusses.

The frightened butler rounded the parapet corner, but he could never have anticipated what he found. Before him a young woman in a flowery-patterned pink and grey silken dress was leaning against one of the chimney-stacks. She was braced against the brickwork, taking full advantage of the cover afforded by the parapet wall, upon which she was resting a rifle. Julia was zeroing in the Garand just as she'd been taught, held tightly by the addition of a leather strap wrapped around her arm and shoulder to give extra steadiness. Her pink and grey dress was hitched up around her long thighs, the high-heeled shoes removed and cast aside, as was her wide-brimmed hat and matching bag. She was too busy concentrating on a final fingertip adjustment of the telescopic sight and checking for windage to notice the old butler approach.

'No!' he screamed.

Julia dropped her aim and spun around on impulse, firing from the hip, releasing a single shot. The rifle shot up in her hands. Travelling at two thousand eight hundred feet per second, the powerful .30 explosive bullet caught the old man in the chest, throwing him high against the pitched roof. He tried desperately to cry out to her, but it was no use: his chest was gone; nothing worked any longer. The girl stared at him with a blank expression; there was no hatred in her heart, nor was there any regret at what she had done. He slithered downwards back into the roof-gully, leaving a bright red trail on the black slate tiles as his body slowly crumpled to a halt. Julia was no longer looking at him; he was an irrelevance. Already she was preparing her aim again. The crowds below were totally oblivious to the drama above; the noise of the brass band, constant cheering and clapping more than muffled the noise of the rifle.

The telescopic sight zeroed precisely on to the Queen's head. First trigger pressure was taken up through her gloved fingers. The target was still clear; now for the second and final pressure. The shot would be perfect. Her breathing, despite the interruption, was controlled. It was now only a matter of placing the shot and then following on to the remaining members of the Windsor household, for now they were all closely congregated at the VIP enclosure, standing in line as the various foreign ambassadors and visiting dignitaries filed along, each being formally introduced by the Queen's equerry. It would be like shooting sitting ducks at a funfair. She needed five perfect shots, and she still had six explosive cartridges left in the rifle.

Ivanov had already found the second policeman; his body

had been propped up against the parapet wall to give an air of normality when viewed from the ground. The policeman had taken a single shot through the neck. Ivanov saw the rifle-barrel of the Garand projecting from the other side of the brick chimney. He kept low, moving fast along the wide gutter-line beside the parapet wall. There, further on beyond the chimney, lay the old butler. There was no time to spare in trying a sudden dash to disarm the girl. Ivanov acted quickly and fired two shots at the protruding rifle. It was an almost impossible shot at twenty-five yards. The first shot went slightly high, but the second slammed into the brick chimney, splintering a corner brick just above, showering Julia in dust and debris.

In that tenth of a second the rifle had discharged and the masonry dust had also unsettled Julia's view. It was another second before she could follow through the telescopic sight to the next target, but she was not viewing the correct position. Even allowing for the recoil of the rifle, she should never have lost sight of the target position. There could only be one explanation; she realized the falling masonry had marred the shot. In the close magnification of the sights her overall view was somewhat obscured; she had to look away from the gun-sight to find the target again.

The Queen's body was obscured by numerous officials and bodyguards as they swarmed around. Someone screamed far below. Ivanov fired again; more masonry was blasted loose just above Julia's head. There were more screams from the crowds below as people started to realize what was happening. Julia discounted her assailant, taking aim once again. Through the telescopic sights she saw the man's body more clearly; he was lying beside an overturned wheelchair. He was not one of the Windsors. She had missed. Already the police and SAS bodyguards had encircled the royal group, the black umbrellas were being hastily raised aloft by various aides to block the sniper's view. Police were rushing through the grounds in every direction. She had failed.

Ivanov was already over the ridge-line and making his way along an adjacent gully to position himself behind the young woman. Julia was tempted to empty the remaining ammunition into the VIP enclosure and damn the consequences, but she followed Sister Marianne's advice. The rifle, having no further use, was to be left there on the roof. But now there was someone else up there, too, and whoever it was would pay for what had happened. She left her shoes, hat, and bag behind and rounded the chimney-stack. Her attacker was nowhere to be seen, which fuelled her frustration and rage further.

'Come out and face me!' she screamed, her blue eyes ablaze with a twisted madness.

By her shouts Ivanov pinpointed her position instantly. He eased up the short distance until he was just under the ridge-tiles. There was only a little time before the roof would be crawling with police and the military.

'Come on!' she yelled again.

Ivanov could wait no longer. From lying on his back with his knees bent, he sprang up and round, hooking his left upper arm over the ridge and taking aim with his right hand. Julia identified her target instantly, but on recognizing Ivanov she hesitated. Ivanov fired once. Julia's left shoulder was ripped open. She fell back into the parapet, almost losing her balance and falling over. There were sudden screams from the crowd far below as the Garand rifle dropped from her grip, bouncing off the coping-stone towards the terrace. She leant against the four-foot wall, her weight supported on her right side; her ashen face broke into tears.

'Why?' Julia began to cry as she looked up at him. 'Why did it have to be me? I never wanted this!' She seemed like a broken doll; the very last vestige of confidence had vanished in her dark lake of insecurity. She got no response. She stared at the bloody mess that was once her shoulder; the wound was bleeding profusely. 'I just wanted her to love me! Can you understand that?' She began to laugh. Ivanov recognized the evil chuckle instantly; she was Mary Garand's daughter beyond any shadow of a doubt. Julia looked again at the bloodstain now enlarging on her pink and grey silk dress. 'Hey, Tucker! Red doesn't suit me!' She laughed again.

Ivanov had a job to do; he had to remind himself of that. He began to take aim once more, but still doubting what he had to do. Suddenly his mind was made up for him. Still laughing, Julia climbed precariously on top of the parapet. She looked down at the swarming crowd below. She stood there swaying slightly, more through shock than through fear. Then she glanced back at Ivanov.

'Aren't you going to kiss me goodbye?' She was crying now; it reminded Ivanov of a child, and for an instant he wanted to shut his mind to everything bad that had happened and just take her into his arms again.

'I could have loved you, you know.' She almost choked the words out, and with that she was gone from his view. There was a tumultuous roar from the crowd below in the palace gardens and then what seemed to be a collective gasp of horror.

Before reinforcements reached the roof-top Ivanov had vanished. Police helicopters circled overhead. The Scots Guards had been reinforced by a further detachment of soldiers mustered from Chelsea Barracks. It was not until after seven o'clock that evening that every guest had been processed through the police incident control point established in the forecourt at the front of the palace. Norma Martin had long since been taken off by ambulance suffering from severe shock. By 9 p.m. the Royal family had already left by helicopter for the increased security of Windsor Castle.

No one had noticed the police dispatch-rider leaving the palace by the side-gate just after 5 p.m. as he began filtering his way through the congested rush-hour traffic in the direction of New Scotland Yard. The fact that he never arrived there appeared to go unregistered until after ten o'clock the same evening when a semi-naked man was discovered inside a pantry off the main palace kitchens, gagged and trussed up like a turkey. It took the embarrassed police motorcyclist almost half an hour to convince the detectives investigating the case that he was in fact their colleague.

What made it even more embarrassing was the morning edition of the *Sun*, which carried an article on page two entitled 'The Case of the Missing Police Motorcycle', tying in the apparent theft from Buckingham Palace to where it was found later the same night; in the children's farm at London Zoo. The *Sun*'s editor thought the photograph of the British alpine goat chewing a rather bent radio aerial on the back of the motor cycle most becoming, although the humour of the picture was deemed to be a toss-up with the other photograph obtained from a nearby enclosure where a chimpanzee was found to be wearing a discarded police motorcyclist's helmet.

Apart from the obvious humour and detailed presumptive analysis carried out by most of the morning papers, all, without exception, carried a photograph of the Spanish ambassador to the Court of St James, the paraplegic murdered during the assassination attempt on Her Majesty The Queen. The solemn features of Señor Juan P. Lopez were displayed on nearly every front page.

THE KREMLIN, MOSCOW
That same day

The Soviet President summoned Rozhkov to his office. The KGB colonel was a man he could trust, the only individual with nothing to gain out of the entire affair. The KGB officer walked positively into the office. Although only five feet two inches tall, he carried himself well; there was a hint of a slight swagger in his walk, the confidence of a man who knew his job. Of course the Soviet President was banking on exactly that.

'Comrade President.' Yosif Nikolayevich Rozhkov stood firmly to attention, smartly dressed in a navy double-breasted suit, his black hair creamed backwards as always, his pencil moustache trimmed impeccably as ever. He reminded the President of a Latin American dancer he had once seen in an old Hollywood movie. He greeted the man warmly.

'Colonel Rozhkov, thank you for coming at such short notice. It is good to see you once again.'

'Comrade President, it is me that is honoured at being summoned here. If I can ever be of service to you personally, you know I will.'

'Even if it means going against Chairman Glazkov?'

'That also.' The little colonel gave no impression of hesitation.

The Soviet leader sat forward. 'Colonel, I have need of your

481

expertise once again. You came to me the last time several weeks ago. Now I must come to you on a matter of the utmost delicacy.'

The little man's eyes narrowed.

GORKI
The next day

Yuri Shalimov, Minister for Economic Development and Planning, was visiting a new factory complex on the northern outskirts of the city of Gorki two hundred and fifty miles east of Moscow. He was being shown round the complex by the site manager. If a red carpet could have been rolled out across the factory floor for the visiting Minister for Economic Development and Planning, the site manager would have done so; after all, he had done everything else to impress his esteemed visitor.

The minister had moved into the latest building site at the rear of the massive industrial chemical plant when the man approached. Barely anyone took any notice of the diminutive figure walking across the wet concrete floor of the unfinished factory building. The minister was busy over a large table that had been set in the middle of the factory extension, studying architectural and civil engineering drawings presented for his perusal by the site manager. Gathered around were the main project architect and three engineers all dressed in their white overalls and yellow safety-helmets. The little man was now only metres away from the huddled group, and still no one had taken any notice of the additional presence.

'Comrade Minister Shalimov?' The voice came from directly behind Yuri Shalimov. He turned around slowly; from the look on his face he was clearly annoyed at being interrupted.

'Can't you see I'm busy?' He took in the little man in the grey overcoat.

'Minister Shalimov, I am Colonel Yosif Nikolayevich Rozhkov of the Committee of State Security.' Rozhkov displayed his identification.

Shalimov hesitated and then excused himself from the group

The men continued talking together, eager to resolve their structural problem before the minister returned to the table.

'What is it, Colonel?' Shalimov's voice sounded more than aggressive, he was not in the habit of being questioned publicly, even by the KGB!

'Can we speak alone?'

'I am a busy man, Colonel, and your chairman happens to be a personal friend and colleague of mine.' The implication was obvious.

'And he is also blackmailing you, Colonel Minister.' Rozhkov let his words sink in. 'A little matter of some "unforeseen works below ground-level" at a stadium under construction in Ryazan. That was how you described spending the extra million roubles in your report, was it not?'

'Colonel, you don't know what you're talking about!' Shalimov was doing well to hide his rising nervousness – just, and no more.

'It was in 1983, if I remember; then, three months after you filed and presented your final report to the Politburo, your wife was spending money like it was going out of fashion,' Rozhkov continued in his usual quiet tone. He knew just which strings to pull; it was his job to get people to admit to things they themselves could hardly bear to remember.

'You speak of my wife!' Heads turned at the table. Shalimov quietened his tone a little. 'My wife received an inheritance following the death of her father. Not that it's any of your business!' A further show of anger now. Rozhkov was at the last hurdle. Give a man enough options and he'd do the job for you himself.

'Your wife's inheritance totalled twenty thousand roubles. A substantial sum, I agree; but inside four months she had spent twice that figure, Comrade Minister.'

'Who are you, damn you? What do you want of me?'

'Your time, comrade, that is all.'

Shalimov's screwed-up features matched the confusion of his pounding brain cells. 'My time?' He answered quietly now.

'Just enough time to explain how long Chairman Glazkov has been blackmailing you over this.'

Shalimov hesitated, then he looked back at the group of men

still working around the table just a few metres away. Then he looked back at the KGB colonel.

'And if I do?'

'I have it on the highest authority that you are a good man, Yuri Viktorovich. Good men cannot go to the wall.'

Shalimov's heart raced; he understood exactly the bullet-pitted wall the little man referred to. 'You still haven't said what will happen to me!'

'Comrade Minister, think of what will happen if you *don't* make a full and private confession. I already have the facts in my possession.'

'Very well,' sighed the minister, almost reduced to tears. 'I shall tell you everything. That *pogannyi pes* Glazkov has had his claws into me long enough!'

The little colonel nodded his agreement.

THE KREMLIN, MOSCOW
Minutes later

The Soviet Ministers for Agriculture and Mining, Anatoly Bishovets and Alexander Konstantinov, begrudgingly went on to the Kremlin as asked. Neither man expected what was in store. They were both shown into the presidential offices, automatically expecting to be greeted by the Soviet President. Instead seventy-five-year-old Suzlov stood alone in the office suite.

'Comrades!' smiled Suzlov. The doors shut behind both men. 'In the absence of our President may I suggest you both join me in a little light conversation?' He gestured for both ministers to sit on one of the green leather settees. Bishovets was just about to speak up when Suzlov continued: 'I would love to have a discussion on fish.' Suzlov redirected his words to the other man. 'I believe, Konstantinov, that fly fishing is your hobby. Am I correct?' Suzlov smiled; he was the only one to do so.

THE PRESIDENTIAL SUITE, THE KREMLIN, MOSCOW
Later that night

And we have something else, Mikhail.' Suzlov was on the edge
f his seat next to the President's desk.

'What?' enquired the Soviet President.

'An entire facility at Viliuisk, built at an inestimable cost,
nvolving the operation and control of spy satellites with an
bility to jam any hostile satellite known to man.'

'Incredible! But why has the Poliburo never known of this?'
he Soviet President was now on the edge of his own seat.

'It is a GRU facility, under Grechko and Mikhailov's per-
onal control.'

'And you say no one else knows of this. What of the scien-
sts, the technicians working there?'

'All under guard by a garrison of six hundred troops, literally
risoners of their own success,' continued Suzlov.

'And the launch facility? Surely they couldn't launch these
atellites without anyone knowing; it just isn't possible!'

'It is. They used the launch site at Verkhoyansk, only about
our hundred miles away from the Viliuisk facility! The satel-
tes were sent up in semi-sealed units; there were four of them
ltogether. The launching facility at Verkhoyansk knew nothing
f their real cargo; they believed that they were sending up
eather and Arctic survey satellites. Our normal monitoring
ations here in the Soviet Union and elsewhere got one signal
the one Mikhailov wanted them to. The real information was
eing fed down all the time to Viliuisk. I have spoken to the
cientist in charge of the programme.'

'Who is he?' the President demanded.

'A remarkable young man called Suvorov. He has been held
virtual prisoner at Viliuisk for the last three years by Mikhai-
v's men. He was under the care of General Vladimir Pavlov-
h Chernyavin; even the general himself was a virtual prisoner
f his own situation. A virtual prisoner or not, Suvorov was
ill required in scientific circles to attend the Moscow and Len-
agrad Institutes for seminars; it was during one of these poorly
upervised visits from Viliuisk that he managed to pass on to

the KGB what was in fact happening. He felt it was wrong tha
the State was unaware of what was going on.'

'So no one can blame his motives.' The Soviet leader shook
his head.

'But perhaps his choice. He came to the attention of Glaz
kov. Red Bear was quietly reprogrammed as part of a KGF
experiment – or, at least, that was what Suvorov was led to
believe. Under the protective umbrella afforded by the satellite
system Glazkov had his controlled terrorists trained in Liby
and later in Cyprus. It was perfect for his purpose. The KGF
had long since discovered through one of their terrorist contact
about the existence of the old Opus 49 transmitter and origina
codes. Unknown to the person who had them, Glazkov ha
the codes broken just enough to develop his plans. Then he
began to manipulate the person who had the transmitter:
deranged woman, the wife of an activate used by a GRU
sleeper based in Ireland. The woman wanted just two things
to hurt the British establishment and also to harm the Sovie
Union whom she blamed for the destruction of her family an
the death of her husband.'

'And her husband – he was killed in 1972?' the Presiden
recalled.

'Da. The woman managed to escape the British authoritie
by masquerading as a nun ever since. She had a child by thi
man, a little girl, just two years old when her father died. Th
child was reared separately but not independently from the ol
nun. The woman must have been absolutely and totally crazy
she actually manipulated the very policeman leading the man
hunt for her husband to take the child and adopt it!'

'What depravity.' The President turned his head away i
disgust.

'Not as depraved as what the KGB did next. They helpe
train the child, by then a young woman, using the cover of
terrorist group they controlled. Glazkov had only to wait fo
the right moment, then under the charade of this woman'
vengeance he began to mount his operation – not to damag
the British or Soviet governments as the woman imagined, bu
to draw the GRU into a carefully woven trap.'

'And to usurp my authority and position for himself,' nodded the Soviet President.

'Exactly as we first anticipated days ago.' Suzlov stood up and began stretching his painful arthritic knee-joints. 'If Glazkov hadn't been found out, he'd have had the entire membership of the Politburo at his feet.' Suzlov noticed the appearance of a smile on the President's face.

'Mikhail, something tells me you were one step ahead of even me.'

'What none of your files revealed was the relationship between Colonel Ivanov and Comrade Minister Polyansky.' The President afforded himself a little grin.

'Valeri Polyansky? He knew Ivanov?' Suzlov was indeed shocked.

'A family friend; apparently a close friend of Ivanov's uncle. Ivanov went to him just before he left Moscow; he didn't appreciate what he was getting himself into, and he wanted to confide in someone. He believed our Minister for Internal Affairs was well placed to do just that, and of course he was quite right, but not for the reasons he suspected; he could never have imagined in a hundred years that the entire episode was dug up and orchestrated by our chairman of the KGB.' The President rose and crossed to a tall window overlooking the river. 'Polyansky is an honest man; what's more, he hates Glazkov. After witnessing Glazkov's attempt to usurp control at the Politburo meeting he came to me, more to save Colonel Ivanov than anything else. All the pieces started to fit – all, that is, except one: General Grechko.' The President turned to look his friend in the eye.

'Grechko? What about him?' urged Suzlov.

'I couldn't understand his behaviour in all of this. Sanctioning Ivanov to go to England in the first instance was a highly dangerous move. But then I remembered something I'd been told by a KGB friend.'

Suzlov's eyes widened. 'We actually have friends in the KGB?'

'I do. Colonel Yosif Nikolayevich Rozhkov, a little man with a great deal of ability. When I worked in Kirov in 1969 he helped me clean up a notorious Mafia black-market ring; we've

been friends ever since. He called me in when some peculia
things were happening concerning Mikhailov visiting a retire
GRU general called Vlasov.'

'I remember him. He should have taken over the GRU afte
Kurakin's death, shouldn't he?' quizzed Suzlov.

'Indeed he should, but he was blackmailed into resigning.
The President frowned.

'By whom?' Suzlov's eyes narrowed.

'It wasn't clear at the start, but after Glazkov's involvemen
became obvious I had Rozhkov dig deeper. Vlasov's male nurs
is a KGB agent; after Mikhailov's visit it was quite easy fo
him to get the old general to open up. It appears Grechko wa
one of the group of officers used by Kurakin to set up hi
original operation all those years ago. Apparently he was on
of the officers in the dacha that was destroyed by Vlasov's kille
squad. He survived by diving out through a rear window jus
as the first hand-grenades were tossed inside.'

'And to keep Grechko quiet Vlasov had to quit?' Suzlo
turned his head from side to side in disbelief.

'Not such an affable old soldier after all.'

'None of them are,' retorted Suzlov. 'Loyalty seems t
stretch just to themselves.'

'Peter, I want Glazkov stripped of his office. I also want
full tribunal to judge his actions.'

'Already in hand.' Suzlov moved a few steps away from th
desk. 'Shall I have him brought in now?'

The Soviet President simply nodded. Suzlov shuffled ou
Seconds later Glazkov was brought in through the open doors
his hands cuffed to the front, and surrounded by four KG
Kremlin guards and their young officer.

'Leave us,' insisted the President. The soldiers filed out, leav
ing Glazkov standing alone in the middle of the office. 'Now
comrade, you and I both know you are finished, but first yo
are going to face the fullest humiliation of your life.'

The Politburo met in a closed night session with the inner circle of eight. The Soviet President sat down last as usual. The atmosphere was tense. The rift between the GRU and the KGB had split the entire Politburo.

'Comrades. I address you this morning on the gravest of matters. As you are all aware, the GRU operation originally code-named Opus 49 has been creating much difficulty for us in the United Kingdom and Ireland.' The President motioned for one of the secretaries to turn on the cassette tape recorder on a side-table.

'Listen carefully and judge for yourselves.'

Glazkov glared straight in front, now minus his shackles. The tape began to turn silently, then a subdued voice broke the silence.

'I am François Jean Debré . . . I am thirty-one years old . . . I am a member of the Paris brigade of Action Directe.' The voice was tired and sounded weary.

'How long have you been an active terrorist?' The inquisitor's voice sounded unrelenting.

'Since the Sorbonne. Ten, maybe eleven years.' The voice seemed austere now.

'Why were you sent to England?'

'England?' The terrorist's voice sounded dry and thirsty. 'In England we were to kill them all.'

'All? Who is all?' insisted the inquisitor.

'The NATO heads of state at the conference.' The Frenchman's voice appeared to weaken.

'The conference at Chevering Hall?'

'*Oui.*'

'Why were you to kill them?'

'Orders. I don't know. Really I don't.' Debré seemed almost to plead now. Suzlov cringed slightly. What methods had Grechko used to get his man to talk? Whatever they had been, drugged or not, the terrorist still sounded fearful.

'Who gave you the orders, Debré?' insisted the inquisitor.

'George did. He told me.' Debré groaned.

'Who is this George?'

'Lebanese. He's with the Hezbollah.'

'And do you know where this George gets his authority and orders?'

'*Non.*'

'Why not?' There was more than the tone of a threat in the question. Silence. Then a sickening scream, followed by a man's voice crying like a blubbering child.

'I didn't need to know! I don't know! I don't!'

The Soviet President's disgust was evident; he indicated for the recording to be stopped. Then he began to address them again but looking directly at the KGB chairman.

'I now hand you over to Defence Minister Andrei Malik.'

It was the first time in weeks that Malik had been allowed back into a Politburo meeting. While under investigation, protocol directed him to abstain from all sessions. Glazkov sat in silence. He already knew that Malik had been summoned to get his official dismissal, as did the elderly Defence Minister. They both at last were going to share something in common and endure this final humiliation.

'Comrades, that recording was made after the arrest of a terrorist who took part in an attack on the heads of state of the NATO countries at Chevering Hall in England a few days ago. The attack was kept silent, unlike the associated attack on the British royal family at Buckingham Palace later on the very same day. The man you listened to is called François Debré, a French terrorist; you heard his admission. The terrorist plot to kill the heads of state was thwarted by a Spetsnaz detachment sent on to British soil with my authority!' Heads began to turn all around the table. 'I take the responsibility no one else. As you just heard, he admitted to his superior being one George, a Lebanese terrorist, who I know to be a KGB agent under the personal control of Comrade Chairman Glazkov.'

Glazkov reddened; his eyes were fixed on the table in front of him. Malik patted a file. 'It is all here for your inspection comrades.'

'The attempt on the lives of the royal family especially hurt me!' interjected the President. 'I have visited them, dined with them in the very location chosen to be their execution-place!

He raised his voice almost into a shout as he glared at Glazkov. 'Before we go into the sphere of blame I must say this of what has happened. I feel certain that none of this would have occurred if not for the stupidity of our predecessors in high office. The GRU were wrong to try to stop this with a clandestine operation; our future peace negotiations could have been shattered as a result of their unauthorized action. The correct and proper method would have been to place their information before us here at the Politburo. *We* decide! Not individual members!' He banged his hands on the table. 'From the evidence it is also perfectly clear that Comrade Glazkov, for undoubtedly personal reasons that he will explain later to an investigative tribunal, used some of his organization's more seedy elements to develop the situation. I would have liked to think that in some distorted way he believed he was helping this country, but I fear he was only helping to further his own control. I have spoken to him before this meeting, and he offered his resignation forthwith from both the Politburo and the KGB. Likewise I feel it appropriate to ask this gathering to support me in asking Comrade Marshal Malik for his resignation from both the Politburo and the Army.' Heads nodded in agreement, including the Defence Minister himself. It was not every day one was offered a pension deal including a dacha on the Black Sea. 'I think it appropriate that both comrades should go quietly without publicity and immediately.' Again a movement of heads. Glazkov and Malik stood up. Glazkov left the table first, then Malik donned his cap and saluted his President for the last time. He was acknowledged with a single nod of the head by the Soviet leader. Both men then walked out to be met by waiting Kremlin guards. The large double doors closed again, and the President continued to address the diminished group.

'Comrades, the control of both the KGB and the GRU must now be discussed, and for the first time it will be done in front of a full Politburo meeting. No one in the Soviet Union can have any doubt as to our openness in discussing the matter. In the mean time I have directed that a deputy of the KGB stand in under strict liaison with Comrade Suzlov. I will personally take charge of our defence forces in the interim. In the case of the GRU I must inform you that General Grechko has stood down on medical grounds, although still under investigation by the appropriate authorities. First Deputy Chief Mikhailov has been placed under arrest and is to face a military court for his actions in this affair; therefore I recommend the temporary appointment of another respected and revered military mind to the post of chief of the Second Chief Directorate. I hereby recommend Comrade General Chernyavin, a well-trusted and respected member of our Party.' The remaining members of the Politburo's inner sanctum applauded the recommendation robustly. Suzlov was first to rise, followed by the others; he smiled down warmly at his friend. Things were now changing, and faster than any of them had ever dreamt.

Later that night the burly and newly promoted Colonel-General Chernyavin marched into the President's office suite alongside the diminutive and also newly promoted General Rozhkov of the KGB.

'Comrades,' greeted their leader. Suzlov stood at his friend's side along with the Minister for Internal Affairs, General Valeri Polyansky.

Both newly promoted officers saluted, not quite in unison but close enough.

'Thank you both for coming so soon to the Kremlin.' Both smiled their approval, Chernyavin glad to have escaped the indeterminate posting at Viliuisk and little Rozhkov still floating on air after being promoted over the heads of at least ten senior KGB officers.

'You both understand that your tenure is temporary. However, under the new structure that I propose, I see no reason why you both should not remain *in situ*.'

Suzlov moved from beside the President's green leather-topped desk. He went across to a baroque walnut side-cabinet, brought out the champagne glasses and removed a bottle of vintage Krug from the ice-bucket.

'And now I think we should drink to your newfound roles and indeed the future,' continued the President as he moved over to Suzlov and lifted the first glasses, handing them round

THE PRESIDENTIAL SUITE,
THE KREMLIN, MOSCOW
Twelve hours later

Peter Suzlov found the Soviet President in full discussion with a delegation of young Komsomol deputies from the People's Congress. He had to wait nearly thirty minutes outside the presidential office while the Soviet supremo finished addressing the group and bade them all farewell. After the ten young party members filed out the elderly academic finally got his friend alone.

'Mikhail, do you recall what I told you once about being rounded up by Lavrenty Beria during the Stalinist purges?'

'*Da.*' The President frowned.

'It was to do with me refusing to help him and his internal secret police and their programme.'

'What programme?' The facial lines deepened.

'They were stripping all our best university linguists and recruiting them for something. I found out about it by accident when one of my students came to me. That was when Beria heard about it. The student concerned was a young man of eighteen; he disappeared, presumed lifted by the Narodny Komissariat Vnutrennikh Del, and I was hauled in for interrogation by Beria personally.'

'A rare honour.'

'And a painful one, but I got by. It was between what the young student told me and what Beria wanted that I began to realize what he was up to.'

'And what *was* he up to?' The President was almost becoming impatient.

'An élitist group of young people, all brilliant in one area: linguistics. Beria was conducting an experiment; he was getting these chosen young people not only to speak but also to act as other nationalities. Psychologically and in every way he was creating the typical English man or woman, perhaps a German or a Canadian or even an American.'

'Why?'

'I found out only today when I read this file.' He handed across the blue and red KGB case-file on Nadine.

'And who, may I ask, is Nadine?'

'A KGB "illegal", a young Russian orphan girl swept up into Beria's experimental programme and created into a stereotypic young English woman assuming an identity profile created for her. Sent to England to enrol later at Cambridge University and obtain an Honours degree. Then on to the British civil service, leading her into GCHQ.'

'That is sick!'

'That is not all. The KGB got Nadine to allow herself to be recruited by the GRU.'

'What are you saying!'

'Nadine, alias Wolverine as the GRU called her, was acting as a KGB spy on our own Military Intelligence! Now, that is what I call a sick system.'

'You mean we have agents out there, spying on each of our other agents?'

'All down to Beria and continued by each successive chairman of the KGB ever since.'

'And we have allowed this to happen!' The President groaned audibly. 'This madness must end! I insist.'

'It will, I assure you, given time.'

The next day

The President sat studiously at his desk inspecting the agricultural survey reports giving crop expectations over the next two years. The door opened. Peter Suzlov walked in, his tall, lean figure identifiable at a glance.

'May I steal a moment of your precious time, Mikhail?' His voice was, as always, sounding like fatherly advice.

'Come in, my friend.' The Soviet leader set his fountain-pen aside and relaxed in his high-backed chair.

'We have had another message along the lines of this Opus 49 thing.'

The Soviet President's eyes widened noticeably.

'Here, read it for yourself. It's from this Colonel Ivanov that Grechko sent to England.'

494

The President sat forward and examined the sheet of paper set before him.

I. I WILL NOT BE RETURNING. 2. I WANT GUARANTEE FOR NADINE. 3. I ALSO WANT GUARANTEE FROM ARCHANGEL PERSONALLY.

'Who is this Archangel?' the President asked.

'Apparently it's a code-word once used for our illustrious late Comrade Khrushchev. Clearly Ivanov must have picked it up from some of the files he researched.'

'In other words he means me, Peter.'

'He means you, Mikhail.' Suzlov paused a moment. 'And I think he's right. If he returns, it could spell extreme difficulty for us; and he has served you well.'

'Then, the West gets a new citizen,' sighed the President. 'And this Nadine – is this the one whose file I saw yesterday?'

'The same. They are both clearly concerned that there will be no witch-hunt.'

'That is understandable, but what I find difficult to understand is how this Ivanov is going to live outside the Soviet Union,' frowned the President.

'If I know anything about Ivanov, he's already a citizen of the world; he wouldn't have made the decision lightly. I was checking one of the Geneva accounts he used; it's now closed, but he had almost a million in US currency transferred out of it last week.'

'How do we let him know we agree?'

'I'll take care of that. But what of this Nadine woman?'

'Peter, you now have overall executive authority over both the KGB and GRU – you sort it out, old friend.' The President patted the file he was studying. 'I have other matters to attend to.'

Suzlov smiled. 'That is what old friends are for.'

Several days later *Pravda* was published with a number of typographical errors on the sixth page. The first link in the communications chain had been forged.

SURREY
Three days later

Sir Peter Churchman received a letter in his personal mail to his Surrey home. It read:

Dear Peter,
As you will know by now, I have gone. I can assure you that in no way will this require the upheaval of new security measures or a witch-hunt inside Cheltenham. Just accept I'm gone and gone for ever. Don't try to find me.

You may also know by now that Colonel Frazer Holbeck was a Soviet agent. He was also a murderer; he killed Charlie Younger. You may handle that any way you wish, but just remember: dig too deep, and it will become public knowledge that we were lovers at one time. You will understand what that means; at minimum the suicide of your career, and you are too vain to let that happen, aren't you?

Undoubtedly by now you will also have seen the file I left on the Rip Van Winkle affair. If you want the transmitter, it's in an old foxhole close to the bank of the Arun river. I'm not going to tell you exactly where it is; that's up to you and all the flat-footed police search-teams you'll undoubtedly employ to find it! Finally, if you are wise, you'll destroy this letter immediately.

Goodbye,
Antonia

The head of GCHQ strolled from the breakfast room and into the lobby, past his wife as she instructed her daily woman. Once inside the lounge he shut the door and crossed over to the Adam fireplace. Two seconds later the letter was no more.

'Goodbye, Antonia,' he whispered as he stood watching the letter wrinkle up and change colour in the flames of the coal fire. 'Bitch!' he growled through clenched teeth.

THE KREMLIN, MOSCOW
Two days later

Suzlov met the President in the main banqueting-hall at the Kremlin just before the commencement of the state dinner that evening. He guided his friend out of earshot of the gathering crowd.

'I have spoken again to this Ivanov.'

'Well?'

'A rare breed, Mikhail. A pity he cannot return to us.'

'He understands, Peter, that if he returned he could be used by hostile elements in either the GRU or the KGB for their own ends. None of us can afford that.'

'He wants something.'

'I suspected as much. Let me guess. The KGB woman?'

Suzlov nodded.

'Will she not lead the KGB to him? Can she be trusted?'

'If I, as the new governing head of both the GRU and the KGB, ordered it, how could she refuse?'

The Soviet President smiled.

'I have your permission, then?'

'Peter. As you have so often said yourself, it does not hurt to do some things behind the back at times. The less I know the better. Now, I am starving!' The President adjusted his dinner-jacket and headed towards the top banqueting-table. Everywhere the gathered comrades began to clap as he approached. Suddenly he had risen again in the popularity charts. The aid package just announced by the United States was a breakthrough both politically and financially. Now there would be food in the shops. The Soviet economy was back on the road to recovery, and it was all thanks to a little-known research establishment in Viliuisk; the Americans no longer had the upper hand with their Star Wars programme and a hurried deal had been struck.

NOGINSK MILITARY PRISON,
EASTERN OUTSKIRTS OF MOSCOW

Alexei Vladimirovich Mikhailov was hurriedly stripped of all title and responsibility. The military tribunal took exactly four minutes to deliver its judgement. The ashen-faced Mikhailov stood alone in the room, stripped of his English-tailored clothing and now wearing only a grey shirt and military-issue denim trousers. He was a pathetic-looking and insignificant figure without his finery; his last remaining confidence had vanished during the hours of solitary confinement in Noginsk Military Prison while awaiting the outcome of the earlier hearing that same day.

Of course the outcome was inevitable; it just made the waiting all that more painful to the fallen angel. He waited between the two burly GRU uniformed prison guards while the tribunal president, a bald-headed and dumpy-looking general from the Northern Command Region, read aloud the findings of the tribunal. The words echoed through Mikhailov's head; nothing seemed to register any more. He stood there, mouth open, holding up the beltless and oversize trousers, as the final sentence was read out.

'. . . and accordingly this tribunal sentences you, Alexei Vladimirovich Mikhailov, to the supreme punishment.'

The supreme punishment. Mikhailov knew exactly what that meant. He was about to utter a protest when his judge spoke again. He felt his chest tighten as the words echoed forth.

'Take the prisoner away.'

The two guards led him away handcuffed and broken. They walked for what seemed like an eternity down a maze of vaulted and whitewashed corridors, past an empty cell whose door was still marked up in chalk: 'Prisoner 231 – Petrov.'

He was led on past the stone steps leading to the inner courtyard and on down a further short flight of steps. Even though he expected it, Mikhailov's eyes widened in horror when he saw the sign on the door: 'Furnace Room'.

He had to be dragged through, crying now and calling out in vain. The young, newly promoted GRU captain in charge of the execution ignored his pleas. Viktor Romanov was enjoying the first task they'd given him in his new rank.

JAMAICA
The following month

Ivanov was sitting on the veranda of the house overlooking Port Royal and beyond to Kingston harbour with its pale blue sparkling water. He had been in the West Indies now for just over a week. He was feeling relaxed, casually dressed in a blue short-sleeved shirt and broad white slacks with open leather sandals. He heard the car engine before he saw the taxi, a small cloud of white dust announcing its imminent arrival as it wound up the steep drive between the palm trees and thick vegetation.

The red and white cab drove through the stone-pillared gates and stopped just below the veranda. He remained seated. He listened to the car door open and close and the noise of someone opening a creaky car-boot, presumably to lift the baggage out. Seconds later the taxi drove off through the gates again. The footsteps on the concrete steps leading to the veranda were light, yet each step echoed around the quiet courtyard announcing progression. He saw her head first. Gone were the black-rimmed glasses. Then her shoulders, no longer hidden under the drab business-suit. Instead her auburn hair was slightly tinted and flicked outwards. She was wearing a low-cut pale-blue summer dress and walked with a confidence she'd just rediscovered.

'You took your time.' He saluted her with a glass of champagne.

'I hope you have another one of those for me!' Antonia Travis smiled warmly before rushing into his arms.

ST DOMINIC'S NURSING HOME FOR MEN, DUBLIN

Quietly he sat there, as always, never moving voluntarily, never speaking. The glass door in the partition wall opened. The chief nursing officer looked in at the patient. Just for a second he imagined he saw a tear begin to fill the patient's eye. Desmond O'Leary shrugged off the idea. Sure they had to put drops in Harry Adams's eyes every day, just to stop them from drying up. He closed the door quietly and went on up the isolation ward. If he'd taken the time to stay a while longer, he'd have seen he was wrong; he'd have seen the tear trickle slowly from the patient's right eye.

Guzman and Apollo were standing next to the glass door, Jamie Lee was laughing in the corner, as always Ripcord was still cracking jokes. They were urging him on now; they were as much a part of him as his own family. Another tear now. He shouldn't have thought about that; his buddies were all fading now, but they'd be back, they always came back . . .

A day later Harry Garand's right hand started to tremble. After all these years he was reawakening . . .

All Pan Books are available at your local bookshop or newsagent, or can be ordered direct from the publisher. Indicate the number of copies required and fill in the form below.

Send to: Pan C. S. Dept
                Macmillan Distribution Ltd
                Houndmills Basingstoke RG21 2XS

or phone: 0256 29242, quoting title, author and Credit Card number.

Please enclose a remittance* to the value of the cover price plus £1.00 for the first book plus 50p per copy for each additional book ordered.

*Payment may be made in sterling by UK personal cheque, postal order, sterling draft or international money order, made payable to Pan Books Ltd.

Alternatively by Barclaycard/Access/Amex/Diners

Card No.   ☐☐☐☐☐☐☐☐☐☐☐☐☐☐☐☐

Expiry Date   ☐☐☐☐☐☐

_____

                         Signature

Applicable only in the UK and BFPO addresses.

While every effort is made to keep prices low, it is sometimes necessary to increase prices at short notice. Pan Books reserve the right to show on covers and charge new retail prices which may differ from those advertised in the text or elsewhere.

NAME AND ADDRESS IN BLOCK LETTERS PLEASE

....

Name _____

Address_____

_____

_____

_____

                                                    3/87